BY R

RUDYARD KIPLING
writer, journalist and i
remains one of the be colonial
experience in India.

Born in Bombay in 1865, Rudyard Joseph Kipling was the son of John Lockwood Kipling, the author and illustrator of *Beast and Man in India* and Alice, sister-in-law to the painter and designer Sir Edward Burne-Jones. In 1871 Kipling was brought with his younger sister to England, where he lived for five unhappy years with an elderly relative in Southsea. This period was later recalled with some bitterness in the short story *Baa, Baa, Black Sheep*. In 1878 Kipling went to study at the United Services College, a minor public school for the sons of service officers. While there, he began writing verse and had a privately published volume appear in 1881. His series of schoolboy stories entitled *Stalky and Co.* (1899) depict his time there, with the character Beetle being something of a self-portrait. After leaving school Kipling worked as a journalist in India from 1882 to 1889, and during this time he produced a body of work – stories, sketches and poems – which had become known in England and had made him famous by the time he settled in London in 1889. *Departmental Ditties*, *Plain Tales from the Hills* and *Soldiers Three* added to Kipling's growing reputation. His second collection of poems *Barrack Room Ballads* appeared in 1892 and contained some of his most famous verse; 'Mandalay', 'Gunga Din' and 'Danny Deever'. In 1892 Kipling married Caroline Balestier, the sister of his American agent and for the next four years they lived in Vermont. During this time Kipling wrote the book for which he is best known, *The Jungle Book*, and it was published to immediate acclaim in 1894. Kipling returned to England in 1896, finally settling at 'Bateman's' in Sussex in 1902. *Kim*, which is generally considered his masterpiece, was published in 1901 and was shortly followed by another of his successful books

for children, *Just So Stories*. Kipling still travelled widely and experienced war at first hand when he went to South Africa in 1900. Kipling's reports about the Boer War were startling, but his strong views on violence and strengthening imperialism antagonized the anti-imperialists at home who accused him of jingoism and of being a war-monger. Widely regarded as the unofficial Poet Laureate (Kipling refused this accolade along with many other civil honours) he was, in 1907, the first English writer to be awarded the Nobel Prize. His work became gradually more sombre as the Great War approached and this is reflected in later stories such as *A Diversity of Creatures* (1917), *Debits and Credits* (1926) and *Limits and Renewals* (1932). The death of his only son in 1915 also contributed to a new inwardness of vision. Kipling died in 1936 and is buried in Westminster Abbey. An unfinished autobiography entitled *Something of Myself* was published posthumously.

Kim was written twelve years after Kipling had left India, and was first published in 1901. Set in India at the time of the British Raj, it contrasts, through the relationship between Kim and the lama, the exotic Indian landscape and its colourful people with the colonial experience.

Readers may also find the following books of interest: Kingsley Amis, *Rudyard Kipling and His World* (1975); Charles Carrington, *Rudyard Kipling: His Life and Work* (1970); R. L. Green, *Kipling: The Critical Heritage* (1971); Rudyard Kipling, *Something of Myself* (1936; reissued 1977); Harold Orel, *Rudyard Kipling: Interviews and Recollections* (1983); Norman Page, *A Kipling Companion* (1984); J. I. M. Stewart, *Rudyard Kipling* (1976); and Angus Wilson, *The Strange Ride of Rudyard Kipling* (1977).

PENGUIN POPULAR CLASSICS

KIM

RUDYARD KIPLING

PENGUIN BOOKS
A PENGUIN/GODFREY CAVE EDITION

PENGUIN BOOKS

Published by the Penguin Group
Penguin Books Ltd, 27 Wrights Lane, London w8 5tz, England
Penguin Books USA Inc., 375 Hudson Street, New York, New York 10014, USA
Penguin Books Australia Ltd, Ringwood, Victoria, Australia
Penguin Books Canada Ltd, 10 Alcorn Avenue, Toronto, Ontario, Canada m4v 3b2
Penguin Books (NZ) Ltd, 182–190 Wairau Road, Auckland 10, New Zealand

Penguin Books Ltd, Registered Offices: Harmondsworth, Middlesex, England

First published 1901
Published in Penguin Popular Classics 1994
3 5 7 9 10 8 6 4 2

Printed in England by Clays Ltd, St Ives plc
Filmset in 10/13 Linotron Palatino

NORTH-WEST INDIA

Mountain areas ⌇⌇⌇⌇ Roads ═══

0 100 200 300 miles
0 100 200 300 400 500 km

Balkh

AFGHANISTAN

N.W. FRONTIER PROV.

Peshawur

Quetta

BALUCHISTAN

30°N

SIND

Karachi

R. Indus

Sukkur

R. Indus

KATHIAWAR

20°N

Bombay

70°E

KARAKORUM MTS

KASHMIR

Abbottabad

Srinagar

Leh

Rawalpindi

R. Jhelum

Chilianwallah

Chilianwallah

Chenab

Pathankot

Han-le

SPITI

KULU

TIBET

PUNJAB

Lahore

Amritzar

Rampur

Chitri

R. Ravi

Jullundur

Kotgarh

Ferozepore

Ludhiana

Simla

Mussoorie

R. Sutluj

Balka

S. WALIKS

Umballa

Saharunpore

NEPAL

Delhi

Bikanir

GRAND TRUNK

UNITED PROVINCES

RAJPUTANA

Alighur

R. Ganges

Jeysalmir

Agra

Lucknow

Jodhpur

Ajmir

RHINE & GANGES ROAD

R. Jumna

R. Lunee

Benares

Chitor

Chunar

80°E

GRAND TRUNK ROAD

Mhow

R. Narbada

R. Tapti

CHAPTER

1

O ye who tread the Narrow Way
By Tophet-flare to Judgement Day,
Be gentle when 'the heathen' pray
To Buddha at Kamakura!

Buddha at Kamakura

He sat, in defiance of municipal orders, astride the gun
Zam-Zammah on her brick platform opposite the old
Ajaib-Gher – the Wonder House, as the natives call
the Lahore Museum. Who hold Zam-Zammah, that
'fire-breathing dragon', hold the Punjab; for the great
green-bronze piece is always first of the conqueror's
loot.

There was some justification for Kim – he had kicked
Lala Dinanath's boy off the trunnions – since the English
held the Punjab and Kim was English. Though he was
burned black as any native; though he spoke the vernacu-
lar by preference, and his mother-tongue in a clipped
uncertain singsong; though he consorted on terms of
perfect equality with the small boys of the bazaar; Kim
was white – a poor white of the very poorest. The
half-caste woman who looked after him (she smoked
opium, and pretended to keep a secondhand furniture
shop by the square where the cheap cabs wait) told the
missionaries that she was Kim's mother's sister; but his
mother had been nursemaid in a colonel's family and had
married Kimball O'Hara, a young colour-sergeant of the

Mavericks, an Irish regiment. He afterwards took a post on the Sind, Punjab, and Delhi Railway, and his regiment went home without him. The wife died of cholera in Ferozepore, and O'Hara fell to drink and loafing up and down the line with the keen-eyed three-year-old baby. Societies and chaplains, anxious for the child, tried to catch him, but O'Hara drifted away, till he came across the woman who took opium and learned the taste from her, and died as poor whites do in India. His estate at death consisted of three papers – one he called his *'ne varietur'* because those words were written below his signature thereon, and another his 'clearance certificate'. The third was Kim's birth certificate. Those things, he was used to say, in his glorious opium hours, would yet make little Kimball a man. On no account was Kim to part with them, for they belonged to a great piece of magic – such magic as men practised over yonder behind the museum, in the big blue and white Jadoo-Gher – the Magic House, as we name the Masonic Lodge. It would, he said, all come right some day, and Kim's horn would be exalted between pillars – monstrous pillars – of beauty and strength. The Colonel himself, riding on a horse, at the head of the finest regiment in the world, would attend to Kim – little Kim that should have been better off than his father. Nine hundred first-class devils, whose God was a Red Bull on a green field, would attend to Kim, if they had not forgotten O'Hara – poor O'Hara that was gang foreman on the Ferozepore line. Then he would weep bitterly in the broken rush chair on the veranda. So it came about after his death that the woman sewed parchment, paper, and birth certificate into a leather amulet-case which she strung round Kim's neck.

'And some day,' she said, confusedly remembering O'Hara's prophecies, 'there will come for you a great Red Bull on a green field, and the Colonel riding on his tall horse, yes, and' – dropping into English – 'nine hundred devils.'

'Ah,' said Kim, 'I shall remember. A Red Bull and a Colonel on a horse will come, but first, my father said, will come the two men making ready the ground for these matters. That is how my father said they always did; and it is always so when men work magic.'

If the woman had sent Kim up to the local Jadoo-Gher with those papers, he would, of course, have been taken over by the Provincial Lodge and sent to the Masonic Orphanage in the Hills; but what she had heard of magic she distrusted. Kim, too, held views of his own. As he reached the years of indiscretion, he learned to avoid missionaries and white men of serious aspect who asked who he was, and what he did. For Kim did nothing with an immense success. True, he knew the wonderful walled city of Lahore from the Delhi Gate to the outer Fort Ditch; was hand in glove with men who led lives stranger than anything Haroun al Raschid dreamed of; and he lived in a life wild as that of the Arabian Nights, but missionaries and secretaries of charitable societies could not see the beauty of it. His nickname through the wards was 'Little Friend of all the World'; and very often, being lithe and inconspicuous, he executed commissions by night on the crowded house-tops for sleek and shiny young men of fashion. It was intrigue, of course – he knew that much, as he had known all evil since he could speak – but what he loved was the game for its own sake – the stealthy prowl through the dark gullies and lanes, the

crawl up a water-pipe, the sights and sounds of the women's world on the flat roofs, and the headlong flight from house-top to house-top under cover of the hot dark. Then there were holy men, ash-smeared *fakirs* by their brick shrines under the trees at the riverside, with whom he was quite familiar – greeting them as they returned from begging tours, and, when no one was by, eating from the same dish. The woman who looked after him insisted with tears that he should wear European clothes – trousers, a shirt, and a battered hat. Kim found it easier to slip into Hindu or Muhammadan garb when engaged on certain businesses. One of the young men of fashion – he who was found dead at the bottom of a well on the night of the earthquake – had once given him a complete suit of Hindu kit, the costume of a low-caste street boy, and Kim stored it in a secret place under some baulks in Nila Ram's timber-yard, beyond the Punjab High Court, where the fragrant deodar logs lie seasoning after they have driven down the Ravi. When there was business or frolic afoot, Kim would use his properties, returning at dawn to the veranda, all tired out from shouting at the heels of a marriage procession, or yelling at a Hindu festival. Sometimes there was food in the house, more often there was not, and then Kim went out again to eat with his native friends.

As he drummed his heels against Zam-Zammah he turned now and again from his king-of-the-castle game with little Chota Lal and Abdullah the sweetmeat-seller's son, to make a rude remark to the native policeman on guard over the rows of shoes at the museum door. The big Punjabi grinned tolerantly: he knew Kim of old. So did the water-carrier, sluicing water on the dry road from

his goatskin bag. So did Jawahir Singh, the museum carpenter, bent over new packing-cases. So did everybody in sight except the peasants from the country, hurrying up to the Wonder House to view the things that men made in their own province and elsewhere. The museum was given up to Indian arts and manufactures, and anybody who sought wisdom could ask the Curator to explain.

'Off! Off! Let me up!' cried Abdullah, climbing up Zam-Zammah's wheel.

'Thy father was a pastry-cook, Thy mother stole the ghee,' sang Kim. 'All Mussulmans fell off Zam-Zammah long ago!'

'Let *me* up!' shrilled little Chota Lal in his gilt-embroidered cap. His father was worth perhaps half a million sterling, but India is the only democratic land in the world.

'The Hindus fell of Zam-Zammah too. The Mussulmans pushed them off. Thy father was a pastry-cook –'

He stopped; for there shuffled round the corner, from the roaring Motee Bazaar, such a man as Kim, who thought he knew all castes, had never seen. He was nearly six feet high, dressed in fold upon fold of dingy stuff like horse-blanketing, and not one fold of it could Kim refer to any known trade or profession. At his belt hung a long open-work iron pen-case and a wooden rosary such as holy men wear. On his head was a gigantic sort of tam-o'-shanter. His face was yellow and wrinkled, like that of Fook Shing, the Chinese bootmaker in the bazaar. His eyes turned up at the corners and looked like little slits of onyx.

'Who is that?' said Kim to his companions.

11

'Perhaps it is a man,' said Abdullah, finger in mouth, staring.

'Without doubt,' returned Kim; 'but he is no man of India that *I* have ever seen.'

'A priest, perhaps,' said Chota Lal, spying the rosary. 'See! He goes into the Wonder House!'

'Nay, nay,' said the policeman, shaking his head. 'I do not understand your talk.' The constable spoke Punjabi. 'O friend of all the World, what does he say?'

'Send him hither,' said Kim, dropping from Zam-Zammah, flourishing his bare heels. 'He is a foreigner, and thou art a buffalo.'

The man turned helplessly and drifted towards the boys. He was old, and his woollen gaberdine still reeked of the stinking artemisia of the mountain passes.

'O Children, what is that big house?' he said in very fair Urdu.

'The Ajaib-Gher, the Wonder House!' Kim gave him no title – such as Lala or Mian. He could not divine the man's creed.

'Ah! The Wonder House! Can any enter?'

'It is written above the door – all can enter.'

'Without payment?'

'I go in and out. *I* am no banker,' laughed Kim.

'Alas! I am an old man. I did not know.' Then, fingering his rosary, he half turned to the museum.

'What is your caste? Where is your house? Have you come far?' Kim asked.

'I came by Kulu – from beyond the Kailas – but what know you? From the Hills where' – he sighed – 'the air and water are fresh and cool.'

'Aha! Khitai [a Chinaman],' said Abdullah proudly.

12

Fook Shing had once chased him out of his shop for spitting at the joss above the boots.

'Pahari [a hillman],' said little Chota Lal.

'Aye, child – a hillman from hills thou'lt never see. Didst hear of Bhotiyal [Tibet]? I am no Khitai, but a Bhotiya [Tibetan], since you must know – a lama – or, say, a guru in your tongue.'

'A guru from Tibet,' said Kim. 'I have not seen such a man. They be Hindus in Tibet, then?'

'We be followers of the Middle Way, living in peace in our lamasseries, and I go to see the Four Holy places before I die. Now do you, who are children, know as much as I do who am old.' He smiled benignantly on the boys.

'Hast thou eaten?'

He fumbled in his bosom and drew forth a worn wooden begging-bowl. The boys nodded. All priests of their acquaintance begged.

'I do not wish to eat yet.' He turned his head like an old tortoise in the sunlight. 'Is it true that there are many images in the Wonder House of Lahore?' He repeated the last words as one making sure of an address.

'That is true,' said Abdullah. 'It is full of heathen *būts*. Thou also art an idolater.'

'Never mind *him*,' said Kim. 'That is the government's house and there is no idolatry in it, but only a sahib with a white beard. Come with me and I will show.'

'Strange priests eat boys,' whispered Chota Lal.

'And he is a stranger and a *būt-parast* [idolater],' said Abdullah, the Muhammadan.

Kim laughed. 'He is new. Run to your mothers' laps, and be safe. Come!'

13

Kim clicked round the self-registering turnstile; the old man followed and halted amazed. In the entrance-hall stood the larger figures of the Greco-Buddhist sculptures done, savants know how long since, by forgotten workmen whose hands were feeling, and not unskilfully, for the mysteriously transmitted Grecian touch. There were hundreds of pieces, friezes of figures in relief, fragments of statues and slabs crowded with figures that had encrusted the brick walls of the Buddhist *stupas* and *viharas* of the North Country and now, dug up and labelled, made the pride of the museum. In open-mouthed wonder the lama turned to this and that, and finally checked in rapt attention before a large alto-relief representing a coronation or apotheosis of the Lord Buddha. The Master was represented seated on a lotus the petals of which were so deeply undercut as to show almost detached. Round him was an adoring hierarchy of kings, elders, and old-time Buddhas. Below were lotus-covered waters with fishes and water-birds. Two butterfly-winged *dewas* held a wreath over his head; above them another pair supported an umbrella surmounted by the jewelled headdress of the Bodhisat.

'The Lord! The Lord! It is Sakya Muni himself,' the lama half sobbed; and under his breath began the wonderful Buddhist invocation:

> 'To Him the Way, the Law, apart
> Whom Maya held beneath her heart,
> Ananda's Lord, the Bodhisat.'

'And he is here! The Most Excellent Law is here also. My pilgrimage is well begun. And what work! What work!'

'Yonder is the sahib,' said Kim, and dodged sideways among the cases of the arts and manufactures wing. A white-bearded Englishman was looking at the lama, who gravely turned and saluted him and after some fumbling drew forth a notebook and a scrap of paper.

'Yes, that is my name,' smiling at the clumsy, childish print.

'One of us who had made pilgrimage to the Holy Places – he is now Abbot of the Lung-Cho Monastery – gave it me,' stammered the lama. 'He spoke of these.' His lean hand moved tremulously round.

'Welcome, then, O lama from Tibet. Here be the images, and I am here' – he glanced at the lama's face – 'to gather knowledge. Come to my office awhile.' The old man was trembling with excitement.

The office was but a little wooden cubicle partitioned off from the sculpture-lined gallery. Kim laid himself down, his ear against a crack in the heat-split cedar door, and, following his instinct, stretched out to listen and watch.

Most of the talk was altogether above his head. The lama, haltingly at first, spoke to the Curator of his own lamassery, the Such-zen, opposite the Painted Rocks, four months' march away. The Curator brought out a huge book of photos and showed him that very place, perched on its crag, overlooking the gigantic valley of many-hued strata.

'Ay, ay!' The lama mounted a pair of horn-rimmed spectacles of Chinese work. 'Here is the little door through which we bring wood before winter. And thou – the English know of these things? He who is now Abbot of Lung-Cho told me, but I did not believe. The Lord – the

Excellent One – he has honour here too? And his life is known?'

'It is all carven upon the stones. Come and see, if thou art rested.'

Out shuffled the lama to the main hall, and, the Curator beside him, went through the collection with the reverence of a devotee and the appreciative instinct of a craftsman.

Incident by incident in the beautiful story he identified on the blurred stone, puzzled here and there by the unfamiliar Greek convention, but delighted as a child at each new trove. Where the sequence failed, as in the Annunciation, the Curator supplied it from his mound of books French and German, with photographs and reproductions.

Here was the devout Asita, the pendant of Simeon in the Christian story, holding the Holy Child on his knee while mother and father listened; and here were incidents in the legend of the cousin Devadatta. Here was the wicked woman who accused the Master of impurity, all confounded; here was the teaching in the Deer-park; the miracle that stunned the fire-worshippers; here was the Bodhisat in royal state as a prince; the miraculous birth; the death at Kusinagara, where the weak disciple fainted; while there were almost countless repetitions of the meditation under the Bodhi tree; and the adoration of the alms-bowl was everywhere. In a few minutes the Curator saw that his guest was no mere bead-telling mendicant, but a scholar of parts. And they went at it all over again, the lama taking snuff, wiping his spectacles, and talking at railway speed in a bewildering mixture of Urdu and Tibetan. He had heard of the travels of the Chinese

pilgrims, Fu-Hiouen and Hwen-Tsiang, and was anxious to know if there was any translation of their record. He drew in his breath as he turned helplessly over the pages of Beal and Stanislas Julien. ''Tis all here. A treasure locked.' Then he composed himself reverently to listen to fragments hastily rendered into Urdu. For the first time he heard of the labours of European scholars, who by the help of these and a hundred other documents have identified the Holy Places of Buddhism. Then he was shown a mighty map, spotted and traced with yellow. The brown finger followed the Curator's pencil from point to point. Here was Kapilavastu, here the Middle Kingdom, and here Mahabodhi, the Mecca of Buddhism; and here was Kusinagara, sad place of the Holy One's death. The old man bowed his head over the sheets in silence for a while, and the Curator lit another pipe. Kim had fallen asleep. When he waked, the talk, still in spate, was more within his comprehension.

'And thus it was, O Fountain of Wisdom, that I decided to go to the Holy Places which his foot had trod – to the Birthplace, even to Kapila; then to Mahabodhi, which is Buddh Gaya – to the Monastery – to the Deer-park – to the place of his death.'

The lama lowered his voice. 'And I come here alone. For five – seven – eighteen – forty years it was in my mind that the Old Law was not well followed; being overlaid, as thou knowest, with devildom, charms, and idolatry. Even as the child outside said but now. Ay, even as the child said, with *būt parasti*.'

'So it comes with all faiths.'

'Thinkest thou? The books of my lamassery I read, and they were dried pith; and the later ritual with which we of

17

the Reformed Law have cumbered ourselves – that, too, had no worth to these old eyes. Even the followers of the Excellent One are at feud on feud with one another. It is all illusion. Ay, *maya*, illusion. But I have another desire' – the seamed yellow face drew within three inches of the Curator, and the long forefinger nail tapped on the table. 'Your scholars, by these books, have followed the Blessed Feet in all their wanderings; but there are things which they have not sought out. I know nothing – nothing do I know – but I go to free myself from the Wheel of Things by a broad and open road.' He smiled with most simple triumph. 'As a pilgrim to the Holy Places I acquire merit. But there is more. Listen to a true thing. When our gracious Lord, being as yet a youth, sought a mate, men said, in his father's court, that he was too tender for marriage. Thou knowest?'

The Curator nodded, wondering what would come next.

'So they made the triple trial of strength against all comers. And at the test of the Bow, our Lord first breaking that which they gave him, called for such a bow as none might bend. Thou knowest?'

'It is written. I have read.'

'And, overshooting all other marks, the arrow passed far and far beyond sight. At the last it fell; and, where it touched earth, there broke out a stream which presently became a River, whose nature, by our Lord's benefi- cence, and that merit he acquired ere he freed himself, is that whoso bathes in it washes away all taint and speckle of sin.'

'So it is written,' said the Curator sadly.

The lama drew a long breath. 'Where is that River? Fountain of Wisdom, where fell the arrow?'

'Alas, my brother, I do not know,' said the Curator.

'Nay, if it please thee to forget – the one thing only that thou hast not told me. Surely thou must know? See, I am an old man! I ask with my head between thy feet, O Fountain of Wisdom. We *know* he drew the bow! We *know* the arrow fell! We *know* the stream gushed! Where, then, is the River? My dream told me to find it. So I came. I am here. But where is the River?'

'If I knew, think you I would not cry it aloud?'

'By it one attains freedom from the Wheel of Things,' the lama went on, unheeding. 'The River of the Arrow! Think again! Some little stream, maybe – dried in the heats? But the Holy One would never so cheat an old man.'

'I do not know. I do not know.'

The lama brought his thousand-wrinkled face once more a handsbreadth from the Englishman's. 'I see thou dost not know. Not being of the Law, the matter is hid from thee.'

'Ay – hidden – hidden.'

'We are both bound, thou and I, my brother. But I' – he rose with a sweep of the soft thick drapery – 'I go to cut myself free. Come also!'

'I am bound,' said the Curator. 'But whither goest thou?'

'First to Kashi [Benares]: where else? There I shall meet one of the pure faith in a Jain temple of that city. He also is a Seeker in secret, and from him haply I may learn. Maybe he will go with me to Buddh Gaya. Thence north and west to Kapilavastu, and there will I seek for the

River. Nay, I will seek everywhere as I go – for the place is not known where the arrow fell.'

'And how wilt thou go? It is a far cry to Delhi, and farther to Benares.'

'By road and the trains. From Pathânkot, having left the hills, I came hither in a *te-rain*. It goes swiftly. At first I was amazed to see those tall poles by the side of the road snatching up and snatching up their threads' – he illustrated the stoop and whirl of a telegraph-pole flashing past the train. 'But later, I was cramped and desired to walk, as I am used.'

'And thou art sure of thy road?' said the Curator.

'Oh, for that one but asks a question and pays money, and the appointed persons despatch all to the appointed place. That much I knew in my lamassery from sure report,' said the lama proudly.

'And when dost thou go?' The Curator smiled at the mixture of old-world piety and modern progress that is the note of India today.

'As soon as may be. I follow the places of his life till I come to the River of the Arrow. There is, moreover, a written paper of the hours of the trains that go south.'

'And for food?' Lamas, as a rule, have a good store of money somewhere about them, but the Curator wished to make sure.

'For the journey, I take up the Master's begging-bowl. Yes. Even as he went so go I, forsaking the ease of my monastery. There was with me when I left the hills a *chela* [disciple] who begged for me as the Rule demands, but halting in Kulu awhile a fever took him and he died. I have now no *chela*, but I will take the alms-bowl and thus enable the charitable to acquire merit.' He nodded his

head valiantly. Learned doctors of a lamassery do not beg, but the lama was an enthusiast in this quest.

'Be it so,' said the Curator, smiling. 'Suffer me now to acquire merit. We be craftsmen together, thou and I. Here is a new book of white English paper: here be sharpened pencils two and three – thick and thin, all good for a scribe. Now lend me thy spectacles.'

The Curator looked through them. They were heavily scratched, but the power was almost exactly that of his own pair, which he slid into the lama's hand, saying: 'Try these.'

'A feather! A very feather upon the face!' The old man turned his head delightedly and wrinkled up his nose. 'How scarcely do I feel them! How clearly do I see!'

'They be *bilaur* – crystal – and will never scratch. May they help thee to thy River, for they are thine.'

'I will take them and the pencils and the white note-book,' said the lama, 'as a sign of friendship between priest and priest – and now –' He fumbled at his belt, detached the open work iron pen-case, and laid it on the Curator's table. 'That is for a memory between thee and me – my pen-case. It is something old – even as I am.'

It was a piece of ancient design, Chinese, of an iron that is not smelted these days; and the collector's heart in the Curator's bosom had gone out to it from the first. For no persuasion would the lama resume his gift.

'When I return, having found the River, I will bring thee a written picture of the Padma Samthora – such as I used to make on silk at the lamassery. Yes – and of the Wheel of Life,' he chuckled, 'for we be craftsmen together, thou and I.'

The Curator would have detained him: they are few in

the world who still have the secret of the conventional brush-pen Buddhist pictures which are, as it were, half written and half drawn. But the lama strode out, head high in air, and pausing an instant before the great statue of a Bodhisat in meditation, brushed through the turnstiles.

Kim followed like a shadow. What he had overheard excited him wildly. This man was entirely new to all his experience, and he meant to investigate further, precisely as he would have investigated a new building or a strange festival in Lahore city. The lama was his trove, and he purposed to take possession. Kim's mother had been Irish too.

The old man halted by Zam-Zammah and looked round till his eye fell on Kim. The inspiration of his pilgrimage had left him for a while, and he felt old, forlorn, and very empty.

'Do not sit under that gun,' said the policeman loftily.

'Huh! Owl!' was Kim's retort on the lama's behalf. 'Sit under that gun if it please thee. When didst thou steal the milk-woman's slippers, Dunnoo?'

That was an utterly unfounded charge sprung on the spur of the moment, but it silenced Dunnoo, who knew that Kim's clear yell could call up legions of bad bazaar boys if need arose.

'And whom didst thou worship within?' said Kim affably, squatting in the shade beside the lama.

'I worshipped none, child. I bowed before the Excellent Law.'

Kim accepted this new god without emotion. He knew already a few score.

'And what dost thou do?'

'I beg. I remember now it is long since I have eaten or drunk. What is the custom of charity in this town? In silence, as we do of Tibet, or speaking aloud?'

'Those who beg in silence starve in silence,' said Kim, quoting a native proverb. The lama tried to rise, but sank back again, sighing for his disciple, dead in faraway Kulu. Kim watched – head to one side, considering and interested.

'Give me the bowl. I know the people of this city – all who are charitable. Give, and I will bring it back filled.'

Simply as a child the old man handed him the bowl.

'Rest, thou. *I* know the people.'

He trotted off to the open shop of a *kunjri*, a low-caste vegetable-seller, which lay opposite the belt-tramway line down the Motee Bazaar. She knew Kim of old.

'Oho, hast thou turned yogi with thy begging-bowl?' she cried.

'Nay,' said Kim proudly. 'There is a new priest in the city – a man such as I have never seen.'

'Old priest – young tiger,' said the woman angrily. 'I am tired of new priests! They settle on our wares like flies. Is the father of my son a well of charity to give to all who ask?'

'No,' said Kim. 'Thy man is rather *yagi* [bad-tempered] than yogi [a holy man]. But this priest is new. The sahib in the Wonder House has talked to him like a brother. O my mother, fill me this bowl. He waits.'

'That bowl indeed! That cow-bellied basket! Thou hast as much grace as the holy bull of Shiv. He has taken the best of a basket of onions already, this morn; and for-sooth, I must fill thy bowl. He comes here again.'

The huge, mouse-coloured Brahmini bull of the ward

was shouldering his way through the many-coloured crowd, a stolen plantain hanging out of his mouth. He headed straight for the shop, well knowing his privileges as a sacred beast, lowered his head, and puffed heavily along the line of baskets ere making his choice. Up flew Kim's hard little heel and caught him on his moist blue nose. He snorted indignantly, and walked away across the tram-rails, his hump quivering with rage.

'See! I have saved more than the bowl will cost thrice over. Now, mother, a little rice and some dried fish atop – yes, and some vegetable curry.'

A growl came out of the back of the shop, where a man lay.

'He drove away the bull,' said the woman in an undertone. 'It is good to give to the poor.' She took the bowl and returned it full of hot rice.

'But my yogi is not a cow,' said Kim gravely, making a hole with his fingers in the top of the mound. 'A little curry is good, and a fried cake, and a morsel of conserve would please him, I think.'

'It is a hole as big as thy head,' said the woman fretfully. But she filled it, none the less, with good, steaming vegetable curry, clapped a fried cake atop, and a morsel of clarified butter on the cake, dabbed a lump of sour tamarind conserve at the side; and Kim looked at the load lovingly.

'That is good. When I am in the bazaar the bull shall not come to this house. He is a bold beggar-man.'

'And thou?' laughed the woman. 'But speak well of bulls. Hast thou not told me that some day a Red Bull will come out of a field to help thee? Now hold all straight and ask for the holy man's blessing upon me. Perhaps, too,

24

he knows a cure for my daughter's sore eyes. Ask him that also, O thou Little Friend of all the World.'

But Kim had danced off ere the end of the sentence, dodging pariah dogs and hungry acquaintances.

'Thus do we beg who know the way of it,' said he proudly to the lama, who opened his eyes at the contents of the bowl. 'Eat now and – I will eat with thee. Ohé, *bhisti!*' he called to the water-carrier, sluicing the crotons by the museum. 'Give water here. We men are thirsty.'

'We men!' said the *bhisti*, laughing. 'Is one skinful enough for such a pair? Drink, then, in the name of the Compassionate.'

He loosed a thin stream into Kim's hands, who drank native-fashion; but the lama must needs pull out a cup from his inexhaustible upper draperies and drink ceremonially.

'*Pardesi* [a foreigner],' Kim explained, as the old man delivered in an unknown tongue what was evidently a blessing.

They ate together in great content, clearing the begging-bowl. Then the lama took snuff from a portentous wooden snuff-gourd, fingered his rosary awhile, and so dropped into the easy sleep of age, as the shadow of Zam-Zammah grew long.

Kim loafed over to the nearest tobacco-seller, a rather lively young Muhammadan woman, and begged a rank cigar of the brand that they sell to students of the Punjab University who copy English customs. Then he smoked and thought, knees to chin, under the belly of the gun, and the outcome of his thoughts was a sudden and stealthy departure in the direction of Nila Ram's timber-yard.

The lama did not wake till the evening life of the city had begun with lamp-lighting and the return of white-robed clerks and subordinates from the government offices. He stared dizzily in all directions, but none looked at him save a Hindu urchin in a dirty turban and Isabella-coloured clothes. Suddenly he bowed his head on his knees and wailed.

'What is this?' said the boy, standing before him. 'Hast thou been robbed?'

'It is my new *chela* [disciple] that is gone away from me, and I know not where he is.'

'And what like of man was thy disciple?'

'It was a boy who came to me in place of him who died, on account of the merit which I had gained when I bowed before the Law within there.' He pointed towards the museum. 'He came upon me to show me a road which I had lost. He led me into the Wonder House, and by his talk emboldened me to speak to the Keeper of the Images, so that I was cheered and made strong. And when I was faint with hunger he begged for me, as would a *chela* for his teacher. Suddenly was he sent. Suddenly has he gone away. It was in my mind to have taught him the Law upon the road to Benares.'

Kim stood amazed at this, because he had overheard the talk in the museum, and knew that the old man was speaking the truth, which is a thing a native on the road seldom presents to a stranger.

'But I see now that he was but sent for a purpose. By this I know that I shall find a certain River for which I seek.'

'The River of the Arrow?' said Kim, with a superior smile.

'Is this yet another Sending?' cried the lama. 'To none have I spoken of my search, save to the Priest of the Images. Who art thou?'

'Thy *chela*,' said Kim simply, sitting on his heels. 'I have never seen any one like to thee in all this my life. I go with thee to Benares. And, too, I think that so old a man as thou, speaking the truth to chance-met people at dusk, is in great need of a disciple.'

'But the River – the River of the Arrow?'

'Oh, that I heard when thou wast speaking to the Englishman. I lay against the door.'

The lama sighed. 'I thought thou hadst been a guide permitted. Such things fall sometimes – but I am not worthy. Thou dost not, then, know the River?'

'Not I.' Kim laughed uneasily. 'I go to look for – for a bull – a Red Bull on a green field who shall help me.' Boy-like, if an acquaintance had a scheme, Kim was quite ready with one of his own; and, boy-like, he had really thought for as much as twenty minutes at a time of his father's prophecy.

'To what, child?' said the lama.

'God knows, but so my father told me. I heard thy talk in the Wonder House of all those new strange places in the Hills, and if one so old and so little – so used to truth-telling – may go out for the small matter of a river, it seemed to me that I too must go a-travelling. If it is our fate to find those things we shall find them – thou, thy River; and I, my Bull, and the Strong Pillars and some other matters that I forget.'

'It is not pillars but a Wheel from which I would be free,' said the lama.

'That is all one. Perhaps they will make me a king,' said Kim, serenely prepared for anything.

'I will teach thee other and better desires upon the road,' the lama replied in the voice of authority. 'Let us go to Benares.'

'Not by night. Thieves are abroad. Wait till the day.'

'But there is no place to sleep.' The old man was used to the order of his monastery, and though he slept on the ground, as the Rule decrees, preferred a decency in these things.

'We shall get good lodging at the Kashmir Serai,' said Kim, laughing at his perplexity. 'I have a friend there. Come!'

The hot and crowded bazaars blazed with light as they made their way through the press of all the races in upper India, and the lama mooned through it like a man in a dream. It was his first experience of a large manufacturing city, and the crowded tramcar with its continually squealing brakes frightened him. Half pushed, half towed, he arrived at the high gate of the Kashmir Serai: that huge open square over against the railway station, surrounded with arched cloisters, where the camel and horse caravans put up on their return from central Asia. Here were all manner of northern folk, tending tethered ponies and kneeling camels; loading and unloading bales and bundles; drawing water for the evening meal at the creaking well windlasses; piling grass before the shrieking, wild-eyed stallions; cuffing the surly caravan dogs; paying off camel-drivers; taking on new grooms; swearing, shouting, arguing, and chaffering in the packed square. The cloisters, reached by three or four masonry steps, made a haven of refuge around this turbulent sea.

Most of them were rented to traders, as we rent the arches of a viaduct; the space between pillar and pillar being bricked or boarded off into rooms, which were guarded by heavy wooden doors and cumbrous native padlocks. Locked doors showed that the owner was away, and a few rude – sometimes very rude – chalk or paint scratches told where he had gone. Thus: 'Lutuf Ullah is gone to Kurdistan.' Below, in coarse verse: 'O Allah, who sufferest lice to live on the coat of a Kabuli, why hast thou allowed this louse Lutuf to live so long?'

Kim, fending the lama between excited men and excited beasts, sidled along the cloisters to the far end, nearest the railway station, where Mahbub Ali, the horse-trader, lived when he came in from that mysterious land beyond the Passes of the North.

Kim had had many dealings with Mahbub in his little life – especially between his tenth and his thirteenth year – and the big burly Afghan, his beard dyed scarlet with lime (for he was elderly and did not wish his grey hairs to show), knew the boy's value as a gossip. Sometimes he would tell Kim to watch a man who had nothing whatever to do with horses: to follow him for one whole day and report every soul with whom he talked. Kim would deliver himself of this tale at evening, and Mahbub would listen without a word or gesture. It was intrigue of some kind, Kim knew; but its worth lay in saying nothing whatever to any one except Mahbub, who gave him beautiful meals all hot from the cookshop at the head of the serai, and once as much as eight annas in money.

'He is here,' said Kim, hitting a bad-tempered camel on

the nose. 'Ohé, Mahbub Ali!' He halted at a dark arch and slipped behind the bewildered lama.

The horse-trader, his deep, embroidered Bokhariot belt unloosed, was lying on a pair of silk carpet saddle-bags, pulling lazily at an immense silver hookah. He turned his head very slightly at the cry; and seeing only the tall silent figure, chuckled in his deep chest.

'Allah! A lama! A Red Lama! It is far from Lahore to the Passes. What dost thou do here?'

The lama held out the begging-bowl mechanically.

'God's curse on all unbelievers!' said Mahbub. 'I do not give to a lousy Tibetan; but ask my Baltis over yonder behind the camels. They may value your blessings. Oh, horse-boys, here is a countryman of yours. See if he be hungry.'

A shaven, crouching Balti, who had come down with the horses, and who was nominally some sort of de-graded Buddhist, fawned upon the priest, and in thick gutturals besought the Holy One to sit at the horse-boys' fire.

'Go!' said Kim, pushing him lightly, and the lama strode away, leaving Kim at the edge of the cloister.

'Go!' said Mahbub Ali, returning to his hookah. 'Little Hindu, run away. God's curse on all unbelievers! Beg from those of my tail who are of thy faith.'

'Maharaj,' whined Kim, using the Hindu form of address, and thoroughly enjoying the situation; 'my father is dead – my mother is dead – my stomach is empty.'

'Beg from my men among the horses, I say. There must be some Hindus in my tail.'

'Oh, Mahbub Ali, but am *I* a Hindu?' said Kim in English.

The trader gave no sign of astonishment, but looked under shaggy eyebrows.

'Little Friend of all the World,' said he, 'what is this?'

'Nothing. I am now that holy man's disciple; and we go a pilgrimage together – to Benares, he says. He is quite mad, and I am tired of Lahore city. I wish new air and water.'

'But for whom dost thou work? Why come to me?' The voice was harsh with suspicion.

'To whom else should I come? I have no money. It is not good to go about without money. Thou wilt sell many horses to the officers. They are very fine horses, these new ones: I have seen them. Give me a rupee, Mahbub Ali, and when I come to my wealth I will give thee a bond and pay.'

'Um!' said Mahbub Ali, thinking swiftly. 'Thou hast never before lied to me. Call that lama – stand back in the dark.'

'Oh, our tales will agree,' said Kim, laughing.

'We go to Benares,' said the lama, as soon as he understood the drift of Mahbub Ali's questions. 'The boy and I. I go to seek for a certain River.'

'Maybe – but the boy?'

'He is my disciple. He was sent, I think, to guide me to that River. Sitting under a gun was I when he came suddenly. Such things have befallen the fortunate to whom guidance was allowed. But I remember now, he said he was of this world – a Hindu.'

'And his name?'

'That I did not ask. Is he not my disciple?'

'His country – his race – his village? Mussulman – Sikh – Hindu – Jain – low caste or high?'

'Why should I ask? There is neither high nor low in the Middle Way. If he is my *chela* – does – will – can any one take him from me? For, look you, without him I shall not find my River.' He wagged his head solemnly.

'None shall take him from thee. Go, sit among my Baltis,' said Mahbub Ali, and the lama drifted off, soothed by the promise.

'Is he not quite mad?' said Kim, coming forward to the light again. 'Why should I lie to thee, Hajji?'

Mahbub puffed his hookah in silence. Then he began, almost whispering: 'Umballa is on the road to Benares – if indeed ye two go there.'

'Tck! Tck! I tell thee he does not know how to lie – as we two know.'

'And if thou wilt carry a message for me as far as Umballa, I will give thee money. It concerns a horse – a white stallion which I have sold to an officer upon the last time I returned from the passes. But then – stand nearer and hold up hands as begging – the pedigree of the white stallion was not fully established, and that officer, who is now at Umballa, bade me make it clear.' (Mahbub here described the house and the appearance of the officer.) 'So the message to that officer will be: 'The pedigree of the white stallion is fully established.' By this will he know that thou comest from me. He will then say 'What proof hast thou?" and thou wilt answer: "Mahbub Ali has given me the proof."'

'And all for the sake of a white stallion,' said Kim, with a giggle, his eyes aflame.

'That pedigree I will give thee now – in my own fashion

32

– and some hard words as well.' A shadow passed behind Kim, and a feeding camel. Mahbub Ali raised his voice.

'Allah! Art thou the only beggar in the city? Thy mother is dead. Thy father is dead. So is it with all of them. Well, well –' He turned as feeling on the floor beside him and tossed a flap of soft, greasy Mussulman bread to the boy. 'Go and lie down among my horse-boys for tonight – thou and the lama. Tomorrow I may give thee service.'

Kim slunk away, his teeth in the bread, and, as he expected, he found a small wad of folded tissue-paper wrapped in oilskin, with three silver rupees – enormous largesse. He smiled and thrust money and paper into his leather amulet-case. The lama, sumptuously fed by Mahbub's Baltis, was already asleep in a corner of one of the stalls. Kim lay down beside him and laughed. He knew he had rendered a service to Mahbub Ali, and not for one little minute did he believe the tale of the stallion's pedigree.

But Kim did not suspect that Mahbub Ali, known as one of the best horse-dealers in the Punjab, a wealthy and enterprising trader, whose caravans penetrated far and far into the Back of Beyond, was registered in one of the locked books of the Indian Survey Department as C25 1B. Twice or thrice yearly C25 would send in a little story, baldly told but most interesting, and generally – it was checked by the statements of R17 and M4 – quite true. It concerned all manner of out-of-the-way mountain principalities, explorers of nationalities other than English, and the gun trade – was, in brief, a small portion of that vast mass of 'information received' on which the Indian

government acts. But, recently, five confederated kings, who had no business to confederate, had been informed by a kindly Northern Power that there was a leakage of news from their territories into British India. So those kings' prime ministers were seriously annoyed and took steps, after the oriental fashion. They suspected, among many others, the bullying, red-bearded horse-dealer whose caravans ploughed through their fastnesses belly-deep in snow. At least, his caravan that season had been ambushed and shot at twice on the way down, when Mahbub's men accounted for three strange ruffians who might, or might not, have been hired for the job. Therefore Mahbub had avoided halting at the insalubrious city of Peshawar, and had come through without stop to Lahore, where, knowing his country-people, he anticipated curious developments.

And there was that on Mahbub Ali which he did not wish to keep an hour longer than was necessary – a wad of closely folded tissue-paper, wrapped in oilskin – an impersonal, unaddressed statement, with five microscopic pin-holes in one corner, that most scandalously betrayed the five confederated kings, the sympathetic Northern Power, a Hindu banker in Peshawar, a firm of gun-makers in Belgium, and an important, semi-independent Muhammadan ruler to the south. This last was R17's work, which Mahbub had picked up beyond the Dora Pass and was carrying in for R17, who, owing to circumstances over which he had no control, could not leave his post of observation. Dynamite was milky and innocuous beside that report of C25; and even an Oriental, with an Oriental's views of the value of time, could see that the sooner it was in the proper hands the better.

34

Mahbub had no particular desire to die by violence, because two or three family blood-feuds across the border hung unfinished on his hands, and when these scores were cleared he intended to settle down as a more or less virtuous citizen. He had never passed the serai gate since his arrival two days ago, but had been ostentatious in sending telegrams to Bombay, where he banked some of his money; to Delhi, where a sub-partner of his own clan was selling horses to the agent of a Rajputana state; and to Umballa, where an Englishman was excitedly demanding the pedigree of a white stallion. The public letter-writer, who knew English, composed excellent telegrams, such as: – 'Creighton, Laurel Bank, Umballa. – Horse is Arabian as already advised. Sorrowful delayed pedigree which am translating.' And later to the same address: 'Much sorrowful delay. Will forward pedigree.' To his sub-partner at Delhi he wired: 'Lutuf Ullah. – Have wired two thousand rupees your credit Luchman Narain's bank.' This was entirely in the way of trade, but every one of those telegrams was discussed and re-discussed, by parties who conceived themselves to be interested, before they went over to the railway station in charge of a foolish Balti, who allowed all sorts of people to read them on the road.

When, in Mahbub's own picturesque language, he had muddied the wells of inquiry with the stick of precaution, Kim had dropped on him, sent from Heaven; and, being as prompt as he was unscrupulous, Mahbub Ali, used to taking all sorts of gusty chances, pressed him into service on the spot.

A wandering lama with a low-caste boy-servant might attract a moment's interest as they wandered about

India, the land of pilgrims; but no one would suspect them or, what was more to the point, rob.

He called for a new light-ball to his hookah, and considered the case. If the worst came to the worst, and the boy came to harm, the paper would incriminate nobody. And he would go up to Umballa leisurely and – at a certain risk of exciting fresh suspicion – repeat his tale by word of mouth to the people concerned.

But R17's report was the kernel of the whole affair, and it would be distinctly inconvenient if that failed to come to hand. However, God was great, and Mahbub Ali felt he had done all he could for the time being. Kim was the one soul in the world who had never told him a lie. That would have been a fatal blot on Kim's character if Mahbub had not known that to others, for his own ends or Mahbub's business, Kim could lie like an Oriental.

Then Mahbub Ali rolled across the serai to the Gate of the Harpies who paint their eyes and trap the stranger, and was at some pains to call on the one girl who, he had reason to believe, was a particular friend of a smooth-faced Kashmiri pundit who had waylaid his simple Balti in the matter of the telegrams. It was an utterly foolish thing to do; because they fell to drinking perfumed brandy against the Law of the Prophet, and Mahbub grew wonderfully drunk, and the gates of his mouth were loosened, and he pursued the Flower of Delight with the feet of intoxication till he fell flat among the cushions, where the Flower of Delight, aided by a smooth-faced Kashmiri pundit, searched him from head to foot most thoroughly.

About the same hour Kim heard soft feet in Mahbub's deserted stall. The horse-trader, curiously enough, had

left his door unlocked, and his men were busy celebrating their return to India with a whole sheep of Mahbub's bounty. A sleek young gentleman from Delhi, armed with a bunch of keys which the Flower had unshackled from the senseless one's belt, went through every single box, bundle, mat, and saddlebag in Mahbub's possession even more systematically than the Flower and the pundit were searching the owner.

'And I think,' said the Flower scornfully an hour later, one rounded elbow on the snoring carcass, 'that he is no more than a pig of an Afghan horse-dealer, with no thought except women and horses. Moreover, he may have sent it away by now – if ever there were such a thing.'

'Nay – in a matter touching Five Kings it would be next his black heart,' said the pundit. 'Was there nothing?'

The Delhi man laughed and resettled his turban as he entered. 'I searched between the soles of his slippers as the Flower searched his clothes. This is not the man but another. I leave little unseen.'

'They did not say he was the very man,' said the pundit thoughtfully. 'They said, "Look if he be the man, since our counsels are troubled."'

'That north country is full of horse-dealers as an old coat of lice. There is Sikander Khan, Nur Ali Beg, and Farrukh Shah – all heads of *kafilas* [caravans] – who deal there,' said the Flower.

'They have not yet come in,' said the pundit. 'Thou must ensnare them later.'

'Phew!' said the Flower with deep disgust, rolling Mahbub's head from her lap. 'I earn my money. Farrukh Shah is a bear, Ali Beg a swashbuckler, and old Sikander

37

Khan – yaie! Go! I sleep now. This swine will not stir till dawn.'

When Mahbub woke, the Flower talked to him severely on the sin of drunkenness. Asiatics do not wink when they have outmanoeuvred an enemy, but as Mahbub Ali cleared his throat, tightened his belt, and staggered forth under the early morning stars, he came very near to it.

'What a colt's trick!' said he to himself. 'As if every girl in Peshawar did not use it! But 'twas prettily done. Now God he knows how many more there be upon the Road who have orders to test me – perhaps with the knife. So it stands that the boy must go to Umballa – and by rail – for the writing is something urgent. I abide here, following the Flower and drinking wine as an Afghan coper should.'

He halted at the stall next but one to his own. His men lay there heavy with sleep. There was no sign of Kim or the lama.

'Up!' He stirred a sleeper. 'Whither went those who lay here last even – the lama and the boy? Is aught missing?'

'Nay,' grunted the man, 'the old madman rose at second cockcrow saying he would go to Benares, and the young one led him away.'

'The curse of Allah on all unbelievers!' said Mahbub heartily, and climbed into his own stall, growling in his beard.

But it was Kim who wakened the lama – Kim with one eye laid against a knot-hole in the planking, who had seen the Delhi man's search through the boxes. This was no common thief that turned over letters, bills, and saddles – no mere burglar who ran a little knife sideways

into the soles of Mahbub's slippers, or picked the seams of the saddlebags so deftly. At first Kim had been minded to give the alarm – the long-drawn *cho-or – choor!* [thief! thief!] that sets the serai ablaze of nights; but he looked more carefully, and, hand on amulet, drew his own conclusions.

'It must be the pedigree of that made-up horse lie,' said he, 'the thing that I carry to Umballa. Better that we go now. Those who search bags with knives may presently search bellies with knives. Surely there is a woman behind this. Hai! Hai!' in a whisper to the light-sleeping old man. 'Come. It is time – time to go to Benares.'

The lama rose obediently, and they passed out of the serai like shadows.

CHAPTER

2

And whoso will, from Pride released,
Contemning neither creed nor priest,
May feel the Soul of all the East
 About him at Kamakura.

 Buddha at Kamakura

They entered the fort-like railway station, black in the end of night; the electrics sizzling over the goods-yard where they handle the heavy northern grain traffic.

'This is the work of devils!' said the lama, recoiling from the hollow echoing darkness, the glimmer of rails between the masonry platforms, and the maze of girders above. He stood in a gigantic stone hall paved, it seemed, with the sheeted dead – third-class passengers who had taken their tickets overnight and were sleeping in the waiting-rooms. All hours of the twenty-four are alike to Orientals, and their passenger traffic is regulated accordingly.

'This is where the fire-carriages come. One stands behind that hole' – Kim pointed to the ticket-office – 'who will give thee a paper to take thee to Umballa.'

'But we go to Benares,' he replied petulantly.

'All one. Benares then. Quick: she comes!'

'Take thou the purse.'

The lama, not so well used to trains as he had pretended, started as the 3.25 a.m. southbound roared in. The sleepers sprang to life, and the station filled with

clamour and shoutings, cries of water and sweetmeat vendors, shouts of native policemen, and shrill yells of women gathering up their baskets, their families, and their husbands.

'It is the train – only the *te-rain*. It will not come here. Wait!' Amazed at the lama's immense simplicity (he had handed him a small bag full of rupees), Kim asked and paid for a ticket to Umballa. A sleepy clerk grunted and flung out a ticket to the next station, just six miles distant.

'Nay,' said Kim, scanning it with a grin. 'This may serve for farmers, but I live in the city of Lahore. It was cleverly done, babu. Now give the ticket to Umballa.'

The babu scowled and dealt the proper ticket.

'Now another to Amritzar,' said Kim, who had no notion of spending Mahbub Ali's money on anything so crude as a paid ride to Umballa. 'The price is so much. The small money in return is just so much. I know the ways of the *te-rain* . . . Never did yogi need *chela* as thou dost,' he went on merrily to the bewildered lama. 'They would have flung thee out at Mian Mir but for me. This way! Come!' He returned the money, keeping only one anna in each rupee of the price of the Umballa ticket as his commission – the immemorial commission of Asia.

The lama jibbed at the open door of a crowded third-class carriage. 'Were it not better to walk?' said he weakly.

A burly Sikh artisan thrust forth his bearded head. 'Is he afraid? Do not be afraid. I remember the time when *I* was afraid of the *te-rain*. Enter! This thing is the work of the government.'

'I do not fear,' said the lama. 'Have ye room within for two?'

'There is no room even for a mouse,' shrilled the wife of a well-to-do cultivator – a Hindu Jat from the rich Jullundur district. Our night trains are not as well looked after as the day ones, where the sexes are very strictly kept to separate carriages.

'Oh, mother of my son, we can make space,' said the blue-turbaned husband. 'Pick up the child. It is a holy man, seest thou?'

'And my lap full of seventy times seven bundles! Why not bid him sit on my knee, Shameless? But men are ever thus!' She looked round for approval. An Amritzar courtesan near the window sniffed behind her head drapery.

'Enter! Enter!' cried a fat Hindu moneylender, his folded account-book in a cloth under his arm. With an oily smirk: 'It is well to be kind to the poor.'

'Ay, at seven per cent a month with a mortgage on the unborn calf,' said a young Dogra soldier going south on leave; and they all laughed.

'Will it travel to Benares?' said the lama.

'Assuredly. Else why should we some? Enter, or we are left,' cried Kim.

'See!' shrilled the Amritzar girl. 'He has never entered a train. Oh, see!'

'Nay, help,' said the cultivator, putting out a large brown hand and hauling him in. 'Thus is it done, father.'

'But – but – I sit on the floor. It is against the Rule to sit on a bench,' said the lama. 'Moreover, it cramps me.'

'I say,' began the moneylender, pursing his lips, 'that there is not one rule of right living which these *te-rains* do not cause us to break. We sit, for example, side by side with all castes and peoples.'

'Yea, and with most outrageously shameless ones,' said the wife, scowling at the Amritzar girl making eyes at the young sepoy.

'I said we might have gone by cart along the road,' said the husband, 'and thus saved some money.'

'Yes – and spent twice over what we saved on food by the way. That was talked out ten thousand times.'

'Ay, by ten thousand tongues,' grunted he.

'The Gods help us poor women if we may not speak. Oho! He is of that sort which may not look at or reply to a woman.' For the lama, constrained by his Rule, took not the faintest notice of her. 'And his disciple is like him?'

'Nay, mother,' said Kim most promptly. 'Not when the woman is well-looking and above all charitable to the hungry.'

'A beggar's answer,' said the Sikh laughing. 'Thou hast brought it on thyself, sister!' Kim's hands were crooked in supplication.

'And whither goest thou?' said the woman, handing him the half of a cake from a greasy package.

'Even to Benares.'

'Jugglers belike?' the young soldier suggested. 'Have ye any tricks to pass the time? Why does not that yellow man answer?'

'Because,' said Kim stoutly, 'he is holy, and thinks upon matters hidden from thee.'

'That may be well. We of the Ludhiana Sikhs' – he rolled it out sonorously – 'do not trouble our heads with doctrine. We fight.'

'My sister's brother's son is *naik* [corporal] in that regiment,' said the Sikh craftsman quietly. 'There are also some Dogra companies there.' The soldier glared, for a

Dogra is of other caste than a Sikh, and the banker tittered.

'They are all one to me,' said the Amritzar girl.

'That we believe,' snorted the cultivator's wife malignantly.

'Nay, but all who serve the Sirkar with weapons in their hands are, as it were, one brotherhood. There is one brotherhood of the caste, but beyond that again' – she looked round timidly – 'the bond of the *pulton* – the regiment – eh?'

'My brother is in a Jat regiment,' said the cultivator. 'Dogras be good men.'

'*Thy* Sikhs at least were of that opinion,' said the soldier, with a scowl at the placid old man in the corner. '*Thy* Sikhs thought so when our two companies came to help them at the Pirzai Kotal in the face of eight Afridi standards on the ridge not three months gone.'

He told the story of a border action in which the Dogra companies of the Ludhiana Sikhs had acquitted themselves well. The Amritzar girl smiled; for she knew the tale was to win her approval.

'Alas!' said the cultivator's wife at the end. 'So their villages were burnt and their little children made homeless?'

'They had marked our dead. They paid a great payment after we of the Sikhs had schooled them. So it was. Is this Amritzar?'

'Ay, and here they cut our tickets,' said the banker, fumbling at his belt.

The lamps were paling in the dawn when the half-caste guard came round. Ticket-collecting is a slow business in

44

the East, where people secrete their tickets in all sorts of curious places. Kim produced his and was told to get out.

'But I go to Umballa,' he protested. 'I go with this holy man.'

'Thou canst go to Jehannum for aught I care. This ticket is only to Amritzar. Out!'

Kim burst into a flood of tears, protesting that the lama was his father and his mother, that he was the prop of the lama's declining years, and that the lama would die without his care. All the carriage bade the guard be merciful – the banker was specially eloquent here – but the guard hauled Kim on to the platform. The lama blinked – he could not overtake the situation – and Kim lifted up his voice and wept outside the carriage window.

'I am very poor. My father is dead – my mother is dead. O charitable ones, if I am left here, who shall tend that old man?'

'What – what is this?' the lama repeated. 'He must go to Benares. He must come with me. He is my *chela*. If there is money to be paid –'

'Oh, be silent,' whispered Kim; 'are we rajahs to throw away good silver when the world is so charitable?'

The Amritzar girl stepped out with her bundles and it was on her that Kim kept his watchful eye. Ladies of that persuasion, he knew, were generous.

'A ticket – a little *tikkut* to Umballa – O Breaker of Hearts!' She laughed. 'Hast thou no charity?'

'Does the holy man come from the north?'

'From far and far in the north he comes,' cried Kim. 'From among the hills.'

'There is snow among the pine-trees in the north – in

the hills there is snow. My mother was from Kulu. Get thee a ticket. Ask him for a blessing.'

'Ten thousand blessings,' shrilled Kim. 'O Holy One, a woman has given us in charity so that I can come with thee – a woman with a golden heart. I run for the *tikkut*.'

The girl looked up at the lama, who had mechanically followed Kim to the platform. He bowed his head that he might not see her, and muttered in Tibetan as she passed on with the crowd.

'Light come – light go,' said the cultivator's wife viciously.

'She has acquired merit,' returned the lama. 'Beyond doubt it was a nun.'

'There be ten thousand such nuns in Amritzar alone. Return, old man, or the *te-rain* may depart without thee,' cried the banker.

'Not only was it sufficient for the ticket, but for a little food also,' said Kim, leaping to his place. 'Now eat, Holy One. Look. Day comes!'

Golden, rose, saffron, and pink, the morning mists smoked away across the flat green levels. All the rich Punjab lay out in the splendour of the keen sun. The lama flinched a little as the telegraph-posts swung by.

'Great is the speed of the *te-rain*,' said the banker, with a patronizing grin. 'We have gone farther since Lahore than thou couldst walk in two days: at even, we shall enter Umballa.'

'And that is still far from Benares,' said the lama wearily, mumbling over the cakes that Kim offered. They all unloosed their bundles and made their morning meal. Then the banker, the cultivator, and the soldier prepared their pipes and wrapped the compartment in choking,

acrid smoke, spitting and coughing and enjoying them-selves. The Sikh and the cultivator's wife chewed *pan*; the lama took snuff and told his beads, while Kim, cross-legged, smiled over the comfort of a full stomach.

'What rivers have ye by Benares?' said the lama of a sudden to the carriage at large.

'We have Gunga,' returned the banker, when the little titter had subsided.

'What others?'

'What other than Gunga?'

'Nay, but in my mind was the thought of a certain River of healing.'

'That is Gunga. Who bathes in her is made clean and goes to the Gods. Thrice have I made pilgrimage to Gunga.' He looked round proudly.

'There was need,' said the young sepoy drily, and the travellers' laugh turned against the banker.

'Clean – to return again to the Gods,' the lama muttered. 'And to go forth on the round of lives anew – still tied to the Wheel.' He shook his head testily. 'But maybe there is a mistake. Who, then, made Gunga in the beginning?'

'The Gods. Of what known faith art thou?' the banker said, appalled.

'I follow the Law – the Most Excellent Law. So it was the Gods that made Gunga. What like of Gods were they?'

The carriage looked at him in amazement. It was inconceivable that any one should be ignorant of Gunga.

'What – what is thy God?' said the moneylender at last.

'Hear!' said the lama, shifting the rosary to his hand.

'Hear: for I speak of him now! O people of Hind, listen!'

He began in Urdu the tale of the Lord Buddha, but, borne by his own thoughts, slid into Tibetan and long-droned texts from a Chinese book of the Buddha's life. The gentle, tolerant folk looked on reverently. All India is full of holy men stammering gospels in strange tongues; shaken and consumed in the fires of their own zeal; dreamers, babblers, and visionaries: as it has been from the beginning and will continue to the end.

'Um!' said the soldier of the Ludhiana Sikhs. 'There was a Muhammadan regiment lay next to us at the Pirzai Kotal, and a priest of theirs – he was, as I remember, a *naik* – when the fit was on him, spake prophecies. But the mad all are in God's keeping. His officers overlooked much in that man.'

The lama fell back on Urdu, remembering that he was in a strange land. 'Hear the tale of the Arrow which our Lord loosed from the bow,' he said.

This was much more to their taste, and they listened curiously while he told it. 'Now, O people of Hind, I go to seek that River. Know ye aught that may guide me, for we be all men and women in evil case.'

'There is Gunga – and Gunga alone – who washes away sin,' ran the murmur round the carriage.

'Though past question we have good Gods Jullundur way,' said the cultivator's wife, looking out of the window. 'See how they have blessed the crops.'

'To search every river in the Punjab is no small matter,' said her husband. 'For me, a stream that leaves good silt on my land suffices, and I thank Bhumia, the God of the Homestead.' He shrugged one knotted, bronzed shoulder.

'Think you our Lord came so far north?' said the lama turning to Kim.

'It may be,' Kim replied soothingly, as he spat red *pan* juice on the floor.

'The last of the Great Ones,' said the Sikh with authority, 'was Sikander Julkarn [Alexander the Great]. He paved the streets of Jullundur and built a great tank near Umballa. That pavement holds to this day; and the tank is there also. I never heard of thy God.'

'Let thy hair grow long and talk Punjabi,' said the young soldier jestingly to Kim, quoting a northern proverb. 'That is all that makes a Sikh.' But he did not say this very loud.

The lama sighed and shrank into himself, a dingy, shapeless mass. In the pauses of their talk they could hear the low droning – '*Om mane pudme hum! Om mane pudme hum!*' – and the thick click of the wooden rosary beads.

'It irks me,' he said at last. 'The speed and the clatter irk me. Moreover, my *chela*, I think that maybe we have overpassed that River.'

'Peace, peace,' said Kim. 'Was not the River near Benares? We are yet far from the place.'

'But – if our Lord came north, it may be any one of these little ones that we have run across.'

'I do not know.'

'But thou wast sent to me – wast thou sent to me? – for the merit I had acquired over yonder at Such-zen. From beside the cannon didst thou come – bearing two faces – and two garbs.'

'Peace. One must not speak of these things here,' whispered Kim. 'There was but one of me. Think again

49

and thou wilt remember. A boy – a Hindu boy – by the great green cannon.'

'But was there not also an Englishman with a white beard – holy among images – who himself made more sure my assurance of the River of the Arrow?'

'He – we – went to the Ajaib-Gher in Lahore to pray before the Gods there,' Kim explained to the openly listening company. 'And the sahib of the Wonder House talked to him – yes, this is truth – as a brother. He is a very holy man, from far beyond the Hills. Rest, thou. In time we come to Umballa.'

'But my River – the River of my healing?'

'And then, if it please thee, we will go hunting for that River on foot. So that we miss nothing – not even a little rivulet in a field-side.'

'But thou hast a Search of thine own?' The lama – very pleased that he remembered so well – sat bolt upright.

'Ay,' said Kim, humouring him. The boy was entirely happy to be out chewing *pan* and seeing new people in the great good-tempered world.

'It was a bull – a Red Bull that shall come and help thee – and carry thee – whither? I have forgotten. A Red Bull on a green field, was it not?'

'Nay, it will carry me nowhere,' said Kim. 'It is but a tale I told thee.'

'What is this?' The cultivator's wife leaned forward, her bracelets clinking on her arm. 'Do ye both dream dreams? A Red Bull on a green field, that shall carry thee to the heavens – or what? Was it a vision? Did one make a prophecy? *We* have a Red Bull in our village behind Jullundur city, and he grazes by choice in the very greenest of our fields!'

'Give a woman an old wife's tale and a weaver bird a leaf and a thread, they will weave wonderful things,' said the Sikh. 'All holy men dream dreams, and by following holy men their disciples attain that power.'

'A Red Bull on a green field, was it?' the lama repeated. 'In a former life it may be thou hast acquired merit, and the Bull will come to reward thee.'

'Nay – nay – it was but a tale one told to me – for a jest belike. But I will seek the Bull about Umballa, and thou canst look for thy River and rest from the clatter of the train.'

'It may be that the Bull knows – that he is sent to guide us both,' said the lama, hopefully as a child. Then to the company, indicating Kim: 'This one was sent to me but yesterday. He is not, I think, of this world.'

'Beggars a plenty have I met, and holy men to boot, but never such a yogi nor such a disciple,' said the woman.

Her husband touched his forehead lightly with one finger and smiled. But the next time the lama would eat they took care to give him of their best.

And at last – tired, sleepy, and dusty – they reached Umballa city station.

'We abide here upon a lawsuit,' said the cultivator's wife to Kim. 'We lodge with my man's cousin's younger brother. There is room also in the courtyard for thy yogi and for thee. Will – will he give me a blessing?'

'O holy man! A woman with a heart of gold gives us lodging for the night. It is a kindly land, this land of the south. See how we have been helped since the dawn!'

The lama bowed his head in benediction.

'To fill my cousin's younger brother's house with

wastrels –' the husband began, as he shouldered his heavy bamboo staff.

'Thy cousin's younger brother owes my father's cousin something yet on his daughter's marriage-feast,' said the woman crisply. 'Let him put their food to that account. The yogi will beg, I doubt not.'

'Ay, I beg for him,' said Kim, anxious only to get the lama under shelter for the night, that he might seek Mahbub Ali's Englishman and deliver himself of the white stallion's pedigree.

'Now,' said he, when the lama had come to an anchor in the inner courtyard of a decent Hindu house behind the cantonments, 'I go away for a while – to – to buy us victual in the bazaar. Do not stray abroad till I return.'

'Thou wilt return? Thou wilt surely return?' The old man caught at his wrist. 'And thou wilt return in this very same shape? Is it too late to look tonight for the River?'

'Too late and too dark. Be comforted. Think how far thou art on the road – an hundred miles from Lahore already.'

'Yea – and farther from my monastery. Alas! It is a great and terrible world.'

Kim stole out and away, as unremarkable a figure as ever carried his own and a few score thousand other folk's fate slung round his neck. Mahbub Ali's directions left him little doubt of the house in which his Englishman lived; and a groom, bringing a dog-cart home from the club, made him quite sure. It remained only to identify his man, and Kim slipped through the garden hedge and hid in a clump of plumed grass close to the veranda. The house blazed with lights, and servants moved about tables dressed with flowers, glass and silver. Presently

forth came an Englishman, dressed in black and white, humming a tune. It was too dark to see his face, so Kim, beggarwise, tried an old experiment.

'Protector of the Poor!'

The man backed towards the voice.

'Mahbub Ali says –'

'Hah! What says Mahbub Ali?' He made no attempt to look for the speaker, and that showed Kim that he knew.

'The pedigree of the white stallion is fully established.'

'What proof is there?' The Englishman switched at the rose hedge in the side of the drive.

'Mahbub Ali has given me this proof.' Kim flipped the wad of folded paper into the air, and it fell on the path beside the man, who put his foot on it as a gardener came round the corner. When the servant passed he picked it up, dropped a rupee – Kim could hear the clink – and strode into the house, never turning round. Swiftly Kim took up the money; but, for all his training, he was Irish enough by birth to reckon silver the least part of any game. What he desired was the visible effect of action; so, instead of slinking away, he lay close in the grass and wormed nearer to the house.

He saw – Indian bungalows are open through and through – the Englishman return to a small dressing-room, in a corner of the veranda, that was half office, littered with papers and despatch-boxes, and sit down to study Mahbub Ali's message. His face, by the full ray of the kerosene lamp, changed and darkened, and Kim, used as every beggar must be to watching countenances, took good note.

'Will! Will, dear!' called a woman's voice. 'You ought to be in the drawing-room. They'll be here in a minute.'

The man still read intently.

'Will!' said the voice, five minutes later. '*He*'s come. I can hear the troopers in the drive.'

The man dashed out bareheaded as a big landau with four native troopers behind it halted at the veranda, and a tall, black-haired man, erect as an arrow, swung out, preceded by a young officer who laughed pleasantly.

Flat on his belly lay Kim, almost touching the high wheels. His man and the black stranger exchanged two sentences.

'Certainly, sir,' said the young officer promptly. 'Everything waits while a horse is concerned.'

'We shan't be more than twenty minutes,' said Kim's man. 'You can do the honours – keep 'em amused, and all that.'

'Tell one of the troopers to wait,' said the tall man, and they both passed into the dressing-room together as the landau rolled away. Kim saw their heads bent over Mahbub Ali's message, and heard the voices – one low and deferential, the other sharp and decisive.

'It isn't a question of weeks. It is a question of days – hours almost,' said the elder. 'I'd been expecting it for some time, but this' – he tapped Mahbub Ali's paper – 'clinches it. Grogan's dining here tonight, isn't he?'

'Yes, sir, and Macklin too.'

'Very good. I'll speak to them myself. The matter will be referred to the Council, of course, but this is a case where one is justified in assuming that we take action at once. Warn the Pindi and Peshawar brigades. It will disorganize all the summer reliefs, but we can't help that. This comes of not smashing them thoroughly the first time. Eight thousand should be enough.'

'What about artillery, sir?'

'I must consult Macklin.'

'Then it means war?'

'No. Punishment. When a man is bound by the action of his predecessor –'

'But C25 may have lied.'

'He bears out the other's information. Practically, they showed their hand six months back. But Devenish would have it there was a chance of peace. Of course they used it to make themselves stronger. Send off those telegrams at once – the new code, not the old – mine and Wharton's. I don't think we need keep the ladies waiting any longer. We can settle the rest over the cigars. I thought it was coming. It's punishment – not war.'

As the trooper cantered off, Kim crawled round to the back of the house, where, going on his Lahore experiences, he judged there would be food – and information. The kitchen was crowded with excited scullions, one of whom kicked him.

'Aie,' said Kim, feigning tears. 'I came only to wash dishes in return for a bellyful.'

'All Umballa is on the same errand. Get hence. They go in now with the soup. Think you that we who serve Creighton Sahib need strange scullions to help us through a big dinner?'

'It is a very big dinner,' said Kim, looking at the plates.

'Small wonder. The guest of honour is none other than the Jang-i-Lat-Sahib [the Commander-in-Chief] '

'Ho!' said Kim, with the correct guttural note of wonder. He had learned what he wanted, and when the scullion turned he was gone.

'And all that trouble,' said he to himself, thinking as

usual in Hindustani, 'for a horse's pedigree! Mahbub Ali should have come to me to learn a little lying. Every time before that I have borne a message it concerned a woman. Now it is men. Better. The tall man said that they will loose a great army to punish some one – somewhere – the news goes to Pindi and Peshawar. There are also guns. Would I had crept nearer. It is big news!'

He returned to find the cultivator's cousin's younger brother discussing the family lawsuit in all its bearings with the cultivator and his wife and a few friends, while the lama dozed. After the evening meal some one passed him a water-pipe; and Kim felt very much of a man as he pulled at the smooth coconut-shell, his legs spread abroad in the moonlight, his tongue clicking in remarks from time to time. His hosts were most polite; for the cultivator's wife had told them of his vision of the Red Bull, and of his probable descent from another world. Moreover, the lama was a great and venerable curiosity. The family priest, an old, tolerant Sarsut Brahmin, dropped in later, and naturally started a theological argument to impress the family. By creed, of course, they were all on their priest's side, but the lama was the guest and the novelty. His gentle kindliness, and his impressive Chinese quotations, that sounded like spells, delighted them hugely; and in this sympathetic, simple air, he expanded like the Bodhisat's own lotus, speaking of his life in the great hills of Such-zen, before, as he said, 'I rose up to seek enlightenment.'

Then it came out that in those worldly days he had been a master-hand at casting horoscopes and nativities; and the family priest led him on to describe his methods; each giving the planets names that the others could not

understand, and pointing upwards as the big stars sailed across the dark. The children of the house tugged un-rebuked at his rosary; and he clean forgot the Rule which forbids looking at women as he talked of enduring snows, landslips, blocked passes, the remote cliffs where men find sapphires and turquoise, and that wonderful upland road that leads at last into Great China itself.

'How thinkest thou of this one?' said the cultivator aside to the priest.

'A holy man – a holy man indeed. His Gods are not the Gods, but his feet are upon the Way,' was the answer. 'And his methods of nativities, though that is beyond thee, are wise and sure.'

'Tell me,' said Kim lazily, 'whether I find my Red Bull on a green field, as was promised me.'

'What knowledge hast thou of thy birth hour?' the priest asked, swelling with importance.

'Between first and second cockcrow of the first night in May.'

'Of what year?'

'I do not know; but upon the hour that I cried first fell the great earthquake in Srinagar which is in Kashmir.' This Kim had from the woman who took care of him, and she again from Kimball O'Hara. The earthquake had been felt in India, and for long stood a leading date in the Punjab.

'Ai!' said a woman excitedly. This seemed to make Kim's supernatural origin more certain. 'Was not such an one's daughter born then –'

'And her mother bore her husband four sons in four years – all likely boys,' cried the cultivator's wife, sitting outside the circle in the shadow.

'None reared in the knowledge,' said the family priest, 'forget how the planets stood in their houses upon that night.' He began to draw in the dust of the courtyard. 'At least thou hast good claim to a half of the House of the Bull. How runs thy prophecy?'

'Upon a day,' said Kim, delighted at the sensation he was creating, 'I shall be made great by means of a Red Bull on a green field, but first there will enter two men making all things ready.'

'Yes: thus ever at the opening of a vision. A thick darkness that clears slowly; anon one enters with a broom making ready the place. Then begins the Sight. Two men – thou sayest? Ay, ay. The sun, leaving the House of the Bull, enters that of the Twins. Hence the two men of the prophecy. Let us now consider. Fetch me a twig, little one.'

He knitted his brows, scratched, smoothed out, and scratched again in the dust mysterious signs – to the wonder of all save the lama, who, with fine instinct, forbore to interfere.

At the end of half an hour, he tossed the twig from him with a grunt.

'Hm! Thus say the stars. Within three days come the two men to make all things ready. After them follows the Bull; but the sign over against him is the sign of war and armed men.'

'There was indeed a man of the Ludhiana Sikhs in the carriage from Lahore,' said the cultivator's wife hopefully.

'Tck! Armed men – many hundreds. What concern hast thou with war?' said the priest to Kim. 'Thine is a red and angry sign of war to be loosed very soon.'

'None – none,' said the lama earnestly. 'We seek only peace and our River.'

Kim smiled, remembering what he had overheard in the dressing-room. Decidedly he was a favourite of the stars.

The priest brushed his foot over the rude horoscope. 'More than this I cannot see. In three days comes the Bull to thee, boy.'

'And my River, my River,' pleaded the lama. 'I had hoped his Bull would lead us both to the River.'

'Alas, for that wondrous River, my brother,' the priest replied. 'Such things are not common.'

Next morning, though they were pressed to stay, the lama insisted on departure. They gave Kim a large bundle of good food and nearly three annas in copper money for the needs of the road, and with many blessings watched the two go southward in the dawn.

'Pity it is that these and such as these could not be freed from the Wheel of Things,' said the lama.

'Nay, then would only evil people be left on the earth, and who would give us meat and shelter?' quoth Kim, stepping merrily under his burden.

'Yonder is a small stream. Let us look,' said the lama, and he led from the white road across the fields; walking into a very hornets'-nest of pariah dogs.

CHAPTER

3

Yea, voice of every Soul that clung
To Life that strove from rung to rung
When Devadatta's rule was young,
 The warm wind brings Kamakura.

Buddha at Kamakura

Behind them an angry farmer brandished a bamboo pole. He was a market-gardener, Arain by caste, growing vegetables and flowers for Umballa city, and well Kim knew the breed.

'Such an one,' said the lama, disregarding the dogs, 'is impolite to strangers, intemperate of speech and uncharitable. Be warned by his demeanour, my disciple.'

'Ho, shameless beggars!' shouted the farmer. 'Begone! Get hence!'

'We go,' the lama returned, with quiet dignity. 'We go from these unblessed fields.'

'Ah,' said Kim, sucking in his breath. 'If the next crops fail, thou canst only blame thine own tongue.'

The man shuffled uneasily in his slippers. 'The land is full of beggars,' he began, half apologetically.

'And by what sign didst thou know that we would beg from thee,'O Mali?' said Kim tartly, using the name that a market-gardener least likes. 'All we sought was to look at that river beyond the field there.'

'River, forsooth!' the man snorted. 'What city do ye hail from not to know a canal-cut? It runs as straight as an

arrow, and I pay for the water as though it were molten silver. There is a branch of a river beyond. But if ye need water I can give that – and milk.'

'Nay, we will go to the river,' said the lama, striding out.

'Milk and a meal,' the man stammered, as he looked at the strange tall figure. 'I – I would not draw evil upon myself – or my crops. But beggars are so many in these hard days.'

'Take notice.' The lama turned to Kim. 'He was led to speak harshly by the red mist of anger. That clearing from his eyes, he becomes courteous and of an affable heart. May his fields be blessed! Beware not to judge men too hastily, O farmer.'

'I have met holy ones who would have cursed thee from hearthstone to byre,' said Kim to the abashed man. 'Is he not wise and holy? I am his disciple.'

He cocked his nose in the air loftily and stepped across the narrow field borders with great dignity.

'There is no pride,' said the lama, after a pause, 'there is no pride among such as follow the Middle Way.'

'But thou hast said he was low-caste and discourteous.'

'Low-caste I did not say, for how can that be which is not? Afterwards he amended his discourtesy, and I forgot the offence. Moreover, he is as we are, bound upon the Wheel of Things; but he does not tread the way of deliverance.' He halted at a little runlet among the fields, and considered the hoof-pitted bank.

'Now, how wilt thou know thy River?' said Kim, squatting in the shade of some tall sugarcane.

'When I find it, an enlightenment will surely be given. This, I feel, is not the place. O littlest among the waters, if

only thou couldst tell me where runs my River! But be thou blessed to make the fields bear!'

'Look! Look!' Kim sprang to his side and dragged him back. A yellow-and-brown streak glided from the purple rustling stems to the bank, stretched its neck to the water, drank, and lay still – a big cobra with fixed, lidless eyes.

'I have no stick – I have no stick,' said Kim. 'I will get me one and break his back.'

'Why? He is upon the Wheel as we are – a life ascending or descending – very far from deliverance. Great evil must the soul have done that is cast into this shape.'

'I hate all snakes,' said Kim. No native training can quench the white man's horror of the serpent.

'Let him live out his life.' The coiled thing hissed and half opened its hood. 'May thy release come soon, brother!' the lama continued placidly. 'Hast *thou* knowledge, by chance, of my River?'

'Never have I seen such a man as thou art,' Kim whispered, overwhelmed. 'Do the very snakes understand thy talk?'

'Who knows?' He passed within a foot of the cobra's poised head. It flattened itself among the dusty coils.

'Come, thou!' he called over his shoulder.

'Not I,' said Kim. 'I go round.'

'Come. He does no hurt.'

Kim hesitated for a moment. The lama backed his order by some droned Chinese quotation which Kim took for a charm. He obeyed and bounded across the rivulet, and the snake, indeed, made no sign.

'Never have I seen such a man.' Kim wiped the sweat from his forehead. 'And now, whither go we?'

'That is for thee to say. I am old, and a stranger – far

from my own place. But that the *rêl*-carriage fills my he\
with noises of devil drums I would go in it to Benares now\
. . . Yet by so going we may miss the River. Let us find
another river.'

Where the hard-worked soil gives three and even four
crops a year – through patches of sugarcane, tobacco,
long white radishes, and nol-kol, all that day they
strolled on, turning aside to every glimpse of water;
rousing village dogs and sleeping villages at noonday;
the lama replying to the volleyed questions with an
unswerving simplicity. They sought a River – a River of
miraculous healing. Had any one knowledge of such a
stream? Sometimes men laughed, but more often heard
the story out to the end and offered them a place in the
shade, a drink of milk, and a meal. The women were
always kind, and the little children as children are the
world over, alternately shy and venturesome. Evening
found them at rest under the village tree of a mud-walled,
mud-roofed hamlet, talking to the headman as the cattle
came in from the grazing grounds and the women pre-
pared the day's last meal. They had passed beyond
the belt of market-gardens round hungry Umballa,
and were among the mile-wide green of the staple
crops.

He was a white-bearded and affable elder, used to
entertaining strangers. He dragged out a string bed-
stead for the lama, set warm cooked food before him,
prepared him a pipe, and, the evening ceremonies
being finished in the village temple, sent for the village
priest.

Kim told the older children tales of the size and beauty
of Lahore, of railway travel, and such-like city things,

while the men talked, slowly as their cattle chew the cud.

'I cannot fathom it,' said the headman at last to the priest. 'How readest thou this talk?' The lama, his tale told, was silently telling his beads.

'He is a Seeker,' the priest answered. 'The land is full of such. Remember him who came only last month – the *fakir* with the tortoise?'

'Ay, but that man had right and reason, for Krishna himself appeared in a vision promising him Paradise without the burning-pyre if he journeyed to Prayag. This man seeks no god who is within my knowledge.'

'Peace, he is old: he comes from far off, and he is mad,' the smooth-shaven priest replied. 'Hear me.' He turned to the lama. 'Three *koss* [six miles] to the westward runs the great road to Calcutta.'

'But I would go to Benares – to Benares.'

'And to Benares also. It crosses all streams on this side of Hind. Now my word to thee, Holy One, is rest here till tomorrow. Then take the road' (it was the Grand Trunk Road he meant) 'and test each stream that it overpasses; for, as I understand, the virtue of thy River lies neither in one pool nor place, but throughout its length. Then, if thy Gods will, be assured that thou wilt come upon thy freedom.'

'That is well said.' The lama was much impressed by the plan. 'We will begin tomorrow, and a blessing on thee for showing old feet such a near road.' A deep, singsong Chinese half-chant closed the sentence. Even the priest was impressed, and the headman feared an evil spell: but none could look at the lama's simple, eager face and doubt him long.

'Seest thou my *chela*?' he said, diving into his snuff-

gourd with an important sniff. It was his duty to repay courtesy with courtesy.

'I see – and hear.' The headman rolled his eye where Kim was chatting to a girl in blue as she laid crackling thorns on a fire.

'He also has a Search of his own. No river, but a Bull. Yea, a Red Bull on a green field will some day raise him to honour. He is, I think, not altogether of this world. He was sent of a sudden to aid me in this search, and his name is Friend of all the World.'

The priest smiled. 'Ho, there, Friend of all the World,' he cried across the sharp-smelling smoke, 'what art thou?'

'This Holy One's disciple,' said Kim.

'He says thou art a *būt* [a spirit].'

'Can *būts* eat?' said Kim, with a twinkle. 'For I am hungry.'

'It is no jest,' cried the lama. 'A certain astrologer of that city whose name I have forgotten –'

'That is no more than the city of Umballa where we slept last night,' Kim whispered to the priest.

'Ay, Umballa was it? He cast a horoscope and declared that my *chela* should find his desire within two days. But what said he of the meaning of the stars, Friend of all the World?'

Kim cleared his throat and looked around at the village grey-beards.

'The meaning of my star is war,' he replied pompously.

Somebody laughed at the little tattered figure strutting on the brickwork plinth under the great tree. Where a native would have lain down, Kim's white blood set him upon his feet.

65

'Ay, war,' he answered.

'That is a sure prophecy,' rumbled a deep voice. 'For there is always war along the border – as I know.'

It was an old, withered man, who had served the government in the days of the Mutiny as a native officer in a newly raised cavalry regiment. The government had given him a good holding in the village, and though the demands of his sons, now grey-bearded officers on their own account, had impoverished him, he was still a person of consequence. English officials – deputy commissioners even – turned aside from the main road to visit him, and on those occasions he dressed himself in the uniform of ancient days, and stood up like a ramrod.

'But this shall be a great war – a war of eight thousand.' Kim's voice shrilled across the quick-gathering crowd, astonishing himself.

'Redcoats or our own regiments?' the old man snapped, as though he were asking an equal. His tone made men respect Kim.

'Redcoats,' said Kim at a venture. 'Redcoats and guns.'

'But – but the astrologer said no word of this,' cried the lama, snuffing prodigiously in his excitement.

'But I know. The word has come to me, who am this Holy One's disciple. There will rise a war – a war of eight thousand redcoats. From Pindi and Peshawar they will be drawn. This is sure.'

'The boy has heard bazaar-talk,' said the priest.

'But he was always by my side,' said the lama. 'How should he know? *I* did not know.'

'He will make a clever juggler when the old man is dead,' muttered the priest to the headman. 'What new trick is this?'

66

'A sign. Give me a sign,' thundered the old soldier suddenly. 'If there were war my sons would have told me.'

'When all is ready, thy sons, doubt not, will be told. But it is a long road from thy sons to the man in whose hands these things lie.' Kim warmed to the game, for it reminded him of experiences in the letter-carrying line, when, for the sake of a few pice, he pretended to know more than he knew. But now he was playing for larger things – the sheer excitement and the sense of power. He drew a new breath and went on.

'Old man, give *me* a sign. Do underlings order the goings of eight thousand redcoats – with guns?'

'No.' Still the old man answered as though Kim were an equal.

'Dost thou know who he is, then, that gives the order?'

'I have seen him.'

'To know again?'

'I have known him since he was a lieutenant in the *top-khana* [the artillery].'

'A tall man. A tall man with black hair, walking thus?' Kim took a few paces in a stiff, wooden style.

'Ay. But that any one may have seen.' The crowd were breathless-still through all this talk.

'That is true,' said Kim. 'But I will say more. Look now. First the great man walks thus. Then he thinks thus.' (Kim drew a forefinger over his forehead and downwards till it came to rest by the angle of the jaw.) 'Anon he twitches his fingers thus. Anon he thrusts his hat under his left armpit.' Kim illustrated the motion and stood like a stork.

The old man groaned, inarticulate with amazement; and the crowd shivered.

'So – so – so. But what does he when he is about to give an order?'

'He rubs the skin at the back of his neck – thus. Then falls one finger on the table and he makes a small sniffing noise through his nose. Then he speaks, saying: "Loose such and such a regiment. Call out such guns."'

The old man rose stiffly and saluted.

'"For"' – Kim translated into the vernacular the clinching sentences he had heard in the dressing-room at Umballa – '"For," says he, "we should have done this long ago. It is not war – it is a chastisement. Snff!"'

'Enough. I believe. I have seen him thus in the smoke of battles. Seen and heard. It is he!'

'I saw no smoke' – Kim's voice shifted to the rapt sing-song of the wayside fortune-teller. 'I saw this in darkness. First came a man to make things clear. Then came horsemen. Then came he, standing in a ring of light. The rest followed as I have said. Old man, have I spoken truth?'

'It is he. Past all doubt it is he.'

The crowd drew a long, quavering breath, staring alternately at the old man, still at attention, and ragged Kim against the purple twilight.

'Said I not – said I not he was from the other world?' cried the lama proudly. 'He is the Friend of all the World. He is the Friend of the Stars!'

'At least it does not concern us,' a man cried. 'O thou young soothsayer, if the gift abides with thee at all seasons, I have a red-spotted cow. She may be sister to thy Bull for aught I know –'

'Or I care,' said Kim. 'My stars do not concern themselves with thy cattle.'

'Nay, but she is very sick,' a woman struck in. 'My man is a buffalo, or he would have chosen his words better. Tell me if she recover?'

Had Kim been at all an ordinary boy, he would have carried on the play; but one does not know Lahore city, and least of all the *fakirs* by the Taksali Gate, for thirteen years without also knowing human nature.

The priest looked at him sideways, something bitterly – a dry and blighting smile.

'Is there no priest, then, in the village? I thought I had seen a great one even now,' cried Kim.

'Ay – but –' the woman began.

'But thou and thy husband hoped to get the cow cured for a handful of thanks.' The shot told: they were notoriously the closest-fisted couple in the village. 'It is not well to cheat the temples. Give a young calf to thine own priest, and, unless thy Gods are angry past recall, she will give milk within a month.'

'A master-beggar art thou,' purred the priest approvingly. 'Not the cunning of forty years could have done better. Surely thou hast made the old man rich?'

'A little flour, a little butter and a mouthful of cardamoms.' Kim retorted, flushed with the praise, but still cautious – 'Does one grow rich on that? And, as thou canst see, he is mad. But it serves me while I learn the road at least.'

He knew what the *fakirs* of the Taksali Gate were like when they talked among themselves, and copied the very inflection of their lewd disciples.

'Is his Search, then, truth or a cloak to other ends? It may be treasure.'

'He is mad – many times mad. There is nothing else.'

Here the old soldier hobbled up and asked if Kim would accept his hospitality for the night. The priest recommended him to do so, but insisted that the honour of entertaining the lama belonged to the temple – at which the lama smiled guilelessly. Kim glanced from one face to the other, and drew his own conclusions.

'Where is the money?' he whispered, beckoning the old man off into the darkness.

'In my bosom. Where else?'

'Give it me. Quietly and swiftly give it me.'

'But why? Here is no ticket to buy.'

'Am I thy *chela*, or am I not? Do I not safeguard thy old feet about the ways? Give me the money and at dawn I will return it.' He slipped his hand above the lama's girdle and brought away the purse.

'Be it so – be it so.' The old man nodded his head. 'This is a great and terrible world. I never knew there were so many men alive in it.'

Next morning the priest was in a very bad temper, but the lama was quite happy; and Kim had enjoyed a most interesting evening with the old man, who brought out his cavalry sabre and, balancing it on his dry knees, told tales of the Mutiny and young captains thirty years in their graves, till Kim dropped off to sleep.

'Certainly the air of this country is good,' said the lama. 'I sleep lightly, as do all old men; but last night I slept unwaking till broad day. Even now I am heavy.'

'Drink a draught of hot milk,' said Kim, who had

70

carried not a few such remedies to opium-smokers of his acquaintance. 'It is time to take the Road again.'

'The long Road that overpasses all the rivers of Hind,' said the lama gaily. 'Let us go. But how thinkest thou, *chela*, to recompense these people, and especially the priest, for their great kindness? Truly they are *būt-parast*, but in other lives, maybe, they will receive enlightenment. A rupee to the temple? The thing which is no more than stone and red paint, but the heart of man we must acknowledge when and where it is good.'

'Holy One, hast thou ever taken the Road alone?' Kim looked up sharply, like the Indian crows so busy about the fields.

'Surely, child: from Kulu to Pathânkot – from Kulu, where my first *chela* died. When men were kind to us we made offerings, and all men were well-disposed throughout all the Hills.'

'It is otherwise in Hind,' said Kim drily. 'Their Gods are many-armed and malignant. Let them alone.'

'I would set thee on thy road for a little, Friend of all the World – thou and thy yellow man.' The old soldier ambled up the village street, all shadowy in the dawn, on a gaunt, scissor-hocked pony. 'Last night broke up the fountains of remembrance in my so-dried heart, and it was as a blessing to me. Truly there is war abroad in the air. I smell it. See! I have brought my sword.'

He sat long-legged on the little beast, with the big sword at his side – hand dropped on the pommel – staring fiercely over the flat lands towards the north. 'Tell me again how he showed in thy vision. Come up and sit behind me. The beast will carry two.'

'I am this Holy One's disciple,' said Kim, as they

cleared the village-gate. The villagers seemed almost sorry to be rid of them, but the priest's farewell was cold and distant. He had wasted some opium on a man who carried no money.

'That is well spoken. I am not much used to holy men, but respect is always good. There is no respect in these days – not even when a commissioner sahib comes to see me. But why should one whose star leads him to war follow a holy man?'

'But he *is* a holy man,' said Kim earnestly. 'In truth, and in talk and in act, holy. He is not like the others. I have never seen such an one. We be not fortune-tellers, or jugglers, or beggars.'

'*Thou* art not. That I can see. But I do not know that other. He marches well, though.'

The first freshness of the day carried the lama forward with long, easy, camel-like strides. He was deep in meditation, mechanically clicking his rosary.

They followed the rutted and worn country road that wound across the flat between the great dark-green mango groves, the line of the snow-capped Himalayas faint to the eastward. All India was at work in the fields, to the creaking of well wheels, the shouting of plough-men behind their cattle, and the clamour of the crows. Even the pony felt the good influence and almost broke into a trot as Kim laid a hand on the stirrup-leather.

'It repents me that I did not give a rupee to the shrine,' said the lama on the last bead of his eighty-one.

The old soldier growled in his beard, so that the lama for the first time was aware of him.

'Seekest thou the River also?' said he, turning.

'The day is new,' was the reply. 'What need of a river

save to water at before sundown? I come to show thee a short lane to the Big Road.'

'That is a courtesy to be remembered, O man of good will. But why the sword?'

The old soldier looked as abashed as a child interrupted in his game of make-believe.

'The sword,' he said, fumbling it. 'Oh, that was a fancy of mine – an old man's fancy. Truly the police orders are that no man must bear weapons throughout Hind, but' – he cheered up and slapped the hilt – 'all the constabeels hereabout know me.'

'It is not a good fancy,' said the lama. 'What profit to kill men?'

'Very little – as I know; but if evil men were not now and then slain it would not be a good world for weaponless dreamers. I do not speak without knowledge who have seen the land from Delhi south awash with blood.'

'What madness was that, then?'

'The Gods, who sent it for a plague, alone know. A madness ate into all the army, and they turned against their officers. That was the first evil, but not past remedy if they had then held their hands. But they chose to kill the sahib's wives and children. Then came the sahibs from over the sea and called them to most strict account.'

'Some such rumour, I believe, reached me once long ago. They called it the Black Year, as I remember.'

'What manner of life hast thou led, not to know the Year? A rumour indeed! All earth knew, and trembled.'

'Our earth never shook but once – upon the day that the Excellent One received Enlightenment.'

'Umph! I saw Delhi shake at least; and Delhi is the navel of the world.'

73

'So they turned against women and children? That was a bad deed, for which the punishment cannot be avoided.'

'Many strove to do so, but with very small profit. I was then in a regiment of cavalry. It broke. Of six hundred and eighty sabres stood fast to their salt – how many, think you? Three. Of whom I was one.'

'The greater merit.'

'Merit! We did not consider it merit in those days. My people, my friends, my brothers fell from me. They said: "The time of the English is accomplished. Let each strike out a little holding for himself." But I had talked with the men of Sobraon, of Chilianwallah, of Moodkee and Ferozeshah. I said: "Abide a little and the wind turns. There is no blessing in this work." In those days I rode seventy miles with an English memsahib and her babe on my saddle-bow. (Wow! That was a horse fit for a man!) I placed them in safety, and back came I to my officer – the one that was not killed of our five. "Give me work," said I, "for I am an outcast among my own kin, and my cousin's blood is wet on my sabre." "Be content," said he. "There is great work forward. When this madness is over there is a recompense."'

'Ay, there is a recompense when the madness is over, surely?' the lama muttered half to himself.

'They did not hang medals in those days on all who by accident had heard a gun fired. No! In nineteen pitched battles was I; in six-and-forty skirmishes of horse; and in small affairs without number. Nine wounds I bear; a medal and four clasps and the medal of an Order, for my captains, who are now generals, remembered me when the Kaisar-i-Hind had accomplished fifty years of her

reign, and all the land rejoiced. They said: "Give him the Order of Berittish India." I carry it upon my neck now. I have also my *jaghir* [holding] from the hands of the state – a free gift to me and mine. The men of the old days – they are now commissioners – come riding to me through the crops – high upon horses so that all the village sees – and we talk out the old skirmishes, one dead man's name leading to another.'

'And after?' said the lama.

'Oh, afterwards they go away, but not before my village has seen.'

'And at the last what wilt thou do?'

'At the last I shall die.'

'And after?'

'Let the Gods order it. I have never pestered them with prayers. I do not think they will pester me. Look you, I have noticed in my long life that those who eternally break in upon those above with complaints and reports and bellowings and weepings are presently sent for in haste, as our colonel used to send for slack-jawed down-country men who talked too much. No, I have never wearied the Gods. They will remember this, and give me a quiet place where I can drive my lance in the shade, and wait to welcome my sons: I have no less than three – Rissaldar-majors all – in the regiments.'

'And they likewise, bound upon the Wheel, go forth from life to life – from despair to despair,' said the lama below his breath, 'hot, uneasy, snatching.'

'Ay,' the old soldier chuckled. 'Three Rissaldar-majors in three regiments. Gamblers a little, but so am I. They must be well mounted; and one cannot take the horses as in the old days one took women. Well, well, my

holding can pay for all. How thinkest thou? It is a well-watered strip, but my men cheat me. I do not know how to ask save at the lance's point. Ugh! I grow angry and I curse them, and they feign penitence, but behind my back I know they call me a toothless old ape.'

'Hast thou never desired any other thing?'

'Yes – yes – a thousand times! A straight back and a close-clinging knee once more; a quick wrist and a keen eye; and the marrow that makes a man. Oh, the old days – the good days of my strength!'

'That strength is weakness.'

'It has turned so; but fifty years since I could have proved it otherwise,' the old soldier retorted, driving his stirrup-edge into the pony's lean flank.

'But I know a River of great healing.'

'I have drunk Gunga-water to the edge of dropsy. All she gave me was a flux, and no sort of strength.'

'It is not Gunga. The River that I know washes from all taint of sin. Ascending the far bank one is assured of Freedom. I do not know thy life, but thy face is the face of the honourable and courteous. Thou has clung to thy Way, rendering fidelity when it was hard to give, in that Black Year of which I now remember other tales. Enter now upon the Middle Way, which is the path to Freedom. Hear the Most Excellent Law, and do not follow dreams.'

'Speak, then, old man,' the soldier smiled, half saluting. 'We be all babblers at our age.'

The lama squatted under the shade of a mango, whose shadow played checkerwise over his face; the soldier sat stiffly on the pony; and Kim, making sure that there were

no snakes, lay down in the crotch of the twisted roots.

There was a drowsy buzz of small life in hot sunshine, a cooing of doves, and a sleepy drone of well wheels across the fields. Slowly and impressively the lama began. At the end of ten minutes the old soldier slid from his pony, to hear better as he said, and sat with the reins round his wrist. The lama's voice faltered – the periods lengthened. Kim was busy watching a grey squirrel. When the little scolding bunch of fur, close pressed to the branch, disappeared, preacher and audience were fast asleep, the old officer's strong-cut head pillowed on his arm, the lama's thrown back against the tree bole, where it showed like yellow ivory. A naked child toddled up, stared, and, moved by some quick impulse of reverence, made a solemn little obeisance before the lama – only the child was so short and fat that it toppled over sideways, and Kim laughed at the sprawling, chubby legs. The child, scared and indignant, yelled aloud.

'Hai! Hai!' said the soldier, leaping to his feet. 'What is it? What orders? . . . It is . . . a child! I dreamed it was an alarm. Little one – little one – do not cry. Have I slept? That was discourteous indeed!'

'I fear! I am afraid!' roared the child.

'What is it to fear? Two old men and a boy? How wilt thou ever make a soldier, Princeling?'

The lama had waked too, but, taking no direct notice of the child, clicked his rosary.

'What is that?' said the child, stopping a yell midway. 'I have never seen such things. Give them me.'

'Aha,' said the lama, smiling, and trailing a loop of it on the grass:

77

'This is a handful of cardamoms,
 This is a lump of *ghee*:
This is millet and chillies and rice,
 A supper for thee and me!'

The child shrieked with joy, and snatched at the dark, glancing beads.

'Oho!' said the old soldier. 'Whence hadst thou that song, despiser of this world?'

'I learned it in Pathânkot – sitting on a doorstep,' said the lama shyly. 'It is good to be kind to babes.'

'As I remember, before the sleep came on us, thou hadst told me that marriage and bearing were darkeners of the true light, stumbling-blocks upon the Way. Do children drop from Heaven in thy country? Is it the Way to sing them songs?'

'No man is all perfect,' said the lama gravely, re-coiling the rosary. 'Run now to thy mother, little one.'

'Hear him!' said the soldier to Kim. 'He is ashamed for that he has made a child happy. There was a very good householder lost in thee, my brother. Hai, child!' He threw it a pice. 'Sweetmeats are always sweet.' And as the little figure capered away into the sunshine: 'They grow up and become men. Holy One, I grieve that I slept in the midst of thy preaching. Forgive me.'

'We be two old men,' said the lama. 'The fault is mine. I listened to thy talk of the world and its madness, and one fault led to the next.'

'Hear him! What harm do thy Gods suffer from play with a babe? And that song was very well sung. Let us go on and I will sing thee the song of Nikal Seyn before Delhi – the old song.'

And they fared out from the gloom of the mango tope,

the old man's high, shrill voice ringing across the field, as wail by long-drawn wail he unfolded the story of Nikal Seyn [Nicholson] – the song that men sing in the Punjab to this day. Kim was delighted, and the lama listened with deep interest.

'"Ahi! Nikal Seyn is dead – he died before Delhi! Lances of the North, take vengeance for Nikal Seyn."' He quavered it out to the end, marking the trills with the flat of his sword on the pony's rump.

'And now we come to the Big Road,' said he, after receiving the compliments of Kim; for the lama was markedly silent. 'It is long since I have ridden this way, but thy boy's talk stirred me. See, Holy One – the Great Road which is the backbone of all Hind. For the most part it is shaded, as here, with four lines of trees; the middle road – all hard – takes the quick traffic. In the days before rail-carriages, the sahibs travelled up and down here in hundreds. Now there are only country-carts and such-like. Left and right is the rougher road for the heavy carts – grain and cotton and timber, fodder, lime and hides. A man goes in safety here – for at every few *koss* is a police-station. The police are thieves and extortioners (I myself would patrol it with cavalry – young recruits under a strong captain), but at least they do not suffer any rivals. All castes and kinds of men move here. Look! Brahmins and chumars, bankers and tinkers, barbers and bunnias, pilgrims and potters – all the world going and coming. It is to me as a river from which I am withdrawn like a log after a flood.'

And truly the Grand Trunk Road is a wonderful spectacle. It runs straight, bearing without crowding India's traffic for fifteen hundred miles – such a river of life as

nowhere else exists in the world. They looked at the green-arched, shade-flecked length of it, the white breadth speckled with slow-pacing folk; and the two-roomed police-station opposite.

'Who bears arms against the law?' a constable called out laughingly, as he caught sight of the soldier's sword. 'Are not the police enough to destroy evil-doers?'

'It was because of the police I bought it,' was the answer. 'Does all go well in Hind?'

'Rissaldar Sahib, all goes well.'

'I am like an old tortoise, look you, who puts his head out from the bank and draws it in again. Ay, this is the Road of Hindustan. All men come by this way . . .'

'Son of a swine, is the soft part of the road meant for thee to scratch thy back upon? Father of all the daughters of shame and husband of ten thousand virtueless ones, thy mother was devoted to a devil, being led thereto by her mother. Thy aunts have never had a nose for seven generations! Thy sister – What owl's folly told thee to draw thy carts across the road? A broken wheel? Then take a broken head and put the two together at leisure!'

The voice and a venomous whip-cracking came out of a pillar of dust fifty yards away, where a cart had broken down. A thin, high Kathiawar mare, with eyes and nostrils aflame, rocketed out of the jam, snorting and wincing as her rider bent her across the road in chase of a shouting man. He was tall and grey-bearded, sitting the almost mad beast as a piece of her, and scientifically lashing his victim between plunges.

The old man's face lit with pride. 'My child!' said he briefly, and strove to rein the pony's neck to a fitting arch.

'Am I to be beaten before the police?' cried the carter. 'Justice! I will have Justice –'

'Am I to be blocked by a shouting ape who upsets ten thousand sacks under a young horse's nose? That is the way to ruin a mare.'

'He speaks truth. He speaks truth. But she follows her man close,' said the old man. The carter ran under the wheels of his cart and thence threatened all sorts of vengeance.

'They are strong men, thy sons,' said the policeman serenely, picking his teeth.

The horseman delivered one last vicious cut with his whip and came on at a canter.

'My father!' He reined back ten yards and dismounted.

The old man was off his pony in an instant, and they embraced as do father and son in the East.

CHAPTER

4

Good Luck, she is never a lady,
But the cursedest quean alive,
Tricksy, wincing, and jady –
Kittle to lead or drive.
Greet her – she's hailing a stranger!
Meet her – she's busking to leave!
Let her alone for a shrew to the bone
And the hussy comes plucking your sleeve!
 Largesse! Largesse, O Fortune!
 Give or hold at your will.
 If I've no care for Fortune,
 Fortune must follow me still!

The Wishing-Caps

Then, lowering their voices, they spoke together. Kim came to rest under a tree, but the lama tugged impatiently at his elbow.

'Let us go on. The River is not here.'

'*Hai mai!* Have we not walked enough for a little? Our River will not run away. Patience, and he will give us a dole.'

'This,' said the old soldier suddenly, 'is the Friend of the Stars. He brought me the news yesterday. Having seen the very man himself, in a vision, giving orders for the war.'

'Hm!' said his son, all deep in his broad chest. 'He came by a bazaar rumour and made profit of it.'

His father laughed. 'At least he did not ride to me begging for a new charger, and the Gods know how

many rupees. Are thy brothers' regiments also under orders?'

'I do not know. I took leave and came swiftly to thee in case –'

'In case they ran before thee to beg. O gamblers and spendthrifts all! But thou hast never yet ridden in a charge. A good horse is needed there, truly. A good follower and a good pony also for the marching. Let us see – let us see.' He thrummed on the pommel.

'This is no place to cast accounts in, my father. Let us go to thy house.'

'At least pay the boy, then: I have no pice with me, and he brought auspicious news. Ho! Friend of all the World, a war is toward as thou hast said.'

'Nay, as I know, *the* war,' returned Kim composedly.

'Eh?' said the lama, fingering his beads, all eager for the road.

'My master does not trouble the stars for hire. We brought the news – bear witness, we brought the news, and now we go.' Kim half crooked his hand at his side.

The son tossed a silver coin through the sunlight, grumbling something about beggars and jugglers. It was a four-anna piece, and would feed them well for some days. The lama, seeing the flash of the metal, droned a blessing.

'Go thy way, Friend of all the World,' piped the old soldier, wheeling his scrawny mount. 'For once in all my days I have met a true prophet – who was not in the army.'

Father and son swung round together: the old man sitting as erect as the younger.

A Punjabi constable in yellow linen trousers slouched across the road. He had seen the money pass.

'Halt!' he cried in impressive English. 'Know ye not that there is a *takkus* of two annas a head, which is four annas, on those who enter the Road from this side-road. It is the order of the Sirkar, and the money is spent for the planting of trees and the beautification of the ways.'

'And the bellies of the police,' said Kim, skipping out of arm's reach. 'Consider for a while, man with a mud head. Think you we came from the nearest pond like the frog, thy father-in-law. Hast thou ever heard the name of thy brother?'

'And who was he? Leave the boy alone,' cried a senior constable, immensely delighted, as he squatted down to smoke his pipe in the veranda.

'He took a label from a bottle of *belaitee-pani* [soda-water], and affixing it to a bridge, collected taxes for a month from those who passed, saying that it was the Sirkar's order. Then came an Englishman and broke his head. Ah, brother, I am a town crow, not a village crow!'

The policeman drew back abashed, and Kim hooted at him all down the road.

'Was there ever such a disciple as I?' he cried merrily to the lama. 'All earth would have picked thy bones within ten mile of Lahore city if I had not guarded thee.'

'I consider in my own mind whether thou art a spirit, sometimes, or sometimes an evil imp,' said the lama, smiling slowly.

'I am thy *chela*.' Kim dropped into step at his side – that indescribable gait of the long-distance tramp all the world over.

'Now let us walk,' muttered the lama, and to the click

of his rosary they walked in silence mile upon mile. The lama, as usual, was deep in meditation, but Kim's bright eyes were open wide. This broad, smiling river of life, he considered, was a vast improvement on the cramped and crowded Lahore streets. There were new people and new sights at every stride – castes he knew and castes that were altogether out of his experience.

They met a troop of long-haired, strong-scented Sansis with baskets of lizards and other unclean food on their backs, their lean dogs sniffing at their heels. These people kept their own side of the road, moving at a quick, furtive jog-trot, and all other castes gave them ample room; for the Sansi is deep pollution. Behind them, walking wide and stiffly across the strong shadows, the memory of his leg-irons still on him, strode one newly released from the jail; his full stomach and shiny skin to prove that the government fed its prisoners better than most honest men could feed themselves. Kim knew that walk well, and made broad jest of it as they passed. Then an Akali, a wild-eyed, wild-haired Sikh devotee in the blue-checked clothes of his faith, with polished steel quoits glistening on the cone of his tall blue turban, stalked past, returning from a visit to one of the independent Sikh states, where he had been singing the ancient glories of the Khalsa to college-trained princelings in top-boots and white-cord breeches. Kim was careful not to irritate that man; for the Akali's temper is short and his arm quick. Here and there they met or were overtaken by the gaily dressed crowds of whole villages turning out to some local fair; the women, with their babes on their hips, walking behind the men, the older boys prancing on sticks of sugarcane, dragging rude brass models of

locomotives such as they sell for a halfpenny, or flashing the sun into the eyes of their betters from cheap toy mirrors. One could see at a glance what each had bought; and if there were any doubt it needed only to watch the wives comparing, brown arm against brown arm, the newly purchased dull glass bracelets that come from the north-west. These merry-makers stepped slowly, calling one to the other and stopping to haggle with sweetmeat-sellers, or to make a prayer before one of the wayside shrines – sometimes Hindu, sometimes Mussulman – which the low-caste of both creeds share with beautiful impartiality. A solid line of blue, rising and falling like the back of a caterpillar in haste, would swing up through the quivering dust and trot past to a chorus of quick cackling. That was a gang of *changars* – the women who have taken all the embankments of all the northern railways under their charge – a flat-footed, big-bosomed, strong-limbed, blue-petticoated clan of earth-carriers, hurrying north on news of a job, and wasting no time by the road. They belong to the caste whose men do not count, and they walked with squared elbows, swinging hips, and heads on high, as suits women who carry heavy weights. A little later a marriage procession would strike into the Grand Trunk with music and shoutings, and a smell of marigold and jasmine stronger even than the reek of the dust. One could see the bride's litter, a blur of red and tinsel, staggering through the haze, while the bridegroom's bewreathed pony turned aside to snatch a mouthful from a passing fodder-cart. Then Kim would join the Kentish-fire of good wishes and bad jokes, wishing the couple a hundred sons and no daughters, as the saying is. Still more interesting and more to be

shouted over it was when a strolling juggler with some half-trained monkeys, or a panting, feeble bear, or a woman who tied goat's horns to her feet, and with these danced on a slack-rope, set the horses to shying and the women to shrill, long-drawn quavers of amazement.

The lama never raised his eyes. He did not note the moneylender on his goose-rumped pony, hastening along to collect the cruel interest; or the long-shouting, deep-voiced little mob – still in military formation – of native soldiers on leave, rejoicing to be rid of their breeches and puttees, and saying the most outrageous things to the most respectable women in sight. Even the seller of Ganges water he did not see, and Kim expected that he would at least buy a bottle of that precious stuff. He looked steadily at the ground, and strode as steadily hour after hour, his soul busied elsewhere. But Kim was in the seventh heaven of joy. The Grand Trunk at this point was built on an embankment to guard against winter floods from the foothills, so that one walked, as it were, a little above the country, along a stately corridor, seeing all India spread out to left and right. It was beautiful to behold the many-yoked grain and cotton wagons crawling over the country roads: one could hear their axles, complaining a mile away, coming nearer, till with shouts and yells and bad words they climbed up the steep incline and plunged on to the hard main road, carter reviling carter. It was equally beautiful to watch the people, little clumps of red and blue and pink and white and saffron, turning aside to go to their own villages, dispersing and growing small by twos and threes across the level plain. Kim felt these things, though he could not give tongue to his feelings, and so contented himself with

buying peeled sugarcane and spitting the pith gener-
ously about his path. From time to time the lama took
snuff, and at last Kim could endure the silence no longer.

'This is a good land – the land of the south!' said he.
'The air is good; the water is good. Eh?'

'And they are all bound upon the Wheel,' said the
lama. 'Bound from life after life. To none of these has the
Way been shown.' He shook himself back to this world.

'And now we have walked a weary way,' said Kim.
'Surely we shall soon come to a *parao* [a resting-place].
Shall we stay there? Look, the sun is sloping.'

'Who will receive us this evening?'

'That is all one. The country is full of good folk.
Besides,' – he sunk his voice beneath a whisper – 'we
have money.'

The crowd thickened as they neared the resting-place
which marked the end of their day's journey. A line of
stalls selling very simple food and tobacco, a stack of
firewood, a police-station, a well, a horse-trough, a few
trees, and, under them, some trampled ground dotted
with the black ashes of old fires, are all that mark a *parao*
on the Grand Trunk; if you except the beggars and the
crows – both hungry.

By this time the sun was driving broad golden spokes
through the lower branches of the mango trees; the
parakeets and doves were coming home in their hun-
dreds; the chattering, grey-backed Seven Sisters, talking
over the day's adventures, walked back and forth in twos
and threes almost under the feet of the travellers; and
shufflings and scufflings in the branches showed that the
bats were ready to go out on the night picket. Swiftly the
light gathered itself together, painted for an instant the

faces and the cart-wheels and the bullocks' horns as red as blood. Then the night fell, changing the touch of the air, drawing a low, even haze, like a gossamer veil of blue, across the face of the country and bringing out, keen and distinct, the smell of wood-smoke and cattle and the good scent of wheaten cakes cooked on ashes. The evening patrol hurried out of the police-station with important coughings and reiterated orders; and a live charcoal ball in the cup of a wayside carter's hookah glowed red while Kim's eye mechanically watched the last flicker of the sun on the brass tweezers.

The life of the *parao* was very like that of the Kashmir Serai on a small scale. Kim dived into the happy Asiatic disorder which, if you only allow time, will bring you everything that a simple man needs.

His wants were few, because, since the lama had no caste scruples, cooked food from the nearest stall would serve; but, for luxury's sake, Kim bought a handful of dung-cakes to build a fire. All about, coming and going round the little flames, men cried for oil, or grain, or sweetmeats, or tobacco, jostling one another while they waited their turn at the well; and under the men's voices you heard from halted, shuttered carts the high squeals and giggles of women whose faces should not be seen in public.

Nowadays, well-educated natives are of opinion that when their womenfolk travel – and they visit a good deal – it is better to take them quickly by rail in a properly screened compartment; and that custom is spreading. But there are always those of the old rock who hold by the use of their forefathers; and, above all, there are always the old women – more conservative than the men – who

towards the end of their days go a pilgrimage. They, being withered and undesirable, do not, under certain circumstances, object to unveiling. After their long seclusion, during which they have always been in business touch with a thousand outside interests, they love the bustle and stir of the open road, the gatherings at the shrines, and the infinite possibilities of gossip with like-minded dowagers. Very often it suits a long-suffering family that a strong-tongued, iron-willed old lady should disport herself about India in this fashion; for certainly pilgrimage is grateful to the Gods. So all about India, in the most remote places as in the most public, you find some knot of grizzled servitors in nominal charge of an old lady who is more or less curtained and hid away in a bullock-cart. Such men are staid and discreet, and when a European or a high-caste native is near will net their charge with most elaborate precautions; but in the ordinary haphazard chances of pilgrimage the precautions are not taken. The old lady is, after all, intensely human, and lives to look upon life.

Kim marked down a gaily ornamented *ruth* or family bullock-cart, with a broidered canopy of two domes, like a double-humped camel, which had just been drawn into the *parao*. Eight men made its retinue, and two of the eight were armed with rusty sabres – sure signs that they followed a person of distinction, for the common folk do not bear arms. An increasing cackle of complaints, orders, and jests, and what to a European would have been bad language, came from behind the curtains. Here was evidently a woman used to command.

Kim looked over the retinue critically. Half of them were thin-legged, grey-bearded Ooryas from down

country. The other half were duffle-clad, felt-hatted hill-men of the north; and that mixture told its own tale, even if he had not overheard the incessant sparring between the two divisions. The old lady was going south on a visit – probably to a rich relative, most probably to a son-in-law, who had sent up an escort as a mark of respect. The hillmen would be of her own people – Kulu or Kangra folk. It was quite clear that she was not taking her daughter down to be wedded, or the curtains would have been laced home and the guard would have allowed no one near the car. A merry and a high-spirited dame, thought Kim, balancing the dung-cake in one hand, the cooked food in the other, and piloting the lama with a nudging shoulder. Something might be made out of the meeting. The lama would give no help, but, as a conscientious *chela*, Kim was delighted to beg for two.

He built his fire as close to the cart as he dared, waiting for one of the escort to order him away. The lama dropped wearily to the ground, much as a heavy fruit-eating bat cowers, and returned to his rosary.

'Stand farther off, beggar!' The order was shouted in broken Hindustani by one of the hillmen.

'Huh! It is only a *pahari* [a hillman],' said Kim over his shoulder. 'Since when have the hill-asses owned all Hindustan?'

The retort was a swift and brilliant sketch of Kim's pedigree for three generations.

'Ah!' Kim's voice was sweeter than ever, as he broke the dung-cake into fit pieces. 'In *my* country we call that the beginning of love-talk.'

A harsh, thin cackle behind the curtains put the hill-man on his mettle for a second shot.

'Not so bad – not so bad,' said Kim with calm. 'But have a care, my brother, lest we – *we*, I say – be minded to give a curse or so in return. And our curses have the knack of biting home.'

The Ooryas laughed; the hillman sprang forward threateningly. The lama suddenly raised his head, bringing his huge tam-o'-shanter hat into the full light of Kim's new-started fire.

'What is it?' said he.

The man halted as though struck to stone. 'I – I – am saved from a great sin,' he stammered.

'The foreigner has found him a priest at last,' whispered one of the Ooryas.

'*Hai!* Why is that beggar-brat not well beaten?' the old woman cried.

The hillman drew back to the cart and whispered something to the curtain. There was dead silence, then a muttering.

'This goes well,' thought Kim, pretending neither to see nor hear.

'When – when – he has eaten' – the hillman fawned on Kim – 'it – it is requested that the Holy One will do the honour to talk to one who would speak to him.'

'After he has eaten he will sleep,' Kim returned loftily. He could not quite see what new turn the game had taken, but stood resolute to profit by it. 'Now I will get him his food.' The last sentence, spoken loudly, ended with a sigh as of faintness.

'I – I myself and the others of my people will look to that – if it is permitted.'

'It is permitted,' said Kim, more loftily than ever. 'Holy One, these people will bring us food.'

'The land is good. All the country of the south is good –
a great and a terrible world,' mumbled the lama drowsily.

'Let him sleep,' said Kim, 'but look to it that we are well
fed when he wakes. He is a very holy man.'

Again one of the Ooryas said something con-
temptuously.

'He is not a *fakir*. He is not a down-country beggar,'
Kim went on severely, addressing the stars. 'He is the
most holy of holy men. He is above all castes. I am his
chela.'

'Come here!' said the flat thin voice behind the curtain;
and Kim came, conscious that eyes he could not see were
staring at him. One skinny brown finger heavy with rings
lay on the edge of the cart, and the talk went this way:

'Who is that one?'

'An exceedingly holy one. He comes from far off. He
comes from Tibet.'

'Where in Tibet?'

'From behind the snows – from a very far place. He
knows the stars; he makes horoscopes; he reads nativi-
ties. But he does not do this for money. He does it for
kindness and great charity. I am his disciple. I am called
also the Friend of the Stars.'

'Thou art no hillman.'

'Ask him. He will tell thee I was sent to him from the
stars to show him an end to his pilgrimage.'

'Humph! Consider, brat, that I am an old woman and
not altogether a fool. Lamas I know, and to these I give
reverence, but thou art no more a lawful *chela* than this
my finger is the pole of this wagon. Thou art a casteless
Hindu – a bold and unblushing beggar, attached, belike,
to the Holy One for the sake of gain.'

'Do we not all work for gain?' Kim changed his tone promptly to match that altered voice. 'I have heard' – this was a bow drawn at a venture – 'I have heard –'

'What hast thou heard?' she snapped, rapping with the finger.

'Nothing that I well remember, but some talk in the bazaars, which is doubtless a lie, that even rajahs – small hill rajahs –'

'But none the less of good Rajput blood.'

'Assuredly of good blood. That these even sell the more comely of their womenfolk for gain. Down south they sell them – to zemindars and such-all of Oudh.'

If there be one thing in the world that the small hill rajahs deny it is just this charge; but it happens to be one thing that the bazaars believe, when they discuss the mysterious slave traffics of India. The old lady explained to Kim, in a tense, indignant whisper, precisely what manner and fashion of malignant liar he was. Had Kim hinted this when she was a girl, he would have been pommelled to death that same evening by an elephant. This was perfectly true.

'*Ahai!* I am only a beggar's brat, as the Eye of Beauty has said,' he wailed in extravagant terror.

'Eye of Beauty, forsooth! Who am I that thou shouldst fling beggar endearments at me?' And yet she laughed at the long-forgotten word. 'Forty years ago that might have been said, and not without truth. Ay, thirty years ago. But it is the fault of this gadding up and down Hind that a king's widow must jostle all the scum of the land, and be made a mock by beggars.'

'Great Queen,' said Kim promptly, for he heard her shaking with indignation, 'I am even what the Great

Queen says I am; but none the less is my master holy. He has not yet heard the Great Queen's order that –'

'Order? I order a Holy One – a Teacher of the Law – to come and speak to a woman? Never!'

'Pity my stupidity. I thought it was given as an order –'

'It was not. It was a petition. Does this make all clear?'

A silver coin clicked on the edge of the cart. Kim took it and salaamed profoundly. The old lady recognized that, as the eyes and the ears of the lama, he was to be propitiated.

'I am but the Holy One's disciple. When he has eaten perhaps he will come.'

'Oh, villain and shameless rogue!' The jewelled forefinger shook itself at him reprovingly; but he could hear the old lady's chuckle.

'Nay, what is it?' he said, dropping into his most caressing and confidential tone – the one, he well knew, that few could resist. 'Is – is there any need of a son in thy family? Speak freely, for we priests –' That last was a direct plagiarism from a *fakir* by the Taksali Gate.

'We priests! Thou art not yet old enough to –' She checked the joke with another laugh. 'Believe me, now and again, we women, O priest, think of other matters than sons. Moreover, my daughter has borne her man-child.'

'Two arrows in the quiver are better than one; and three are better still.' Kim quoted the proverb with a meditative cough, looking discreetly earthward.

'True – oh, true. But perhaps that will come. Certainly those down-country Brahmins are utterly useless. I sent gifts and monies and gifts again to them, and they prophesied.'

95

'Ah,' drawled Kim, with infinite contempt, 'they prophesied!' A professional could have done no better.

'And it was not until I remembered my own Gods that my prayers were heard. I chose an auspicious hour, and – perhaps the Holy One has heard of the Abbot of the Lung-Cho lamassery. It was to him I put the matter, and behold in the due time all came about as I desired. The Brahmin in the house of the father of my daughter's son has since said that it was through *his* prayers – which is a little error that I will explain to him when we reach our journey's end. And so afterwards I go to Buddh Gaya, to make *shraddha* for the father of my children.'

'Thither go we.'

'Doubly auspicious,' chirruped the old lady. 'A second son at least!'

'O Friend of all the World!' The lama had waked, and, simply as a child bewildered in a strange bed, called for Kim.

'I come! I come, Holy One!' He dashed to the fire, where he found the lama already surrounded by dishes of food, the hillmen visibly adoring him and the southerners looking sourly.

'Go back! Withdraw!' Kim cried. 'Do we eat publicly like dogs?' They finished the meal in silence, each turned a little from the other, and Kim topped it with a native-made cigarette.

'Have I not said an hundred times that the south is a good land? Here is a virtuous and high-born widow of a hill rajah on pilgrimage, she says, to Buddh Gaya. She it is sends us those dishes; and when thou art well rested she would speak to thee.'

'Is this also thy work?' The lama dipped deep into his snuff-gourd.

'Who else watched over thee since our wonderful journey began?' Kim's eyes danced in his head as he blew the rank smoke through his nostrils and stretched him on the dusty ground. 'Have I failed to oversee thy comforts, Holy One?'

'A blessing on thee.' The lama inclined his solemn head. 'I have known many men in my so long life, and disciples not a few. But to none among men, if so be thou art woman-born, has my heart gone out as it has to thee – thoughtful, wise, and courteous; but something of a small imp.'

'And I have never seen such a priest as thou.' Kim considered the benevolent yellow face wrinkle by wrinkle. 'It is less than three days since we took the road together, and it is as though it were a hundred years.'

'Perhaps in a former life it was permitted that I should have rendered thee some service. Maybe' – he smiled – 'I freed thee from a trap; or, having caught thee on a hook in the days when I was not enlightened, cast thee back into the river.'

'Maybe,' said Kim quietly. He had heard this sort of speculation again and again, from the mouths of many whom the English would not consider imaginative. 'Now, as regards that woman in the bullock-cart, I think she needs a second son for her daughter.'

'That is no part of the Way,' sighed the lama. 'But at least she is from the Hills. Ah, the Hills, and the snow of the Hills!'

He rose and stalked to the cart. Kim would have given his ears to come too, but the lama did not invite him; and

the few words he caught were in an unknown tongue, for they spoke some common speech of the mountains. The woman seemed to ask questions which the lama turned over in his mind before answering. Now and again he heard the singsong cadence of a Chinese quotation. It was a strange picture that Kim watched between drooped eyelids. The lama, very straight and erect, the deep folds of his yellow clothing slashed with black in the light of the *parao* fires precisely as a knotted tree-trunk is slashed with the shadows of the low sun, addressed a tinsel and làcquered *ruth* which burned like a many-coloured jewel in the same uncertain light. The patterns on the gold-worked curtains ran up and down, melting and re-forming as the folds shook and quivered to the night wind; and when the talk grew more earnest the jewelled forefinger snapped out little sparks of light between the embroideries. Behind the cart was a wall of uncertain darkness speckled with little flames and alive with half-caught forms and faces and shadows. The voices of early evening had settled down to one soothing hum whose deepest note was the steady chumping of the bullocks above their chopped straw, and whose highest was the tinkle of a Bengali dancing-girl's *sitar*. Most men had eaten and pulled deep at their gurgling, grunting hookahs, which in full blast sound like bull-frogs.

At last the lama returned. A hillman walked behind him with a wadded cotton quilt and spread it carefully by the fire.

'She deserves ten thousand grandchildren,' thought Kim. 'None the less, but for me, these gifts would not have come.'

'A virtuous woman – and a wise one.' The lama slack-

ened off, joint by joint, like a slow camel. 'The world is full of charity to those who follow the Way.' He flung a fair half of the quilt over Kim.

'And what said she?' Kim rolled up in his share of it.

'She asked me many questions and propounded many problems – the most of which were idle tales which she had heard from devil-serving priests who pretend to follow the Way. Some I answered, and some I said were foolish. Many wear the Robe, but few keep the Way.'

'True. That is true.' Kim used the thoughtful, conciliatory tone of those who wish to draw confidences.

'But by her lights she is most right-minded. She desires greatly that we should go with her to Buddh Gaya; her road being ours, as I understand, for many days' journey to the southward.'

'And?'

'Patience a little. To this I said that my Search came before all things. She had heard many foolish legends, but this great truth of my River she had never heard. Such are the priests of the lower hills! She knew the Abbot of Lung-Cho, but she did not know of my River – nor the tale of the Arrow.'

'And?'

'I spoke therefore of the Search, and of the Way, and of matters that were profitable; she desiring only that I should accompany her and make prayer for a second son.'

'Aha! "We women" do *not* think of anything save children,' said Kim sleepily.

'Now, since our roads run together for a while, I do not

99

see that we in any way depart from our Search if so be we accompany her – at least as far as – I have forgotten the name of the city.'

'*Ohé!*' said Kim, turning and speaking in a sharp whisper to one of the Ooryas a few yards away. 'Where is your master's house?'

'A little behind Saharunpore, among the fruit gardens.' He named the village.

'That was the place,' said the lama. 'So far, at least, we can go with her.'

'Flies go to carrion,' said the Oorya, in an abstracted voice.

'For the sick cow a crow; for the sick man a Brahmin.' Kim breathed the proverb impersonally to the shadow-tops of the trees overhead.

The Oorya grunted and held his peace.

'So then we go with her, Holy One?'

'Is there any reason against? I can still step aside and try all the rivers that the road overpasses. She desires that I should come. She very greatly desires it.'

Kim stifled a laugh in the quilt. When once that imperious old lady had recovered from her natural awe of a lama he thought it probable that she would be worth listening to.

He was nearly asleep when the lama suddenly quoted a proverb: 'The husbands of the talkative have a great reward hereafter.' Then Kim heard him snuff thrice, and dozed off, still laughing.

The diamond-bright dawn woke men and crows and bullocks together. Kim sat up and yawned, shook himself, and thrilled with delight. This was seeing the world in real truth; this was life as he would have it – bustling

and shouting, the buckling of belts, and beating of bullocks and creaking of wheels, lighting of fires and cooking of food, and new sights at every turn of the approving eye. The morning mist swept off in a whorl of silver, the parrots shot away to some distant river in shrieking green hosts: all the well wheels within earshot went to work. India was awake, and Kim was in the middle of it, more awake and more excited than any one, chewing on a twig that he would presently use as a toothbrush; for he borrowed right- and left-handedly from all the customs of the country he knew and loved. There was no need to worry about food – no need to spend a cowrie at the crowded stalls. He was the disciple of a holy man annexed by a strong-willed old lady. All things would be prepared for them, and when they were respectfully invited so to do they would sit and eat. For the rest – Kim giggled here as he cleaned his teeth – his hostess would rather heighten the enjoyment of the road. He inspected her bullocks critically, as they came up grunting and blowing under the yokes. If they went too fast – it was not likely – there would be a pleasant seat for himself along the pole; the lama would sit beside the driver. The escort, of course, would walk. The old lady, equally of course, would talk a great deal, and by what he had heard that conversation would not lack salt. She was already ordering, haranguing, rebuking, and, it must be said, cursing her servants for delays.

'Get her her pipe. In the name of the Gods, get her her pipe and stop her ill-omened mouth,' cried an Oorya, tying up his shapeless bundles of bedding. 'She and the parrots are alike. They screech in the dawn.'

'The lead bullocks! *Hai!* Look to the lead bullocks!'

They were backing and wheeling as a grain-cart's axle caught them by the horns. 'Son of an owl, where dost thou go?' This to the grinning carter.

'*Ai! Yai! Yai!* That within there is the Queen of Delhi going to pray for a son,' the man called back over his high load. 'Room for the Queen of Delhi and her Prime Minister the grey monkey climbing up his own sword!' Another cart loaded with bark for a down-country tannery followed close behind, and its driver added a few compliments as the *ruth*-bullocks backed and backed again.

From behind the shaking curtains came one volley of invective. It did not last long, but in kind and quality, in blistering, biting appropriateness, it was beyond anything that even Kim had heard. He could see the carter's bare chest collapse with amazement, as the man salaamed reverently to the voice, leaped from the pole, and helped the escort haul their volcano on to the main road. Here the voice told him truthfully what sort of wife he had wedded, and what she was doing in his absence.

'Oh, *shabash*!' murmured Kim, unable to contain himself, as the man slunk away.

'Well done, indeed? It is a shame and a scandal that a poor woman may not go to make prayer to her Gods except she be jostled and insulted by all the refuse of Hindustan – that she must eat *gâli* [abuse] as men eat ghee. But I have yet a wag left to my tongue – a word or two well spoken that serves the occasion. And *still* am I without my tobacco! Who is the one-eyed and luckless son of shame that has not yet prepared my pipe?'

It was hastily thrust in by a hillman, and a trickle of thick smoke from each corner of the curtains showed that peace was restored.

If Kim had walked proudly the day before, disciple of a holy man, today he paced with tenfold pride in the train of a semi-royal procession, with a recognized place under the patronage of an old lady of charming manners and infinite resource. The escort, their heads tied up native-fashion, fell in on either side the cart, shuffling enormous clouds of dust.

The lama and Kim walked a little to one side; Kim chewing his stick of sugarcane, and making way for no one under the status of a priest. They could hear the old lady's tongue clack as steadily as a rice husker. She bade the escort tell her what was going on on the road; and so soon as they were clear of the *parao* she flung back the curtains and peered out, her veil a third across her face. Her men did not eye her directly when she addressed them, and thus the proprieties were more or less observed.

A dark, sallowish District Superintendent of Police, faultlessly uniformed, an Englishman, trotted by on a tired horse, and, seeing from her retinue what manner of person she was, chaffed her.

'O mother,' he cried, 'do they do this in the zenanas? Suppose an Englishman came by and saw that thou hadst no nose?'

'What?' she shrilled back. 'Thine own mother has no nose? Why say so, then, on the open road?'

It was a fair counter. The Englishman threw up his hand with the gesture of a man hit at swordplay. She laughed and nodded.

'Is this a face to tempt virtue aside?' She withdrew all her veil and stared at him.

It was by no means lovely, but as the man gathered up his reins he called it a Moon of Paradise, a Disturber of Integrity, and a few other fantastic epithets which doubled her up with mirth.

'That is a *nut-cut* [rogue],' she said. 'All police-constables are *nut-cuts*; but the police-wallahs are the worst. *Hai*, my son, thou hast never learned all that since thou camest from *Belait* [Europe]. Who suckled thee?'

'A *pahareen* – a hillwoman of Dalhousie, my mother. Keep thy beauty under a shade – O Dispenser of Delights,' and he was gone.

'These be the sort' – she took a fine judicial tone, and stuffed her mouth with *pan* – 'These be the sort to oversee justice. They know the land and the customs of the land. The others, all new from Europe, suckled by white women and learning our tongues from books, are worse than the pestilence. They do harm to kings.' Then she told a long, long tale to the world at large, of an ignorant young policeman who had disturbed some small hill rajah, a ninth cousin of her own, in the matter of a trivial land-case, winding up with a quotation from a work by no means devotional.

Then her mood changed, and she bade one of the escort ask whether the lama would walk alongside and discuss matters of religion. So Kim dropped back into the dust and returned to his sugarcane. For an hour or more the lama's tam-o'-shanter showed like a moon through the haze; and, from all he heard, Kim gathered that the old woman wept. One of the Ooryas half apologized for his rudeness overnight, saying that he had never known

his mistress of so bland a temper and he ascribed it to the presence of the strange priest. Personally, he believed in Brahmins, though, like all natives, he was acutely aware of their cunning and their greed. Still, when Brahmins but irritated with begging demands the mother of his master's wife, and when she sent them away so angry that they cursed the whole retinue (which was the real reason of the second offside bullock going lame, and of the pole breaking the night before), he was prepared to accept any priest of any other denomination in or out of India. To this Kim assented with wise nods, and bade the Oorya observe that the lama took no money, and that the cost of his and Kim's food would be repaid a hundred times in the good luck that would attend the caravan henceforward. He also told stories of Lahore city, and sang a song or two which made the escort laugh. As a town-mouse well acquainted with the latest songs by the most fashionable composers – they are women for the most part – Kim had a distinct advantage over men from a little fruit village behind Saharunpore, but he let that advantage be inferred.

At noon they turned aside to eat, and the meal was good, plentiful, and well-served on plates of clean leaves, in decency, out of drift of the dust. They gave the scraps to certain beggars, that all requirements might be fulfilled, and sat down to a long, luxurious smoke. The old lady had retreated behind her curtains, but mixed most freely in the talk, her servants arguing with and contradicting her as servants do throughout the East. She compared the cool and the pines of the Kangra and Kulu hills with the dust and the mangoes of the south; she told a tale of some old local Gods at the edge of her husband's

territory; she roundly abused the tobacco which she was then smoking, reviled all Brahmins, and speculated without reserve on the coming of many grandsons.

CHAPTER
5

Here come I to my own again –
Fed, forgiven, and known again –
Claimed by bone of my bone again,
 And sib to flesh of my flesh!
The fatted calf is dressed for me,
But the husks have greater zest for me . . .
I think my pigs will be best for me,
 So I'm off to the styes afresh.

The Prodigal Son

Once more the lazy, string-tied, shuffling procession got under way, and she slept till they reached the next halting-stage. It was a very short march, and time lacked an hour to sundown, so Kim cast about for means of amusement.

'But why not sit and rest?' said one of the escort. 'Only the devils and the English walk to and fro without reason.'

'Never make friends with the Devil, a monkey, or a boy. No man knows what they will do next,' said his fellow.

Kim turned a scornful back – he did not want to hear the old story how the Devil played with the boys and repented of it – and walked idly across country.

The lama strode after him. All that day, whenever they passed a stream, he had turned aside to look at it, but in no case had he received any warning that he had found his River. Insensibly, too, the comfort of speaking to

some one in a reasonable tongue, and of being properly considered and respected as her spiritual adviser by a well-born woman, had weaned his thoughts a little from the Search. And further, he was prepared to spend serene years in his quest; having nothing of the white man's impatience, but a great faith.

'Where goest thou?' he called after Kim.

'Nowhither – it was a small march, and all this' – Kim waved his hands abroad – 'is new to me.'

'She is beyond question a wise and a discerning woman. But it is hard to meditate when –'

'All women are thus.' Kim spoke as might have Solomon.

'Before the lamassery was a broad platform,' the lama muttered, looping up the well-worn rosary, 'of stone. On that I have left the marks of my feet – pacing to and fro with these.'

He clicked the beads, and began the '*Om mane pudme hum*'s of his devotion; grateful for the cool, the quiet, and the absence of dust.

One thing after another drew Kim's idle eye across the plain. There was no purpose in his wanderings, except that the build of the huts near by seemed new, and he wished to investigate.

They came out on a broad tract of grazing ground, brown and purple in the afternoon light, with a heavy clump of mangoes in the centre. It struck Kim as curious that no shrine stood in so eligible a spot: the boy was observing as any priest for these things. Far across the plain walked side by side four men, made small by the distance. He looked intently under his curved palms and caught the sheen of brass.

'Soldiers. White soldiers!' said he. 'Let us see.'

'It is always soldiers when thou and I go out alone together. But I have never seen the white soldiers.'

'They do no harm except when they are drunk. Keep behind this tree.'

They stepped behind the thick trunks in the cool dark of the mango tope. Two little figures halted; the other two came forward uncertainly. They were the advance-party of a regiment on the march, sent out, as usual, to mark the camp. They bore five-foot sticks with fluttering flags, and called to each other as they spread over the flat earth.

At last they entered the mango grove, walking heavily.

'It's here or hereabouts – officers' tents under the trees, I take it, an' the rest of us can stay outside. Have they marked out for the baggage-waggons behind?'

They cried again to their comrades in the distance, and the rough answer came back faint and mellowed.

'Shove the flag in here, then,' said one.

'What do they prepare?' said the lama, wonderstruck. 'This is a great and a terrible world. What is the device on the flag?'

A soldier thrust a stave within a few feet of them, grunted discontentedly, pulled it up again, conferred with his companion, who looked up and down the shaded cave of greenery, and returned it.

Kim stared with all his eyes, his breath coming short and sharp between his teeth. The soldiers stamped off into the sunshine.

'O Holy One!' he gasped. 'My horoscope! The drawing in the dust by the priest at Umballa! Remember what he said. First come two – *ferashes* – to make all things ready – in a dark place, as it is always at the beginning of a vision.'

'But this is not vision,' said the lama. 'It is the world's illusion, and no more.'

'And after them comes the Bull – the Red Bull on the green field. Look! It is he!'

He pointed to the flag that was snap-snapping in the evening breeze not ten feet away. It was no more than an ordinary camp marking-flag; but the regiment, always punctilious in matters of millinery, had charged it with the regimental device, the Red Bull, which is the crest of the Mavericks – the great Red Bull on a background of Irish green.

'I see, and now I remember,' said the lama. 'Certainly it is thy Bull. Certainly, also, the two men came to make all ready.'

'They are soldiers – white soldiers. What said the priest? "The sign over against the Bull is the sign of war and armed men." Holy One, this thing touches my Search.'

'True. It is true.' The lama stared fixedly at the device that flamed like a ruby in the dusk. 'The priest at Umballa said that thine was the sign of war.'

'What is to do now?'

'Wait. Let us wait.'

'Even now the darkness clears,' said Kim. It was only natural that the descending sun should at last strike through the tree-trunks, across the grove, filling it with mealy gold light for a few minutes; but to Kim it was crown of the Umballa Brahmin's prophecy.

'Hark!' said the lama. 'One beats a drum – far off!'

At first the sound, carrying diluted through the still air, resembled the beating of an artery in the head. Soon a sharpness was added.

'Ah! The music,' Kim explained. He knew the sound of a regimental band, but it amazed the lama.

At the far end of the plain a heavy, dusty column crawled in sight. Then the wind brought the tune:

> We crave your condescension
> To tell you what we know
> Of marching in the Mulligan Guards
> To Sligo Port below!

Here broke in the shrill-tongued fifes:

> We shouldered arms,
> We marched – we marched away.
> From Phoenix Park
> We marched to Dublin Bay.
> The drums and the fifes,
> Oh, sweetly they did play,
> As we marched – marched – marched – with the
> Mulligan Guards!

It was the band of the Mavericks playing the regiment to camp; for the men were route-marching with their baggage. The rippling column swung into the level – carts behind it – divided left and right, ran about like an ant-hill, and . . .

'But this is sorcery!' said the lama.

The plain dotted itself with tents that seemed to rise, all spread, from the carts. Another rush of men invaded the grove, pitched a huge tent in silence, ran up yet eight or nine more by the side of it, unearthed cooking-pots, pans, and bundles, which were taken possession of by a crowd of native servants; and behold the mango tope turned into an orderly town as they watched!

'Let us go,' said the lama, sinking back afraid, as the fires twinkled and white officers with jingling swords stalked into the mess-tent.

'Stand back in the shadow. No one can see beyond the light of the fire,' said Kim, his eyes still on the flag. He had never before watched the routine of a seasoned regiment pitching camp in thirty minutes.

'Look! look! look!' clucked the lama. 'Yonder comes a priest.'

It was Bennett, the Church of England Chaplain of the regiment, limping in dusty black. One of his flock had made some rude remarks about the Chaplain's mettle; and to abash him Bennett had marched step by step with the men that day. The black dress, gold cross on the watch-chain, the hairless face, and the soft, black wide-awake hat would have marked him as a holy man anywhere in all India. He dropped into a camp-chair by the door of the mess-tent and slid off his boots. Three or four officers gathered round him, laughing and joking over his exploit.

'The talk of white men is wholly lacking in dignity,' said the lama, who judged only by tone. 'But I have considered the countenance of that priest, and I think he is learned. Is it likely that he will understand our talk? I would talk to him of my Search.'

'Never speak to a white man till he is fed,' said Kim, quoting a well-known proverb. 'They will eat now, and – and I do not think they are good to beg from. Let us go back to the resting-place. After we have eaten we will come again. It certainly was a Red Bull – *my* Red Bull.'

They were both noticeably absent-minded when the

old lady's retinue set their meal before them; so none broke their reserve, for it is not lucky to annoy guests.

'Now,' said Kim, picking his teeth, 'we will return to that place; but thou, O Holy One, must wait a little way off, because thy feet are heavier than mine and I am anxious to see more of that Red Bull.'

'But how canst thou understand the talk? Walk slowly. The road is dark,' the lama replied uneasily.

Kim put the question aside. 'I marked a place near to the trees,' said he, 'where thou canst sit till I call. Nay,' as the lama made some sort of protest, 'remember this is *my* Search – the Search for my Red Bull. The sign in the stars was not for thee. I know a little of the customs of white soldiers, and I always desire to see some new things.'

'What dost thou not know of this world?' The lama squatted obediently in a little hollow of the ground not a hundred yards from the hump of the mango trees dark against the star-powdered sky.

'Stay till I call.' Kim flitted into the dusk. He knew that in all probability there would be sentries round the camp, and smiled to himself as he heard the thick boots of one. A boy who can dodge over the roofs of Lahore city on a moonlight night, using every little patch and corner of darkness to discomfit his pursuer, is not likely to be checked by a line of well-trained soldiers. He paid them the compliment of crawling between a couple, and, running and halting, crouching and dropping flat, worked his way toward the lighted mess-tent where, close pressed behind the mango tree, he waited till some chance word should give him a returnable lead.

The one thing now in his mind was further information as to the Red Bull. For aught he knew, and Kim's limi-

tations were as curious and sudden as his expansions, the men, the nine hundred thorough devils of his father's prophecy, might pray to the beast after dark, as Hindus pray to the Holy Cow. That at least would be entirely right and logical, and the padre with the gold cross would be therefore the man to consult in the matter. On the other hand, remembering sober-faced padres whom he had avoided in Lahore city, the priest might be an inquisitive nuisance who would bid him learn. But had it not been proven at Umballa that his sign in the high heavens portended war and armed men? Was he not the Friend of the Stars as well as of all the World, crammed to the teeth with dreadful secrets? Lastly – and firstly as the under-current of all his quick thoughts – this adventure, though he did not know the English word, was a stupendous lark – a delightful continuation of his old flights across the house-tops, as well as the fulfilment of sublime prophecy. He lay belly-flat and wriggled towards the mess-tent door, a hand on the amulet round his neck.

It was as he suspected. The sahibs prayed to their God; for in the centre of the mess-table – its sole ornament when they were on the line of march – stood a golden bull fashioned from old-time loot of the Summer Palace at Peking – a red-gold bull with lowered head, ramping upon a field of Irish green. To him the sahibs held out their glasses and cried aloud confusedly.

Now the Reverend Arthur Bennett always left mess after that toast, and being rather tired by his march his movements were more abrupt than usual. Kim, with slightly raised head, was still staring at his totem on the table, when the Chaplain stepped on his right shoulder-blade. Kim flinched under the leather, and, rolling side-

ways, brought down the Chaplain, who, ever a man of action, caught him by the throat and nearly choked the life out of him. Kim then kicked him desperately in the stomach. Mr Bennett gasped and doubled up, but without relaxing his grip, rolled over again, and silently hauled Kim to his own tent. The Mavericks were incurable practical jokers; and it occurred to the Englishman that silence was best till he had made complete inquiry.

'Why, it's a boy!' he said, as he drew his prize under the light of the tent-pole lantern, then shaking him severely cried: 'What were you doing? You're a thief. *Choor? Mallum?*' His Hindustani was very limited, and the ruffled and disgusted Kim intended to keep to the character laid down for him. As he recovered his breath he was inventing a beautifully plausible tale of his relations to some scullion, and at the same time keeping a keen eye on and a little under the Chaplain's left arm-pit. The chance came; he ducked for the doorway, but a long arm shot out and clutched at his neck, snapping the amulet string and closing on the amulet.

'Give it me. Oh, give it me. Is it lost? Give me the papers.'

The words were in English – the tinny, saw-cut English of the native-bred, and the Chaplain jumped.

'A scapular,' said he, opening his hand. 'No, some sort of heathen charm. Why – why, do you speak English? Little boys who steal are beaten. You know that?'

'I do not – I did not steal.' Kim danced in agony like a terrier at a lifted stick. 'Oh, give it me. It is my charm. Do not thieve it from me.'

The Chaplain took no heed, but, going to the tent door, called aloud. A fattish, clean-shaven man appeared.

'I want your advice, Father Victor,' said Bennett. 'I found this boy in the dark outside the mess-tent. Ordinarily, I should have chastized him and let him go, because I believe him to be a thief. But it seems he talks English, and he attaches some sort of value to a charm round his neck. I thought perhaps you might help me.'

Between himself and the Roman Catholic Chaplain of the Irish contingent lay, as Bennett believed, an unbridgeable gulf, but it was noticeable that whenever the Church of England dealt with a human problem she was very likely to call in the Church of Rome. Bennett's official abhorrence of the Scarlet Woman and all her ways was only equalled by his private respect for Father Victor.

'A thief talking English, is it? Let's look at his charm. No, it's not a scapular, Bennett.' He held out his hand.

'But have we any right to open it? A sound whipping –'

'I did *not* thieve,' protested Kim. 'You have hit me kicks all over my body. Now give me my charm and I will go away.'

'Not quite so fast. We'll look first,' said Father Victor, leisurely rolling out poor Kimball O'Hara's '*ne varietur*' parchment, his clearance-certificate, and Kim's baptismal certificate. On this last O'Hara – with some confused idea that he was doing wonders for his son – had scrawled scores of times: 'Look after the boy. Please look after the boy' – signing his name and regimental number in full.

'Powers of Darkness below!' said Father Victor, passing all over to Mr Bennett. 'Do you know what these things are?'

'Yes,' said Kim. 'They are mine, and I want to go away.'

'I do not quite understand,' said Mr Bennett. 'He probably brought them on purpose. It may be a begging trick of some kind.'

'I never saw a beggar less anxious to stay with his company, then. There's the makings of a gay mystery here. Ye believe in Providence, Bennett?'

'I hope so.'

'Well, I believe in miracles, so it comes to the same thing. Powers of Darkness! Kimball O'Hara! And his son! But then he's a native, and I saw Kimball married myself to Annie Shott. How long have you had these things, boy?'

'Ever since I was a little baby.'

Father Victor stepped forward quickly and opened the front of Kim's upper garment. 'You see, Bennett, he's not very black. What's your name?'

'Kim.'

'Or Kimball?'

'Perhaps. Will you let me go away?'

'What else?'

'They call me Kim Rishti ke. That is Kim of the Rishti.'

'What is that – "Rishti"?'

'*Eye*-rishti – that was the regiment – my father's.'

'Irish – oh, I see.'

'Yess. That was how my father told me. My father, he has lived.'

'Has lived where?'

'Has lived. Of *course* he is dead – gone out.'

'Oh! That's your abrupt way of putting it, is it?'

Bennett interrupted. 'It is possible I have done the boy

117

an injustice. He is certainly white, though evidently neglected. I am sure I must have bruised him. I do not think spirits –'

'Get him a glass of sherry, then, and let him squat on the cot. Now, Kim,' continued Father Victor, 'no one is going to hurt you. Drink that down and tell us about yourself. The truth, if you've no objection.'

Kim coughed a little as he put down the empty glass, and considered. This seemed a time for caution and fancy. Small boys who prowl about camps are generally turned out after a whipping. But he had received no stripes; the amulet was evidently working in his favour, and it looked as though the Umballa horoscope and the few words that he could remember of his father's maunderings fitted in most miraculously. Else why did the fat padre seem so impressed, and why the glass of hot yellow drink from the lean one?

'My father, he is dead in Lahore city since I was very little. The woman, she kept *kabarri* shop near where the hire-carriages are.' Kim began with a plunge, not quite sure how far the truth would serve him.

'Your mother?'

'*No!*' – with a gesture of disgust. 'She went out when I was born. My father, he got these papers from the Jadoo-Gher – what do you call that?' (Bennett nodded) 'because he was in – good standing. What do you call that?' (again Bennett nodded). 'My father told me that. He said, too, and also the Brahmin who made the drawing in the dust at Umballa two days ago, *he* said, that I shall find a Red Bull on a green field and that the Bull shall help me.'

'A phenomenal little liar,' muttered Bennett.

118

'Powers of Darkness below, what a country!' murmured Father Victor. 'Go on, Kim.'

'I did *not* thieve. Besides, I am just now disciple of a very holy man. He is sitting outside. We saw two men come with flags, making the place ready. That is *always* so in a dream, or on account of a – a – prophecy. So I knew it was come true. I saw the Red Bull on the green field, and my father he said: "Nine hundred *pukka* devils and the Colonel riding on a horse will look after you when you find the Red Bull!" I did not know what to do when I saw the Bull, but I went away and I came again when it was dark. I wanted to see the Bull again, and I saw the Bull again with the – the sahibs praying to it. I think the Bull shall help me. The holy man said so too. He is sitting outside. Will you hurt him, if I call him a shout now? He is very holy. He can witness to all the things I say, and he knows I am not a thief.'

'"Sahibs praying to a bull!" What in the world do you make of that?' said Bennett. '"Disciple of a holy man!" Is the boy mad?'

'It's O'Hara's boy, sure enough. O'Hara's boy leagued with all the Powers of Darkness. It's very much what his father would have done – if he was drunk. We'd better invite the holy man. He may know something.'

'He does not know anything,' said Kim. 'I will show you him if you come. He is my master. Then afterwards we can go.'

'Powers of Darkness!' was all that Father Victor could say, as Bennett marched off, with a firm hand on Kim's shoulder.

They found the lama where he had dropped.

'The Search is at an end for me,' shouted Kim in the

vernacular. 'I have found the Bull, but God knows what comes next. They will not hurt you. Come to the fat priest's tent with this thin man and see the end. It is all new, and they cannot talk Hindi. They are only uncurried donkeys.'

'Then it is not well to make a jest of their ignorance,' the lama returned. 'I am glad if thou art rejoiced, *chela*.'

Dignified and unsuspicious, he strode into the little tent, saluted the Churches as a churchman, and sat down by the open charcoal brazier. The yellow lining of the tent reflected in the lamplight made his face red-gold.

Bennett looked at him with the triple-ringed uninterest of the creed that lumps nine-tenths of the world under the title of 'heathen'.

'And what was the end of the Search? What gift has the Red Bull brought?' The lama addressed himself to Kim.

'He says, "What are you going to do?"' Bennett was staring uneasily at Father Victor, and Kim, for his own ends, took upon himself the office of interpreter.

'I do not see what concern this *fakir* has with the boy, who is probably his dupe or his confederate,' Bennett began. 'We cannot allow an English boy – Assuming that he is the son of a Mason, the sooner he goes to the Masonic Orphanage the better.'

'Ah! That's your opinion as secretary to the regimental lodge,' said Father Victor; 'but we might as well tell the old man what we are going to do. He doesn't look like a villain.'

'My experience is that one can never fathom the oriental mind. Now, Kimball, I wish you to tell this man what I say – word for word.'

Kim gathered the import of the next few sentences and began thus:

'Holy One, the thin fool who looks like a camel says that I am the son of a sahib.'

'But how?'

'Oh, it is true. I knew it since my birth, but *he* could only find it out by rending the amulet from my neck and reading all the papers. He thinks that once a sahib is always a sahib, and between the two of them they purpose to keep me in this regiment or to send me to a *madrissah* [a school]. It has happened before. I have always avoided it. The fat fool is of one mind and the camel-like one of another. But that is no odds. I may spend one night here and perhaps the next. It has happened before. Then I will run away and return to thee.'

'But tell them that thou art my *chela*. Tell them how thou didst come to me when I was faint and bewildered. Tell them of our Search, and they will surely let thee go now.'

'I have already told them. They laugh, and they talk of the police.'

'What are you saying?' asked Mr Bennett.

'Oah. He only says that if you do not let me go it will stop him in his business – his ur-gent private af-fairs.' This last was a reminiscence of some talk with a Eurasian clerk in the Canal Department, but it only drew a smile, which nettled him. 'And if you *did* know what his business was you would not be in such a beastly hurry to interfere.'

'What is it then?' said Father Victor, not without feeling, as he watched the lama's face.

'There is a River in this country which he wishes to find

121

so veree much. It was put out by an Arrow which –' Kim tapped his foot impatiently as he translated in his own mind from the vernacular to the clumsy English. 'Oah, it was made by our Lord God Buddha, you know, and if you wash there you are washed away from all your sins and made as white as cotton wool.' (Kim had heard mission-talk in his time.) 'I am his disciple, and we *must* find that River. It is so veree valuable to us.'

'Say that again,' said Bennett. Kim obeyed, with amplifications.

'But this is gross blasphemy!' cried the Church of England.

'Tck! Tck!' said Father Victor sympathetically. 'I'd give a good deal to be able to talk the vernacular. A river that washes away sin! And how long have you two been looking for it?'

'Oh, many days. Now we wish to go away and look for it again. It is not here, you see.'

'I see,' said Father Victor gravely. 'But he can't go on in that old man's company. It would be different, Kim, if you were not a soldier's son. Tell him that the Regiment will take care of you and make you as good a man as your – as good a man as can be. Tell him that if he believes in miracles he must believe that –'

'There is no need to play on his credulity,' Bennett interrupted.

'I'm doing no such thing. He must believe that the boy's coming here – to his own regiment – in search of his Red Bull is in the nature of a miracle. Consider the chances against it, Bennett. This one boy in all India, and our regiment of all others on the line o' march for him to meet with! It's predestined on the face of

it. Yes, tell him it's *Kismet*. *Kismet, mallum?* [Do you understand?]'

He turned towards the lama, to whom he might as well have talked of Mesopotamia.

'They say,' – the old man's eye lighted at Kim's speech – 'they say that the meaning of my horoscope is now accomplished, and that being led back – though as thou knowest I went out of curiosity – to these people and their Red Bull I must needs go to a *madrissah* and be turned into a sahib. Now I make pretence of agreement, for at the worst it will be but a few meals eaten away from thee. Then I will slip away and follow down the road to Saharunpore. Therefore, Holy One, keep with that Kulu woman – on no account stray far from her cart till I come again. Past question, my sign is of war and of armed men. See how they have given me wine to drink and set me upon a bed of honour! My father must have been some great person. So if they raise me to honour among them, good. If not, good again. However it goes, I will run back to thee when I am tired. But stay with the Rajputni, or I shall miss thy feet . . . Oah yess,' said the boy, 'I have told him everything you tell me to say.'

'And I cannot see any need why he should wait,' said Bennett, feeling in his trouser pocket. 'We can investigate the details later – and I will give him a ru–'

'Give him time. Maybe he's fond of the lad,' said Father Victor, half arresting the clergyman's motion.

The lama dragged forth his rosary and pulled his huge hat-brim over his eyes.

'What can he want now?'

'He says' – Kim put up one hand. 'He says: Be quiett. He wants to speak to me by himself. You see, you do not

know one little word of what he says, and I think if you talk he will perhaps give you very bad curses. When he takes those beads like that, you see, he always wants to be quiett.'

The two Englishmen sat overwhelmed, but there was a look in Bennett's eye that promised ill for Kim when he should be relaxed to the religious arm.

'A sahib and the son of a sahib –' The lama's voice was harsh with pain. 'But no white man knows the land and the customs of the land as thou knowest. How comes it this is true?'

'What matter, Holy One? – but remember it is only for a night or two. Remember, I can change swiftly. It will all be as it was when I first spoke to thee under Zam-Zammah the great gun –'

'As a boy in the dress of white men – when I first went to the Wonder House. And a second time thou wast a Hindu. What shall the third incarnation be?' He chuckled drearily. 'Ah, *chela*, thou hast done a wrong to an old man because my heart went out to thee.'

'And mine to thee. But how could I know that the Red Bull would bring me to this business?'

The lama covered his face afresh, and nervously rattled the rosary. Kim squatted beside him and laid hold upon a fold of his clothing.

'Now it is understood that the boy is a sahib?' he went on in a muffled tone. 'Such a sahib as was he who kept the images in the Wonder House.' The lama's experience of white men was limited. He seemed to be repeating a lesson. 'So then it is not seemly that he should do other than as the sahibs do. He must go back to his own people.'

'For a day and a night and a day,' Kim pleaded.

'No, ye don't!' Father Victor saw Kim edging towards the door, and interposed a strong leg.

'I do not understand the customs of white men. The Priest of the Images in the Wonder House in Lahore was more courteous than the thin one here. This boy will be taken from me. They will make a sahib of my disciple? Woe to me! How shall I find my River? Have *they* no disciples? Ask.'

'He says he is very sorree that he cannot find the River now any more. He says, Why have you no disciples, and stop bothering him? He wants to be washed of his sins.'

Neither Bennett nor Father Victor found any answer ready.

Said Kim in English, distressed for the lama's agony: 'I think if you will let me go now we will walk away quietly and not steal. We will look for that River like before I was caught. I wish I did not come here to find the Red Bull and all that sort of thing. I do not want it.'

'It's the very best day's work you ever did for yourself, young man,' said Bennett.

'Good heavens, I don't know how to console him,' said Father Victor, watching the lama intently. 'He can't take the boy away with him, and yet he's a good man – I'm sure he's a good man. Bennett, if you give him that rupee he'll curse you root and branch!'

They listened to each other's breathing – three – five full minutes. Then the lama raised his head, and looked forth across them into space and emptiness.

'And I am a Follower of the Way,' he said bitterly. 'The sin is mine and the punishment is mine. I made believe to myself – for now I see it was but make-belief – that thou

wast sent to me to aid in the Search. So my heart went out to thee for thy charity and thy courtesy and the wisdom of thy little years. But those who follow the Way must permit not the fire of any desire or attachment, for that is all illusion. As says . . .' He quoted an old, old Chinese text, backed it with another, and reinforced these with a third. 'I stepped aside from the Way, my *chela*. It was no fault of thine. I delighted in the sight of life, the new people upon the roads, and in thy joy at seeing these things. I was pleased with thee who should have considered my Search and my Search alone. Now I am sorrowful because thou art taken away and my River is far from me. It is the Law which I have broken!'

'Powers of Darkness below!' said Father Victor, who, wise in the confessional, heard the pain in every sentence.

'I can see now that the sign of the Red Bull was a sign for me as well as for thee. All desire is red – and evil. I will do penance and find my River alone.'

'At least go back to the Kulu woman,' said Kim, 'otherwise thou wilt be lost upon the roads. She will feed thee till I run back to thee.'

The lama waved a hand to show that the matter was finally settled in his mind.

'Now,' – his tone altered as he turned to Kim – 'what will they do with thee? At least I may, acquiring merit, wipe out past ill.'

'Make me a sahib – so they think. The day after tomorrow I return. Do not grieve.'

'Of what sort? Such an one as this or that man?' He pointed to Father Victor. 'Such an one as those I saw this evening – men wearing swords and stamping heavily?'

'Maybe.'

'That is not well. These men follow desire and come to emptiness. Thou must not be of their sort.'

'The Umballa priest said that my star was war,' Kim interjected. 'I will ask these fools – but there is truly no need. I will run away this night, for all I wanted to see the new things.'

Kim put two or three questions in English to Father Victor, translating the replies to the lama.

Then: 'He says, "You take him from me and you cannot say what you will make him." He says, "Tell me before I go, for it is not a small thing to make a child."'

'You will be sent to a school. Later on, we shall see. Kimball, I suppose you'd like to be a soldier?'

'*Gorah-log* [white-folk]. No-ah! No-ah!' Kim shook his head violently. There was nothing in his composition to which drill and routine appealed. 'I will *not* be a soldier.'

'You will be what you're told to be,' said Bennett; 'and you should be grateful that we're going to help you.'

Kim smiled compassionately. If these men lay under the delusion that he would do anything that he did not fancy, so much the better.

Another long silence followed. Bennett fidgeted with impatience, and suggested calling a sentry to evict the *fakir*.

'Do they give or sell learning among the sahibs? Ask them,' said the lama, and Kim interpreted.

'They say that money is paid to the teacher – but that money the Regiment will give . . . What need? It is only for a night.'

'And – the more money is paid the better learning is given?' The lama disregarded Kim's plans for an early

flight. 'It is no wrong to pay for learning. To help the ignorant to wisdom is always a merit.' The rosary clicked furiously as an abacus. Then he faced his oppressors.

'Ask them for how much money do they give a wise and suitable teaching? And in what city is that teaching given?'

'Well,' said Father Victor in English, when Kim had translated, 'that depends. The Regiment would pay for you all the time you are at the Military Orphanage; or you might go on the Punjab Masonic Orphanage's list (not that he or you 'ud understand what that means): but the best schooling a boy can get in India is, of course, at St Xavier's in Partibus at Lucknow.' This took some time to interpret, for Bennett wished to cut it short.

'He wants to know how much?' said Kim placidly.

'Two or three hundred rupees a year.' Father Victor was long past any sense of amazement. Bennett, impatient, did not understand.

'He says: "Write that name and the money upon a paper and give it him." And he says you must write your name below, because he is going to write a letter in some days to you. He says you are a good man. He says the other man is a fool. He is going away.'

The lama rose suddenly. 'I follow my Search,' he cried, and was gone.

'He'll run slap into the sentries,' cried Father Victor, jumping up as the lama stalked out; 'but I can't leave the boy.' Kim made swift motion to follow, but checked himself. There was no sound of challenge outside. The lama had disappeared.

Kim settled himself composedly on the Chaplain's cot. At least the lama had promised that he would stay with

the Rajput woman from Kulu, and the rest was of the smallest importance. It pleased him that the two padres were so evidently excited. They talked long in undertones, Father Victor urging some scheme on Mr Bennett, who seemed incredulous. All this was very new and fascinating, but Kim felt sleepy. They called men into the tent – one of them certainly was the Colonel, as his father had prophesied – and they asked him an infinity of questions, chiefly about the woman who looked after him, all of which Kim answered truthfully. They did not seem to think the woman a good guardian.

After all, this was the newest of his experiences. Sooner or later, if he chose, he could escape into great, grey, formless India, beyond tents and padres and colonels. Meantime, if the sahibs were to be impressed, he would do his best to impress them. He too was a white man.

After much talk that he could not comprehend, they handed him over to a sergeant, who had strict instructions not to let him escape. The Regiment would go on to Umballa, and Kim would be sent up, partly at the expense of the Lodge and in part by subscription, to a place called Sanawar.

'It's miraculous past all whooping, Colonel,' said Father Victor, when he had talked without a break for ten minutes. 'His Buddhist friend has levanted after taking my name and address. I can't quite make out whether he'll pay for the boy's education or whether he is preparing some sort of witchcraft on his own account.' Then to Kim: 'You'll live to be grateful to your friend the Red Bull yet. We'll make a man of you at Sanawar – even at the price o' making you a Protestant.'

'Certainly – most certainly,' said Bennett.

'But you will not go to Sanawar,' said Kim.

'But we *will* go to Sanawar, little man. That's the order of the Commander-in-Chief, who's a trifle more important than O'Hara's son.'

'You will not go to Sanawar. You will go to thee War.'

There was a shout of laughter from the full tent.

'When you know your own regiment a trifle better you won't confuse the line of march with line of battle, Kim. We hope to go to "thee War" sometime.'

'Oah, I know all thatt.' Kim drew his bow again at a venture. If they were not going to the war, at least they did not know what he knew of the talk in the veranda at Umballa.

'I know you are not at thee war now; but I tell *you* that as soon as you get to Umballa you will be sent to the war – the new war. It is a war of eight thousand men, besides the guns.'

'That's explicit. D'you add prophecy to your other gifts? Take him along, sergeant. Take up a suit for him from the Drums, an' take care he doesn't slip through your fingers. Who says the age of miracles is gone by? I think I'll go to bed. My poor mind's weakening.'

At the far end of the camp, silent as a wild animal, an hour later sat Kim, newly washed all over, in a horrible stuff suit that rasped his arms and legs.

'A most amazin' young bird,' said the sergeant. 'He turns up in charge of a yellow-headed buck-Brahmin priest, with his father's Lodge certificates round his neck, talkin' God knows what all of a red bull. The buck-Brahmin evaporates without explanations, an' the bhoy sets cross-legged on the Chaplain's bed prophesyin'

bloody war to the men at large. Injia's a wild land for a
God-fearin' man. I'll just tie his leg to the tent-pole in case
he'll go through the roof. What did ye say about the war?'

'Eight thousand men, besides guns,' said Kim. 'Very
soon you will see.'

'You're a consolin' little imp. Lie down between the
Drums an' go to bye-bye. Those two boys will watch your
slumbers.'

CHAPTER
6

> Now I remember comrades –
> Old playmates on new seas –
> Whenas we traded orpiment
> Among the savages.
> Ten thousand leagues to southward,
> And thirty years removed –
> They knew not noble Valdez,
> But me they knew and loved.

<div align="right">Song of Diego Valdez</div>

Very early in the morning the white tents came down and disappeared as the Mavericks took a side-road to Umballa. It did not skirt the resting-place, and Kim, trudging beside a baggage-cart under fire of comments from soldiers' wives, was not so confident as over-night. He discovered that he was closely watched – Father Victor on the one side, and Mr Bennett on the other.

In the forenoon the column checked. A camel orderly handed the Colonel a letter. He read it, and spoke to a major. Half a mile in the rear, Kim heard a hoarse and joyful clamour rolling down on him through the thick dust. Then some one beat him on the back, crying: 'Tell us how ye knew, ye little limb of Satan? Father dear, see if ye can make him tell.'

A pony ranged alongside, and he was hauled on to the priest's saddle-bow.

'Now, my son, your prophecy of last night has come

true. Our orders are to entrain at Umballa for the Front tomorrow.'

'What is thatt?' said Kim, for *'front'* and *'entrain'* were newish words to him.

'We are going to "thee War", as you called it.'

'Of course you are going to thee War. I said last night.'

'Ye did; but, Powers o' Darkness, how did ye know?'

Kim's eyes sparkled. He shut his lips, nodded his head and looked unspeakable things. The Chaplain moved on through the dust, and privates, sergeants, and subalterns called one another's attention to the boy. The Colonel, at the head of the column, stared at him curiously. 'It was probably some bazaar rumour,' he said; 'but even then –' He referred to the paper in his hand. 'Hang it all, the thing was only decided within the last forty-eight hours.'

'Are there many more like you in India?' said Father Victor, 'or are you by way o' being a *lusus naturae*?'

'Now I have told you,' said the boy, 'will you let me go back to my old man? If he has not stayed with that woman from Kulu, I am afraid he will die.'

'By what I saw of him he's as well able to take care of himself as you. No. Ye've brought us luck, an' we're goin' to make a man of you. I'll take ye back to your baggage-cart and ye'll come to me this evening.'

For the rest of the day Kim found himself an object of distinguished consideration among a few hundred white men. The story of his appearance in camp, the discovery of his parentage, and his prophecy, had lost nothing in the telling. A big, shapeless white woman on a pile of bedding asked him mysteriously whether he thought her husband would come back from the war. Kim reflected

gravely, and said that he would, and the woman gave
him food. In many respects, this big procession that
played music at intervals – this crowd that talked and
laughed so easily – resembled a festival in Lahore city. So
far, there was no sign of hard work, and he resolved
to lend the spectacle his patronage. At evening there
came out to meet them bands of music, and played the
Mavericks into camp near Umballa railway station. That
was an interesting night. Men of other regiments came to
visit the Mavericks. The Mavericks went visiting on their
own account. Their pickets hurried forth to bring them
back, met pickets of strange regiments on the same duty;
and, after a while, the bugles blew madly for more
pickets with officers to control the tumult. The Mavericks
had a reputation for liveliness to live up to. But they fell in
on the platform next morning in perfect shape and condi-
tion; and Kim, left behind with the sick, women, and
boys, found himself shouting farewells excitedly as the
trains drew away. Life as a sahib was amusing so far; but
he touched it with a cautious hand. Then they marched
him back in charge of a drummer-boy to empty, lime-
washed barracks, whose floors were covered with rub-
bish and string and paper, and whose ceilings gave back
his lonely footfall. Native-fashion, he curled himself up
on a stripped cot and went to sleep. An angry man
stumped down the veranda, woke him up, and said he
was a schoolmaster. This was enough for Kim, and he
retired into his shell. He could just puzzle out the various
English police notices in Lahore city, because they
affected his comfort; and among the many guests of the
woman who looked after him had been a queer German
who painted scenery for the Parsee travelling theatre. He

told Kim that he had been 'on the barricades in Forty-eight', and therefore – at least that was how it struck Kim – he would teach the boy to write in return for food. Kim had been kicked as far as single letters, but did not think well of them.

'I do not know anything. Go away!' said Kim, scenting evil. Hereupon the man caught him by the ear, dragged him to a room in a far-off wing where a dozen drummer-boys were sitting on forms, and told him to be still if he could do nothing else. This he managed very success-fully. The man explained something or other with white lines on a black board for at least half an hour, and Kim continued his interrupted nap. He much disapproved of the present aspect of affairs, for this was the very school and discipline he had spent two thirds of his young life in avoiding. Suddenly a beautiful idea occurred to him, and he wondered that he had not thought of it before.

The man dismissed them, and first to spring through the veranda into the open sunshine was Kim.

''Ere, you! 'Alt! Stop!' said a high voice at his heels. 'I've got to look after you. My orders are not to let you out of my sight. Where are you goin'?'

It was the drummer-boy who had been hanging round him all the forenoon – a fat and freckled person of about fourteen, and Kim loathed him from the soles of his boots to his cap ribbons.

'To the bazaar – to get sweets – for you,' said Kim, after thought.

'Well, the bazaar's out o' bounds. If we go there we'll get a dressing-down. You come back.'

'How near can we go?' Kim did not know what bounds meant, but he wished to be polite – for the present.

''Ow near? 'Ow far, you mean! We can go as far as that tree down the road.'

'Then I will go there.'

'All right. I ain't goin'. It's too 'ot. I can watch you from 'ere. It's no good runnin' away. If you did, they'd spot you by your clothes. That's regimental stuff you're wearing. There ain't a picket in Umballa wouldn't 'ead you back quicker than you started out.'

This did not impress Kim as much as the knowledge that his raiment would tire him out if he tried to run. He slouched to the tree at the corner of a bare road leading towards the bazaar, and eyed the natives passing. Most of them were barrack servants of the lowest caste. Kim hailed a sweeper, who promptly retorted with a piece of unnecessary insolence, in the natural belief that the European boy could not follow it. The low, quick answer undeceived him. Kim put his fettered soul into it, thankful for the late chance to abuse somebody in the tongue he knew best. 'And now, go to the nearest letter-writer in the bazaar and tell him to come here. I would write a letter.'

'But – but what manner of white man's son art thou to need a bazaar letter-writer? Is there not a schoolmaster in the barracks?'

'Ay; and Hell is full of the same sort. Do my order, you – you Od! Thy mother was married under a basket! Servant of Lal Beg' (Kim knew the God of the sweepers), 'run on my business or we will talk again.'

The sweeper shuffled off in haste. 'There is a white boy by the barracks waiting under a tree who is not a white boy,' he stammered to the first bazaar letter-writer he came across. 'He needs thee.'

'Will he pay?' said that spruce scribe, gathering up his desk and pens and sealing-wax all in order.

'I do not know. He is not like other boys. Go and see. It is well worth.'

Kim danced with impatience when the slim young Kayeth hove in sight. As soon as his voice could carry he cursed him volubly.

'First I will take my pay,' the letter-writer said. 'Bad words have made the price higher. But who art thou, dressed in that fashion, to speak in this fashion?'

'Aha! That is in the letter which thou shalt write. Never was such a tale. But I am in no haste. Another writer will serve me. Umballa city is full of them as is Lahore.'

'Four annas,' said the writer, sitting down and spreading his cloth in the shade of a deserted barrack wing.

Mechanically Kim squatted beside him – squatted as only the natives can – in spite of the abominable clinging trousers.

The writer regarded him sideways.

'That is the price to ask of sahibs,' said Kim. 'Now fix me a true one.'

'An anna and a half. How do I know, having written the letter, that thou wilt not run away?'

'I must not go beyond this tree, and there is also the stamp to be considered.'

'I get no commission on the price of the stamp. Once more, what manner of white boy art thou?'

'That shall be said in the letter, which is to Mahbub Ali, the horse-dealer in the Kashmir Serai, at Lahore. He is my friend.'

'Wonder on wonder!' murmured the letter-writer, dipping a reed in the inkstand. 'To be written in Hindi?'

'Assuredly. To Mahbub Ali then. Begin! "I have come down with the old man as far as Umballa in the train. At Umballa I carried the news of the bay mare's pedigree."' After what he had seen in the garden, he was not going to write of white stallions.

'Slower a little. What has a bay mare to do . . . Is it Mahbub Ali, the great dealer?'

'Who else? I have been in his service. Take more ink. Again. "As the order was, so I did it. We then went on foot towards Benares, but on the third day we found a certain regiment." Is that down?'

'Ay, *pulton*,' murmured the writer all ears.

'"I went into their camp and was caught, and by means of the charm about my neck, which thou knowest, it was established that I was the son of some man in the regiment: according to the prophecy of the Red Bull, which thou knowest was common talk of our bazaar."' Kim waited for this shaft to sink into the letter-writer's heart, cleared his throat, and continued: '"A priest clothed me and gave me a new name . . . One priest, however, was a fool. The clothes are very heavy, but I am a sahib and my heart is heavy too. They send me to a school and beat me. I do not like the air and water here. Come then and help me, Mahbub Ali, or send me some money, for I have not sufficient to pay the writer who writes this."'

'"Who writes this." It is my own fault that I was tricked. Thou art as clever as Husain Bux that forged the Treasury stamps at Nucklao. But what a tale! What a tale! Is it true by any chance?'

'It does not profit to tell lies to Mahbub Ali. It is better to help his friends by lending them a stamp. When the money comes I will repay.'

The writer grunted doubtfully, but took a stamp out of his desk, sealed the letter, handed it over to Kim, and departed. Mahbub Ali's was a name of power in Umballa.

'That is the way to win a good account with the Gods,' Kim shouted after him.

'Pay me twice over when the money comes,' the man cried over his shoulder.

'What was you bukkin' to that nigger about?' said the drummer-boy when Kim returned to the veranda. 'I was watchin' you.'

'I was only talkin' to him.'

'You talk the same as a nigger, don't you?'

'No-ah! No-ah! I onlee speak a little. What shall we do now?'

'The bugles 'll go for dinner in arf a minute. My Gawd! I wish I'd gone up to the Front with the Regiment. It's awful doin' nothin' but school down 'ere. Don't you 'ate it?'

'Oah yess!'

'I'd run away if I knew where to go to, but, as the men say, in this bloomin' Injia you're only a prisoner at large. You can't desert without bein' took back at once. I'm fair sick of it.'

'You have been in *Be* – England?'

'W'y, I only come out last troopin' season with my mother. I should think I *'ave* been in England. What a ignorant little beggar you are! You was brought up in the gutter, wasn't you?'

'Oah yess. Tell me something about England. My father he came from there.'

Though he would not say so, Kim of course disbelieved

every word the drummer-boy spoke about the Liverpool suburb which was his England. It passed the heavy time till dinner – a most unappetizing meal served to the boys and a few invalids in a corner of a barrack-room. But that he had written to Mahbub Ali, Kim would have been almost depressed. The indifference of native crowds he was used to; but this strong loneliness among white men preyed on him. He was grateful when, in the course of the afternoon, a big soldier took him over to Father Victor, who lived in another wing across another dusty parade-ground. The priest was reading an English letter written in purple ink. He looked at Kim more curiously than ever.

'An' how do you like it, my son, as far as you've gone? Not much, eh? It must be hard – very hard on a wild animal. Listen now. I've an amazin' epistle from your friend.'

'Where is he? Is he well? Oah! If he knows to write me letters, it is all right.'

'You're fond of him, then?'

'*Of* course I am fond of him. He was fond of me.'

'It seems so by the look of this. He can't write English, can he?'

'Oah no. Not that I know, but *of* course he found a letter-writer who can write English veree well, and so he wrote. I *do* hope you understand.'

'That accounts for it. D'you know anything about his money affairs?' Kim's face showed that he did not.

'How can I tell?'

'That's what I'm askin'. Now listen if you can make head or tail o' this. We'll skip the first part . . . It's written from Jagadhir Road . . . "Sitting on wayside in grave

meditation, trusting to be favoured with your Honour's applause of present step, which recommend your Honour to execute for Almighty God's sake. Education is greatest blessing if of best sorts. Otherwise no earthly use." Faith, the old man's hit the bull's-eye that time! "If your Honour condescending giving my boy best educations Xavier" (I suppose that's St Xavier's in Partibus) "in terms of our conversation dated in your tent 15th instant" (a business-like touch there!) "then Almighty God blessing your Honour's succeedings to third an' fourth generation and" – now listen! – "confide in your Honour's humble servant for adequat remuneration per hoondi per annum three hundred rupees a year to one expensive education St Xavier, Lucknow, and allow small time to forward same per hoondi sent to any part of India as your Honour shall address yourself. This servant of your Honour has presently no place to lay crown of his head, but going to Benares by train on account of persecution of old woman talking so much and unanxious residing Saharunpore in any domestic capacity." Now what in the world does that mean?'

'She has asked him to be her *puro* – her clergyman – at Saharunpore, *I* think. He would not do that on account of his River. She *did* talk.'

'It's clear to you, is it? It beats me altogether. "So going to Benares, where will find address and forward rupees for boy who is apple of eye, and for Almighty God's sake execute this education, and your petitioner as in duty bound shall ever awfully pray. Written by Sobrao Satai, Failed Entrance Allahabad University, for Venerable Teshoo Lama the priest of Such-zen looking for a River, address care of Tirthankars' Temple, Benares. P.M. –

Please note boy is apple of eye, and rupees shall be sent per hoondi three hundred per annum. For God Almighty's sake." Now, is that ravin' lunacy or a business proposition? I ask you, because I am fairly at my wit's end.'

'He says he will give me three hundred rupees a year? So he will give me them.'

'Oh, that's the way you look at it, is it?'

'*Of* course. If he says so!'

The priest whistled; then he addressed Kim as an equal.

'I don't believe it; but we'll see. You were goin' off today to the Military Orphanage at Sanawar, where the Regiment would keep you till you were old enough to enlist. Ye'd be brought up to the Church of England. Bennett arranged for that. On the other hand, if ye go to St Xavier's ye'll get a better education an' – an' can have the religion. D'ye see my dilemma?'

Kim saw nothing save a vision of the lama going south in a train with none to beg for him.

'Like most people, I'm going to temporize. If your friend sends the money from Benares – Powers of Darkness below, where's a street-beggar to raise three hundred rupees? – ye'll go down to Lucknow and I'll pay your fare, because I can't touch the subscription-money if I intend, as I do, to make ye a Catholic. If he doesn't, ye'll go to the Military Orphanage at the Regiment's expense. I'll allow him three days' grace, though I don't believe it at all. Even then, if he fails in his payments later on . . . but it's beyond me. We can only walk one step at a time in this world, praise God! An' they sent Bennett to the Front an' left me behind. Bennett can't expect everything.'

'Oah yess,' said Kim vaguely.

The priest leaned forward. 'I'd give a month's pay to find what's goin' on inside that little round head of yours.'

'There is nothing,' said Kim, and scratched it. He was wondering whether Mahbub Ali would send him as much as a whole rupee. Then he could pay the letter-writer and write letters to the lama at Benares. Perhaps Mahbub Ali would visit him next time he came south with horses. Surely he must know that Kim's delivery of the letter to the officer at Umballa had caused the great war which the men and boys had discussed so loudly over the barrack dinner-tables. But if Mahbub Ali did not know this, it would be very unsafe to tell him so. Mahbub Ali was hard upon boys who knew, or thought they knew, too much.

'Well, till I get further news.' – Father Victor's voice interrupted the reverie. 'Ye can run along now and play with the other boys. They'll teach ye something – but I don't think ye'll like it.'

The day dragged to its weary end. When he wished to sleep he was instructed how to fold up his clothes and set out his boots; the other boys deriding. Bugles waked him in the dawn; the schoolmaster caught him after breakfast, thrust a page of meaningless characters under his nose, gave them senseless names, and whacked him without reason. Kim meditated poisoning him with opium borrowed from a barrack sweeper, but reflected that, as they all ate at one table in public (this was particularly revolting to Kim, who preferred to turn his back on the world at meals), the stroke might be dangerous. Then he attempted running off to the village where the priest had

tried to drug the lama – the village where the old soldier lived. But far-seeing sentries at every exit headed back the little scarlet figure. Trousers and jacket crippled body and mind alike, so he abandoned the project and fell back, oriental-fashion, on time and chance. Three days of torment passed in the big, echoing white rooms. He walked out of afternoons under escort of the drummer-boy, and all he heard from his companion were the few useless words which seemed to make two thirds of the white man's abuse. Kim knew and despised them all long ago. The boy resented his silence and lack of interest by beating him, as was only natural. He did not care for any of the bazaars which were in bounds. He styled all natives 'niggers'; yet servants and sweepers called him abominable names to his face, and, misled by their deferential attitude, he never understood. This somewhat consoled Kim for the beatings.

On the morning of the fourth day a judgement over-took that drummer. They had gone out together towards Umballa racecourse. He returned alone, weeping, with news that young O'Hara, to whom he had been doing nothing in particular, had hailed a scarlet-bearded nigger on horseback; that the nigger had then and there laid into him with a peculiarly adhesive quirt, picked up young O'Hara, and borne him off at full gallop. These tidings came to Father Victor and he drew down his long upper lip. He was already sufficiently startled by a letter from the Temple of the Tirthankars at Benares, enclosing a native banker's note of hand for three hundred rupees, and an amazing prayer to 'Almighty God'. The lama would have been more annoyed than the priest had he

known how the bazaar letter-writer had translated his phrase 'to acquire merit'.

'Powers of Darkness below!' Father Victor fumbled with the note. 'An' now he's off with another of his peep-o'-day friends. I don't know whether it will be a greater relief to me to get him back or to have him lost. He's beyond my comprehension. How the Divil – yes, *he's* the man I mean – can a street-beggar raise money to educate white boys?'

Three miles off, on Umballa racecourse, Mahbub Ali, reining a grey Kabuli stallion with Kim in front of him, was saying:

'But, Little Friend of all the World, there is *my* honour and reputation to be considered. All the officer-sahibs in all the regiments, and all Umballa, know Mahbub Ali. Men saw me pick thee up and chastise that boy. We are seen now from far across this plain. How can I take thee away, or account for thy disappearing if I set thee down and let thee run off into the crops? They would put me in jail. Be patient. Once a sahib, always a sahib. When thou art a man – who knows? – thou wilt be grateful to Mahbub Ali.'

'Take me beyond their sentries where I can change this red. Give me money and I will go to Benares and be with my lama again. I do not want to be a sahib, and remember I *did* deliver that message.'

The stallion bounded wildly. Mahbub Ali had incautiously driven home the sharp-edged stirrup. (He was not the new sort of fluent horse-dealer who wears English boots and spurs.) Kim drew his own conclusions from that betrayal.

'That was a small matter. It lay on the straight road to

Benares. I and the sahib have by this time forgotten it. I send so many letters and messages to men who ask questions about horses, I cannot well remember one from the other. Was it some matter of a bay mare that Peters Sahib wished the pedigree of?'

Kim saw the trap at once. If he had said 'bay mare' Mahbub would have known by his very readiness to fall in with the amendment that the boy suspected something. Kim replied therefore:

'Bay mare. No. I do not forget my messages thus. It was a white stallion.'

'Ay, so it was. A white Arab stallion. But thou didst write "bay mare" to me.'

'Who cares to tell truth to a letter-writer?' Kim answered, feeling Mahbub's palm on his heart.

'Hi! Mahbub, you old villain, pull up!' cried a voice, and an Englishman raced alongside on a little polo-pony. 'I've been chasing you half over the country. That Kabuli of yours can go. For sale, I suppose?'

'I have some young stuff coming on made by Heaven for the delicate and difficult polo-game. He has no equal. He –'

'Plays polo and waits at table. Yes. We know all that. What the deuce have you got there?'

'A boy,' said Mahbub gravely. 'He was being beaten by another boy. His father was once a white soldier in the big war. The boy was a child in Lahore city. He played with my horses when he was a babe. Now I think they will make him a soldier. He has been newly caught by his father's regiment that went up to the war last week. But I do not think he wants to be a soldier. I take him for a ride. Tell me where thy barracks are and I will set thee there.'

'Let me go. I can find the barracks alone.'

'And if thou runnest away who will say it is not my fault?'

'He'll run back to his dinner. Where has he to run to?' the Englishman asked.

'He was born in the land. He has friends. He goes where he chooses. He is a *chabuk sawai* [a sharp chap]. It needs only to change his clothing, and in a twinkling he would be a low-caste Hindu boy.'

'The deuce he would!' The Englishman looked critically at the boy as Mahbub headed towards the barracks. Kim ground his teeth. Mahbub was mocking him, as faithless Afghans will; for he went on:

'They will send him to a school and put heavy boots on his feet and swaddle him in these clothes. Then he will forget all he knows. Now, which of the barracks is thine?'

Kim pointed – he could not speak – to Father Victor's wing, all staring white near by.

'Perhaps he will make a good soldier,' said Mahbub reflectively. 'He will make a good orderly at least. I sent him to deliver a message once from Lahore. A message concerning the pedigree of a white stallion.'

Here was deadly insult on deadlier injury – and the sahib to whom he had so craftily given that war-waking letter heard it all. Kim beheld Mahbub Ali frying in flame for his treachery, but for himself he saw one long grey vista of barracks, schools, and barracks again. He gazed imploringly at the clear-cut face in which there was no glimmer of recognition; but even at this extremity it never occurred to him to throw himself on the white man's mercy or to denounce the Afghan. And Mahbub

stared deliberately at the Englishman, who stared as deliberately at Kim, quivering and tongue-tied.

'My horse is well trained,' said the dealer. 'Others would have kicked, Sahib.'

'Ah,' said the Englishman at last, rubbing his pony's damp withers with his whip-butt. 'Who makes the boy a soldier?'

'He says the Regiment that found him, and especially the Padre-sahib of the regiment.'

'There is the Padre!' Kim choked as bare-headed Father Victor sailed down upon them from the veranda.

'Powers o' Darkness below, O'Hara! How many more mixed friends do you keep in Asia?' he cried, as Kim slid down and stood helplessly before him.

'Good morning, Padre,' the Englishman said cheerily. 'I know you by reputation well enough. Meant to have come over and called before this. I'm Creighton.'

'Of the Ethnological Survey?' said Father Victor. The Englishman nodded. 'Faith, I'm glad to meet you then; an' I owe you thanks for bringing back the boy.'

'No thanks to me, Padre. Besides, the boy wasn't going away. You don't know old Mahbub Ali.' The horse-dealer sat impassive in the sunlight. 'You will when you have been in the station a month. He sells us all our crocks. That boy is rather a curiosity. Can you tell me anything about him?'

'Can I tell you?' puffed Father Victor. 'You'll be the one man that could help me in my quandaries. Tell you! Powers o' Darkness, I'm bursting to tell some one who knows something o' the native!'

A groom came round the corner. Colonel Creighton raised his voice, speaking in Urdu. 'Very good, Mahbub

Ali, but what is the use of telling me all those stories about the pony? Not one pie more than three hundred and fifty rupees will I give.'

'The Sahib is a little hot and angry after riding,' the horse-dealer returned, with a leer of a privileged jester. 'Presently, he will see my horse's points more clearly. I will wait till he has finished his talk with the Padre. I will wait under that tree.'

'Confound you!' The Colonel laughed. 'That comes of looking at one of Mahbub's horses. He's a regular old leech, Padre. Wait, then, if thou hast so much time to spare, Mahbub. Now I'm at your service, Padre. Where is the boy? Oh, he's gone off to collogue with Mahbub. Queer sort of boy. Might I ask you to send my mare round under cover?'

He dropped into a chair which commanded a clear view of Kim and Mahbub Ali in conference beneath the tree. The Padre went indoors for cheroots.

Creighton heard Kim say bitterly: 'Trust a Brahmin before a snake, and a snake before an harlot, and an harlot before a Pathan, Mahbub Ali.'

'That is all one.' The great red beard wagged solemnly. 'Children should not see a carpet on the loom till the pattern is made plain. Believe me, Friend of all the World, I do thee great service. They will not make a soldier of thee.'

'You crafty old sinner!' thought Creighton. 'But you're not far wrong. That boy mustn't be wasted if he is as advertised.'

'Excuse me half a minute,' cried the Padre from within, 'but I'm getting the documents in the case.'

'If through me the favour of this bold and wise Colonel

149

Sahib comes to thee, and thou art raised to honour, what thanks wilt thou give Mahbub Ali when thou art a man?'

'Nay, nay! I begged thee to let me take the Road again, where I should have been safe; and thou hast sold me back to the English. What will they give thee for blood-money?'

'A cheerful young demon!' The Colonel bit his cigar, and turned politely to Father Victor.

'What are the letters that the fat priest is waving before the Colonel? Stand behind the stallion as though looking at my bridle!' said Mahbub Ali.

'A letter from my lama which he wrote from Jagadhir Road, saying that he will pay three hundred rupees by the year for my schooling.'

'Oho! Is old Red Hat of that sort? At which school?'

'God knows. I think in Nucklao.'

'Yes. There is a big school there for the sons of sahibs – and half-sahibs. I have seen it when I sell horses there. So the lama also loved the Friend of all the World?'

'Ay; and *he* did not tell lies, or return me to captivity.'

'Small wonder the Padre does not know how to un-ravel the thread. How fast he talks to the Colonel Sahib!' Mahbub Ali chuckled. 'By Allah!' – the keen eyes swept the veranda for an instant – 'thy lama has sent what to me looks like a note of hand. I have had some few dealings in *hoondis*. The Colonel Sahib is looking at it.'

'What good is all this to me?' said Kim wearily. 'Thou wilt go away, and they will return me to those empty rooms where there is no good place to sleep and where the boys beat me.'

'I do not think that. Have patience, child. All Pathans are not faithless – except in horse-flesh.'

Five – ten – fifteen minutes passed, Father Victor talking energetically or asking questions which the Colonel answered.

'Now I've told you everything that I know about the boy from beginnin' to end; and it's a blessed relief to me. Did ye ever hear the like?'

'At any rate, the old man has sent the money. Gobind Sahai's notes of hand are good from here to China,' said the Colonel. 'The more one knows about natives the less can one say what they will or won't do.'

'That's consolin' – from the head of the Ethnological Survey. It's this mixture of Red Bulls and Rivers of Healing (poor heathen, God help him!) an' notes of hand and Masonic certificates. Are you a Mason, by any chance?'

'By Jove, I am, now I come to think of it. That's an additional reason,' said the Colonel absently.

'I'm glad ye see a reason in it. But as I said, it's the mixture o' things that's beyond me. An' his prophesyin' to our Colonel, sitting on my bed with his little shimmy torn open showing his white skin; an' the prophecy comin' true! They'll cure all that nonsense at St Xavier's, eh?'

'Sprinkle him with holy water,' the Colonel laughed.

'On my word, I fancy I ought to sometimes. But I'm hoping he'll be brought up as a good Catholic. All that troubles me is what'll happen if the old beggar-man –'

'Lama, lama, my dear sir; and some of them are gentlemen in their own country.'

'The lama, then, fails to pay next year. He's a fine business head to plan on the spur of the moment, but

he's bound to die some day. An' takin' a heathen's money to give a child a Christian education –'

'But he said explicitly what he wanted. As soon as he knew the boy was white he seems to have made his arrangements accordingly. I'd give a month's pay to hear how he explained it all at the Tirthankars' Temple at Benares. Look here, Padre, I don't pretend to know much about natives, but if he says he'll pay, he'll pay – dead or alive. I mean, his heirs will assume the debt. My advice to you is, send the boy down to Lucknow. If your Anglican Chaplain thinks you've stolen a march on him –'

'Bad luck to Bennett! He was sent to the Front instead o' me. Doughty certified me medically unfit. I'll ex-communicate Doughty if he comes back alive! Surely Bennett ought to be content with –'

'Glory, leaving you the religion. Quite so! As a matter of fact I don't think Bennett will mind. Put the blame on me. I – er – strongly recommend sending the boy to St Xavier's. He can go down on pass as a soldier's orphan, so the railway fare will be saved. You can buy him an outfit from the regimental subscription. The Lodge will be saved the expense of his education, and that will put the Lodge in a good temper. It's perfectly easy. I've got to go down to Lucknow next week. I'll look after the boy on the way – give him in charge of my servants, and so on.'

'You're a good man.'

'Not in the least. Don't make that mistake. The lama has sent us money for a definite end. We can't very well return it. We shall have to do as he says. Well, that's settled, isn't it? Shall we say that, Tuesday next, you'll hand him over to me at the night train south?

That's only three days. He can't do much harm in three days.'

'It's a weight off my mind, but – this thing here?' – he waved the note of hand – 'I don't know Gobind Sahai: or his bank, which may be a hole in the wall.'

'*You*'ve never been a subaltern in debt. I'll cash it if you like, and send you the vouchers in proper order.'

'But with all your own work too! It's askin' –'

'It's not the least trouble indeed. You see, as an ethnologist, the thing's very interesting to me. I'd like to make a note of it for some government work that I'm doing. The transformation of a regimental badge like your Red Bull into a sort of fetish that the boy follows is very interesting.'

'But I can't thank you enough.'

'There's one thing you can do. All we ethnological men are as jealous as jackdaws of one another's discoveries. They're of no interest to any one but ourselves, of course, but you know what book-collectors are like. Well, don't say a word, directly or indirectly, about the Asiatic side of the boy's character – his adventures and his prophecy, and so on. I'll worm them out of the boy later on and – you see?'

'I do. Ye'll make a wonderful account of it. Never a word will I say to any one till I see it in print.'

'Thank you. That goes straight to an ethnologist's heart. Well, I must be getting back to my breakfast. Good Heavens! Old Mahbub here still?' He raised his voice, and the horse-dealer came out from under the shadow of the tree. 'Well, what is it?'

'As regards that young horse,' said Mahbub, 'I say that when a colt is born to be a polo-pony, closely following

the ball without teaching – when such a colt knows the game by divination – then I say it is a great wrong to break that colt to a heavy cart, Sahib!'

'So say I also, Mahbub. The colt will be entered for polo only. (These fellows think of nothing in the world but horses, Padre.) I'll see you tomorrow, Mahbub, if you've anything likely for sale.'

The dealer saluted, horseman-fashion, with a sweep of the off hand. 'Be patient a little, Friend of all the World,' he whispered to the agonized Kim. 'Thy fortune is made. In a little while thou goest to Nucklao, and – here is something to pay the letter-writer. I shall see thee again, I think, many times,' and he cantered off down the road.

'Listen to me,' said the Colonel from the veranda, speaking in the vernacular. 'In three days thou wilt go with me to Lucknow, seeing and hearing new things all the while. Therefore sit still for three days and do not run away. Thou wilt go to school at Lucknow.'

'Shall I meet my Holy One there?' Kim whimpered.

'At least Lucknow is nearer to Benares than Umballa. It may be thou wilt go under my protection. Mahbub Ali knows this, and he will be angry if thou returnest to the Road now. Remember – much has been told me which I do not forget.'

'I will wait,' said Kim, 'but the boys will beat me.'

Then the bugles blew for dinner.

CHAPTER
7

Unto whose use the pregnant suns are poised
 With idiot moons and stars retracting stars?
Creep thou betweene – thy coming's all unnoised.
 Heaven hath her high, as Earth her baser, wars.
Heir to these tumults, this affright, that fraye
(By Adam's fathers', own, sin bound alway);
 Peer up, draw out thy horoscope and say
 Which planet mends thy threadbare fate or mars!

Sir John Christie

In the afternoon the red-faced schoolmaster told Kim that he had been 'struck off the strength,' which conveyed no meaning to him till he was ordered to go away and play. Then he ran to the bazaar, and found the young letter-writer to whom he owed a stamp.

'Now I pay,' said Kim royally, 'and now I need another letter to be written.'

'Mahbub Ali is in Umballa,' said the writer jauntily. He was, by virtue of his office, a bureau of general misinformation.

'This is not to Mahbub, but to a priest. Take thy pen and write quickly. "To Teshoo Lama, the Holy One from Bhotiyal seeking for a River, who is now in the Temple of the Tirthankars at Benares." Take more ink! "In three days I am to go down to Nucklao to the school at Nucklao. The name of the school is Xavier. I do not know where that school is, but it is at Nucklao."'

'But I know Nucklao,' the writer interrupted. 'I know the school.'

'Tell him where it is, and I give half an anna.'

The reed pen scratched busily. 'He cannot mistake.' The man lifted his head. 'Who watches us across the street?'

Kim looked up hurriedly and saw Colonel Creighton in tennis flannels.

'Oh, that is some sahib who knows the fat priest in the barracks. He is beckoning me.'

'What dost thou?' said the Colonel, when Kim trotted up.

'I – I am not running away. I send a letter to my Holy One at Benares.'

'I had not thought of that. Hast thou said that I take thee to Lucknow?'

'Nay, I have not. Read the letter, if there be a doubt.'

'Then why hast thou left out my name in writing to that Holy One?' The Colonel smiled a queer smile. Kim took his courage in both hands.

'It was said once to me that it is inexpedient to write the names of strangers concerned in any matter, because by the naming of names many good plans are brought to confusion.'

'Thou hast been well taught,' the Colonel replied, and Kim flushed. 'I have left my cheroot-case in the Padre's veranda. Bring it to my house this even.'

'Where is the house?' said Kim. His quick wit told him that he was being tested in some fashion or another, and he stood on guard.

'Ask any one in the big bazaar.' The Colonel walked on.

'He has forgotten his cheroot-case,' said Kim, return-ing. 'I must bring it to him this evening. That is all my letter except, thrice over, "Come to me! Come to me! Come to me!" Now I will pay for a stamp and put it in the post.' He rose to go, and as an afterthought asked: 'Who is that angry-faced sahib who lost the cheroot-case?'

'Oh, he is only Creighton Sahib – a very foolish sahib, who is a colonel sahib without a regiment.'

'What is his business?'

'God knows. He is always buying horses which he cannot ride, and asking riddles about the works of God – such as plants and stones and the customs of the people. The dealers call him the father of fools, because he is so easily cheated about a horse. Mahbub Ali says he is madder than most other sahibs.'

'Oh!' said Kim, and departed. His training had given him some small knowledge of character, and he argued that fools are not given information which leads to calling out eight thousand men besides guns. The Commander-in-Chief of all India does not talk, as Kim had heard him talk, to fools. Nor would Mahbub Ali's tone have changed, as it did every time he mentioned the Colonel's name, if the Colonel had been a fool. Consequently – and this set Kim to skipping – there was a mystery some-where, and Mahbub Ali probably spied for the Colonel much as Kim had spied for Mahbub. And, like the horse-dealer, the Colonel evidently respected people who did not show themselves to be too clever.

He rejoiced that he had not betrayed his knowledge of the Colonel's house; and when, on his return to barracks, he discovered that no cheroot-case had been left behind, he beamed with delight. Here was a man after his own

heart – a tortuous and indirect person playing a hidden game. Well, if he could be a fool, so could Kim.

He showed nothing of his mind when Father Victor, for three long mornings, discoursed to him of an entirely new set of Gods and Godlings – notably of a Goddess called Mary, who, he gathered, was one with Bibi Miriam of Mahbub Ali's theology. He betrayed no emotion when, after the lecture, Father Victor dragged him from shop to shop buying articles of outfit, nor when envious drummer-boys kicked him because he was going to a superior school did he complain, but awaited the play of circumstances with an interested soul. Father Victor, good man, took him to the station, put him into an empty second-class next to Colonel Creighton's first, and bade him farewell with genuine feeling.

'They'll make a man o' you, O'Hara, at St Xavier's – a white man, an' I hope, a good man. They know all about your comin', an' the Colonel will see that ye're not lost or mislaid anywhere on the road. I've given you a notion of religious matters – at least I hope so – and you'll remember, when they ask you your religion, that you're a Cath'lic. Better say Roman Cath'lic, tho' I'm not fond of the word.'

Kim lit a rank cigarette – he had been careful to buy a stock in the bazaar – and lay down to think. This solitary passage was very different from that joyful down-journey in the third-class with the lama. 'Sahibs get little pleasure of travel,' he reflected. '*Hai mai!* I go from one place to another as it might be a kick-ball. It is my *Kismet*. No man can escape his *Kismet*. But I am to pray to Bibi Miriam, and I am a sahib.' He looked at his boots ruefully. 'No; I am Kim. This is the great world, and I am

only Kim. Who is Kim?' He considered his own identity, a thing he had never done before, till his head swam. He was one insignificant person in all this roaring whirl of India, going southward to he knew not what fate.

Presently the Colonel sent for him, and talked for a long time. So far as Kim could gather, he was to be diligent and enter the Survey of India as a chain-man. If he were very good, and passed the proper examinations, he would be earning thirty rupees a month at seventeen years old, and Colonel Creighton would see that he found suitable employment.

Kim pretended at first to understand perhaps one word in three of this talk. Then the Colonel, seeing his mistake, turned to fluent and picturesque Urdu and Kim was contented. No man could be a fool who knew the language so intimately, who moved so gently and silently, and whose eyes were so different from the dull fat eyes of other sahibs.

'Yes, and thou must learn how to make pictures of roads and mountains and rivers – to carry these pictures in thine eye till a suitable time comes to set them down upon paper. Perhaps some day, when thou art a chain-man, I may say to thee when we are working together: "Go across those hills and see what lies beyond." Then one will say: "There are bad people living in those hills who will slay the chain-man if he be seen to look like a sahib." What then?'

Kim thought. Would it be safe to return the Colonel's lead?

'I would tell what that other man had said.'

'But if I answered: "I will give thee a hundred rupees for knowledge of what is behind those hills – for a picture

of a river and a little news of what the people say in the villages there"?'

'How can I tell? I am only a boy. Wait till I am a man.' Then, seeing the Colonel's brow clouded, he went on: 'But I think I should in a few days earn the hundred rupees.'

'By what road?'

Kim shook his head resolutely. 'If I said how I would earn them, another man might hear and forestall me. It is not good to sell knowledge for nothing.'

'Tell now.' The Colonel held up a rupee. Kim's hand half reached towards it, and dropped.

'Nay, Sahib; nay. I know the price that will be paid for the answer, but I do not know why the question is asked.'

'Take it for a gift, then,' said Creighton, tossing it over. 'There is a good spirit in thee. Do not let it be blunted at St Xavier's. There are many boys there who despise the black men.'

'Their mothers were bazaar-women,' said Kim. He knew well there is no hatred like that of the half-caste for his brother-in-law.

'True; but thou art a sahib and the son of a sahib. Therefore, do not at any time be led to contemn the black men. I have known boys newly entered into the service of the government who feigned not to understand the talk or the customs of black men. Their pay was cut for ignorance. There is no sin so great as ignorance. Remember this.'

Several times in the course of the long twenty-four hours' run south did the Colonel send for Kim, always developing this latter text.

'We be all on one lead-rope, then,' said Kim at last, 'the

Colonel, Mahbub Ali, and I – when I become a chain-man. He will use me as Mahbub Ali employed me, I think. That is good, if it allows me to return to the Road again. This clothing grows no easier by wear.'

When they came to the crowded Lucknow station there was no sign of the lama. He swallowed his disappointment, while the Colonel bundled him into a *ticca-gharri* with his neat belongings and despatched him alone to St Xavier's.

'I do not say farewell, because we shall meet again,' he cried. 'Again, and many times, if thou art one of good spirit. But thou art not yet tried.'

'Not when I brought thee' – Kim actually dared to use the *tum* of equals – 'a white stallion's pedigree that night?'

'Much is gained by forgetting, little brother,' said the Colonel, with a look that pierced through Kim's shoulder-blades as he scuttled into the carriage.

It took him nearly five minutes to recover. Then he sniffed the new air appreciatively. 'A rich city,' he said. 'Richer than Lahore. How good the bazaars must be! Coachman, drive me a little through the bazaars here.'

'My order is to take thee to the school.' The driver used the 'thou', which is rudeness when applied to a white man. In the clearest and most fluent vernacular Kim pointed out his error, climbed on to the box-seat, and, perfect understanding established, drove for a couple of hours up and down, estimating, comparing, and enjoying. There is no city – except Bombay, the queen of all – more beautiful in her garish style than Lucknow, whether you see her from the bridge over the river, or from the top of the Imambara looking down on the gilt umbrellas of the Chutter Munzil, and the trees in which

the town is bedded. Kings have adorned her with fantastic buildings, endowed her with charities, crammed her with pensioners, and drenched her with blood. She is the centre of all idleness, intrigue, and luxury, and shares with Delhi the claim to talk the only pure Urdu.

'A fair city – a beautiful city.' The driver, as a Lucknow man, was pleased with the compliment, and told Kim many astounding things where an English guide would have talked of the Mutiny.

'Now we will go to the school,' said Kim at last. The great old school of St Xavier's in Partibus, block on block of low white buildings, stands in vast grounds over against the Gumti River, at some distance from the city.

'What like of folk are they within?' said Kim.

'Young sahibs – all devils. But to speak truth, and I drive many of them to and fro from the railway station, I have never seen one that had in him the making of a more perfect devil than thou – this young sahib whom I am now driving.'

Naturally, for he was never trained to consider them in any way improper, Kim had passed the time of day with one or two frivolous ladies at upper windows in a certain street, and naturally, in the exchange of compliments, had acquitted himself well. He was about to acknowledge the driver's last insolence, when his eye – it was growing dusk – caught a figure in the long sweep of wall.

'Stop!' he cried. 'Stay here. I do not go to the school at once.'

'But what is to pay me for this coming and recoming?' said the driver petulantly. 'Is the boy mad? Last time it was a dancing-girl. This time it is a priest.'

Kim was in the road headlong, patting the dusty feet beneath the yellow robe.

'I have waited here a day and a half,' the lama's level voice began. 'Nay, I had a disciple with me. He that was my friend at the Temple of the Tirthankars gave me a guide for this journey. I came from Benares in the *te-rain*, when thy letter was given me. Yes, I am well fed. I need nothing.'

'But why didst thou not stay with the Kulu woman, O Holy One? In what way didst thou get to Benares? My heart has been heavy since we parted.'

'The woman wearied me by constant flux of talk and requiring charms for children. I separated myself from that company, permitting her to acquire merit by gifts. She is at least a woman of open hands, and I made a promise to return to her house if need arose. Then, perceiving myself alone in this great and terrible world, I bethought me of the *te-rain* to Benares, where I knew one abode in the Tirthankars' Temple who was a Seeker, even as I.'

'Ah! Thy River,' said Kim. 'I had forgotten the River.'

'So soon, my *chela*? I have never forgotten it. But when I had left thee it seemed better that I should go to the Temple and take counsel, for, look you, India is very large, and it may be that wise men before us, some two or three, have left a record of the place of our River. There is debate in the Temple of the Tirthankars on this matter; some saying one thing, and some another. They are courteous folk.'

'So be it; but what dost thou do now?'

'I acquire merit in that I help thee, my *chela*, to wisdom. The priest of that body of men who serve the Red Bull

wrote me that all should be as I desired for thee. I sent the
money to suffice for one year, and then I came, as thou
seest me, to watch for thee going up into the Gates of
Learning. A day and a half have I waited – not because I
was led by any affection towards thee – that is no part of
the Way – but, as they said at the Tirthankars' Temple,
because, money having been paid for learning, it was
right that I should oversee the end of the matter. They
resolved my doubts most clearly. I had a fear that,
perhaps, I came because I wished to see thee – misguided
by the Red Mist of affection. It is not so . . . Moreover, I
am troubled by a dream.'

'But surely, Holy One, thou hast not forgotten the
Road and all that befell on it. Surely it was a little to see
me that thou didst come?'

'The horses are cold, and it is past their feeding-time,'
whined the driver.

'Go to Jehannum and abide there with thy reputation-
less aunt!' Kim snarled over his shoulder. 'I am all alone
in this land; I know not where I go nor what shall befall
me. My heart was in that letter I sent thee. Except for
Mahbub Ali, and he is a Pathan, I have no friend save
thee, Holy One. Do not altogether go away.'

'I have considered that also,' the lama replied, in a
shaking voice. 'It is manifest that from time to time I shall
acquire merit – if before that I have not found my River –
by assuring myself that thy feet are set on wisdom. What
they will teach thee I do not know, but the priest wrote
me that no son of a sahib in all India will be better taught
than thou. So from time to time, therefore, I will come
again. Maybe thou wilt be such a sahib as he who gave
me those spectacles' – the lama wiped them elaborately –

164

'in the Wonder House at Lahore. That is my hope, for he was a Fountain of Wisdom – wiser than many abbots . . . Again, maybe thou wilt forget me and our meetings.'

'If I eat thy bread,' cried Kim passionately, 'how shall I ever forget thee?'

'No – no.' He put the boy aside. 'I must go back to Benares. From time to time, now that I know the customs of letter-writers in this land, I will send thee a letter, and from time to time I will come and see thee.'

'But whither shall I send my letters?' wailed Kim, clutching at the robe, all forgetful that he was a sahib.

'To the Temple of the Tirthankars at Benares. That is the place I have chosen till I find my River. Do not weep; for, look you, all desire is illusion and a new binding upon the Wheel. Go up to the Gates of Learning. Let me see thee go . . . Dost thou love me? Then go, or my heart cracks . . . I will come again. Surely I will come again.'

The lama watched the *ticca-gharri* rumble into the compound, and strode off, snuffing between each long stride.

'The Gates of Learning' shut with a clang.

The country-born and -bred boy has his own manners and customs, which do not resemble those of any other land; and his teachers approach him by roads which an English master would not understand. Therefore you would scarcely be interested in Kim's experiences as a St Xavier's boy among two or three hundred precocious youths, most of whom had never seen the sea. He suffered the usual penalties for breaking out of bounds when there was cholera in the city. This was before he had learned to write fair English, and so was obliged to

find a bazaar letter-writer. He was, of course, indicted for smoking and for the use of abuse more full-flavoured than even St Xavier's had ever heard. He learned to wash himself with the Levitical scrupulosity of the native-born, who in his heart considers the Englishman rather dirty. He played the usual tricks on the patient coolies pulling the punkahs in the sleeping-rooms where the boys threshed through the hot nights telling tales till the dawn; and quietly he measured himself against his self-reliant mates.

They were sons of subordinate officials in the railway, telegraph, and canal services; of warrant-officers, sometimes retired and sometimes acting as commanders-in-chief to a feudatory rajah's army; of captains of the Indian Marine, government pensioners, planters, presidency shopkeepers, and missionaries. A few were cadets of the old Eurasian houses that have taken strong root in Dhurrumtollah – Pereiras, De Souzas, and D'Silvas. Their parents could well have educated them in England, but they loved the school that had served their own youth, and generation followed sallow-hued generation at St Xavier's. Their homes ranged from Howrah of the railway people to abandoned cantonments like Monghyr and Chunar; lost tea-gardens Shillong way; villages where their fathers were large landholders in Oudh or the Deccan; mission-stations a week from the nearest railway line; seaports a thousand miles south, facing the brazen Indian surf; and cinchona plantations south of all. The mere story of their adventures, which to them were no adventures, on their road to and from school would have crisped a Western boy's hair. They were used to jogging off alone through a hundred miles of jungle,

where there was always the delightful chance of being delayed by tigers; but they would no more have bathed in the English Channel in an English August than their brothers across the world would have lain still while a leopard snuffed at their palanquin. There were boys of fifteen who had spent a day and a half on an islet in the middle of a flooded river, taking charge, as by right, of a camp of frantic pilgrims returning from a shrine. There were seniors who had requisitioned a chance-met rajah's elephant in the name of St Francis Xavier, when the rains once blotted out the cart-track that led to their father's estate, and had all but lost the huge beast in a quicksand. There was a boy, who, he said, and none doubted, had helped his father to beat off with rifles from the veranda a rush of Akas in the days when those head-hunters were bold against lonely plantations.

And every tale was told in the even, passionless voice of the native-born, mixed with quaint reflections, borrowed unconsciously from native foster-mothers, and turns of speech that showed they had been that instant translated from the vernacular. Kim watched, listened, and approved. This was not insipid, single-word talk of drummer-boys. It dealt with a life he knew and in part understood. The atmosphere suited him, and he throve by inches. They gave him a white drill suit as the weather warmed, and he rejoiced in the new-found bodily comforts as he rejoiced to use his sharpened mind over the tasks they set him. His quickness would have delighted an English master; but at St Xavier's they know the first rush of minds developed by sun and surroundings, as they know the half-collapse that sets in at twenty-two or twenty-three.

None the less he remembered to hold himself lowly. When tales were told of hot nights, Kim did not sweep the board with his reminiscences; for St Xavier's looks down on boys who 'go native altogether'. One must never forget that one is a sahib, and that some day, when examinations are passed, one will command natives. Kim made a note of this, for he began to understand where examinations led.

Then came the holidays from August to October – the long holidays imposed by the heat and the rains. Kim was informed that he would go north to some station in the hills behind Umballa, where Father Victor would arrange for him.

'A barrack-school?' said Kim, who had asked many questions and thought more.

'Yes, I suppose so,' said the master. 'It will not do you any harm to keep you out of mischief. You can go up with young De Castro as far as Delhi.'

Kim considered it in every possible light. He had been diligent, even as the Colonel advised. A boy's holiday was his own property – of so much the talk of his companions had advised him – and a barrack-school would be torment after St Xavier's. Moreover – this was magic worth anything else – he could write. In three months he had discovered how men can speak to each other without a third party, at the cost of half an anna and a little knowledge. No word had come from the lama, but there remained the Road. Kim yearned for the caress of soft mud squishing up between the toes, as his mouth watered for mutton stewed with butter and cabbages, for rice speckled with strong-scented cardamoms, for the saffron-tinted rice, garlic and onions, and the forbidden

greasy sweetmeats of the bazaars. They would feed him raw beef on a platter at the barrack-school, and he must smoke by stealth. But again, he was a sahib and was at St Xavier's, and that pig Mahbub Ali . . . No, he would not test Mahbub's hospitality – and yet . . . He thought it out alone in the dormitory, and came to the conclusion he had been unjust to Mahbub.

The school was empty; nearly all the masters had gone away; Colonel Creighton's railway pass lay in his hand, and Kim puffed himself that he had not spent Colonel Creighton's or Mahbub's money in riotous living. He was still lord of two rupees seven annas. His new bullock-trunk, marked 'K. O'H.', and bedding-roll lay in the empty sleeping-room. 'Sahibs are always tied to their baggage,' said Kim, nodding at them. 'You will stay here.' He went out into the warm rain, smiling sinfully, and sought a certain house whose outside he had noted down some time before . . .

'Arré! Dost thou know what manner of women we be in this quarter? Oh, shame!'

'Was I born yesterday?' Kim squatted native-fashion on the cushions of that upper room. 'A little dye-stuff and three yards of cloth to help out a jest. Is it too much to ask?'

'Who is she? Thou art full young, as sahibs go, for this devilry.'

'Oh, she? She is the daughter of a certain schoolmaster of a regiment in the cantonments. He has beaten me twice because I went over their wall in these clothes. Now I would go as a gardener's boy. Old men are very jealous.'

'That is true. Hold thy face still while I dab on the juice.'

'Not too black, *Naikan*. I would not appear to her as a *hubshi* [nigger].'

'Oh, love makes nought of these things. And how old is she?'

'Twelve years, I think,' said the shameless Kim. 'Spread it also on the breast. It may be her father will tear my clothes off me, and if I am piebald –' he laughed.

The girl worked busily, dabbing a twist of cloth into a little saucer of brown dye that holds longer than any walnut juice.

'Now send out and get me a cloth for the turban. Woe is me, my head is all unshaved! And he will surely knock off my turban.'

'I am not a barber, but I will make shift. Thou was born to be a breaker of hearts! All this disguise for one evening? Remember, the stuff does not wash away.' She shook with laughter till her bracelets and anklets jingled. 'But who is to pay me for this? Huneefa herself could not have given thee better stuff.'

'Trust in the Gods, my sister,' said Kim gravely, screwing his face round as the stain dried. 'Besides, hast thou ever helped to paint a sahib thus before?'

'Never indeed. But a jest is not money.'

'It is worth much more.'

'Child, thou art beyond all dispute the most shameless son of Shaitan that I have ever known to take up a poor girl's time with this play, and then to say: "Is not the jest enough?" Thou wilt go very far in this world.' She gave him the dancing-girls' salutation in mockery.

'All one. Make haste and rough-cut my head.' Kim shifted from foot to foot, his eyes ablaze with mirth as he

thought of the fat days before him. He gave the girl four annas, and ran down the stairs in the likeness of a low-caste Hindu boy – perfect in every detail. A cook-shop was his next point of call, where he feasted in extravagance and greasy luxury.

On Lucknow station platform he watched young De Castro, all covered with prickly-heat, get into a second-class compartment. Kim patronized a third, and was the life and soul of it. He explained to the company that he was assistant to a juggler who had left him behind sick with fever, and that he would pick up his master at Umballa. As the occupants of the carriage changed, he varied this tale, or adorned it with all the shoots of a budding fancy, the more rampant for being held off native speech so long. In all India that night was no human being so joyful as Kim. At Umballa he got out and headed eastward, plashing over the sodden fields to the village where the old soldier lived.

About this time Colonel Creighton at Simla was advised from Lucknow by wire that young O'Hara had disappeared. Mahbub Ali was in town selling horses, and to him the Colonel confided the affair one morning cantering round Annandale racecourse.

'Oh, that is nothing,' said the horse-dealer. 'Men are like horses. At certain times they need salt, and if that salt is not in the mangers they will lick it up from the earth. He has gone back to the Road again for a while. The *madrissah* wearied him. I knew it would. Another time, I will take him upon the Road myself. Do not be troubled, Creighton Sahib. It is as though a polo-pony, breaking loose, ran out to learn the game alone.'

'Then he is not dead, think you?'

'Fever might kill him. I do not fear for the boy otherwise. A monkey does not fall among trees.'

Next morning, on the same course, Mahbub's stallion ranged alongside the Colonel.

'It is as I had thought,' said the horse-dealer. 'He has come through Umballa at least, and there he has written a letter to me, having learned in the bazaar that I was here.'

'Read,' said the Colonel, with a sigh of relief. It was absurd that a man of his position should take an interest in a little country-bred vagabond; but the Colonel remembered the conversation in the train, and often in the past few months had caught himself thinking of the queer, silent, self-possessed boy. His evasion, of course, was the height of insolence, but it argued some resource and nerve.

Mahbub's eyes twinkled as he reined out into the centre of the cramped little plain, where none could come near unseen.

'"The Friend of the Stars, who is the Friend of all the World—"'

'What is this?'

'A name we give him in Lahore city. "The Friend of all the World takes leave to go his own places. He will come back upon the appointed day. Let the box and the bedding-roll be sent for; and if there has been a fault let the Hand of Friendship turn aside the Whip of Calamity." There is yet a little more, but –'

'No matter, read.'

'"Certain things are not known to those who eat with forks. It is better to eat with both hands for a while. Speak soft words to those who do not understand this that the return may be propitious." Now the manner in which

that was cast is, of course, the work of the letter-writer, but see how wisely the boy has devised the matter of it so that no hint is given except to those who know!'

'Is this the Hand of Friendship to avert the Whip of Calamity?' laughed the Colonel.

'See how wise is the boy. He would go back to the Road again, as I said. Not knowing yet thy trade –'

'I am not at all sure of that,' the Colonel muttered.

'He turns to me to make a peace between you. Is he not wise? He says he will return. He is but perfecting his knowledge. Think, Sahib! He has been three months at the school. And he is not mouthed to that bit. For my part, I rejoice. The pony learns the game.'

'Ay, but another time he must not go alone.'

'Why? He went alone before he came under the Colonel Sahib's protection. When he comes to the Great Game he must go alone – alone, and at peril of his head. *Then*, if he spits, or sneezes, or sits down other than as the people do whom he watches, he may be slain. Why hinder him now? Remember how the Persians say: The jackal that lives in the wilds of Mazanderan can only be caught by the hounds of Mazanderan.'

'True. It is true, Mahbub Ali. And if he comes to no harm, I do not desire anything better. But it is great insolence on his part.'

'He does not tell me, even, whither he goes,' said Mahbub. 'He is no fool. When his time is accomplished he will come to me. It is time the healer of pearls took him in hand. He ripens too quickly – as sahibs reckon.'

This prophecy was fulfilled to the letter a month later. Mahbub had gone down to Umballa to bring up a fresh consignment of horses, and Kim met him on the Kalka

road at dusk riding alone, begged an alms of him, was sworn at, and replied in English. There was nobody within earshot to hear Mahbub's gasp of amazement.

'Oho! And where hast thou been?'

'Up and down – down and up.'

'Come under a tree, out of the wet, and tell.'

'I stayed for a while with an old man near Umballa; anon with a household of my acquaintance in Umballa. With one of these I went as far as Delhi to the southward. That is a wondrous city. Then I drove a bullock for a *teli* [an oilman] coming north; but I heard of a great feast forward in Patiala, and thither went I in the company of a firework-maker. It was a great feast' (Kim rubbed his stomach). 'I saw rajahs, and elephants with gold and silver trappings; and they lit all the fireworks at once, whereby eleven men were killed, my firework-maker among them, and I was blown across a tent but took no harm. Then I came back to the *rêl* with a Sikh horseman, to whom I was groom for my bread; and so here.'

'*Shabash!*' said Mahbub Ali.

'But what does the Colonel Sahib say? I do not wish to be beaten.'

'The Hand of Friendship has averted the Whip of Calamity; but another time, when thou takest the Road it will be with me. This is too early.'

'Late enough for me. I have learned to read and to write English a little at the *madrissah*. I shall soon be altogether a sahib.'

'Hear him!' laughed Mahbub, looking at the little drenched figure dancing in the wet. 'Salaam – Sahib,' and he saluted ironically. 'Well, art tired of the Road, or wilt

thou come on to Umballa with me and work back with the horses?'

'I will come with thee, Mahbub Ali.'

CHAPTER

8

Something I owe to the soil that grew –
 More to the life that fed –
But most to Allah Who gave me two
 Separate sides to my head.

I would go without shirts or shoes,
 Friends, tobacco or bread
Sooner than for an instant lose
 Either side of my head.

The Two-Sided Man

'Then in God's name take blue for red,' said Mahbub, alluding to the Hindu colour of Kim's disreputable turban.

Kim countered with the old proverb, 'I will change my faith and my bedding, but *thou* must pay for it.'

The dealer laughed till he nearly fell from his horse. At a shop on the outskirts of the city the change was made, and Kim stood up, externally at least, a Muhammadan.

Mahbub hired a room over against the railway station, sent for a cooked meal of the finest with almond-curd sweetmeats [*balushai* we call it] and fine-chopped Lucknow tobacco.

'This is better than some other meat that I ate with the Sikh,' said Kim, grinning as he squatted, 'and assuredly they give no such victuals at my *madrissah*.'

'I have a desire to hear of that same *madrissah*.' Mahbub stuffed himself with great boluses of spiced mutton fried

in fat with cabbage and golden-brown onions. 'But tell me first, altogether and truthfully, the manner of thy escape. For, O Friend of all the World,' – he loosed his cracking belt – 'I do not think it is often that a sahib and the son of a sahib runs away from there.'

'How should they? They do not know the land. It was nothing,' said Kim, and began his tale. When he came to the disguisement and the interview with the girl in the bazaar, Mahbub Ali's gravity went from him. He laughed aloud and beat his hand on his thigh.

'*Shabash! Shabash!* Oh, well done, little one! What will the healer of turquoises say to this? Now, slowly, let us hear what befell afterwards – step by step, omitting nothing.'

Step by step then, Kim told his adventures between coughs as the full-flavoured tobacco caught his lungs.

'I said,' growled Mahbub Ali to himself, 'I *said* it was the pony breaking out to play polo. The fruit is ripe already – except that he must learn his distances and his pacings, and his rods and his compasses. Listen now. I have turned aside the Colonel's whip from thy skin, and that is no small service.'

'True.' Kim puffed serenely. 'That is all true.'

'But it is not to be thought that this running out and in is any way good.'

'It was my holiday, Hajji. I was a slave for many weeks. Why should I not run away when the school was shut? Look, too, how I, living upon my friends or working for my bread, as I did with the Sikh, have saved the Colonel Sahib a great expense.'

Mahbub's lips twitched under his well-pruned Muhammadan moustache.

'What are a few rupees' – the Pathan threw out his open hand carelessly –' to the Colonel Sahib? He spends them for a purpose, not in any way for love of thee.'

'That,' said Kim slowly, 'I knew a very long time ago.'

'Who told?'

'The Colonel Sahib himself. Not in those many words, but plainly enough for one who is not altogether a mud-head. Yea, he told me in the *te-rain* when we went down to Lucknow.'

'Be it so. Then I will tell thee more, Friend of all the World, though in the telling I lend thee my head.'

'It was forfeit to me,' said Kim, with deep relish, 'in Umballa, when thou didst pick me up on the horse after the drummer-boy beat me.'

'Speak a little plainer. All the world may tell lies save thou and I. For equally is thy life forfeit to me if I chose to raise my finger here.'

'And this is known to me also,' said Kim, readjusting the live charcoal-ball on the weed. 'It is a very sure tie between us. Indeed, thy hold is surer even than mine; for who would miss a boy beaten to death, or, it may be, thrown into a well by the roadside? Many people here and in Simla and across the passes behind the Hills would, on the other hand, say: "What has come to Mahbub Ali?" if he were found dead among his horses. Surely, too, the Colonel Sahib would make inquiries. But again' – Kim's face puckered with cunning – 'he would not make overlong inquiry, lest people should ask. "What has this Colonel Sahib to do with that horse-dealer?" But I – if I lived –'

'As thou wouldst surely die –'

'Maybe; but I say, *if* I lived, I, and I alone, would know

that one had come by night, as a common thief perhaps, to Mahbub Ali's bulkhead in the serai, and there had slain him, either before or after that thief had made a full search into his saddlebags and between the soles of his slippers. Is that news to tell to the Colonel, or would he say to me – (I have not forgotten when he sent me back for a cigar-case that he had *not* left behind him) – "What is Mahbub Ali to me"?'

Up went a gout of heavy smoke. There was a long pause: then Mahbub Ali spoke in admiration: 'And with these things on thy mind, dost thou lie down and rise again among all the sahibs' little sons at the *madrissah* and meekly take instruction from thy teachers?'

'It is an order,' said Kim blandly. 'Who am I to dispute an order?'

'A most finished Son of Eblis,' said Mahbub Ali. 'But what is this tale of the thief and the search?'

'That which I saw,' said Kim, 'the night that my lama and I lay next thy place in the Kashmir Serai. The door was left unlocked, which I think is not thy custom, Mahbub. He came in as one assured that thou wouldst not soon return. My eye was against a knot-hole in the plank. He searched as it were for something – not a rug, not stirrups, nor a bridle, nor brass pots – something little and most carefully hid. Else why did he prick with an iron between the soles of thy slippers?'

'Ha!' Mahbub Ali smiled gently. 'And seeing these things, what tale didst thou fashion to thyself, Well of the Truth?'

'None. I put my hand upon my amulet, which lies always next to my skin, and, remembering the pedigree of a white stallion that I had bitten out of a piece of

Mussulmani bread, I went away to Umballa perceiving that a heavy trust was laid upon me. At that hour, had I chosen, thy head was forfeit. It needed only to say to that man, "I have here a paper concerning a horse which I cannot read." And then?' Kim peered at Mahbub under his eyebrows.

'Then thou wouldst have drunk water twice – perhaps thrice, afterwards. I do not think more than thrice,' said Mahbub simply.

'It is true. I thought of that a little, but most I thought that I loved thee, Mahbub. Therefore I went to Umballa, as thou knowest, but (and this thou dost not know) I lay hid in the garden grass to see what Colonel Creighton Sahib might do upon reading the white stallion's pedigree.'

'And what did he?' for Kim had bitten off the conversation.

'Dost *thou* give news for love, or dost thou sell it?' Kim asked.

'I sell and – I buy.' Mahbub took a four-anna piece out of his belt and held it up.

'Eight!' said Kim, mechanically following the huckster instinct of the East.

Mahbub laughed, and put away the coin. 'It is too easy to deal in that market, Friend of all the World. Tell me for love. Our lives lie in each other's hand.'

'Very good. I saw the Jang-i-Lat Sahib [the Commander-in-Chief] come to a big dinner. I saw him in Creighton Sahib's office. I saw the two read the white stallion's pedigree. I heard the very orders given for the opening of a great war.'

'Hah!' Mahbub nodded with deepest eyes afire. 'The

180

game is well played. That war is done now, and the evil, we hope, nipped before the flower – thanks to me – and thee. What didst thou later?'

'I made the news as it were a hook to catch me victual and honour among the villagers in a village whose priest drugged my lama. But I bore away the old man's purse, and the Brahmin found nothing. So next morning he was angry. Ho! Ho! And I also used the news when I fell into the hands of that white regiment with their Bull!'

'That was foolishness.' Mahbub scowled. 'News is not meant to be thrown about like dung-cakes, but used sparingly – like *bhang*.'

'So I think now, and moreover, it did me no sort of good. But that was very long ago' – he made as to brush it all away with a thin brown hand – 'and since then, and especially in the nights under the punkah at the *madrissah*, I have thought very greatly.'

'Is it permitted to ask whither the Heaven-born's thought might have led?' said Mahbub, with an elaborate sarcasm, smoothing his scarlet beard.

'It is permitted,' said Kim, and threw back the very tone. 'They say at Nucklao that no sahib must tell a black man that he has made a fault.'

Mahbub's hand shot into his bosom, for to call a Pathan a 'black man' [*kala admi*] is a blood-insult. Then he remembered and laughed. 'Speak, Sahib. Thy black man hears.'

'But,' said Kim, 'I am *not* a sahib, and I say I made a fault to curse thee, Mahbub Ali, on that day at Umballa when I thought I was betrayed by a Pathan. I was senseless; for I was but newly caught, and I wished to kill that low-caste drummer-boy. I say now, Hajji, that it was

well done; and I see my road all clear before me to a good service. I will stay in the *madrissah* till I am ripe.'

'Well said. Especially are distances and numbers and the manner of using compasses to be learned in that game. One waits in the Hills above to show thee.'

'I will learn their teaching upon a condition – that my time is given to me without question when the *madrissah* is shut. Ask that for me of the Colonel.'

'But why not ask the Colonel in the sahibs' tongue?'

'The Colonel is the servant of the government. He is sent hither and yon at a word, and must consider his own advancement. (See how much I have already learned at Nucklao!) Moreover, the Colonel I know since three months only. I have known one Mahbub Ali for six years. So! To the *madrissah* I will go. At the *madrissah* I will learn. In the *madrissah* I will be a sahib. But when the *madrissah* is shut, then must I be free and go among my people. Otherwise I die!'

'And who are thy people, Friend of all the World?'

'This great and beautiful land,' said Kim, waving his paw round the little clay-walled room where the oil-lamp in its niche burned heavily through the tobacco smoke. 'And, further, I would see my lama again. And, further, I need money.'

'That is the need of every one,' said Mahbub ruefully. 'I will give thee eight annas, for much money is not picked out of horses' hooves, and it must suffice for many days. As to all the rest, I am well pleased, and no further talk is needed. Make haste to learn, and in three years, or it may be less, thou wilt be an aid – even to me.'

'Have I been such a hindrance till now?' said Kim, with a boy's giggle.

'Do not give answers,' Mahbub grunted. 'Thou art my new horse-boy. Go and bed among my men. They are near the north end of the station, with the horses.'

'They will beat me to the south end of the station if I come without authority.'

Mahbub felt in his belt, wetted his thumb on a cake of Chinese ink, and dabbed the impression on a piece of soft native paper. From Balkh to Bombay men know that rough-ridged print with the old scar running diagonally across it.

'That is enough to show my headman. I come in the morning.'

'By which road?' said Kim.

'By the road from the city. There is but one, and then we return to Creighton Sahib. I have saved thee a beating.'

'Allah! What is a beating when the very head is loose on the shoulders?'

Kim slid out quietly into the night, walked half round the house, keeping close to the walls, and headed away from the station for a mile or so. Then, fetching a wide compass, he worked back at leisure, for he needed time to invent a story if any of Mahbub's retainers asked questions.

They were camped on a piece of waste ground beside the railway, and, being natives, had not, of course, unloaded the two trucks in which Mahbub's animals stood among a consignment of country-breds bought by the Bombay tram-company. The headman, a broken-down, consumptive-looking Muhammadan, promptly challenged Kim, but was pacified at sight of Mahbub's sign-manual.

'The Hajji has of his favour given me service,' said Kim testily. 'If this be doubted, wait till he comes in the morning. Meantime, a place by the fire.'

Followed the usual aimless babble that every low-caste native must raise on every occasion. It died down, and Kim lay out behind the little knot of Mahbub's followers, almost under the wheels of a horse-truck, a borrowed blanket for covering. Now a bed among brickbats and ballast-refuse on a damp night, between overcrowded horses and unwashen Baltis, would not appeal to many white boys; but Kim was utterly happy. Change of scene, service, and surroundings were the breath of his little nostrils, and thinking of the neat white cots of St Xavier's all arow under the punkah gave him joy as keen as the repetition of the multiplication-table in English.

'I am very old,' he thought sleepily. 'Every month I become a year more old. I was very young, and a fool to boot, when I took Mahbub's message to Umballa. Even when I was with that white regiment I was very young and small and had no wisdom. But now I learn every day, and in three years the Colonel will take me out of the *madrissah* and let me go upon the Road with Mahbub hunting for horses' pedigrees, or maybe I shall go by myself; or maybe I shall find the lama and go with him. Yes; that is best. To walk again as a *chela* with my lama when he comes back to Benares.' The thoughts came more slowly and disconnectedly. He was plunging into a beautiful dreamland when his ears caught a whisper, thin and sharp, above the monotonous babble round the fire. It came from behind the iron-skinned horse-truck.

'He is not here, then?'

'Where should he be but roystering in the city. Who

looks for a rat in a frog-pond? Come away. He is not our man.'

'He must not go back beyond the passes a second time. It is the order.'

'Hire some woman to drug him. It is a few rupees only, and there is no evidence.'

'Except the woman. It must be more certain; and remember the price upon his head.'

'Ay, but the police have a long arm, and we are far from the border. If it were in Peshawar, now!'

'Yes – in Peshawar,' the second voice sneered. 'Peshawar, full of his blood-kin – full of bolt-holes and women behind whose clothes he will hide. Yes, Peshawar or Jehannum would suit us equally well.'

'Then what is the plan?'

'O fool, have I not told it a hundred times? Wait till he comes to lie down, and then one sure shot. The trucks are between us and pursuit. We have but to run back over the lines and go our way. They will not see whence the shot came. Wait here at least till the dawn. What manner of *fakir* art thou, to shiver at a little watching?'

'Oho!' thought Kim, behind close-shut eyes. 'Once again it is Mahbub. Indeed a white stallion's pedigree is not a good thing to peddle to sahibs! Or maybe Mahbub has been selling other news. Now what is to do, Kim? I know not where Mahbub houses, and if he comes here before the dawn they will shoot him. That would be no profit for thee, Kim. And this is not a matter for the police. That would be no profit for Mahbub; and' – he giggled almost aloud – 'I do not remember any lesson at Nucklao which will help me. Allah! Here is Kim and yonder are they. First, then, Kim must wake and go

185

away, so that they shall not suspect. A bad dream wakes a man – thus –'

He threw the blanket off his face, and raised himself suddenly with the terrible, bubbling, meaningless yell of the Asiatic roused by nightmare.

'Urr-urr-urr-urr! Ya-la-la-la-la! *Narain!* The *churel!* The *churel!*'

A *churel* is the peculiarly malignant ghost of a woman who has died in child-bed. She haunts lonely roads, her feet are turned backwards on the ankles, and she leads men to torment.

Louder rose Kim's quavering howl, till at last he leaped to his feet and staggered off sleepily, while the camp cursed him for waking them. Some twenty yards farther up the line he lay down again, taking care that the whisperers should hear his grunts and groans as he recomposed himself. After a few minutes he rolled towards the road and stole away into the thick darkness.

He paddled along swiftly till he came to a culvert, and dropped behind it, his chin on a level with the coping-stone. Here he could command all the night-traffic, himself unseen.

Two or three carts passed, jingling out to the suburbs; a coughing policeman and a hurrying foot-passenger or two who sang to keep off evil spirits. Then rapped the shod feet of a horse.

'Ah! This is more like Mahbub,' thought Kim, as the beast shied at the little head above the culvert.

'Ohé, Mahbub Ali,' he whispered, 'have a care!'

The horse was reined back almost on its haunches, and forced towards the culvert.

'Never again,' said Mahbub, 'will I take a shod horse

for night-work. They pick up all the bones and nails in the city.' He stooped to lift its forefoot, and that brought his head within a foot of Kim's. 'Down – keep down,' he muttered. 'The night is full of eyes.'

'Two men wait thy coming behind the horse-trucks. They will shoot thee at thy lying down, because there is a price on thy head. I heard, sleeping near the horses.'

'Didst thou see them? . . . Hold still, Sire of Devils!' This furiously to the horse.

'No.'

'Was one dressed belike as a *fakir*?'

'One said to the other, "What manner of *fakir* art thou, to shiver at a little watching?"'

'Good. Go back to the camp and lie down. I do not die tonight.'

Mahbub wheeled his horse and vanished. Kim tore back down the ditch till he reached a point opposite his second resting-place, slipped across the road like a weasel, and re-coiled himself in the blanket.

'At least Mahbub knows,' he thought contentedly. 'And certainly he spoke as one expecting it. I do not think those two men will profit by tonight's watch.'

An hour passed, and, with the best will in the world to keep awake all night, he slept deeply. Now and again a night train roared along the metals within twenty feet of him; but he had all the Oriental's indifference to mere noise, and it did not even weave a dream through his slumber.

Mahbub was anything but asleep. It annoyed him vehemently that people outside his tribe and unaffected by his casual amours should pursue him for the life. His first and natural impulse was to cross the line lower

down, work up again, and, catching his wellwishers from behind, summarily slay them. Here, he reflected with sorrow, another branch of the government, totally unconnected with Colonel Creighton, might demand explanations which would be hard to supply; and he knew that south of the border a perfectly ridiculous fuss is made about a corpse or so. He had not been troubled in this way since he sent Kim to Umballa with the message, and hoped that suspicion had been finally diverted.

Then a most brilliant notion struck him.

'The English do eternally tell the truth,' he said, 'therefore we of this country are eternally made foolish. By Allah, I will tell the truth to an Englishman! Of what use is the government police if a poor Kabuli be robbed of his horses in their very trucks. This is as bad as Peshawar! I should lay a complaint at the station. Better still, some young sahib on the railway! They are zealous, and if they catch thieves it is remembered to their honour.'

He tied up his horse outside the station, and strode on to the platform.

'Hullo, Mahbub Ali!' said a young assistant district traffic superintendent who was waiting to go down the line – a tall, tow-haired, horsy youth in dingy white linen. 'What are you doing here? Selling weeds – eh?'

'No; I am not troubled for my horses. I come to look for Lutuf Ullah. I have a truck-load up the line. Could any one take them out without the railway's knowledge?'

'Shouldn't think so, Mahbub. You can claim against us if they do.'

'I have seen two men crouching under the wheels of one of the trucks nearly all the night. *Fakirs* do not steal

horses, so I gave them no more thought. I would find Lutuf Ullah, my partner.'

'The deuce you did? And you didn't bother your head about it? 'Pon my word, it's just almost as well that I met you. What were they like, eh?'

'They were only *fakirs*. They will no more than take a little grain, perhaps, from one of the trucks. There are many up the line. The state will never miss the dole. I came here seeking for my partner, Lutuf Ullah –'

'Never mind your partner. Where are your horse-trucks?'

'A little to this side of the farthest place where they make lamps for the trains.'

'The signal-box? Yes.'

'And upon the rail nearest to the road upon the right-hand side – looking up the line thus. But as regards Lutuf Ullah – a tall man with a broken nose, and a Persian greyhound – Aie!'

'The boy had hurried off to wake up a young and enthusiastic policeman; for, as he said, the railway had suffered much from depredations in the goods-yard. Mahbub Ali chuckled in his dyed beard.

'They will walk in their boots, making a noise, and then they will wonder why there are no *fakirs*. They are very clever boys – Barton Sahib and Young Sahib.'

He waited idly for a few minutes, expecting to see them hurry up the line girt for action. A light engine slid through the station, and he caught a glimpse of young Barton in the cab.

'I did that child an injustice. He is not altogether a fool,' said Mahbub Ali. 'To take a fire-carriage for a thief is a new game!'

When Mahbub Ali came to his camp in the dawn, no one thought it worth while to tell him any news of the night. No one, at least, but one small horse-boy, newly advanced to the great man's service, whom Mahbub called to his tiny tent to assist in some packing.

'It is all known to me,' whispered Kim, bending above saddlebags. 'Two sahibs came up on a *te-rain*. I was running to and fro in the dark on this side of the trucks as the *te-rain* moved up and down slowly. They fell upon two men sitting under this truck – Hajji, what shall I do with this lump of tobacco? Wrap it in paper and put it under the salt-bag? Yes – and struck them down. But one man struck at a sahib with a *fakir's* buck's horn' (Kim meant the conjoined black-buck horns, which are a *fakir's* sole temporal weapon) – 'the blood came. So the other sahib, first smiting his own man senseless, smote the stabber with a short gun which had rolled from the first man's hand. They all raged as though mad together.'

Mahbub smiled with heavenly resignation. 'No! That is not so much *dewanee* [madness, or a case for the civil court – the word can be punned upon both ways] as *nizamut* [a criminal case]. A gun, sayest thou? Ten good years in jail.'

'Then they both lay still, but I think they were nearly dead when they were put on the *te-rain*. Their heads moved thus. And there is much blood on the line. Come and see?'

'I have seen blood before. Jail is the sure place – and assuredly they will give false names, and assuredly no man will find them for a long time. They were unfriends of mine. Thy fate and mine seem on one string. What a tale for the healer of pearls! Now swiftly with the saddle-

bags and the cooking-platter. We will take out the horses and away to Simla.'

Swiftly – as Orientals understand speed – with long explanations, with abuse and windy talk, carelessly, amid a hundred checks for little things forgotten, the untidy camp broke up and led the half-dozen stiff and fretful horses along the Kalka road in the fresh of the rain-swept dawn. Kim, regarded as Mahbub Ali's favourite by all who wished to stand well with the Pathan, was not called upon to work. They strolled on by the easiest of stages, halting every few hours at a wayside shelter. Very many sahibs travel along the Kalka road; and, as Mahbub Ali says, every young sahib must needs esteem himself a judge of a horse, and, though he be over head in debt to the moneylender, must make as if to buy. That was the reason that sahib after sahib, rolling along in a stage-carriage, would stop and open talk. Some would even descend from their vehicles and feel the horses' legs; asking inane questions, or, through sheer ignorance of the vernacular, grossly insulting the imperturbable trader.

'When first I dealt with sahibs, and that was when Colonel Soady Sahib was Governor of Fort Abazai and flooded the Commissioner's camping-ground for spite,' Mahbub confided to Kim as the boy filled his pipe under a tree, 'I did not know how greatly they were fools, and this made me wroth. As thus –' and he told Kim a tale of an expression, misused in all innocence, that doubled Kim up with mirth. 'Now I see, however' – he exhaled smoke slowly – 'that it is with them as with all men – in certain matters they are wise, and in others most foolish. Very foolish it is to use the wrong word to a stranger; for

191

though the heart may be clean of offence, how is the stranger to know that? He is more like to search truth with a dagger.'

'True. True talk,' said Kim solemnly. 'Fools speak of a cat when a woman is brought to bed, for instance. I have heard them.'

'Therefore, in one situate as thou art, it particularly behoves thee to remember this with both kinds of faces. Among sahibs, never forgetting thou art a sahib; among the folk of Hind, always remembering thou art –' He paused, with a puzzled smile.

'What am I? Mussulman, Hindu, Jain, or Buddhist? That is a hard knot.'

'Thou art beyond question an unbeliever, and therefore thou wilt be damned. So says my Law – or I think it does. But thou art also my Little Friend of all the World, and I love thee. So says my heart. This matter of creeds is like horseflesh. The wise man knows horses are good – that there is a profit to be made from all; and for myself – but that I am a good *Sunni* and hate the men of Tirah – I could believe the same of all the Faiths. Now manifestly a Kathiawar mare taken from the sands of her birthplace and removed to the west of Bengal founders – nor is even a Balkh stallion (and there are no better horses than those of Balkh, were they not so heavy in the shoulder) of any account in the great northern deserts beside the snow-camels I have seen. Therefore I say in my heart the Faiths are like the horses. Each has merit in its own country.'

'But my lama said altogether a different thing.'

'Oh, he is an old dreamer of dreams from Bhotiyal. My heart is a little angry, Friend of all the World, that thou shouldst see such worth in a man so little known.'

'It is true, Hajji; but that worth do I see, and to him my heart is drawn.'

'And his to thine, I hear. Hearts are like horses. They come and they go against bit or spur. Shout Gul Sher Khan yonder to drive in that bay stallion's pickets more firmly. We do not want a horse fight at every resting-stage, and the dun and the black will be locked in a little . . . Now hear me. Is it necessary to the comfort of thy heart to see that lama?'

'It is one part of my bond,' said Kim. 'If I do not see him, and if he is taken from me, I will go out of that *madrissah* in Nucklao and, and – once gone, who is to find me again?'

'It is true. Never was colt held on a lighter heel-rope than thou.' Mahbub nodded his head.

'Do not be afraid.' Kim spoke as though he could have evanished on the moment. 'My lama has said that he will come to see me at the *madrissah* –'

'A beggar and his bowl in the presence of those young sa—'

'Not all!' Kim cut in with a snort. 'Their eyes are blued and their nails are blackened with low-caste blood, many of them. Sons of *mehteranees* – brothers-in-law to the *bhungi* [sweeper].'

We need not follow the rest of the pedigree; but Kim made his little point clearly and without heat, chewing a piece of sugarcane the while.

'Friend of all the World,' said Mahbub, pushing over the pipe for the boy to clean, 'I have met many men, women, and boys, and not a few sahibs. I have never in all my days met such an imp as thou art.'

'And why? When I always tell thee the truth.'

'Perhaps the very reason, for this is a world of danger to honest men.' Mahbub Ali hauled himself off the ground, girt in his belt, and went over to the horses.

'Or sell it?'

There was that in the tone that made Mahbub halt and turn. 'What new devilry?'

'Eight annas, and I will tell,' said Kim, grinning. 'It touches thy peace.'

'O Shaitan!' Mahbub gave the money.

'Rememberest thou the little business of the thieves in the dark, down yonder at Umballa?'

'Seeing they sought my life, I have not altogether forgotten. Why?'

'Rememberest thou the Kashmir Serai?'

'I will twist thy ears in a moment – Sahib.'

'No need – Pathan. Only, the second *fakir*, whom the sahibs beat senseless, was the man who came to search thy bulkhead at Lahore. I saw his face as they helped him on the engine. The very same man.'

'Why didst thou not tell before?'

'Oh, he will go to jail, and be safe for some years. There is no need to tell more than is necessary at any one time. Besides, I did not then need money for sweetmeats.'

'*Allah kerim!*' said Mahbub Ali. 'Wilt thou some day sell my head for a few sweetmeats if the fit takes thee?'

Kim will remember till he dies that long, lazy journey from Umballa, through Kalka and the Pinjore Gardens near by, up to Simla. A sudden spate in the Gugger River swept down one horse (the most valuable, be sure), and nearly drowned Kim among the dancing boulders. Farther up the road the horses were stampeded by a

government elephant, and being in high condition of grass food, it cost a day and a half to get them together again. Then they met Sikandar Khan coming down with a few unsaleable screws – remnants of his string – and Mahbub, who has more of horse-coping in his little fingernail than Sikandar Khan in all his tents, must needs buy two of the worst, and that meant eight hours' laborious diplomacy and untold tobacco. But it was all pure delight – the wandering road, climbing, dipping, and sweeping about the growing spurs; the flush of the morning laid along the distant snows; the branched cacti, tier upon tier on the stony hillsides; the voices of a thousand water channels; the chatter of the monkeys; the solemn deodars, climbing one after another with downdrooped branches; the vista of the plains rolled out far beneath them; the incessant twanging of the tonga-horns and the wild rush of the led horses when a tonga swung round a curve; the halts for prayers (Mahbub was very religious in dry-washings and bellowings when time did not press); the evening conferences by the halting-places, when camels and bullocks chewed solemnly together and the stolid drivers told the news of the Road – all these things lifted Kim's heart to song within him.

'But, when the singing and dancing is done,' said Mahbub Ali, 'comes the Colonel Sahib's, and that is not so sweet.'

'A fair land – a most beautiful land is this of Hind – and the land of the Five Rivers is fairer than all,' Kim half chanted. 'Into it I will go again if Mahbub Ali or the Colonel lift hand or foot against me. Once gone, who shall find me? Look, Hajji, is yonder the city of Simla? Allah, what a city!'

'My father's brother, and he was an old man when Mackerson Sahib's well was new at Peshawar, could recall when there were but two houses in it.'

He led the horses below the main road into the lower Simla bazaar – the crowded rabbit-warren that climbs up from the valley to the Town Hall at an angle of forty-five. A man who knows his way there can defy all the police of India's summer capital, so cunningly does veranda communicate with veranda, alley-way with alley-way, and bolt-hole with bolt-hole. Here live those who minister to the wants of the glad city – *jhampanis* who pull the pretty ladies' rickshaws by night and gamble till the dawn; grocers, oil-sellers, curio-vendors, firewood-dealers, priests, pickpockets, and native employees of the government. Here are discussed by courtesans the things which are supposed to be profoundest secrets of the India Council; and here gather all the sub-sub-agents of half the native states. Here, too, Mahbub Ali rented a room, much more securely locked than his bulkhead at Lahore, in the house of a Muhammadan cattle-dealer. It was a place of miracles, too, for there went in at twilight a Muhammadan horse-boy, and there came out an hour later a Eurasian lad – the Lucknow girl's dye was of the best – in badly fitting shop-clothes.

'I have spoken with Creighton Sahib,' quoth Mahbub Ali,' and a second time has the Hand of Friendship averted the Whip of Calamity. He says that thou hast altogether wasted sixty days upon the Road, and it is too late, therefore, to send thee to any hill-school.'

'I have said that my holidays are my own. I do not go to school twice over. That is one part of my bond.'

'The Colonel Sahib is not yet aware of that contract.

Thou art to lodge in Lurgan Sahib's house till it is time to go again to Nucklao.'

'I had sooner lodge with thee, Mahbub.'

'Thou dost not know the honour. Lurgan Sahib himself asked for thee. Thou wilt go up the hill and along the road atop, and there thou must forget for a while that thou hast ever seen or spoken to me, Mahbub Ali, who sells horses to Creighton Sahib, whom thou dost not know. Remember this order.'

Kim nodded. 'Good,' said he, 'and who is Lurgan Sahib? Nay' – he caught Mahbub's sword-keen glance – 'indeed I have never heard his name. Is he by chance' – he lowered his voice – 'one of us?'

'What talk is this of *us*, Sahib?' Mahbub Ali returned, in the tone he used towards Europeans. 'I am a Pathan; thou art a sahib and the son of a sahib. Lurgan Sahib has a shop among the European shops. All Simla knows it. Ask there . . . and, Friend of all the World, he is one to be obeyed to the last wink of his eyelashes. Men say he does magic, but that should not touch thee. Go up the hill and ask. Here begins the Great Game.'

CHAPTER
9

S'doaks was son of Yelth the wise –
 Chief of the Raven clan.
Itswoot the Bear had him in care
 To make him a medicine-man.

He was quick and quicker to learn –
 Bold and bolder to dare:
He danced the dread Kloo-Kwallie Dance
 To tickle Itswoot the Bear!

Oregon Legend

Kim flung himself wholeheartedly upon the next turn of the wheel. He would be a sahib again for a while. In that idea, so soon as he had reached the broad road under Simla Town Hall, he cast about for one to impress. A Hindu child, some ten years old, squatted under a lamp-post.

'Where is Mr Lurgan's house?' demanded Kim.

'I do not understand English,' was the answer, and Kim shifted his speech accordingly.

'I will show.'

Together they set off through the mysterious dusk, full of the noises of a city below the hillside, and the breath of a cool wind in deodar-crowned Jakko, shouldering the stars. The house lights, scattered on every level, made, as it were, a double firmament. Some were fixed, others belonged to the rickshaws of the careless, open-spoken English folk, going out to dinner.

'It is here,' said Kim's guide, and halted in a veranda flush with the main road. No door stayed them, but a curtain of beaded reeds that split up the lamplight beyond.

'He is come,' said the boy, in a voice little louder than a sigh, and vanished. Kim felt sure that the boy had been posted to guide him from the first, but, putting a bold face on it, parted the curtain. A black-bearded man, with a green shade over his eyes, sat at a table, and, one by one, with short, white hands, picked up globules of light from a tray before him, threaded them on a glancing silken string, and hummed to himself the while. Kim was conscious that beyond the circle of light the room was full of things that smelt like all the temples of all the East. A whiff of musk, a puff of sandalwood, and a breath of sickly jessamine oil caught his opened nostrils.

'I am here,' said Kim at last, speaking in the vernacular: the smells made him forget that he was to be a sahib.

'Seventy-nine, eighty, eighty-one,' the man counted to himself, stringing pearl after pearl so quickly that Kim could scarcely follow his fingers. He slid off the green shade and looked fixedly at Kim for a full half-minute. The pupils of the eye dilated and closed to pin-pricks, as if at will. There was a *fakir* by the Taksali Gate who had just this gift and made money by it, especially when cursing silly women. Kim stared with interest. His disreputable friend could further twitch his ears, almost like a goat, and Kim was disappointed that this new man could not imitate him.

'Do not be afraid,' said Lurgan Sahib suddenly.

'Why should I fear?'

'Thou wilt sleep here tonight, and stay with me till it is time to go again to Nucklao. It is an order.'

'It is an order,' Kim repeated. 'But where shall I sleep?'

'Here, in this room.' Lurgan Sahib waved his hand towards the darkness behind him.

'So be it,' said Kim composedly. 'Now?'

He nodded and held the lamp above his head. As the light swept them, there leaped out from the walls a collection of Tibetan devil-dance masks, hanging above the fiend-embroidered draperies of those ghastly functions – horned masks, scowling masks, and masks of idiotic terror. In a corner, a Japanese warrior, mailed and plumed, menaced him with a halberd, and a score of lances and *khandas* and *kuttars* gave back the unsteady gleam. But what interested Kim more than all these things – he had seen devil-dance masks at the Lahore Museum – was a glimpse of the soft-eyed Hindu child who had left him in the doorway, sitting cross-legged under the table of pearls with a little smile on his scarlet lips.

'I think that Lurgan Sahib wishes to make me afraid. And I am sure that that devil's brat below the table wishes to see me afraid. This place,' he said aloud, 'is like a Wonder House. Where is my bed?'

Lurgan Sahib pointed to a native quilt in a corner by the loathsome masks, picked up the lamp, and left the room black.

'Was that Lurgan Sahib?' Kim asked as he cuddled down. No answer. He could hear the Hindu boy breathing, however, and, guided by the sound, crawled across the floor, and cuffed into the darkness, crying: 'Give answer, devil! Is this the way to lie to a sahib?'

From the darkness he fancied he could hear the echo of a chuckle. It could not be his soft-fleshed companion, because he was weeping. So Kim lifted up his voice and called aloud: 'Lurgan Sahib! O Lurgan Sahib! Is it an order that thy servant does not speak to me?'

'It is an order.' The voice came from behind him and he started.

'Very good. But remember,' he muttered, as he re-sought the quilt, 'I will beat thee in the morning. I do not love Hindus.'

That was no cheerful night; the room being over-full of voices and music. Kim was waked twice by some one calling his name. The second time he set out in search, and ended by bruising his nose against a box that certainly spoke with a human tongue, but in no sort of human accent. It seemed to end in a tin trumpet and to be joined by wires to a smaller box on the floor – so far, at least, as he could judge by touch. And the voice, very hard and whirring, came out of the trumpet. Kim rubbed his nose and grew furious, thinking, as usual, in Hindi.

'This with a beggar from the bazaar might be good, but – I am a sahib and the son of a sahib and, which is twice as much more beside, a student of Nucklao. Yess' (here he turned to English), 'a boy of St Xavier's. Damn Mr Lurgan's eyes! – It is some sort of machinery like a sewing-machine. Oh, it is a *great* cheek of him – we are not frightened that way at Lucknow – No!' Then in Hindi: 'But what does *he* gain? He is only a trader – I am in his shop. But Creighton Sahib is a colonel – and I think Creighton Sahib gave orders that it should be done. *How* I will beat that Hindu in the morning! What is this?'

The trumpet-box was pouring out a string of the most

elaborate abuse that even Kim had ever heard, in a high uninterested voice, that for a moment lifted the short hairs of his neck. When the vile thing drew breath, Kim was reassured by the soft, sewing-machine-like whirr.

'*Chûp!* [Be still]' he cried, and again he heard a chuckle that decided him. '*Chûp* – or I break your head.'

The box took no heed. Kim wrenched at the tin trumpet and something lifted with a click. He had evidently raised a lid. If there were a devil inside, now was its time, for – he sniffed – thus did the sewing-machines of the bazaar smell. He would clean that *shaitan*. He slipped off his jacket, and plunged it into the box's mouth. Something long and round bent under the pressure, there was a whirr and the voice stopped – as voices must if you ram a thrice-doubled coat on to the wax cylinder and into the works of an expensive phonograph. Kim finished his slumbers with a serene mind.

In the morning he was aware of Lurgan Sahib looking down on him.

'Oah!' said Kim, firmly resolved to cling to his sahib-dom. 'There was a box in the night that gave me bad talk. So I stopped it. Was it your box?'

The man held out his hand.

'Shake hands, O'Hara,' he said. 'Yes, it was my box. I keep such things because my friends the rajahs like them. That one is broken, but it was cheap at the price. Yes, my friends, the kings, are very fond of toys – and so am I sometimes.'

Kim looked him over out of the corners of his eyes. He was a sahib in that he wore sahib's clothes; the accent of his Urdu, the intonation of his English, showed that he

was anything but a sahib. He seemed to understand what moved in Kim's mind ere the boy opened his mouth, and he took no pains to explain himself as did Father Victor or the Lucknow masters. Sweetest of all – he treated Kim as an equal on the Asiatic side.

'I am sorry you cannot beat my boy this morning. He says he will kill you with a knife or poison. He is jealous, so I have put him in the corner and I shall not speak to him today. He has just tried to kill me. You must help me with the breakfast. He is almost too jealous to trust, just now.'

Now a genuine imported sahib from England would have made a great to-do over this tale. Lurgan Sahib stated it as simply as Mahbub Ali was used to record his little affairs in the north.

The back veranda of the shop was built out over the sheer hillside, and they looked down into their neighbours' chimney-pots, as is the custom of Simla. But even more than the purely Persian meal cooked by Lurgan Sahib with his own hands, the shop fascinated Kim. The Lahore Museum was larger, but here were more wonders – ghost-daggers and prayer-wheels from Tibet; turquoise and raw amber necklaces; green jade bangles; curiously packed incense-sticks in jars crusted over with raw garnets; the devil-masks of overnight and a wall full of peacock-blue draperies; gilt figures of Buddha, and little portable lacquer altars; Russian samovars with turquoises on the lid; egg-shell china sets in quaint octagonal cane boxes; yellow ivory crucifixes – from Japan of all places in the world, so Lurgan Sahib said; carpets in dusty bales, smelling atrociously, pushed back behind torn and rotten screens of geometrical work; Persian

water-jugs for the hands after meals; dull copper incense-burners neither Chinese nor Persian, with friezes of fantastic devils running round them; tarnished silver belts that knotted like raw hide; hairpins of jade, ivory, and plasma; arms of all sorts and kinds, and a thousand other oddments were cased, or piled, or merely thrown into the room, leaving a clear space only round the rickety deal table, where Lurgan Sahib worked.

'Those things are nothing,' said his host, following Kim's glance. 'I buy them because they are pretty, and sometimes I sell – if I like the buyer's look. My work is on the table – some of it.'

It blazed in the morning light – all red and blue and green flashes, picked out with the vicious blue-white spurt of a diamond here and there. Kim opened his eyes.

'Oh, they are quite well, those stones. It will not hurt them to take the sun. Besides, they are cheap. But with sick stones it is very different.' He piled Kim's plate anew. 'There is no one but *me* can doctor a sick pearl and re-blue turquoises. I grant you opals – any fool can cure an opal – but for a sick pearl there is only me. Suppose I were to die! Then there would be no one . . . Oh no! *You* cannot do anything with jewels. It will be quite enough if you understand a little about the turquoise – some day.'

He moved to the end of the veranda to refill the heavy, porous clay water-jug from the filter.

'Do you want drink?'

Kim nodded. Lurgan Sahib, fifteen feet off, laid one hand on the jar. Next instant, it stood at Kim's elbow, full to within half an inch of the brim – the white cloth only showing, by a small wrinkle, where it had slid into place.

'Wah!' said Kim in most utter amazement. 'That

204

is magic.' Lurgan Sahib's smile showed that the compliment had gone home.

'Throw it back.'

'It will break.'

'I say, throw it back.'

Kim pitched it at random. It fell short and crashed into fifty pieces, while the water dripped through the rough veranda boarding.

'I said it would break.'

'All one. Look at it. Look at the largest piece.'

That lay with a sparkle of water in its curve, as it were a star on the floor. Kim looked intently. Lurgan Sahib laid one hand gently on the nape of his neck, stroked it twice or thrice, and whispered: 'Look! It shall come to life again, piece by piece. First the big piece shall join itself to two others on the right and the left – on the right and the left. Look!'

To save his life, Kim could not have turned his head. The light touch held him as in a vice, and his blood tingled pleasantly through him. There was one large piece of the jar where there had been three, and above them the shadowy outline of the entire vessel. He could see the veranda through it, but it was thickening and darkening with each beat of his pulse. Yet the jar – how slowly the thoughts came! – the jar had been smashed before his eyes. Another wave of prickling fire raced down his neck, as Lurgan Sahib moved his hand.

'Look! It is coming into shape,' said Lurgan Sahib.

So far Kim had been thinking in Hindi, but a tremor came on him, and with an effort like that of a swimmer before sharks, who hurls himself half out of the water, his mind leaped up from a darkness that was

swallowing it and took refuge in – the multiplication-table in English!

'Look! It is coming into shape,' whispered Lurgan Sahib.

The jar had been smashed – yess, smashed – not the native word, he would not think of that – but smashed – into fifty pieces, and twice three was six, and thrice three was nine, and four times three was twelve. He clung desperately to the repetition. The shadow outline of the jar cleared like a mist after rubbing eyes. There were the broken shards; there was the spilt water drying in the sun, and through the cracks of the veranda showed, all ribbed, the white house wall below – and thrice twelve was thirty-six!

'Look! Is it coming into shape?' asked Lurgan Sahib.

'But it *is* smashed – smashed,' he gasped – Lurgan Sahib had been muttering softly for the last half-minute. Kim wrenched his head aside. 'Look! *Dekho!* It is there as it was there.'

'It is there as it was there,' said Lurgan, watching Kim closely while the boy rubbed his neck. 'But you are the first of a many who has ever seen it so.' He wiped his broad forehead.

'Was that more magic?' Kim asked suspiciously. The tingle had gone from his veins; he felt unusually wide awake.

'No, that was not magic. It was only to see if there was – a flaw in a jewel. Sometimes very fine jewels will fly all to pieces if a man holds them in his hand, and knows the proper way. That is why one must be careful before one sets them. Tell me, did you see the shape of the pot?'

'For a little time. It began to grow like a flower from the ground.'

'And then what did you do? I mean, how did you think?'

'Oah! I knew it was broken, and so, I think, that was what I thought – and it *was* broken.'

'Hm! Has any one ever done that same sort of magic to you before?'

'If it was,' said Kim, 'do you think I should let it again? I should run away.'

'And now you are not afraid – eh?'

'Not now.'

Lurgan Sahib looked at him more closely than ever. 'I shall ask Mahbub Ali – not now, but some days later,' he muttered. 'I am pleased with you – yes; and I am pleased with you – no. You are the first that ever saved himself. I wish I knew what it was that . . . But you are right. You should not tell that – not even to me.'

He turned into the dusky gloom of the shop, and sat down at the table, rubbing his hands softly. A small, husky sob came from behind a pile of carpets. It was the Hindu child obediently facing towards the wall. His thin shoulders worked with grief.

'Ah! He is jealous, so jealous. I wonder if he will try to poison me again in my breakfast, and make me cook it twice.'

'*Kubbee – kubbee nahin*' [Never – never. No!], came the broken answer.

'And whether he will kill this other boy?'

'*Kubbee – kubbee nahin.*'

'What do *you* think he will do?' He turned suddenly on Kim.

'Oah! I do not know. Let him go, perhaps. Why did he want to poison you?'

'Because he is so fond of me. Suppose you were fond of some one, and you saw some one come, and the man you were fond of was more pleased with him than he was with you, what would you do?'

Kim thought. Lurgan repeated the sentence slowly in the vernacular.

'I should not poison that man,' said Kim reflectively, 'but I should beat that boy – *if* that boy was fond of my man. But first I would ask that boy if it were true.'

'Ah! He thinks every one must be fond of me.'

'Then I think he is a fool.'

'Hearest thou?' said Lurgan Sahib to the shaking shoulders. 'The sahib's son thinks thou art a little fool. Come out, and next time thy heart is troubled, do not try white arsenic quite so openly. Surely the Devil Dasim was lord of our tablecloth that day! It might have made me ill, child, and then a stranger would have guarded the jewels. Come!'

The child, heavy-eyed with much weeping, crept out from behind the bale and flung himself passionately at Lurgan Sahib's feet, with an extravagance of remorse that impressed even Kim.

'I will look into the ink-pools – I will faithfully guard the jewels! Oh, my Father and my Mother, send *him* away!' He indicated Kim with a backward jerk of his bare heel.

'Not yet – not yet. In a little while he will go away again. But now he is at school – at a new *madrissah* – and thou shalt be his teacher. Play the Play of the Jewels against him. I will keep tally.'

The child dried his tears at once, and dashed to the

back of the shop, whence he returned with a copper tray.

'Give me!' he said to Lurgan Sahib. 'Let them come from thy hand, for he may say that I knew them before.'

'Gently – gently,' the man replied, and from a drawer under the table dealt a half-handful of clattering trifles into the tray.

'Now,' said the child, waving an old newspaper. 'Look on them as long as thou wilt, stranger. Count and, if need be, handle. One look is enough for *me*.' He turned his back proudly.

'But what is the game?'

'When thou hast counted and handled and art sure thou canst remember them all, I cover them with this paper, and thou must tell over the tally to Lurgan Sahib. *I* will write mine.'

'Oah!' The instinct of competition waked in his breast. He bent over the tray. There were but fifteen stones on it. 'That is easy,' he said after a minute. The child slipped the paper over the winking jewels and scribbled in a native account-book.

'There are under that paper five blue stones – one big, one smaller, and three small,' said Kim, all in haste. 'There are four green stones, and one with a hole in it; there is one yellow stone that I can see through, and one like a pipe-stem. There are two red stones, and – and – I made the count fifteen, but two I have forgotten. No! Give me time. One was of ivory, little and brownish; and – and – give me time . . .'

'One – two' – Lurgan Sahib counted him out up to ten. Kim shook his head.

'Hear my count!' the child burst in, trilling with laughter. 'First, are two flawed sapphires – one of two

ruttees and one of four as I should judge. The four-ruttee sapphire is chipped at the edge. There is one Turkestan turquoise, plain with black veins, and there are two inscribed – one with a Name of God in gilt, and the other being cracked across, for it came out of an old ring, I cannot read. We have now all five blue stones. Four flawed emeralds there are, but one is drilled in two places, and one is a little carven –'

'Their weights?' said Lurgan Sahib impassively.

'Three – five – five – and four ruttees as I judge it. There is one piece of old greenish pipe amber, and a cut topaz from Europe. There is one ruby of Burma, of two ruttees, without a flaw, and there is a balas-ruby, flawed, of two ruttees. There is a carved ivory from China representing a rat sucking an egg; and there is last – ah ha! – a ball of crystal as big as a bean set on a gold leaf.'

He clapped his hands at the close.

'He is thy master,' said Lurgan Sahib, smiling.

'Huh! He knew the names of the stones,' said Kim, flushing. 'Try again! With common things such as he and I both know.'

They heaped the tray again with odds and ends gathered from the shop, and even the kitchen, and every time the child won, till Kim marvelled.

'Bind my eyes – let me feel once with my fingers, and even *then* I will leave thee open-eyed behind,' he challenged.

Kim stamped with vexation when the lad made his boast good.

'If it were men – or horses,' he said, 'I could do better. This playing with tweezers and knives and scissors is too little.'

'Learn first – teach later,' said Lurgan Sahib. 'Is he thy master?'

'Truly. But how is it done?'

'By doing it many times over till it is done perfectly – for it is worth doing.'

The Hindu boy, in highest feather, actually patted Kim on the back.

'Do not despair,' he said. 'I myself will teach thee.'

'And I will see that thou art well taught,' said Lurgan Sahib, still speaking in the vernacular, 'for except my boy here – it was foolish of him to buy so much white arsenic when, if he had asked, I could have given it – except my boy here I have not in a long time met with one better worth teaching. And there are ten days more ere thou canst return to Nucklao where they teach nothing at the long price. We shall, I think, be friends.'

They were a most mad ten days, but Kim enjoyed himself too much to reflect on their craziness. In the morning they played the Jewel Game – sometimes with veritable stones, sometimes with piles of swords and daggers, sometimes with photographs of natives. Through the afternoons he and the Hindu boy would mount guard in the shop, sitting dumb behind a carpet-bale or a screen and watching Mr Lurgan's many and very curious visitors. There were small rajahs, escorts coughing in the veranda, who came to buy curiosities – such as phonographs and mechanical toys. There were ladies in search of necklaces, and men, it seemed to Kim – but his mind may have been vitiated by early training – in search of the ladies; natives from independent and feudatory courts whose ostensible business was the repair of

broken necklaces – rivers of light poured out upon the table – but whose true end seemed to be to raise money for angry maharanees or young rajahs. There were babus to whom Lurgan Sahib talked with austerity and authority, but at the end of each interview he gave them money in coined silver and currency and currency notes. There were occasional gatherings of long-coated theatrical natives who discussed metaphysics in English and Bengali, to Mr Lurgan's great edification. He was always interested in religions. At the end of the day, Kim and the Hindu boy – whose name varied at Lurgan's pleasure – were expected to give a detailed account of all that they had seen and heard – their view of each man's character, as shown in his face, talk, and manner, and their notions of his real errand. After dinner, Lurgan Sahib's fancy turned more to what might be called dressing-up, in which game he took a most informing interest. He could paint faces to a marvel; with a brush dab here and a line there changing them past recognition. The shop was full of all manner of dresses and turbans, and Kim was apparelled variously as a young Muhammadan of good family, an oilman, and once – which was a joyous evening – as the son of an Oudh landholder in the fullest of full dress. Lurgan Sahib had a hawk's eye to detect the least flaw in the make-up; and lying on a worn teak-wood couch, would explain by the half-hour together how such and such a caste talked, or walked, or coughed, or spat, or sneezed, and, since 'hows' matter little in this world, the 'why' of everything. The Hindu child played this game clumsily. That little mind, keen as an icicle where tally of jewels was concerned, could not temper itself to enter another's soul; but a demon in Kim woke up and

sang with joy as he put on the changing dresses, and changed speech and gesture therewith.

Carried away by enthusiasm, he volunteered to show Lurgan Sahib one evening how the disciples of a certain caste of *fakir*, old Lahore acquaintances, begged doles by the roadside; and what sort of language he would use to an Englishman, to a Punjabi farmer going to a fair, and to a woman without a veil. Lurgan Sahib laughed immensely, and begged Kim to stay as he was, immobile for half an hour – cross-legged, ash-smeared, and wild-eyed in the back room. At the end of that time entered a hulking, obese babu whose stockinged legs shook with fat, and Kim opened on him with a shower of wayside chaff. Lurgan Sahib – this annoyed Kim – watched the babu and not the play.

'I think,' said the babu heavily, lighting a cigarette, 'I am of opeenion that it is most extra-ordinary and effeecient performance. Except that you had told me I should have opined that – that – that you were pulling my legs. How soon can he become approximately effeecient chain-man? Because *then* I shall indent for him.'

'That is what he must learn at Lucknow.'

'Then order him to be jolly-dam'-quick. Goodnight, Lurgan.' The babu swung out with the gait of a bogged cow.

When they were telling over the day's list of visitors, Lurgan Sahib asked Kim who he thought the man might be.

'God knows!' said Kim cheerily. The tone might almost have deceived Mahbub Ali, but it failed entirely with the healer of sick pearls.

'That is true. God, He knows; but I wish to know what you think.'

Kim glanced sideways at his companion, whose eye had a way of compelling truth.

'I – I think he will want me when I come from the school, but' – confidentially, as Lurgan Sahib nodded approval – 'I do not understand how *he* can wear many dresses and talk many tongues.'

'Thou wilt understand many things later. He is a writer of tales for a certain colonel. His honour is great only in Simla, and it is noticeable that he has no name, but only a number and a letter – that is a custom among us.'

'And is there a price upon his head too – as upon Mah – all the others?'

'Not yet; but if a boy rose up who is now sitting here and went – look, the door is open! – as far as a certain house with a red-painted veranda, behind that which was the old theatre in the Lower Bazaar, and whispered through the shutters: "Hurree Chunder Mookerjee bore the bad news of last month", that boy might take away a belt full of rupees.'

'How many?' said Kim promptly.

'Five hundred – a thousand – as many as he might ask for.'

'Good. And for how long might such a boy live after the news was told?' He smiled merrily at Lurgan Sahib's very beard.

'Ah! That is to be well thought of. Perhaps if he were very clever, he might live out the day – but not the night. By no means the night.'

'Then what is the babu's pay if so much is put upon his head?'

'Eighty – perhaps a hundred – perhaps a hundred and fifty rupees; but the pay is the least part of the work. From time to time, God causes men to be born – and thou art one of them – who have a lust to go abroad at the risk of their lives and discover news – today it may be of far-off things, tomorrow of some hidden mountain, and the next day of some nearby men who have done a foolishness against the state. These souls are very few; and of these few, not more than ten are of the best. Among these ten I count the babu, and that is curious. How great, therefore, and desirable must be a business that brazens the heart of a Bengali!'

'True. But the days go slowly for me. I am yet a boy, and it is only within two months I learned to write Angrezi. Even now I cannot read it well. And there are yet years and years and long years before I can be even a chain-man.'

'Have patience, Friend of all the World' – Kim started at the title. 'Would I had a few of the years that so irk thee. I have proved thee in several small ways. This will not be forgotten when I make my report to the Colonel Sahib.' Then, changing suddenly into English with a deep laugh:

'By Jove! O'Hara, I think there is a great deal in you; but you must not become proud and you must not talk. You must go back to Lucknow and be a good little boy and mind your book, as the English say, and perhaps, next holidays if you care, you can come back to me!' Kim's face fell. 'Oh, I mean *if* you like. I know where you want to go.'

Four days later a seat was booked for Kim and his small trunk at the rear of a Kalka tonga. His companion was the whale-like babu, who, with a fringed shawl wrapped

round his head, and his fat openwork-stockinged left leg tucked under him, shivered and grunted in the morning chill.

'How comes it that this man is one of *us*?' thought Kim, considering the jelly back as they jolted down the road; and the reflection threw him into most pleasant day-dreams. Lurgan Sahib had given him five rupees – a splendid sum – as well as the assurance of his protection if he worked. Unlike Mahbub, Lurgan Sahib had spoken most explicitly of the reward that would follow obedi-ence, and Kim was content. If only, like the babu, he could enjoy the dignity of a letter and a number – and a price upon his head! Some day he would be all that and more. Some day he might be almost as great as Mahbub Ali! The house-tops of his search should be half India; he would follow kings and ministers, as in the old days he had followed *vakils* and lawyers' touts across Lahore city for Mahbub Ali's sake. Meantime, there was the present, and not at all unpleasant, fact of St Xavier's immediately before him. There would be new boys to condescend to, and there would be tales of holiday adventures to hear. Young Martin, son of the tea-planter at Manipur, had boasted that he would go to war, with a rifle, against the head-hunters. That might be, but it was certain young Martin had not been blown half across the forecourt of a Patiala palace by an explosion of fireworks; nor had he . . . Kim fell to telling himself the story of his own adventures through the last three months. He could paralyse St Xavier's – even the biggest boys who shaved – with the recital, were that permitted. But it was, of course, out of the question. There would be a price upon his head in good time, as Lurgan Sahib had assured him;

and if he talked foolishly now, not only would that price never be set, but Colonel Creighton would cast him off – and he would be left to the wrath of Lurgan Sahib and Mahbub Ali – for the short space of life that would remain to him.

'So I should lose Delhi for the sake of a fish,' was his proverbial philosophy. It behoved him to forget his holidays (there would always remain the fun of inventing imaginary adventures) and, as Lurgan Sahib had said, to work.

Of all the boys hurrying back to St Xavier's, from Sukkur in the sands to Galle beneath the palms, none was so filled with virtue as Kimball O'Hara, jiggeting down to Umballa behind Hurree Chunder Mookerjee, whose name on the books of one section of the Ethnological Survey was R17.

And if additional spur were needed, the babu supplied it. After a huge meal at Kalka, he spoke uninterruptedly. Was Kim going to school? Then he, an MA of Calcutta University, would explain the advantages of education. There were marks to be gained by due attention to Latin and Wordsworth's *Excursion* (all this was Greek to Kim). French, too, was vital, and the best was to be picked up in Chandernagore, a few miles from Calcutta. Also a man might go far, as he himself had done, by strict attention to plays called *Lear* and *Julius Caesar*, both much in demand by examiners. *Lear* was not so full of historical allusions as *Julius Caesar*; the book cost four annas, but could be bought second-hand in Bow Bazaar for two. Still more important than Wordsworth, or the eminent authors, Burke and Hare, was the art and science of mensuration. A boy who had passed his examination in these branches

– for which, by the way, there were no cram books – could, by merely marching over a country with a compass and a level and a straight eye, carry away a picture of that country which might be sold for large sums in coined silver. But as it was occasionally inexpedient to carry about measuring-chains, a boy would do well to know the precise length of his own foot-pace, so that when he was deprived of what Hurree Chunder called 'adventitious aids' he might still tread his distances. To keep count of thousands of paces, Hurree Chunder's experience had shown him nothing more valuable than a rosary of eighty-one or a hundred and eight beads, for 'it was divisible and sub-divisible into many multiples and sub-multiples'. Through the volleying drifts of English, Kim caught the general trend of the talk, and it interested him very much. Here was a new craft that a man could tuck away in his head; and by the look of the large wide world unfolding itself before him, it seemed that the more a man knew the better for him.

Said the babu when he had talked for an hour and a half, 'I hope some day to enjoy your offeecial acquaintance. *Ad interim*, if I may be pardoned that expression, I shall give you this betel-box, which is highly valuable article and cost me two rupees only four years ago.' It was a cheap, heart-shaped thing with three compartments for carrying the eternal betel-nut, lime and *pan*-leaf; but it was filled with little tabloid-bottles. 'That is reward of merit for your performance in character of that holy man. You see, you are so young you think you will last for ever and not take care of your body. It is great nuisance to go sick in the middle of business. I am fond of drugs myself, and they are handy to cure poor people too. These are

good departmental drugs – quinine and so on. I give it you for souvenir. Now goodbye. I have urgent private business here by the roadside.'

He slipped out noiselessly as a cat, on the Umballa road, hailed a passing cart and jingled away, while Kim, tongue-tied, twiddled the brass betel-box in his hands.

The record of a boy's education interests few save his parents, and, as you know, Kim was an orphan. It is written in the books of St Xavier's in Partibus that a report of Kim's progress was forwarded at the end of each term to Colonel Creighton and to Father Victor, from whose hands duly came the money for his schooling. It is further recorded in the same books that he showed a great aptitude for mathematical studies as well as map-making, and carried away a prize (*The Life of Lord Lawrence*, tree-calf, two vols, nine rupees, eight annas) for proficiency therein; and the same term played in St Xavier's eleven against the Alighur Muhammadan College, his age being fourteen years and ten months. He was also re-vaccinated (from which we may assume that there had been another epidemic of smallpox at Lucknow) about the same time. Pencil notes on the edge of an old muster-roll record that he was punished several times for 'conversing with improper persons', and it seems that he was once sentenced to heavy pains for 'absenting himself for a day in the company of a street beggar'. That was when he got over the gate and pleaded with the lama through a whole day down the banks of the Gumti to accompany him on the Road next holidays – for one month – for a little week; and the lama set his face as a flint against it,

averring that the time had not yet come. Kim's business, said the old man as they ate cakes together, was to get all the wisdom of the sahibs and then he would see. The Hand of Friendship must in some way have averted the Whip of Calamity, for six weeks later Kim seems to have passed an examination in elementary surveying 'with great credit', his age being fifteen years and eight months. From this date the record is silent. His name does not appear in the year's batch of those who entered for the subordinate Survey of India, but against it stand the words 'removed on appointment'.

Several times in those three years, cast up at the Temple of the Tirthankars in Benares the lama, a little thinner and a shade yellower, if that were possible, but gentle and untainted as ever. Sometimes it was from the south that he came – from south of Tuticorin, whence the wonderful fire-boats go to Ceylon where are priests who know Pali; sometimes it was from the wet green west and the thousand cotton-factory chimneys that ring Bombay; and once from the north, where he had doubled back eight hundred miles to talk for a day with the Keeper of the Images in the Wonder House. He would stride to his cell in the cool, cut marble – the priests of the Temple were good to the old man – wash off the dust of travel, make prayer, and depart for Lucknow, well accustomed now to the ways of the rail, in a third-class carriage. Returning, it was noticeable, as his friend the Seeker pointed out to the head-priest, that he ceased for a while to mourn the loss of his River, or to draw wondrous pictures of the Wheel of Life, but preferred to talk of the beauty and wisdom of a certain mysterious *chela* whom no man of the Temple had ever seen. Yes, he had

followed the traces of the Blessed Feet throughout all India. (The Curator has still in his possession a most marvellous account of his wanderings and meditations.) There remained nothing more in life but to find the River of the Arrow. Yet it was shown to him in his dreams that it was a matter not to be undertaken with any hope of success unless that seeker had with him the one *chela* appointed to bring the event to a happy issue, and versed in great wisdom – such wisdom as white-haired Keepers of Images possess. For example, (here came out the snuff-gourd, and the kindly Jain priests made haste to be silent):

'Long and long ago, when Devadatta was King of Benares – let all listen to the *Jâtaka*! – an elephant was captured for a time by the king's hunters and, ere he broke free, beringed with a grievous leg-iron. This he strove to remove with hate and frenzy in his heart, and hurrying up and down the forests, besought his brother-elephants to wrench it asunder. One by one, with their strong trunks, they tried and failed. At the last they gave it as their opinion that the ring was not to be broken by any bestial power. And in a thicket, new-born, wet with the moisture of birth, lay a day-old calf of the herd whose mother had died. The fettered elephant, forgetting his own agony, said: "If I do not help this suckling it will perish under our feet." So he stood above the young thing, making his legs buttresses against the uneasily moving herd; and he begged milk of a virtuous cow, and the calf throve, and the ringed elephant was the calf's guide and defence. Now the days of an elephant – let all listen to the *Jâtaka*! – are thirty-five years to his full strength, and through thirty-five rains the ringed

elephant befriended the younger, and all the while the fetter ate into the flesh.

'Then one day the young elephant saw the half-buried iron, and turning to the elder said: "What is this?" "It is even my sorrow," said he who had befriended him. Then that other put out his trunk and in the twinkling of an eyelash abolished the ring, saying: "The appointed time has come." So the virtuous elephant who had waited temperately and done kind acts was relieved, at the appointed time, by the very calf whom he had turned aside to cherish – let all listen to the *Jâtaka*! – for the Elephant was Ananda, and the Calf that broke the ring was none other than the Lord himself . . .'

Then he would shake his head benignly, and over the ever-clicking rosary point out how free that elephant-calf was from the sin of pride. He was as humble as a *chela* who, seeing his master sitting in the dust outside the Gates of Learning, overleapt the gates (though they were locked) and took his master to his heart in the presence of the proud-stomached city. Rich would be the reward of such a master and such a *chela* when the time came for them to seek freedom together!

So did the lama speak, coming and going across India as softly as a bat. A sharp-tongued old woman in a house among the fruit trees behind Saharunpore honoured him as the woman honoured the prophet, but his chamber was by no means upon the wall. In an apartment of the forecourt overlooked by cooing doves he would sit, while she laid aside her useless veil and chattered of spirits and fiends of Kulu, of grandchildren unborn, and of the free-tongued brat who had talked to her in the resting-place. Once, too, he strayed alone from the Grand Trunk

Road below Umballa to the very village whose priest had tried to drug him; but the kind Heaven that guards lamas sent him at twilight through the crops, absorbed and unsuspicious, to the Rissaldar's door. Here was like to have been a grave misunderstanding, for the old soldier asked him why the Friend of the Stars had gone that way only six days before.

'That may not be,' said the lama. 'He has gone back to his own people.'

'He sat in that corner telling a hundred merry tales five nights ago,' his host insisted. 'True, he vanished somewhat suddenly in the dawn after foolish talk with my granddaughter. He grows apace, but he is the same Friend of the Stars as brought me true word of the war. Have ye parted?'

'Yes – and no,' the lama replied. 'We – we have not altogether parted, but the time is not ripe that we should take the Road together. He acquires wisdom in another place. We must wait.'

'All one – but if it were not the boy, how did he come to speak so continually of thee?'

'And what said he?' asked the lama eagerly.

'Sweet words – an hundred thousand – that thou art his father and mother and such all. Pity that he does not take the Queen's service. He is fearless.'

This news amazed the lama, who did not then know how religiously Kim kept to the contract made with Mahbub Ali and perforce ratified by Colonel Creighton . . .

'There is no holding the young pony from the game,' said the horse-dealer when the Colonel pointed out that vagabonding over India in holiday time was absurd. 'If

permission be refused to go and come as he chooses, he will make light of the refusal. Then who is to catch him? Colonel Sahib, only once in a thousand years is a horse born so well fitted for the game as this our colt. And we need men.'

Your tiercel's too long at hack, Sire. He's no eyass
But a passage-hawk that footed ere we caught him,
Dangerously free o' the air. Faith! were he mine
(As mine's the glove he binds to for his tirings)
I'd fly him with a make-hawk. He's in yarak
Plumed to the very point – so manned, so
 weathered . . .
Give him the firmament God made him for,
And what shall take the air of him?

 Gow's Watch

Lurgan Sahib did not use as direct speech, but his advice
tallied with Mahbub's; and the upshot was good for Kim.
He knew better now than to leave Lucknow city in native
garb, and if Mahbub were anywhere within reach of a
letter, it was to Mahbub's camp he headed, and made his
change under the Pathan's wary eye. Could the little
Survey paintbox that he used for map-tinting in term-
time have found a tongue to tell of holiday doings, he
might have been expelled. Once Mahbub and he went
together as far as the beautiful city of Bombay, with three
truck-loads of tram-horses, and Mahbub nearly melted
when Kim proposed a sail in a dhow across the Indian
Ocean to buy Gulf Arabs, which, he understood from a
hanger-on of the dealer Abdul Rahman, fetched better
prices than mere Kabulis.

 He dipped his hand into the dish with that great trader
when Mahbub and a few co-religionists were invited to a

big Haj dinner. They came back by way of Karachi by sea, when Kim took his first experience of sea-sickness on the fore-hatch of a coasting-steamer, well persuaded he had been poisoned. The babu's famous drug-box proved useless, though Kim had restocked it at Bombay. Mahbub had business at Quetta, and there Kim, as Mahbub admitted, earned his keep, and perhaps a little over, by spending four curious days as scullion in the house of a fat Commissariat sergeant, from whose office-box, in an auspicious moment, he removed a little vellum ledger which he copied out – it seemed to deal entirely with cattle and camel sales – by moonlight, lying behind an outhouse, all through one hot night. Then he returned the ledger to its place, and, at Mahbub's word, left that service unpaid, rejoining him six miles down the road, the clean copy in his bosom.

'That soldier is a small fish,' Mahbub Ali explained, 'but in time we shall catch the larger one. He only sells oxen at two prices – one for himself and one for the government – which I do not think is a sin.'

'Why could not I take away the little book and be done with it?'

'Then he would have been frightened, and he would have told his master. Then we should miss, perhaps, a great number of new rifles which seek their way up from Quetta to the north. The Game is so large that one sees but a little at a time.'

'Oho!' said Kim, and held his tongue. That was in the monsoon holidays, after he had taken the prize for mathematics. The Christmas holidays he spent – deducting ten days for private amusements – with Lurgan Sahib, where he sat for the most part in front of a roaring

wood-fire – Jakko road was four feet deep in snow that year – and – the small Hindu had gone away to be married – helped Lurgan to thread pearls. He made Kim learn whole chapters of the Koran by heart, till he could deliver them with the very roll and cadence of a mullah. Moreover, he told Kim the names and properties of many native drugs, as well as the runes proper to recite when you administer them. And in the evenings he wrote charms on parchment – elaborate pentagrams crowned with the names of devils – Murra, and Awan the Companion of Kings – all fantastically written in the corners. More to the point, he advised Kim as to the care of his own body, the cure of fever-fits, and simple remedies of the Road. A week before it was time to go down, Colonel Creighton Sahib – this was unfair – sent Kim a written examination-paper that concerned itself solely with rods and chains and links and angles.

Next holidays he was out with Mahbub, and here, by the way, he nearly died of thirst, plodding through the sand on a camel to the mysterious city of Bikanir, where the wells are four hundred feet deep, and lined throughout with camel-bone. It was not an amusing trip from Kim's point of view, because – in defiance of the contract – the Colonel ordered him to make a map of that wild, walled city; and since Muhammadan horse-boys and pipe-tenders are not expected to drag survey-chains round the capital of an independent native state, Kim was forced to pace all his distances by means of a bead rosary. He used the compass for bearings as occasion served – after dark chiefly, when the camels had been fed – and by the help of his little Survey paintbox of six colour-cakes and three brushes, he achieved something

not remotely unlike the city of Jeysulmir. Mahbub laughed a great deal, and advised him to make up a written report as well; and in the back of the big account-book that lay under the flap of Mahbub's pet saddle Kim fell to work.

'It must hold everything that thou hast seen or touched or considered. Write as though the Jang-i-Lat Sahib himself had come by stealth with a vast army outsetting to war.'

'How great an army?'

'Oh, half a lakh of men.'

'Folly! Remember how few and bad were the wells in the sand. Not a thousand thirsty men could come near by here.'

'Then write that down – also all the old breaches in the walls – and whence the firewood is cut – and what is the temper and disposition of the king. I stay here till all my horses are sold. I will hire a room by the gateway, and thou shalt be my accountant. There is a good lock to the door.'

The report in its unmistakable St Xavier's running script, and the brown, yellow and lake-daubed map, was on hand a few years ago (a careless clerk filed it with the rough notes of E23's second Seistan survey), but by now the pencil characters must be almost illegible. Kim translated it, sweating under the light of an oil-lamp, to Mahbub, the second day of their return-journey. The Pathan rose and stooped over his dappled saddlebags.

'I knew it would be worthy a dress of honour, and so I made one ready,' he said smiling. 'Were I Amir of Afghanistan (and some day we may see him), I would fill thy mouth with gold.' He laid the garments formally at Kim's

feet. There was a gold-embroidered Peshawar turban-cap, rising to a cone, and a big turban-cloth ending in a fringe of gold. There was a Delhi embroidered waistcoat to slip over a milky white shirt, fastening to the right, ample and flowing; green pyjamas with twisted silk waist-string; and that nothing might be lacking russia-leather slippers, smelling divinely, with arrogantly curled tips.

'Upon a Wednesday, and in the morning, to put on new clothes is auspicious,' said Mahbub solemnly. 'But we must not forget the wicked folk in the world. So!'

He capped all the splendour, that was taking Kim's delighted breath away, with a mother-of-pearl, nickel-plated, self-extracting .450 revolver.

'I had thought of a smaller bore, but reflected that this takes government bullets. A man can always come by those – especially across the border. Stand up and let me look.' He clapped Kim on the shoulder. 'May you never be tired, Pathan! Oh, the hearts to be broken! Oh, the eyes under the eyelashes, looking sideways!'

Kim turned about, pointed his toes, stretched, and felt mechanically for the moustache that was just beginning. Then he stooped towards Mahbub's feet to make proper acknowledgement with fluttering, quick-patting hands; his heart too full for words. Mahbub forestalled and embraced him.

'My son,' said he, 'what need of words between us? But is not the little gun a delight? All six cartridges come out at one twist. It is borne in the bosom next the skin, which, as it were, keeps it oiled. Never put it elsewhere, and please God, thou shalt some day kill a man with it.'

'*Hai mai!*' said Kim ruefully. 'If a sahib kills a man he is hanged in the jail.'

'True: but one pace beyond the border, men are wiser. Put it away; but fill it first. Of what use is a gun unfed?'

'When I go back to the *madrissah* I must return it. They do not allow little guns. Thou wilt keep it for me?'

'Son, I am wearied of that *madrissah*, where they take the best years of a man to teach him what he can only learn upon the Road. The folly of the sahibs has neither top nor bottom. No matter. Maybe thy written report shall save thee further bondage; and God he knows we need men more and more in the Game.'

They marched, jaw-bound against blowing sand, across the salt desert to Jodhpur, where Mahbub and his handsome nephew Habib Ullah did much trading; and then sorrowfully, in European clothes, which he was fast outgrowing, Kim went second-class to St Xavier's. Three weeks later, Colonel Creighton, pricing Tibetan ghost-daggers at Lurgan's shop, faced Mahbub Ali openly mutinous. Lurgan Sahib operated as support in reserve.

'The pony is made – finished – mouthed and paced, Sahib! From now on, day by day, he will lose his manners if he is kept at tricks. Drop the rein on his back and let go,' said the horse-dealer. 'We need him.'

'But he is so young, Mahbub – not more than sixteen – is he?'

'When I was fifteen, I had shot my man and begot my man, Sahib.'

'You impenitent old heathen!' Creighton turned to Lurgan. The black beard nodded assent to the wisdom of the Afghan's dyed scarlet.

'*I* should have used him long ago,' said Lurgan. 'The

younger the better. That is why I always have my really valuable jewels watched by a child. You sent him to me to try. I tried him in every way: he is the only boy I could not make to see things.'

'In the crystal – in the ink-pool?' demanded Mahbub.

'No. Under my hand, as I told you. That has never happened before. It means that he is strong enough – but you think it skittles, Colonel Creighton – to make any one do anything he wants. And that is three years ago. I have taught him a good deal since, Colonel Creighton. I think you waste him now.'

'Hmm! Maybe you're right. But, as you know, there is no Survey work for him at present.'

'Let him out – let him go,' Mahbub interrupted. 'Who expects any colt to carry heavy weight at first? Let him run with the caravans – like our white camel-colts – for luck. I would take him myself, but –'

'There is a little business where he would be most useful – in the south,' said Lurgan, with peculiar suavity, dropping his heavy blued eyelids.

'E23 has that in hand,' said Creighton quickly. 'He must not go down there. Besides, he knows no Turki.'

'Only tell him the shape and the smell of the letters we want and he will bring them back,' Lurgan insisted.

'No. That is a man's job,' said Creighton.

It was a wry-necked matter of unauthorized and incendiary correspondence between a person who claimed to be the ultimate authority in all matters of the Muhammadan religion throughout the world, and a younger member of a royal house who had been brought to book for kidnapping women within British territory. The Muslim Archbishop had been emphatic and over-arrogant;

the young prince was merely sulky at the curtailment of his privileges, but there was no need he should continue a correspondence which might some day compromise him. One letter indeed had been procured, but the finder was later found dead by the roadside in the habit of an Arab trader, as E23, taking up the work, duly reported.

These facts, and a few others not to be published, made both Mahbub and Creighton shake their heads.

'Let him go out with his Red Lama,' said the horse-dealer with visible effort. 'He is fond of the old man. He can learn his paces by the rosary at least.'

'I have had some dealings with the old man – by letter,' said Colonel Creighton, smiling to himself. 'Whither goes he?'

'Up and down the land, as he has these three years. He seeks a River of Healing. God's curse upon all –' Mahbub checked himself. 'He beds down at the Temple of the Tirthankars or at Buddh Gaya when he is in from the Road. Then he goes to see the boy at the *madrissah*, as we know, for the boy was punished for it twice or thrice. He is quite mad, but a peaceful man. I have met him. The babu also has had dealings with him. We have watched him for three years. Red Lamas, are not so common in Hind that one loses track.'

'Babus are very curious,' said Lurgan meditatively. 'Do you know what Hurree Babu really wants? He wants to be made a member of the Royal Society by taking ethnological notes. I tell you, I tell him about the lama everything which Mahbub and the boy have told me. Hurree Babu goes down to Benares – at his own expense, I think.'

'I don't,' said Creighton briefly. He had paid Hurree's

travelling expenses, out of a most lively curiosity to learn what the lama might be.

'And he applies to the lama for information on lamaism, and devil-dances, and spells and charms, several times in these few years. Holy Virgin! I could have told him all that yee-ars ago. I think Hurree Babu is getting too old for the Road. He likes better to collect manners and customs information. Yes, he wants to be an FRS.'

'Hurree thinks well of the boy, doesn't he?'

'Oh, very indeed – we have had some pleasant evenings at my little place – but I think it would be waste to throw him away with Hurree on the ethnological side.'

'Not for a first experience. How does that strike you, Mahbub? Let the boy run with the lama for six months. After that we can see. He will get experience.'

'He has it already, Sahib – as a fish controls the water he swims in. But for every reason it will be well to loose him from the school.'

'Very good, then,' said Creighton, half to himself. 'He can go with the lama, and if Hurree Babu cares to keep an eye on them so much the better. He won't lead the boy into any danger as Mahbub would. Curious – his wish to be an FRS. Very human, too. He *is* best on the ethnological side – Hurree.'

No money and no preferment would have drawn Creighton from his work on the Indian Survey, but deep in his heart also lay the ambition to write 'FRS' after his name. Honours of a sort he knew could be obtained by ingenuity and the help of friends, but, to the best of his belief, nothing save work – papers representing a life of it – took a man into the Society which he had bombarded for years with monographs on strange Asiatic cults and

unknown customs. Nine men out of ten would flee from a Royal Society soirée in extremity of boredom; but Creighton was the tenth, and at times his soul yearned for the crowded rooms in easy London where silver-haired, bald-headed gentlemen who know nothing of the army move among spectroscopic experiments, the lesser plants of the frozen tundras, electric flight-measuring machines, and apparatus for slicing into fractional millimetres the left eye of the female mosquito. By all right and reason, it was the Royal Geographical that should have appealed to him, but men are as chancy as children in their choice of playthings. So Creighton smiled, and thought the better of Hurree Babu, moved by like desire.

He dropped the ghost-dagger and looked up at Mahbub.

'How soon can we get the colt from the stable?' said the horse-dealer, reading his eyes.

'Hmm! If I withdraw him by order now – what will he do, think you? I have never before assisted at the teaching of such an one.'

'He will come to me,' said Mahbub promptly. 'Lurgan Sahib and I will prepare him for the Road.'

'So be it, then. For six months he shall run at his choice. But who will be his sponsor?'

Lurgan slightly inclined his head. 'He will not tell anything, if that is what you are afraid of, Colonel Creighton.'

'It's only a boy, after all.'

'Ye-es; but first, he has nothing to tell; and secondly, he knows what would happen. Also, he is very fond of Mahbub, and of me a little.'

'Will he draw pay?' demanded the practical horse-dealer.

'Food and water allowance only. Twenty rupees a month.'

One advantage of the Secret Service is that it has no worrying audit. That Service is ludicrously starved, of course, but the funds are administered by a few men who do not call for vouchers or present itemized accounts. Mahbub's eyes lighted with almost a Sikh's love of money. Even Lurgan's impassive face changed. He considered the years to come when Kim would have been entered and made to the Great Game that never ceases day and night, throughout India. He foresaw honour and credit in the mouths of a chosen few, coming to him from his pupil. Lurgan Sahib had made E23 what E23 was, out of a bewildered, impertinent, lying little North-West Province man.

But the joy of these masters was pale and smoky beside the joy of Kim when St Xavier's head called him aside, with word that Colonel Creighton had sent for him.

'I understand, O'Hara, that he has found you a place as an assistant chain-man in the Canal Department: that comes of taking up mathematics. It is great luck for you, for you are only sixteen; but of course you understand that you do not become *pukka* [permanent] till you have passed the autumn examination. So you must not think you are going out into the world to enjoy yourself, or that your fortune is made. There is a great deal of hard work before you. Only, if you succeed in becoming *pukka*, you can rise, you know, to four hundred and fifty a month.' Whereat the Principal gave him much good advice as to

his conduct, and his manners, and his morals; and others, his elders, who had not been wafted into billets, talked as only Anglo-Indian lads can, of favouritism and corruption. Indeed, young Cazalet, whose father was a pensioner at Chunar, hinted very broadly that Colonel Creighton's interest in Kim was directly paternal; and Kim, instead of retaliating, did not even use language. He was thinking of the immense fun to come, of Mahbub's letter of the day before, all neatly written in English, making appointment for that afternoon in a house the very name of which would have crisped the Principal's hair with horror . . .

Said Kim to Mahbub in Lucknow railway station that evening, above the luggage-scales: 'I feared lest, at the last, the roof would fall upon me and cheat me. Is it indeed all finished, O my father?'

Mahbub snapped his fingers to show the utterness of that end, and his eyes blazed like red coals.

'Then where is the pistol that I may wear it?'

'Softly! A half-year, to run without heel-ropes. I begged that much from Colonel Creighton Sahib. At twenty rupees a month. Old Red Hat knows that thou art coming.'

'I will pay thee *dustoorie* (commission) on my pay for three months,' said Kim gravely. 'Yea, two rupees a month. But first we must get rid of these.' He plucked his thin linen trousers and dragged at his collar. 'I have brought with me all that I need on the Road. My trunk has gone up to Lurgan Sahib's.'

'Who sends his salaams to thee – Sahib.'

'Lurgan Sahib is a very clever man. But what dost thou do?'

'I go north again, upon the Great Game. What else? Is thy mind still set on following old Red Hat?'

'Do not forget he made me that I am – though he did not know it. Year by year, he sent the money that taught me.'

'I would have done as much – had it struck my thick head,' Mahbub growled. 'Come away. The lamps are lit now, and none will mark thee in the bazaar. We go to Huneefa's house.'

On the way thither, Mahbub gave him much the same sort of advice as his mother gave to Lemuel, and curiously enough, Mahbub was exact to point out how Huneefa and her likes destroyed kings.

'And I remember,' he quoted maliciously, 'one who said, "Trust a snake before an harlot, and an harlot before a Pathan, Mahbub Ali." Now, excepting as to Pathans, of whom I am one, all that is true. Most true is it in the Great Game, for it is by means of women that all plans come to ruin and we lie out in the dawning with our throats cut. So it happened to such a one.' He gave the reddest particulars.

'Then why –?' Kim paused before a filthy staircase that climbed to the warm darkness of an upper chamber, in the ward that is behind Azim Ullah's tobacco-shop. Those who know it call it the Bird-cage – it is so full of whisperings and whistlings and chirrupings.

The room, with its dirty cushions and half-smoked hookahs, smelt abominably of stale tobacco. In one corner lay a huge and shapeless woman clad in greenish gauzes, and decked, brow, nose, ear, neck, wrist, arm, waist and ankle, with heavy native jewellery. When she turned it was like the clashing of copper pots. A lean cat

in the balcony outside the window mewed hungrily. Kim checked, bewildered, at the door-curtain.

'Is that the new stuff, Mahbub?' said Huneefa lazily, scarce troubling to remove the mouthpiece from her lips. 'O Buktanoos!' – like most of her kind, she swore by the djinns – 'O Buktanoos! He is very good to look upon.'

'That is part of the selling of the horse,' Mahbub explained to Kim, who laughed.

'I have heard that talk since my Sixth Day,' he replied, squatting by the light. 'Whither does it lead?'

'To protection. Tonight we change thy colour. This sleeping under roofs has blanched thee like an almond. But Huneefa has the secret of a colour that catches. No painting of a day or two. Also, we fortify thee against the chances of the Road. That is *my* gift to thee, my son. Take out all metals on thee and lay them here. Make ready, Huneefa.'

Kim dragged forth his compass, Survey paintbox, and the new-filled medicine-box. They had all accompanied his travels, and boy-like he valued them immensely.

The woman rose slowly and moved with her hands a little spread before her. Then Kim saw that she was blind. 'No, no,' she muttered, 'the Pathan speaks truth – my colour does not go in a week or a month, and those whom I protect are under strong guard.'

'When one is far off and alone, it would not be well to grow blotched and leprous of a sudden,' said Mahbub. 'When thou wast with me I could oversee the matter. Besides, a Pathan is a fair-skin. Strip to the waist now and look how thou art whitened.' Huneefa felt her way back from an inner room. 'It is no matter, she cannot see.' He took a pewter bowl from her ringed hand.

The dye-stuff showed blue and gummy. Kim experimented on the back of his wrist, with a dab of cotton wool; but Huneefa heard him.

'No, no,' she cried, 'the thing is not done thus, but with the proper ceremonies. The colouring is the least part. I give thee the full protection of the Road.'

'*Jadoo* [magic]?' said Kim, with a half start. He did not like the white, sightless eyes. Mahbub's hand on his neck bowed him to the floor, nose within an inch of the boards.

'Be still. No harm comes to thee, my son. I am thy sacrifice!'

He could not see what the woman was about, but heard the clish-clash of her jewellery for many minutes. A match lit up the darkness; he caught the well-known purr and fizzle of grains of incense. Then the room filled with smoke – heavy, aromatic, and stupefying. Through growing drowse he heard the names of devils – of Zulbazan, Son of Eblis, who lives in bazaars and *paraos*, making all the sudden lewd wickedness of wayside halts; of Dulhan, invisible about mosques, the dweller among the slippers of the Faithful, who hinders folk from their prayers; and Musboot, Lord of lies and panic. Huneefa, now whispering in his ear, now talking as from an immense distance, touched him with horrible soft fingers, but Mahbub's grip never shifted from his neck till, relaxing with a sigh, the boy lost his senses.

'Allah! How he fought! We should never have done it but for the drugs. That was his white blood, I take it,' said Mahbub testily. 'Go on with the *dawut* [invocation]. Give him full protection.'

'*O Hearer! Thou that hearest with ears, be present. Listen, O*

Hearer!' Huneefa moaned, her dead eyes turned to the west. The dark room filled with moanings and snortings.

From the outer balcony, a ponderous figure raised a round bullet head and coughed nervously.

'Do not interrupt this ventriloquial necromanciss, my friend,' it said in English. 'I opine that it is very disturbing to you, but no enlightened observer is jolly-well upset.'

'. . . I will lay a plot for their ruin! O Prophet, bear with the unbelievers. Let them alone awhile!' Huneefa's face, turned to the northward, worked horribly, and it was as though voices from the ceiling answered her.

Hurree Babu returned to his notebook, balanced on the windowsill, but his hand shook. Huneefa, in some sort of drugged ecstasy, wrenched herself to and fro as she sat crosslegged by Kim's still head, and called upon devil after devil, in the ancient order of the ritual, binding them to avoid the boy's every action.

'With Him are the keys of the Secret Things! None knoweth them beside Himself. He knoweth that which is in the dry land and in the sea!' Again broke out the unearthly whistling responses.

'I – I apprehend it is not at all malignant in its operation?' said the babu, watching the throat muscles quiver and jerk as Huneefa spoke with tongues. 'It – it is not likely that she has killed the boy? If so, I decline to be witness at the trial . . . What was the last hypothetical devil mentioned?'

'Babuji,' said Mahbub in the vernacular. 'I have no regard for the devils of Hind, but the Sons of Eblis are far otherwise, and whether they be *jumalee* [well-affected] or *jullalee* [terrible] they love not Kafirs.'

'Then you think I had better go?' said Hurree

Babu, half rising. 'They are, of course, dematerialized phenomena. Spencer says –'

Huneefa's crisis passed, as these things must, in a paroxysm of howling, with a touch of froth at the lips. She lay spent and motionless beside Kim, and the crazy voices ceased.

'Wah! That work is done. May the boy be better for it; and Huneefa is surely a mistress of *dawut*. Help haul her aside, Babu. Do not be afraid.'

'How am I to fear the absolutely non-existent?' said Hurree Babu, talking English to reassure himself. It is an awful thing still to dread the magic that you contemptuously investigate – to collect folklore for the Royal Society with a lively belief in all Powers of Darkness.

Mahbub chuckled. He had been out with Hurree on the Road ere now. 'Let us finish the colouring,' said he. 'The boy is well protected if – if the Lords of the Air have ears to hear. I am a Sufi [free-thinker], but when one can get blind-sides of a woman, a stallion, or a devil, why go round to invite a kick? Set him upon the way, Babu, and see that old Red Hat does not lead him beyond our reach. I must get back to my horses.'

'All raight,' said Hurree Babu. 'He is at present curious spectacle.'

About third cockcrow, Kim woke after a sleep of thousands of years. Huneefa, in her corner, snored heavily, but Mahbub was gone.

'I hope you were not frightened,' said an oily voice at his elbow. 'I superintended entire operation, which was most interesting from ethnological point of view. It was high-class *dawut*.'

'Huh!' said Kim, recognizing Hurree Babu, who smiled ingratiatingly.

'And also I had honour to bring down from Lurgan your present costume. I am not in the habit offeecially of carrying such gauds to subordinates, but' – he giggled – 'your case is noted as exceptional on the books. I hope Mr Lurgan will note my action.'

Kim yawned and stretched himself. It was good to turn and twist within loose clothes once again.

'What is this?' He looked curiously at the heavy duffle-stuff loaded with the scents of the far north.

'Oho! That is inconspicuous dress of *chela* attached to service of lamaistic lama. *Com*plete in every particular,' said Hurree Babu, rolling into the balcony to clean his teeth at a goglet. 'I am of opeenion it is not your old gentleman's precise releegion, but rather sub-variant of same. I have contributed rejected notes to *Asiatic Quarterly Review* on these subjects. Now it is curious that the old gentleman himself is totally devoid of releegiosity. He is not a dam' particular.'

'Do you know him?'

Hurree Babu held up his hand to show he was engaged in the prescribed rites that accompany tooth-cleaning and such things among decently bred Bengalis. Then he recited in English an Arya-Somaj prayer of a theistical nature, and stuffed his mouth with *pan* and betel.

'Oah yes. I have met him several times at Benares, and also at Buddh Gaya, to interrogate him on releegious points and devil-worship. He is pure agnostic – same as me.'

Huneefa stirred in her sleep, and Hurree Babu jumped

nervously to the copper incense-burner, all black and discoloured in morning-light, rubbed a finger in the accumulated lampblack, and drew it diagonally across his face.

'Who has died in thy house?' asked Kim in the vernacular.

'None. But she may have the Evil Eye – that sorceress,' the babu replied.

'What dost thou do now, then?'

'I will set thee on thy way to Benares, if thou goest thither, and tell thee what must be known by Us.'

'I go. At what hour runs the *te-rain*?' He rose to his feet, looked round the desolate chamber and at the yellow-wax face of Huneefa as the low sun stole across the floor. 'Is there money to be paid that witch?'

'No. She has charmed thee against all devils and all dangers – in the name of her devils. It was Mahbub's desire.' In English: 'He is highly obsolete, *I* think, to indulge in such supersteetion. Why, it is all ventri*lo*quy. Belly-speak – eh?'

Kim snapped his fingers mechanically to avert whatever evil – Mahbub, he knew, meditated none – might have crept in through Huneefa's ministrations; and Hurree giggled once more. But as he crossed the room he was careful not to step in Huneefa's blotched, squat shadow on the boards. Witches – when their time is on them – can lay hold of the heels of a man's soul if he does that.

'Now you must well listen,' said the babu when they were in the fresh air. 'Part of these ceremonies which we witnessed they include supply of effeecient amulet to those of our Department. If you feel in your neck you will

243

find one small silver amulet, verree cheap. That is *ours*. Do you understand?'

'Oah yes, *hawa-dilli* [a heart-lifter],' said Kim, feeling at his neck.

'Huneefa she makes them for two rupees twelve annas with – oh, all sorts of exorcisms. They are quite common, except they are partially black enamel, and there is a paper inside each one full of names of local saints and such things. *Thatt* is Huneefa's lookout, you see? Huneefa makes them onlee for us, but in case she does not, when we get them we put in, before issue, one small piece of turquoise. Mr Lurgan he gives them. There is no other source of supply; but it was me invented all this. It is strictly unoffeecial of course, but convenient for subordinates. Colonel Creighton he does not know. He is European. The turquoise is wrapped in the paper . . . Yes, that is road to railway station . . . Now suppose you go with the lama, or with me, I hope, some day, or with Mahbub. Suppose we get into a dam'-tight place. I am a fearful man – most fearful – but I tell you I have been in dam'-tight places more than hairs on my head. You say: "I am Son of the Charm." Verree good.'

'I do not understand quite. We must not be heard talking English here.'

'That is all raight. I am only babu showing off my English to you. All we babus talk English to show off,' said Hurree, flinging his shoulder-cloth jauntily. 'As I was about to say, "Son of the Charm" means that you may be member of the *Sat Bhai* – the Seven Brothers, which is Hindi *and* Tantric. It is popularly supposed to be extinct Society, but I have written notes to show it is still extant. You see, it is all my invention. Verree good. *Sat*

Bhai has many members, and perhaps before they jolly-well-cut-your-throat they may give you just a chance for life. That is useful, anyhow. And moreover, these foolish natives – if they are not too excited – they always stop to think before they kill a man who says he belongs to any speecific organization. You see? You say then when you are in tight place, "I am Son of the Charm", and you get – perhaps – ah – your second wind. That is only in extreme instances, or to open negotiations with a stranger. Can you quite see? Verree good. But suppose now, I, or any one of the Department, come to you dressed quite different. You would not know me at all unless I choose, I bet you. Some day I will prove it. I come as Ladakhi trader – oh, anything – and I say to you: "You want to buy precious stones?" You say: "Do I look like a man who buys precious stones?" Then I say: "Even verree poor man can buy a turquoise or *tarkeean*."'

'That is *kichree* – vegetable curry,' said Kim.

'Of course it is. You say: "Let me see the *tarkeean*." Then I say: "It was cooked by a woman, and perhaps it is bad for your caste." Then you say: "There is no caste when men go to – look for *tarkeean*." You stop a little between those words, "to – look." That is thee whole secret. The little stop before the words.'

Kim repeated the test sentence.

'That is all right. Then I will show you my turquoise if there is time, and then you know who I am, and then we exchange views and documents and those-all things. And so it is with any other man of us. We talk sometimes about turquoises and sometimes about *tarkeean*, but always with that little stop in the words. It is verree easy. First, "Son of the Charm", if you are in a tight place.

Perhaps that may help you – perhaps not. Then what I have told you about the *tarkeean*, if you want to transact offeecial business with a strange man. Of course, at present, you have no offeecial business. You are – ah ha! – super-numerary on probation. Quite unique specimen. If you were Asiatic of birth you might be employed right off; but this half-year of leave is to make you de-Englishized, you see? The lama he expects you, because I have demi-offeecially informed him you have passed all your examinations, and will soon obtain government appointment. Oh ho! You are on acting-allowance, you see: so if you are called upon to help Sons of the Charm mind you jolly-well try. Now I shall say goodbye, my dear fellow, and I hope you – ah – will come out top-side all raight.'

Hurree Babu stepped back a pace or two into the crowd at the entrance of Lucknow station and – was gone. Kim drew a deep breath and hugged himself all over. The nickel-plated revolver he could feel in the bosom of his sad-coloured robe, the amulet was on his neck; begging-gourd, rosary, and ghost-dagger (Mr Lurgan had forgotten nothing) were all to hand, with medicine, paintbox, and compass, and in a worn old purse-belt embroidered with porcupine-quill patterns lay a month's pay. Kings could be no richer. He bought sweetmeats in a leaf-cup from a Hindu trader, and ate them with glad rapture till a policeman ordered him off the steps.

CHAPTER
11

Give the man who is not made
 To his trade
Swords to fling and catch again,
Coins to ring and snatch again,
Men to harm and cure again,
Snakes to charm and lure again –
He'll be hurt by his own blade,
By his serpents disobeyed,
By his clumsiness bewrayed,
By the people mocked to scorn –
 So 'tis not with juggler born!
Pinch of dust or withered flower,
 Chance-flung fruit or borrowed staff,
Serve his need and shore his power,
 Bind the spell, or loose the laugh!
 But a man who, etc.

The Juggler's Song, Op. 15

Followed a sudden natural reaction.

'Now am I alone – all alone,' he thought. 'In all India is no one so alone as I! If I die today, who shall bring the news – and to whom? If I live and God is good, there will be a price upon my head, for I am a Son of the Charm – I, Kim.'

A very few white people, but many Asiatics, can throw themselves into amazement as it were by repeating their own names over and over again to themselves, letting the mind go free upon speculation as to what is called personal identity. When one grows older, the power,

usually, departs, but while it lasts it may descend upon a man at any moment.

'Who is Kim – Kim – Kim?'

He squatted in a corner of the clanging waiting-room, rapt from all other thoughts; hands folded in lap, and pupils contracted to pin-points. In a minute – in another half-second – he felt he would arrive at the solution of the tremendous puzzle; but here, as always happens, his mind dropped away from those heights with the rush of a wounded bird, and passing his hand before his eyes, he shook his head.

A long-haired Hindu *bairagi* [holy man], who had just bought a ticket, halted before him at that moment and stared intently.

'I also have lost it,' he said sadly. 'It is one of the Gates to the Way, but for me it has been shut many years.'

'What is the talk?' said Kim, abashed.

'Thou wast wondering there in thy spirit what manner of thing thy soul might be. The seizure came of a sudden. *I* know. Who should know but I? Whither goest thou?'

'Toward Kashi [Benares].'

'There are no Gods there. I have proved them. I go to Prayag [Allahabad] for the fifth time – seeking the Road to Enlightenment. Of what faith art thou?'

'I too am a Seeker,' said Kim, using one of the lama's pet words. 'Though' – he forgot his northern dress for the moment – 'though Allah alone knoweth what I seek.'

The old fellow slipped the *bairagi's* crutch under his armpit and sat down on a patch of ruddy leopard's skin as Kim rose at the call for the Benares train.

'Go in hope, little brother,' he said. 'It is a long road to the feet of the One; but thither do we all travel.'

Kim did not feel so lonely after this, and ere he had sat out twenty miles in the crowded compartment, was cheering his neighbours with a string of most wonderful yarns about his own and his master's magical gifts.

Benares struck him as a peculiarly filthy city, though it was pleasant to find how his cloth was respected. At least one third of the population prays eternally to some group or other of the many million deities, and so reveres every sort of holy man. Kim was guided to the Temple of the Tirthankars, about a mile outside the city, near Sarnath, by a chance-met Punjabi farmer – a Kamboh from Jullundur way who had appealed in vain to every God of his homestead to cure his small son, and was trying Benares as a last resort.

'Thou art from the north?' he asked, shouldering through the press of the narrow, stinking streets much like his own pet bull at home.

'Ay, I know the Punjab. My mother was a *pahareen*, but my father came from Amritzar – by Jandiala,' said Kim, oiling his ready tongue for the needs of the Road.

'Jandiala – Jullundur? Oho! Then we be neighbours in some sort, as it were.' He nodded tenderly to the wailing child in his arms. 'Whom dost thou serve?'

'A most holy man at the Temple of the Tirthankars.'

'They are all most holy and – most greedy,' said the Jat with bitterness. 'I have walked the pillars and trodden the temples till my feet are flayed, and the child is no whit better. And the mother being sick too . . . Hush, then, little one . . . We changed his name when the fever came. We put him into girl's clothes. There was nothing we did not do, except – I said to his mother when she bundled me off to Benares – she should have come with me – I *said*

249

Sakhi Sarwar Sultan would serve us best. We know His generosity, but these down-country Gods are strangers.'

The child turned on the cushion of the huge corded arms and looked at Kim through heavy eyelids.

'And was it all worthless?' Kim asked, with easy interest.

'All worthless – all worthless,' said the child, lips cracking with fever.

'The Gods have given him a good mind, at least,' said the father proudly. 'To think he should have listened so cleverly. Yonder is thy Temple. Now I am a poor man – many priests have dealt with me – but my son is my son, and if a gift to thy master can cure him – I am at my very wits' end.'

Kim considered for a while, tingling with pride. Three years ago he would have made prompt profit on the situation and gone his way without a thought; but now, the very respect the Jat paid him proved that he was a man. Moreover, he had tasted fever once or twice already, and knew enough to recognize starvation when he saw it.

'Call him forth and I will give him a bond on my best yoke, so that the child is cured.'

Kim halted at the carved outer door of the temple. A white-clad Oswal banker from Ajmir, his sins of usury new wiped out, asked him what he did.

'I am *chela* to Teshoo Lama, an Holy One from Bhotiyal – within there. He bade me come. I wait. Tell him.'

'Do not forget the child,' cried the importunate Jat over his shoulder, and then bellowed in Punjabi: 'O Holy One – O disciple of the Holy One – O Gods above all the Worlds – behold affliction sitting at the gate!' That cry is

so common in Benares that the passers never turned their heads.

The Oswal, at peace with mankind, carried the message into the darkness behind him, and the easy, uncounted Eastern minutes slid by; for the lama was asleep in his cell, and no priest would wake him. When the click of his rosary again broke the hush of the inner court where the calm images of the Arhats stand, a novice whispered, 'Thy *chela* is here,' and the old man strode forth, forgetting the end of that prayer.

Hardly had the tall figure shown in the doorway than the Jat ran before him, and, lifting up the child, cried: 'Look upon this, Holy One; and if the Gods will, he lives – he lives!'

He fumbled in his waist-belt and drew out a small silver coin.

'What is now?' The lama's eyes turned to Kim. It was noticeable he spoke far clearer Urdu than long ago, under Zam-Zammah; but the father would allow no private talk.

'It is no more than a fever,' said Kim. 'The child is not well fed.'

'He sickens at everything, and his mother is not here.'

'If it be permitted, I may cure, Holy One.'

'What! Have they made thee a healer? Wait here,' said the lama, and he sat down by the Jat upon the lowest step of the temple, while Kim, looking out of the corner of his eyes, slowly opened the little betel-box. He had dreamed dreams at school of returning to the lama as a sahib – of chaffing the old man before he revealed himself – boy's dreams all. There was more drama in this abstracted, brow-puckered search through the tabloid-bottles, with a

pause here and there for thought and a muttered invocation between whiles. Quinine he had in tablets, and dark brown meat-lozenges – beef most probably, but that was not *his* business. The little thing would not eat, but it sucked at a lozenge greedily, and said it liked the salt taste.

'Take then these six.' Kim handed them to the man. 'Praise the Gods, and boil three in milk; other three in water. After he has drunk the milk give him this' (it was the half ᵒᶠ a quinine pill), 'and wrap him warm. Give him the water of the other three, and the other half of this white pill when he wakes. Meantime, here is another brown medicine that he may suck at on the way home.'

'Gods, what wisdom!' said the Kamboh, snatching.

It was as much as Kim could remember of his own treatment in a bout of autumn malaria – if you except the patter that he added to impress the lama.

'Now go! Come again in the morning.'

'But the price – the price,' said the Jat, and threw back his sturdy shoulders. 'My son is my son. Now that he will be whole again, how shall I go back to his mother and say I took help by the wayside and did not even give a bowl of curds in return?'

'They are alike, these Jats,' said Kim softly. 'The Jat stood on his dunghill and the king's elephants went by. "O driver," said he, "what will you sell those little donkeys for?"'

The Jat burst into a roar of laughter, stifled with apologies to the lama. 'It is the saying of my own country – the very talk of it. So are we Jats all. I will come tomorrow with the child; and the blessing of the Gods of the Homesteads – who are good little Gods – be on you both

. . . Now, son, we grow strong again. Do not spit it out, little Princeling! King of my Heart, do not spit it out, and we shall be strong men, wrestlers and club-wielders, by morning.'

He moved away, crooning and mumbling. The lama turned to Kim, and all the loving old soul of him looked out through his narrow eyes.

'To heal the sick is to acquire merit; but first one gets knowledge. That was wisely done, O Friend of all the World.'

'I was made wise by thee, Holy One,' said Kim, forgetting the little play just ended; forgetting St Xavier's; forgetting his white blood; forgetting even the Great Game as he stooped, Muhammadan-fashion, to touch his master's feet in the dust of the Jain temple. 'My teaching I owe to thee. I have eaten thy bread three years. My time is finished. I am loosed from the schools. I come to thee.'

'Herein is my reward. Enter! Enter! And is all well?' They passed to the inner court, where the afternoon sun sloped golden across. 'Stand that I may see. So!' He peered critically. 'It is no longer a child, but a man, ripened in wisdom, walking as a physician. I did well – I did well when I gave thee up to the armed men on that black night. Dost thou remember our first day under Zam-Zammah?'

'Ay,' said Kim. 'Dost thou remember when I leapt off the carriage the first day I went to—'

'The Gates of Learning? Truly. And the day that we ate the cakes together at the back of the river by Nucklao. Aha! Many times hast thou begged for me, but that day I begged for thee.'

'Good reason,' quoth Kim. 'I was then a scholar in the Gates of Learning, and attired as a sahib. Do not forget, Holy One,' he went on playfully, 'I am still a sahib – by thy favour.'

'True. And a sahib in most high esteem. Come to my cell, *chela*.'

'How is that known to thee?'

The lama smiled. 'First by means of letters from the kindly priest whom we met in the camp of armed men; but he is now gone to his own country, and I sent the money to his brother.' Colonel Creighton, who had succeeded to the trusteeship when Father Victor went to England with the Mavericks, was hardly the Chaplain's brother. 'But I do not well understand sahibs' letters. They must be interpreted to me. I chose a surer way. Many times when I returned from my Search to this Temple, which has always been a nest to me, there came one seeking Enlightenment – a man from Leh – that had been, he said, a Hindu, but wearied of all those Gods.' The lama pointed to the Arhats.

'A fat man?' said Kim, a twinkle in his eye.

'Very fat; but I perceived in a little his mind was wholly given up to useless things – such as devils and charms and the form and fashion of our tea-drinkings in the monasteries, and by what road we initiated the novices. A man abounding in questions; but he was a friend of thine, *chela*. He told me that thou wast on the road to much honour as a scribe. And I see thou art a physician.'

'Yes, that am I – a scribe, when I am a sahib, but it is set aside when I come as thy disciple. I have accomplished the years appointed for a sahib.'

'As it were a novice?' said the lama, nodding his head.

'Art thou freed from the schools? I would not have thee unripe.'

'I am all free. In due time I take service under the government as a scribe –'

'Not as a warrior. That is well.'

'But first I come to wander – with thee. Therefore I am here. Who begs for thee, these days?' he went on quickly. The ice was thin.

'Very often I beg myself; but, as thou knowest, I am seldom here, except when I come to look again at my disciple. From one end to another of Hind have I travelled afoot and in the *te-rain*. A great and a wonderful land! But here, when I put in, is as though I were in my own Bhotiyal.'

He looked round the little clean cell complacently. A low cushion gave him a seat, on which he had disposed himself in the cross-legged attitude of the Bodhisat emerging from meditation; a black teak-wood table, not twenty inches high, set with copper tea-cups, was before him. In one corner stood a tiny altar, also of heavily carved teak, bearing a copper-gilt image of the seated Buddha and fronted by a lamp, an incense-holder, and a pair of copper flower-pots.

'The Keeper of the Images in the Wonder House acquired merit by giving me these a year since,' he said, following Kim's eye. 'When one is far from one's own land such things carry remembrance; and we must reverence the Lord for that he showed the Way. See!' He pointed to a curiously built mound of coloured rice crowned with a fantastic metal ornament. 'When I was abbot in my own place – before I came to better knowledge – I made that offering daily. It is the Sacrifice of the

Universe to the Lord. Thus do we of Bhotiyal offer all the world daily to the Excellent Law. And I do it even now, though I know that the Excellent One is beyond all pinchings and pattings.' He snuffed from his gourd.

'It is well done, Holy One,' Kim murmured, sinking at ease on the cushions, very happy and rather tired.

'And also,' the old man chuckled, 'I write pictures of the Wheel of Life. Three days to a picture. I was busied on it – or it may be I shut my eyes a little – when they brought word of thee. It is good to have thee here: I will show thee my art – not for pride's sake, but because thou must learn. The sahibs have not *all* this world's wisdom.'

He drew from under the table a sheet of strangely scented yellow Chinese paper, the brushes, and slab of Indian ink. In cleanest, severest outline he had traced the Great Wheel with its six spokes, whose centre is the conjoined Hog, Snake, and Dove (Ignorance, Anger, and Lust), and whose compartments are all the Heavens and Hells, and all the chances of human life. Men say that the Bodhisat himself first drew it with grains of rice upon dust, to teach his disciples the cause of things. Many ages have crystallized it into a most wonderful convention crowded with hundreds of little figures whose every line carries a meaning. Few can translate the picture-parable; there are not twenty in all the world who can draw it surely without a copy: of those who can both draw and expound are but three.

'I have a little learned to draw,' said Kim. 'But this is a marvel beyond marvels.'

'I have written it for many years,' said the lama. 'Time was when I could write it all between one lamp-lighting

and the next. I will teach thee the art – after due preparation; and I will show thee the meaning of the Wheel.'

'We take the Road, then?'

'The Road and our Search. I was but waiting for thee. It was made plain to me in a hundred dreams – notably one that came upon the night of the day that the Gates of Learning first shut – that without thee I should never find my River. Again and again, as thou knowest, I put this from me, fearing an illusion. Therefore I would not take thee with me that day at Lucknow, when we ate the cakes. I would not take thee till the time was ripe and auspicious. From the hills to the sea, from the sea to the hills have I gone, but it was vain. Then I remembered the *Jâtaka*.'

He told Kim the story of the elephant with the leg-iron, as he had told it so often to the Jain priests.

'Further testimony is not needed,' he ended serenely. 'Thou wast sent for an aid. That aid removed, my Search came to naught. Therefore we will go out again together, and our Search is sure.'

'Whither go we?'

'What matters, Friend of all the World? The Search, I say, is sure. If need be, the River will break from the ground before us. I acquired merit when I sent thee to the Gates of Learning, and gave thee the jewel that is Wisdom. Thou didst return, I saw even now, a follower of Sakyamuni, the Physician, whose altars are many in Bhotiyal. It is sufficient. We are together, and all things are as they were – Friend of all the World – Friend of the Stars – my *chela*!'

Then they talked of matters secular; but it was notice-

able that the lama never demanded any details of life at St Xavier's, nor showed the faintest curiosity as to the manners and customs of sahibs. His mind moved all in the past, and he revived every step of their wonderful first journey together, rubbing his hands and chuckling, till it pleased him to curl himself up into the sudden sleep of old age.

Kim watched the last dusty sunshine fade out of the court, and played with his ghost-dagger and rosary. The clamour of Benares, oldest of all earth's cities awake before the Gods, day and night, beat round the walls as the sea's roar round a breakwater. Now and again, a Jain priest crossed the court, with some small offering to the images, and swept the path about him lest by chance he should take the life of a living thing. A lamp twinkled, and there followed the sound of a prayer. Kim watched the stars as they rose one after another in the still, sticky dark, till he fell asleep at the foot of the altar. That night he dreamed in Hindustani, with never an English word . . .

'Holy One, there is the child to whom we gave the medicine,' he said, about three o'clock in the morning, when the lama, also waking from dreams, would have fared forth on pilgrimage. 'The Jat will be here at the light.'

'I am well answered. In my haste I would have done a wrong.' He sat down on the cushions and returned to his rosary. 'Surely old folk are as children,' he said pathetically. 'They desire a matter – behold, it must be done at once, or they fret and weep! Many times when I was upon the Road I have been ready to stamp with my feet at the hindrance of an ox-cart in the way, or a mere cloud of

dust. It was not so when I was a man – a long time ago. None the less it is wrongful—'

'But thou art indeed old, Holy One.'

'The thing was done. A Cause was put out into the world, and, old or young, sick or sound, knowing or unknowing, who can rein in the effect of that Cause? Does the Wheel hang still if a child spin it – or a drunkard? *Chela*, this is a great and a terrible world.'

'I think it good,' Kim yawned. 'What is there to eat? I have not eaten since yesterday even.'

'I had forgotten thy need. Yonder is good Bhotiyal tea and cold rice.'

'We cannot walk far on such stuff.' Kim felt all the European's lust for flesh-meat, which is not accessible in a Jain temple. Yet, instead of going out at once with the begging-bowl, he stayed his stomach on slabs of cold rice till the full dawn. It brought the farmer, voluble, stuttering with gratitude.

'In the night the fever broke and the sweat came,' he cried. 'Feel here – his skin is fresh and new! He esteemed the salt lozenges, and took milk with greed.' He drew the cloth from the child's face, and it smiled sleepily at Kim. A little knot of Jain priests, silent but all-observant, gathered by the temple door. They knew, and Kim knew that they knew, how the old lama had met his disciple. Being courteous folk, they had not obtruded themselves overnight by presence, word, or gesture. Wherefore Kim repaid them as the sun rose.

'Thank the Gods of the Jains, brother,' he said, not knowing how those gods were named. 'The fever is indeed broken.'

'Look! See!' The lama beamed in the background upon

his hosts of three years. 'Was there ever such a *chela*? He follows our Lord the Healer.'

Now the Jains officially recognize all the gods of the Hindu creed, as well as the Lingam and the Snake. They wear the Brahminical thread; they adhere to every claim of Hindu caste-law. But, because they knew and loved the lama, because he was an old man, because he sought the Way, because he was their guest, and because he collogued long of nights with the head-priest – as free-thinking a metaphysician as ever split one hair into seventy – they murmured assent.

'Remember,' – Kim bent over the child – 'this trouble may come again.'

'Not if thou hast the proper spell,' said the father.

'But in a little while we go away.'

'True,' said the lama to all the Jains. 'We go now together upon the Search whereof I have often spoken. I waited till my *chela* was ripe. Behold him! We go north. Never again shall I look upon this place of my rest, O people of good will.'

'But I am not a beggar.' The cultivator rose to his feet, clutching the child.

'Be still. Do not trouble the Holy One,' a priest cried.

'Go,' Kim whispered. 'Meet us again under the big railway bridge, and for the sake of all the Gods of our Punjab, bring food – curry, pulse, cakes fried in fat, and sweetmeats. Specially sweetmeats. Be swift!'

The pallor of hunger suited Kim very well as he stood, tall and slim, in his sad-coloured, sweeping robes, one hand on his rosary and the other in the attitude of benediction, faithfully copied from the lama. An English observer might have said that he looked rather like the

young saint of a stained-glass window, whereas he was but a growing lad faint with emptiness.

Long and formal were the farewells, thrice ended and thrice renewed. The Seeker – he who had invited the lama to that haven from far-away Tibet, a silver-faced hairless ascetic – took no part in it, but meditated, as always, alone among the images. The others were very human; pressing small comforts upon the old man – a betel-box, a fine new iron pen-case, a food-bag, and such-like – warning him against the dangers of the world without, and prophesying a happy end to the Search. Meantime Kim, lonelier than ever, squatted on the steps, and swore to himself in the language of St Xavier's.

'But it is my own fault,' he concluded. 'With Mahbub, I ate Mahbub's bread, or Lurgan Sahib's. At St Xavier's, three meals a day. Here I must jolly-well look out for myself. Besides, I am not in good training. *How* I could eat a plate of beef now! . . . Is it finished, Holy One?'

The lama, both hands raised, intoned a final blessing in ornate Chinese. 'I must lean on thy shoulder,' said he, as the temple gates closed. 'We grow stiff, I think.'

The weight of a six-foot man is not light to steady through miles of crowded streets, and Kim, loaded down with bundles and packages for the way, was glad to reach the shadow of the railway bridge.

'Here we eat,' he said resolutely, as the Kamboh, blue-robed and smiling, hove in sight, a basket in one hand and the child on the other.

'Fall to, Holy Ones!' he cried from fifty yards. (They were by the shoal under the first bridge-span, out of sight of hungry priests.) 'Rice and good curry, cakes all warm and well scented with *hing* [asafoetida], curds and sugar.

King of my fields,' – this to the small son – 'let us show these holy men that we Jats of Jullundur can pay a service . . . I had heard the Jains would eat nothing that they had not cooked, but truly' – he looked away politely over the broad river – 'where there is no eye there is no caste.'

'And we,' said Kim, turning his back and heaping a leaf-platter for the lama, 'are beyond all castes.'

They gorged themselves on the good food in silence. Nor till he had licked the last of the sticky sweetstuff from his little finger did Kim note that the Kamboh too was girt for travel.

'If our roads lie together,' he said roughly, 'I go with thee. One does not often find a worker of miracles, and the child is still weak. But I am not altogether a reed.' He picked up his *lathi* – a five-foot male-bamboo ringed with bands of polished iron – and flourished it in the air. 'The Jats are called quarrelsome, but that is not true. Except when we are crossed, we are like our own buffaloes.'

'So be it,' said Kim. 'A good stick is a good reason.'

The lama gazed placidly upstream, where in long, smudged perspective the ceaseless columns of smoke go up from the burning-ghats by the river. Now and again, despite all municipal regulations, the fragment of a half-burned body bobbed by on the full current.

'But for thee,' said the Kamboh to Kim, drawing the child into his hairy breast, 'I might today have gone thither – with this one. The priests tell us that Benares is holy – which none doubt – and desirable to die in. But I do not know their Gods, and they ask for money; and when one has done one worship a shaved-head vows it is of none effect except one do another. Wash here! Wash

there! Pour, drink, lave, and scatter flowers – but always pay the priests. No, the Punjab for me, and the soil of the Jullundur-*doab* for the best soil in it.'

'I have said many times – in the Temple, I think – that if need be, the River will open at our feet. We will therefore go north,' said the lama, rising. 'I remember a pleasant place, set about with fruit trees, where one can walk in meditation – and the air is cooler there. It comes from the Hills and the snow of the Hills.'

'What is the name?' said Kim.

'How should I know? Didst thou not – no, that was after the army rose out of the earth and took thee away. I abode there in meditation in a room against the dovecot – except when she talked eternally.'

'Oho! the woman from Kulu. That is by Saharunpore.' Kim laughed.

'How does the spirit move thy master? Does he go afoot, for the sake of past sins?' the Jat demanded cautiously. 'It is a far cry to Delhi.'

'No,' said Kim. 'I will beg a *tikkut* for the *te-rain*.' One does not own to the possession of money in India.

'Then, in the name of the Gods, let us take the fire-carriage. My son is best in his mother's arms. The government has brought on us many taxes, but it gives us one good thing – the *te-rain* that joins friends and unites the anxious. A wonderful matter is the *te-rain*.'

They all piled into it a couple of hours later, and slept through the heat of the day. The Kamboh plied Kim with ten thousand questions as to the lama's walk and work in life, and received some curious answers. Kim was content to be where he was, to look out upon the flat north-western landscape, and to talk to the changing

mob of fellow-passengers. Even today, tickets and ticket-clipping are dark oppression to Indian rustics. They do not understand why, when they have paid for a magic piece of paper, strangers should punch great pieces out of the charm. So, long and furious are the debates between travellers and Eurasian ticket-collectors. Kim assisted at two or three with grave advice, meant to darken counsel and to show off his wisdom before the lama and the admiring Kamboh. But at Somna Road the Fates sent him a matter to think upon. There tumbled into the compartment, as the train was moving off, a mean, lean little person – a Mahratta, so far as Kim could judge by the cock of the tight turban. His face was cut, his muslin upper garment was badly torn, and one leg was bandaged. He told them that a country-cart had upset and nearly slain him: he was going to Delhi, where his son lived. Kim watched him closely. If, as he asserted, he had been rolled over and over on the earth, there should have been signs of gravel-rash on the skin. But all his injuries seemed clean cuts, and a mere fall from a cart could not cast a man into such extremity of terror. As, with shaking fingers, he knotted up the torn cloth about his neck he laid bare an amulet of the kind called a keeper-up of the heart. Now, amulets are common enough, but they are not generally strung on square-plaited copper wire, and still fewer amulets bear black enamel on silver. There were none except the Kamboh and the lama in the compartment, which luckily was of an old type with solid ends. Kim made as to scratch in his bosom, and thereby lifted his own amulet. The Mahratta's face changed altogether at the sight, and he disposed the amulet fairly on his breast.

'Yes,' he went on to the Kamboh, 'I was in haste, and the cart, driven by a bastard, bound its wheel in a water-cut, and besides the harm done to me there was lost a full dish of *tarkeean*. I was not a Son of the Charm [a lucky man] that day.'

'That was a great loss,' said the Kamboh, withdrawing interest. His experience of Benares had made him suspicious.

'Who cooked it?' said Kim.

'A woman.' The Mahratta raised his eyes.

'But all women can cook *tarkeean*,' said the Kamboh. 'It is a good curry, as I know.'

'Oh yes, it is a good curry,' said the Mahratta.

'And cheap,' said Kim. 'But what about caste?'

'Oh, there is no caste where men go to – look for *tarkeean*,' the Mahratta replied, in the prescribed cadence. 'Of whose service art thou?'

'Of the service of this Holy One.' Kim pointed to the happy, drowsy lama, who woke with a jerk at the well-loved word.

'Ah, he was sent from Heaven to aid me. He is called the Friend of all the World. He is also called the Friend of the Stars. He walks as a physician – his time being ripe. Great is his wisdom.'

'And a Son of the Charm,' said Kim under his breath, as the Kamboh made haste to prepare a pipe lest the Mahratta should beg.

'And who is *that*?' the Mahratta asked, glancing sideways nervously.

'One whose child I – we have cured, who lies under great debt to us – Sit by the window, man from Jullundur. Here is a sick one.'

265

'Humph! *I* have no desire to mix with chance-met wastrels. *My* ears are not long. *I* am not a woman wishing to overhear secrets.' The Jat slid himself heavily into a far corner.

'Art thou anything of a healer? I am ten leagues deep in calamity,' cried the Mahratta, picking up the cue.

'This man is cut and bruised all over. I go about to cure him,' Kim retorted. 'None interfered between thy babe and me.'

'I am rebuked,' said the Kamboh meekly. 'I am thy debtor for the life of my son. Thou art a miracle-worker – I know it.'

'Show me the cuts.' Kim bent over the Mahratta's neck, his heart nearly choking him; for this was the Great Game with a vengeance. 'Now, tell thy tale swiftly, brother, while I say a charm.'

'I came from the south, where my work lay. One of us they slew by the roadside. Hast thou heard?' Kim shook his head. He, of course, knew nothing of E23's predecessor, slain down south in the habit of an Arab trader. 'Having found a certain letter which I was sent to seek, I came away. I escaped from the city and ran to Mhow. So sure was I that none knew, I did not change my face. At Mhow a woman brought charge against me of theft of jewellery in that city which I had left. Then I saw the cry was out against me. I ran from Mhow by night, bribing the police, who had been bribed to hand me over without question to my enemies in the south. Then I lay in old Chitor city a week, a penitent in a temple, but I could not get rid of the letter which was my charge. I buried it under the Queen's Stone, at Chitor, in the place known to us all.'

Kim did not know, but not for worlds would he have broken the thread.

'At Chitor, look you, I was all in kings' country; for Kotah to the east is beyond the Queen's law, and east again lie Jaipur and Gwalior. Neither love spies, and there is no justice. I was hunted like a wet jackal; but I broke through at Bandakui, where I heard there was a charge against me of murder in the city I had left – of the murder of a boy. They have both the corpse and the witnesses waiting.'

'But cannot the government protect?'

'We of the Game are beyond protection. If we die, we die. Our names are blotted from the book. That is all. At Bandakui, where lives one of us, I thought to slip the scent by changing my face, and so made me a Mahratta. Then I came to Agra, and would have turned back to Chitor to recover the letter. So sure I was I had slipped them. Therefore I did not send a *tar* [telegram] to any one saying where the letter lay. I wished the credit of it all.'

Kim nodded. He understood that feeling well.

'But at Agra, walking in the streets, a man cried a debt against me, and approaching with many witnesses, would hale me to the courts then and there. Oh, they are clever in the south! He recognized me as his agent for cotton. May he burn in Hell for it!'

'And wast thou?'

'O fool! I was the man they sought for the matter of the letter! I ran into the Fleshers' Ward and came out by the House of the Jew, who feared a riot and pushed me forth. I came afoot to Somna Road – I had only money for my *tikkut* to Delhi – and there, while I lay in a ditch with a

267

fever, one sprang out of the bushes and beat me and cut me and searched me from head to foot. Within earshot of the *te-rain* it was!'

'Why did he not slay thee out of hand?'

'They are not so foolish. If I am taken in Delhi at the instance of lawyers, upon a proven charge of murder, my body is handed over to the state that desires it. I go back guarded, and then – I die slowly for an example to the rest of us. The south is not my country. I run in circles – like a goat with one eye. I have not eaten for two days. I am marked' – he touched the filthy bandage on his leg – 'so that they will know me at Delhi.'

'Thou art safe in the *te-rain*, at least.'

'Live a year at the Great Game and tell me that again! The wires will be out against me at Delhi, describing every tear and rag upon me. Twenty – a hundred, if need be – will have seen me slay that boy. And thou art useless!'

Kim knew enough of native methods of attack not to doubt that the case would be deadly complete – even to the corpse. The Mahratta twitched his fingers with pain from time to time. The Kamboh in his corner glared sullenly; the lama was busy over his beads; and Kim, fumbling doctor-fashion at the man's neck, thought out his plan between invocations.

'Hast thou a charm to change my shape? Else I am dead. Five – ten minutes alone, if I had not been so pressed, and I might –'

'Is he cured yet, miracle-worker?' said the Kamboh jealously. 'Thou hast chanted long enough.'

'Nay. There is no cure for his hurts, as I see, except he sit for three days in the habit of a *bairagi*.' This is a

common penance, often imposed on a fat trader by his spiritual teacher.

'One priest always goes about to make another priest,' was the retort. Like most grossly superstitious folk, the Kamboh could not keep his tongue from deriding his Church.

'Will thy son be a priest, then? It is time he took more of my quinine.'

'We Jats are all buffaloes,' said the Kamboh, softening anew.

Kim rubbed a fingertip of bitterness on the child's trusting little lips. 'I have asked for nothing,' he said sternly to the father, 'except food. Dost thou grudge me that? I go to heal another man. Have I thy leave – Prince?'

Up flew the man's huge paws in supplication. 'Nay – nay. Do not mock me thus.'

'It pleases me to cure this sick one. Thou shalt acquire merit by aiding. What colour ash is there in thy pipe-bowl? White. That is auspicious. Was there raw turmeric among thy foodstuffs?'

'I – I –'

'Open thy bundle!'

It was the usual collection of small oddments: bits of cloth, quack medicines, cheap fairings, a clothful of *atta* – greyish, rough-ground native flour – twists of down-country tobacco, tawdry pipe-stems, and a packet of curry-stuff, all wrapped in a quilt. Kim turned it over with the air of a wise warlock, muttering a Muhammadan invocation.

'This is wisdom I learned from the sahibs,' he whispered to the lama; and here, when one thinks of his training at Lurgan's, he spoke no more than the truth.

'There is a great evil in this man's fortune, as shown by the Stars, which – which troubles him. Shall I take it away?'

'Friend of the Stars, thou hast done well in all things. Let it be at thy pleasure. Is it another healing?'

'Quick! Be quick!' gasped the Mahratta. 'The train may stop.'

'A healing against the shadow of death,' said Kim, mixing the Kamboh's flour with the mingled charcoal and tobacco ash in the red-earth bowl of the pipe. E23, without a word, slipped off his turban and shook down his long black hair.

'That is my food – priest,' the Jat growled.

'A buffalo in the temple! Hast thou dared to look even thus far?' said Kim. 'I must do mysteries before fools; but have a care for thine eyes. Is there a film before them already? I save the babe, and for return thou – oh, shameless!' The man flinched at the direct gaze, for Kim was wholly in earnest. 'Shall I curse thee, or shall I –' He picked up the outer cloth of the bundle and threw it over the bowed head. 'Dare so much as to think a wish to see, and – and – even I cannot save thee. Sit! Be dumb!'

'I am blind – dumb. Forbear to curse! Co – come, child; we will play a game of hiding. Do not, for my sake, look from under the cloth.'

'I see hope,' said E23. 'What is thy scheme?'

'This comes next,' said Kim, plucking the thin body-shirt. E23 hesitated, with all a north-west man's dislike of baring his body.

'What is caste to a cut-throat?' said Kim, rending it to the waist. 'We must make thee a yellow Saddhu all over. Strip – strip swiftly, and shake thy hair over thine eyes

while I scatter the ash. Now, a caste-mark on thy fore-head.' He drew from his bosom the little Survey paintbox and a cake of crimson lake.

'Art thou only a beginner?' said E23, labouring literally for the dear life, as he slid out of his body-wrappings and stood clear in the loincloth while Kim splashed in a noble caste-mark on the ash-smeared brow.

'But two days entered to the Game, brother,' Kim replied. 'Smear more ash on the bosom.'

'Hast thou met – a physician of sick pearls?' He switched out his long, tight-rolled turban-cloth and, with swiftest hands, rolled it over and under about his loins into the intricate devices of a Saddhu's cincture.

'Hah! Dost thou know his touch, then? He was my teacher for a while. We must bar thy legs. Ash cures wounds. Smear it again.'

'I was his pride once, but thou art almost better. The Gods are kind to us! Give me *that*.'

It was a tin box of opium pills among the rubbish of the Jat's bundle. E23 gulped down a half handful. 'They are good against hunger, fear, and chill. And they make the eyes red too,' he explained. 'Now I shall have heart to play the Game. We lack only a Saddhu's tongs. What of the old clothes?'

Kim rolled them small, and stuffed them into the slack folds of his tunic. With a yellow-ochre paint cake he smeared the legs and the breast, great streaks against the background of flour, ash, and turmeric.

'The blood on them is enough to hang thee, brother.'

'Maybe; but no need to throw them out of the window . . . It is finished.' His voice thrilled with a boy's pure delight in the Game. 'Turn and look, O Jat!'

'The Gods protect us,' said the hooded Kamboh, emerging like a buffalo from the reeds. 'But – whither went the Mahratta? What hast thou done?'

Kim had been trained by Lurgan Sahib; and E23, by virtue of his business, was no bad actor. In place of the tremulous, shrinking trader there lolled against the corner an all but naked, ash-smeared, ochre-barred, dusty-haired Saddhu, his swollen eyes – opium takes quick effect on an empty stomach – luminous with insolence and bestial lust, his legs crossed under him, Kim's brown rosary round his neck, and a scant yard of worn, flowered chintz on his shoulders. The child buried his face in his amazed father's arms.

'Look up, Princeling! We travel with warlocks, but they will not hurt thee. Oh, do not cry . . . What is the sense of curing a child one day and killing him with fright the next?'

'The child will be fortunate all his life. He has seen a great healing. When I was a child I made clay men and horses.'

'I have made them too. Sír Banás, he comes in the night and makes them all alive at the back of our kitchen-midden,' piped the child.

'And so thou art not frightened at anything. Eh, Prince?'

'I was frightened because my father was frightened. I felt his arms shake.'

'Oh, chicken-man!' said Kim, and even the abashed Jat laughed. 'I have done a healing on this poor trader. He must forsake his gains and his account-books, and sit by the wayside three nights to overcome the malignity of his enemies. The stars are against him.'

'The fewer moneylenders the better, say I; but, Saddhu or no Saddhu, he should pay for my stuff on his shoulders.'

'So? But that is thy child on thy shoulder – given over to the burning-ghat not two days ago. There remains one thing more. I did this charm in thy presence because need was great. I changed his shape and his soul. None the less, if, by any chance, O man from Jullundur, thou rememberest what thou hast seen, either among the elders sitting under the village tree, or in thine own house, or in company of thy priest when he blesses thy cattle, a murrain will come among the buffaloes, and a fire in thy thatch, and rats in thy corn-bin, and the curse of our Gods upon thy fields that they may be barren before thy feet and after thy ploughshare.' This was part of an old curse picked up from a *fakir* by the Taksali Gate in the days of Kim's innocence. It lost nothing by repetition.

'Cease, Holy One! In mercy, cease!' cried the Jat. 'Do not curse the household. I saw nothing! I heard nothing! I am thy cow!' and he made to grab at Kim's bare foot beating rhythmically on the carriage floor.

'But since thou hast been permitted to aid me in the matter of a pinch of flour and a little opium and such trifles as I have honoured by using in my art, so will the Gods return a blessing,' and he gave it at length, to the man's immense relief. It was one that he had learned from Lurgan Sahib.

The lama stared through his spectacles as he had not stared at the business of disguisement.

'Friend of the Stars,' he said at last, 'thou hast acquired great wisdom. Beware that it does not give birth to pride

273

No man having the Law before his eyes speaks hastily of any matter which he has seen or encountered.'

'No – no – no, indeed,' cried the farmer, fearful lest the master should be minded to improve on the pupil. E23, with relaxed mouth, gave himself up to the opium that is meat, tobacco, and medicine to the spent Asiatic.

So, in a silence of awe and great miscomprehension, they slid into Delhi about lamp-lighting time.

CHAPTER
12

Who hath desired the Sea – the sight of salt-water unbounded?
The heave and the halt and the hurl and the crash of the
 comber wind-hounded?
The sleek-barrelled swell before storm – grey, foamless,
 enormous, and growing?
Stark calm on the lap of the Line – or the crazy-eyed hurricane
 blowing?
His Sea in no showing the same – his Sea and the same 'neath
 all showing –
 His Sea that his being fulfils?
So and no otherwise – so and no otherwise hill-men desire
 their Hills!

The Sea and the Hills

'I have found my heart again,' said E23, under cover of
the platform's tumult. 'Hunger and fear make men
dazed, or I might have thought of this escape before. I
was right. They come to hunt for me. Thou hast saved my
head.'

A group of yellow-trousered Punjab policemen,
headed by a hot and perspiring young Englishman,
parted the crowd about the carriages. Behind them,
inconspicuous as a cat, ambled a small fat person who
looked like a lawyer's tout.

'See the young sahib reading from a paper. My descrip-
tion is in his hand,' said E23. 'They go carriage by
carriage, like fisher-folk netting a pool.'

When the procession reached their compartment, E23
was counting his beads with a steady jerk of the wrist;

while Kim jeered at him for being so drugged as to have lost the ringed fire-tongs which are the Saddhu's distinguishing mark. The lama, deep in meditation, stared straight before him; and the farmer, glancing furtively, gathered up his belongings.

'Nothing here but a parcel of holy-bolies,' said the Englishman aloud, and passed on amid a ripple of uneasiness; for native police mean extortion to the native all India over.

'The trouble now,' whispered E23, 'lies in sending a wire as to the place where I hid that letter I was sent to find. I cannot go to the *tar*-office in this guise.'

'Is it not enough I have saved thy neck?'

'Not if the work be left unfinished. Did never the healer of sick pearls tell thee so? Comes another sahib! Ah!'

This was a tallish, sallowish District Superintendent of Police – belt, helmet, polished spurs and all – strutting and twirling his dark moustache.

'What fools are these police sahibs!' said Kim genially.

E23 glanced up under his eyelids. 'It is well said,' he muttered in a changed voice. 'I go to drink water. Keep my place.'

He blundered out almost into the Englishman's arms, and was bad-worded in clumsy Urdu.

'*Tum mut?* You drunk? You mustn't bang about as though Delhi station belonged to you, my friend.'

E23, not moving a muscle of his countenance, answered with a stream of the filthiest abuse, at which Kim naturally rejoiced. It reminded him of the drummer-boys and the barrack-sweepers at Umballa in the terrible time of his first schooling.

'My good fool,' the Englishman drawled. *'Nickle-jao!* Go back to your carriage.'

Step by step, withdrawing deferentially, and dropping his voice, the yellow Saddhu clomb back to the carriage, cursing the DSP to remotest posterity by – here Kim almost jumped – by the curse of the Queen's Stone, by the writing under the Queen's Stone and by an assortment of Gods with wholly new names.

'I don't know what you're saying' – the Englishman flushed angrily – 'but it's some piece of blasted impertinence. Come out of that!'

E23, affecting to misunderstand, gravely produced his ticket, which the Englishman wrenched angrily from his hand.

'Oh, *zoolum*! What oppression!' growled the Jat from his corner. 'All for the sake of a jest too.' He had been grinning at the freedom of the Saddhu's tongue. 'Thy charms do not work well today, Holy One!'

The Saddhu followed the policeman, fawning and supplicating. The ruck of passengers, busy with their babies and their bundles, had not noticed the affair. Kim slipped out behind him; for it flashed through his head that he had heard this angry, stupid sahib discoursing loud personalities to an old lady near Umballa three years ago.

'It is well,' the Saddhu whispered, jammed in the calling, shouting, bewildered press – a Persian greyhound between his feet and a cageful of yelling hawks under charge of a Rajput falconer in the small of his back. 'He has gone now to send word of the letter which I hid. They told me he was in Peshawar. I might have known that he is like the crocodile – always at the

other ford. He has saved me from present calamity, but I owe my life to thee.'

'Is he also one of us?' Kim ducked under a Mewar camel-driver's greasy armpit and cannoned off a covey of jabbering Sikh matrons.

'Not less than the greatest. We are both fortunate! I will make report to him of what thou hast done. I am safe under his protection.'

He bored through the edge of the crowd besieging the carriages, and squatted by the bench near the telegraph-office.

'Return, or they take thy place! Have no fear for the work, brother – or my life. Thou hast given me a breathing-space, and Strickland Sahib has pulled me to land. We may work together at the Game yet. Farewell!'

Kim hurried to his carriage: elated, bewildered, but a little nettled in that he had no key to the secrets about him.

'I am only a beginner at the Game, that is sure. *I* could not have leaped into safety as did the Saddhu. He knew it was darkest under the lamp. *I* could not have thought to tell news under pretence of cursing . . . and how clever was the sahib! No matter, I saved the life of one . . . Where is the Kamboh gone, Holy One?' he whispered, as he took his seat in the now crowded compartment.

'A fear gripped him,' the lama replied, with a touch of tender malice. 'He saw thee change the Mahratta to a Saddhu in the twinkling of an eye, as a protection against evil. That shook him. Then he saw the Saddhu fall sheer into the hands of the *polis* – all the effect of thy art. Then he gathered up his son and fled; for he said that thou didst change a quiet trader into an impudent bandier of

words with sahibs, and he feared a like fate. Where is the Saddhu?'

'With the *polis*,' said Kim . . . 'Yet I saved the Kamboh's child.'

The lama snuffed blandly.

'Ah, *chela*, see how thou art overtaken! Thou didst cure the Kamboh's child solely to acquire merit. But thou didst put a spell on the Mahratta with prideful workings – I watched thee – and with sidelong glances to bewilder an old old man and a foolish farmer: whence calamity and suspicion.'

Kim controlled himself with an effort beyond his years. Not more than any other youngster did he like to eat dirt or to be misjudged, but he saw himself in a cleft stick. The train rolled out of Delhi into the night.

'It is true,' he murmured. 'Where I have offended thee I have done wrong.'

'It is more, *chela*. Thou hast loosed an act upon the world, and as a stone thrown into a pool so spread the consequences thou canst not tell how far.'

This ignorance was well both for Kim's vanity and for the lama's peace of mind, when we think that there was then being handed in at Simla a code-wire reporting the arrival of E23 at Delhi, and, more important, the where-abouts of a letter he had been commissioned to – abstract. Incidentally, an over-zealous policeman had arrested, on charge of murder done in a far southern state, a horribly indignant Ajmir cotton-broker, who was explaining himself to a Mr Strickland on Delhi platform, while E23 was paddling through byways into the locked heart of Delhi city. In two hours several telegrams had reached the angry minister of a southern state reporting that all trace

279

of a somewhat bruised Mahratta had been lost; and by the time the leisurely train halted at Saharunpore the last ripple of the stone Kim had helped to heave was lapping against the steps of a mosque in far-away Roum – where it disturbed a pious man at prayers.

The lama made his in ample form near the dewy bougainvillea trellis near the platform, cheered by the clear sunshine and the presence of his disciple. 'We will put these things behind us,' he said, indicating the brazen engine and the gleaming track. 'The jolting of the *te-rain* – though a wonderful thing – has turned my bones to water. We will use clean air henceforward.'

'Let us go to the Kulu woman's house' said Kim, and stepped forth cheerily under the bundles. Early morning Saharunpore way is clean and well scented. He thought of the other mornings at St Xavier's, and it topped his already thrice-heaped contentment.

'Where is this new haste born from? Wise men do not run about like chickens in the sun. We have come hundreds upon hundreds of *koss* already, and, till now, I have scarcely been alone with thee an instant. How canst thou receive instruction all jostled of crowds? How can I, whelmed by a flux of talk, meditate upon the Way?'

'Her tongue grows no shorter with the years, then?' The disciple smiled.

'Nor her desire for charms. I remember once when I spoke of the Wheel of Life' – the lama fumbled in his bosom for his latest copy – 'she was only curious about the devils that besiege children. She shall acquire merit by entertaining us – in a little while – at an after-occasion – softly, softly. Now we will wander loose-foot, waiting upon the Chain of Things. The Search is sure.'

So they travelled very easily across and among the broad bloomful fruit-gardens – by way of Aminabad, Sahaigunge, Akrola of the Ford, and little Phulesa – the line of the Siwaliks always to the north, and behind them again the snows. After long, sweet sleep under the dry stars came the lordly, leisurely passage through a waking village – begging-bowl held forth in silence, but eyes roving in defiance of the Law from sky's edge to sky's edge. Then would Kim return soft-footed through the dust to his master under the shadow of a mango tree or the thinner shade of a white Doon *siris*, to eat and drink at ease. At midday, after talk and a little wayfaring, they slept; meeting the world refreshed when the air was cooler. Night found them adventuring into new territory – some chosen village spied three hours before across the fat land, and much discussed upon the road.

There they told their tale – a new one each evening so far as Kim was concerned – and there were they made welcome, either by priest or headman, after the custom of the kindly East.

When the shadows shortened and the lama leaned more heavily upon Kim, there was always the Wheel of Life to draw forth, to hold flat under wiped stones, and with a long straw to expound cycle by cycle. Here sat the Gods on high – and they were dreams of dreams. Here was our Heaven and the world of the demi-Gods – horsemen fighting among the hills. Here were the agonies done upon the beasts, souls ascending or descending the ladder and therefore not to be interfered with. Here were the Hells, hot and cold, and the abodes of tormented ghosts. Let the *chela* study the troubles that come from overeating – bloated stomach and burning

bowels. Obediently, then, with bowed head and brown finger alert to follow the pointer, did the *chela* study; but when they came to the Human World, busy and profitless, that is just above the Hells, his mind was distracted; for by the roadside trundled the very Wheel itself, eating, drinking, trading, marrying, and quarrelling – all warmly alive. Often the lama made the living pictures the matter of his text, bidding Kim – too ready – note how the flesh takes a thousand thousand shapes, desirable or detestable as men reckon, but in truth of no account either way; and how the stupid spirit, bond-slave to the Hog, the Dove, and the Serpent – lusting after betel-nut, a new yoke of oxen, women, or the favour of kings – is bound to follow the body through all the Heavens and all the Hells, and strictly round again. Sometimes a woman or a poor man, watching the ritual – it was nothing else – when the great yellow chart was unfolded, would throw a few flowers or a handful of cowries upon its edge. It sufficed these humble ones that they had met a Holy One who might be moved to remember them in his prayers.

'Cure them if they are sick,' said the lama, when Kim's sporting instincts woke. 'Cure them if they have fever, but by no means work charms. Remember what befell the Mahratta.'

'Then all doing is evil?' Kim replied, lying out under a big tree at the fork of the Doon road, watching the little ants run over his hand.

'To abstain from action is well – except to acquire merit.'

'At the Gates of Learning we were taught that to abstain from action was unbefitting a sahib. And I am a sahib.'

'Friend of all the World,' – the lama looked directly at Kim – 'I am an old man – pleased with shows as are children. To those who follow the Way there is neither black nor white, Hind nor Bhotiyal. We be all souls seeking escape. No matter what thy wisdom learned among sahibs, when we come to my River thou wilt be freed from all illusion – at my side. *Hai!* my bones ache for that River, as they ached in the *te-rain*; but my spirit sits above my bones, waiting. The Search is sure!'

'I am answered. Is it permitted to ask a question?'

The lama inclined his stately head.

'I ate thy bread for three years – as thou knowest. Holy One, whence came –?'

'There is much wealth, as men count it, in Bhotiyal,' the lama returned with composure. 'In my own place I have the illusion of honour. I ask for that I need. I am not concerned with the account. That is for my monastery. *Ai!* The black high seats in the monastery, and the novices all in order!'

And he told stories, tracing with a finger in the dust, of the immense and sumptuous ritual of avalanche-guarded cathedrals; of processions and devil-dances; of the changing of monks and nuns into swine; of holy cities fifteen thousand feet in the air; of intrigue between monastery and monastery; of voices among the hills, and of that mysterious mirage that dances on dry snow. He spoke even of Lhasa and of the Dalai Lama, whom he had seen and adored.

Each long, perfect day rose behind Kim for a barrier to cut him off from his race and his mother-tongue. He slipped back to thinking and dreaming in the vernacular, and mechanically followed the lama's ceremonial observ-

ances at eating, drinking, and the like. The old man's mind turned more and more to his monastery as his eyes turned to the steadfast snows. His River troubled him nothing. Now and again, indeed, he would gaze long and long at a tuft or a twig, expecting, he said, the earth to cleave and deliver its blessing; but he was content to be with his disciple, at ease in the temperate wind that comes down from the Doon. This was not Ceylon, nor Buddh Gaya, nor Bombay, nor some grass-tangled ruins that he seemed to have stumbled upon two years ago. He spoke of those places as a scholar removed from vanity, as a Seeker walking in humility, as an old man, wise and temperate, illumining knowledge with brilliant insight. Bit by bit, disconnectedly, each tale called up by some wayside thing, he spoke of all his wanderings up and down Hind; till Kim, who had loved him without reason, now loved him for fifty good reasons. So they enjoyed themselves in high felicity, abstaining, as the Rule demands, from evil words, covetous desires; not overeating, not lying on high beds, nor wearing rich clothes. Their stomachs told them the time, and the people brought them their food, as the saying is. They were lords of the villages of Aminabad, Sahaigunge, Akrola of the Ford, and little Phulesa, where Kim gave the soulless woman a blessing.

But news travels fast in India, and too soon shuffled across the crop-land, bearing a basket of fruits with a box of Kabul grapes and gilt oranges, a white-whiskered servitor – a lean, dry Oorya – begging them to bring the honour of their presence to his mistress, distressed in her mind that the lama had neglected her so long.

'Now do I remember' – the lama spoke as though it

were a wholly new proposition. 'She is virtuous, but an inordinate talker.'

Kim was sitting on the edge of a cow's manger, telling stories to a village smith's children.

'She will only ask for another son for her daughter. I have not forgotten her,' he said. 'Let her acquire merit. Send word that we will come.'

They covered eleven miles through the fields in two days, and were overwhelmed with attentions at the end; for the old lady held a fine tradition of hospitality, to which she forced her son-in-law, who was under the thumb of his women-folk and bought peace by borrowing of the moneylender. Age had not weakened her tongue or her memory, and from a discreetly barred upper window, in the hearing of not less than a dozen servants, she paid Kim compliments that would have flung European audiences into unclean dismay.

'But thou art still the shameless beggar-brat of the *parao*,' she shrilled. 'I have not forgotten thee. Wash ye and eat. The father of my daughter's son is gone away awhile. So we poor women are dumb and useless.'

For proof, she harangued the entire household unsparingly till food and drink were brought; and in the evening – the smoke-scented evening, copper-dun and turquoise across the fields – it pleased her to order her palanquin to be set down in the untidy forecourt by smoky torchlight; and there, behind not too closely drawn curtains, she gossiped.

'Had the Holy One come alone, I should have received him otherwise; but with this rogue, who can be too careful?'

285

'Maharanee,' said Kim, choosing as always the amplest title, 'is it my fault that none other than a sahib – a *polis*-sahib – called the Maharanee whose face he –'

'Chutt! That was on the pilgrimage. When we travel – thou knowest the proverb.'

'Called the Maharanee a Breaker of Hearts and a Dispenser of Delights?'

'To remember that! It was true. So he did. That was in the time of the bloom of my beauty.' She chuckled like a contented parrot above the sugar lump. 'Now tell me of thy goings and comings – as much as may be without shame. How many maids, and whose wives, hang upon thine eyelashes? Ye hail from Benares? I would have gone there again this year, but my daughter – we have only two sons. Phaii! Such is the effect of these low plains. Now in Kulu men are elephants. But I would ask thy Holy One – stand aside, rogue – a charm against most lamentable windy colics that in mango-time overtake my daughter's eldest. Two years back he gave me a powerful spell.'

'Oh, Holy One!' said Kim, bubbling with mirth at the lama's rueful face.

'It is true. I gave her one against wind.'

'Teeth – teeth – teeth,' snapped the old woman.

'"Cure them if they are sick,"' Kim quoted relishingly, '"but by no means work charms. Remember what befell the Mahratta."'

'That was two rains ago; she wearied me with her continual importunity.' The lama groaned as the Unjust Judge had groaned before him. 'Thus it comes – take note, my *chela* – that even those who would follow the

286

Way are thrust aside by idle women. Three days through, when the child was sick, she talked to me.'

'*Arré!* and to whom else should I talk? The boy's mother knew nothing, and the father – in the nights of the cold weather it was – "Pray to the Gods," said he, forsooth, and turning over, snored!'

'I gave her the charm. What is an old man to do?'

'"To abstain from action is well – except to acquire merit."'

'Ah, *chela*, if thou desertest me, I am all alone.'

'He found his milk-teeth easily at any rate,' said the old lady. 'But all priests are alike.'

Kim coughed severely. Being young, he did not approve of her flippancy. 'To importune the wise out of season is to invite calamity.'

'There is a talking mynah' – the thrust came back with the well-remembered snap of the jewelled forefinger – 'over the stables which has picked up the very tone of the family priest. Maybe I forget honour to my guests, but if ye had seen *him* double his fists into his belly, which was like a half-grown gourd, and cry: "Here is the pain!" ye would forgive. I am half minded to take the *hakim's* medicine. He sells it cheap, and certainly it makes him as fat as Shiv's own bull. *He* does not deny remedies, but I doubted for the child because of the inauspicious colour of the bottles.'

The lama, under cover of the monologue, had faded out into the darkness towards the room prepared.

'Thou hast angered him, belike,' said Kim.

'Not he. He is wearied, and I forgot, being a grandmother. (None but a grandmother should ever oversee a child. Mothers are only fit for bearing.) Tomorrow, when

he sees how my daughter's son is grown, he will write the charm. Then, too, he can judge of the new *hakim's* drugs.'

'Who is the *hakim*, Maharanee?'

'A wanderer, as thou art, but a most sober Bengali from Dacca – a master of medicine. He relieved me of an oppression after meat by means of a small pill that wrought like a devil unchained. He travels about now, vending preparations of great value. He has even papers, printed in Angrezi, telling what things he has done for weak-backed men and slack women. He has been here four days; but hearing ye were coming (*hakims* and priests are snake and tiger the world over) he has, as I take it, gone to cover.'

While she drew breath after this volley, the ancient servant, sitting unrebuked on the edge of the torchlight, muttered: 'This house is a cattle-pound, as it were, for all charlatans and – priests. Let the boy stop eating mangoes . . . but who can argue with a grandmother?' He raised his voice respectfully: 'Sahiba, the *hakim* sleeps after his meat. He is in the quarters behind the dovecot.'

Kim bristled like an expectant terrier. To outface and down-talk a Calcutta-taught Bengali, a voluble Dacca drug-vendor, would be a good game. It was not seemly that the lama, and incidentally himself, should be thrown aside for such an one. He knew those curious bastard English advertisements at the backs of native newspapers. St Xavier's boys sometimes brought them in by stealth to snigger over among their mates; for the language of the grateful patient recounting his symptoms is most simple and revealing. The Oorya, not unanxious to

play off one parasite against the other, slunk away towards the dovecot.

'Yes,' said Kim, with measured scorn. 'Their stock-in-trade is a little coloured water and a very great shamelessness. Their prey are broken-down kings and overfed Bengalis. Their profit is in children – who are not yet born.'

The old lady chuckled. 'Do not be envious. Charms are better, eh? *I* never gainsaid it. See that thy Holy One writes me a good amulet by the morning.'

'None but the ignorant deny' – a thick, heavy voice boomed through the darkness, as a figure came to rest squatting – 'None but the ignorant deny the value of charms. None but the ignorant deny the value of medicines.'

'A rat found a piece of turmeric. Said he: "I will open a grocer's shop,"' Kim retorted.

Battle was fairly joined now, and they heard the old lady stiffen to attention.

'The priest's son knows the names of his nurse and three Gods. Says he: "Hear me, or I will curse you by the three million Great Ones."' Decidedly this invisible had an arrow or two in his quiver. He went on: 'I am but a teacher of the alphabet. I have learned all the wisdom of the sahibs.'

'The sahibs never grow old. They dance and they play like children when they are grandfathers. A strong-backed breed,' piped the voice inside the palanquin.

'I have, too, our drugs which loosen humours of the head in hot and angry men. *Sinà* well compounded when the moon stands in the proper House; yellow earths I have – *arplan* from China that makes a man renew his youth and astonish his household; saffron from Kashmir,

and the best salep of Kabul. Many people have died before –'

'That I surely believe,' said Kim.

'They knew the value of my drugs. I do not give *my* sick the mere ink in which a charm is written, but hot and rending drugs which descend and wrestle with the evil.'

'Very mightily they do so,' sighed the old lady.

The voice launched into an immense tale of misfortune and bankruptcy, studded with plentiful petitions to the government. 'But for my fate, which overrules all, I had been now in government employ. I bear a degree from the great school at Calcutta – whither, maybe, the son of this house shall go.'

'He shall indeed. If our neighbour's brat can in a few years be made an FA' (First Arts – she used the English word, of which she had heard so often), 'how much more shall children clever as some that I know bear away prizes at rich Calcutta.'

'Never,' said the voice, 'have I seen such a child! Born in an auspicious hour, and – but for that colic which, alas! turning into black cholers, may carry him off like a pigeon – destined to many years, he is enviable.'

'*Hai mai!*' said the old lady. 'To praise children is inauspicious, or I could listen to this talk. But the back of the house is unguarded, and even in this soft air men think themselves to be men, and women we know . . . The child's father is away too, and I must be *chowkedar* [watchman] in my old age. Up! Up! Take up the palanquin. Let the *hakim* and the young priest settle between them whether charms or medicine most avail. Ho! worthless people, fetch tobacco for the guests, and – round the homestead go I!'

The palanquin reeled off, followed by straggling torches and a horde of dogs. Twenty villages knew the Sahiba – her failings, her tongue, and her large charity. Twenty villages cheated her after immemorial custom, but no man would have stolen or robbed within her jurisdiction for any gift under heaven. None the less, she made great parade of her formal inspections, the riot of which could be heard half-way to Mussoorie.

Kim relaxed, as one augur must when he meets another. The *hakim*, still squatting, slid over his hookah with a friendly foot, and Kim pulled at the good weed. The hangers-on expected grave professional debate, and perhaps a little free doctoring.

'To discuss medicine before the ignorant is of one piece with teaching the peacock to sing,' said the *hakim*.

'True courtesy,' Kim echoed, 'is very often in-attention.'

These, be it understood, were company-manners, designed to impress.

'Hi! I have an ulcer on my leg,' cried a scullion. 'Look at it!'

'Get hence! Remove!' said the *hakim*. 'Is it the habit of the place to pester honoured guests? Ye crowd in like buffaloes.'

'If the Sahiba knew –' Kim began.

'*Ai! Ai!* Come away. They are meat for our mistress. When her young Shaitan's colics are cured perhaps we poor people may be suffered to –'

'The mistress fed thy wife when thou wast in jail for breaking the moneylender's head. Who speaks against her?' The old servitor curled his white moustaches savagely in the young moonlight. '*I* am responsible

for the honour of this house. Go!' and he drove the underlings before him.

Said the *hakim*, hardly more than shaping the words with his lips: 'How do you do, Mister O'Hara? I am jolly glad to see you again.'

Kim's hand clenched about the pipe-stem. Anywhere on the open road, perhaps, he would not have been astonished; but here, in this quiet backwater of life, he was not prepared for Hurree Babu. It annoyed him, too, that he had been hoodwinked.

'Ah ha! I told you at Lucknow – *resurgam* – I shall rise again and you shall not know me. How much did you bet – eh?'

He chewed leisurely upon a few cardamom seeds, but he breathed uneasily.

'But why come here, Babuji?'

'Ah! *Thatt* is the question, as Shakespeare hath it. I come to congratulate you on your extraordinary effeecient performance at Delhi. Oah! I tell you we are all proud of you. It was verree neat and handy. Our mutual friend, he is old friend of mine. He has been in some dam' tight places. Now he will be in some more. He told me; I tell Mr Lurgan; and he is pleased you graduate so nicely. All the Department is pleased.'

For the first time in his life, Kim thrilled to the clean pride (it can be a deadly pitfall, none the less) of depart-mental praise – ensnaring praise from an equal of work appreciated by fellow-workers. Earth has noth-ing on the same plane to compare with it. But, cried the Oriental in him, babus do not travel far to retail compliments.

'Tell thy tale, Babu,' he said authoritatively.

'Oah, it is nothing. Onlee I was at Simla when the wire came in about what our mutual friend said he had hidden, and old Creighton –' He looked to see how Kim would take this piece of audacity.

'The Colonel Sahib,' the boy from St Xavier's corrected.

'*Of* course. He found me at a loose string, and I had to go down to Chitor to find that beastly letter. I do not like the south – too much railway travel; but I drew good travelling allowance. Ha! Ha! I meet our mutual at Delhi on the way back. He lies quiett just now, and says Saddhu disguise suits him to the ground. Well, there I hear what you have done so well, so quickly, upon the instantaneous spur of the moment. I tell our mutual you take the bally bun, by Jove! It was splendid. I come to tell you so.'

'Umm!'

The frogs were busy in the ditches, and the moon slid to her setting. Some happy servant had gone out to commune with the night and to beat upon a drum. Kim's next sentence was in the vernacular.

'How didst thou follow us?'

'Oah. Thatt was nothing. I know from our mutual friend you go to Saharunpore. So I come on. Red Lamas are not inconspicuous persons. I buy myself my drug-box, and I am very good doctor really. I go to Akrola of the Ford, and hear all about you and I talk here and talk there. All the common people know what you do. I knew when the hospitable old lady sent the *dooli*. They have great recollections of the old lama's visits here. I know old ladies cannot keep their hands from medicines. So I am a doctor, and – you hear my talk? *I* think it is verree good. My word, Mister O'Hara, they know about you and the

lama for fifty miles – the common people. So I come. Do you mind?'

'Babuji,' said Kim, looking up at the broad, grinning face, 'I am a sahib.'

'My dear Mister O'Hara –'

'And I hope to play the Great Game.'

'You are subordinate to me departmentally at present.'

'Then why talk like an ape in a tree? Men do not come after one from Simla and change their dress, for the sake of a few sweet words. I am not a child. Talk Hindi and let us get to the yolk of the egg. Thou art here – speaking not one word of truth in ten. Why art thou here? Give a straight answer.'

'That is so verree disconcerting of the Europeans, Mister O'Hara. *You* should know a heap better at your time of life.'

'But I want to know,' said Kim, laughing. 'If it is the Game, I may help. How can I do anything if you *bukh* [babble] all round the shop?'

Hurree Babu reached for the pipe, and sucked it till it guggled again.

'Now I will speak vernacular. You sit tight, Mister O'Hara . . . It concerns the pedigree of a white stallion.'

'Still? That was finished long ago.'

'When every one is dead the Great Game is finished. Not before. Listen to me till the end. There were five kings who prepared a sudden war three years ago, when thou wast given the stallion's pedigree by Mahbub Ali. Upon them, because of that news, and ere they were ready, fell our army.'

'Ay – eight thousand men with guns. I remember that night.'

'But the war was not pushed. That is the government custom. The troops were recalled because the government believed the five kings were cowed; and it is not cheap to feed men among the high passes. Hilás and Bunár – rajahs with guns – undertook for a price to guard the passes against all coming from the north. They protested both fear and friendship.' He broke off with a giggle into English: 'Of course, I tell you this unoffeecially to elucidate political situation, Mister O'Hara. Offeecially, I am debarred from criticizing any action of superiors. Now I go on – This pleased the government, anxious to avoid expense, and a bond was made for so many rupees a month that Hilás and Bunár should guard the passes as soon as the state's troops were withdrawn. At that time – it was after we two met – I, who had been selling tea in Leh, became a clerk of accounts in the army. When the troops were withdrawn, I was left behind to pay the coolies who made new roads in the Hills. This road-making was part of the bond between Bunár, Hilás, and the government.'

'So? And then?'

'I tell you, it was jolly-beastly cold up there too, after summer,' said Hurree Babu confidentially. 'I was afraid these Bunár men would cut my throat every night for thee pay-chest. My native sepoy-guard, they laughed at me! By Jove! I was such a fearful man. Nevar mind thatt. I go on colloquially . . . I send word many times that these two kings were sold to the north; and Mahbub Ali, who was yet farther north, amply confirmed it. Nothing was done. Only my feet were frozen, and a toe dropped off. I sent word that the roads for which I was paying money to

the diggers were being made for the feet of strangers and enemies.'

'For?'

'For the Russians. The thing was an open jest among the coolies. Then I was called down to tell what I knew by speech of tongue. Mahbub came south too. See the end! Over the passes this year after snow-melting' – he shivered afresh – 'come two strangers under cover of shooting wild goats. They bear guns, but they bear also chains and levels and compasses.'

'Oho! The things get clearer.'

'They are well received by Hilás and Bunár. They make great promises; they speak as the mouthpiece of a kaisar with gifts. Up the valleys, down the valleys go they, saying, "Here is a place to build a breastwork; here can ye pitch a fort. Here can ye hold the road against an army" – the very roads for which I paid out the rupees monthly. The government knows, but does nothing. The three other kings, who were *not* paid for guarding the passes, tell them by runner of the bad faith of Bunár and Hilás. When all the evil is done, look you – when those two strangers with the levels and the compasses make the five kings to believe that a great army will sweep the passes tomorrow or the next day – hill-people are all fools – comes the order to me, Hurree Babu, "Go north and see what those strangers do." I say to Creighton Sahib, "This is not a lawsuit, that we go about to collect evidence."' Hurree returned to his English with a jerk: '"By Jove," I said, "why the dooce do you not issue demi-offeecial orders to some brave man to poison them, for an example? It is, if you permit the observation, most reprehensible laxity on your part." And Colonel

296

Creighton, he laughed at me! It is all your beastly English pride. You think no one dare conspire! That is all tommy-rott.'

Kim smoked slowly, revolving the business, so far as he understood it, in his quick mind.

'Then thou goest forth to follow the strangers?'

'No. To meet them. They are coming in to Simla to send their horns and heads to be dressed at Calcutta. They are exclusively sporting gentlemen, and they are allowed special faceelities by the government. Of course, we always do that. It is our British pride.'

'Then what is to fear from them?'

'By Jove, they are not black people. I can do all sorts of things with black people, of course. They are Russians, and highly unscrupulous people. I – I do not want to consort with them without a witness.'

'Will they kill thee?'

'Oah, thatt is nothing. I am good enough Herbert Spencerian, I trust, to meet little thing like death, which is all in my fate, you know. But – but they may beat me.'

'Why?'

Hurree Babu snapped his fingers with irritation. 'Of *course* I shall affeeliate myself to their camp in super-numerary capacity as perhaps interpreter, or person mentally impotent and hungree, or some such thing. And then I must pick up what I can, I suppose. That is as easy for me as playing Mister Doctor to the old lady. Onlee – onlee – you see, Mister O'Hara, I am unfortu-nately Asiatic, which is serious detriment in some respects. And *all*-so I am Bengali – a fearful man.'

'God made the Hare and the Bengali. What shame?' said Kim, quoting the proverb.

'It was process of Evolution, I think, from Primal Necessity, but the fact remains in all the *cui bono*. I am, oh, awfully fearful! – I remember once they wanted to cut off my head on the road to Lhasa. (No, I have never reached to Lhasa.) I sat down and cried, Mister O'Hara, anticipating Chinese tortures. I do not suppose these two gentlemen will torture me, but I like to provide for possible contingency with European assistance in emergency. He coughed and spat out the cardamoms. 'It is purely unoffeecial indent, to which you can say "No, Babu." If you have no pressing engagement with your old man – perhaps you might divert him; perhaps I can seduce his fancies – I should like you to keep in departmental touch with me till I find those sporting coves. I have great opeenion of you since I met my friend at Delhi. And also I will embody your name in my offeecial report when matter is finally adjudicated. It will be a great feather in your cap. That is why I come really.'

'Humph! The end of the tale, I think, is true; but what of the fore-part?'

'About the five kings? Oah! there is ever so much truth in it. A lots more than you would suppose,' said Hurree earnestly. 'You come – eh? I go from here straight into the Doon. It is verree verdant and painted meads. I shall go to Mussoorie – to good old Munsoorie Pahar, as the gentlemen and ladies say. Then by Rampur into Chini. That is the only way they can come. I do not like waiting in the cold, but we must wait for them. I want to walk with them to Simla. You see, one Russian is a Frenchman, and I know my French pretty well. I have friends in Chandernagore.'

'*He* would certainly rejoice to see the Hills again,' said

Kim meditatively. 'All his speech these ten days past has been of little else. If we go together –'

'Oah! We can be quite strangers on the road, if your lama prefers. I shall just be four or five miles ahead. There is no hurry for Hurree – thatt is an Europe pun, ha! ha! – and you come after. There is plenty of time; they will plot and survey and map, of course. I shall go tomorrow, and you the next day, if you choose. Eh? You go think on it till morning. By Jove, it is near morning now.' He yawned ponderously, and with never a civil word lumbered off to his sleeping-place. But Kim slept little, and his thoughts ran in Hindustani:

'Well is the Game called great! I was four days a scullion at Quetta, waiting on the wife of the man whose book I stole. And that was part of the Great Game! From the south – God knows how far – came up the Mahratta, playing the Great Game in fear of his life. Now I shall go far and far into the north playing the Great Game. Truly, it runs like a shuttle throughout all Hind. And my share and my joy' – he smiled to the darkness – 'I owe to the lama here. Also to Mahbub Ali – also to Creighton Sahib, but chiefly to the Holy One. He is right – a great and a wonderful world – and I am Kim – Kim – Kim – alone – one person – in the middle of it all. But I will see these strangers with their levels and chains . . .'

'What was the upshot of last night's babble?' said the lama after his orisons.

'There came a strolling seller of drugs – a hanger-on of the Sahiba's. Him I abolished by arguments and prayers, proving that our charms are worthier than his coloured waters.'

'Alas, my charms! Is the virtuous woman still bent upon a new one?'

'Very strictly.'

'Then it must be written, or she will deafen me with her clamour.' He fumbled at his pen-case.

'In the Plains,' said Kim, 'are always too many people. In the Hills, as I understand, there are fewer.'

'Oh! the Hills, and the snows upon the Hills.' The lama tore off a tiny square of paper fit to go in an amulet. 'But what dost thou know of the Hills?'

'They are very close.' Kim thrust open the door and looked at the long, peaceful line of the Himalayas flushed in morning-gold. 'Except in the dress of a sahib, I have never set foot among them.'

The lama snuffed the wind wistfully.

'If we go north,' – Kim put the question to the waking sunrise – 'would not much midday heat be avoided by walking among the lower hills at least? . . . Is the charm made, Holy One?'

'I have written the names of seven silly devils – not one of whom is worth a grain of dust in the eye. Thus do foolish women drag us from the Way!'

Hurree Babu came out from behind the dovecot, washing his teeth with ostentatious ritual. Full-fleshed, heavy-haunched, bull-necked, and deep-voiced, he did not look like a 'fearful man'. Kim signed almost imperceptibly that matters were in good train, and when the morning toilet was over, Hurree Babu, in flowery speech, came to do honour to the lama. They ate, of course, apart, and afterwards the old lady, more or less veiled behind a window, returned to the vital business of green-mango colics in the young. The lama's knowledge of medicine

was, of course, sympathetic only. He believed that the dung of a black horse, mixed with sulphur, and carried in a snake-skin, was a sound remedy for cholera; but the symbolism interested him far more than the science. Hurree Babu deferred to these views with enchanting politeness, so that the lama called him a courteous physician. Hurree Babu replied that he was no more than an inexpert dabbler in the mysteries; but at least – he thanked the Gods therefore – he knew when he sat in the presence of a master. He himself had been taught by the sahibs, who do not consider expense, in the lordly halls of Calcutta; but, as he was ever first to acknowledge, there lay a wisdom behind earthly wisdom – the high and lonely lore of meditation. Kim looked on with envy. The Hurree Babu of his knowledge – oily, effusive, and nervous – was gone; gone, too, was the brazen drug-vendor of overnight. There remained – polished, polite, attentive – a sober, learned son of experience and adversity, gathering wisdom from the lama's lips. The old lady confided to Kim that these rare levels were beyond her. She liked charms with plenty of ink that one could wash off in water, swallow, and be done with. Else what was the use of the Gods? She liked men and women, and she spoke of them – of kinglets she had known in the past; of her own youth and beauty; of the depredations of leopards and the eccentricities of love Asiatic; of the incidence of taxation, rack-renting, funeral ceremonies, her son-in-law (this by allusion, easy to be followed), the care of the young, and the age's lack of decency. And Kim, as interested in the life of this world as she soon to leave it, squatted with his feet under the hem of his robe, drinking all in, while the lama

demolished one after another every theory of body-curing put forward by Hurree Babu.

At noon the Babu strapped up his brass-bound drug-box, took his patent-leather shoes of ceremony in one hand, a gay blue-and-white umbrella in the other, and set off northwards to the Doon, where, he said, he was in demand among the lesser kings of those parts.

'We will go in the cool of the evening, *chela*,' said the lama. 'That doctor, learned in physic and courtesy, affirms that the people among these lower hills are devout, generous, and much in need of a teacher. In a very short time – so says the *hakim* – we come to cool air and the smell of pines.'

'Ye go to the Hills? And by Kulu road? Oh, thrice happy!' shrilled the old lady. 'But that I am a little pressed with the care of the homestead I would take palanquin . . . but that would be shameless, and my reputation would be cracked. Ho! Ho! I know the road – every march of the road I know. Ye will find charity throughout – it is not denied to the well-looking. I will give orders for provision. A servant to set you forth upon your journey? No . . . Then I will at least cook ye good food.'

'What a woman is the Sahiba!' said the white-bearded Oorya, when a tumult rose by the kitchen quarters. 'She has never forgotten a friend: she has never forgotten an enemy in all her years. And her cookery – wah!' He rubbed his slim stomach.

There were cakes, there were sweetmeats, there was cold fowl stewed to rags with rice and prunes – enough to burden Kim like a mule.

'I am old and useless,' she said. 'None now love me –

and none respect – but there are few to compare with me when I call on the Gods and squat to my cooking-pots. Come again, O people of good will. Holy One and disciple, come again. The room is always prepared; the welcome is always ready . . . See the women do not follow thy *chela* too openly. *I* know the women of Kulu. Take heed, *chela*, lest he run away when he smells his Hills again . . . *Hai!* Do not tilt the rice bag upside down . . . Bless the household, Holy One, and forgive thy servant her stupidities.'

She wiped her red old eyes on a corner of her veil, and clucked throatily.

'Women talk,' said the lama at last, 'but that is a woman's infirmity. I gave her a charm. She is upon the Wheel and wholly given over to the shows of this life, but none the less, *chela*, she is virtuous, kindly, hospitable – of a whole and zealous heart. Who shall say she does not acquire merit?'

'Not I, Holy One,' said Kim, reslinging the bountiful provision on his shoulders. 'In my mind – behind my eyes – I have tried to picture such an one altogether freed from the Wheel – desiring nothing, causing nothing – a nun, as it were.'

'And, O imp?' The lama almost laughed aloud.

'I cannot make the picture.'

'Nor I. But there are many, many millions of lives before her. She will get wisdom a little it may be, in each one.'

'And will she forget how to make stews with saffron upon that road?'

'Thy mind is set on things unworthy. But she has skill. I am refreshed all over. When we reach the lower hills I

shall be yet stronger. The *hakim* spoke truly to me this morn when he said a breath from the snows blows away twenty years from the life of a man. We will go up into the Hills – the high hills – up to the sound of snow-waters and the sound of the trees – for a little while. The *hakim* said that at any time we may return to the Plains, for we do no more than skirt the pleasant places. The *hakim* is full of learning; but he is in no way proud. I spoke to him – when thou wast talking to the Sahiba – of a certain dizziness that lays hold upon the back of my neck in the night, and he said it rose from excessive heat – to be cured by cool air. Upon consideration, I marvelled that I had not thought of such a simple remedy.'

'Didst thou tell him of thy Search?' said Kim, a little jealously. He preferred to sway the lama by his own speech – not through the wiles of Hurree Babu.

'Assuredly. I told him of my dream, and of the manner by which I had acquired merit by causing thee to be taught wisdom.'

'Thou didst not say I was a sahib?'

'What need? I have told thee many times we be but two souls seeking escape. He said – and he is just herein – that the River of Healing will break forth even as I dreamed – at my feet, if need be. Having found the Way, seest thou, that shall free me from the Wheel, need I trouble to find a way about the mere fields of the earth – which are illusion? That were senseless. I have my dreams, night upon night repeated; I have the *Jâtaka*; and I have thee, Friend of all the World. It was written in thy horoscope that a Red Bull on a green field – I have not forgotten – should bring thee to honour. Who but I saw that prophecy accomplished? Indeed, I was the instrument. Thou

shalt find me my River, being in return the instrument. The Search is sure!'

He set his ivory-yellow face, serene and untroubled, towards the beckoning Hills; his shadow shouldering far before him in the dust.

Who hath desired the Sea – the immense and contemptuous
 surges?
The shudder, the stumble, the swerve ere the star-stabbing
 bowsprit emerges –
The orderly clouds of the Trades and the ridged roaring
 sapphire thereunder –
Unheralded cliff-lurking flaws and the head-sails'
 low-volleying thunder?
His Sea in no wonder the same – his Sea and the same in each
 wonder –
 His Sea that his being fulfils?
So and no otherwise – so and no otherwise hill-men desire
 their Hills!

 The Sea and the Hills

'Who goes to the Hills goes to his mother.' They had
crossed the Siwaliks and the half-tropical Doon, left
Mussoorie behind them, and headed north along the
narrow hill roads. Day after day they struck deeper into
the huddled mountains, and day after day Kim watched
the lama return to a man's strength. Among the terraces
of the Doon he had leaned on the boy's shoulder, ready
to profit by wayside halts. Under the great ramp to
Mussoorie he drew himself together as an old hunter
faces a well-remembered bank, and where he should
have sunk exhausted swung his long draperies about
him, drew a deep double lungful of the diamond air, and
walked as only a hillman can. Kim, plains-bred and
plains-fed, sweated and panted astonished. 'This is *my*

country,' said the lama. 'Beside Such-zen, this is flatter than a rice field'; and with steady, driving strokes from the loins he strode upwards. But it was on the steep downhill marches, three thousand feet in three hours, that he went utterly away from Kim, whose back ached with holding back, and whose big toe was nigh cut off by his grass sandal-string. Through the speckled shadow of the great deodar forests; through oak feathered and plumed with ferns; birch, ilex, rhododendron, and pine, out on to the bare hillsides' slippery sunburnt grass, and back into the woodlands' coolth again, till oak gave way to bamboo and palm of the valley, the lama swung untiring.

Glancing back in the twilight at the huge ridges behind him and the faint, thin line of the road whereby they had come, he would lay out, with a hillman's generous breadth of vision, fresh marches for the morrow; or, halting in the neck of some uplifted pass that gave on Spiti and Kulu, would stretch out his hands yearningly towards the high snows of the horizon. In the dawns they flared windy-red above stark blue, as Kedarnath and Badrinath – kings of that wilderness – took the first sunlight. All day long they lay like molten silver under the sun, and at evening put on their jewels again. At first they breathed temperately upon the travellers, winds good to meet when one crawled over some gigantic hog's back; but in a few days, at a height of nine or ten thousand feet, those breezes bit; and Kim kindly allowed a village of hillmen to acquire merit by giving him a rough blanket-coat. The lama was mildly surprised that any one should object to the knife-edged breezes which had cut the years off his shoulders.

'These are but the lower hills, *chela*. There is no cold till we come to the true Hills.'

'Air and water are good, and the people are devout enough, but the food is very bad,' Kim growled; 'and we walk as though we were mad – or English. It freezes at night, too.'

'A little, maybe; but only enough to make old bones rejoice in the sun. We must not always delight in soft beds and rich food.'

'We might at the least keep to the road.'

Kim had all a plainsman's affection for the well-trodden track, not six feet wide, that snaked among the mountains; but the lama, being Tibetan, could not refrain from short cuts over spurs and the rims of gravel-strewn slopes. As he explained to his limping disciple, a man bred among mountains can prophesy the course of a mountain road, and though low-lying clouds might be a hindrance to a short-cutting stranger, they made no earthly difference to a thoughtful man. Thus, after long hours of what would be reckoned very fair mountaineering in civilized countries, they would pant over a saddle-back, sidle past a few landslips, and drop through forest at an angle of forty-five on to the road again. Along their track lay the villages of the hill-folk – mud and earth huts, timbers now and then rudely carved with an axe – clinging like swallows' nests against the steeps, huddled on tiny flats half-way down a three-thousand-foot glissade; jammed into a corner between cliffs that funnelled and focused every wandering blast; or, for the sake of summer pasture, cowering down on a neck that in winter would be ten feet deep in snow. And the people – the sallow, greasy, duffle-clad people, with short bare legs

and faces almost Esquimo – would flock out and adore. The Plains – kindly and gentle – had treated the lama as a holy man among holy men. But the Hills worshipped him as one in the confidence of all their devils. Theirs was an almost obliterated Buddhism, overlaid with a nature-worship fantastic as their own landscapes, elaborate as the terracing of their tiny fields; but they recognized the big hat, the clicking rosary, and the rare Chinese texts for great authority; and they respected the man beneath the hat.

'We saw thee come down over the black Breasts of Eua,' said a Betah who gave them cheese, sour milk, and stone-hard bread one evening. 'We do not use that often – except when calving cows stray in summer. There is a sudden wind among those stones that casts men down on the stillest day. But what should such folk care for the Devil of Eua!'

Then did Kim, aching in every fibre, dizzy with looking down, footsore with cramping desperate toes into in-adequate crannies, take joy in the day's march – such joy as a boy of St Xavier's who had won the quarter-mile on the flat might take in the praises of his friends. The hills sweated the ghee and sugar suet off his bones; the dry air, taken sobbingly at the head of cruel passes, firmed and built out his upper ribs; and the tilted levels put new hard muscles into calf and thigh.

They meditated often on the Wheel of Life – the more so since, as the lama said, they were freed from its visible temptations. Except the grey eagle and an occasional far-seen bear grubbing and rooting on the hillside; a vision of a furious painted leopard met at dawn in a still valley devouring a goat; and now and again a bright-

coloured bird, they were alone with the winds and the grass singing under the wind. The women of the smoky huts over whose roofs the two walked as they descended the mountains, were unlovely and unclean, wives of many husbands, and afflicted with goitre. The men were woodcutters when they were not farmers – meek, and of an incredible simplicity. But that suitable discourse might not fail, Fate sent them, overtaking and overtaken upon the road, the courteous Dacca physician, who paid for his food in ointments good for goitre and counsels that restore peace between men and women. He seemed to know these hills as well as he knew the hill dialects, and gave the lama the lie of the land towards Ladakh and Tibet. He said they could return to the Plains at any moment. Meantime, for such as loved mountains, yonder road might amuse. This was not all revealed in a breath, but at evening encounters on the stone threshing-floors, when, patients disposed of, the doctor would smoke and the lama snuff, while Kim watched the wee cows grazing on the house-tops, or threw his soul after his eye across the deep blue gulfs between range and range. And there were talks apart in the dark woods, when the doctor would seek herbs, and Kim, as budding physician, must accompany him.

'You see, Mister O'Hara, I do not know what the deuce-an'-all I shall do when I find our sporting friends; but if you will kindly keep within sight of my umbrella, which is fine fixed point for cadastral survey, I shall feel much better.'

Kim looked out across the jungle of peaks. 'This is not my country, *hakim*. Easier, I think, to find one louse in a bearskin.'

'Oah, thatt is my strong points. There is no hurry for Hurree. They were at Leh not so long ago. They said they had come down from the Karakorum with their heads and horns and all. I am onlee afraid they will have sent back all their letters and compromising things from Leh into Russian territoree. Of course they will walk away as far to the east as possible – just to show that they were never among the western states. You do not know the Hills?' He scratched with a twig on the earth. 'Look! They should have come in by Srinagar or Abbottabad. *Thatt* is their short road – down the river by Bunji and Astor. But they have made mischief in the west. So' – he drew a furrow from left to right – 'they march and they march away east to Leh (ah! it is cold there), and down the Indus to Han-lé (I know that road), and then down, you see, to Bushahr and Chini valley. That is ascertained by process of elimination, and also by asking questions from people that I cure so well. Our friends have been a long time playing about and producing impressions. So they are well known from far off. You will see me catch them somewhere in Chini valley. Please keep your eye on the umbrella.'

It nodded like a wind-blown harebell down the valleys and round the mountain sides, and in due time the lama and Kim, who steered by compass, would overhaul it, vending ointments and powders at eventide. 'We came by such and such a way!' The lama would throw a careless finger backward at the ridges, and the umbrella would expend itself in compliments.

They crossed a snowy pass in cold moonlight, when the lama, mildly chaffing Kim, went through up to his knees, like a bactrian camel – the snow-bred, shag-haired

sort that come into the Kashmir Serai. They dipped across beds of light snow and snow-powdered shale, where they took refuge from a gale in a camp of Tibetans hurrying down tiny sheep, each laden with a bag of borax. They came out upon grassy shoulders still snow-speckled, and through forest, to grass anew. For all their marchings, Kedarnath and Badrinath were not impressed; and it was only after days of travel that Kim, uplifted upon some insignificant ten-thousand-foot hummock, could see that a shoulder-knot or horn of the two great lords had – ever so slightly – changed outline.

At last they entered a world within a world – a valley of leagues where the high hills were fashioned of the mere rubble and refuse from off the knees of the mountains. Here one day's march carried them no farther, it seemed, than a dreamer's clogged pace bears him in a nightmare. They skirted a shoulder painfully for hours, and, behold, it was but an outlying boss in an outlying buttress of the main pile! A rounded meadow revealed itself, when they had reached it, for a vast tableland running far into the valley. Three days later, it was a dim fold in the earth to the southward.

'Surely the Gods live here!' said Kim, beaten down by the silence and the appalling sweep and dispersal of the cloud-shadows after rain. 'This is no place for men!'

'Long and long ago,' said the lama, as to himself, 'it was asked of the Lord whether the world were everlasting. To this the Excellent One returned no answer . . . When I was in Ceylon, a wise Seeker confirmed that from the Gospel which is written in Pali. Certainly, since we know the way to Freedom, the question were unprofitable, but – look, and know illusion, *chela*! These are the

true Hills! They are like my hills by Such-zen. Never were such hills!'

Above them, still enormously above them, earth towered away towards the snow-line, where from east to west across hundreds of miles, ruled as with a ruler, the last of the bold birches stopped. Above that, in scarps and blocks upheaved, the rocks strove to fight their heads above the white smother. Above these again, changeless since the world's beginning, but changing to every mood of sun and cloud, lay out the eternal snow. They could see blots and blurs on its face where storm and wandering wullie-wa got up to dance. Below them, as they stood, the forest slid away in a sheet of blue-green for mile upon mile; below the forest was a village in its sprinkle of terraced fields and steep grazing grounds. Below the village they knew, though a thunderstorm worried and growled there for the moment, a pitch of twelve or fifteen hundred feet gave to the moist valley where the streams gather that are the mothers of young Sutluj.

As usual, the lama had led Kim by cow-track and by-road, far from the main route along which Hurree Babu, that 'fearful man', had bucketed three days before through a storm to which nine Englishmen out of ten would have given full right of way. Hurree was no game-shot – the snick of a trigger made him change colour – but, as he himself would have said, he was 'fairly effeecient stalker', and he had raked the huge valley with a pair of cheap binoculars to some purpose. Moreover, the white of worn canvas tents against green carries far. Hurree Babu had seen all he wanted to see when he sat on the threshing-floor of Ziglaur, twenty miles away as

the eagle flies, and forty by road – that is to say, two small dots which one day were just below the snow-line, and the next had moved downward perhaps six inches on the hillside. Once cleaned out and set to the work, his fat bare legs could cover a surprising amount of ground, and this was the reason why, while Kim and the lama lay in a leaky hut at Ziglaur till the storm should be overpast, an oily, wet, but always smiling Bengali, talking the best of English with the vilest of phrases, was ingratiating himself with two sodden and rather rheumatic foreigners. He had arrived, revolving many wild schemes, on the heels of a thunderstorm which had split a pine over against their camp, and so convinced a dozen or two forcibly impressed baggage-coolies the day was inauspicious for farther travel that with one accord they had thrown down their loads and jibbed. They were subjects of a hill rajah who farmed out their services, as is the custom, for his private gain; and, to add to their personal distresses, the strange sahibs had already threatened them with rifles. The most of them knew rifles and sahibs of old: they were trackers and *shikarris* of the northern valleys, keen after bear and wild goat; but they had never been thus treated in their lives. So the forest took them to her bosom, and, for all oaths and clamour, refused to restore. There was no need to feign madness or – the babu had thought of another means of securing a welcome. He wrung out his wet clothes, slipped on his patent-leather shoes, opened the blue-and-white umbrella, and with mincing gait and a heart beating against his tonsils appeared as 'agent for His Royal Highness the Rajah of Rampur, gentlemen. What can I do for you, please?'

The gentlemen were delighted. One was visibly

French, the other Russian, but they spoke English not much inferior to the babu's. They begged his kind offices. Their native servants had gone sick at Leh. They had hurried on because they were anxious to bring the spoils of the chase to Simla ere the skins grew moth-eaten. They bore a general letter of introduction (the babu salaamed to it orientally) to all government officials. No, they had not met any other shooting-parties *en route*. They did for themselves. They had plenty of supplies. They only wished to push on as soon as might be. At this he waylaid a cowering hillman among the trees, and after three minutes' talk and a little silver (one cannot be economical upon state service, though Hurree's heart bled at the waste) the eleven coolies and the three hangers-on reappeared. At least the babu would be a witness to their oppression.

'My royal master, he will be much annoyed, but these people are onlee common people and grossly ignorant. If your honours will kindly overlook unfortunate affair, I shall be much pleased. In a little while rain will stop and we can then proceed. You have been shooting, eh? That is fine performance!'

He skipped nimbly from one *kilta* to the next, making pretence to adjust each conical basket. The Englishman is not, as a rule, familiar with the Asiatic, but he would not strike across the wrist a kindly babu who had accidentally upset a *kilta* with a red oilskin top. On the other hand, he would not press drink upon a babu were he never so friendly, nor would he invite him to meat. The strangers did all these things, and asked many questions – about women mostly – to which Hurree returned gay and unstudied answers. They gave him a glass of whitish

fluid like to gin, and then more; and in a little time his gravity departed from him. He became thickly treasonous, and spoke in terms of sweeping indecency of a government which had forced upon him a white man's education and neglected to supply him with a white man's salary. He babbled tales of oppression and wrong till the tears ran down his cheeks for the miseries of his land. Then he staggered off, singing love-songs of Lower Bengal, and collapsed upon a wet tree-trunk. Never was so unfortunate a product of English rule in India more unhappily thrust upon aliens.

'They are all just of that pattern,' said one sportsman to the other in French. 'When we get into India proper thou wilt see. I should like to visit his rajah. One might speak the good word there. It is possible that he has heard of us and wishes to signify his goodwill.'

'We have not time. We must get into Simla as soon as may be,' his companion replied. 'For my own part, I wish our reports had been sent back from Hilás, or even Leh.'

'The English post is better and safer. Remember we are given all facilities – and Name of God! – they gave them to us too! Is it unbelievable stupidity?'

'It is pride – pride that deserves and will receive punishment.'

'Yes! To fight a fellow-continental in our game is something. There is a risk attached, but these people – bah! It is too easy.'

'Pride – all pride, my friend.'

'Now what the deuce is good of Chandernagore being so close to Calcutta and all,' said Hurree, snoring open-mouthed on the sodden moss, 'if I cannot understand

their French? They talk so particularly fast! It would have been much better to cut their beastly throats.'

When he presented himself again he was racked with a headache – penitent, and volubly afraid that in his drunkenness he might have been indiscreet. He loved the British government – it was the source of all prosperity and honour, and his master at Rampur held the very same opinion. Upon this the men began to deride him and to quote past words, till step by step, with deprecating smirks, oily grins, and leers of infinite cunning, the poor babu was beaten out of his defences and forced to speak – truth. When Lurgan was told the tale later, he mourned aloud that he could not have been in the place of the stubborn, inattentive coolies, who with grass mats over their heads and the raindrops puddling in their footprints, waited on the weather. All the sahibs of their acquaintance – rough-clad men joyously returning year after year to their chosen gullies – had servants and cooks and orderlies, very often hillmen. These sahibs travelled without any retinue. Therefore they were poor sahibs, and ignorant; for no sahib in his senses would follow a Bengali's advice. But the Bengali, appearing from somewhere, had given them money, and could make shift with their dialect. Used to comprehensive ill-treatment from their own colour, they suspected a trap somewhere, and stood by to run if occasion offered.

Then through the new-washed air, steaming with delicious earth-smells, the babu led the way down the slopes – walking ahead of the coolies in pride; walking behind the foreigners in humility. His thoughts were many and various. The least of them would have interested his companions beyond words. But he was an

317

agreeable guide, ever keen to point out the beauties of his royal master's domain. He peopled the hills with anything they had a mind to slay – thar, ibex, or markhor, and bear by Elisha's allowance. He discoursed of botany and ethnology with unimpeachable inaccuracy, and his store of local legends – he had been a trusted agent of the state for fifteen years, remember – was inexhaustible.

'Decidedly this fellow is an original,' said the taller of the two foreigners. 'He is like the nightmare of a Viennese courier.'

'He represents in little India in transition – the monstrous hybridism of East and West,' the Russian replied. 'It is *we* who can deal with Orientals.'

'He has lost his own country and has not acquired any other. But he has a most complete hatred of his conquerors. Listen. He confided to me last night,' said the other.

Under the striped umbrella Hurree Babu was straining ear and brain to follow the quick-poured French, and keeping both eyes on a *kilta* full of maps and documents – an extra-large one with a double red oilskin cover. He did not wish to steal anything. He only desired to know what to steal, and, incidentally, how to get away when he had stolen it. He thanked all the Gods of Hindustan, and Herbert Spencer, that there remained some valuables to steal.

On the second day the road rose steeply to a grass spur above the forest; and it was here, about sunset, that they came across an aged lama – but they called him a bonze – sitting cross-legged above a mysterious chart held down by stones, which he was explaining to a young man, evidently a neophyte, of singular, though unwashen,

beauty. The striped umbrella had been sighted half a march away, and Kim had suggested a halt till it came up to them.

'Ha!' said Hurree Babu, resourceful as Puss-in-Boots. 'That is eminent local holy man. Probably subject of my royal master.'

'What is he doing? It is very curious.'

'He is expounding holy picture – *all* hand-worked.'

The two men stood bareheaded in the wash of the afternoon sunlight low across the gold-coloured grass. The sullen coolies, glad of the check, halted and slid down their loads.

'Look!' said the Frenchman. 'It is like a picture for the birth of a religion – the first teacher and the first disciple. Is he a Buddhist?'

'Of some debased kind,' the other answered. 'There are no true Buddhists among the Hills. But look at the folds of the drapery. Look at his eyes – how insolent! Why does this make one feel that we are so young a people?' The speaker struck passionately at a tall weed. 'We have nowhere left our mark yet. Nowhere! *That*, do you understand, is what disquiets me.' He scowled at the placid face, and the monumental calm of the pose.

'Have patience. We shall make your mark together – we and you young people. Meantime, draw his picture.'

The babu advanced loftily; his back out of all keeping with his deferential speech, or his wink towards Kim.

'Holy One, these be sahibs. My medicines cured one of a flux, and I go into Simla to oversee his recovery. They wish to see thy picture –'

'To heal the sick is always good. This is the Wheel of Life,' said the lama, 'the same I showed thee in the hut at Ziglaur when the rain fell.'

'And to hear thee expound it.'

The lama's eyes lighted at the prospect of new listeners. 'To expound the Most Excellent Way is good. Have they any knowledge of Hindi, such as had the Keeper of Images?'

'A little, maybe.'

Hereat, simply as a child engrossed with a new game, the lama threw back his head and began the full-throated invocation of the Doctor of Divinity ere he opens the full doctrine. The strangers leaned on their alpenstocks and listened. Kim, squatting humbly, watched the red sunlight on their faces, and the blend and parting of their long shadows. They wore un-English leggings and curious girt-in belts that reminded him hazily of the pictures in a book in St Xavier's library: *The Adventures of a Young Naturalist in Mexico* was its name. Yes, they looked very like the wonderful M. Sumichrast of that tale, and very unlike the 'highly unscrupulous folk' of Hurree Babu's imagining. The coolies, earth-coloured and mute, crouched reverently some twenty or thirty yards away, and the babu, the slack of his thin gear snapping like a marking-flag in the chill breeze, stood by with an air of happy proprietorship.

'These are the men,' Hurree whispered, as the ritual went on and the two whites followed the grass-blade sweeping from Hell to Heaven and back again. 'All their books are in the large *kilta* with the reddish top – books and reports and maps – and I have seen a king's letter that either Hilás or Bunár has written. They guard it most

carefully. They have sent nothing back from Hilás or Leh. That is sure.'

'Who is with them?'

'Only the *beegar*-coolies. They have no servants. They are so close they cook their own food.'

'But what am I to do?'

'Wait and see. Only if any chance comes to me thou wilt know where to seek for the papers.'

'This were better in Mahbub Ali's hands than a Bengali's,' said Kim scornfully.

'There are more ways of getting to a sweetheart than butting down a wall.'

'See here the Hell appointed for avarice and greed. Flanked upon the one side by Desire and on the other by Weariness.' The lama warmed to his work, and one of the strangers sketched him in the quick-fading light.

'That is enough,' the man said at last brusquely. 'I cannot understand him, but I want that picture. He is a better artist than I. Ask him if he will sell it.'

'He says "No, sar,"' the babu replied. The lama, of course, would no more have parted with his chart to a casual wayfarer than an archbishop would pawn the holy vessels of the cathedral. All Tibet is full of cheap reproductions of the Wheel; but the lama was an artist, as well as a wealthy abbot in his own place.

'Perhaps in three days, or four, or ten, if I perceive that the sahib is a Seeker and of good understanding, I may myself draw him another. But *this* was used for the initiation of a novice. Tell him so, *hakim*.'

'He wishes it now – for money.'

The lama shook his head slowly and began to fold up

the Wheel. The Russian, on his side, saw no more than an unclean old man haggling over a dirty piece of paper. He drew out a handful of rupees, and snatched half-jestingly at the chart, which tore in the lama's grip. A low murmur of horror went up from the coolies – some of whom were Spiti men and, by their lights, good Buddhists. The lama rose at the insult; his hand went to the heavy iron pen-case that is the priest's weapon, and the babu danced in agony.

'Now you see – you see why I wanted witnesses. They are highly unscrupulous people. Oh, sar! sar! You must *not* hit holy man!'

'*Chela!* He has defiled the Written Word!'

It was too late. Before Kim could ward him off, the Russian struck the old man full on the face. Next instant he was rolling over and over downhill with Kim at his throat. The blow had waked every unknown Irish devil in the boy's blood, and the sudden fall of his enemy did the rest. The lama dropped to his knees, half-stunned; the coolies under their loads fled up the hill as fast as plainsmen run across the level. They had seen sacrilege unspeakable, and it behoved them to get away before the Gods and devils of the hills took vengeance. The French-man ran towards the lama, fumbling at his revolver with some notion of making him a hostage for his companion. A shower of cutting stones – hillmen are very straight shots – drove him away, and a coolie from Ao-chung snatched the lama into the stampede. All came about as swiftly as the sudden mountain darkness.

'They have taken the baggage and all the guns,' yelled the Frenchman, firing blindly into the twilight.

'All right, sar! All right! Don't shoot. I go to rescue,'

and Hurree, pounding down the slope, cast himself bodily upon the delighted and astonished Kim, who was banging his breathless foe's head against a boulder.

'Go back to the coolies,' whispered the babu in his ear. 'They have the baggage. The papers are in the *kilta* with the red top, but look through all. Take their papers, and specially the *murasla* [king's letter]. Go! The other man comes!'

Kim tore uphill. A revolver bullet rang on a rock by his side, and he cowered partridge-wise.

'If you shoot,' shouted Hurree, 'they will descend and annihilate us. I have rescued the gentleman, sar. This is particularly dangerous.'

'By Jove!' Kim was thinking hard in English. 'This is dam'-tight place, but *I* think it is self-defence.' He felt in his bosom for Mahbub's gift, and uncertainly – save for a few practice shots in the Bikanir desert, he had never used the little gun – pulled trigger.

'What did I say, sar!' The babu seemed to be in tears. 'Come down here and assist to resuscitate. We are all up a tree, I tell you.'

The shots ceased. There was a sound of stumbling feet, and Kim hurried upward through the gloom, swearing like a cat – or a country-bred.

'Did they wound thee, *chela*?' called the lama above him.

'No. And thou?' He dived into a clump of stunted firs.

'Unhurt. Come away. We go with these folk to Shamlegh-under-the-Snow.'

'But not before we have done justice,' a voice cried. 'I have got the sahibs' guns – all four. Let us go down.'

'He struck the Holy One – we saw it! Our cattle will be

barren – our wives will cease to bear! The snows will slide upon us as we go home . . . Atop of all other oppression too!'

The little fir clump filled with clamouring coolies – panic-stricken, and in their terror capable of anything. The man from Ao-chung clicked the breech-bolt of his gun impatiently, and made as to go downhill.

'Wait a little, Holy One; they cannot go far. Wait till I return,' said he.

'It is this person who has suffered wrong,' said the lama, his hand over his brow.

'For that very reason,' was the reply.

'If this person overlooks it, your hands are clean. Moreover, ye acquire merit by obedience.'

'Wait, and we will all go to Shamlegh together,' the man insisted.

For a moment, for just so long as it needs to stuff a cartridge into a breech-loader, the lama hesitated. Then he rose to his feet, and laid a finger on the man's shoulder.

'Hast thou heard? *I* say there shall be no killing – I who was Abbot of Such-zen. Is it any lust of thine to be re-born as a rat, or a snake under the eaves – a worm in the belly of the most mean beast? Is it thy wish to –'

The man from Ao-chung fell to his knees, for the voice boomed like a Tibetan devil-gong.

'Ai! ai!' cried the Spiti men. 'Do not curse us – do not curse him. It was but his zeal, Holy One! . . . Put down the rifle, fool!'

'Anger on anger! Evil on evil! There will be no killing. Let the priest-beaters go in bondage to their own acts. Just and sure is the Wheel, swerving not a hair! They will

be born many times – in torment.' His head drooped, and he leaned heavily on Kim's shoulder.

'I have come near to great evil, *chela*,' he whispered in that dead hush under the pines. 'I was tempted to loose the bullet; and truly, in Tibet there would have been a heavy and a slow death for them . . . He struck me across the face . . . upon the flesh . . .' He slid to the ground, breathing heavily, and Kim could hear the over-driven heart bump and check.

'Have they hurt him to the death?' said the Ao-chung man, while the others stood mute.

Kim knelt over the body in deadly fear. 'Nay,' he cried passionately, 'this is only a weakness.' Then he remembered that he was a white man, with a white man's camp-fittings at his service. 'Open the *kiltas*! The sahibs may have a medicine.'

'Oho! Then I know it,' said the Ao-chung man with a laugh. 'Not for five years was I Yankling Sahib's *shikarri* without knowing that medicine. I too have tasted it. Behold!'

He drew from his breast a bottle of cheap whisky – such as is sold to explorers at Leh – and cleverly forced a little between the lama's teeth.

'So I did when Yankling Sahib twisted his foot beyond Astor. Aha! I have already looked into their baskets – but we will make fair division at Shamlegh. Give him a little more. It is good medicine. Feel! His heart goes better now. Lay his head down and rub a little on his chest. If he had waited quietly while I accounted for the sahibs this would never have come. But perhaps the sahibs may chase us here. Then it would not be wrong to shoot them with their own guns, heh?'

'One is paid, I think, already,' said Kim between his teeth. 'I kicked him in the groin as we went downhill. Would I had killed him!'

'It is well to be brave when one does not live in Rampur,' said one whose hut lay within a few miles of the rajah's rickety palace. 'If we get a bad name among the sahibs, none will employ us as *shikarris* any more.'

'Oh, but these are not Angrezi sahibs – not merry-minded men like Fostum Sahib or Yankling Sahib. They are foreigners – they cannot speak Angrezi as do sahibs.'

Here the lama coughed and sat up, groping for the rosary.

'There shall be no killing,' he murmured. 'Just is the Wheel! Evil on evil –'

'Nay, Holy One. We are all here.' The Ao-chung man timidly patted his feet. 'Except by thy order, no one shall be slain. Rest awhile. We will make a little camp here, and later, as the moon rises, we go to Shamlegh-under-the-Snow.'

'After a blow,' said a Spiti man sententiously, 'it is best to sleep.'

'There is, as it were, a dizziness at the back of my neck, and a pinching in it. Let me lay my head on thy lap, *chela*. I am an old man, but not free from passion . . . We must think of the Cause of Things.'

'Give him a blanket. We dare not light a fire lest the sahibs see.'

'Better get away to Shamlegh. None will follow us to Shamlegh.'

This was the nervous Rampur man.

'I have been Fostum Sahib's *shikarri*, and I am Yankling Sahib's *shikarri*. I should have been with Yankling Sahib

now but for this cursed *beegar* [the *corvée*]. Let two men watch below with the guns lest the sahibs do more foolishness. *I* shall not leave this Holy One.'

They sat down a little apart from the lama, and, after listening awhile, passed round a water-pipe whose receiver was an old Day and Martin blacking-bottle. The glow of the red charcoal as it went from hand to hand lit up the narrow, blinking eyes, the high Chinese cheek-bones, and the bull throats that melted away into the dark duffle folds round the shoulders. They looked like kobolds from some magic mine – gnomes of the hills in conclave. And while they talked, the voices of the snow-waters round them diminished one by one as the night-frost choked and clogged the runnels.

'How he stood up against us!' said a Spiti man admiring. 'I remember an old ibex, out Ladakh way, that Dupont Sahib missed on a shoulder-shot, seven seasons back, standing up just like him. Dupont Sahib was a good *shikarri*.'

'Not as good as Yankling Sahib.' The Ao-chung man took a pull at the whisky bottle and passed it over. 'Now hear me – unless any other man thinks he knows more.'

The challenge was not taken up.

'We go to Shamlegh when the moon rises. There we will fairly divide the baggage between us. I am content with this new little rifle and all its cartridges.'

'Are the bears only bad on thy holding?' said a mate, sucking at his pipe.

'No; but musk-pods are worth six rupees apiece now, and thy women can have the canvas of the tents and some of the cooking-gear. We will do all that at Shamlegh before dawn. Then we all go our ways, remembering that

we have never seen or taken service with these sahibs, who may, indeed, say that we have stolen their baggage.'

'That is well for thee, but what will our rajah say?'

'Who is to tell him? Those sahibs, who cannot speak our talk, or the babu, who for his own ends gave us money? Will *he* lead an army against us? What evidence will remain? That we do not need we shall throw on Shamlegh-midden, where no man has yet set foot.'

'Who is at Shamlegh this summer?' The place was only a grazing centre of three or four huts.

'The Woman of Shamlegh. *She* has no love for sahibs, as we know. The others can be pleased with little presents; and here is enough for us all.' He patted the fat sides of the nearest basket.

'But – but –'

'I have said they are not true sahibs. *All* their skins and heads were bought in the bazaar at Leh. I know the marks. I showed them to ye last march.'

'True. They were all bought skins and heads. Some had even the moth in them.'

That was a shrewd argument, and the Ao-chung man knew his fellows.

'If the worst comes to the worst, I shall tell Yankling Sahib, who is a man of a merry mind, and he will laugh. We are not doing any wrong to any sahibs whom we know. *They* are priest-beaters. They frightened us. We fled! Who knows where we dropped the baggage? Do ye think Yankling Sahib will permit down-country police to wander all over the hills, disturbing his game? It is a far cry from Simla to Chini, and farther from Shamlegh to Shamlegh-midden.'

'So be it, but I carry the big *kilta*. The basket with the red top that the sahibs pack themselves every morning.'

'Thus it is proved,' said the Shamlegh man adroitly, 'that they are sahibs of no account. Who ever heard of Fostum Sahib, or Yankling Sahib, or even the little Peel Sahib that sits up at nights to shoot serow – I say, who ever heard of these sahibs coming into the hills without a down-country cook, and a bearer, and – and all manner of well-paid, high-handed and oppressive folk in their tail? How can *they* make trouble? What of the *kilta*?'

'Nothing, but that it is full of the Written Word – books and papers in which they wrote, and strange instruments, as of worship.'

'Shamlegh-midden will take them all.'

'True! But how if we insult the sahibs' Gods thereby? I do not like to handle the Written Word in that fashion. And their brass idols are beyond my comprehension. It is no plunder for simple hill-folk.'

'The old man still sleeps. Hst! We will ask his *chela*.' The Ao-chung man refreshed himself, and swelled with pride of leadership.

'We have here,' he whispered, 'a *kilta* whose nature we do not know.'

'But I do,' said Kim cautiously. The lama drew breath in natural, easy sleep, and Kim had been thinking of Hurree's last words. As a player of the Great Game, he was disposed just then to reverence the babu. 'It is a *kilta* with a red top full of very wonderful things, not to be handled by fools.'

'I said it; I said it,' cried the bearer of that burden. 'Thinkest thou it will betray us?'

'Not if it be given to me. I can draw out its magic. Otherwise it will do great harm.'

'A priest always takes his share.' Whisky was demoralizing the Ao-chung man.

'It is no matter to me,' Kim answered, with the craft of his mother-country. 'Share it among you, and see what comes!'

'Not I. I was only jesting. Give the order. There is more than enough for us all. We go our way from Shamlegh in the dawn.'

They arranged and rearranged their artless little plans for another hour, while Kim shivered with cold and pride. The humour of the situation tickled the Irish and the Oriental in his soul. Here were the emissaries of the dread Power of the North, very possibly as great in their own land as Mahbub or Colonel Creighton, suddenly smitten helpless. One of them, he privately knew, would be lame for a time. They had made promises to kings. Tonight they lay out somewhere below him, chartless, foodless, tentless, gunless – except for Hurree Babu, guideless. And this collapse of their Great Game (Kim wondered to whom they would report it), this panicky bolt into the night, had come about through no craft of Hurree's or contrivance of Kim's, but simply, beautifully, and inevitably as the capture of Mahbub's *fakir* friends by the zealous young policeman at Umballa.

'They are there – with nothing; and, by Jove, it is cold! I am here with all their things. Oh, they will be angry! I am sorry for Hurree Babu.'

Kim might have saved his pity, for though at that moment the Bengali suffered acutely in the flesh, his soul was puffed and lofty. A mile down the hill, on the edge of

the pine forest, two half-frozen men – one powerfully sick at intervals – were varying mutual recriminations with the most poignant abuse of the babu, who seemed distraught with terror. They demanded a plan of action. He explained that they were very lucky to be alive; that their coolies, if not then stalking them, had passed beyond recall; that the rajah, his master, was ninety miles away, and, so far from lending them money and a retinue for the Simla journey, would surely cast them into prison if he heard that they had hit a priest. He enlarged on this sin and its consequences till they bade him change the subject. Their one hope, said he, was unostentatious flight from village to village till they reached civilization; and, for the hundredth time dissolved in tears, he demanded of the high stars why the sahibs 'had beaten holy man'.

Ten steps would have taken Hurree into the creaking gloom utterly beyond their reach – to the shelter and food of the nearest village, where glib-tongued doctors were scarce. But he preferred to endure cold, belly-pinch, bad words, and occasional blows in the company of his honoured employers. Crouched against a tree-trunk, he sniffed dolefully.

'And have you thought,' said the uninjured man hotly, 'what sort of spectacle we shall present wandering through these hills among these aborigines?'

Hurree Babu had thought of little else for some hours, but the remark was not to his address.

'We cannot wander! I can hardly walk,' groaned Kim's victim.

'Perhaps the holy man will be merciful in loving-kindness, sar, otherwise –'

'I promise myself a peculiar pleasure in emptying my revolver into that young bonze when next we meet,' was the unchristian answer.

'Revolvers! Vengeance! Bonzes!' Hurree crouched lower. The war was breaking out afresh. 'Have you no consideration for our loss? The baggage! The baggage!' He could hear the speaker literally dancing on the grass. 'Everything we bore! Everything we have secured! Our gains! Eight months' work! Do you know what that means? "Decidedly it is we who can deal with Orientals!" Oh, you have done well.'

They fell to it in several tongues, and Hurree smiled. Kim was with the *kiltas*, and in the *kiltas* lay eight months of good diplomacy. There was no means of communicating with the boy, but he could be trusted. For the rest, Hurree could so stage-manage the journey through the hills that Hilás, Bunár, and four hundred miles of hill roads should tell the tale for a generation. Men who cannot control their own coolies are little respected in the Hills, and the hillman has a very keen sense of humour.

'If I had done it myself,' thought Hurree, 'it would not have been better; and, by Jove, now I think of it, of course I arranged it myself. How quick I have been! Just when I ran downhill I thought it! Thee outrage was accidental, but onlee me could have worked it – ah – for all it was dam'-well worth. Consider the moral effect upon these ignorant peoples! No treaties – no papers – no written documents at all – and *me* to interpret for them. How I shall laugh with the Colonel! I wish I had their papers also: but you cannot occupy two places in space simultaneously. Thatt is axiomatic.'

CHAPTER
14

My brother kneels (so saith Kabir)
 To stone and brass in heathen wise,
But in my brother's voice I hear
 My own unanswered agonies.
His God is as his Fates assign –
His prayer is all the world's – and mine.

 The Prayer

At moonrise the cautious coolies got under way. The lama, refreshed by his sleep and the spirit, needed no more than Kim's shoulder to bear him along – a silent, swift-striding man. They held the shale-sprinkled grass for an hour, swept round the shoulder of an immortal cliff, and climbed into a new country entirely blocked off from all sight of Chini valley. A huge pasture-ground ran up fan-shaped to the living snow. At its base was perhaps half an acre of flat land, on which stood a few soil and timber huts. Behind them – for, hill-fashion, they were perched on the edge of all things – the ground fell sheer two thousand feet to Shamlegh-midden, where never yet man has set foot.

The men made no motion to divide the plunder till they had seen the lama bedded down in the best room of the place, with Kim shampooing his feet, Muhammadan-fashion.

'We will send food,' said the Ao-chung man, 'and the red-topped *kilta*. By dawn there will be none to give

evidence, one way or the other. If anything is not needed in the *kilta* – see here!'

He pointed through the window – opening into space that was filled with moonlight reflected from the snow – and threw out an empty whisky bottle.

'No need to listen for the fall. This is the world's end,' he said, and went out. The lama looked forth, a hand on either sill, with eyes that shone like yellow opals. From the enormous pit before him white peaks lifted themselves yearning to the moonlight. The rest was as the darkness of interstellar space.

'These,' he said slowly, 'are indeed my Hills. Thus should a man abide, perched above the world, separated from delights, considering vast matters.'

'Yes; if he has a *chela* to prepare tea for him, and to fold a blanket for his head, and to chase out calving cows.'

A smoky lamp burned in a niche, but the full moonlight beat it down; and by the mixed light, stooping above the food cups and bags, Kim moved like a tall ghost.

'*Ai!* But now I have let the blood cool, my head still beats and drums, and there is a cord round the back of my neck.'

'No wonder. It was a strong blow. May he who dealt it –'

'But for my own passions there would have been no evil.'

'What evil? Thou hast saved the sahibs from the death they deserved a hundred times.'

'The lesson is not well learnt, *chela*.' The lama came to rest on a folded blanket, as Kim went forward with his evening routine. 'The blow was but a shadow upon a shadow. Evil in itself – my legs weary apace these latter

days! – it met evil in me – anger, rage, and a lust to return evil. These wrought in my blood, woke tumult in my stomach, and dazzled my ears.' Here he drank scalding block-tea ceremonially, taking the hot cup from Kim's hand. 'Had I been passionless, the evil blow would have done only bodily evil – a scar, or a bruise – which is illusion. But my mind was *not* abstracted, for rushed in straightway a lust to let the Spiti men kill. In fighting that lust, my soul was torn and wrenched beyond a thousand blows. Not till I had repeated the Blessings' (he meant the Buddhist Beatitudes) 'did I achieve calm. But the evil planted in me by that moment's carelessness works out to its end. Just is the Wheel, swerving not a hair! Learn the lesson, *chela*.'

'It is too high for me,' Kim muttered. 'I am still all shaken. I am glad I hurt the man.'

'I felt that, sleeping upon thy knees, in the wood below. It disquieted me in my dreams – the evil in thy soul working through to mine. Yet on the other hand' – he loosed his rosary – 'I have acquired merit by saving two lives – the lives of those that wronged me. Now I must see into the Cause of Things. The boat of my soul staggers.'

'Sleep, and be strong. That is wisest.'

'I meditate. There is a need greater than thou knowest.'

Till the dawn, hour after hour, as the moonlight paled on the high peaks, and that which had been belted blackness on the sides of the far hills showed as tender green forest, the lama stared fixedly at the wall. From time to time he groaned. Outside the barred door, where discomfited kine came to ask for their old stable, Shamlegh and the coolies gave itself up to plunder and riotous

living. The Ao-chung man was their leader, and once they had opened the sahibs' tinned foods and found that they were very good they dared not turn back. Shamlegh kitchen-midden took the dunnage.

When Kim, after a night of bad dreams, stole forth to brush his teeth in the morning chill, a fair-coloured woman with turquoise-studded headgear drew him aside.

'The others have gone. They left thee this *kilta* as the promise was. I do not love sahibs, but thou wilt make us a charm in return for it. We do not wish little Shamlegh to get a bad name on account of the – accident. I am the Woman of Shamlegh.' She looked him over with bold, bright eyes, unlike the usual furtive glance of hillwomen.

'Assuredly. But it must be done in secret.'

She raised the heavy *kilta* like a toy and slung it into her own hut.

'Out and bar the door! Let none come near till it is finished,' said Kim.

'But afterwards – we may talk?'

Kim tilted the *kilta* on the floor – a cascade of survey-instruments, books, diaries, letters, maps, and queerly scented native correspondence. At the very bottom was an embroidered bag covering a sealed, gilded, and illu-minated document such as one king sends to another. Kim caught his breath with delight, and reviewed the situation from a sahib's point of view.

'The books I do not want. Besides, they are logarithms – survey, I suppose.' He laid them aside. 'The letters I do not understand, but Colonel Creighton will. They must all be kept. The maps – they draw better maps than me – *of* course. All the native letters – oho! – and particularly

the *murasla*.' He sniffed the embroidered bag. 'That must be from Hilás or Bunár, and Hurree Babu spoke truth. By Jove! It is a fine haul. I wish Hurree could know . . . The rest must go out of the window.' He fingered a superb prismatic compass and the shiny top of a theodolite. But after all, a sahib cannot very well steal, and the things might be inconvenient evidence later. He sorted out every scrap of manuscript, every map, and the native letters. They made one softish slab. The three locked ferril-backed books, with five worn pocket-books, he put aside.

'The letters and the *murasla* I must carry inside my coat and under my belt, and the handwritten books I must put into the food-bag. It will be very heavy. No. I do not think there is anything more. If there is, the coolies have thrown it down the *khud*, so *thatt* is all right. Now you go too.' He repacked the *kilta* with all he meant to lose, and hove it up on to the windowsill. A thousand feet below lay a long, lazy, round-shouldered bank of mist, as yet untouched by the morning sun. A thousand feet below that was a hundred-year-old pine-forest. He could see the green tops looking like a bed of moss when a wind eddy thinned the cloud.

'No! I don't think any one will go after *you*!'

The wheeling basket vomited its contents as it dropped. The theodolite hit a jutting cliff ledge and exploded like a shell; the books, inkstands, paintboxes, compasses, and rulers showed for a few seconds like a swarm of bees. Then they vanished; and, though Kim, hanging half out of the window, strained his young ears, never a sound came up from the gulf.

'Five hundred – a thousand rupees could not buy

337

them,' he thought sorrowfully. 'It was verree wasteful, but I have all their other stuff – everything they did – I hope. Now how the deuce am I to tell Hurree Babu, and *whatt* the deuce am I to do? And my old man is sick. I must tie up the letters in oilskin. That is something to do first – else they will get all sweated . . . And I am all alone!' He bound them into a neat packet, swedging down the stiff, sticky oilskin at the corners, for his roving life had made him as methodical as an old hunter in matters of the road. Then with double care he packed away the books at the bottom of the food-bag.

The woman rapped at the door.

'But thou hast made no charm,' she said, looking about.

'There is no need.' Kim had completely overlooked the necessity for a little patter-talk. The woman laughed at his confusion irreverently.

'None – for thee. Thou canst cast a spell by the mere winking of an eye. But think of us poor people when thou art gone! They were all too drunk last night to hear a woman. Thou art not drunk?'

'I am a priest.' Kim had recovered himself, and, the woman being aught but unlovely, thought best to stand on his office.

'I warned them that the sahibs will be angry and will make an inquisition and a report to the rajah. There is also the babu with them. Clerks have long tongues.'

'Is that all thy trouble?' The plan rose fully formed in Kim's mind, and he smiled ravishingly.

'Not all,' quoth the woman, putting out a hard brown hand all covered with turquoises set in silver.

'I can finish that in a breath,' he went on quickly. 'The

babu is the very *hakim* (thou hast heard of him?) who was wandering among the hills by Ziglaur. I know him.'

'He will tell for the sake of a reward. Sahibs cannot distinguish one hillman from another, but babus have eyes for men – and women.'

'Carry a word to him from me.'

'There is nothing I would not do for thee.'

He accepted the compliment calmly, as men must in lands where women make the love, tore a leaf from a notebook, and with a patent indelible pencil wrote in gross Shikast – the script that bad little boys use when they write dirt on walls: 'I have everything that they have written: their pictures of the country, and many letters. Especially the *murasla*. Tell me what to do. I am at Shamlegh-under-the-Snow. The old man is sick.'

'Take this to him. It will altogether shut his mouth. He cannot have gone far.'

'Indeed no. They are still in the forest across the spur. Our children went to watch them when the light came, and have cried the news as they moved.'

Kim looked his astonishment; but from the edge of the sheep-pasture floated a shrill, kite-like trill. A child tending cattle had picked it up from a brother or sister on the far side of the slope that commanded Chini valley.

'My husbands are also out there gathering wood.' She drew a handful of walnuts from her bosom, split one neatly, and began to eat. Kim affected blank ignorance.

'Dost thou not know the meaning of the walnut – priest?' she said coyly, and handed him the half-shells.

'Well thought of.' He slipped the piece of paper between them quickly. 'Hast thou a little wax to close them on this letter?'

The woman sighed aloud, and Kim relented.

'There is no payment till service has been rendered. Carry this to the babu, and say it was sent by the Son of the Charm.'

'*Ai!* Truly! Truly! By a magician – who is like a sahib.'

'Nay, a Son of the Charm: and ask if there be any answer.'

'But if he offer a rudeness? I – I am afraid.'

Kim laughed. 'He is, I have no doubt, very tired and very hungry. The Hills make cold bedfellows. *Hai*, my' – it was on the tip of his tongue to say Mother, but he turned it to Sister – 'though art a wise and witty woman. By this time all the villages know what has befallen the sahibs – eh?'

'True. News was at Ziglaur by midnight, and by tomorrow should be at Kotgarh. The villages are both afraid and angry.'

'No need. Tell the villages to feed the sahibs and pass them on, in peace. We must get them quietly away from our valleys. To steal is one thing – to kill another. The babu will understand, and there will be no after-complaints. Be swift. I must tend my master when he wakes.'

'So be it. After service – thou hast said? – comes the reward. I am the Woman of Shamlegh, and I hold from the rajah. I am no common bearer of babes. Shamlegh is thine: hoof and horn and hide, milk and butter. Take or leave.'

She turned resolutely uphill, her silver necklaces clicking on her broad breast, to meet the morning sun fifteen hundred feet above them. This time Kim thought in the

vernacular as he waxed down the oilskin edges of the packets.

'How can a man follow the Way or the Great Game when he is so-always pestered by women? There was the girl at Akrola of the Ford: and there was the scullion's wife behind the dovecot – not counting the others – and now comes this one! When I was a child it was well enough, but now I am a man and they will not regard me as a man. Walnuts, indeed! Ho! ho! It is almonds in the plains!'

He went out to levy on the village – not with a begging-bowl, which might do for down-country, but in the manner of a prince. Shamlegh's summer population is only three families – four women and eight or nine men. They were all full of tinned meats and mixed drinks, from ammoniated quinine to white vodka, for they had taken their full share in the overnight loot. The neat continental tents had been cut up and shared long ago, and there were patent aluminium saucepans abroad.

But they considered the lama's presence a perfect safeguard against all consequences, and impenitently brought Kim of their best – even to a drink of *chang* – the barley-beer that comes from Ladakh way. Then they thawed out in the sun, and sat with their legs hanging over infinite abysses, chattering, laughing, and smoking. They judged India and its government solely from their experience of wandering sahibs who had employed them or their friends as *shikarris*. Kim heard tales of shots missed upon ibex, serow, or markhor, by sahibs twenty years in their graves – every detail lighted from behind like twigs on tree-tops seen against lightning. They told him of their little diseases, and, more important, the

diseases of their tiny, sure-footed cattle; of trips as far as Kotgarh, where the strange missionaries live, and beyond even to marvellous Simla, where the streets are paved with silver, and any one, look you, can get service with the sahibs, who ride about in two-wheeled carts and spend money with a spade. Presently, grave and aloof, walking very heavily, the lama joined himself to the chatter under the eaves, and they gave him great room. The thin air refreshed him, and he sat on the edge of precipices with the best of them, and, when talk languished, flung pebbles into the void. Thirty miles away, as the eagle flies, lay the next range, seamed and channelled and pitted with little patches of brush – forests, each a day's dark march. Behind the village, Shamlegh hill itself cut off all view to southward. It was like sitting in a swallow's nest under the eaves of the roof of the world.

From time to time the lama stretched out his hand, and with a little low-voiced prompting would point out the road to Spiti and north across the Parungla.

'Beyond, where the hills lie thickest, lies De-ch'en' (he meant Han-lé), 'the great monastery. s'Tag-stan-ras-ch'en built it, and of him there runs this tale.' Whereupon he told it: a fantastic piled narrative of bewitchment and miracles that set Shamlegh a-gasping. Turning west a little, he speered for the green hills of Kulu, and sought Kailung under the glaciers. 'For thither came I in the old, old day. From Leh I came, over the Baralachi.'

'Yes, yes; we know it,' said the far-faring people of Shamlegh.

'And I slept two nights with the priests of Kailung. These are the Hills of my delight! Shadows blessed above

all other shadows! There my eyes opened on this world; there my eyes were opened to this world; there I found Enlightenment; and there I girt my loins for my Search. Out of the Hills I came – the high Hills and the strong winds. Oh, just is the Wheel!' He blessed them in detail – the great glaciers, the naked rocks, the piled moraines and tumbled shale; dry upland, hidden salt-lake, age-old timber and fruitful water-shot valley one after the other, as a dying man blesses his folk; and Kim marvelled at his passion.

'Yes – yes. There is no place like our Hills,' said the people of Shamlegh. And they fell to wondering how a man could live in the hot terrible plains where the cattle run as big as elephants, unfit to plough on a hillside; where village touches village, they had heard, for a hundred miles; where folk went about stealing in gangs, and what the robbers spared the police carried utterly away.

So the still forenoon wore through, and at the end of it Kim's messenger dropped from the steep pasture as unbreathed as when she had set out.

'I sent a word to the *hakim*,' Kim explained, while she made reverence.

'He joined himself to the idolaters? Nay, I remember he did a healing upon one of them. He has acquired merit, though the healed employed his strength for evil. Just is the Wheel! What of the *hakim*?'

'I feared that thou hadst been bruised and – and I knew he was wise.' Kim took the waxed walnut-shell and read in English on the back of his note: 'Your favour received. Cannot get away from present company at present, but shall take them into Simla. After which, hope to rejoin

343

you. Inexpedient to follow angry gentlemen. Return by same road you came, and will overtake. Highly gratified about correspondence due to my forethought.' 'He says, Holy One, that he will escape from the idolaters, and will return to us. Shall we wait awhile at Shamlegh, then?'

The lama looked long and lovingly upon the hills and shook his head.

'That may not be, *chela*. From my bones outward I do desire it, but it is forbidden. I have seen the Cause of Things.'

'Why? When the Hills give thee back thy strength day by day? Remember we were weak and fainting down below there in the Doon.'

'I became strong to do evil and to forget. A brawler and a swashbuckler upon the hillsides was I.' Kim bit back a smile. 'Just and perfect is the Wheel, swerving not a hair. When I was a man – a long time ago – I did pilgrimage to Guru Ch'wan among the poplars' (he pointed Bhotan-wards), 'where they keep the Sacred Horse.'

'Quiet, be quiet!' said Shamlegh, all arow. 'He speaks of Jam-lin-nin-k'or, the Horse That Can Go round the World in a Day.'

'I speak to my *chela* only,' said the lama, in gentle reproof, and they scattered like frost on south eaves of a morning. 'I did not seek truth in those days, but the talk of doctrine. All illusion! I drank the beer and ate the bread of Guru Ch'wan. Next day one said: "We go out to fight Sangor Gutok down the valley to discover" (mark again how lust is tied to anger!) "which abbot shall bear rule in the valley and take the profit of the prayers they print at Sangor Gutok." I went, and we fought a day.'

'But how, Holy One?'

'With our long pen-cases as I could have shown . . . I say, we fought under the poplars, both abbots and all the monks, and one laid open my forehead to the bone. See!' He tilted back his cap and showed a puckered silvery scar. 'Just and perfect is the Wheel! Yesterday the scar itched, and after fifty years I recalled how it was dealt and the face of him who dealt it; dwelling a little in illusion. Followed that which thou didst see – strife and stupidity. Just is the Wheel! The idolater's blow fell upon the scar. Then I was shaken in my soul: my soul was darkened, and the boat of my soul rocked upon the waters of illusion. Not till I came to Shamlegh could I meditate upon the Cause of Things, or trace the running grass roots of Evil. I strove all the long night.'

'But, Holy One, thou art innocent of all evil. May I be thy sacrifice!'

Kim was genuinely distressed at the old man's sorrow, and Mahbub Ali's phrase slipped out unawares.

'In the dawn,' the lama went on more gravely, ready rosary clicking between the slow sentences, 'came enlightenment. It is here . . . I am an old man . . . hill-bred, hill-fed, never to sit down among my Hills. Three years I travelled through Hind, but – can earth be stronger than Mother Earth? My stupid body yearned to the Hills and the snows of the Hills, from below there. I said, and it is true, my Search is sure. So, at the Kulu woman's house I turned hillward, over-persuaded by myself. There is no blame to the *hakim*. He – following Desire – foretold that the Hills would make me strong. They strengthened me to do evil, to forget my Search. I delighted in life and the lust of life. I desired strong slopes to climb. I cast about to

345

find them. I measured the strength of my body, which is evil, against the high Hills. I made a mock of thee when thy breath came short under Jamnotri. I jested when thou wouldst not face the snow of the pass.'

'But what harm? I *was* afraid. It was just. I am not a hillman; and I loved thee for thy new strength.'

'More than once I remember' – he rested his cheek dolefully on his hand – 'I sought thy praise and the *hakim's* for the mere strength of my legs. Thus evil followed evil till the cup was full. Just is the Wheel! All Hind for three years did me all honour. From the Fountain of Wisdom in the Wonder House to' – he smiled – 'a little child playing by a big gun – the world prepared my road. And why?'

'Because we loved thee. It is only the fever of the blow. I myself am still sick and shaken.'

'No! It was because I was upon the Way – tuned as are *si-nen* [cymbals] to the purpose of the Law. I departed from that ordinance. The tune was broken: followed the punishment. In my own Hills, on the edge of my own country, in the very place of my evil desire, comes the buffet – here!' (He touched his brow.) 'As a novice is beaten when he misplaces the cups, so am I beaten, who was Abbot of Such-zen. No word, look you, but a blow, *chela*.'

'But the sahibs did not know thee, Holy One?'

'We were well matched. Ignorance and Lust met Ignorance and Lust upon the road, and they begat Anger. The blow was a sign to me, who am no better than a strayed yak, that my place is not here. Who can read the Cause of an act is half-way to Freedom! "Back to the path," says the Blow. "The Hills are not for thee. Thou canst not

346

choose Freedom and go in bondage to the delight of life."'

'Would we had never met that cursed Russian!'

'Our Lord himself cannot make the Wheel swing backward. And for my merit that I had acquired I gain yet another sign.' He put his hand in his bosom, and drew forth the Wheel of Life. 'Look! I considered this after I had meditated. There remains untorn by the idolater no more than the breadth of my finger-nail.'

'I see.'

'So much, then, is the span of my life in this body. I have served the Wheel all my days. Now the Wheel serves me. But for the merit I have acquired in guiding thee upon the Way, there would have been added to me yet another life ere I had found my River. Is it plain, *chela*?'

Kim stared at the brutally disfigured chart. From left to right diagonally the rent ran – from the Eleventh House where Desire gives birth to the Child (as it is drawn by Tibetans) – across the human and animal worlds, to the Fifth House – the empty House of the Senses. The logic was unanswerable.

'Before our Lord won Enlightenment' – the lama folded all away with reverence – 'he was tempted. I too have been tempted, but it is finished. The Arrow fell in the Plains – not in the Hills. Therefore, what make we here?'

'Shall we at least wait for the *hakim*?'

'I know how long I shall live in this body. What can a *hakim* do?'

'But thou art all sick and shaken. Thou canst not walk.'

'How can I be sick if I see Freedom?' He rose unsteadily to his feet.

'Then I must get food from the village. Oh, the weary Road!' Kim felt that he too needed rest.

'That is lawful. Let us eat and go. The Arrow fell in the Plains . . . but I yielded to Desire. Make ready, *chela*.'

Kim turned to the woman with the turquoise headgear who had been idly pitching pebbles over the cliff. She smiled very kindly.

'I found him like a strayed buffalo in a cornfield – the babu; snorting and sneezing with cold. He was so hungry that he forgot his dignity and gave me sweet words. The sahibs have nothing.' She flung out an empty palm. 'One is very sick about the stomach. Thy work?'

Kim nodded, with a bright eye.

'I spoke to the Bengali first – and to the people of a nearby village after. The sahibs will be given food as they need it – nor will the people ask money. The plunder is already distributed. The babu makes lying speeches to the sahibs. Why does he not leave them?'

'Out of the greatness of his heart.'

'Was never a Bengali yet had one bigger than a dried walnut. But it is no matter . . . Now as to walnuts. After service comes reward. I have said the village is thine.'

'It is my loss,' Kim began. 'Even now I had planned desirable things in my heart which' – there is no need to go through the compliments proper to these occasions. He sighed deeply . . . 'But my master, led by a vision –'

'Huh! What can old eyes see except a full begging-bowl?'

'– turns from this village to the Plains again.'

'Bid him stay.'

Kim shook his head. 'I know my Holy One, and his

rage if he be crossed,' he replied impressively. 'His curses shake the Hills.'

'Pity they did not save him from a broken head! I heard that thou wast the tiger-hearted one who smote the sahib. Let him dream a little longer. Stay!'

'Hillwoman,' said Kim, with austerity that could not harden the outlines of his young oval face, 'these matters are too high for thee.'

'The Gods be good to us! Since when have men and women been other than men and women?'

'A priest is a priest. He says he will go upon this hour. I am his *chela*, and I go with him. We need food for the road. He is an honoured guest in all the villages, but' – he broke into a pure boy's grin – 'the food here is good. Give me some.'

'What if I do not give it thee? I am the woman of this village.'

'Then I curse thee – a little – not greatly, but enough to remember.' He could not help smiling.

'Thou hast cursed me already by the down-dropped eyelash and the uplifted chin. Curses? What should I care for mere words?' She clenched her hands upon her bosom . . . 'But I would not have thee to go in anger, thinking hardly of me – a gatherer of cow-dung and grass at Shamlegh, but still a woman of substance.'

'I think nothing,' said Kim, 'but that I am grieved to go, for I am very weary; and that we need food. Here is the bag.'

The woman snatched it angrily. 'I was foolish,' said she. 'Who is thy woman in the Plains? Fair or black? I was fair once. Laughest thou? Once, long ago, if thou canst believe, a sahib looked on me with favour. Once, long

ago, I wore European clothes at the mission-house yonder.' She pointed towards Kotgarh. 'Once, long ago, I was Ker-lis-ti-an and spoke English – as the sahibs speak it. Yes. My sahib said he would return and wed me – yes, wed me. He went away – I had nursed him when he was sick – but he never returned. Then I saw that the Gods of the Kerlistians lied, and I went back to my own people . . . I have never set eyes on a sahib since. (Do not laugh at me. The fit is past, little priestling.) Thy face and thy walk and thy fashion of speech put me in mind of my sahib, though thou art only a wandering mendicant to whom I give a dole. Curse me? Thou canst neither curse nor bless!' She set her hands on her hips and laughed bitterly. 'Thy Gods are lies; thy works are lies; thy words are lies. There are no Gods under all the Heavens. I know it . . . But for a while I thought it was my sahib come back, and he was my God. Yes, once I made music on a *pianno* in the mission-house at Kotgarh. Now I give alms to priests who are *heatthen*.' She wound up with the English word, and tied the mouth of the brimming bag.

'I wait for thee, *chela*,' said the lama, leaning against the door-post.

The woman swept the tall figure with her eyes. 'He walk! He cannot cover half a mile. Whither would old bones go?'

At this Kim, already perplexed by the lama's collapse and foreseeing the weight of the bag, fairly lost his temper.

'What is it to thee, woman of ill-omen, where he goes?'

'Nothing – but something to thee, priest with a sahib's face. Wilt thou carry him on thy shoulders?'

'I go to the Plains. None must hinder my return. I have

wrestled with my soul till I am strengthless. The stupid body is spent and we are far from the Plains.'

'Behold!' she said simply, and drew aside to let Kim see his own utter helplessness. 'Curse me. Maybe it will give him strength. Make a charm! Call on thy great God. Thou art a priest.' She turned away.

The lama had squatted limply, still holding by the door-post. One cannot strike down an old man that he recovers again like a boy in a night. Weakness bowed him to the earth, but his eyes that hung on Kim were alive and imploring.

'It is all well,' said Kim. 'It is the thin air that weakens thee. In a little while we go! It is the mountain-sickness. I too am a little sick at stomach,' . . . and he knelt and comforted with such poor words as came first to his lips. Then the woman returned, more erect than ever.

'Thy Gods useless, heh? Try mine. *I* am the Woman of Shamlegh.' She hailed hoarsely, and there came out of a cow-pen her two husbands and three others with a *dooli*, the rude native litter of the Hills, that they use for carrying the sick and for visits of state. 'These cattle' – she did not condescend to look at them – 'are thine for so long as thou shalt need.'

'But we will not go Simla way. We will not go near the sahibs,' cried the first husband.

'They will not run away as the others did, nor will they steal baggage. Two I know for weaklings. Stand to the rear-pole, Sonoo and Taree.' They obeyed swiftly. 'Lower now, and lift in that holy man. I will see to the village and your virtuous wives till ye return.'

'When will that be?'

'Ask the priests. Do not pester me. Lay the food-bag at the foot, it balances better so.'

'Oh, Holy One, thy Hills are kinder than our Plains!' cried Kim, relieved, as the lama tottered to the litter. 'It is a very king's bed – a place of honour and ease. And we owe it to –'

'A woman of ill-omen. I need thy blessings as much as I do thy curses. It is *my* order and none of thine. Lift and away! Here! Hast thou money for the road?'

She beckoned Kim to her hut, and stooped above a battered English cash-box under her cot.

'I do not need anything,' said Kim, angered where he should have been grateful. 'I am already rudely loaded with favours.'

She looked up with a curious smile and laid a hand on his shoulder. 'At least, thank me. I am foul-faced and a hillwoman, but, as thy talk goes, I have acquired merit. Shall I show thee how the sahibs render thanks?' and her hard eyes softened.

'I am but a wandering priest,' said Kim, his eyes lighting in answer. 'Thou needest neither my blessings nor my curses.'

'Nay. But for one little moment – thou canst overtake the *dooli* in ten strides – *if* thou wast a sahib, shall I show thee what thou wouldst do?'

'How if I guess, though?' said Kim, and putting his arm round her waist, he kissed her on the cheek, adding in English: 'Thank you verree much, my dear.'

Kissing is practically unknown among Asiatics, which may have been the reason that she leaned back with wide-open eyes and a face of panic.

'Next time,' Kim went on, 'you must not be so sure of

your heatthen priests. Now I say goodbye.' He held out his hand English-fashion. She took it mechanically. 'Goodbye, my dear.'

'Goodbye, and – and' – she was remembering her English words one by one – 'you will come back again? Goodbye, and – thee God bless you.'

Half an hour later, as the creaking litter jolted up the hill path that leads south-easterly from Shamlegh, Kim saw a tiny figure at the hut door waving a white rag.

'She has acquired merit beyond all others,' said the lama. 'For to set a man upon the way to Freedom is half as great as though she herself had found it.

'Umm,' said Kim thoughtfully, considering the past. 'It may be that I have acquired merit also . . . At least she did not treat me like a child.' He hitched the front of his robe, where lay the slab of documents and maps, re-stowed the precious food-bag at the lama's feet, laid his hand on the litter's edge, and buckled down to the slow pace of the grunting husbands.

'These also acquire merit,' said the lama, after three miles.

'More than that, they shall be paid in silver,' quoth Kim. The Woman of Shamlegh had given it to him; and it was only fair, he argued, that her men should earn it back again.

CHAPTER
15

I'd not give room for an Emperor –
 I'd hold my road for a King.
To the Triple Crown I'd not bow down –
 But this is a different thing!
I'll not fight with the Powers of Air –
 Sentry, pass him through!
Drawbridge let fall – He's the Lord of us all –
 The Dreamer whose dream came true!

<div align="right">The Siege of the Fairies</div>

Two hundred miles north of Chini, on the blue shale of Ladakh, lies Yankling Sahib, the merry-minded man, spy-glassing wrathfully across the ridges for some sign of his pet tracker – a man from Ao-chung. But that renegade, with a new Männlicher rifle and two hundred cartridges, is elsewhere, shooting musk-deer for the market, and Yankling Sahib will learn next season how very ill he has been.

Up the valleys of Bushahr – the far-beholding eagles of the Himalayas swerve at his new blue-and-white gored umbrella – hurries a Bengali, once fat and well-looking, now lean and weather-worn. He has received the thanks of two foreigners of distinction, piloted not unskilfully to Mashobra tunnel, which leads to the great and gay capital of India. It was not his fault that, blanketed by wet mists, he conveyed them past the telegraph-station and European colony of Kotgarh. It was not his fault, but that of the Gods, of whom he discoursed so engagingly, that

he led them into the borders of Nahan, where the rajah of that state mistook them for deserting British soldiery. Hurree Babu explained the greatness and glory, in their own country, of his companions, till the drowsy kinglet smiled. He explained it to every one who asked – many times – aloud – variously. He begged food, arranged accommodation, proved a skilful leech for an injury of the groin – such a blow as one may receive rolling down a rock-covered hillside in the dark – and in all things indispensable. The reason of his friendliness did him credit. With millions of fellow-serfs, he had learned to look upon Russia as the great deliverer from the north. He was a fearful man. He had been afraid that he could not save his illustrious employers from the anger of an excited peasantry. He himself would just as lief hit a holy man as not, but . . . He was deeply grateful and sincerely rejoiced that he had done his 'little possible' towards bringing their venture to – barring the lost baggage – a successful issue. He had forgotten the blows; denied that any blows had been dealt that unseemly first night under the pines. He asked neither pension nor retaining fee, but, if they deemed him worthy, would they write him a testimonial? It might be useful to him later, if others, their friends, came over the passes. He begged them to re-member him in their future greatnesses, for he 'opined subtly' that he, even he, Mohendro Lal Dutt, MA of Calcutta, had 'done the state some service'.

They gave him a certificate praising his courtesy, help-fulness, and unerring skill as a guide. He put it in his waist-belt and sobbed with emotion; they had endured so many dangers together. He led them at high noon along crowded Simla Mall to the Alliance Bank of Simla,

where they wished to establish their identity. Thence he vanished like a dawn-cloud on Jakko.

Behold him, too fine-drawn to sweat, too pressed to vaunt the drugs in his little brass-bound box, ascending Shamlegh slope, a just man made perfect. Watch him, all babudom laid aside, smoking at noon on a cot, while a woman with turquoise-studded headgear points south-easterly across the bare grass. Litters, she says, do not travel as fast as single men, but his birds should now be in the Plains. The holy man would not stay though Lispeth pressed him. The babu groans heavily, girds up his huge loins, and is off again. He does not care to travel after dusk; but his days' marches – there is none to enter them in a book – would astonish folk who mock at his race. Kindly villagers, remembering the Dacca drug-vendor of two months ago, give him shelter against evil spirits of the wood. He dreams of Bengali gods, university text-books of education, and the Royal Society, London, England. Next dawn the bobbing blue-and-white umbrella goes forward.

On the edge of the Doon, Mussoorie well behind them and the Plains spread out in golden dust before, rests a worn litter in which – all the Hills know it – lies a sick lama who seeks a River for his healing. Villages have almost come to blows over the honour of bearing it, for not only has the lama given them blessings, but his disciple good money – full one-third sahibs' prices. Twelve miles a day has the *dooli* travelled, as the greasy, rubbed pole-ends show, and by roads that few sahibs use. Over the Nilang Pass in storm when the driven snow-dust filled every fold of the impassive lama's drapery; between the black horns of Raieng where they heard the whistle of the wild

goats through the clouds; pitching and strained on the
shale below; hard-held between shoulder and clenched
jaw when they rounded the hideous curves of the Cut
Road under Bhagirati; swinging and creaking to the
steady jog-trot of the descent into the Valley of the
Waters; pressed along the steamy levels of that locked
valley; up, up and out again, to meet the roaring gusts off
Kedarnath; set down of middays in the dun gloom of
kindly oak forests; passed from village to village in dawn
chill, when even devotees may be forgiven for swearing
at impatient holy men; or by torchlight, when the least
fearful think of ghosts – the *dooli* has reached her last
stage. The little hill-folk sweat in the modified heat of the
lower Siwaliks, and gather round the priests for their
blessing and their wage.

'Ye have acquired merit,' says the lama. 'Merit greater
than your knowing. And ye will return to the Hills,' he
sighs.

'Surely. The high Hills as soon as may be.' The bearer
rubs his shoulder, drinks water, spits it out again, and
readjusts his grass sandal. Kim – his face is drawn and
tired – pays very small silver from his belt, heaves out the
food-bag, crams an oilskin packet – they are holy writings
– into his bosom, and helps the lama to his feet. The peace
has come again into the old man's eyes, and he does not
look for the hills to fall down and crush him as he did that
terrible night when they were delayed by the flooded
river.

The men pick up the *dooli* and swing out of sight
between the scrub clumps.

The lama raises a hand toward the rampart of the
Himalayas. 'Not with you, O blessed among all hills, fell

the Arrow of Our Lord! And never shall I breathe your airs again!'

'But thou art ten times the stronger man in this good air,' says Kim, for to his wearied soul appeal the well-cropped, kindly Plains. 'Here, or hereabouts, fell the Arrow, yes. We will go very softly, perhaps a *koss* a day, for the Search is sure. But the bag weighs heavy.'

'Ay, our Search is sure. I have come out of great temptation.'

It was never more than a couple of miles a day now, and Kim's shoulders bore all the weight of it – the burden of an old man, the burden of the heavy food-bag with the locked books, the load of the writings on his heart, and the details of the daily routine. He begged in the dawn, set blankets for the lama's meditation, held the weary head on his lap through the noonday heats, fanning away the flies till his wrists ached, begged again in the evenings, and rubbed the lama's feet, who rewarded him with promise of Freedom – today, tomorrow, or, at furthest, the next day.

'Never was such a *chela*. I doubt at times whether Ananda more faithfully nursed Our Lord. And thou art a sahib? When I was a man – a long time ago – I forgot that. Now I look upon thee often, and every time I remember that thou art a sahib. It is strange.'

'Thou hast said there is neither black nor white. Why plague me with this talk, Holy One? Let me rub the other foot. It vexes me. I am *not* a sahib. I am thy *chela*, and my head is heavy on my shoulders.'

'Patience a little! We reach Freedom together. Then thou and I, upon the far bank of the River, will look back

upon our lives as in the Hills we saw our days' marches laid out behind us. Perhaps I was once a sahib.'

"Was never a sahib like thee, I swear it.'

'I am certain the Keeper of the Images in the Wonder House was in past life a very wise abbot. But even his spectacles do not make my eyes see. There fall shadows when I would look steadily. No matter – we know the tricks of the poor stupid carcass – shadow changing to another shadow. I am bound by the illusion of Time and Space. How far came we today in the flesh?'

'Perhaps half a *koss*.' (Three quarters of a mile, and it was a weary march.)

'Half a *koss*. Ha! I went ten thousand thousand in the spirit. How we are all lapped and swathed and swaddled in these senseless things.' He looked at his thin blue-veined hand that found the beads so heavy. '*Chela*, hast thou never a wish to leave me?'

Kim thought of the oilskin packet and the books in the food-bag. If some one duly authorized would only take delivery of them the Great Game might play itself for aught he then cared. He was tired and hot in his head, and a cough that came from the stomach worried him.

'No,' he said almost sternly. 'I am not a dog or a snake to bite when I have learned to love.'

'Thou art too tender towards me.'

'Not that either. I have moved in one matter without consulting thee. I have sent a message to the Kulu woman by that woman who gave us the goat's milk this morn, saying that thou wast a little feeble and wouldst need a litter. I beat myself in my mind that I did not do it when we entered the Doon. We stay in this place till the litter returns.'

359

'I am content. She is a woman with a heart of gold, as thou sayest, but a talker – something of a talker.'

'She will not weary thee. I have looked to that also. Holy One, my heart is very heavy for my many carelessnesses towards thee.' An hysterical catch rose in his throat. 'I have walked thee too far: I have not picked good food always for thee; I have not considered the heat; I have talked to people on the road and left thee alone . . . I have – I have . . . *Hai mai!* But I love thee . . . and it is all too late . . . I was a child . . . Oh, why was I not a man? . . .' Overborne by strain, fatigue, and the weight beyond his years, Kim broke down and sobbed at the lama's feet.

'What a to-do is here!' said the old man gently. 'Thou hast never stepped a hair's breadth from the Way of Obedience. Neglect *me*? Child, I have lived on thy strength as an old tree lives on the lime of a new wall. Day by day, since Shamlegh down, I have stolen strength from thee. *Therefore*, not through any sin of thine, art thou weakened. It is the Body – the silly, stupid Body – that speaks now. Not the assured Soul. Be comforted! Know at least the devils that thou fightest. They are earth-born – children of illusion. We will go to the woman from Kulu. She shall acquire merit in housing us, and specially in tending me. Thou shalt run free till strength returns. I had forgotten the stupid Body. If there be any blame, I bear it. But we are too close to the Gates of Deliverance to weigh blame. I could praise thee, but what need? In a little – in a very little – we shall sit beyond all needs.'

And so he petted and comforted Kim with wise saws and grave texts on that little-understood beast, our Body,

who, being but a delusion, insists on posing as the Soul, to the darkening of the Way, and the immense multiplication of unnecessary devils.

'*Hai! hai!* Let us talk of the woman from Kulu. Think you she will ask for another charm for her grandsons? When I was a young man, a very long time ago, I was plagued with these vapours – and some others – and I went to an abbot – a very holy man and a seeker after truth, though then I knew it not. Sit up and listen, child of my soul! My tale was told. Said he to me, "*Chela*, know this. There are many lies in the world, and not a few liars, but there are no liars like our bodies, except it be the sensations of our bodies." Considering this I was comforted, and of his great favour he suffered me to drink tea in his presence. Suffer me now to drink tea, for I am thirsty.'

With a laugh across his tears, Kim kissed the lama's feet and set about the tea-making.

'Thou leanest on me in the body, Holy One, but I lean on thee for some other things. Dost know it?'

'I have guessed maybe,' and the lama's eyes twinkled. 'We must change that.'

So, when with scufflings and scrapings and a hot air of importance, paddled up nothing less than the Sahiba's pet palanquin sent twenty miles, with that same grizzled old Oorya servant in charge, and when they reached the disorderly order of the long white rambling house behind Saharunpore, the lama took his own measures.

Said the Sahiba cheerily from an upper window, after compliments: 'What is the good of an old woman's advice to an old man? I told thee – I *told* thee, Holy One, to keep

an eye upon the *chela*. How didst thou do it? Never
answer me! *I* know. He has been running among the
women. Look at his eyes – hollow and sunk – and the
Betraying Line from the nose down! He has been sifted
out! Fie! Fie! And a priest, too!'

Kim looked up, over-weary to smile, shaking his head
in denial.

'Do not jest,' said the lama. 'That time is done. We are
here upon great matters. A sickness of soul took me in the
Hills, and him a sickness of the body. Since then I have
lived upon his strength – eating him.'

'Children together – young and old,' she sniffed, but
forbore to make any new jokes. 'May this present hospi-
tality restore ye! Hold awhile and I will come to gossip of
the high good Hills.'

At evening time – her son-in-law was returned, so she
did not need to go on inspection round the farm – she
won to the meat of the matter, explained low-voicedly by
the lama. The two old heads nodded wisely together.
Kim had reeled to a room with a cot in it, and was dozing
soddenly. The lama had forbidden him to set blankets or
get food.

'I know – I know. Who but I?' she cackled. 'We who go
down to the burning-ghats clutch at the hands of those
coming up from the River of Life with full water-jars –
yes, brimming water-jars. I did the boy wrong. He lent
thee his strength? It is true that the old eat the young
daily. Stands now we must restore him.'

'Thou hast many times acquired merit –'

'*My* merit. What is it? Old bag of bones making curries
for men who do not ask "Who cooked this?" Now if it
were stored up for my grandson –'

'He that had the belly-pain?'

'To think the Holy One remembers *that*! I must tell his mother. It is most singular honour! "He that had the belly-pain" – straightway the Holy One remembered. She will be proud.'

'My *chela* is to me as is a son to the unenlightened.'

'Say grandson, rather. Mothers have not the wisdom of our years. If a child cries they say the heavens are falling. Now a grandmother is far enough separated from the pain of bearing and the pleasure of giving the breast to consider whether a cry is wickedness pure or the wind. And since thou speakest once again of wind, when last the Holy One was here, maybe I offended in pressing for charms.'

'Sister,' said the lama, using that form of address a Buddhist monk may sometimes employ towards a nun, 'if charms comfort thee –'

'They are better than ten thousand doctors.'

'I say, if they comfort thee, I who was Abbot of Suchzen, will make as many as thou mayest desire. I have never seen thy face –'

'*That* even the monkeys who steal our loquats count for a gain. Hee! hee!'

'But as he who sleeps there said,' – he nodded at the shut door of the guest-chamber across the forecourt – 'thou hast a heart of gold . . . And he is in the spirit my very "grandson" to me.'

'Good! I am the Holy One's cow.' This was pure Hinduism, but the lama never heeded. 'I am old. I have borne sons in the body. Oh, once I could please men! Now I can cure them.' He heard her armlets tinkle as though she bared arms for action. 'I will take over the boy

and dose him, and stuff him, and make him all whole. *Hai! hai!* We old people know something yet.'

Wherefore when Kim, aching in every bone, opened his eyes, and would go to the cook-house to get his master's food, he found strong coercion about him, and a veiled old figure at the door, flanked by the grizzled manservant, who told him very precisely the things that he was on no account to do.

'Thou must have? Thou shalt have nothing. What? A locked box in which to keep holy books? Oh, that is another matter. Heavens forbid I should come between a priest and his prayers! It shall be brought, and thou shalt keep the key.'

They pushed the coffer under his cot, and Kim shut away Mahbub's pistol, the oilskin packet of letters, and the locked books and diaries, with a groan of relief. For some absurd reason their weight on his shoulders was nothing to their weight on his poor mind. His neck ached under it of nights.

'Thine is a sickness uncommon in youth these days: since young folk have given up tending their betters. The remedy is sleep, and certain drugs,' said the Sahiba; and he was glad to give himself up to the blankness that half menaced and half soothed him.

She brewed drinks, in some mysterious Asiatic equivalent to the still-room – drenches that smelt pestilently and tasted worse. She stood over Kim till they went down, and inquired exhaustively after they had come up. She laid a taboo upon the forecourt, and enforced it by means of an armed man. It is true he was seventy odd, that his scabbarded sword ceased at the hilt; but he represented the authority of the Sahiba, and loaded

wains, chattering servants, calves, dogs, hens, and the like, fetched a wide compass by those parts. Best of all, when the body was cleared, she cut out from the mass of poor relations that crowded the back of the buildings – household dogs, we name them – a cousin's widow, skilled in what Europeans, who know nothing about it, call massage. And the two of them, laying him east and west, that the mysterious earth-currents which thrill the clay of our bodies might help and not hinder, took him to pieces all one long afternoon – bone by bone, muscle by muscle, ligament by ligament, and lastly, nerve by nerve. Kneaded to irresponsible pulp, half hypnotized by the perpetual flick and readjustment of the uneasy *chudders* that veiled their eyes, Kim slid ten thousand miles into slumber – thirty-six hours of it – sleep that soaked like rain after drought.

Then she fed him, and the house spun to her clamour. She caused fowls to be slain; she sent for vegetables, and the sober, slow-thinking gardener, nigh as old as she, sweated for it; she took spices, and milk, and onion, with little fish from the brooks – anon limes for sherbets, fat quails from the pits, then chicken livers upon a skewer, with sliced ginger between.

'I have seen something of the world,' she said over the crowded trays, 'and there are but two sorts of women in it – those who take the strength out of a man and those who put it back. Once I was that one, and now I am this. Nay – do not play the priestling with me. Mine was but a jest. If it does not hold good now, it will when thou takest the road again. Cousin,' – this to the poor relation, never wearied of extolling her patroness's charity – 'he is getting a bloom on the skin of a new-curried horse. Our

work is like polishing jewels to be thrown to a dance-girl – eh?'

Kim sat up and smiled. The terrible weakness had dropped from him like an old shoe. His tongue itched for free speech again, and but a week back the lightest word clogged it like ashes. The pain in his neck (he must have caught it from the lama) had gone with the heavy dengue-aches and the evil taste in the mouth. The two old women, a little, but not much, more careful about their veils now, clucked as merrily as the hens that had entered pecking through the open door.

'Where is my Holy One?' he demanded.

'Hear him! Thy Holy One is well,' she snapped viciously. 'Though that is none of *his* merit. Knew I a charm to make him wise, I'd sell my jewels and buy it. To refuse good food that I cooked myself – and go roving into the fields for two nights on an empty belly – and to tumble into a brook at the end of it – call you *that* holiness? Then, when he has nearly broken what thou hast left of my heart with anxiety, he tells me that he has acquired merit. Oh, how like are all men! No, that was not it – he tells me that he is freed from all sin. *I* could have told him that before he wetted himself all over. He is well now – this happened a week ago – but burn me such holiness! A babe of three would do better. Do not fret thyself for the Holy One. He keeps both eyes on thee when he is not wading our brooks.'

'I do not remember to have seen him. I remember that the days and nights passed like bars of white and black, opening and shutting. I was not sick: I was but tired.'

'A lethargy that comes by right some few score years later. But it is done now.'

'Maharanee,' Kim began, but led by the look in her eye, changed it to the title of plain love – 'Mother, I owe my life to thee. How shall I make thanks? Ten thousand blessings upon thy house and –'

'The house be unblessed!' (It is impossible to give exactly the old lady's word.) 'Thank the Gods as a priest if thou wilt, but thank me, if thou carest, as a son. Heavens above! Have I shifted thee and lifted thee and slapped and twisted thy ten toes to find texts flung at my head? Somewhere a mother must have borne thee to break her heart. What used thou to her – son?'

'I had no mother, my mother,' said Kim. 'She died, they tell me, when I was young.'

'*Hai mai!* Then none can say I have robbed her of any right if – when thou takest the road again and this house is but one of a thousand used for shelter and forgotten, after an easy-flung blessing. No matter. I need no blessings, but – but –' She stamped her foot at the poor relation. 'Take up the trays to the house. What is the good of stale food in the room, O woman of ill-omen?'

'I ha – have borne a son in my time too, but he died,' whimpered the bowed sister-figure behind the *chudder*. 'Thou knowest he died! I only waited for the order to take away the tray.'

'It is I that am the woman of ill-omen,' cried the old lady penitently. 'We that go down to the *chattris* [the big umbrellas above the burning-ghats where the priests take their last dues] clutch hard at the bearers of the *chattis* [water-jars – young folk full of the pride of life, she meant; but the pun is clumsy]. When one cannot dance in the festival one must e'en look out of the window, and grandmothering takes all a woman's time. Thy master

367

gives me all the charms I now desire for my daughter's eldest, by reason – is it? – that he is wholly free from sin. The *hakim* is brought very low these days. He goes about poisoning my servants for lack of their betters.'

'What *hakim*, mother?'

'That very Dacca man who gave me the pill which rent me in three pieces. He cast up like a strayed camel a week ago, vowing that he and thou had been blood-brothers together up Kulu way, and feigning great anxiety for thy health. He was very thin and hungry, so I gave orders to have him stuffed too – him and his anxiety!'

'I would see him if he is here.'

'He eats five times a day, and lances boils for my hinds to save himself from an apoplexy. He is so full of anxiety for thy health that he sticks to the cookhouse door and stays himself with scraps. He will keep. We shall never get rid of him.'

'Send him here, mother' – the twinkle returned to Kim's eye for a flash – 'and I will try.'

'I'll send him, but to chase him off is an ill turn. At least he had the sense to fish the Holy One out of the brook; thus, as the Holy One did *not* say, acquiring merit.'

'He is a very wise *hakim*. Send him, mother.'

'Priest praising priest? A miracle! If he is any friend of thine (ye squabbled at your last meeting) I'll hale him here with horse-ropes and – and give him a caste-dinner afterwards, my son . . . Get up and see the world! This lying abed is the mother of seventy devils . . . my son! my son!'

She trotted forth to raise a typhoon off the cookhouse, and almost on her shadow rolled in the babu, robed as to the shoulders like a Roman emperor, jowled like Titus,

bare-headed, with new patent-leather shoes, in highest condition of fat, exuding joy and salutations.

'By Jove, Mister O'Hara, but I *am* jolly-glad to see you. I will kindly shut the door. It is a pity you are sick. Are you very sick?'

'The papers – the papers from the *kilta*. The maps and the *murasla*!' He held out the key impatiently; for the present need on his soul was to get rid of the loot.

'You are quite right. That is correct departmental view to take. You have got everything?'

'All that was handwritten in the *kilta* I took. The rest I threw down the hill.' He could hear the key's grate in the lock, the sticky pull of the slow-rending oilskin, and a quick shuffling of papers. He had been annoyed out of all reason by the knowledge that they lay below him through the sick idle days – a burden incommunicable. For that reason the blood tingled through his body, when Hurree, skipping elephantinely, shook hands again.

'This is fine! This is finest! Mister O'Hara! You have – ha! ha! – swiped the whole bag of tricks – locks, stocks, and barrels. They told me it was eight months' work gone up the spouts! By Jove, how they beat me! . . . Look, here is the letter from Hilás!' He intoned a line or two of Court Persian, which is the language of authorized and un-authorized diplomacy. 'Mister Rajah Sahib has just about put his foot in the holes. He will have to explain offeecially how the deuce-an'-all he is writing love-letters to the Tsar. And they are very clever maps . . . and there is three or four prime ministers of these parts implicated by the correspondence. By Gad, sar! The British government will change the succession in Hilás and Bunár, and nominate new heirs to the throne.

"Trea-son most base" . . . but you do not understand? Eh?'

'Are they in thy hands?' said Kim. It was all he cared for.

'Just you jolly-well bet yourself they are.' He stowed the entire trove about his body, as only Orientals can. 'They are going up to the office too. The old lady thinks I am a permanent fixture here, but I shall go away with these straight off – immediately. Mr Lurgan will be proud man. You are offeecially subordinate to me, but I shall embody your name in my verbal report. It is a pity we are not allowed written reports. We Bengalis excel in thee exact science.' He tossed back the key and showed the box empty.

'Good. That is good. I was very tired. My Holy One was sick, too. And did he fall into –'

'Oah yess. I am his good friend, I tell you. He was behaving very strange when I came down after you, and I thought perhaps he might have the papers. I followed him on his meditations, and to discuss ethnological points also. You see, I am verree small person here nowadays, in comparison with all his charms. By Jove, O'Hara, do you know, he is afflicted with infirmity of fits. Yess, I tell you. Cataleptic, too, if not also epileptic. I found him in such a state under a tree *in articulo mortem*, and he jumped up and walked into a brook and he was nearly drowned but for me. I pulled him out.'

'Because I was not there!' said Kim. 'He might have died.'

'Yes, he might have died, but he is dry now, and asserts he has undergone transfiguration.' The babu tapped his forehead knowingly. 'I took notes of his

statements for Royal Society – *in posse*. You must make haste and be quite well and come back to Simla, and I will tell you all my tale at Lurgan's. It was splendid. The bottoms of their trousers were *quite* torn, and old Nahan Rajah, he thought they were European soldiers deserting.'

'Oh, the Russians? How long were they with thee?'

'One was a Frenchman. Oh, days and days and days! Now all the hill-people believe all Russians are all beggars. By Jove! they had not one dam'-thing that I did not get them. And I told the common people – oah, *such* tales and anecdotes! I will tell you at old Lurgan's when you come up. We will have – ah – a night out! It is feather in both our caps! Yess, and they gave me a certificate. That is creaming joke. You should have seen them at the Alliance Bank identifying themselves! And thank Almighty God you got their papers so well! You do not laugh verree much, but you shall laugh when you are well. Now I will go straight to the railway and get out. You shall have all sorts of credits for your game. When do you come along? We are very proud of you though you gave us great frights. And especially Mahbub.'

'Ay, Mahbub. And where is he?'

'Selling horses in this vi-cinity, of course.'

'Here! Why? Speak slowly. There is a thickness in my head still.'

The babu looked shyly down his nose. 'Well, you see, I am a fearful man, and I do not like responsibility. You were sick, you see, and I did not know where deuce-an'-all the papers were, and if so, how many. So when I had come down here I slipped in private wire to Mahbub – he was at Meerut for races – and I tell him how case stands.

He comes up with his men and he consorts with the lama, and then he calls me a fool, and is very rude –'

'But wherefore – wherefore?'

'That is what *I* ask. I only suggest that if any one steals the papers I should like some good strong, brave men to rob them back again. You see, they are vitally important, and Mahbub Ali he did not know where you were.'

'Mahbub Ali to rob the Sahiba's house? Thou art mad, Babu,' said Kim with indignation.

'I wanted the papers. Suppose she had stole them? It was only practical suggestion, *I* think. You are not pleased, eh?'

A native proverb – unquotable – showed the blackness of Kim's disapproval.

'Well,' – Hurree shrugged his shoulders – 'there is no accounting for thee taste. Mahbub was angry too. He has sold horses all about here, and he says old lady is *pukka* [thorough] old lady and would not condescend to such ungentlemanly things. *I* do not care. I have got the papers, and I was very glad of moral support from Mahbub. I tell you, I am fearful man, but, somehow or other, the more fearful I am the more dam'-tight places I get into. So I was glad you came with me to Chini, and I am glad Mahbub was close by. The old lady she is sometimes very rude to me and my beautiful pills.'

'Allah be merciful!' said Kim on his elbow, rejoicing. 'What a beast of wonder is a babu! And that man walked alone – if he did walk – with robbed and angry foreigners!'

'Oah, thatt was nothing, after they had done beating

me; but if I lost the papers it was pretty-jolly serious. Mahbub he nearly beat me too, and he went and consorted with the lama no end. I shall stick to ethnological investigations henceforwards. Now goodbye, Mister O'Hara. I can catch 4.25 p.m. to Umballa if I am quick. It will be good times when we all tell thee tale up at Mr Lurgan's. I shall report you offeecially better. Goodbye, my dear fallow, and when next you are under thee emotions please do not use the Muhammadan terms with the Tibetan dress.'

He shook hands twice – a babu to his boot-heels – and opened the door. With the fall of the sunlight upon his still triumphant face he returned to the humble Dacca quack.

'He robbed them,' thought Kim, forgetting his own share in the game. 'He tricked them. He lied to them like a Bengali. They gave him a *chit* [a testimonial]. He makes them a mock at the risk of his life – *I* never would have gone down to them after the pistol shots – and then he says he is a fearful man . . . And he *is* a fearful man. I must get into the world again.'

At first his legs bent like bad pipe-stems, and the flood and rush of the sunlit air dazzled him. He squatted by the white wall, the mind rummaging among the incidents of the long *dooli* journey, the lama's weaknesses, and, now that the stimulus of talk was removed, his own self-pity, of which, like the sick, he had great store. The unnerved brain edged away from all the outside, as a raw horse, once rowelled, sidles from the spur. It was enough, amply enough, that the spoil of the *kilta* was away – off his hands – out of his possession. He tried to think of the lama – to wonder why he had stumbled into a brook – but

the bigness of the world, seen between the forecourt gates, swept linked thought aside. Then he looked upon the trees and the broad fields, with the thatched huts hidden among crops – looked with strange eyes unable to take up the size and proportion and use of things – stared for a still half-hour. All that while he felt, though he could not put it into words, that his soul was out of gear with its surroundings – a cog-wheel unconnected with any machinery, just like the idle cog-wheel of a cheap Beheea sugar-crusher laid by in a corner. The breezes fanned over him, the parrots shrieked at him, the noises of the populated house behind – squabbles, orders, and re-proofs – hit on dead ears.

'I am Kim. I am Kim. And what is Kim?' His soul repeated it again and again.

He did not want to cry – had never felt less like crying in his life – but of a sudden easy, stupid tears trickled down his nose, and with an almost audible click he felt the wheels of his being lock up anew on the world without. Things that rode meaningless on the eyeball an instant before slid into proper proportion. Roads were meant to be walked upon, houses to be lived in, cattle to be driven, fields to be tilled, and men and women to be talked to. They were all real and true – solidly planted upon the feet – perfectly comprehensible – clay of his clay, neither more nor less. He shook himself like a dog with a flea in his ear, and rambled out of the gate. Said the Sahiba, to whom watchful eyes reported this move: 'Let him go. I have done my share. Mother Earth must do the rest. When the Holy One comes back from meditation, tell him.'

There stood an empty bullock-cart on a little knoll half a

mile away, with a young banyan tree behind – a lookout, as it were, above some new-ploughed levels; and his eyelids, bathed in soft air, grew heavy as he neared it. The ground was good clean dust – no new herbage that, living, is half-way to death already, but the hopeful dust that holds the seeds of all life. He felt it between his toes, patted it with his palms, and joint by joint, sighing luxuriously, laid him down full length along in the shadow of the wooden-pinned cart. And Mother Earth was as faithful as the Sahiba. She breathed through him to restore the poise he had lost lying so long on a cot cut off from her good currents. His head lay powerless upon her breast, and his opened hands surrendered to her strength. The many-rooted tree above him, and even the dead manhandled wood beside, knew what he sought, as he himself did not know. Hour upon hour he lay deeper than sleep.

Towards evening, when the dust of returning kine made all the horizons smoke, came the lama and Mahbub Ali, both afoot, walking cautiously, for the house had told them where he had gone.

'Allah! What a fool's trick to play in open country!' muttered the horse-dealer. 'He could be shot a hundred times – but this is not the border.'

'And,' said the lama, repeating a many-times-told tale, 'never was such a *chela*. Temperate, kindly, wise, of ungrudging disposition, a merry heart upon the road, never forgetting, learned, truthful, courteous. Great is his reward!'

'I know the boy – as I have said.'

'And he was all of those things?'

'Some of them – but I have not yet found a Red Hat's

charm for making him overly truthful. He has certainly been well nursed.'

'The Sahiba is a heart of gold,' said the lama earnestly. 'She looks upon him as her son.'

'Hmph! Half Hind seems that way disposed. I only wished to see that the boy had come to no harm and was a free agent. As thou knowest, he and I were old friends in the first days of your pilgrimage together.'

'That is a bond between us.' The lama sat down. 'We are at the end of the pilgrimage.'

'No thanks to thee thine was not cut off for good and all a week back. I heard what the Sahiba said to thee when we bore thee up on the cot.' Mahbub laughed, and tugged his newly dyed beard.

'I was meditating upon other matters that tide. It was the *hakim* from Dacca broke my meditations.'

'Otherwise' – this was in Pushtu for decency's sake – 'thou wouldst have ended thy meditations upon the sultry side of Hell – being an unbeliever and an idolater for all thy child's simplicity. But now, Red Hat, what is to be done?'

'This very night,' – the words came slowly, vibrating with triumph – 'this very night he will be as free as I am from all taint of sin – assured as I am, when he quits this body, of Freedom from the Wheel of Things. I have a sign' – he laid his hand above the torn chart in his bosom – 'that my time is short; but I shall have safeguarded him throughout the years. Remember, I have reached Knowledge, as I told thee only three nights back.'

'It must be true, as the Tirah priest said when I stole his cousin's wife, that I am a Sufi [a free-thinker]; for here I sit,' said Mahbub to himself, 'drinking in blasphemy

unthinkable . . . I remember the tale. On that, then, he goes to *Jannatu l'Adn* [the Gardens of Eden]. But how? Wilt thou slay him or drown him in that wonderful river from which the babu dragged thee?'

'I was dragged from no river,' said the lama simply. 'Thou hast forgotten what befell. I found it by Knowledge.'

'Oh, ay. True,' stammered Mahbub, divided between high indignation and enormous mirth. 'I had forgotten the exact run of what happened. Thou didst find it knowingly.'

'And to say that I would take life is – not a sin, but a madness simple. My *chela* aided me to the River. It is his right to be cleansed from sin – with me.'

'Ay, he needs cleansing. But afterwards, old man – afterwards?'

'What matter under all the Heavens? He is sure of Nibban – enlightened – as I am.'

'Well said. I had a fear he might mount Muhammad's Horse and fly away.'

'Nay – he must go forth as a teacher.'

'Aha! Now I see! That is the right gait for the colt. Certainly he must go forth as a teacher. He is somewhat urgently needed as a scribe by the state, for instance.'

'To that end he was prepared. I acquired merit in that I gave alms for his sake. A good deed does not die. He aided me in my Search. I aided him in his. Just is the Wheel, O horse-seller from the North. Let him be a teacher; let him be a scribe – what matter? He will have attained Freedom at the end. The rest is illusion.'

'What matter? When I must have him with me beyond Balkh in six months! I come up with ten lame horses and

three strong-backed men – thanks to that chicken of a babu – to break a sick boy by force out of an old trot's house. It seems that I stand by while a young sahib is hoisted into Allah knows what of an idolater's Heaven by means of old Red Hat. And I am reckoned something of a player of the Game myself! But the madman is fond of the boy; and I must be very reasonably mad too.'

'What is the prayer?' said the lama, as the rough Pushtu rumbled into the red beard.

'No matter at all; but now I understand that the boy, sure of Paradise, can yet enter government service, my mind is easier. I must get to my horses. It grows dark. Do not wake him. I have no wish to hear him call thee master.'

'But he *is* my disciple. What else?'

'He has told me.' Mahbub choked down his touch of spleen and rose laughing. 'I am not altogether of thy faith, Red Hat – if so small a matter concern thee.'

'It is nothing,' said the lama.

'I thought not. Therefore it will not move thee, sinless, new-washed and three parts drowned to boot, when I call thee a good man – a very good man. We have talked together some four or five evenings now, and for all I am a horse-coper I can still, as the saying is, see holiness beyond the legs of a horse. Yea, can see, too, how our Friend of all the World put his hand in thine at the first. Use him well, and suffer him to return to the world as a teacher, when thou hast – bathed his legs, if that be the proper medicine for the colt.

'Why not follow the Way thyself, and so accompany the boy?'

Mahbub stared stupefied at the magnificent insolence

of the demand, which across the border he would have paid with more than a blow. Then the humour of it touched his worldly soul.

'Softly – softly – one foot at a time, as the lame gelding went over the Umballa jumps. I may come to Paradise later – I have workings that way – great motions – and I owe them to thy simplicity. Thou hast never lied?'

'What need?'

'O Allah, hear him! "What need" in this thy world! Nor ever harmed a man?'

'Once – with a pen-case – before I was wise.'

'So? I think the better of thee. Thy teachings are good. Thou hast turned one man that I know from the path of strife.' He laughed immensely. 'He came here open-minded to commit a *dacoity* [a house-robbery with violence]. Yes, to cut, rob, kill, and carry off what he desired.'

'A great foolishness!'

'Oh! black shame too. So he thought after he had seen thee – and a few others, male and female. So he abandoned it; and now he goes to beat a big fat babu man.'

'I do not understand.'

'Allah forbid it! Some men are strong in knowledge, Red Hat. Thy strength is stronger still. Keep it – I think thou wilt. If the boy be not a good servant, pull his ears off.'

With a hitch of his broad Bokhariot belt the Pathan swaggered off into the gloaming, and the lama came down from his clouds so far as to look at the broad back.

'That person lacks courtesy, and is deceived by the shadow of appearances. But he spoke well of my *chela*,

who now enters upon his reward. Let me make the prayer! . . . Wake, O fortunate above all born of women. Wake! It is found!'

Kim came up from those deep wells, and the lama attended his yawning pleasure; duly snapping fingers to head off evil spirits.

'I have slept a hundred years. Where –? Holy One, hast *thou* been here long? I went out to look for thee, but' – he laughed drowsily – 'I slept by the way. I am all well now. Hast thou eaten? Let us go to the house. It is many days since I tended thee. And the Sahiba fed thee well? Who shampooed thy legs? What of the weaknesses – the belly and the neck, and the beating in the ears?'

'Gone – all gone. Dost thou not know?'

'I know nothing, but that I have not seen thee in a monkey's age. Know what?'

'Strange the knowledge did not reach out to thee, when all my thoughts were theeward.'

'I cannot see the face, but the voice is like a gong. Has the Sahiba made a young man of thee by her cookery?'

He peered at the cross-legged figure, outlined jet-black against the lemon-coloured drift of light. So does the stone Bodhisat sit who looks down upon the patent self-registering turnstiles of the Lahore Museum.

The lama held his peace. Except for the click of the rosary and a faint *clop-clop* of Mahbub's retreating feet, the soft, smoky silence of evening in India wrapped them close.

'Hear me! I bring news.'

'But let us –'

Out shot the long yellow hand compelling silence. Kim tucked his feet under his robe-edge obediently.

'Hear me! I bring news! The Search is finished. Comes now the Reward . . . Thus. When we were among the Hills, I lived on thy strength till the young branch bowed and nigh broke. When we came out of the Hills, I was troubled for thee and for other matters which I held in my heart. The boat of my soul lacked direction; I could not see into the Cause of Things. So I gave thee over to the virtuous woman altogether. I took no food. I drank no water. Still I saw not the Way. They pressed food upon me and cried at my shut door. So I removed myself to a hollow under a tree. I took no food. I took no water. I sat in meditation two days and two nights, abstracting my mind; inbreathing and outbreathing in the required manner . . . Upon the second night – so great was my reward – the wise Soul loosed itself from the silly Body and went free. This I have never before attained, though I have stood on the threshold of it. Consider, for it is a marvel!'

'A marvel indeed. Two days and two nights without food! Where was the Sahiba?' said Kim under his breath.

'Yea, my Soul went free, and, wheeling like an eagle, saw indeed that there was no Teshoo Lama nor any other soul. As a drop draws to water, so my Soul drew near to the Great Soul which is beyond all things. At that point, exalted in contemplation, I saw all Hind, from Ceylon in the sea to the Hills, and my own Painted Rocks at Such-zen; I saw every camp and village, to the least, where we have ever rested. I saw them at one time and in one place; for they were within the Soul. By this I knew the Soul had passed beyond the illusion of Time and Space and of Things. By this I knew that I was free. I saw thee lying in thy cot, and I saw thee falling downhill under the idolater – at one time, in one place, in my Soul,

381

which, as I say, had touched the Great Soul. Also I saw the stupid body of Teshoo Lama lying down, and the *hakim* from Dacca kneeled beside, shouting in its ear. Then my Soul was all alone, and I saw nothing, for I was all things, having reached the Great Soul. And I meditated a thousand thousand years, passionless, well aware of the Causes of all Things. Then a voice cried: "What shall come to the boy if thou art dead?" and I was shaken back and forth in myself with pity for thee; and I said: "I will return to my *chela*, lest he miss the Way." Upon this my Soul, which is the Soul of Teshoo Lama, withdrew itself from the Great Soul with strivings and yearnings and retchings and agonies not to be told. As the egg from the fish, as the fish from the water, as the water from the cloud, as the cloud from the thick air, so put forth, so leaped out, so drew away, so fumed up the Soul of Teshoo Lama from the Great Soul. Then a voice cried: "The River! Take heed to the River!" and I looked down upon all the world, which was as I had seen it before – one in time, one in place – and I saw plainly the River of the Arrow at my feet. At that hour my Soul was hampered by some evil or other whereof I was not wholly cleansed, and it lay upon my arms and coiled round my waist; but I put it aside, and I cast forth as an eagle in my flight for the very place of the River. I pushed aside world upon world for thy sake. I saw the River below me – the River of the Arrow – and, descending, the waters of it closed over me; and behold I was again in the body of Teshoo Lama, but free from sin, and the *hakim* from Dacca bore up my head in the waters of the River. It is here! It is behind the mango tope here – even here!'

'*Allah kerim!* Oh, well that the babu was by! Wast thou very wet?'

'Why should I regard? I remember the *hakim* was concerned for the body of Teshoo Lama. He haled it out of the holy water in his hands, and there came afterwards thy horse-seller from the north with a cot and men, and they put the body on the cot and bore it up to the Sahiba's house.'

'What said the Sahiba?'

'I was meditating in that body, and did not hear. So thus the Search is ended. For the merit that I have acquired, the River of the Arrow is here. It broke forth at our feet, as I have said. I have found it. Son of my Soul, I have wrenched my Soul back from the Threshold of Freedom to free thee from all sin – as I am free, and sinless! Just is the Wheel! Certain is our deliverance! Come!'

He crossed his hands on his lap and smiled, as a man may who has won salvation for himself and his beloved.

- The author of Hebrews wrote, "Since then the children share in flesh and blood, He Himself likewise also partook of the same, that through death He might render powerless him who had the power of death, that is the devil; and might deliver those who through fear of death were subject to slavery all their lives" (Hebrews 2:14–15).
- Paul asked, "O death, where is your sting?" (1 Corinthians 15:55).
- John assures us, "And I heard a voice from heaven, saying, 'Write, "Blessed are the dead who die in the Lord from now on."' 'Yes,' says the Spirit, 'that they may rest from their labor, for their deeds follow with them'" (Revelation 14:13).

We do not know who will be next to hear the divine call. Let us be ready when it comes.

Moody Press, a ministry of Moody Bible Institute,
is designed for education, evangelization, and edification.
If we may assist you in knowing more about Christ
and the Christian life, please write us without obligation:
Moody Press, c/o MLM, Chicago, Illinois 60610.

presses your desire to transfer your trust to Christ alone for your eternal salvation. This prayer can be the link that will connect you to God. And if you pray it in faith, God will receive you.

Dear God,

I know that I am a sinner and there is nothing that I can do to save myself. I confess my complete helplessness to forgive my own sin or to work my way to heaven. At this moment I trust Christ alone as the One who bore my sin when He died on the cross. I believe that He did all that ever will be necessary for me to stand in your holy presence.

I thank you that Christ was raised from the dead as a guarantee of my own resurrection. As best as I can, I now transfer my trust to Him. I am grateful that He has promised to receive me despite my many sins and failures.

Father, I take you at your word. I thank you that I can face death now that you are my Savior. Thank you for the assurance that you will walk with me though the deep valley.

> Thank You for hearing this prayer.
> In Jesus' Name. Amen.

Here are some promises that are given to all who trust Christ alone for their entrance into the kingdom.

- Christ said, "I am the resurrection and the life; he who believes in Me shall live even if he dies, and everyone who lives and believes in Me shall never die" (John 11:25).

Whether 'tis nobler in the mind to suffer
The slings and arrows of outrageous fortune,
Or to take arms against a sea of troubles,
And by opposing end them? To die: to sleep;
No more; and by a sleep we say we end
The heart-ache and the thousand natural shocks
That flesh is heir to, 'tis a consummation
Devoutly to be wish'd. To die, to sleep;
To sleep: perchance to dream: ay, there's the rub;
For in that sleep of death what dreams may come
When we have shuffled off this mortal coil.

(III. i. 58–67)

Hamlet finds suicide both attractive and repulsive. If he could be sure that it would rid him of his sea of troubles, he would do it; but he fears that "undiscover'd country from whose bourn / No traveller returns " (III.i.79–80). His present ills might be pleasant in comparison to the fate that would await him.

Compare Hamlet's dilemma with that of Paul:

For to me, to live is Christ, and to die is gain. But if I am to live on in the flesh, this will mean fruitful labor for me; and I do not know which to choose. But I am hard-pressed from both directions, having the desire to depart and be with Christ, for that is very much better; yet to remain on in the flesh is more necessary for your sake. (Philippians 1:21–24)

Hamlet says, "Live or die, I lose!" Paul says, "Live or die, I win!"

What a difference Christ makes!

MAKING SURE

Here is a prayer you can pray, a prayer that ex-

142

shall be able to separate us from the love of God, which is in Jesus Christ our Lord" (Romans 8:38–39). Death is not any more successful than life in separating us from Christ's love.

What is Christ's attitude toward our homecoming? Repeatedly in the New Testament Christ is spoken of as sitting "at the right hand of God." But there is one reference to His leaving His seat and standing; He is welcoming one of His servants home. As Stephen was being stoned, we read that "being full of the Holy Spirit, he gazed intently into heaven and saw the glory of God, and Jesus standing at the right hand of God" (Acts 7:55).

Thus the seated Son of God stood to welcome one of His own into the heavenly realm. A believer's death may be unnoticed on earth, but it is front-page news in heaven. The Son of God takes note. He will be there to welcome us.

D. L. Moody at death caught a glimpse of heaven. Awakening from sleep he said, "Earth recedes, Heaven opens before me. If this is death, it is sweet! There is no valley here. God is calling me and I must go!"

Just before John Bunyan died, he said, "Weep not for me, but for yourselves. I go to the Father of our Lord Jesus Christ, who will through the mediation of His blessed Son receive me though a sinner; there we shall meet to sing the new song and remain everlastingly happy, world without end."

Remember the words of Hamlet in Shakespeare's play? In a moment of deep contemplation he mused, "To be, or not to be: that is the question" (III.i.56). He was contemplating suicide because life had become unbearable. Yet when he thought of where that might lead him, he continued,

Him as the One who did all that we will ever need to stand in God's holy presence. To believe in Christ means that as best we know, we trust Him for all that we need in this life and in the life to come.

How sure can we be that we will spend eternity with God? We can be so sure that death need not terrify us. Yes, there is mystery; yes, we all are apprehensive of taking leave of this body to wake up in the world to come. But when we have trusted Christ, we know that He walks with us through the parted curtain.

In the New Testament, Paul taught that those who belong to Christ can be very sure that they will enter heaven. Though these verses contain some theological words, you will understand what Paul is getting at. "For whom He foreknew, He also predestined to become conformed to the image of His Son, that He might be the first-born among many brethren; and whom He predestined, these He also called; and whom He called, these He also justified; and whom He justified, these He also glorified" (Romans 8:29–30).

We are already glorified! In effect, our arrival in heaven has already taken place. Those whom God chooses to be His—that is, those whom He foreknows and predestinates—these are the ones who are justified, and all of these are guaranteed a safe passage into their heavenly home. None is lost en route; in God's mind they already have their glorified bodies! For God "calls into being that which does not exist" (Romans 4:17).

Here is another promise for those who face death. Paul said that nothing can separate God's children from His love. Then he adds, "For I am convinced that neither death, nor life, nor angels, nor principalities, nor things present, nor things to come, nor powers, nor height, nor depth, nor any other created thing,

credited to our account so that we can enter into heaven immediately at death without so much as an intermediate stop.

When Christ died on the cross, He made a sacrifice for sinners, which God accepted. Though Christ was perfect, God made Him legally guilty of all of our sins. In turn, we receive His righteousness. "He made Him who knew no sin [Christ] to be sin on our behalf, that we might become the righteousness of God in Him" (2 Corinthians 5:21).

What grace!

What this means is that Christ was regarded as a sinner when He bore our sin; we are regarded as saints when we receive His righteousness. Though very imperfect, we are regarded as "the righteousness of God." God has exceedingly high standards, but thanks be, He meets them for us!

Perhaps you think that you have sinned too much to receive such a gift. Well, I want you to know that God is able to save great sinners—criminals, in fact. The amount of our sin is not a barrier; it is our unbelief that cuts us off from God's mercy and pardon.

When we receive Christ's righteousness, another miracle happens to us at the same time. God gives us a new nature; He changes us from the inside out. Christ said to Nicodemus, a Jewish religious leader, "Truly, truly, I say to you, unless one is born again, he cannot see the kingdom of God" (John 3:3). Obviously, we cannot cause ourselves to be born again. That is something that God must do for us.

What must we do to receive the gift of righteousness and a new nature within? The answer is to admit our helplessness, to acknowledge that we are dependent on God's mercy. Then we must transfer all of our trust to Christ as our sin-bearer; *we must believe in*

139

from which also we eagerly wait for a Savior, the Lord Jesus Christ" (Philippians 3:20).

Indeed, the redeemed are spoken of as having been raised with Christ and already seated in heaven (Ephesians 2:6). Because we are legally there we should not expect that crossing the border will be a hassle. What matters is that we have qualifications that are recognized by the "Keeper of the Keys."

Don't imagine for a moment that you will get to heaven without the right credentials. You will not be there because your wife has a right to enter; you will not be there because you have a child who is already there. No, this is an individual matter, and only those with the right document will be allowed entry.

This is just another way of saying that no one can enter into heaven without God's specific approval. Our problem, of course, is that God will not accept us just as we are. We cannot come to heaven's gates hoping for leniency. We cannot come pleading for special favors once we have slipped through the parted curtain. Visas are not available on the other side of the border.

WHAT GOD REQUIRES

How perfect do you have to be to enter into heaven? The answer, quite simply: as perfect as God. In fact, if you are not as perfect as He is, don't even think that you will enter into the kingdom of heaven! Christianity, whether Catholic or Protestant, has always taught that we must be as perfect as God to enter through those pearly gates.

The question, of course, is: How can we as sinners be as perfect as God? The answer: God is able to give us all of His perfections; His righteousness can be

\mathcal{K}NOWING TODAY WHERE YOU WILL BE TOMORROW
What God Requires—Making Sure

Those of us who have traveled in foreign countries know the importance of a passport. Regardless of your status or charisma, that document is what qualifies you for entry and acceptance among the people in a different land.

Though I have lived in the United States for more than twenty-five years, I am still a citizen of Canada. With my Canadian passport, I have no fear that I will be barred from Canada when our family takes a vacation during the summer. My wife and children, who are Americans, enter on the goodwill of the Canadian government; but I enter because I have the legal right to do so.

We need a passport to get into heaven, if that is the country where we wish to go. Those who have such a visa can rejoice in their citizenship long before their arrival. Paul wrote, "For our citizenship is in heaven,

Our future existence is not in the hands of doctors, nor in the hands of disease, nor in the hands of the drunk who runs into our car along the highway. Our life is in the hands of the Almighty, who can use any means He wishes, including the above, to have us brought into the heavenly gates.

Perhaps today our name will be called.

teaching of the New Testament emphasizes that His suffering took place on the cross where His blood was shed. There our debt was paid. As His soul left His body, He found Himself in the presence of God, along with the penitent thief. Three days later, Christ was raised from the dead with a glorified body and later ascended into heaven.

How shall we summarize our understanding of Christ's death? The immediate cause was the anger of the religious leaders and the cooperation of the Romans in carrying out this unjust execution. But the ultimate cause was God. "But the Lord was pleased to crush Him, putting Him to grief" (Isaiah 53:10).

Before his death, John Calvin had the same confidence when he said, "Thou, Lord, bruisest me. But I am abundantly satisfied since it is from Thy hand."

Death can steal nothing from a Christian. Health, wealth, and joy—all of these come in greater abundance when the spirit goes to God.

William Cowper combined both the story of redemption and the story of the penitent thief in his song when he wrote:

> *There is a fountain filled with blood*
> *Drawn from Immanuel's veins;*
> *And sinners, plunged beneath that flood,*
> *Lose all their guilty stains.*

> *The dying thief rejoiced to see*
> *That fountain in His day;*
> *And there may I, though vile as he,*
> *Wash all my sins away.*

> *When this poor lisping, stamm'ring tongue*
> *Lies silent in the grave,*
> *Then in a nobler, sweeter song,*
> *I will sing Thy pow'r to save.*

Father. This teaching has been reinforced by the Apostles' creed, which says "He descended into hell."

On the day of Pentecost, Peter quoted Psalm 16:10 and applied it to Christ: "Because Thou wilt not abandon my soul to Hades, nor allow Thy Holy One to undergo decay" (Acts 2:27). Apparently, Christ's soul did go to sheol or hades. However, we must remember that hades had two regions, one for the righteous and the other for the unrighteous. That Christ went to the righteous side can be shown by quoting His words to the thief hanging on a cross at His left side: "Today you shall be with Me in Paradise" (Luke 23:43).

Since Christ died before the thief did, our Lord was waiting for him; there in paradise they met again, this time to talk about the glories of eternity. The sins that the thief had committed had all been taken away in that moment when he exercised faith in the dying Christ.

Think of the faith that thief had! Humanly speaking, Christ seemed no better off than he himself was. Needless to say, Christ did not look like a Savior while writhing in pain on the cross. Yet there was something about Him that made the thief take notice. Perhaps the thief had heard about Christ long before they met at Golgotha. Or maybe it was the words Christ spoke and the attitude He displayed. Whatever the reason, the thief believed and was saved.

The thief who died on the left side of Christ rejected Him, taunting, "Are You not the Christ? Save Yourself and us!" (Luke 23:39). He thought only about the salvation of his body, not the salvation of his soul. If he died with such defiance as the Scriptures seem to teach, he did not join Christ in paradise.

Christ did not go to hades to suffer for us. All of the

given me" (John 17:11 KJV). When He cried, "It is finished!" the work was accomplished (John 19:30).

Obviously, our death does not accomplish redemption, but it is the means by which we experience the redemption Christ accomplished for us. Death is the doorway by which we can leave the limitations and pains of this existence and enter into the heavenly realm. Our death also serves a divine purpose.

Although we can be thankful for the wonders of modern medicine, there does come a time when believers must answer the call to "come up higher." So often when a Christian becomes ill, we immediately pray for his physical restoration. How can we be so sure that it is not God's time to have him enter into the inheritance that is reserved for him (1 Peter 1:4)?

When a person has lived a long life and has virtually no hope of recovery, we must simply commit him to God rather than use heroic measures to eke out one more day of pitiful existence. The day of our death is the day of our glorification. Death is the grand entrance, the door that swings into eternity. Eventually it will open in God's time and in God's way to let another child come home where he or she belongs.

He Died with the Right Commitment

Death can be a time of trust in God's deliverance. Christ's last comment was "Father, into Thy hands I commit My spirit" (Luke 23:46). Thus He died entrusting Himself to the Father whom He so passionately loved. We too can die committing our eternity into the hands of our Father who is in heaven.

Many Christians believe that Christ descended into hell (or more accurately hades) before He went to the

133

earthy existence. "Truly, truly, I say to you, when you were younger, you used to gird yourself, and walk wherever you wished; but when you grow old, you will stretch out your hands, and someone else will gird you, and bring you where you do not wish to go." Then John adds, "Now this He said, signifying by what kind of death he would glorify God" (John 21:18–19). In old age, Peter was tied to a cross and had his hands stretched out, apparently crucified upside down because he felt unworthy to be crucified in the same way Christ was. Can anyone deny that Christ chose the way in which Peter would die?

Most likely, our death will not be by crucifixion. But here again, we know that the ultimate choice will be made by God. The porter God chooses to summon us will come our way, knock on our door, and it will be time to leave. We are thankful that Christ could say, "And do not fear those who kill the body, but are unable to kill the soul; but rather fear Him who is able to destroy both soul and body in hell" (Matthew 10:28). If we fear God, we need fear nothing else.

When the summons comes, it will be like sitting in a concert enjoying the music, only to have our name called before the performance is finished. It will be like building a house and being told that we are not able to live in it. This abrupt interruption of our plans will, however, lead us to our permanent home.

He Died for the Right Purpose

Christ's death was not simply the tragic end of a beautiful life. Within the will of God, His death accomplished redemption for the people whom God had chosen. Christ refers to these individuals as a gift given to Him from the Father: "Those whom thou hast

families, "God took your child." Some think it is better to say, "Cancer took your child," or, "A drunken driver took your child." But the Christian can see beyond these immediate causes. He knows that God can control diseases and restrain the wicked. The immediate cause of death might be any number of things, but the ultimate cause is God. Yes, wicked men nailed Christ to the cross, yet we read, "But the Lord was pleased to crush Him, putting Him to grief" (Isaiah 53:10).

Let us clearly say that God took the six children of the Willis family. God took the woman whose cancer was discovered too late for treatment. God took the child who was gunned down in a drive-by shooting. And someday God will take you and me.

He Died in the Right Way

We've emphasized that there are many ways to die: disease, accidents, murder, to name a few. The circumstances differ for each individual. In God's plan, Christ was to die on a cross, for this was a symbol of humiliation and an unmistakable sign that He was cursed by God. It was death without dignity.

There was no sanitary hospital room, no blankets that would hide the shame of His bloodstained body. He died without dignity, crucified naked for all to see. Today most people die under heavy sedation so that their exit is made as peaceful as possible. When Christ was offered wine mingled with myrrh, He refused this ancient sedative so that He could be fully aware of His surroundings. He took all the horror that death could offer.

If the time of our death is under divine providential guidance, then so is the means. Christ predicted, for example, how Peter would come to the end of his

ately cause the untimely death of another. Mothers who have abortions, thieves who kill their victims—in these instances God holds people responsible for their actions.

But let us boldly say that even when a believer is murdered by evil men (Jim Elliot serves as an example), such a one dies according to the providential plan of God. If Christ, who was brutally murdered by jealous religious leaders, died as planned by God, why should we think that a believer who is gunned down in a robbery is any less under the care of the Almighty? Car accidents, heart attacks, cancer—all of these are the means used to open the door of heaven to the children of God. The immediate cause of our death is neither haphazard nor arbitrary. The One who knows the number of hairs on our head and sees the sparrow fall has the destiny of every one of our days in His loving hands.

Our death is just as meticulously planned as the death of Christ. There is no combination of evil men, disease, or accident that can kill us as long as God still has work for us to do. To those who walk with faith in God's providence, they die according to God's timetable.

This fact should rid us of false guilt. The mother who thoughtlessly answered "Yes" to her little daughter who asked "May I cross the street?" only to see her hit by a truck—that blessed woman must understand that her little one also died under the providential hand of God. Could the Almighty not have arranged that the truck come to the intersection a moment later or earlier? Or could not the mother have been detained and arrived at a different time? Yes, even accidents occur within the circle of divine providence.

Sometimes ministers are reluctant to tell Christian

Yes, even the crime of the crucifixion was a part of God's good plan. "For truly in this city there were gathered together against Thy holy servant Jesus, whom Thou didst anoint, both Herod and Pontius Pilate, along with the Gentiles and the peoples of Israel, to do whatever Thy hand and Thy purpose predestined to occur" (Acts 4:27–28). They could not act until God's clock struck. The "hour" had to come!

Christ died young, but His work was finished. We don't have to live a long life to do all that God has planned for us to do. Some of God's best servants have died at an early age—early from our standpoint, at the right time from God's. They too have finished the work God gave them to do.

The death of a child seems like mockery since God is taking a life before he or she has the joy of accomplishment. As Jung says, "It is like putting a period before the end of the sentence." But a child's short life can fulfill the will of God. Though we do not understand it, that little one has "finished the work God has given him (or her) to do." Though now in heaven, the little one continues his or her ministry in the life of parents and relatives.

Jim Elliot, who himself was killed at a young age while doing missionary work among the Auca Indians, said, "God is peopling Heaven; why should He limit Himself to old people?"

Why, indeed! If the Almighty wants to reach down and take one of His little lambs, or if He wishes to take a servant in the prime of life, He has that right. We think it cruel only because we cannot see behind the dark curtain.

Of course, looked at from our point of view, we can hasten our own death by bad eating habits and other forms of carelessness. And sometimes people deliber-

that He should depart out of this world to the Father, having loved His own who were in the world, He loved them to the end" (John 13:1). This was the hour into which was compacted the agony of Gethsemane, the betrayal of Judas, and the excruciating death of the cross. Interestingly, three times before this we read that "His hour had not yet come" (John 7:30; 8:20; see also 2:4). Until "the hour" arrived, His enemies were powerless against Him.

What sustained Christ? We read, "Jesus, knowing that the Father had given all things into His hands, and that He had come forth from God, and was going back to God, rose from supper, and laid aside His garments; and taking a towel, He girded Himself about" (John 13:3–4). He had come to earth at an hour appointed by God, and now He was returning on schedule! There was not the slightest possibility that Christ would die sooner than God planned!

Christ died more quickly than most others who were crucified. The soldiers, you recall, did not break his legs because "they saw that He was already dead" (John 19:33). He died between three and six in the afternoon, just as the Passover lambs were being slaughtered. He died at the hour God planned, a striking reminder that He was indeed "the Lamb of God, which taketh away the sin of the world" (John 1:29 KJV).

He was only thirty-three years old, young by today's standards and those of ancient Middle Eastern culture. Why not fifty-three, so that He could have many more years of healing the sick, training the disciples, and preaching the love of God to the multitudes? No doubt people in those days wondered, even as they do today, as to why the righteous often die young whereas the wicked live to a ripe old age.

He agonized as He contemplated becoming identified with the sins of the world. He would soon become legally guilty of adultery, theft, and murder. As the sin-bearer, He knew that His personal holiness would come in contact with the defilement of sin. He was sorrowful unto death as He wrestled with the trauma that awaited Him.

But there was hope, too. His impending death was a doorway leading back to the Father; it was the path to victory. Before He went to Gethsemane, He spoke these words, "And now, glorify Thou me together with Thyself, Father, with the glory which I had with Thee before the world was" (John 17:5). We also read elsewhere that He endured the cross, "for the joy set before Him . . . , despising the shame, and has sat down at the right hand of the throne of God" (Hebrews 12:2). For the short term there was pain; but long term, there was glory and joy.

We should not feel guilty for facing death with apprehension, for Christ Himself experienced emotional agony the night before the horror of the cross. Yet, with the fear came comfort; joy and sorrow existed in the same heart. Death was, after all, the Father's will for Christ, and for us all.

A daughter said of her godly father, who died of cancer, "In his closing days, Dad spent more time in heaven than he did on earth." If we can look beyond the immediate heartache to the eventual glory, there is joy. The exit is grievous; the entrance is joyful.

He Died at the Right Time

The night of His betrayal Christ chose to eat the Passover with His disciples. "Now before the Feast of the Passover, Jesus knowing that His hour had come

Remarkably, Lina had confidence that the death of her father, which many would simply ascribe to the random fate of a wind-blown ship, died under God's loving care. She could write, "The protection of His child and treasure, / Is a charge that on Himself He laid." Far from seeing this incident as a cruel oversight on God's part, she saw in her father's death an expression of loving protection! On the human side, he died because of the unexpected high wave; on the divine side, he died because God wanted him home.

As the time of our death approaches we can take comfort from the example of someone who parted the curtain and returned to tell us what to expect on the other side. Christ is our best example of how to face that final hour that most assuredly will come to us all. He died so that we could die triumphantly.

A LESSON IN HOW TO DIE

We never have to say of a believer, "He departed." Rather, we can say, "He has arrived." Heaven is the Christian's final destination. Thanks to Christ, we can be free from the fear of death. We can take comfort from Christ, who gave us an example of how to face that final hour.

He Died with the Right Attitude

Christ died with a mixture of grief and joy. Listen to His words in Gethsemane, "My soul is deeply grieved, to the point of death; remain here and keep watch with Me" (Matthew 26:38). The disciples failed him, so alone He pleaded with His Father, "My Father, if this cannot pass away unless I drink it, Thy will be done" (v. 42).

somewhere they did not want to go; we all could have suffered a similar fate. We must see that God is bigger than our mistakes; He is bigger than a piece of steel that falls randomly from a truck on the expressway. We must remember that those events that are completely out of our control are firmly within His grasp.

At the age of twenty-six, Lina Sandell Berg was accompanying her father aboard a ship across Lake Vattern in Sweden en route to the city of Gothenburg. The ship unexpectedly gave a sudden lurch and Lina's father, a devout Christian, fell overboard and drowned before the eyes of his devoted daughter. From her broken heart she wrote a song that many of us have often sung. As you read the words, find all the lines that affirm Lina's confidence that her father died within the protection and loving care of God.

> *Day by day and with each passing moment,*
> *Strength I find to meet my trials here;*
> *Trusting in my Father's wise bestowment,*
> *I've no cause for worry or for fear.*
>
> *He whose heart is kind beyond all measure*
> *Gives unto each day what He deems best—*
> *Lovingly, its part of pain and pleasure,*
> *Mingling toil with peace and rest*
>
> *Every day the Lord Himself is near me*
> *With a special mercy for each hour;*
> *All my cares He fain would bear, and cheer me,*
> *He whose name is Counselor and Pow'r.*
>
> *The protection of His child and treasure*
> *Is a charge that on Himself He laid;*
> *"As thy days, your strength shall be in measure,"*
> *This the pledge to me He made.*

is greater than our "if onlys." His providential hand encompasses the whole of our lives, not just the good days but the "bad" days too. We have the word *accident* in our vocabulary; He does not.

Accidents, ill health, or even dying at the hand of an enemy—God uses all of these means to bring His children home. As long as we entrust ourselves to His care, we can be confident that we are dying according to His timetable. We can't control events outside of us; we are, however, responsible for how we react to what happens in the seemingly random events of life. The fact is that God can send any chariot He wishes to fetch us for Himself.

Martha and Mary had their "if onlys" too (John 11:1–44). When Christ was told that His friend Lazarus was sick, He stayed away for two extra days so that Lazarus would already be dead and buried by the time He arrived in Bethany. The sisters individually voiced their complaint, "If only you had been here, my brother would not have died." Yet Christ wanted them to know that Lazarus had died within the will of God; he had died according to the divine schedule.

Nothing is gained by bemoaning the fact that "if we had only known then, things could have been different." We do not have to be like the woman who went to the grave of her husband every morning for fourteen years because she felt guilty. She had convinced her husband to go to a concert; en route they were in an accident and he was killed. Such false guilt is not from God, but is self-generated.

That woman—bless her!—could have spared herself much grief if she had but remembered that we are only humans and only God is God. She couldn't foreknow that the accident was going to happen that evening. We have all encouraged our mates to go

"Every morning we awake we say, this is one more day to prove the faithfulness of God. Every night we say, we are one day closer to seeing our children again." Such is the testimony of this couple who understood that children are a gift of God; and when God wants them back, He has the right to take them to Himself. Job, the Old Testament patriarch, would agree.

We say that the Willis family had an accident, but was not this, from God's perspective, a providential happening? I believe so. What we call an accident might be a well-planned event to God.

Just think of the contingencies, the events that had to converge for the accident to happen. Here are a few: *If only* they had started their trip a minute earlier in the morning—or a minute later. Then again, *if only* the truck had been at different location on the expressway, either a few seconds earlier or later. Or one can say, "*If only* that piece of metal had fallen earlier, or later, or if it had scuttled into the ditch rather than in the middle of the lane of traffic . . ."

With a little bit of ingenuity we could identify a dozen "if onlys." After all, this accident would not have happened unless a number of circumstances had converged at the right time and the right place.

Listen to the conversation at almost any funeral and you will hear some "if onlys."

"*If only* we had called the doctor sooner . . ."

"*If only* there would not have been ice on the highway . . ."

"*If only* we had noticed the lump sooner . . ."

"*If only* they had operated . . ."

"*If only* they had not operated . . ."

Let me encourage you to take those "if onlys" and draw a circle around them. Then label the circle, "The providence of God." The Christian believes that God

they commit suicide they will go to heaven. I routinely tell them that they have other options—suicide is never an honorable way out of a difficulty. Whatever our need is, Christ has given us the resources to cope with the difficulties of life. That might mean making some tough choices, but there is "a way of escape."

Second—and this is important—it is presumptuous to commit suicide on the premise that all will be well on the other side. For one thing, many people who say they are Christians aren't. Thus for them suicide is a doorway to eternal misery. For another, we forget that we are accountable to Christ for the way we lived (and died) on earth. Though Christ will not parade our sins before us, our life will be carefully reviewed. It simply makes no sense to see Christ before He has called our name.

FAITH IN GOD'S PROVIDENCE

On November 8, 1994, Pastor Scott Willis and his wife, Janet, were traveling with six of their nine children on Highway I-94 near Milwaukee when a piece of metal fell off the truck ahead of them. Scott had no choice but to let the object pass under his vehicle; the result was that the rear gas tank exploded and five of the six Willis children died instantly in the flames. The sixth child, Benjamin, died a few hours later.

Scott and Janet were able to get out of the vehicle, sustaining burns from which they would later recover. Standing there watching their children die in the fire, Scott said to Janet, "This is the moment for which we are prepared." The courage of this couple was reported throughout the United States and the world. Christ walked with them through the deep sorrows of this tragedy.

endure such shameful public torture, but death is never pretty.

Another argument for assisting in death is that medical technology has artificially prolonged life. Rather than suffer, we now have doctors who take it upon themselves to help patients grant themselves "self-deliverance."

This is not the place to discuss the fallout of assisted suicide in society. We can only anticipate the pressure that will be placed on the elderly to end it all to save medical costs and to make it easier for their families. Very quickly the *right* to die can become the *responsibility* to die.

Those who do choose suicide (for whatever reason) should remember that death is not the end, but a doorway to an eternal existence. Sad to say, some who find the pain of dying intolerable will awaken in a realm that is even more terrible than earth could ever be. We should welcome death from the hand of God, but not force the hand that brings it.

Just recently a rather well-known pastor committed suicide. He had preached the gospel for many years; no doubt dozens, if not hundreds, were converted under his ministry, and yet there he lay on the grass with self-inflicted gunshot wounds.

Yes, Christians—genuine Christians—sometimes do commit suicide. I believe that such are in heaven by the only route by which any one of us shall make it—*the grace of God.* Of course those who end their own lives die as failures; their last act was murder (their own). And yet because they have come under the shelter of God's protection through Christ, they will be escorted into the heavenly gates.

As a pastor I have frequently had phone calls from distraught people wanting me to assure them that if

have an appointment with him in Sumera tonight."

You and I have an appointment. Perhaps it will be in London, Taipei, or Chicago. Wherever, it is one appointment we will not miss. As C. S. Lewis observed, the statistics on death are impressive—so far it is one out of one!

Cancer, accidents, and a hundred different diseases lurk about waiting for an opportunity to devour us. Death awaits us as the concrete floor awaits the falling light bulb. The first person who ever died was not Adam, the first sinful man; nor Cain, the man who would be a murderer, but Abel, the one who was righteous. We give a wry smile when we hear about the friendly undertaker who signed all of his correspondence, "Eventually yours."

DEATH BY SUICIDE

The suffering that often precedes death can be so excruciating that many people hope to leapfrog over the process of dying to get to death itself. Books explaining how to commit suicide are selling briskly; a growing number of people want to "control their own destiny" rather than be at the mercy of modern medicine. "Dying with dignity," we are told, is our right.

Strictly speaking, no one "dies with dignity." Ever since sin entered into the world and brought death with it, death has always been the final humiliation, the one unalterable fact that confirms our mortality and reduces our bodies to ashes.

Apparently, Jesus Himself hung on the cross naked, exposed to the gawkers outside the city of Jerusalem. We are thankful that none of us will likely have to

*W*HEN THE CURTAIN OPENS FOR YOU

Death by Suicide—Faith in God's Providence—
A Lesson in How to Die

In the Middle East a fable is told of a Baghdad merchant who sent his servant to the marketplace to run an errand. When the servant had completed his assignment and was about to leave the marketplace, he turned a corner and unexpectedly met Lady Death.

The look on her face so frightened him that he left the marketplace and hurried home. He told his master what had happened and requested his fastest horse so that he could get as far from Lady Death as possible— a horse that would take him all the way to Sumera before nightfall.

Later the same afternoon the merchant himself went to the marketplace and met Lady Death. "Why did you startle my servant this morning?" he asked.

"I didn't intend to startle your servant—it was I who was startled," replied Lady Death. "I was surprised to see your servant in Baghdad this morning, because I

do so. Indeed, we read, "He who believes in the Son has eternal life; but he who does not obey the Son shall not see life, but the wrath of God abides on him" (John 3:36). Thankfully, there is a way of escape; we can be forever shielded from the wrath to come!

NOTES

1. John A. Robinson, "Universalism: Is It Heretical?" *Scottish Journal of Theology,* June 1949, 155.

2. Percy Dearmer, *The Legend of Hell* (London: Cassell, 1929), 74–75.

3. Robert Morey, *Death and the Afterlife* (Minneapolis: Bethany, 1984), 90.

4. Walter B. Knight, *Knight's Master Book of New Illustrations* (Grand Rapids: Eerdmans, 1956), 159.

5. Charles Hodge, *Systematic Theology,* vol. 3, pt. 4 (Grand Rapids: Eerdmans, 1956), 159.

6. Warren Wiersbe, *Treasury of the World's Great Sermons* (Grand Rapids: Kregel, 1977), 198–205.

Therefore, it was only the mercy of God that kept them from plunging into the abyss:

> There is nothing that keeps wicked men at any one moment out of hell, but the mere pleasure of God. . . . There is no want in God's power to cast wicked men into hell at any moment. . . . They deserve to be cast into hell, so divine justice never stands in the way. . . . They are now the objects of that very same anger and wrath that is expressed in the torments of hell . . . yea, God is a great deal more angry with great numbers that are now on the earth, yea doubtless with some who reread this book, who it may be are at ease, than he is with many of those who are now in the flames of hell.
>
> Unconverted men walk over the pit of hell on a rotten covering, and there are innumerable places in this covering so weak that they will not bear their weight, and those places are not seen. . . . There is the dreadful pit of the glowing flames of the wrath of God; there is hell's wide gaping mouth open; and you have nothing to stand upon, nor anything to take hold of, there is nothing between you and hell but air; it is only the power and mere pleasure of God that holds you up. . . . His wrath burns against you like fire; he looks upon you as worthy of nothing else than to be thrown into the fire. . . . You hang by the slender thread, with the flames of divine wrath flashing about it and ready every moment to singe it, and burn it asunder.[6]

Powerful!

If reading this chapter has been frightening, the good news is that if God grants you the desire to trust Christ that you might escape hell, you are invited to

before the bird had carried away a single handful of sand. Now let's expand that illustration and think how long it would take the bird to move the Oak Street Beach in Chicago and then the other thousands of beaches around the world. After that, the bird could begin on the mountains and the earth's crust.

By the time the bird transported the entire earth to the far-off planet, eternity would not have officially begun. Strictly speaking, one cannot begin an infinite series, for a beginning implies an end. In other words, we might say that after the bird has done his work, those in eternity will not be one step closer to having their suffering alleviated. There is no such thing as half an eternity.

The most sobering thought that could ever cross our minds is the fact that the rich man in hades referred to above has not yet received the drop of water for which he so desperately longed. Today, as you read this book, he is still there awaiting the final judgment of the lake of fire. Eternity endures, and it endures forever.

A Place of Easy Access but No Exit

Entering hell is easy enough. All that one has to do is neglect Christ, the only one who can save us.

Jonathan Edwards, whom we have already quoted, gave more consideration to the doctrine of hell than any other theologian. His sermon "Sinners in the Hands of an Angry God" kept audiences spellbound, stripping from them any objections or excuses they might have had against the doctrine of hell. He made the point that there are some people now living for whom God has more anger than some who are now in hades (he called it hell) who have already died.

bliss of heaven knowing full well the fate of the wicked in hell.

Though Dante added many of his own ideas to the superstitions of his day when he wrote *The Inferno,* the sign he read in the vestibule of hell does portray the biblical teaching of hopelessness and abandonment.

> *I am the way to the city of woe.*
> *I am the way to a forsaken people.*
> *I am the way into eternal sorrow.*
>
> *Sacred justice moved my architect.*
> *I was raised here by divine omnipotence,*
> *Primordial love and ultimate intellect.*
>
> *Only those elements time cannot wear*
> *Were made before me, and beyond time I stand.*
> *Abandon all hope ye who enter here.*
>
> Canto 3.1–9

Jonathan Edwards pointed out that those in hell will have no reason for entertaining any secret hope that after being in the flames many ages God will take pity on them and release them. God, says Edwards, will not be any more inclined to release them after a million ages than He was at the very first moment. Little wonder, Edwards said, that any description we give of hell can be but a faint representation of the reality!

A Place of Eternity

How long is eternity?

Visualize a bird coming to earth every million years and taking one grain of sand to a distant planet. At that rate it would take thousands of billions of years

the two men, but at least they could speak to one another. But it is unlikely that there will be the opportunity of such communication in hell. For one thing, "Abraham's bosom" was transferred directly into the presence of Christ at the Ascension. For another, we have no suggestion in the New Testament that those who are in hell will be able to communicate with one another.

C. S. Lewis believed there would not be communication in hell, because it was a place of solitude. Jonathan Edwards believed that if unbelievers are next to one another they will only add to each other's agony through expressions of hatred, accusations, and curses. Of one thing we can be absolutely certain: No comfort will be derived from the presence of others. Consumed with the torment of raging, unforgiven sin, those in hell will never find comfort again.

However, the Scriptures teach that those who are in hell will be tormented in the presence of Christ and the holy angels (Revelation 14:10). Nothing is said about whether other people behold the sufferings of the damned, though God often invites righteous people or angels to behold the judgment He inflicts upon the wicked (Psalm 46:8–9; Isaiah 66:23–24; Revelation 19:17–21). The famous British preacher Charles Haddon Spurgeon wrote, "If there be one thing in hell worse than another, it will be seeing the saints in heaven. . . . Husband, there is your wife in heaven and you are among the damned. And do you see your father? Your child is before the throne, and you accursed of God and man are in hell!"

If believers do witness these events, we can be sure that they will agree completely with the justice displayed by God, for then they shall see all things from His point of view. Thus, the righteous can enjoy the

lake of fire. Yet, there is no doubt that some of the characteristics of hades continue, or more accurately, that the suffering of hades is intensified in hell.

A Place of Torment

Usually when we think of hell, we think of fire, since Christ spoke of the "fire of hell." In Revelation we read of "the lake of fire and brimstone."

There is no reason the torments of hell could not include physical fire, since the bodies of those present will have been recreated and made indestructible. Unlike our present bodies, those of the resurrected dead will not burn up or be extinguished. Literal fire is a possibility.

However, as we learned earlier, there is another kind of fire that will be in hell, a fire that may be worse than literal fire. That is the fire of unfulfilled passion, of desires that are never satisfied. Perpetually burning lusts never subside, and the tortured conscience burns but is never sated or appeased. There will be increased desire with decreased satisfaction.

Hell, then, is the raw soul joined to an indestructible body, exposed to its own sin for eternity. Hell is the place of unquenchable, raging guilt, without pain-killers or sedation. Literal fire might be welcomed if only it would cleanse the tormented conscience.

Be assured of this: Neither the devil nor his angels will torment people in hell. Satan and his demons will be among the tormented; they will not be tormentors (Revelation 20:10).

A Place of Abandonment

In hades there was an unbridgeable chasm between

gehenna. The Jews taught, and Christ confirmed, that the wicked would suffer there forever. Body and soul would be in eternal torment.

For years, liberal scholars taught (and some sentimentalists still do) that Christ, who stressed the love of God, could never be party to the doctrine of hell. Yet significantly, of the twelve times the word *gehenna* is used in the New Testament, eleven times it came from the mouth of our Lord. Indeed, He spoke more about hell than about heaven.

The third word is *hades,* a word we have already studied in a previous chapter. I mention it here only because it is translated "hell" in the King James Version of the Bible. Most other translations simply leave it untranslated as "hades," so that it might be properly distinguished from hell.

What will the suffering of hell be like? We must guard against undue speculation since the Scriptures do not describe the torments of hell in specifics. We must not fall into the error of the medievals, who described hell with the vivid details of a guide taking tourists through the Vatican. Yet, Jesus told a story that does give us a glimpse of hell, or more accurately, a glimpse of hades, which is a prelude to the final place of eternal punishment.

CHARACTERISTICS OF HELL

In a previous chapter we referred to Christ's story of the rich man who was in hades while his friend Lazarus was in Abraham's bosom. Christ's point was to show how the fortunes of these men were reversed in the life to come. The rich man was now in torment, the poor man in bliss.

But after the judgment, hades is thrown into the

Hodge asks, "If the highest glory of God and the good of the universe have been promoted by the past sinfulness and misery of men, why may not those objects be promoted by what is declared to be future?"[5]

If our concept of justice differs from God's, we can be quite sure that He will be unimpressed by our attempts to get Him to see things from our point of view. No one is God's counselor; no one instructs or corrects Him. He does not look to us for input on how to run His universe.

GREEK WORDS FOR HELL

The New Testament uses three different Greek words of hell. One is *tartarus,* used in 2 Peter 2:4 for the abode of evil angels who sinned during the time of Noah. "For . . . God did not spare angels when they sinned, but cast them into hell and committed them to pits of darkness, reserved for judgment." In Jude 6 the word *tartarus* is used similarly.

The second and most often used word for hell in the New Testament is *gehenna,* a word for hell already used by the Jews before the time of Christ. The word is derived from the Hebrew "valley of Hinnom" found in the Old Testament (Joshua 15:8; 2 Kings 23:10; Nehemiah 11:30). In that valley outside Jerusalem the Jews gave human sacrifices to pagan deities. There too the garbage of the city was thrown, where it bred worms. That explains why Christ referred to hell as the place where "their worm does not die, and the fire is not quenched" (Mark 9:44, 46, 48).

This picture of an unclean dump where fires and worms never die became to the Jewish mind an appropriate description of the ultimate fate of all idolaters. Thus the word became applied to the ultimate

love and mercy of God; He does not delight in the death of the wicked. But it also has much to say about His justice and the fact that even the wicked in hell will glorify Him. To put it clearly, we must accept God as He is revealed in the Bible, whether He suits our preferences or not.

It is absurd in the extreme to say, "I don't want to be in heaven with a God who sends people to hell . . . I would rather go to hell and defy Him." I can't exaggerate the foolishness of those who think they can oppose God to their own satisfaction or to His detriment! In Psalm 2 we read that God sits in the heavens and laughs at those who think they can defy Him. Like the mouse who thinks it can stand against the farmer's plow or the rowboat poised to thwart the path of an aircraft carrier, it is insanity for man to think that he can oppose the living God, who is angry with sinners and is bent on taking vengeance on those who oppose Him.

Even as we look at the world today, we should not be surprised that God allows multitudes to live in eternal misery. Think of the vast amount of suffering (preventable suffering, if you please) that God has allowed on this earth. An earthquake in Mexico kills twenty thousand, a tidal wave in Bangladesh kills fifty thousand, and famines in the world cause twenty thousand deaths every single day! Who can begin to calculate the amount of emotional pain experienced by babies, children, and adults? Yet we know that strengthening the earth's crust, sending rain, and withholding floods could all be accomplished by a word from the Almighty.

If God has allowed people to live in untold misery for thousands of years, why would it be inconsistent for Him to allow misery to continue forever? Charles

and be united to him again! But it is a fruitless wish. Millions and millions of years would bring me no nearer to the end of my torments than one poor hour. Oh, eternity, eternity! forever and forever! Oh, the insufferable pains of hell![4]

He was quite right in saying that a million years in hell could not purchase salvation. Tragically, he did not cast himself upon the mercy of God in Christ. Since no man's works or sufferings can save him, he must bear the full weight of his sin throughout eternity.

We Cannot Comprehend the Seriousness of Sin

We must confess that we do not know exactly how much punishment is enough for those who have sinned against God. We may think we know what God is like, but we see through a glass darkly. Jonathan Edwards said that the reason we find hell so offensive is because of our insensitivity to sin.

What if, from God's viewpoint, the greatness of sin is determined by the greatness of the One against whom it is committed? Then the guilt of sin is infinite because it is a violation of the character of an infinite Being. What if, in the nature of God, it is deemed that such infinite sins deserve an infinite penalty, a penalty which no one can ever repay?

We must realize that God did not choose the attributes He possesses. Because He has existed from all eternity, His attributes were already determined from eternity past. If God had not possessed love and mercy throughout all eternity, we might have been created by a malicious and cruel being who delighted in watching His creatures suffer perpetual torment. Fortunately, that is not the case. The Bible tells of the

the pain of rejection—all blame will be accurately proportioned.

We all agree that heaven is a comforting doctrine. What is often overlooked is that hell is comforting too. Our newspapers are filled with stories of rape, child abuse, and a myriad of injustices. Every court case ever tried on earth will be reopened; every action and motive will be meticulously inspected and just retribution meted out. In the presence of an all-knowing God there will be no unsolved murders, no unknown child abductor, and no hidden bribe.

Unbelievers Are Eternally Guilty

Hell exists because unbelievers are eternally guilty. The powerful lesson to be learned is that no human being's suffering can ever be a payment for sin. If our suffering could erase even the most insignificant sin, then those in hell would eventually be freed after their debt was paid. But all human goodness and suffering from the beginning of time, if added together, could not cancel so much as a single sin.

> *Could my zeal no respite know,*
> *Could my tears forever flow,*
> *All for sin could not atone;*
> *Thou must save, and Thou alone.*
>
> "Rock of Ages"

Sir Francis Newport, who ridiculed Christianity, is quoted as saying these terrifying words on his deathbed:

Oh, that I was to lie a thousand years upon the fire that never is quenched, to purchase the favor of God,

of Christ is needed for salvation. "And there is salvation in no one else; for there is no other name under heaven that has been given among men, by which we must be saved" (Acts 4:12).

But the light of God in nature and in the human conscience is still a sufficient basis for judgment. Whatever the degree of punishment, it will fit the offense exactly, for God is meticulously just. Those who believe in Christ experience mercy; those who do not (either because they have never heard of Him or because they reject what they know of Him) will receive justice. Either way, God is glorified.

Think of how accurately God will judge every unbeliever! Each day of every life will be analyzed in minute detail. The hidden thoughts and motives of each hour will be replayed, along with all the actions and attitudes. The words spoken in secret will be made public, the intentions of the heart displayed for all to see. They will have no attorney to whom they may appeal, no loopholes by which they can escape. Nothing but bare, indisputable facts.

I believe that the balance of justice will be so accurate that the pornographer will wish he had never published such material, the thief will wish he had earned an honest living, and the adulterer will regret that he lived an immoral life. Faithfulness to his marriage vows would not have earned him a place in heaven, to be sure, but it would have made his existence in hell slightly more bearable.

Before God, no motives will be misinterpreted, no extenuating circumstances thrown out of court. The woman who seduced the man will receive her fair share of punishment, and the man who allowed himself to be seduced will receive his. The parents who abused their child who turned to drugs to escape from

To us as humans, everlasting punishment is dispro-portionate to the offense committed. God appears cruel, unjust, sadistic, and vindictive. The purpose of punishment, we are told, is always redemptive. Reha-bilitation is the goal of all prison sentences. The con-cept of a place where there will be endless punishment without any possibility of parole or reform seems unjust.

How can hell be just? The following observations may not answer all of our questions, but I hope they will help us begin to see hell from God's perspective.

The Judgment Is Based on What They Did

In a previous chapter we learned that hades will eventually be thrown into hell. But before that hap-pens every person will be resurrected and judged individually. "And I saw the dead, the great and the small, standing before the throne, and books were opened; and another book was opened, which is the book of life; and the dead were judged from the things which were written in the books, according to their deeds" (Revelation 20:12).

No one is saved by works, to be sure. As we shall stress in the final chapter of this book, salvation is a gift of God, not of works. But for the unsaved the works are the basis of judgment. In other words, they will be rightly judged on the basis of what they did with what they knew.

Those who live without specific knowledge about Christ will be judged by the light of nature and their own conscience (Romans 1:20; 2:14–16). That does not mean that those who respond to general revela-tion will be automatically saved, for no one lives up to all that he knows. That is why a personal knowledge

the smoke of their torment goes up forever and ever; and they have no rest day and night, those who worship the beast and his image, and whoever receives the mark of his name. (vv. 10–11)

Notice that the fire does not annihilate the wicked but torments them. There, in the presence of the holy angels and the Lamb, there will be no periods of rest during which the wicked are unconscious of torment. They will never slip into peaceful nonexistence.

In Revelation 20 we have a similar scene. The beast and the false prophet have been thrown into the lake of fire, and Satan has been released to deceive the nations for one thousand years. At the end of that period, Satan is cast into the lake of fire. Notice carefully that the beast and the false prophet have not been annihilated during those one thousand years in hell. The fire has not consumed them: "And the devil who deceived them was thrown into the lake of fire and brimstone, where the beast and the false prophet are also; and they will be tormented day and night forever and ever" (v. 10).

Hence, the teachings of universalism and annihilationism come to their deceptive end. Eternal, conscious torment is clearly taught—*there is no other honest interpretation of these passages.*

THE JUSTICE OF GOD

At the root of the debate is the question of whether hell is fair and just. Pinnock, you will recall, lamented that it was difficult enough to explain evil to the unbelieving world without having to explain hell too. Sensitive Christians, he says, cannot believe in eternal, conscious punishment.

9:17, Luke 15:4, and John 6:12, 27. In none of those instances does it mean "to pass out of existence." Morey writes: "There isn't a single instance in the New Testament where apollumi means annihilation in the strict sense of the word."[3] Thayer's *Greek-English Lexicon* defines destruction as "to be delivered up to eternal misery."

Unfortunately, annihilationism simply will not wash. Christ says that the lost will go into "eternal fire," which has been prepared for the devil and his angels. And then He adds, "And these will go away into eternal punishment, but the righteous into eternal life" (Matthew 25:46). Since the same word *eternal* describes both the destiny of the righteous and the wicked, it seems clear that Christ taught that both groups will exist forever, albeit in different places. The same eternal fire that Satan and his hosts experience will be the lot of unbelievers.

In an earlier chapter we learned that the eternal conscious existence of unbelievers was already taught in the Old Testament. Daniel wrote, "And many of those who sleep in the dust of the ground will awake, these to everlasting life, but the others to disgrace and everlasting contempt" (Daniel 12:2). The wicked will experience shame and contempt for as long as the righteous experience bliss.

Finally, the occupants of hell are clearly said to experience eternal misery. Those who worship the beast and have received his mark "will drink of the wine of the wrath of God, which is mixed in full strength in the cup of His anger" (Revelation 14:10). Such will be

> tormented with fire and brimstone in the presence of the holy angels and in the presence of the Lamb. And

Conditional Immortality

Whereas universalism sought to take the "forever" out of hell, we now come to a theory that attempts to take the hell out of forever. Conditional immortality contends that all will not be saved, but neither will any be in conscious torment forever. God resurrects the wicked to judge them; then they are thrown into the fire and consumed. The righteous are granted eternal life, whereas the unbelievers are granted eternal death. Hell is annihilation.

Clark Pinnock of McMaster University in Toronto, Canada, asks how one can imagine for a moment that the God who gave His Son to die on the cross would "install a torture chamber somewhere in the new creation in order to subject those who reject him in everlasting pain?" He observes that it is difficult enough to defend Christianity in light of the problem of evil and suffering without having to explain hell too.

Pinnock believes that the fire of God consumes the lost. Thus God does not raise the wicked to torture them but rather to declare judgment on them and condemn them to extinction, which is the second death. Everlasting punishment, according to Pinnock, means that God sentences the lost to final, definitive death.

Pinnock's favorite text is: "And do not fear those who kill the body, but are unable to kill the soul; but rather fear Him who is able to destroy both soul and body in hell" (Matthew 10:28). He assumes that if a soul is destroyed in hell it is annihilated.

Unfortunately, that interpretation will not survive careful analysis. Robert A. Morey points out in *Death and the Afterlife* that the word *destroyed* as used in the Bible does not mean "to annihilate." The Greek word *apollumi* is used in passages such as Matthew

shall be made alive." Universalists interpret these verses to mean that as all men are condemned for Adam's offense, so all men are justified by Christ's act of righteousness.

Unfortunately, that interpretation fails for two reasons. First, the texts must be interpreted in light of others that clearly teach the eternal misery of unbelievers in hell. We simply do not have the luxury of isolating passages of Scripture.

Second, we must realize that the Bible frequently uses the word *all* in a restricted sense, as pertaining to all in a certain category rather than all without exception. Examples are numerous. Matthew tells us that "all Judea" went out to hear John the Baptist (Matthew 3:5-6). Luke records that a decree went out that "a census be taken of all the inhabited earth" (Luke 2:1). And the disciples of John the Baptist complained that "all" were following Christ (John 3:26). In the passages written by Paul, it is clear that all who are in Adam die, whereas all who are in Christ shall be made alive. The *all* has limitations built into it by the context.

The final death blow to universalism is in Matthew 12:32. Christ is speaking of the unpardonable sin: "It shall not be forgiven him, either in this age, or in the age to come." In Mark 3:29 it is called an "eternal sin," indicating that it begins in this age and is carried on for all eternity without hope of reversal. How could those who have committed this sin be reconciled to God when Scripture clearly says they shall never be forgiven?

Universalism has never been widely accepted by those who take the Scriptures seriously. Obviously if this teaching were true, there would be no pressing reason to fulfill the Great Commission or to urge unbelievers to accept Christ in this life.

ming up of all things in Christ, things in the heavens and things upon the earth" (Ephesians 1:10). And it is God's intention to "reconcile all things to Himself, having made peace through the blood of His cross; through Him, I say, whether things on earth or things in heaven" (Colossians 1:20). The implication, we are told, is that everyone will eventually be brought into the family of God.

Unfortunately, this attractive interpretation has serious weaknesses. If the universalists' interpretation were correct, then Satan would also have to be redeemed, that is, reconciled to God. Yet it is clear that Christ did not die for him (Hebrews 2:16); therefore God would have no just grounds to pardon him, even if he repented.

What is more, the Scriptures explicitly teach that he along with the beast and the false prophet shall be "tormented day and night forever and ever" (Revelation 20:10). Here we have a clear statement that Satan shall never be redeemed but will exist in conscious eternal torment.

Yes, everything will be summed up in Christ. That means that all things will be brought under Christ's direct authority. Christ has completed everything necessary to fulfill God's plan of salvation. The order of nature shall be restored, and justice will prevail throughout the whole universe. As we shall see later, that restoration does not negate the doctrine of hell but instead necessitates it.

Universalists also quote other verses, such as, "So then as through one transgression there resulted condemnation to all men, even so through one act of righteousness there resulted justification of life to all men" (Romans 5:18). A similar passage is 1 Corinthians 15:22: "As in Adam all die, so also in Christ all

ance of such a God. "If such a God exists," he complained, "He is the devil."

To put it simply, to us the punishment of hell does not fit the crime. Yes, all men do some evil and a few do great evils, but nothing that anyone has ever done can justify eternal torment. And to think that millions of good people will be in hell simply because they have not heard of Christ (as Christianity affirms) strains credulity. It's like capital punishment for a traffic violation.

Thus millions of Westerners believe in some kind of afterlife, but it is one of bliss, not misery. Genuine fear of suffering in hell has vanished from the mainstream of Western thought. Few, if any, give prolonged thought to the prospect that some people will be in hell. Fewer yet believe they themselves will be among that unfortunate number.

ALTERNATIVE TEACHINGS

There are two alternative theories that vie for acceptance. One takes the hell out of forever; the other takes the forever out of hell.

Universalism

Universalism is the name given to the belief that eventually all men will arrive safely to heaven. Since Christ died for all people without exception, it follows, they say, that all will eventually be saved. God will overcome every remnant of evil, and all rational creatures (some would even include Satan) will eventually be redeemed.

Here is a verse universalists like to use. Paul taught that in the fullness of time, there would be the "sum-

And yet we read that in the final judgment the unbelieving dead of all the ages stand before God to be judged, "And death and Hades were thrown into the lake of fire. . . . And if anyone's name was not found written in the book of life, he was thrown into the lake of fire" (Revelation 20:14–15). This is but one of many descriptions of hell found in the Bible. What shall we do with this teaching?

REASONS TO DISBELIEVE

This doctrine is often neglected because it is difficult to reconcile hell with the love of God. That millions of people will be in conscious torment forever is beyond the grasp of the human mind. Bishop John A. Robinson, who gained notoriety with his liberal views in *Honest to God,* writes,

> Christ . . . remains on the Cross as long as one sinner remains in hell. . . . In a universe of love there can be no heaven that tolerates a chamber of horrors; no hell for any which does not at the same time make it hell for God. He cannot endure that, for that would be a final mockery of his nature.[1]

The doctrine of hell has driven many people away from Christianity. James Mill expressed what many have felt. "I will call no being good, who is not what I mean by good when I use that word of my fellow creatures; and if there be a Being who can send me to hell for not so calling him, to hell I will go."[2]

One man said that he would not want to be in heaven with a God who sends people to hell. His preference was to be in hell so that he could live in defi-

WHEN HADES IS THROWN INTO HELL

*Reasons to Disbelieve—Alternative Teachings—
The Justice of God—Greek Words for Hell—
Characteristics of Hell*

Hell disappeared. And no one noticed."
With that terse observation, American church historian Martin Marty summarized our attitude toward a vanishing doctrine that received careful attention in previous generations. If you are a churchgoer, ask yourself when you last heard an entire sermon or Sunday school lesson on the topic.

A recent *Newsweek* article says, "Today, hell is theology's H-word, a subject too trite for serious scholarship." Gordon Kaufman of Harvard Divinity School believes we have gone through a transformation of ideas, and he says, "I don't think there can be any future for heaven and hell."

Admittedly, hell is an unpleasant topic. Unbelievers disbelieve in it; most Christians ignore it. Even the staunchly biblical diehards are often silent out of embarrassment. Hell, more than any doctrine of the Bible, seems to be out of step with our times.

And so while your family tends to the your funeral, you are beholding the face of Christ. Though the family weeps at your departure, you would not return to earth even if the choice were given to you. Having seen heaven, you will find that earth has lost all of its attraction. As Tony Evans says, "Have a good time at my funeral, because I'm not going to be there!"

You only wish that those you left behind would know how important it was to be faithful to Christ. Looked at from the other side of the curtain, knowing what is now so clear to you, you wish that you could shout to earth encouraging believers to serve Christ will all their hearts. You wish you had grasped this before the call came for you to come up higher.

Suddenly you realize that not everyone will have your experience. Some people—millions of them—will be lost forever because they did not take advantage of Christ's sacrifice on their behalf. You weep as you think of all the people still on earth who most probably will not be there.

You know that you would weep forever except that God comes to wipe the tears from your eyes.

It will all be true, just as Christ said.

NOTES

1. David Gregg, *The Heaven-Life* (New York: Revell, 1895), 62.

2. Richard Whately, *A View of the Scripture Revelations Concerning a Future State*, 3d ed. (Philadelphia: Lindsay & Blakiston, 1857), 214–15.

3. Wilbur M. Smith, *Biblical Doctrine of Heaven* (Chicago: Moody, 1968), 253.

4. Joseph Seiss, *Lectures on the Apocalypse* (New York: Charles C. Cook, 1901), 3:412–13; quoted in Wilbur Smith, *Biblical Doctrine,* 249.

replaced as one supply burns out; for it is the uncreated light of Him who is light, dispensed by and through the Lamb as the everlasting Lamp, to the home, and hearts, and understandings of His glorified saints.[4]

No Abominations (21:27)

The nations shall bring the honor and glory of God into the city, but we read, "Nothing unclean and no one who practices abomination and lying shall ever come into it, but only those whose names are written in the Lamb's book of life" (21:27). John lists others who will be excluded: immoral people, murderers, idolaters, and the like (21:8; 22:15).

No More Hunger, Thirst, or Heat (7:16)

Those burdens borne by the multitudes of this present world will vanish forever. In their place will be the Tree of Life and the beauty of the paradise of God.

Those things that cast such a pall of gloom over the earth today will be replaced by indescribable happiness in the presence of Divine Glory.

> *Just think of stepping on shore,*
> *And finding it heaven;*
> *Of clasping a hand,*
> *And finding it God's;*
> *Of breathing new air,*
> *And finding it celestial;*
> *Of waking up in glory,*
> *And finding it home.*

"Finally Home," words by Don Wyrtzen;
reprinted with permission, Benson Company, Inc.
Copyright 1971 by Singspiration Music.

And no more emotional pain because of rejection, separation, or abuse.

No Temple (21:22)

Some have been puzzled by that assertion because elsewhere John says that there is a temple in heaven (Revelation 11:19). Wilbur M. Smith points out that the apparent contradiction can be resolved when we realize that the temple and its angelic messengers "continue in action during the time of man's sin and the outpouring of the wrath of God, but after the old earth has disappeared, the temple has no longer any function."[3] The worship in heaven is now carried on directly; God Himself is the shrine, the temple. The former patterns of worship give way to a new, unrestricted order.

No More Sun or Moon (7:16; 21:23; 22:5)

Those planets created by God to give light to the earth have outlived their purpose. God Himself is the light of heaven. "And the city has no need of the sun or of the moon to shine upon it, for the glory of God has illumined it, and its lamp the Lamb" (21:23; see also 7:16). Again we read, "And there shall no longer be any night; and they shall not have need of the light of a lamp nor the light of the sun, because the Lord God shall illumine them; and they shall reign forever and ever" (22:5).

That means that the holy city is interpenetrated with light. Joseph Seiss explains it this way:

> That shining is not from any material combustion, not from any consumption of fuel that needs to be

human ignorance. That is especially true in heaven, where we will have better mental faculties than on earth. In heaven we shall be comforted, not because we know less than we did on earth but because we know more.

It is more likely that God will wipe away all tears by explaining His ultimate purposes. We will look at heaven and hell from His viewpoint and say that He did all things well. If God can be content knowing that unbelievers are in hell, so will we. I expect that all who are in heaven will live with the knowledge that justice was fully served and that God's plan was right. And with such an explanation and perspective, our emotions will mirror those of our heavenly Father. Jonathan Edwards said that heaven will have no pity for hell, not because the saints are unloving but because they are perfectly loving. They will see everything in conformity with God's love, justice, and glory. Thus with both head and heart we will worship the Lord without regret, sorrow, or misgivings about our Father's plan.

No More Pain (21:4)

Come with me as we walk down the corridor of a hospital. Here is a young mother dying of cancer; there is a man gasping for breath, trying to overcome the terror of a heart attack. In the next ward an abused child has just been admitted with burns inflicted by an angry father. For those and countless other emergencies scientists have prepared painkillers to help people make it through life, one day at a time.

In heaven, pain, which is the result of sin, is banished forever. No headaches, slipped discs, or surgery.

No More Crying (7:17; 21:4)

No one could possibly calculate the buckets of tears that are shed every single moment in this hurting world. From the child crying because of the death of a parent to the woman weeping because of a failed marriage—multiply those tears by a million, and you will realize that we live in a crying world.

In heaven, He who wiped away our sins now wipes away our tears. This comment has raised the question of why there would be tears in heaven in the first place. And does the Lord come with a handkerchief and literally wipe away each tear? That is possible. But I think that John means more than that. He wants us to understand that God will give us an explanation for the sorrow we experienced on earth so that we will not have to cry anymore. If that were not so, then the tears might return after He has wiped them away. But being able to view the tearful events of earth from the perspective of heaven will dry up our tears forever.

The question is often asked how we can be happy in heaven if one or more of our relatives is in hell. Can a child, for example, enjoy the glories of eternity knowing that a father or a mother will always be absent from the celebration? Or can a godly mother serve and worship with joy knowing that her precious son will be in torment forever? That question has so vexed the minds of theologians that some have actually asserted that in heaven God will blank out a part of our memory. The child will not know that his parents are lost in hell; the mother will not remember that she had a son.

However, it is unlikely that we will know less in heaven than we do on earth. It is not characteristic of God to resolve a problem by expanding the sphere of

A New Order of Reality

Fortunately, heaven will not have everything. In fact the apostle John lists in Revelation 7, 21, and 22 many different experiences and realities known on earth that will be *absent* there.

No More Sea (21:1)

Throughout the Bible, the word *sea* stands for the nations of the world, usually the rebellious nations. Heaven means that the strife between nations and the seething turmoil that accompanies those struggles will vanish. No broken treaties, no wars, no scandals.

No More Death (21:4)

The hearse will have made its last journey. Today we look at death as a thief that robs us of our earthly existence. It is simply the final act in the deterioration of the human body. As such it is almost universally feared; no one can escape its terrors. Even Christians who have conquered it in Christ may tremble at its fearsome onslaught. But death shall not enter heaven. No funeral services, no tombstones, no tearful good-byes.

No More Sorrow (21:4)

Read the newspaper, and sorrow is written on every page. An automobile accident takes the life of a young father; a child is raped by a madman; a flood in Bangladesh kills twenty thousand. No one can fathom the amount of emotional pain borne by the inhabitants of this world in any single moment. In heaven there will be uninterrupted joy and emotional tranquillity.

expanded. Think of it this way: The intimacy you now enjoy with your family will include all the other saints who are present.

One day some of Christ's friends sent word that His mother and brothers were looking for Him. Christ responded, "Who are My mother and My brothers?" And looking around Him, He said, "Behold, My mother and My brothers! For whoever does the will of God, he is My brother and sister and mother" (Mark 3:33–35).

Think of the implications. We will be just as close to Christ as we are to any member of our present family. Indeed, He is not ashamed to call us His brothers! There will be extended family with greater intimacy than we have known on earth.

Archbishop Richard Whately has an excellent description of the kind of friendship we can expect in heaven.

> I am convinced that the extension and perfection of friendship will constitute a great part of the future happiness of the blest. . . . A wish to see and personally know, for example, the apostle Paul, or John, is the most likely to arise in the noblest and purest mind. I should be sorry to think such a wish absurd and presumptuous, or unlikely ever to be gratified. The highest enjoyment doubtless to the blest will be the personal knowledge of their great and beloved Master. Yet I cannot but think that some part of their happiness will consist in an intimate knowledge of the greatest of His followers also; and of those of them in particular, whose peculiar qualities are, to each, the most peculiarly attractive.[2]

Think of the joys of such a family! And of the infinite time to become better acquainted.

ity over cities. Most scholars believe that will be fulfilled during the millennial kingdom when we shall rule with Christ here on earth. But it is reasonable to assume that there is continuity between the earthly kingdom and the eternal heavenly kingdom. In other words, it may well be that our faithfulness (or unfaithfulness) on earth may have repercussions throughout eternity.

Yes, everyone in heaven will be happy and fulfilled. Everyone will be assigned a place in the administration of the vast heavenly kingdom. But just as there are varied responsibilities in the palace of an earthly king, so in heaven some will be given more prominent responsibilities than others.

Of this we may be certain: Heaven is not a place of inactivity or boredom. It is not, as a Sunday school pupil thought, an interminable worship service where we begin on page one of the hymnal and sing all the way through. God will have productive work for us to do. We will increase our knowledge of Him and His wondrous works. Will not Christ show us the Father that we might be forever satisfied? Will we not then learn to love the Lord our God in ways that we have never been able to do on earth?

We do not know, as some have speculated, whether we shall explore other worlds. Others have suggested that we shall be able to complete many projects begun on earth. Whatever our activity, we can be sure that our infinite heavenly Father will have infinite possibilities.

OUR NEW FAMILY

We have already learned that we will know our earthy family in heaven. But now our family will be

we have already begun. Praise is the language of heaven and the language of the faithful on earth.

Service to the Lord

Though worship shall occupy much of our time in heaven, we will also be assigned responsibilities commensurate with the faithfulness we displayed here on earth: "And His bond-servants shall serve Him; and they shall see His face, and His name shall be on their foreheads" (Revelation 22:3–4).

That word *servant* is found frequently in the book of Revelation, for it pictures a continuation of the relationship we even now have with Christ. However, the word *serve* that appears here is used primarily in the New Testament for service that is carried on within the temple or church (Matthew 4:10; Luke 2:37; Acts 24:14). Thus we shall serve Him in that special, intimate relationship available only to those who are included within the inner circle of the redeemed. David Gregg gives his impression of what that kind of work will be like:

> It is work as free from care and toil and fatigue as is the wing-stroke of the jubilant lark when it soars into the sunlight of a fresh, clear day and, spontaneously and for self-relief, pours out its thrilling carol. Work up there is a matter of self-relief, as well as a matter of obedience to the ruling will of God. It is work according to one's tastes and delight and ability. If tastes vary there, if abilities vary there, then occupations will vary there.[1]

What responsibilities will we have? Christ told a parable that taught that the faithful were given author-

ed upon a throne with twenty-four other thrones occupied by twenty-four elders who worship the King. "From the throne proceed flashes of lightning and sounds and peals of thunder" (Revelation 4:5). And what is the nature of the activity around that throne? There is uninhibited joy and spontaneous worship.

Needless to say, the saints on earth are imperfect. They are beset by quarrels, carnality, and doctrinal deviations. Read a book on church history and you will marvel that the church has survived these two thousand years.

Have you ever wondered what it would be like to belong to a perfect church? That is precisely what John saw when he peered into heaven. Free from the limitations of the flesh and the opposition of the devil, the perfect church is found singing the praises of Christ without self-consciousness or mixed motives.

Repeatedly John sees worship taking place in heaven. Even after the judgment of God is heaped upon unrepentant sinners, the saints join with other created beings to chant the praises of God:

> And a voice came from the throne, saying,
>
> "Give praise to our God, all you His bond-servants, you who fear Him, the small and the great." And I heard, as it were, the voice of a great multitude and as the sound of many waters and as the sound of mighty peals of thunder, saying,
>
> "Hallelujah! For the Lord our God, the Almighty, reigns" (Revelation 19:5–6).

If we want to prepare for our final destination, we should begin to worship God here on earth. Our arrival in heaven will only be a continuation of what

transformed body and mind to behold it with unrestricted admiration.

When Christ said He was preparing a home for us with many mansions, He did not imply, as some have suggested, that He needed plenty of time to do the building. God is able to create the heavenly Jerusalem in a moment of time. But Christ did emphasize that we would be with Him, and we know that His presence will be even more marvelous than our environment.

OUR NEW OCCUPATION

It has been estimated that there are at least forty thousand different occupations in the United States. Yet for all that, only a small percentage of the population is completely satisfied with their responsibilities. Personnel problems, the lack of adequate pay, and wearisome hours of routine tasks are only some of the reasons. Few people, if any, are truly satisfied.

But those problems will be behind us forever in heaven. Each job description will entail two primary responsibilities. First, there will be the worship of God; second, there will be the serving of the Most High in whatever capacity assigned to us.

The Worship of God

Let's try to capture the privilege of worship.

Heaven is first and foremost the dwelling place of God. It is true, of course, that God's presence is not limited to heaven, for He is omnipresent. Solomon perceptively commented, "Behold, heaven and the highest heaven cannot contain Thee, how much less this house which I have built!" (1 Kings 8:27).

Yet in heaven God is localized. John saw God seat-

security and to make sure that it is accessible only through proper entrances.

Second, we notice the twelve gates, each a single pearl (Revelation 21:12–21). That is a reminder that entrance into the city is restricted; only those who belong are admitted, "and nothing unclean and no one who practices abomination and lying, shall ever come into it, but only those whose names are written in the Lamb's book of life" (v. 27).

John gives a further description of those who are outside the city walls. "Outside are the dogs and the sorcerers and the immoral persons and the murderers and the idolaters, and everyone who loves and practices lying" (22:15). There is a sentinel angel at each gate, evidently to make sure that only those who have their names written in the book are admitted.

The twelve gates are divided into four groups; thus three gates face each of the four directions. "There were three gates on the east and three gates on the north and three gates on the south and three gates on the west" (21:13). That is a reminder that the gospel is for all men, and all the tribes of the earth will be represented.

Notice that the saints of the Old Testament and the New are both included. The names of the twelve sons of Israel are written on the gates of the city, and the New Testament apostles have their names inscribed on the foundation stones. Thus the unity of the people of God throughout all ages is evident.

As for the street of the city, it was "pure gold, like transparent glass" (v. 21). It is illuminated by the glory of God, and the Lamb is the lamp. Now we can better understand why Bunyan said that the pilgrims must see the city through a special instrument. Its beauty is simply too much for us to comprehend. We need a

His lambs. As someone has said, there will be a crown awaiting us that no one else can wear, a dwelling place that no one else can enter.

THE MATERIALS OF THE CITY

The details can be written, though hardly imagined. In John Bunyan's *Pilgrim's Progress,* as Christian and Hopeful finally see the City of God, there was such beauty that they fell sick with happiness, crying out, "If you see my Beloved, tell Him I am sick with love." The city was so glorious that they could not yet look upon it directly but had to use an instrument made for that purpose. This, after all, is the dwelling place of God.

John wrote in the Revelation that the city had the glory of God. "Her brilliance was like a very costly stone, as a stone of crystal-clear jasper" (21:11). It is interesting that the city shares some features of the earthly Jerusalem, but we are more impressed with the contrasts. The new Jerusalem is a city of unimaginable beauty and brilliance.

First, there is a wall with twelve foundation stones that encompasses the city. "And the wall of the city had twelve foundation stones, and on them were the twelve names of the twelve apostles of the Lamb" (21:14).

As for the foundation stones on which the wall is built, each is adorned with a different kind of precious stone—the list is in 21:19–20. The jewels roughly parallel the twelve stones in the breastplate of the high priest (Exodus 28:17–20).

The height of the wall is given as seventy-two yards, not very high in comparison to the massive size of the city, but high enough, however, to provide

fire to make room for the new order of creation (2 Peter 3:7–13). This new city came out of heaven because it is part of the heavenly realm.

Let's consider some features of this beautiful permanent home.

THE SIZE OF THE CITY

The dimensions are given as a cube, fifteen hundred miles square. "And the city is laid out as a square, and its length is as great as the width; and he measured the city with the rod, fifteen hundred miles; its length and width and height are equal" (Revelation 21:16).

If we take that literally, heaven will be composed of 396,000 stories (at twenty feet per story) each having an area as big as one half the size of the United States! Divide that into separate condominiums, and you have plenty of room for all who have been redeemed by God since the beginning of time. The Old Testament saints—Abraham, Isaac, and Jacob—they will be there. Then we think of the New Testament apostles and all the redeemed throughout two thousand years of church history—heaven will be the home for all of them. Unfortunately, however, the majority of the world's population will likely not be there. Heaven, as Christ explained, is a special place for special people.

You need not fear that you will be lost in the crowd; nor need you fear being stuck on the thousandth floor when all of the activity is in the downstairs lounge. All you will need to do is to decide where you would like to be, and you will be there! Each occupant will receive individualized attention. The Good Shepherd who calls His own sheep by name will have a special place prepared for each of

company of the redeemed. Those whom you did not know on earth are just as instantly known as those of your earthly friends who often joined you at your favorite restaurant. Your uncle asks about the well-being of some of his relatives, but the primary conversation is about the beauty of Christ, the wonder of God's love, and the undeserved grace that makes you a beneficiary of such blessings.

A little girl who had been looking at pictures of Christ in the evening dreamed about Him at night. In the morning she said, "Oh, He is a hundred times better than the pictures." Now that you see Him, you will agree, I'm sure, that He is much better than our most enchanting dreams.

At your leisure you explore your new home. This, after all, is where you will spend eternity, so it is worth a look. Christ assured the disciples that the place He was preparing had "many dwelling places." There would be plenty of room for all of the redeemed.

In the book of Revelation, we have the best description of the New Jerusalem, which is our permanent home. John writes,

> And I saw a new heaven and a new earth; for the first heaven and the first earth passed away, and there is no longer any sea. And I saw the holy city, new Jerusalem, coming down out of heaven from God, made ready as a bride adorned for her husband. (Revelation 21:1–2)

This city is new—that is, recreated—just as our resurrected bodies are recreated from our earthly bodies. The previous heavens (the atmospheric heavens) and the earth, tainted by sin, will have been obliterated by

\mathscr{L}IVING IN THE NEW JERUSALEM

The Size of the City—The Materials of the City—
Our New Occupation—Our New Family—
A New Order of Reality

You are lying in the hospital surrounded by friends who have tiptoed in and out of your room for the last two days. The doctor has not told you that your death is imminent, because you already know that the end is near. You have had the courage to talk to your family about your funeral, and you are relieved to know that you have done all you could to prepare for this hour. Your bags are packed for the journey.

When you breathe your last, a doctor will come and verify the death. Your family will leave the room, and a sheet will be draped over your body, which will be carried to the temporary morgue. While your family is making funeral arrangements, you have already arrived at your permanent home.

We've already emphasized that we will make the transition into heaven without a break in consciousness. We will meet Christ and be introduced to the

Agent does not expect us to discover the trail for ourselves. Often we say that Christ will meet us on the other side. That is true, of course, but misleading. Let us never forget that He walks with us on this side of the curtain and then guides us through the opening. We will meet Him *there,* because we have met Him *here.*

The tomb is not an entrance to death, but to life. The sepulcher is not an empty vault, but the doorway to heaven. When we die, nothing in God dies, and His faithfulness endures. Little wonder the pagans said of the early church that they carried their dead as if in triumph!

Aristides, a first-century Greek, marveled at the extraordinary success of Christianity and wrote to a friend, "If any righteous man among the Christians passes from this world, they rejoice and offer thanks to God, and they escort his body with songs and thanksgiving as if he were setting out from one place to another nearby."

And so it is. At death believers set out from one place to another. There is reason for sorrowing but "not as those who have no hope." Such confidence makes the unbelievers take notice that Christians die differently.

Christ assures us, "Where I am, there you may be also" (John 14:3).

NOTE

1. Steve Saint, "Did They Have to Die?" *Christianity Today,* 16 September 1996, 26.

eyes could see the spirit world, we might find that we are already at its gates.

Judson B. Palmer relates the story of the Reverend A. D. Sandborn, who preceded him as pastor in a church in Iowa. Reverend Sandborn called on a young Christian woman who was seriously ill. She was bolstered up in bed, almost in a sitting position, looking off in the distance. "Now just as soon as they open the gate I will go in," she whispered.

Then she sank upon her pillow in disappointment. "They have let Mamie go in ahead of me, but soon I will go in."

Moments later she again spoke, "They let Grampa in ahead of me, but next time I will go in for sure."

No one spoke to her and she said nothing more to anyone, and seemed to see nothing except the sights of the beautiful city. Reverend Sandborn then left the house because of the press of other duties.

Later in the day the pastor learned that the young woman had died that morning. He was so impressed with what she had said that he asked the family about the identity of Mamie and Grampa. Mamie was a little girl who had lived near them at one time but later moved to New York State. As for Grampa, he was a friend of the family and had moved somewhere in the Southwest.

Reverend Sandborn then wrote to the addresses given him to inquire about these two individuals. Much to his astonishment he discovered that both Mamie and Grampa had died the morning of September 16, the very hour that the young woman herself had passed into glory.

Death is not the *end* of the road; it is only a *bend* in the road. The road winds only through those paths through which Christ Himself has gone. This Travel

When Peter Marshall was taken by ambulance to a hospital in Washington, D.C., his wife, Catherine, said that at that moment she realized that "life consists not in duration, but in donation."

It is not how long you live but the contribution you make that matters. And yes, these little ones have made their contribution too—they have opened the hearts of their loved ones to the realization that we are all headed toward home.

OUR ENEMY, OUR FRIEND

Why is death such a blessing? Paul said, "Flesh and blood cannot inherit the kingdom of God" (1 Corinthians 15:50). The fact is that you and I can't go to heaven just as we are today. No matter how alert and primed, no matter how neatly we have showered and dressed, we are not fit for heaven. You can't have a decaying body in a permanent home.

Death rescues us from the endlessness of this existence; it is the means by which those who love God finally are brought to Him. Paul had no illusions as to whether heaven was better than earth. He was itching to depart and to be with Christ, which "is far better." Even our heroic attempts to live one day longer with respirators and other high-tech equipment would seem unnecessary if we could see what awaits us.

Only on this side of the curtain is death our enemy. Just beyond the curtain the monster turns out to be our friend. The label "Death" is still on the bottle, but the contents are "Life Eternal." Death is our friend because it reminds us that heaven is near. How near? As near as a heartbeat; as near as an auto accident; as near as a stray bullet; as near as a plane crash. If our

afraid; I am the first and the last, and the living One; and I was dead, and behold, I am alive forevermore, and I have the keys of death and of Hades.'"

"You think the key to your little daughter's casket is in the hands of the keeper of the cemetery," the minister said. "But the key is in the hands of the Son of God, and He will come some morning and use it."

Bob Neudorf wrote "To My Baby":

> *Is it proper to cry*
> *For a baby too small*
> *For a coffin?*
> *Yes, I think it is.*
> *Does Jesus have*
> *My too-small baby*
> *In His tender arms?*
> *Yes, I think He does.*
> *There is so much I do not know*
> *About you—my child—*
> *He, she? quiet or restless?*
> *Will I recognize*
> *Someone I knew so little about,*
> *Yet loved so much?*
> *Yes, I think I will.*
> *Ah, sweet, small child*
> *Can I say*
> *That loving you is like loving God?*
> *Loving—yet not seeing,*
> *Holding—yet not touching,*
> *Caressing—yet separated by the chasm of time.*
> *No tombstone marks your sojourn,*
> *And only God recorded your name.*
> *The banquet was not canceled,*
> *Just moved. Just moved.*
> *Yet a tear remains*
> *Where baby should have been.*

The Alliance Witness,
16 September 1987, 14.
Used by Permission.

among the redeemed. Heaven is not a place for second-class citizens; all handicaps are removed. Heaven is a place of perfection.

The death of an infant, however, causes all of us to struggle with the will and purpose of God. It seems strange that God would grant the gift of life and then cause it to be snuffed out before it could blossom into a stage of usefulness. But we can be sure that there is a purpose in such a life, even if it is not immediately discernible.

James Vernon McGee again says that when a shepherd seeks to lead his sheep to better grass up the winding, thorny mountain paths, he often finds that the sheep will not follow him. They fear the unknown ridges and the sharp rocks. The shepherd will then reach into the flock and take a little lamb on one arm and another on his other arm. Then he starts up the precipitous pathway. Soon the two mother sheep begin to follow, and afterward the entire flock. Thus they ascend the tortuous path to greener pastures.

So it is with the Good Shepherd. Sometimes He reaches into the flock and takes a lamb to Himself. He uses the experience to lead His people, to lift them to new heights of commitment as they follow the little lamb all the way home.

A little girl died in a hotel where she was staying with her father. Since her mother was already dead, just two followed the body to the cemetery—the father and the minister. The man grieved uncontrollably as he took the key and unlocked the casket to look upon the face of his child one last time. Then he closed the casket and handed the key to the keeper of the cemetery.

On the way back the minister quoted Revelation 1:17–18 to the broken-hearted man. "'Do not be

because they are too young to believe, the requirement of personal faith is waived. We do not know at what age they are held personally accountable. It is impossible to suggest an age, since that may vary, depending on the child's capacity and mental development.

There are strong indications that children who die are with the Lord. David lost two sons for whom he grieved deeply. For Absalom, his rebellious son, he wept uncontrollably and refused comfort, for he was uncertain about the young man's destiny. But when the child born to Bathsheba died, he washed, anointed himself, and came into the house of the Lord to worship. He gave this explanation to those who asked about his behavior: "Now he has died; why should I fast? Can I bring him back again? I shall go to him, but he will not return to me" (2 Samuel 12:23).

Christ saw children as being in close proximity to God and the kingdom of heaven. "See that you do not despise one of these little ones, for I say to you, that their angels in heaven continually behold the face of My Father who is in heaven" (Matthew 18:10). Children are close to the heart of God.

Will a baby always be a baby in heaven? James Vernon McGee has made the interesting suggestion that God will resurrect the infants as they are and that the mothers' arms that have ached for them will have the opportunity of holding their little ones. The father who never had the opportunity of holding that little hand will be given that privilege. Thus the children will grow up with their parents.

Whether that will be the case, we do not know. But of this we can be confident: A child in heaven will be complete. Either the child will look as he would have if he were full grown, or else his mental and physical capacities will be enhanced to give him full status

rection, Christ ate fish with His disciples on the shores of Galilee. And, of course, believers will be present at the marriage supper of the Lamb (Revelation 19:7).

THE DEATH OF INFANTS

Just this week I spoke on the phone to a close friend who had lost a baby; little Grace Elizabeth died one-day-old. Since there is continuity between the earthly and heavenly body, will she be an infant forever?

Recently, my wife and I were eagerly anticipating becoming grandparents, but God had other plans. Our granddaughter, Sarah, was stillborn. We have struggled, along with our daughter and son-in-law, wondering what God's purpose might be in our disappointment and grief.

Yes, I believe that our precious Sarah is in heaven, but we must be clear as to why we believe that she and other children will be there. Contrary to popular opinion, children will not be in heaven because they are innocent. Paul taught clearly that children are born under condemnation of Adam's sin (Romans 5:12). Indeed, it is because they are born sinners that they experience death.

Nor should we make a distinction between children who are baptized and those who are not, as if such a ritual can make one a child of God. The idea of infant baptism arose in North Africa years after the New Testament was written. Even if it can be justified theologically as a sign of the covenant (a debatable proposition), there is no evidence whatever that it can give to children the gift of eternal life.

If children are saved (and I believe they shall be), it can only be because God credits their sin to Christ; and

rial forces. Remember how Christ came through closed doors after the resurrection. Keep in mind that the reason the angel rolled the stone from the tomb was not to let Christ out, but to let the disciples in!

Finally, *we are sown a natural body, but we are raised a spiritual body.* To say that we will have a "spiritual body" does not mean that we will just be spirits. Christ's glorified body was so human that He invited the disciples to touch Him and affirmed, "See My hands and My feet, that it is I Myself; touch Me and see, for a spirit does not have flesh and bones as you see that I have" (Luke 24:39).

There will be continuity with a difference. Our future body will be like Christ's resurrection body. "We know that, when He appears, we shall be like Him, because we shall see Him just as He is" (1 John 3:2). Just think of the implications.

The continuity between Christ's earthly and heavenly body was clear to see—for example, the nail prints were in His hands. The disciples recognized Him instantly, and He even ate fish with them at the seashore. But there were also radical changes. He was able to travel from one place to another without physical effort and went through doors without opening them.

Evidently we too shall be able to travel effortlessly. Just as Christ could be in Galilee and then suddenly appear in Judea, so we shall be free from the limitations of terrestrial travel. That does not mean, of course, that we will be omnipresent, as God is; we will be limited to one place at one time. But travel will be swift and effortless.

And yet, to the delight of many people, we shall still eat, not because we are hungry, but because we will delight in the fellowship it affords. After the resur-

permanent bodies for us *ex nihilo,* that is, out of nothing. But if that were so, there would be no need for the doctrine of resurrection. In 1 Corinthians 15 Paul makes four contrasts between our present bodies and our future ones. "It is sown a perishable body, it is raised an imperishable body; it is sown in dishonor, it is raised in glory; it is sown in weakness, it is raised in power; it is sown a natural body, it is raised a spiritual body" (1 Corinthians 15:42–44).

First, *we are sown a perishable body, but we will be raised imperishable.* Like a seed sown in the ground, there is continuity between the acorn and the tree, between the kernel and the stalk. Not every particle that ever was a part of you has to be raised, and God just might add additional material to make up the deficiencies.

In heaven, no one will comment on your age or notice that the years are beginning to take their toll. You will look as young a billion years from now as you will a thousand years from now.

As Dr. Hinson wrote:

> *The stars shall live for a million years,*
> *A million years and a day.*
> *But God and I will live and love*
> *When the stars have passed away.*

Second, *we are sown in dishonor, but raised in power.* When a body is transported to a funeral home it is always covered by a sheet to shield gaping eyes from the ignominy of looking upon the corpse. Every dead body is a reminder of our dishonor, a reminder that we are but frail. But we shall be raised in power.

Third, *we are sown in weakness, but raised in strength.* The resurrection body is not subject to mate-

"lives," or "persons." But the word is often translated "soul" as distinguished from the body. If that is what John meant, it would give credence to the view that souls can take upon themselves shape and bodily characteristics. If that seems strange to us, it may well be that our concept of the soul is too limited.

We cannot be sure which of these views is correct. Of this much we may be certain: *Believers go directly into the presence of Christ at death. They are conscious and in command of all of their faculties.* As D. L. Moody said before he died, "Soon you will read in the papers that Moody is dead. . . . Don't believe it . . . for in that moment I will be more alive than I have ever been."

We do not have to know exactly what kind of body we will have in order to have the assurance that our personalities will continue. We will be the same people we were on earth, will have the same thoughts, feelings, and desires. Though our struggles with sin will be over, we will be aware of who we really are. There will be no doubt in our minds that we have just moved from one place to another without an intermediate stop.

And yet we will await the final resurrection.

THE RESURRECTION BODY

The New Testament doctrine of the resurrection is an affirmation that we are a spiritual and physical unity and that God intends to put us back together again. Although the soul is separable from the body, such a separation is only temporary. If we are to live forever, we must be brought together as a united human being—body, soul, and spirit.

Some Christians assume that God will create new

On the Mount of Transfiguration, Moses and Elijah appeared in some kind of body, though neither yet has his permanent resurrection body. Admittedly, Elijah was taken up to heaven without dying and Moses was buried on Mount Nebo by God, but they also still await the resurrection. Yet there they were, talking, communicating, and evidently recognizable to Peter, James, and John.

The rich man who died and went to hades must have had a body, since he was able to use human speech and wanted his tongue cooled. He had eyes to see and ears to hear. His body, of whatever kind, was sensitive to pain and was recognizable to Lazarus, who was on the other side of the great divide. Usually we think of spirits as unable to perform such functions.

However, we must ask ourselves: If the saints already have bodies in heaven (albeit temporary ones), why does Paul place such an emphasis on the resurrection in his writings? He clearly implies that the saints in heaven today are incomplete and in an unnatural state.

So a second plausible explanation might be that the souls of the departed dead may in some ways have the functions of a body. If that is the case, it would explain how they can communicate with one another and have a visible presence in heaven. These capabilities of the soul are implied in Revelation 6:9–10, which was quoted earlier. The souls that were beneath the altar had a voice with which they were able to cry up to God. And what is more, these souls were actually given white robes to wear as they waited for God to avenge them.

Admittedly the word *psychas* (translated "souls") has a broad meaning and can also be translated

THE INTERMEDIATE STATE

The question on our minds is: What kind of body do the saints have in heaven now? Since the permanent, resurrection body is still future, what kind of an existence do believers have even now as you are reading this book?

Since the resurrection of the body is future, are the present saints in heaven disembodied spirits? Or do they have some kind of temporary "intermediate" body that will be discarded on the day of resurrection—the day when we shall receive our permanent, glorified bodies?

The point of disagreement is over Paul's words in 2 Corinthians 5:1, "For we know that if the earthly tent which is our house is torn down, we have a building from God, a house not made with hands, eternal in the heavens." The question is: To what period in the future does he refer when he speaks of our having "a building from God . . . eternal in the heavens"? Do we have that building [a body] at death, or do we receive it at the future resurrection? Paul shrinks from the idea that his soul would live through a period of nakedness, a time when it would exist without a body.

One explanation is that God creates a body for these believers and that this explains how the redeemed in heaven can relate to Christ and to one another. Since departed believers can sing the praises of God and communicate with one another, it seems that they must have a body in which to do so. What is more, at the point of transition between life and death some have actually testified that they saw departed relatives awaiting their arrival. That points to the conclusion that the saints in heaven already have recognizable bodies.

Knowledge, love, feelings, a desire for justice—all of these are the present experience of those who have gone ahead of us to heaven. Remember that the entire personality simply carries over into the life beyond. Heaven has its differences, but it is populated with your friends, who are still the people who once dwelt on the earth. They are still your friends!

Personal Activities Continue

Yes, in heaven we will rest, but it is not the rest of inactivity. We will most probably continue many of the same kinds of projects we knew on earth. Artists will do art as never before; the scientist just might be invited to continue his or her exploration of God's magnificent creation. The musicians will do music; all of us will continue to learn.

We are, says Maclaren, saplings here, but we shall be transported into our heavenly soil to grow in God's light. Here our abilities are in blossom; there they shall burst forth with fruits of greater beauty. Our death is but the passing from one degree of loving service to another; the difference is like that of the unborn child and the one who has entered into the experiences of a new life. Our love for God will continue, but awakened with new purity and purposefulness.

The famous Puritan writer Jonathan Edwards believed that the saints in heaven would begin by contemplating God's providential care of the church on earth and then move on to other aspects of the divine plan, and thus "the ideas of the saints shall increase to eternity."

The "real you" will be there.

67

would tell us that if we only knew how generous God is, we would do all we could to please him. "For I consider that the sufferings of this present time are not worthy to be compared to the glory that is to be revealed to us" (Romans 8:18). They would tell us to live on earth with heaven in mind.

Personal Feelings Continue

Think of your purest joy on earth; then multiply that many times and you might get catch a glimpse of heaven's euphoria. Even in the Old Testament, David knew enough to write, "In Thy presence is fulness of joy; in Thy right hand there are pleasures forever" (Psalm 16:11). Heaven is the perfecting of the highest moments of our present Christian experience.

What about sorrow? Yes, there will be sorrow until God Himself "shall wipe every tear from their eyes" (Revelation 7:17; 21:4). When we think of the opportunities we squandered, when we consider how imperfectly we loved Christ on earth, we will grieve. Such sorrow will vanish, but for the moment the reality of what could have been will dawn upon us.

If we still question whether the departed spirits experience the same emotions as we, let us read these words:

> And when He broke the fifth seal, I saw underneath the altar the souls of those who had been slain because of the word of God, and because of the testimony which they had maintained; and they cried out with a loud voice, saying, "How long, O Lord, holy and true, wilt Thou refrain from judging and avenging our blood on those who dwell on the earth?" (Revelation 6:9–10)

Our love for God will also be intensified. Here, at last, without distractions, God can be loved, for faith has given way to sight. We will keep loving whatever we loved on earth, apart from sin. In heaven, our affections will be like they were on earth, except more so.

There is no evidence that those in heaven can actually see us on earth, though that might be possible. It is more likely that they can ask for regular updates on how we are doing. I cannot imagine that such a request would be denied.

When her grandfather died, a seven-year-old girl at the Moody Church asked her father, "Can we ask Jesus to get a message to grampa?" He was caught somewhat by surprise but realized that there was nothing in his theology that would cause him to say no. So he responded, "Yes, that might be possible; let's tell Jesus what we want grampa to know."

We might not be sure whether Jesus gave the message to grampa, but we must agree that this little girl's theology was much better than that of millions of other people in the world. She knew that *although we might pray to Jesus to get a message to grampa, we don't pray to grampa to get a message to Jesus!*

We must warn, however, that those who are in heaven cannot communicate with us. In the first chapter I emphasized that the Bible strictly forbids any attempt to communicate with those who have died. We must be satisfied that they are more knowledgeable than we and that someday we will be with them. God has told us all we need to know in this life; we need to entrust our loved ones into His loving care for the life to come.

If those in heaven could talk with us, what would they say? They would urge us to be faithful; they

minds will be redeemed from the limitations sin imposed upon them.

Of course, we will not know everything, for such knowledge belongs only to God. But we shall "know fully," even as we are "fully known" (1 Corinthians 13:12). In heaven, we will know just like we do on earth, except more so. Only our desire to sin will no longer be a part of our being.

Personal Love Continues

Again we are reminded of the rich man who was concerned about his brothers, lest they come to the same place of torment. He not only knew who his brothers were, but he was concerned about them. He loved them so much that he was willing to never see them again if only they would not join him in this place of torment. He would endure isolation if they experienced consolation.

Of course, dear widow, your husband who is in heaven continues to love you as he did on earth. Today he loves you with a fonder, sweeter, purer love. It is a love purified by God. Your child loves you; so does your mother and father. There is no more a break in love than there is in continuity of thought. Death breaks ties on earth but renews them in heaven.

Christ made clear that we will not marry in heaven nor be given in marriage. But that does not mean that we will be sexless. In heaven we will retain our female or male gender. Your mother will be still known as your mother in heaven; your son or daughter will be known as a member of your earthly family. I like what Chet Bitterman said after his missionary son was killed by guerrillas. "We have eight children. And they all are living: one's in heaven and seven are on earth."

powerful business," for you just keep living some-
where else without undue interruption.

YOUR PERSONALITY CONTINUES

We are accustomed to talk about the differences
there will be when we make our transition from earth
to heaven. But there are some similarities too. Given
the fact that our personalities continue, we can expect
continuity. Heaven is the earthly life of the believer
glorified and perfected.

Personal Knowledge Continues

One minute after we die, our minds, our memories,
will be clearer than ever before. In chapter 2 we were
reminded of Jesus' story of the rich man who went to
hades with his memory intact. He knew his family on
earth, pleading, "I have five brothers." Death does not
change what we know; our personalities will just go
on with the same information we have stored in our
minds today.

Think back to your background: your parents,
brothers, sisters, family reunions. Of course, you will
remember all of this and more in heaven. Do you
actually think you might know less in heaven than
you do on earth? Unthinkable!

Once in heaven we will soon get to meet a host of
others, some known to us in this life or through the
pages of church history, others nameless in this world
but equally honored in the world to come. On the
Mount of Transfiguration, three of the disciples met
Moses and Elijah. So far as we know, there was no
need for introductions; no need for name tags. In
heaven there will be intuitive knowledge, for our

self in new surroundings which just now are beyond our imagination. Most probably, you will have seen angels who have been assigned the responsibility of escorting you to your destination, just as the angels who carried Lazarus into "Abraham's bosom."

Back in January of 1956, five young missionaries were speared to death in the jungles of Ecuador. The offenders have now become Christians and have told Steve Saint, the son of one of the martyrs, that they heard and saw what they now believe to be angels while the killings were taking place. A woman hiding at a distance also saw these beings above the trees and didn't know what kind of music it was until she heard a Christian choir on records.[1]

Though such a revelation of angels is rare, this incident is a reminder that these heavenly beings who watch us on earth await us in heaven. Of course our greatest desire is to see Christ, who will be on hand to welcome us, but angels will be on hand too.

Since we are Christ's sheep, He calls us by name, perhaps standing even as He did for Stephen (Acts 7:55). We look into His eyes and see compassion, love, and understanding. Though we are unworthy, we know His welcome is genuine. We see His nail-prints, and this triggers memories that make us fall on our faces in worship. Were it not for His tender hand helping us to our feet, we'd be unable to stand up.

So much is different, yet you are quite the same. You have entered heaven without a break in consciousness. Back on earth our friends will bury our body, but they cannot bury *us*. Personhood survives the death of the body. Just before Stephen died, he said, "Lord, receive my spirit." He did not say, "Receive my body." Death, someone has said, "is

*W*ELCOME!
YOU HAVE ARRIVED!

Your Personality—Your Intermediate State—
Your Resurrection Body—The Death of Infants—
Enemy Turned Friend

When Del Fahsenfeld was battling a rare brain tumor, the doctors assured him in April that he would be dead before Christmas. When I interviewed him, he told me that he wanted to follow God so fully while he still had strength that when weakness came he would be able to endure his suffering with confidence. When you come home at night, he said, "you can manage to get around the house in the darkness because you have been there so often in the light."

When Del died in November of that year, those who were with him reported that he died well. For him, the darkness of death was as the light. He was prepared for that final hour; the Christ he had known for so many years led him through the curtain all the way to the other side.

What can we expect one minute after we die?

While relatives sorrow on earth, you will find your-

> Yea, though I walk through the
> valley of the shadow of death,
> I will fear no evil:
> For thou art with me.
> (Psalm 23:4 KJV)

Death is the chariot our heavenly Father sends to bring us to Himself.

NOTES

1. For a more complete critique of soul sleep, see Robert Morey, *Death and the Afterlife* (Minneapolis: Bethany House, 1984), 199–222.
2. Joseph Bayly, *The View from a Hearse* (Elgin, Ill.: David C. Cook, 1969), 36.

devout men buried Stephen, and made loud lamentation over him" (Acts 8:2).

Joe Bayly, who had three sons who died, wrote of his own experience, "Death wounds us, but wounds are meant to heal. And given time they will. But we must want to be healed. We cannot be like the child who keeps picking the scab from the cut."[2] As Christians, we live with the tension between what is "already ours" and the "not yet" of our experience. Paul said believers should look forward to Christ's return "that you may not grieve, as do the rest who have no hope" (1 Thessalonians 4:13). Grief was expected, but it is different from the grief of the world. There is a difference between tears of hope and tears of hopelessness.

Let those of us who wish to comfort the sorrowing remember that words can have a hollow ring for those who are overwhelmed with grief. Let us by our presence "weep with those who weep" (Romans 12:15). We must say we care much louder with our actions than with our words. Our presence and our tears can say more than words could ever communicate.

Donald Grey Barnhouse, on the way home from the funeral of his first wife, was trying to think of some way of comforting his children. Just then a huge moving van passed by their car and its shadow swept over them. Instantly, Barnhouse asked, "Children, would you rather be run over by a truck or by its shadow?" The children replied, "Of course we'd prefer the shadow!"

To which Barnhouse replied, "Two thousand years ago the truck of death ran over the Lord Jesus . . . now only the shadow of death can run over us!"

fully when their time came. The same God who guides us on earth will escort us all the way to heaven. "With Thy counsel Thou wilt guide me, and afterward receive me to glory" (Psalm 73:24).

When Corrie ten Boom was a girl, her first experience with death came after visiting the home of a neighbor who had just died. When she thought of the fact that her parents would die someday, her father comforted her by asking, "When I go to Amsterdam, when do I give you your ticket?"

"Just before we get on the train."

"Exactly. Just so your heavenly Father will give you exactly what you need when we die—He'll give it to you just when you need it."

Dying grace does not mean that we will be free from sorrow, whether at our own impending death or the death of someone we love. Some Christians have mistakenly thought that grief demonstrates a lack of faith. Thus they have felt it necessary to maintain strength rather than deal honestly with a painful loss.

Good grief is grief that enables us to make the transition to a new phase of existence. The widow must learn to live alone; the parents must bear the loneliness brought on by the death of a child. Grief that deals honestly with the pain is a part of the healing process. Christ wept at the tomb of Lazarus and agonized with "loud crying and tears" in Gethsemane at His own impending death (Hebrews 5:7).

Sorrow and grief are to be expected. If we feel the pain of loneliness when a friend of ours moves from Chicago to Atlanta, why should we not experience genuine grief when a friend leaves us for heaven? Dozens of passages in the Old and New Testaments tell how the saints mourned. When Stephen, the first Christian martyr, was stoned we read, "And some

GOOD GRIEF

Though we are comforted by these images, we still find that death can terrify us. Paul asks, "O death, where is your victory? O death, where is your sting?" (1 Corinthians 15:55). A bee can only sting a man once. Although the insect can still frighten us when the stinger is gone, it can do no damage. Because Christ removed death's sting, it can now only threaten; it cannot make good on its threats.

Will we have grace to face our exit victoriously? I have not had to face my own imminent death; I can't predict how I might react if I were told that I have a terminal disease.

I, for one, would like to have dying grace long before I need it! But the famous English preacher Charles Haddon Spurgeon says that death is the last enemy to be destroyed, and we should leave him to the last. He adds:

> Brother, you do not want dying grace till dying moments. What would be the good of dying grace while you are yet alive? A boat will only be needful when you reach a river. Ask for living grace, and glorify Christ thereby, and then you shall have dying grace when the time comes.
>
> Your enemy is going to be destroyed but not today. . . . Leave the final shock of arms till the last adversary advances, and meanwhile hold your place in the conflict. God will in due time help you to overcome your last enemy, but meanwhile see to it that you overcome the world, the flesh and the devil.

Some believers who thought they could not face death discovered they had the strength to die grace-

Most of us find comfort in being told that we are going to go on living; Paul was comforted when he was told that he soon would be dying! He kept referring to death as that which was "far better."

The fact that we don't view death with optimism just might be because we think of death as taking us *from* our home rather than bringing us *to* our home! Unlike Paul, we have become so attached to our tent that we just don't want to move.

The old song says it best:

> *This world is not my home,*
> *I'm just a pass'n through.*
> *My treasures are laid up*
> *Somewhere beyond the blue.*

To die is to go home to heaven; to live is to exist in a foreign country on earth. Someday we'll understand this distinction much better; for now the future is ours by faith.

In the Old Testament there is a beautiful story of a man who apparently was taken to heaven without dying. "And Enoch walked with God; and he was not, for God took him" (Genesis 5:24). A little girl who described what she had learned in Sunday school said to her mother, "One day Enoch and God took a long walk together until Enoch said it was getting late. And the Lord said, 'We are now closer to my home than we are to yours . . . Why don't you just come to my home tonight?'"

When we are closer to heaven than earth, we'll just keep walking all the way to God's home. Home is where we belong.

The King James translation "many mansions" elicits the vision of a ranch-style home with a fifty-acre front yard and limousines parked in the driveway. But that word *abode* really means "dwelling place," a place that we can call home.

We should not think that Christ has been working for two thousand years getting heaven ready for us. It has been facetiously suggested that since Christ was a carpenter on earth, he has been exercising His trade in glory, working to finish the rooms for our arrival.

As God, He didn't have to get a head start. He can create our future home in a moment of time. Christ's point is simply that just as a mother prepares for the arrival of her son who has been at sea, so Christ awaits our arrival in heaven. Heaven is called home, for it is where we belong.

Paul wrote that in this world we are "at home" in the body, but in the world to come we will be "at home" with the Lord (2 Corinthians 5:6–8). And he left no doubt as to which home he prefers. "We are of good courage, I say, and prefer rather to be absent from the body and to be at home with the Lord" (v. 8). Understandably, he preferred the mansion to the tent.

After I left home I never feared returning. In fact, I often was so lonely in college I could hardly wait until Christmas break so that I could join my parents and siblings to get caught up on our friendship. There sitting around the table, I found love, acceptance, and comfort when I needed it. Home sweet home.

Why should we fear death if it is the route to our final home? Jesus assures us that there is nothing to fear; in fact, the knowledge that we shall die gives us the courage and hope to live triumphantly in this world!

John Drummond tells the story of a sea captain who was asked to visit a dying man in a hospital. When the captain reached the sick man's room, he noticed decorated flags of different colors surrounding his bed. As they talked, the captain learned that both of them had actually served on the same ship many years earlier.

"What do these flags mean?" the captain wondered.

"Have you forgotten the symbols?" the dying man asked.

Then he continued. "These flags mean that the ship is ready to sail and is awaiting orders," the dying man replied.

Our flags must always be flying, for we know neither the day nor the hour of our departure. Some are given more notice than others, but all must go when the Celestial Clock strikes.

Thankfully, we can be ready to embark on the last leg of our voyage. Christ leads His own safely into the harbor.

A PERMANENT HOME

In a sense, to speak of heaven as our home is not a figure of speech; heaven *is* our home. Jesus, you will recall, spoke of leaving His disciples to build a mansion for them in the world beyond.

> In My Father's house are many dwelling places; if it were not so, I would have told you; for I go to prepare a place for you. And if I go and prepare a place for you, I will come again, and receive you unto Myself; that where I am, there you may be also. (John 14:2–3)

was imminent. He said good-bye, but only for the time being. He would not return to Timothy, but Timothy would soon·cross over and they would meet again.

The author of Hebrews picks up on the same imagery and says that we can flee to Christ to lay hold of the hope set before us. He adds, "This hope we have as an anchor of the soul, a hope both sure and steadfast and one which enters within the veil, where Jesus has entered as a forerunner for us" (Hebrews 6:19–20). That means that we do not cast our anchor on anything within ourselves. We seek our security neither in feelings nor experiences. Our anchor is fastened to Christ, who is within the Holy of Holies where He resides now that His blood bought our salvation.

Philip Mauro suggests that the picture here is that of the forerunner used in ancient times to help a vessel enter the harbor safely. He would jump from the ship, wade to the harbor, and fasten the strong rope of the ship to a rock along the shore. Then, by means of a winch, the vessel was brought in.

Just so, our forerunner has gone to heaven, where He stands ready to guide us safely into the Holy of Holies. We are fastened to a rock that cannot be moved. Let the storms tear our sails to shreds; let the floors creak; let the gusts of wind attempt to blow us off course; let the tides overwhelm us; we shall arrive safely into the port. Each day we are pulled a notch closer to the harbor by the One who proved He is more powerful than death.

We have an anchor that keeps the soul
Steadfast and sure while the billows roll,
Fastened to the Rock which cannot move,
Grounded firm and deep in the Saviour's love.

uncomfortable they become, the more willing they are to move into a house. Thus the persecuted and infirm long for heaven, while those who are healthy and fulfilled wish to postpone death indefinitely. But the time will come when even the strongest among us will have to leave the tent behind.

Some people act as if they intend to live in this body forever, not realizing that it is about to collapse around them. A tent reminds us that we are only pilgrims here on earth, en route to our final home. Someone has said that we should not drive in our stakes too deeply, for we are leaving in the morning!

A SAILING SHIP

Paul also speaks of death as the sailing of a ship. In a passage already quoted, he wrote, "But I am hard-pressed from both directions, having the desire to depart and to be with Christ, for that is very much better" (Philippians 1:23). That word *depart* was used for the loosing of an anchor. A. T. Robertson translates it, "To weigh anchor and put out to sea."

Thanks to Christ, Paul was ready to embark on this special journey that would take him to his heavenly destination. Christ had already successfully navigated to the other side and was waiting with a host of Paul's friends. Of course, he had some friends on this side too; that's why he added, "Yet to remain on in the flesh is more necessary for your sake" (v. 24).

Paul's bags were packed. But for now the Captain said, "Wait!" A few years later, Paul was closer to leaving earth's shore. Again he spoke of death as his departure: "For I am already being poured out as a drink offering, and the time of my departure has come" (2 Timothy 4:6). The signal for him to push off

The book of Revelation describes those who follow the beast [Antichrist] as those who "have no rest day or night" (Revelation 14:11); but as for those who belong to the Lord, "Blessed are the dead who die in the Lord from now on . . . that they may rest from their labors, for their deeds follow with them" (v. 13). Believers find their death to be the joyous rest of fulfillment. And their deeds follow after them, never to be lost in the annals of eternity. Like a pebble thrown into a pool whose ripples continue in ever-widening circles, so the deeds of the godly will reverberate for all of eternity. Blessed are the dead who die in the Lord!

"As for me, I shall behold Thy face in righteousness; I will be satisfied with Thy likeness when I awake" (Psalm 17:15).

Rest at last!

A COLLAPSING TENT

Paul spoke of death as the dismantling of a tent. "For we know that if the earthly tent which is our house is torn down, we have a building from God, a house not made with hands, eternal in the heavens" (2 Corinthians 5:1).

Our present body is like a tent where our spirit dwells; it is a temporary structure. Tents deteriorate in the face of changing weather and storms. If used regularly, they often need repairs. A tattered tent is a sign that we will soon have to move. Death takes us from the tent to the palace; it is changing our address from earth to heaven.

You've met camping enthusiasts who want to camp out most of the year. They can do that, of course, until the rains come or the snow begins to fly. The more

from the body and to be at home with the Lord" (2 Corinthians 5:8). There is no fair way to interpret this except to understand that he expected to be with Christ immediately after he died.

Sleep is used as a picture of death in the New Testament because the body sleeps until the day of resurrection, not the soul. Sleep is used as a picture of death because it is a means of rejuvenation. We look forward to sleep when we feel exhausted and our work is done. Furthermore, we do not fear falling asleep, for we have the assurance that we shall awaken in the morning; we have proved a thousand times that daylight will come.

Just last night I arrived home from a speaking engagement at 2:30 A.M. I was so exhausted, my last recollection was putting my head on the pillow. I longed for the sleep that came quickly and peacefully. This morning I am refreshed, able to continue the work I had begun days ago. Sleep is a welcome experience for those who need not fear the morning.

The difference, of course, is that we have never had the experience of death, so we aren't sure exactly what it will be like to awaken in eternity. But of this we can be certain: Those who die in the Lord need not fear the unknown, for they fall asleep to awaken in the arms of God.

It is difficult to fall asleep when you are not tired. Just so, those of us who enjoy good health, a fulfilling vocation, and a wholesome family life do not look forward to "falling asleep in Jesus." But the day will come when it will no longer be our choice; we will have to obey our summons. If we should live long enough to be weary of life, falling asleep will be more inviting. Indeed, many of the saints looked forward with increasing joy to the day of their final rest.

tent with the fact that though he died and was buried by God, he was not *un*conscious but able to converse with Christ. When Stephen was about to die, he did not ask the grave to receive him, but said, "Lord Jesus, receive my spirit!" (Acts 7:59). Clearly he was not looking forward to an unconscious existence, but awaited the immediate bliss of heaven and fellowship with Christ.

Then there is the story of the dying thief, to whom Christ said, "Truly I say to you, today you shall be with Me in Paradise" (Luke 23:43). Ignoring both the rules of grammar and syntax, those who believe in soul sleep say that the word *today* refers only to the time that Christ spoke the words. They interpret Christ's words to say, "Verily, I say to you today, you shall be with me in paradise." So, the argument goes, the thief was not going to paradise on that day; it was just that Christ made a promise to him on that day!

The problem is that Greek scholars agree that this rearranging of the words is "grammatically senseless."[1] It was already rather obvious that Christ was speaking to the thief on that day (could Christ have been speaking to him yesterday or tomorrow?). Clearly, Christ was comforting the thief by telling him that they would yet meet in paradise *before the end of that very day*. To force any other meaning on the text because of a preconceived idea that the soul sleeps is a disservice to the plain sense of Scripture.

Paul certainly expected to be with Christ when he died. He writes that he has a great desire "to depart and to be with Christ, for that is very much better" (Philippians 1:23). Paul does not long for death so that his soul can sleep; he longs for death because he knows he will be with Christ, which is far better. Again he writes that his preference is "to be absent

debt on the cross, and the resurrection was our receipt. His resurrection was the "proof of purchase."

A little girl was asked whether she feared walking through the cemetery. She replied, "No, I'm not afraid, for my home is on the other side!" An exodus need never be feared if it is the route to a better land.

A RESTFUL SLEEP

When Christ entered the home of the ruler of the synagogue, He comforted the crowd by saying that the ruler's daughter was not dead, but sleeping (Luke 8:52). On another occasion, when He began His trip to Bethany He said to the disciples, "Our friend Lazarus has fallen asleep; but I go, that I may awaken him out of sleep" (John 11:11).

Paul used the same figure of speech when he taught that some believers would not see death but would be caught up to meet Christ. "Behold, I tell you a mystery; we shall not all sleep, but we shall all be changed" (1 Corinthians 15:51). Not everyone shall die; some will live until the return of Christ. Death, then, is spoken of as a restful sleep.

As you are probably aware, there are those who teach "soul sleep," that is, the belief that no one is conscious at death because the soul sleeps until the resurrection of the body. Although this view has had some able defenders, it suffers from the difficulty of having to reinterpret many clear passages of Scripture in order to make this doctrine fit.

Moses certainly did not "sleep" until the day of resurrection but was fully conscious when He appeared on the Mount of Transfiguration. To say, as some do, that he already was resurrected, is to make an assumption that is not found in the Bible. We should be con-

exodus. There on the Mount of Transfiguration Moses and Elijah appeared with Christ and "were speaking of His departure which He was about to accomplish at Jerusalem" (Luke 9:31). That word *departure* in Greek is *exodus,* from which we get our word exit. The second book of the Old Testament is called Exodus because it gives the details regarding the exit of the children of Israel from Egypt.

Just as Moses led his people out of slavery, so now Christ passed through His own Red Sea, routing the enemies and preparing to lead His people to the Promised Land. His exodus is proof that He can safely conduct us all the way from earth to heaven.

There was nothing fearful about taking the journey from Egypt to Canaan; the people simply had to follow Moses, the servant of God. Once they had gone through the Red Sea, Canaan lay on the other side. If you have a qualified leader, you can enjoy the journey.

Neither is it fearful for us to make our final exodus, for we are following our leader, who has gone on ahead. When the curtain parts, we shall not only find Him on the other side but discover that He is the One who led us toward the curtain in the first place.

Just before His death, Christ told the disciples He was going where they could not come. Peter, who did not like what he heard, wanted to follow Christ everywhere. But Christ's response was, "Where I go, you cannot follow Me now; but you shall follow later" (John 13:36).

Yes, now that He has died and been raised to heaven, we all shall follow Him. What gives us courage is the knowledge that He does not ask us to go where He Himself has not gone. He who made a successful exit will make our exit successful also. Christ paid our

door to let you in. Similarly, death is the means by which our bodies are put to rest while our spirits are escorted through the gates of heaven. Death itself brings us to the gate, but then it is opened by One who says, "He who is holy, who is true, who has the key of David, who opens and no one will shut, and who shuts and no one opens" (Revelation 3:7). If the Drake prides itself in twenty-four-hour doorman service, would the Good Shepherd do any less?

Christ came, wrote the author of Hebrews, that "through death He might render powerless him who had the power of death, that is, the devil; and might deliver those who through fear of death were subject to slavery all their lives" (Hebrews 2:14–15). Satan does not have the power of death in the sense that he determines the day that a believer dies. But he has used the *fear* of death to keep Christians in bondage, unable to approach the curtain with a tranquillity borne of the "full assurance of faith."

In the next chapters I shall discuss more specifically what we can expect when the curtain parts for those who are at peace with God through Christ. For now, I want to provide comfort by describing five figures of speech that help us understand how death is viewed in the New Testament. For those who are prepared, the journey need not be feared.

Death in the New Testament is transformed from a monster to a minister. What at first seems to box us in, frees us to go to God. Here are some words of comfort that will help us soften the blow.

A DEPARTURE

Jesus, whose courage in the face of death is a model for us, referred to His death as a departure, an

That is why Paul classified death as one of the possessions of the Christian. "For all things belong to you, whether Paul or Apollos or Cephas or the world or life or death or things present or things to come; all things belong to you, and you belong to Christ; and Christ belongs to God" (1 Corinthians 3:21–23). We should not be surprised that death is listed as one of the gifts that belongs to us. Only death can give us the gift of eternity.

When persecutions came to the Christian church during the heady days of the Roman Empire, the believers realized that the pagans could take many things from them: wealth, food, friends, and health, to name a few. But they could not rid Christians of the gift of death that would escort them into the presence of God. Indeed, God often used the pagans to give His children that special present without which no man can see the Lord.

Think of how powerless death actually is! Rather than rid us of our wealth, it introduces us to "riches eternal." In exchange for poor health, death gives us a right to the Tree of Life that is for "the healing of the nations" (Revelation 22:2). Death might temporarily take our friends from us, but only to introduce us to that land in which there are no good-byes.

That is why Christ could say, "And do not fear those who kill the body, but are unable to kill the soul; but rather fear Him who is able to destroy both soul and body in hell" (Matthew 10:28). The body might temporarily be the possession of cancer or evil men, but these enemies cannot prevent the soul from going to God. When the executioners have done their worst, God will be shown to have done His best.

Just drive up to the Drake Hotel in Chicago and a valet will park your car and a doorman will open the

transferred your trust to a qualified Savior, perhaps years ago.

No doubt you will vacillate between despair and hope, denial and determination. Perhaps you will have more concern for those you leave behind than you do for yourself. Not a one of us can predict how we might react when it is our turn to hear the dreadful news.

And yet the Bible presents an entirely different picture of death that should give us hope. After Adam and Eve sinned, they died spiritually as well as physically. Sending them out of the garden, far from being an act of cruelty, was actually proof of God's kindness. We read, "'Lest he stretch out his hand, and take also from the tree of life, and eat, and live forever'—therefore the Lord God sent him out from the garden of Eden, to cultivate the ground from which he was taken" (Genesis 3:22–23).

If Adam and Eve had eaten of the other special tree of the garden—the Tree of Life—they would have been immortalized in their sinful condition. They never would have qualified for the heaven that God wanted them to enjoy. Imagine living forever as sinners, with no possibility of redemption and permanent transformation. Although they would never have had to face the finality of death, they would have been condemned to a pitiful existence.

Thus God prevented Adam and Eve from eternal sinfulness by giving them the gift of death, the ability to exit this life and arrive safely in the wondrous life to come. Death, though it would appear to be man's greatest enemy, would in the end, prove to be his greatest friend. Only through death can we go to God (unless, of course, we are still living when Christ returns).

\mathscr{T}HE ASCENT INTO GLORY

A Departure—A Restful Sleep—
A Collapsing Tent—A Sailing Ship—
A Permanent Home—Good Grief

The doctor has just told you news that you thought could only be true about someone else. Your worst suspicions regarding that lump have been confirmed: you have a rare form of cancer, which almost certainly is terminal. The surgeon tells you that you have at most a year to live.

Where do you turn for comfort? To your family and friends, yes; you need them more now than ever. They sit in stunned silence when you give them the news, and they assure you of their prayers and love. You know you will not have to walk through these dark days alone.

Of course you also turn to God. You have come to know Christ personally and have lived your life with single-minded devotion to Him and His agenda. You know the promises of God by memory. In a sense, you have been prepared for this hour ever since you

courage, I say, and prefer rather to be absent from the body and to be at home with the Lord" (2 Corinthians 5:8). The good news is that we can have the same confidence.

One day on a talk show a woman called with this question: "My father, though religious, died without believing in Christ as his Savior. . . . Is there something I can do to get him out of where I think he probably went?"

I replied, "I have some good news and some bad news. First, the bad news: no, there is nothing you can do to change the eternal destiny of your father. The good news is that whatever God does will be just . . . not one single fact will be overlooked in judging your father's fate . . . there is no possibility that the information will be misinterpreted or the penalty unfairly administered." (This will be more fully discussed in the chapter on hell.)

So far we have learned that death has two faces: to the unbeliever the very thought of death is terrifying, or at least it should be. But for those who have made their peace with God, death is a blessing. Death is a means of redemption, a doorway into a blissful eternity. Just what that means will be clarified in future chapters.

When the curtain parts for us, nothing can keep us from answering the summons. One minute after we die we will be either elated or terrified. And it will be too late to reroute our travel plans.

But now we turn to a much brighter side of death.

NOTE

1. For a more complete discussion of sheol and hades, see *Death and the Afterlife,* by Robert A. Morey (Minneapolis: Bethany, 1984), 72–87.

THE DESCENT INTO GLOOM

believers are said to go directly into heaven. In other words, the two regions of hades no longer exist side-by-side; Abraham's bosom is in heaven today. Hades, as far as we know, now has only one region, and that is where unbelievers enter.

Hades, then, is still an abode for departed spirits, a temporary intermediate state where those who have not received God's forgiveness must wait until further notice. When they hear their names called, the news that awaits them will not be encouraging.

THE PURGATORY OF MEDIEVAL THEOLOGY

Hades is not purgatory. We've learned that those who are in hades have no possibility of entering heaven. In contrast, purgatory is believed to have an exit. After the soul is purified by the sufferings of purgatory, we are told that it goes to God. *Purgatory* might be defined as a temporary place where those who have died as penitent are purified from sin by punishment.

The doctrine of purgatory is not found in the Bible but was accepted as a tradition in medieval times because of a faulty doctrine of salvation. The belief was that nobody (or almost nobody) was righteous enough to enter into heaven at death; thus there must be a place where men and women are purged from their sins to prepare them for heavenly perfections. Purgatory, the theory went, may last for a few years or millions of years (depending on the level of righteousness one has attained), but eventually it would come to an end and the penitent could enter heaven.

Thanks be, purgatory is unnecessary. As we shall see in a future chapter, when Christ's righteousness is credited to us, we can go directly to heaven. The apostle Paul, you might recall, wrote, "We are of good

goes, "A man convinced against his will is of the same opinion still."

I think back to the rich man buried in Chicago. He too had a keen memory; he thought of the family he had left behind. While I was scouring about looking for a parking space at the funeral home and discussing the service with his weeping widow and self-assured son, the man whose death brought us together was thinking fondly of his children. He thought back to how he had treated his wife; he remembered those with whom he had done business.

The beautiful words said at his eulogy, had he heard them, would have brought him shame. The shallow opinions of men now rose to mock him. He, too, I'm sure, had the plaintive hope that his family would repent so that they might not have to join him! If only *he,* and not his son, had been able to tell me what to say at his funeral!

Fourth, *let us not forget that the rich man of Luke 16 was not yet in hell, but hades.* Because the King James Version often translated both *sheol* and *hades* as hell, this has needlessly confused two different kinds of regions. The Bible is clear that no one is yet in hell today. Someday, hades will be thrown into hell, but that has as yet not happened (Revelation 20:14).

Peter has just finished expounding on the judgment of disobedient angels, then adds, "The Lord knows how to rescue godly men from trials and to hold the unrighteous for the day of judgment, while continuing their punishment" (2 Peter 2:9 NIV). The tense of the verb attests that the punishment is ongoing, though the final judgment is yet future.

What about the believer, Lazarus? He was in that region of sheol, or hades, which is called here "Abraham's bosom." But after the Ascension of Christ

important, he knew exactly what his brothers would have to do if they were to avoid his own fate! If they would *repent,* they would be kept from joining him in misery.

Incredibly, the man suddenly became interested in missions! He asked Abraham to warn his five brothers that they might not come to the same place of torment. And when Abraham said no, because they had Moses and the Prophets, this man replied, "No, Father Abraham, but if someone goes to them from the dead, they will repent!" (v. 30).

Unforgiven sin, the rich man knew, led quite logically to a place of agony. And if his brothers were to escape his distress, they would have to do something about their predicament while they were alive on earth. With heightened perception and a better understanding, he could see that his relationship with the Almighty should have been his highest priority.

We might think this man would have preferred to have his brothers join him in hades for the sake of companionship. But he was more than willing to never see them again if only he knew that they would be on the other side of the gulf where Lazarus and Abraham were meeting for the first time. Apparently, even in hades there is compassion, a natural human concern about the fate of those who are loved.

Abraham's answer is instructive. "If they do not listen to Moses and the Prophets, neither will they be persuaded if someone rises from the dead" (v. 31).

How true! When Christ told this story, He had not yet been put to death and resurrected. Yet He taught that His resurrection was the only sign that He would give to the world. But today, even though the evidence for His resurrection is overwhelming, many men and women still do not believe. As the saying

desires that were neither satisfied nor quenched.

Second, *the eternal destiny of this man was irrevocably fixed.* "Between us and you there is a great chasm fixed, in order that those who wish to come over from here to you may not be able, and that none may cross over from there to us" (Luke 16:26). Whereas the relatives on earth can leave the funeral home, go out for dinner, and plan a vacation, their friend in hades is confined, without any possibility of escape.

As M. R. DeHaan put it, "Once we have passed through the door of death we can't pick up our suitcase and move out because we don't like the accommodations." In hades, then, there is monotony; here is the isolation of boredom and triviality. No challenges can be undertaken; no goals set; no pleasures sampled.

While I was preaching that short sermon, the man whose body lay in that beautiful casket was fully aware that he was hemmed in; his future was no longer under his control. He had an overwhelming realization that his destiny was irrevocably fixed. And as we shall see, in the future his predicament will yet become worse, never better.

Third, *this man knew himself well enough to know that what he was experiencing was fair and just.* In hades his entire life was present to him; his transfer into the nether world did not diminish, but only heightened, his self-awareness. He begged Abraham to send Lazarus back to his father's house, "for I have five brothers—that he may warn them, lest they also come to this place of torment" (v. 28).

We have reason to think that this man believed that what was happening to him was just for two reasons. First, he says nothing about how unfair it is for him to be there. He complains about the pain, but he does not complain about injustice. Second, and more

focus on the fate of the rich man, trying to understand his predicament while his family was still enjoying the creature comforts of earth. Though we can be quite sure his family didn't know it, he was in acute distress.

My mind goes back to the shipping magnate at whose funeral I spoke in Chicago. Both he and the rich man in the parable, and millions like them, have discovered too late that their worldly influence could not save them; nor could their wealth and reputation extricate them from this bind. Instead of victors, they were now victims; rather than bragging about their freedom, they now had to confess their enslavement.

First, *the man in hades was fully conscious immediately after death.* Memory, speaking, pain, and bliss—all of these were a part of his experience. The rich man said, "Father Abraham, have mercy on me, and send Lazarus, that he may dip the tip of his finger in water and cool off my tongue; for I am in agony in this flame" (v. 24). In hades, an alcoholic will thirst for a drop of liquor, but none will be given to him. The drug addict will crave a shot of heroin, but will not receive it. The immoral man will burn with sexual desire, but never be satisfied.

Perpetually burning lusts never subside, and the tortured conscience aches but is never sedated. There will be increased desire with decreased satisfaction. In Proverbs, we read of the insatiable desires of both the nether world and a man's lusts: "Sheol and Abaddon are never satisfied, nor are the eyes of a man ever satisfied" (Proverbs 27:20).

So while we listened attentively to the obituary read in that funeral home in Chicago, the one whose memory was respectfully honored was in pain; he had smoldering needs that were unmet. He had inflamed

Remember the context. A rich man who habitually dressed in purple and fine linen and lived in splendor every day died and his soul was taken to hades. A beggar named Lazarus who lay at the rich man's gate also died and was carried into Abraham's bosom (the blissful region of hades). Now the description of the hereafter begins:

> And in Hades [the Greek translation of the Old Testament *sheol*] he lifted up his eyes, being in torment, and saw Abraham far away, and Lazarus in his bosom. And he cried out and said, 'Father Abraham, have mercy on me, and send Lazarus, that he may dip the tip of his finger in water and cool off my tongue; for I am in agony in this flame.' But Abraham said, 'Child, remember that during your life you received your good things, and likewise Lazarus bad things; but now he is being comforted here, and you are in agony. And besides all this, between us and you there is a great chasm fixed, in order that those who wish to come over from here to you may not be able, and that none may cross over from there to us.' (Luke 16:23–26)

It would be a mistake to think that this tormented man ended in hades because he was rich! Elsewhere in the New Testament we are clearly taught that our riches or lack of them do not dictate our eternal destiny. Remember, Christ told this story to jolt greedy Pharisees into the realization that their riches cannot save them; poor people might be better off in the life to come. (Exactly what determines where we will spend eternity will be discussed later in this book.)

Christ described the radically different destinies of a believer and unbeliever. For our purposes, let us

If the door to the afterlife is open but a crack in the Old Testament, it is thrown wide open in the New. Here we have detailed descriptions of both the righteous and the unbelievers after death. Based on this information, we are better able to answer the question of what we can expect one minute after we have breathed our last.

HADES IN THE NEW TESTAMENT

We've learned that the Hebrew word *sheol* is used for the realm of the dead in the Old Testament. The New Testament, however, was written in Greek, and there we find sheol translated by the Greek word *hades*. In fact, when the whole of the Old Testament was translated into Greek before the time of Christ, *sheol* was always translated "hades." Similarly, when the New Testament quotes Old Testament texts, *sheol* is always translated "hades"; they are one and the same.

The New Testament pulls back the curtain so that we can see into hades (or sheol) with more clarity. As we might expect, just like *sheol,* the word *hades* is never used of the grave, but always refers to the world of departed spirits. Here we are given some very specific details about what hades is like, both for those who die as believers as well as those who die as unbelievers. At least some of the mystery disappears as God parts the curtain for us.

Christ accepted the rabbis' understanding that sheol, or hades, had two compartments. To emphasize to the greedy Pharisees how the fortunes of rich people might someday be reversed in the world to come, he told a story that takes us behind the veil which separates the dead from the living.

best explained by remembering that sheol has two different kinds of inhabitants. "This is the way of those who are foolish. . . . As sheep they are appointed for Sheol; death shall be their shepherd; and the upright shall rule over them in the morning; and their form shall be for Sheol to consume, so that they have no habitation. But God will redeem my soul from the power of Sheol; for He will receive me" (Psalm 49:13–15). Other Old Testament passages make a similar contrast (Job 24:19; Psalms 9:17; 16:10; 31:17; 55:15).

Perhaps one of the clearest expressions of immortality in the Old Testament comes from the book of Daniel. "And many of those who sleep in the dust of the ground will awake, these to everlasting life, but the others to disgrace and everlasting contempt" (Daniel 12:2). Daniel not only believed that there were two classes of people who would live either in bliss or contempt, but that their bodies would also arise some day. This is an explicit reference to the New Testament doctrine of the resurrection of the body.

The Old Testament makes a sharp distinction between the wicked and the righteous, with the clear implication that they have separate destinies in the afterlife. Though this division of sheol is not expressly stated, later rabbis clearly taught that sheol has two compartments.

Sheol, then, is a general term for the nether world, the region of departed spirits. As the scholar B. B. Warfield wrote, "Israel from the beginning of its recorded history cherished the most settled conviction of the persistence of the soul in life after death. . . . The body is laid in the grave and the soul departs for sheol." Here the righteous and the wicked enter, though when they arrive, they do not have the same experience.

34

their inhabitants. Naked is Sheol before Him and Abaddon has no covering" (Job 26:5–6).

Third, *after death one can be united with his ancestors in sheol.* Jacob went down into sheol and was "gathered to his people" (Genesis 49:33). Abraham was assured by the Lord that he would go down to his fathers in peace (Genesis 15:15). Some have interpreted this as simply a reference to the fact that the bones of a particular family were often buried together. But the clear implication is that there would be a reunion of some kind in the world beyond.

That the word *sheol* refers to the realm of departed spirits seems unmistakable. What seems equally clear is that those who entered this region did not all have the same experience. For some, it was a region of gloom; but for others, it was a place where they would dwell with God.

Asaph, the author of many of the psalms, wrote, "Nevertheless I am continually with Thee; Thou has taken hold of my right hand. With Thy counsel Thou wilt guide me, and afterward receive me to glory. Whom have I in heaven but Thee? And besides Thee, I desire nothing on earth" (Psalm 73:23–25). He expected to see the glory of God at death; indeed, he speaks about heaven.

Fourth, *there are hints in the Old Testament that sheol has different regions.* Both the wicked and the righteous are said go to sheol. Jacob went into sheol, but so did the rebellious people, such as Korah and Dathan. This explains why there is a "lower region." The Lord says, "For a fire is kindled in My anger, and burns to the lowest part of Sheol, and consumes the earth with its yield, and sets on fire the foundations of the mountains" (Deuteronomy 32:22).

The reason there are two different realms in sheol is

departed spirits who were conscious, either in bliss or torment. The word *sheol* never means just the grave.

For the purpose of greater clarity, more recent translations of the Bible sometimes do not attempt to use an English equivalent to translate *sheol*. They simply let the Hebrew word stand as it is. For example, in the very first use of the word in the Old Testament, the *New American Standard Bible* quotes Jacob as saying, "Surely I will go down to Sheol in mourning for my son" (Genesis 37:35).

So here are some facts we should know in order to understand what the Old Testament means by the word *sheol*.[1]

First, *there is a clear distinction between the grave, where the body rests, and sheol, where the spirits of the dead gather.* Although graves are usually in shallow earth or even above the earth, sheol is always thought of as down under, somewhere in a hollow part of the earth. Isaiah writes that when the king is overthrown, "Sheol from beneath is excited over you to meet you when you come; it arouses for you the spirits of the dead, all the leaders of the earth; it raises all the kings of the nations from their thrones" (Isaiah 14:9; see also v. 10). Sheol is not impersonal; it is a place of activity.

Second, *sheol is often spoken of as a shadowy place of darkness, a place that is not a part of this existence.* Another prophet, Ezekiel, says that Tyre will be "[brought] down with those who go down to the pit, to the people of old, and I shall make you dwell in the lower parts of the earth, like the ancient waste places, with those who go down to the pit [sheol], so that you will not be inhabited; but I shall set glory in the land of the living" (Ezekiel 26:20).

Job speaks of the inhabitants of sheol as in pain. "The departed spirits tremble under the waters and

32

understand as much as we do with the light of the New Testament, but clearly they knew that the soul survived the life of the body. In fact, a belief in the consciousness of the afterlife was so universally accepted by all cultures that the biblical writers simply assumed it was so. All that they did was clarify what God had already revealed through natural revelation.

Let's take a tour of the data.

THE SHEOL OF THE OLD TESTAMENT

The most important word in the Old Testament that speaks of the afterlife is the Hebrew word *sheol,* which occurs sixty-five times in the Old Testament. In the King James Version of the Bible it is translated "hell" thirty-one times, "grave" thirty-one times, and "pit" three times. This inconsistency in translation has caused some to be confused regarding what *sheol* really means.

First, we must remember that elsewhere in the Bible sheol is clearly distinguished from hell (I'll comment more on this later). And second, just because it is sometimes translated "grave," this does not mean that it refers *only* to the grave. Some people who believe that it refers to the grave and nothing more assume that when we die, we just die like a dog.

Not so. Of course, *sheol* can be translated "grave" in some contexts, because the word includes the concept of the grave. But what seems clear is that the writers of the Old Testament believed that to go to sheol was not only to go to the grave but also to experience a conscious afterlife.

There is a Hebrew word that can only be translated "grave" [*kever*], but the writers often preferred the word *sheol* because it encompassed the region of

apparently had made millions of dollars in the ship-
ping industry, but he was to be cremated on that very
day, after a rather long eulogy but a very short sermon.

What did he experience one minute after he died?
Of course I can't be this man's judge. Only God
knows whether or not he had come to trust Christ as
his Savior, even in the closing minutes of his life. But,
for the purposes of illustration, we can assume that he
died as an unbeliever, just as his son had said. If so,
what was this man experiencing even as we gathered
in the funeral parlor to honor his memory? What
would we have seen if we could have looked beyond
the elegant casket?

To give a complete answer to this question, we
must embark on a quick tour of the Old Testament
teaching regarding the afterlife and then take a further
step into the New Testament. When we are finished,
we will have a fairly good understanding of what was
happening to this man in the region of death, even as
his family was frantically seeking for a minister to
make his funeral appropriately religious. What we will
discover is both mysterious and frightening.

Death, we must remember, is the consequence of
Adam and Eve's disobedience in the Garden of Eden.
God had warned them that if they ate the forbidden
fruit they would die. And die they did. They died *spir-
itually* in that they were separated from God and tried
to hide from Him. They also began to die *physically,*
as their bodies began the journey to the grave. And if
Adam and Eve had not been redeemed by God, they
would have died *eternally,* which is the third form of
death. From the original disobedience in Eden, death
in all of its forms began its trek throughout the world.

The Old Testament goes on to unfold God's revela-
tion of the afterlife. Of course, those writers didn't

\mathcal{T}HE DESCENT INTO GLOOM

Sheol—Hades—Purgatory

One day I received a call from a distraught family who wanted a minister to do a quick funeral. I say "quick" because they asked me to speak for only a few minutes. "We don't want anything religious," the son told me, "and nothing you will do will be too short."

I asked him why it was so important for the funeral to be brief. He told me his family was not religious; his father who had died suddenly had never attended church. They did not believe in God; the only reason I was called was because a relative thought a minister should be present.

I made a deal with him. Yes, I would be brief; but I would have to tell the guests what I believed about death in general and Christ in particular. He reluctantly agreed.

If there is one word that characterized that funeral, it was the word *hopelessness*. Here was a man who

glimpses of the regions of death come into view. This will prepare us for the much clearer revelation given in the New Testament. Though we have no right to peer behind the curtain and report what we have found, we can gratefully accept all that God has shown to us in His Word.

What follows in the next chapters of this book is His revelation, not our observation. God parts the curtain so that we can glimpse inside.

Let us find out what is there.

NOTES

1. Tom Howard, *Christianity Today,* 29 March 1974, 31.

2. Martha Smilgis, "Hollywood Goes to Heaven," *Time,* 3 June 1991, 70.

3. James A. Pike, *The Other Side* (New York: Doubleday, 1968), 115.

4. Raymond Moody, *Life After Life* (Covington, Ga.: Mockingbird, 1975).

5. Melvin Morse, *Closer to the Light* (New York: Ivy, 1990), 33.

6. Betty J. Eadie and Curtis Taylor, *Embraced by the Light* (Placerville, Calif.: Gold Leaf, 1992).

7. Ibid.

8. Philip J. Swihart, *The Edge of Death* (Downers Grove, Ill.: InverVarsity, 1978).

9. Maurice S. Rawlings, *Beyond Death's Door* (Nashville: Nelson, 1978).

the "religion of the resuscitated," who report only the utopian idea that death leads to a higher degree of consciousness for all people regardless of their religion or beliefs. We must remember that all near-death reports are from those who might have died clinically but have not experienced biological or irreversible death. None has been resurrected. Whether the experience is positive or negative, it must always be evaluated by a more reliable authority.

Personally, I am much more concerned about what I will experience after death than what I will experience when I am near death. It's not the *transition* but the *destination* that really counts. Thus, to discover what really lies on the other side, we must find a more credible map, a more certain authority than people who go only to the threshold of the life beyond and give us their reports.

We will do much better if we trust someone who was actually dead, not someone who was just near death. Christ, as we shall see, is the only One who is qualified to tell us what we can expect on the other side. He was dead—so dead that His body became cold and was put into a tomb. Three days later He was raised from the dead with a glorified body. Here is someone whose opinion can be trusted. To John this risen Christ said, "Do not be afraid; I am the first and the last, and the living One; and I was dead, and behold, I am alive forevermore, and I have the keys of death and Hades" (Revelation 1:17–18).

Reliable information does not come to us by trying to peer behind the partially open curtain. God alone knows what really lies on the other side of the veil. And that is why we can do no better than study what the Bible has to say about the Great Beyond.

We begin with the Old Testament, where the first

Light" they met gives everyone an unconditional welcome.

One woman reported that when she crossed the line between life and death she met Christ, who took her for a walk. He explained that all the religions of the world were paths to the same destination. There was a Buddhist path, a Hindu path, an Islamic path, and of course, a Christian path. But, like spokes in a wheel, all of them led to the central hub of heaven. In other words, everyone will be saved. This has always been Satan's most believable lie.

As for the widely reported experiences of seeing light, we should remember that since God is light, it is understandable that Satan duplicates light of his own. We cannot emphasize too strongly that he wishes to disguise himself as an "angel of light" (2 Corinthians 11:14). And of course, many unsuspecting souls simply assume that this "being" who radiates light is kind and benevolent; in an age of "feel good" religion they can't imagine that it is anyone else but Christ.

Although positive near-death experiences are widely reported, I must point out that other research indicates that many have dark and foreboding experiences. In *The Edge of Death,* by Philip J. Swihart,[8] and *Beyond Death's Door,* by Maurice Rawlings,[9] there are accounts of those who tell terrifying stories of the life beyond. Some have seen a lake of fire or abysmal darkness, along with tormented persons—all of whom are awaiting judgment. These reports, the authors contend, are more accurate because they were gained through interviews almost immediately following near-death and resuscitation. These dark experiences, the writers say, are often lost to the memory after a short period of time.

We cannot overstate the deception perpetuated by

be classified as a near-death experience, or perhaps even a "revived from death" experience.

If Stephen saw our Lord before he died, and if Paul died and was caught up into paradise, it is just possible that other believers might also have such a vision. Reports of seeing Christ or relatives long dead might have some validity. We should not expect such experiences, but they could happen.

The problem, of course, is that we cannot accept without scrutiny what people claim to have seen behind the curtain. Near-death experiences may or may not reflect the true conditions of life beyond death. They must be carefully evaluated to see whether they conform to the biblical picture of the hereafter. Also, the prior beliefs of those who report what they have seen and heard are essential in evaluating what was experienced.

Remember—and this is important—Satan would try to duplicate the same positive experiences for unbelievers that God gave to Stephen and Paul. The Great Deceiver wants to have people think that one's relationship with Jesus Christ has no bearing on the beauty and bliss that awaits everyone. If it is true that angels await those who have been made righteous by Christ, it is understandable that demonic spirits would await those who enter eternity without God's forgiveness and acceptance.

We know that at least some positive near-death experiences are demonic, for they sharply contradict the teaching of the Bible. First, some like Betty Eadie tell us that the Jesus they met assured them that everyone will have an equally blissful welcome into the life beyond. Second, we are told that there is no judgment, no rigorous examination of a person's life. Several of the people explicitly mention that the "being of

nothing to offend her. There was no reason to regret past deeds, for we as humans are not sinful creatures; indeed, human "spirit beings" assisted the heavenly Father at creation. Thankfully, the world is not filled with tragedy as we suppose, and in the presence of Christ, Eadie concluded, "I knew that I was worthy to embrace Him."[7]

What do these experiences prove? Apparently, they do confirm that at death the soul separates from the body. A few patients not only looked back and saw doctors hover around their body, but could see what was going on in other places in the hospital. This, it seems, is impossible unless the soul had actually left the body and could review earth from a different perspective.

We have reason to believe that a person may see Christ in the twilight zone between life and death. Before Stephen was stoned God gave him a glimpse into heaven. Stephen said, "Behold, I see the heavens opened up and the Son of Man standing at the right hand of God" (Acts 7:56). This experience was unique in that it happened before Stephen died, not at death. Here was positive encouragement that heaven was waiting to receive him!

The apostle Paul had a similar experience, though some think that he actually died when he was caught up into paradise, where he heard "inexpressible words, which a man is not permitted to speak" (2 Corinthians 12:4). Since he said it happened fourteen years before writing these words to the church at Corinth, there is at least some evidence that the event coincided with his experience at Lystra, where he was stoned and dragged out of the city presumed dead (Acts 14:19–20). If he did die and then revived, this account could

in almost all instances very positive. Typical is the account of a sixteen-year-old boy who was rushed to the hospital with a very severe kidney problem. While in the admitting room, he slumped over in his chair. A nurse searched for his pulse but found none. Thankfully, he was eventually resuscitated. Later he told of a supernatural experience:

> I reached a certain point in the tunnel where lights suddenly began flashing all around me. They made me certain that I was in some kind of tunnel, and the way I moved past them, I knew I was going hundreds of miles an hour.
>
> At this point I also noticed that there was somebody with me. He was about seven feet tall and wore a long white gown with a simple belt tied at the waist. His hair was golden, and although he didn't say anything, I wasn't afraid because I could feel him radiating peace and love.
>
> No, he wasn't the Christ, but I knew that he was sent from Christ. It was probably one of his angels or someone else sent to transport me to Heaven.[5]

More recently, Betty Eadie, in *Embraced by the Light*,[6] gives a fantastic account of her visit to the "other side." She claims to have seen Christ and thus even dedicated her book to him: "To the Light, my Lord and Savior Jesus Christ, to whom I owe all that I have. He is the 'staff' that I lean on; without Him I would fail." Yet it becomes clear that the Christ she tells us about is not the Jesus of the New Testament.

Eadie's Jesus is a benevolent being of light that surrounded her in such a way that she could not tell where her "light" stopped and his began. Jesus, she tells us, is separate from the Father and would do

few months old, have reportedly babbled blasphemies and obscenities they could never have personally learned in their short lifetimes.

Occultism, of whatever variety, is not a reliable source of information regarding what happens after death. It proves only the existence of a spirit world, a world of deception and dark intelligence. God considers all forms of occultism an abomination (Leviticus 19:31; Deuteronomy 18:9–12; Isaiah 8:19–20; 1 Corinthians 10:14–22).

Neither Shirley MacLaine nor any other guru is qualified to tell us about eternity. No one can prove that he or she has had the experience of being recycled from another existence. The curtain opens when we go in, but once it is firmly closed, it will not open to let us return.

NEAR-DEATH EXPERIENCES

Some people claim to have died and returned to their bodies to give us information on the life beyond. In 1976, Raymond Moody, in *Life After Life*,[4] recorded the interviews of many who were near death but were successfully resuscitated. Their stories, for the most part, had many similar elements: the patient would hear himself being pronounced dead; he would be out of his body, watching the doctors work over his corpse. While in this state, he would meet relatives or friends who had died and then encounter a "being of light." When he knows that he must return to his body, he does so reluctantly because the experience of love and peace has engulfed him.

Melvin Morse, in *Closer to the Light,* recounts the stories of children who have had near-death experiences. Again, their stories are remarkably similar, and

22

This doctrine teaches that we just keep being recycled; death is nothing more than a transition from one body to another. Thus Shirley MacLaine claims we can eliminate the fear of death by proclaiming that it does not exist. Through contacts in the spirit world, she has discovered that in a previous existence she was a princess in Atlantis, an Inca in Peru, and even was a child raised by elephants. In some previous existences, she was male; in others, female.

A woman I met on a plane told me that as a child she had detailed knowledge of a house in Vermont that she had never visited. Later, as an adult, she visited the house, and the details coincided with her visions. She was then convinced she had lived there during the eighteenth century. I pointed out that there is no such thing as a transmigration of souls, but there is a transmigration of demons. She was getting knowledge about an eighteenth-century family from evil spirits.

"But," she protested, "I have nothing to do with evil spirits; I communicate only with good ones!"

"How do you tell the difference between good spirits and evil ones?" I asked.

"I communicate only with those spirits that come to me clothed in light."

I reminded her of 2 Corinthians 11:13–14, "For such men are false apostles, deceitful workers, disguising themselves as apostles of Christ. And no wonder, for even Satan disguises himself as an angel of light." Yes, light indeed!

Her experiences and similar ones do not prove reincarnation, but rather confirm that people of all ages can become the victims of demonic influence. There is evidence that even children sometimes inherit the demonically induced traits of their parents or ancestors. This would explain why some children, a

demons need to relocate. Often they choose to stay in the place where the death took place (this seems particularly true in the case of violent deaths, such as murder or suicide). They will take the name and characteristics of the deceased person and make occasional appearances under these pretenses. Such entities (as they are frequently called today) are evil spirits who often pose as "friendly ghosts."

To try to contact the dead is to invite fellowship with hosts of darkness pretending to be helpful angels of light. Isaiah the prophet warned the people that to consult a medium was to turn one's back on God. "And when they say to you, 'Consult the mediums and the spiritists who whisper and mutter,' should not a people consult their God? Should they consult the dead on behalf of the living? To the law and to the testimony! If they do not speak according to this word, it is because they have no dawn [light]" (Isaiah 8:19–20).

The point, of course, is that all information about life after death that comes from spiritists or channelers is unreliable. Those who turn to the occult world for knowledge of death are misled. Yes, there is life after death, but we cannot learn the details from demons, whose chief delight is to confuse and deceive. No wonder the theology allegedly given by Pike's son was so convoluted.

We have no right to try to peek behind the curtain by communicating with those on the other side. Once the curtain has opened to admit a fellow traveler, it closes and we must not try to peek behind the veil.

REINCARNATION

Another form of occultism that purports to give information about life after death is reincarnation.

from the dead, but not by the witch of Endor. God Himself seems to have done this miracle; only such a surprising act can explain the medium's terror (1 Samuel 28:3–25).

We must remember that the voice of Samuel did not speak through the lips of this medium. Samuel and Saul spoke to one another directly because of this surprising miracle. What is more, the Almighty was displeased with Saul's desperate attempt to consult the dead prophet. No wonder Saul heard a prophecy of judgment that he and his sons would die the very next day—a prophecy that was fulfilled. Attempting to talk with the dead is consistently condemned by God (Deuteronomy 18:11–12).

So you can be quite sure that no one has ever talked to your dead uncle, cousin, or grandmother. There are, however, spirits that impersonate the dead. Their trickery is compounded because they may actually talk about love, the value of religion, or make favorable references to Christ. And of course they know enough about the one who has died to deceive the unwary.

This ability of demonic spirits to masquerade as the personality of the dead helps us understand haunted houses. While I was staying in a hotel near Calgary, a local newspaper carried a story saying that there were at least two ghosts in the beautiful building. One of the employees showed us a marble staircase where one of these ghosts lived (verified by the testimony of employees). A new bride had stumbled down the stairs years ago and hit her head, resulting in her death. We were told that her spirit now lives on the stairs, appearing with some regularity.

How do we explain this phenomenon? When a person who is inhabited by evil spirits dies, these

CHANNELING

Some people claim to have talks with the dead. In his book *The Other Side,* Bishop James A. Pike described in detail how he made contact with his son, who had committed suicide. Using a spirit medium, the bishop had what he believed to be several extensive conversations with the boy.

"I failed the test, I can't face you, can't face life," Pike's son reportedly said. "I'm confused. . . . I am not in purgatory, but something like Hell, here, . . . yet nobody blames me here."[3] Jesus, the boy said, was an example but not a Savior.

A surprise was the alleged appearance in spirit of a friend, Paul Tillich, a well-known German-American theologian who had died several months before. Pike was caught off guard when he discerned his deceased friend's German accent passing through the lips of the medium (or channeler).

How should this evidence be interpreted? Liberal theologian that he was, Pike did not realize that demons impersonate the dead to create the illusion that the living can communicate with the dead. These spirits have astonishing knowledge of the dead person's life since they carefully observe individuals while they are living. Through the power of deception, they can mimic a deceased person's voice, personality, and even appearance. The King James Version actually translates the word *medium* as those who have "familiar spirits" (Leviticus 19:31; 20:6, 27; Deuteronomy 18:11), suggesting the familiarity some demons have with individuals.

Sometimes the story of Samuel and Saul is used to justify communication with the dead. In this remarkable instance, Samuel was apparently brought back

fided to friends that he saw a "bright white light" that eased his fears and made him look forward to what awaited him on the other side. He died calmly, anticipating what he called "quite an experience."

Reincarnation, altered states of consciousness, and glad reunions in a metaphysical place such as heaven are popular themes at the box office. Larry Gordon, chief executive of Largo Entertainment, says, "People are looking for something that makes them feel good. We all want to believe that death isn't so bad."[2] Dozens of movies portray the enchantment of the life beyond. One advertised, "There is at least one laugh on the other side."

Fear of death has been supplanted by blissful feelings about a hereafter where everyone ends happily reunited. There is no judgment, no careful review of one's life. To be sure, death has mystery, we are told, but is not to be dreaded. Given this positive assessment of the Great Beyond, we should not be surprised that some people want to hasten their arrival at this destination.

How legitimate are reported glimpses from behind the parted curtain? Many are convinced that the immortality of the soul is now confirmed by paranormal experiences that can have no other explanation but that the soul survives the death of the body. We might agree that the soul does survive the death of the body, but how much reliable information can be transmitted back to earth by those who tell us what they have seen and heard from the other side?

Let us evaluate three different kinds of evidence that are sometimes used to assure us that all will be well as we make our own exits through the mysterious veil.

those who face death. No matter that death is common to the human race; each person must face this ultimate ignominy individually. No one can endure this moment for us. Friends and family can walk only as far as the curtain; the dying one must disappear behind the veil alone.

Understandably, Jacquelyn was apprehensive as she faced the closed partition. She thought about the mystery that lay back of the shrouded veil. She wished for some insight, some glimpse into the future that would assure her that she did not have to be afraid. Yet neither her curiosity nor her desire to live kept her from slipping through the curtain and going into the night alone. Will she find herself fully conscious in some dark cavern seeking companionship but finding none?

Tom Howard says that when we face death we are like a hen before a cobra, incapable of doing anything at all in the presence of the very thing that seems to call for the most drastic and decisive action. "There is, in fact, nothing we can do," he writes. "Say what we will, dance how we will, we will soon enough be a heap of ruined feathers and bones, indistinguishable from the rest of the ruins that lie about. It will not appear to matter in the slightest whether we met the enemy with equanimity, shrieks, or a trumped-up gaiety, *there we will be.*"[1]

Naturally, we would like to know in advance what we can expect on the other side. Human nature being what it is, we grasp for some clue, some hint we might glean from those who are about to cross the boundary. We are particularly anxious to hear a good word, the assurance that all will be well. When television actor Michael Landon ("Little House On the Prairie" and "Bonanza") lay on his deathbed, he con-

ATTEMPTING TO PEEK BEHIND THE CURTAIN

Channeling—Reincarnation—
Near Death Experiences

During the last few months of her struggle with cancer, Jacquelyn Helton kept a diary. Her thoughts and feelings would become a legacy for her husband, Tom, and her eighteen-month-old daughter, Jennifer.

In her diary she wonders what death would be like? What clothes should she wear for burial? She thinks of her daughter. Who will love her? Put her to sleep? In her writings, she tells Jennifer that when it hurts, she should remember that her mother would have cared. Then she thinks of her husband and the needs he will have after she is gone.

Finally she cries out, "What is the matter with you, God? My family is not a bunch of Boy Scouts who can figure all these things out for themselves—you're some kind of idiot to pull something like this!"

Denial, anger, fear, depression, and helpless resignation—all of these feelings erupt in the souls of

elation, just a desire to accurately explain what the Bible has to say.

I pray God will help me make heaven so inviting that those who are ready to enter will scarcely be able to wait. I pray also, that I shall make hell so fearsome that those who are not ready to die shall quickly come to trust the only One who can shield them from "the wrath to come."

Death, our enemy, can be our friend when God gives us the final call. We can be glad He has given us a shaft of light to illumine the darkness. Death is not a hopeless plunge into the vast unknown.

So, what can we expect *one minute after we die?*

NOTE

1. C. S. Lewis, "The Weight of Glory," in *The Weight of Glory and Other Addresses,* rev. and exp. ed. (New York: Macmillan, 1980), 18–19.

permanent; if we are wise, we will spend our time preparing for that which lasts forever. What is life but preparation for eternity?

Recently, I read a tragic story about people enjoying themselves on the top stories of a tall apartment building not knowing that there was a fire burning on the lower floors. Just so, many are enjoying life, comfortably ignoring the fact that their death is not only inevitable, but much nearer than they think. Though there are many uncertainties in our lives, we can count on this: Whatever we strive for in this world must of necessity be temporary. Indeed, this world and all we have accumulated will eventually be burned up.

The other day I was browsing in the travel section of a bookstore. Potential travelers were buying maps and guidebooks on Hawaii and Europe. Some were purchasing booklets to help them learn some phrases of a foreign language. No doubt they had saved their money, blocked out their vacation schedules, and purchased airline tickets. All that just for a two-week journey.

I wondered how many of them were giving at least that much attention to their final destination. I wondered how many were reading the guidebook, studying the map, and trying to learn the language of heaven. Europe and Hawaii seemed so much more real than the unseen realm of the dead. And yet, even as they planned their vacations, they were en route to a more distant destination.

The purpose of this book is to study what the Bible has to say about the life beyond. Many who read it will be comforted; others will be disturbed; and everyone, I hope, will be instructed. I claim no special rev-

Pause, stranger, when you pass me by
As you are now, so once was I
As I am now, so you will be
So prepare for death and follow me

An unknown passerby read those words and underneath scratched this reply:

To follow you I'm not content
Until I know which way you went

In recent days I have conducted two funerals. The first was that of a Christian woman who had distinguished herself by a life of sacrificial service for Christ. The triumph of the family was striking; there was irrepressible joy mixed with the sorrow.

The second was that of an apparent unbeliever who was killed in a highway accident. The grief of the relatives was marked by desperation and hopelessness. They refused to be comforted.

You and I shall follow these two people to the grave. Unless Christ should return in our lifetime, we all shall pass through that iron gate described by Hamlet as "the undiscover'd country from whose bourn / No traveller returns" (III.i. 79–80).

Thinking about our final destination gives us perspective. Visualize a measuring tape extending from earth to the farthest star. Our stay here is but a hair line, almost invisible to the length of the tape. Strictly speaking, no distance can be compared to eternity. No matter how endless we visualize eternity to be, our conception is never endless enough.

Every one of us wants to make wise investments, to get the "biggest bang for our buck," as the saying goes. The best investments are those that are safe and

Those who find themselves in heaven will be surrounded with friends whom they have known on earth. Friendships, once rudely interrupted by death, will continue where they left off. Every description of heaven they have ever heard will pale in the light of reality. All this, *forever.*

Others—indeed many others—will be shrouded in darkness, a region of deprivation and unending regret. There, with their memories and feelings fully intact, images of their life on earth will return to haunt them. They will think back to their friends, family and relatives; they will brood over opportunities they squandered and intuitively know that their future is both hopeless and unending. For them, death will be far worse than they imagined.

And so while relatives and friends plan your funeral —deciding on a casket, a burial plot, and who the pallbearers shall be—you will be more alive than you have ever been. You will either see God on His throne surrounded by angels and redeemed humanity, or you will feel an indescribable weight of guilt and abandonment. There is no destination midway between these two extremes; just gladness or gloom.

Nor will it be possible to transfer from one region to another. No matter how endless the ages, no matter how heartfelt the cries, no matter how intense the suffering, your travel plans are limited to your present abode. Those who find themselves in the lower gloomy regions shall never enter the gates that lead to endless light and ecstasy. They will discover that the beautiful words spoken in their eulogy bear no resemblance to the reality that now confronts them. If only their friends could see them now!

I'm told that there is a cemetery in Indiana that has an old tombstone bearing this epitaph:

INTRODUCTION

𝒲ELCOME
TO ETERNITY

One minute after you slip behind the parted curtain, you will either be enjoying a personal welcome from Christ or catching your first glimpse of gloom as you have never known it. Either way, your future will be irrevocably fixed and eternally unchangeable.

"Every human being," says C. S. Lewis, "is in the process of becoming a noble being; noble beyond imagination. Or else, alas, a vile being beyond redemption." He exhorts us to remember that "the dullest and most uninteresting person you can talk to may one day be a creature which, if you saw it now, you would be strongly tempted to worship, or else a horror and a corruption such as you now meet, if at all, only in a nightmare. . . . There are no *ordinary* people . . . It is immortals whom we joke with, work with, marry, snub and exploit—immortal horrors or everlasting splendors."[1]

\mathscr{C}ONTENTS

*In loving memory of our
precious stillborn granddaughter, Sarah,
who even now beholds the face
of our Father who is in heaven*

Portions adapted from Salt & Light Pocket Guides:
 © 1992 *Coming to Grips with Death & Dying*
 © 1992 *Coming to Grips with Heaven*
 © 1992 *Coming to Grips with Hell*

All Scripture quotations, unless indicated, are taken from the *New American Standard Bible,* © 1960, 1962, 1963, 1968, 1971, 1972, 1973, 1975, and 1977, by The Lockman Foundation, La Habra, Calif. Used by permission.

Scripture quotations marked (NIV) are taken from the *Holy Bible: New International Version®*. NIV®. Copyright © 1973, 1978, 1984 by International Bible Society. Used by permission of Zondervan Publishing House. All rights reserved.

The "NIV" and "New International Version" trademarks are registered in the United States Patent and Trademark Office by International Bible Society. Use of either trademark requires the permission of International Bible Society.

Scripture quotations marked (KJV) are taken from the King James Version.

ISBN: 0-8024-6312-6

5 7 9 10 8 6 4

Printed in the United States of America

*A Preview of Your
Final Destination*

ONE MINUTE *After* You Die

Erwin W. Lutzer

MOODY PRESS
CHICAGO

ONE
MINUTE
After
You Die

About the Author

Rebecca Adler lives in Texas and writes mysteries set in *far* West Texas, filled with sweet, Southern-fried flavor, delicious suspense, and scrumptious Tex-Mex recipes. She is the author of *Here Today, Gone Tamale* (book one in the Taste of Texas Mystery series). Visit her online at AuthorRebeccaAdler.com.

✒ Josie's Favorite Peach Margarita

Makes 1 cocktail

1 ounce peach schnapps
1 ounce cranberry juice
1½ ounces margarita mix
1 ounce tequila
½ ounce raspberry liqueur
¼ cup lime juice

Shake all ingredients together in a cocktail shaker. Serve on the rocks (use plenty of ice) in a salted or sugared margarita glass.

✒The Cogburn Hotel's Chocolate Chip Pecan Cookies

Makes about 4 dozen

Prep time: 15 minutes. Cook time: 10 minutes

2½ cups all-purpose flour
1 teaspoon salt
1 teaspoon baking soda
1 cup butter (2 sticks)
¾ cup sugar
¾ cup brown sugar, packed
1 teaspoon vanilla
2 eggs
2 cups chocolate chips
1 cup coarsely chopped pecans

Preheat the oven to 375 degrees F.

In a bowl, combine the flour, salt, and baking soda. Set aside.

In a large mixing bowl, cream together the butter and sugars until combined. Add the eggs and vanilla and mix well. Gradually stir the flour mixture into the butter-sugar mixture.

Stir in the chocolate chips and pecans. Spoon the dough onto an ungreased cookie sheet by tablespoons. Bake for 10 to 12 minutes, or until the edges are golden brown.

In a large nonstick pan, melt the butter over medium-high heat. Add the fillets, and cook 3 to 4 minutes on each side, or until well-browned and the fish flakes when pierced with a fork.

Serve each fillet with Golden Rum–Butter Sauce, a lemon wedge, and a parsley sprig, if desired.

Golden Rum–Butter Sauce

 3 tablespoons butter
 1 shallot, minced
 1 clove garlic, minced
 2 tablespoons rum
 1 teaspoon honey
 ½ teaspoon salt
 2 tablespoons fresh lemon juice
 2 tablespoons fresh orange juice

Melt the butter in a small pan over medium-high heat. Stir in the minced shallot and garlic. Cook, stirring occasionally, until the shallot is tender.

Reduce the heat to low. Whisk in the rum slowly, and then add the honey, salt, lemon juice, and orange juice. Cook for 1 minute, stirring occasionally.

Serve warm.

Variation

You may substitute fresh lemon juice for the rum.

Preheat the oven to 450 degrees F. Grease a large baking dish.

Pour the oil in a small skillet, and heat tortillas one at a time. Keep them wrapped in a cloth after heating until all are heated. Pour ½ cup of chili gravy in the baking dish.

Place ¼ cup of the cheese and 1 tablespoon of the onion in the center of each tortilla and roll it. Place the rolled tortillas in the baking dish, seam side down.

Pour the remaining gravy over the rolled tortillas. Sprinkle the remaining cheese and onions on top. Bake for 10 minutes, or until the sauce is bubbly and the cheese is melted.

✒ Senora Mari's Pecan-Crusted Tilapia

Makes 4 servings

Prep time: 15 minutes. Cook time: 8 minutes

½ cup pecan halves
4 fresh tilapia fillets, about 6 ounces each
1 teaspoon salt
½ teaspoon garlic powder
¼ teaspoon black pepper
3 tablespoons butter
Golden Rum–Butter Sauce (see recipe)
lemon wedges, for garnish
fresh parsley sprigs, for garnish

Chop the pecans until fine and pour into a shallow bowl. Sprinkle the fish fillets with the salt, garlic powder, and pepper. Dredge the fish in the finely chopped pecans.

✒ Carlos's Cheese Enchiladas

Chili Gravy

Makes 2 cups

Prep time: 20 minutes

¼ cup vegetable oil
¼ cup all-purpose flour
½ teaspoon black pepper
1 teaspoon salt
1 teaspoon garlic powder
2 teaspoons ground cumin
½ teaspoon dried oregano
2 tablespoons chili powder
2 cups beef broth, chicken broth, or water

In a skillet over medium-high heat, heat the oil. Stir in the flour and continue stirring for 3 to 4 minutes, or until it makes a light brown roux.

Add the black pepper, salt, garlic powder, cumin, oregano, and chili powder and continue to cook for 1 minute, stirring constantly. Add the broth or water, stirring until the sauce thickens. Turn the heat to low and simmer for 15 minutes. Add water as needed to the desired thickness.

Cheese Enchiladas

Makes 4 servings

Prep time: 20 minutes. Cook time: 10 minutes

½ cup vegetable oil
8 corn tortillas
3 cups shredded cheddar cheese
1 medium onion, diced
2 cups chili gravy

1 large green chile pepper, seeded and diced
2 large tomatoes, peeled and diced
1 teaspoon kosher salt
1 cup fresh lime juice
½ lime
½ cup fresh cilantro, chopped
tortilla chips or tortilla chip strips, for topping

In a large pot, combine the chicken broth, chicken breasts, red onion, garlic, black pepper, and thyme and bring to a boil. Reduce the heat and simmer until the chicken breasts are no longer pink in the center and the juices run clear. Remove the cooked chicken and shred, and then return it to the simmering pot.

Heat the oil in a pan over medium heat. Cook the green onions and chile pepper in the oil until tender. Add the tomatoes and continue cooking until soft. Add the mixture to the pot with the chicken soup.

Season with the salt. Return the soup to a simmer.

Add the lime juice and ½ lime. Cook 10 minutes. Remove from the heat and remove the lime half. Add the cilantro.

Serve with tortilla chips.

Add the diced onion, jalapeños, cilantro, and black pepper. Peppers vary individually in their hotness. Start with half of one pepper and add more to your desired degree of hotness.

Cover with plastic wrap and chill. Refrigerate until ready to serve.

Tip: Refrigerating tomatoes can hurt their flavor. If you want to add chopped tomato to your guacamole, add it immediately before serving.

Serve with tortilla chips.

Variation

For a quick guacamole take ¼ cup salsa and mix it in with your mashed avocados.

Milagro's Sopa de Lima (Mexican Lime Soup)

Makes 8 servings

Prep time: 20 minutes. Cook time: 45 minutes

9 cups chicken broth
5 skinless, boneless chicken breasts
1 large red onion, quartered
5 cloves garlic, chopped
1 teaspoon black pepper
½ teaspoon dried thyme or 2 sprigs fresh thyme
1 tablespoon vegetable oil
4 green onions, chopped

Recipes

🌿 Simple Guacamole

Be careful handling jalapeños. Wash your hands thoroughly after handling and do not touch your eyes or the area near your eyes with your hands for several hours.

2 ripe avocados
1 tablespoon fresh lime juice or lemon juice
½ teaspoon salt (optional)
¼ cup of diced red onion
2 jalapeño peppers, seeds removed, finely chopped
2 tablespoons cilantro, finely chopped
dash of black pepper
½ ripe tomato, seeds and pulp removed, diced (optional)
tortilla chips

Cut the avocados in half. Remove the seeds. Carefully score the inside of the avocado with a blunt knife and scoop out the flesh. Place in a bowl.

Mash the avocado with a fork. (Guacamole should be chunky.)

Sprinkle with the lime (or lemon) juice and salt.

glanced around the table, enjoying the rapt attention. "You married him and had lots of babies."

Everyone hooted, including Gretchen Cruz. Her laugh was a surprise, light and flirtatious as fairy wings.

Lightfoot glanced at Gretchen and Ryan did the same. When I turned to see if Patti had noticed, I caught her studying the unaware deputy with a wistful look of her own.

Detective Quint Lightfoot. It made sense. He had a knack for playing his cards close to his chest and placating the local political powers around him.

With a smile, I scooped Lenny up from the floor and placed him on my lap. I missed Austin, but I no longer missed the *Gazette.* I was finding more exciting news stories here in little old Broken Boot. Go figure.

"To Josie," the table of friends agreed, lifting their glasses.

"She's the best darn detective in Big Bend County." Patti tried to smile as she blinked away tears.

"The best darn detective in Big Bend County," my friends and family echoed as one.

"Uh-hum," Senora Mari said, clinking her fork against her glass.

"Yip, yip," Lenny said from beneath my chair.

"Don't insult the Indian." She raised her water glass in Lightfoot's direction.

"Speaking of insulting," I interrupted, careful not to offend my proud *abuela*. "The term is *Native American*."

She gave me a look of disapproval and then turned back to him. "I was going to say, He's the detective and she's the writer, just like on TV."

His gaze narrowed, piercing the elderly woman at the opposite end of the table. "I'm not a detective tonight," he said in his rich baritone, "but I will be one next week."

"You applying for a promotion?" Ryan joked.

"Sheriff Wallace put me up for it. I found out this morning I was approved."

The table whooped in approval and raised their glasses. "To Detective Lightfoot."

He lifted his glass and flashed the table one of his rare but brilliant smiles. My heart fluttered in surprise.

"Yip," Lenny said.

"To Lenny," I cheered.

The room rang in response. "To Lenny."

"Yip, yip, yip," he said, jumping into the air.

Everyone laughed, including Aunt Linda.

"I had a dream," Senora Mari began.

"I can't wait to hear this one."

I glanced around the table and found smiles of anticipation on everyone's face.

"In my dream, you met a man here at Milagro." She

I hesitated, hoping Lightfoot wouldn't get his nose out of joint that I was hogging all the attention. "She was pregnant with Clark's baby."

"*¡Ay, no!*" Uncle Eddie cried.

"How awful," Aunt Linda murmured.

"Did the poor guy know?" Ryan asked.

I exchanged glances with Patti. "Britney made sure to tell him right before she smashed him over the head with Patti's guitar."

"What I don't understand," Patti said, "is how she knew where to find him."

"Don't look at me." I gestured to Lightfoot. "He's the expert."

The somber deputy took a moment to gather his thoughts. "Clark and Britney were texting back and forth all night. At one point, she demanded to know where he was." He shot Patti an apologetic look. "Clark told her he was at your place."

Patti nodded and quietly stabbed a roasted tomato with her fork.

"I don't get it," Aunt Linda said.

"Phone records?" I interrupted, before Lightfoot could respond.

"We found the second phone Britney used that night in the Dumpster at Two Boots, and, boy, was it ripe." The deputy made a face.

We all laughed at his comical expression.

"Sad, sad. What will they do with the baby?" Senora Mari asked.

"Well, she *said* she was pregnant with Jeff Clark's baby." I caught Patti's eye. "She's lied about everything else. Why not lie about that too?"

"Hoping for a lighter sentence, if you ask me." Lightfoot continued eating with a disgusted shake of his head.

We'd partaken of a couple of tortillas of savory wonderfulness when Patti lifted her glass. "To Josie."

Anthony and Lily fussed over Patti, both racing to the bar to see who could place a drink in her hand first. As Lily set a pint of Revolver beer in front of my newly freed friend, I cornered Anthony.

"Where's Lucinda?" By the time I remembered to talk to Senora Mari, Anthony's would-be bride had arrived and gone straight to Casa Martinez.

"She is resting from her journey," he said. His smile was beatific.

"What do you think of her?"

"I think," he leaned close, so that no one—especially Senora Mari—could overhear, "that she is very beautiful." And he blushed.

The cowbell over the front door rang.

"Back here," I called.

With an unexpectedly shy smile, Gretchen Cruz gave a nod to the table. I found her a chair and squeezed it in between Ryan and Detective Lightfoot. From their appreciative glances, I knew my plan would work beautifully.

Call me masochistic if you want, but if I had to throw other women in the way of the two most eligible bachelors in Broken Boot, I would. You might call me pigheaded, but I didn't want to think about men, dating, or anything else that reeked of romance for a good, long time.

There were no tamales at the table, but I chowed on the refrieds and fajitas. *Awesome.*

Ryan wiped his mouth. "What I don't understand about this whole thing is why this Britney woman wanted to kill Jeff Clark."

"It was all about wanting her husband to have the fame and fortune, right, Josie?" Uncle Eddie spread his arms wide as if to deliver a lawyerly argument.

"Yes and no. Turns out Britney had a secret she didn't want her fiancé, Clay, to uncover." I looked at Lightfoot, and he frowned.

"Which was?" Ryan leaned in.

place of honor in the center of the table, a version created from pushing all the tables together into the middle of the restaurant.

"She's here," Senora Mari cried, hurrying toward the kitchen.

In response, the kitchen doors swung open and my aunt and uncle entered, each carrying an aromatic platter of succulent grilled fajita chicken, steak, and shrimp.

The crowd at the table whooped in delight.

Patti's eyes lit up, but dimmed when she spotted what each tray bore.

As they placed their trays in the center of the table, Senora Mari entered bearing a platter of her own. She placed it in front of our special guest.

Patti's expression brightened. Before her lay the most gorgeous roasted peppers, onions, tomatoes, eggplant, and cobs of corn.

I followed with family-style helpings of charro beans, vegan black beans, and refrieds with mouth-watering cheese and onions on top.

Patti sighed. "There is a God," she groaned with a reverence I'd yet to hear from her on Sundays.

Ryan laughed and slapped her on the back from his seat beside her. "You're free to eat all the veggies you want. Just make sure you leave the meat for me."

"You got it. Just stay away from me."

He leaned in and gave her a one-armed squeeze. "I can't do that. I'm so happy you're free."

"Well, make sure you breathe that stinky meat breath on someone else when you're through."

"Corn or flour?" Deputy Lightfoot asked from the end of the table, holding up a dish of tortillas in each hand.

"Neither," Patti said as she stabbed a red pepper and onion onto her fork.

Everyone chuckled, including Wilhelmina and Heather from the tour bus, and a hardy Dustin Akers.

cops. We hired someone to clean up the living room, who swore they'd make it better than new."

"Which isn't saying much. I need to go home, Jos. I'll come over soon, but I've got to go home." There was a quiet desperation in her voice.

I squeezed her hand and fought back tears. The family and friends from Milagro and Two Boots would wait. They were so excited to see her, there would be nothing to forgive.

A few minutes later, she stared at the house she'd lived in her entire life as if she were in a dream—as if counting every brick and windowpane.

"Do you want me to come in?" I asked as I turned off the engine.

She wet her lips. "No."

She stepped out, slammed the door, and walked away. Seconds later, she knocked on my window. I rolled it down. "Thanks, Jos. I appreciate everything you did." She screwed up her mouth as her face turned red. "I thought for sure I was next."

I shook my head.

"Bad things come in threes—that's what my Granny Roberts always said. "First Mommy and then Daddy. I just knew I'd be next."

I blinked rapidly as my eyes welled with tears. "What sentimental, superstitious claptrap."

She laughed.

"Now go get ready. You'd better be at Milagro in an hour, or we're going to *all* come over here and drag you out."

"Yes, ma'am."

I drove away with a smile on my face.

True to her word, Patti appeared in the Milagro dining room within the hour. Her hair was wet and her face was powdered her usual ghostly shade. She'd applied her cat-eye liner, and all her earrings and facial piercings were in place.

"You call this a party?" she asked with her usual sarcasm.

Everyone whooped and clapped.

Senora Mari rushed up and pulled her by the hand to the

"Is my jeep still outside?"

"No, we drove it back to Uncle Eddie's. Didn't want them to impound it or steal it for parts while you were gone."

She clapped me on the back and started for the exit. "Good thinking. That would have really hacked me off."

"Miss?" Gretchen Cruz's cousin called from behind her counter. "She needs to sign for her property."

Patti eyed the exit and the stack of papers on the counter. As she turned to me, I noticed her breathing was rapid. She swallowed two times.

"You can do this," I said, giving her arm a squeeze. "You're almost free."

She shook her head and swallowed one last time. "No problem." She spun toward the counter, picked up the pen, and began to scribble her name as if they'd lock her back inside if she didn't finish in sixty seconds or less.

The clerk added Patti's paperwork to a tower of files on her desk.

"Is that it?" Goth Girl demanded.

The other woman raised her eyebrows. "Yes, ma'am. You're free."

"Woo hoo!" Patti shouted, to the surprise of everyone in the room. Several heads snapped around to watch her bolt for the door, with me hurrying along behind her like a friendly puppy. We hit the road like Thelma and Louise—at the beginning of the movie, before horrible things happened to them and they drove themselves off a cliff into the Grand Canyon.

"I need a shower," she groaned.

"You'll have to make it quick."

She turned in her seat to glare. "There had better not be a crowd of people waiting to congratulate me."

"Uh . . ."

"You take me home." Her face fell. "Guess I can't take a shower in my own bathroom or sleep in my own bed without remembering Jeff there."

"Aunt Linda, Senora Mari, and I cleaned up after the

Chapter 23

On Monday morning, I parked once again in a metal chair, studying the mundane actions of those blessed to have the benefits of a government job. Their faces wore masks of smug boredom as they went from one task to another, never varying their speed: slow.

From the far side of the room, a dark-haired woman entered. She was tall and slim, her skin unusually pale, gleaming from the fluorescents overhead. She wore jeans, black combat boots, and a skintight black T-shirt.

"Patti," I cried, and rushed to her. My eyes stung with tears and my throat tightened. I threw my arms around her and squeezed. She stood rock still, and then lifted her arms and hugged me back.

After a few seconds, she gave me a gentle push. "Hey, calm down. It's not as if I was in Huntsville." She lifted her arms at her sides and spun around. "No flesh wounds or puncture marks."

I could feel my cheeks cramp from smiling so hard. "What now? What do you want to do? Where do you want to go?"

"I backed into the tour bus, and that's a fact." She turned first to one side of the crowd and then the other. "Clay will vouch for me. Just ask him."

"I'm sure he will," Lightfoot muttered. He grabbed one of her arms, and Deputy Barnes took ahold of the other. "Come along with me, ma'am. You can write it all down for us at the station."

Britney realized her mistake. "Wilhelmina will vouch for me as well. She was on the bus that next morning. She can tell you I don't have good night vision." She glanced at the crowd and smiled weakly. "Can't help it, but that's the way the good Lord made me."

"Make sure you include the part where you killed Jeff Clark so your fiancé could take over as lead singer before the band hit the big time," I muttered.

Her mouth fell open like a trout struggling to breathe, her eyes wide and fearful. Suddenly, she fought free of Barnes's grasp. "I didn't kill Jeff Clark," she said in a voice as clear and cold as Barton Springs, "so Clay could become the lead singer of some second-rate band. One-hit wonders, the mess of them." She stared down the crowd and lifted her chin. "I killed him because he's the sorry son of a gun who got me pregnant."

Everyone within earshot froze, as if her confession had turned us to pillars of disbelief. Why was she broadcasting her crime to the world? Had she gone over the edge for the last time?

Instead of anger, I felt only sorrow. I didn't know where to look. "I'm sorry."

"Huh. Sure you are." She stepped forward and clenched her fists at her side. With another step, she was so close I could see the sweat droplets running off the end or her nose. She raised a finger and pointed it at me. "Just make sure you spell my name right in that small-town tabloid of yours."

A siren bleated. The crowd parted, and a sheriff's cruiser pulled up to the field.

"Tell her she's not going anywhere," I hollered to the first deputy on the scene. After a few steps, I realized it was Lightfoot.

"Did you hurt yourself?" Ryan asked, his forehead wrinkling with concern.

"I'm fine." I straightened my shoulders and hurried to the runaway blonde.

Britney, playing the part of the injured party beautifully, took the hand Lightfoot offered and straightened her clothing. "Officer," she whimpered, "that woman is a murderer."

Lightfoot gave me a quick once-over. "She's no more a murderer than I am."

She turned on the Scarlett O'Hara act. "You saw her," she said to the players and coaches gathered around. "She chased me all over the stadium, threatening to . . ." She sobbed, she sniffed, she batted her wet eyelashes. "Why, she threatened to run me over with her car and then shoot me for good measure."

Lightfoot blinked. "That's the craziest thing I've ever heard tell of."

"Speaking of running things over with your car . . . What happened to your taillight? Did you back into something as you left Patti's house?" It wasn't the smartest remark I could've made or the swiftest retort, but my adrenaline was pumping.

"I don't know what you're talking about."

"The gold Range Rover," I pointed toward the parking lot, "that you painted and sold so you wouldn't get caught."

"I don't have a Range Rover. *Katy*, Jeff's witch of an ex-wife owns one of those."

"What's the matter?" I demanded. "Were you jealous of her and her kids?" This woman had ruined my friend's life. I wanted her to pay.

Britney's face turned so red, I thought she was going to start whistling like a teakettle. She scrunched up her face.

hometown team. She must have run track in school. I swear she ran the fifty-yard dash in five seconds flat.

That lunatic was sprinting across the football field in front of God and all his children, as if chased by the devil himself.

Behind me, I heard voices gaining momentum. Words like *crazy, gun, woman.*

Realizing that I couldn't lie about the gun without serious consequences, I took off after her. "Briiiitneey," I screamed, nearly busting a gut.

The hometown team was halfway across the field when five large players separated themselves from the pack. They ran straight for me. I saw them point in my direction and then in hers. At the last second, they veered off, chasing the blond bullet as she headed for the end zone and the parking lot beyond.

From the corner of my eye, I saw the crowd rise. The roar from the stands overwhelmed me and drove me on. Britney passed the twenty-five-yard line, the twenty, and the fifteen.

I collapsed onto the field, my lungs in my throat. I lifted my head to watch her cross the goal line. That was when the players picked up speed and tackled her at the five-yard line.

Funny how the promise of *tamales* had worked in my favor.

Sirens wailed in the background. From my arms, Lenny whimpered.

"Sorry, boy." I rained kisses on his head. "You were awesome."

I struggled to my knees. I had to make it to those kicking legs and broken high heels before the bruisers let her go. That would be just like her to slither out of sight when no one was looking.

"Josie, are you all right?"

A strong hand grasped my arm and lifted me to my feet. It was Ryan. "I . . . have . . . to get . . ." This breathing was harder than I remembered. I waved toward the players, who were carefully lifting themselves off the grounded female.

I won't ever forget that day. I ran so fast, I burned a hole in the sole of my Vans.

The herd passed. Again I caught just a glimpse of a blond head of hair. I turned this way and that. No striped blondes. The home-team side of the field was empty. At the opposite fence, another group of cheerleaders and fans formed a tunnel to welcome their hometown warriors.

She popped up along the visitors' sideline, trying to hide behind the players. She hadn't seen us approach.

Slowly we wove in and out of the spectators like two ninjas, moving closer and closer to our prey. I had one last opportunity to stop her before she slipped away, taking Patti's only chance for vindication with her. Whatever I said had to be powerful enough to stop her in her tracks.

"And now," the announcer said, "let's welcome your hometown West Texas Armadillos."

"Why did you kill Jeff Clark?" I bellowed.

In that split second, between the announcer's proclamation and the band's fight song, Britney froze. Her face turned deathly white, her hands fisted at her sides, her chest heaved. She opened her mouth—

And the fight song filled the air.

Her red mouth moved, words coming out that I couldn't hear.

I sprang toward her, but she turned and ran like a yellow-bellied coward.

"Let's go," I cried.

"Yip, yip," Lenny said.

"Hey, get off the field." A boy bearing a rack of water bottles stood in our way. "What do you think you're doing?" he yelled, his stubbly chin waving in the air.

I didn't think. "See that crazy woman?" I swung an arm in Britney's direction. "I think she's got a gun."

Lord help me. I'd lied. Again.

Britney's mouth was no longer moving because her feet were carrying her across the field, right into the path of the

"As if," the renegade cried, righting herself and continuing with her escape.

"Hey, she's knocked everything over," a young voice in the crowd wailed.

"Sorry about that, mister," I said on my way past.

"Yip, yip."

"I just want to ask you some questions," I hollered, hoping she would slow down before she caused someone to drop a hot dog or break a hip.

Lenny and I hit the track that surrounded the field and lost her. I hurried on a few feet, craning my neck to see through the crowd. Then I stopped and took stock.

"Yip," Lenny said.

I spun to search back along the track going the other way. That smaller crowd was heading toward the visitors' section.

"Yip, yip," Lenny said.

She'd removed her hood, cap, and sunglasses, but I recognized her tracksuit. She turned her head.

It was Britney. *Oh my God.*

Slowly, I started toward her. "No need to worry," I said, trying to sound as pleasant as I could with a dozen people between us. "I only want to ask you where I can buy—"

"Leave me alone," she growled.

Two men, both wearing purple and white Mohawk wigs, turned around, and in doing so blocked her from our view. "Would you two stop acting like total idiots?" the heavier one demanded.

"Yip," Lenny said.

"He's right," added his friend.

From the corner of my eye, I saw Britney sprint around the far curve of the track.

I heard the stadium announcer say, "Let's welcome the Fort Davis Prairie Dogs." The visitors went wild. Through a tunnel of cheerleaders waving glittery pom-poms in the air charged a herd of young men intent on intimidating their opponents, running straight for us.

Without planning or thinking, I leapt. "Hey, girl. It's me."
I slowed to a hurried walk. After all, I didn't want to scare
her away.

Her jaw dropped and she froze.

"I was coming to the game—great team, by the way—
and happened to see you talking to that incredible Niles
Williams."

Her feet had yet to move, but I could see she was about
to spring into action.

"I was so sorry to hear that he broke his ankle. Did he
tell you all about it?"

"Uh, no." She eyed me up and down, probably figuring
she could outrun me. How dare she assume curvy girls can't
run fast?

"Well, he and I got to talking earlier this week about . . .
what kind of vehicle I should buy. My Prius—you know
the yellow one from the Milagro parking lot?—is on its
last leg."

"Is that so?" Then she made a huge mistake. She smiled
and removed her purse strap from her right shoulder and
placed it over her head and her left shoulder, which meant
one thing: she was ready to run.

I raised a hand as if to calm a nervous filly. "I wonder if
you could help me out."

The muscles in her body tensed.

"Was that your Range Rover—?"

"No," she cried, and then spun on her high heels and
bolted like a wild mustang.

"Yip," Lenny cried.

We ran, dodging enthusiastic football fans, their coolers
and baby strollers, and their grandmothers' walkers. In a
moment of clarity, I reached down and tucked Lenny to my
side like a football.

Katy collided with a display of blue foam fingers and
yellow pennants.

"Watch yourself, young woman," the elderly merchant
cried. "You better git back here and straighten this mess out."

Lenny whined.

"Shh. I understand, little buddy."

Niles, in full uniform, and a woman wearing sunglasses, a hooded tracksuit, and a West Texas cap were making an exchange. The young man leaned heavily on his crutches as he passed over a few bills.

The woman glanced nervously around the parking lot, gave him a tight-lipped smile, and handed over a folded piece of paper. I'd wager my Prius it was the title. Niles must have grown impatient waiting for her to follow through on the repairs. The taillight was still broken.

I looked around. How had Katy arrived? Perhaps someone was waiting nearby to give her a ride home?

Lenny whined.

He'd held it as long as he could. "That's okay, pal. I don't think anyone will notice." The back tire of the minivan would dry in minutes.

It was time to confront Katy about the broken taillight.

Suddenly Niles hopped on one foot, readjusted his crutches, and hurried toward the stadium with surprising speed. Like a master champion of the three-legged race, he had those crutches flying. Too bad he'd broken his ankle; he was a heck of an athlete.

Lenny and I dropped back behind a silver van. I raised a finger to my lips. "Ssh. Stealth is of the essence." My long-haired accomplice remained silent.

I peered around the corner, revealing only one eye and the side of my face—a trick I learned in grade school playing hide-and-go-seek.

Katy was gone. I jumped out, turned in a circle, and spotted her, already yards ahead of me, cruising for the entrance gate to the stadium. I hurried after her, praying my irregular running regime would keep me from falling to the ground in a disheveled heap.

Lenny pulled ahead. "Yip," he urged.

"I'm trying," I whispered.

Katy turned around and saw us.

"And what does it all mean?"

We steered our way around two baby strollers and the various parents and siblings that accompanied them. At the gate, I purchased our tickets and set out to find the home team section and the seats Uncle Eddie had described.

The marching Armadillos gave a final fanfare, screamed a war cry, and ran for the sidelines as the drum section beat a warlike cadence. There was, unfortunately, another thirty minutes to go before the game started.

I glanced at the sidelines and found Ryan farther down the field, making battle plans of his own with two of his assistants. As we approached our seats, I craned my neck in an effort to find Niles on the bench, which was impossible because the players blocked my view as they stood around in full pads and uniforms.

As we climbed the bleachers, folks smiled and waved at Lenny. In return, he lifted his head and preened, so very proud of his West Texas shirt. Uncle Eddie was seated on the end of a row about halfway up, thank God. Lenny looked at me and I looked at him. We weren't squeezing into those seats until we absolutely had to. My knees might be young, but years of playing softball had made sitting in tight quarters for a long stretch more than a mite uncomfortable.

We went strolling around the track until I had a clear view of the bench. No Niles Williams. After a thorough study of the players on the sidelines, we found no player of Niles Williams's significant girth, with crutches or without.

"Yip, yip," Lenny complained, giving me a certain panicky look.

"You got it, buddy." We made a beeline for the exit.

The excited fans forced us to one side while we swam against the tide toward the parking lot to give Lenny a doggie pit stop.

After a quick examination of our options, I headed for a break of trees and scraggly grass. One row of cars and trucks remained when I hit the brakes. Under the same live oak tree rested Niles Williams's new Range Rover.

"Yip."

"And a young man dressed like a . . ." Her brow creased in concentration. After a few seconds, she threw her hands up. "*Oh, Dios*, what are those called?"

"What did he look like?"

"A sissy. He wore a dress."

Uncle Eddie popped his head in the driver's door. "If you two are going to sit out here and have a séance, I'm going in for the preshow."

"Leave the door open," I said, catching him with his hand on the doorframe. A slight breeze was in the air due to the approaching sunset, but Senora Mari and I would cook in the 89-degree temperatures with the door closed. Plus, I didn't want to be stuck out in the parking lot for more than a quick five-minute conversation.

"*Adiós.*" Uncle Eddie hurried away, two bleacher seats under one arm, my cooler and an umbrella under the other.

Jeff Clark was no sissy. "A dress?" I prodded.

"No. More like . . . a robe. With tassels."

"Yip."

"You don't mean a sorcerer's robe, do you?" I asked.

"No." She closed her eyes and then popped them open. "Sandals on his feet that had those thingies." She made a crisscrossing motion around one of her legs.

"Roman? Greek?"

She tut-tutted and opened the passenger door. "One of those two. He carried a sword and a shield, like in that movie with Russell Crowe."

Now we were getting down to it. Senora Mari was a huge *Gladiator* fan.

"I get it." I opened my door, grabbed my bag and Lenny, and slid down to the ground. Quickly I helped my *abuela* step down without falling and retrieved her sun hat from beneath the seat. "What was that all about? Some guy with a sword wants to fight?" We strolled between the parked cars, aiming for the entrance gate. "And what about the baby?"

"Poor thing. All blue from the cold."

regional music fans to the area. Heck, we'd seen a boost in ticket sales from the Jeff Clark Band alone.

We passed the turnoff to the jail. "Should we stop by and see Patti?" I had been derelict in my visits, but only because I was trying so hard to get her out. We'd talked over the phone the past three days. Five-minute phone calls, I discovered, either flew by like a shaft of lightning or dragged on with nothing new to say, like a conversation with a total stranger your friend thought you should meet because you were suited for each other. Not that I knew anything about that.

"Visiting hours are over," Senora Mari said.

I checked my watch with more than a twinge of guilt. Six o'clock. "How'd you know?"

She shrugged. "I am here because of my dream."

Careful not to crowd Lenny, I leaned closer. "Give us all the gory details."

Uncle Eddie frowned and turned on the radio.

"In my dream . . ." Senora Mari turned to glare at her son.

"I've heard it before, *Mami*."

The slap she gave his hand had some heft. "Josie has not heard it before."

"Yip," Lenny said.

"We want to hear it," I said, placing my hand on my uncle's shoulder. "Who was in your dream this time? Did Jeff Clark schedule a return engagement?"

In the distance, the West Texas campus came into view. On the hillside above the administration building, a distinctive *WT*, formed from large white rocks, rested in the scrub.

"Jeff Sexy Clark was not present."

Uncle Eddie swerved into a parking space, jumped out, and began unloading the back. A drumline cadence punctuated the air, echoing from the small stadium and spilling out into the surrounding neighborhoods.

"Who made an appearance, *Abuela*?"

"A baby."

my bills. I worked the lunch shift, walked my dog, squeezed him into his West Texas tee, and loaded up the car with his necessities and an old bleacher cushion Uncle Eddie no longer used.

"Jo Jo," Uncle Eddie called from the foot of my apartment stairs.

"Yo," I answered, gathering our water bottles and locking the door.

"Ride with me and *Mami*." Uncle Eddie never missed a game.

"Who?"

Lenny and I met him at the bottom of the stairs. He grabbed the small cooler from my hand and headed for the back door. "*Mami* is insisting on coming with us."

"What'd you do this time?" His mother hated football and compared sitting in the bleachers to working in the fields all day, picking chile peppers.

"Wasn't me. This has something to do with one of her cockamamie dreams."

"Look at you, you football fan, you." Without rolling my eyes—though it required some effort on my part—I climbed into the backseat of the truck. Senora Mari, bedecked in one of my uncle's West Texas jerseys and pearls, waited in the shotgun seat.

"*Hola*, Jo Jo. Why's the dog coming?"

"He likes it outside—makes him think he's a dog, not a human. Gets him back to his roots."

"Yip, yip," Lenny said, wagging his tail and jumping up on my lap.

I wanted to ask about the jersey, but I hated to see her overreact by taking it off.

As we drove out of the parking lot, two cars passed us coming in. Things were shaping up for a good dinner service. We'd seen a boost the past weekend. The city council could pat themselves on the back. The Homestead Days Music Festival had done the deed, bringing tourists and

Chapter 22

On weekends, the population of Broken Boot had one thing on their minds: West Texas football. No one cared that the only cowboys in sight were those that rode American quarter horses and wore ropers. The Dallas Cowboys and the Houston Texans had their place: the flat-screen on Sunday and Monday nights.

The Broken Boot community lapped up local football like thirsty dogs. Folks who loved the pigskin could worship it on Friday nights by going to the local high school games, and on Saturdays by supporting the West Texas University Armadillos, who occasionally played on Thursdays for broadcast on the smaller sports cable networks.

Since I'd been home, Ryan had harangued, begged, and attempted to shame me into attending one of his games, quite unsuccessfully too, until this week. Obviously, I wasn't a huge fan of football and guys in weird uniforms. But it was Ryan, and he had come through by giving me the tip about the Land Rover.

Saturday, I needed a break from part-time journalism, which had managed to increase my anxiety without paying

what I already knew: that Clay Conley lies, and so does that Ken Price character."

"What do you mean?"

"I heard him tell your uncle that Katy Bonham was going to be a star, and she'd put Two Boots on the map if he let her play."

"Enough said." Perhaps Price planned to whisk Katy and her children off to Los Angeles, and perhaps time would flow backwards so that she and Jeff Clark would never have divorced. For her sake, I hoped it was the latter.

My bubble burst so fast, my head nearly spun from disappointment. All the information I'd collected was rubbish.

After we awarded the Arizonian the cash prize, I thanked the judges on Uncle Eddie's behalf. I searched through the crowd for Lightfoot and thought of my best friend, Patti Perez, Broken Boot's only Goth Princess. I had no doubt she would've won if she'd been free to compete.

Then it struck me. That was how Katy Bonham, Jeff's ex, had slipped into the competition. She'd stolen Patti's place. My stomach soured as I thought about Goth Girl sitting in jail, desperate for hope, while that neophyte stood on stage in her place.

I eventually found Lightfoot outside in his cruiser. I knocked on the window and gestured for him to roll it down. "So, Clay didn't leave the table the night of the murder—got it?"

He raised an eyebrow. "That's what you said."

"And he was willing to cover for Britney. Are you going to interview her?"

"No need."

"Why not, *Sheriff* Lightfoot? Fill me in."

"According to the coroner, Jeff wasn't killed at twelve thirty in the morning—more like five," Lightfoot said.

"Well, dad gum." I shared with him the text message I'd received from Victoria Pappas, Patti's next-door neighbor.

"What's that mean?" he asked.

"It means my theory's been shot to *H-E*-double-toothpicks and back."

He said, "What was Jeff Clark's ex-wife's name again?"

"Katy Bonham. You know, she very well could've walked across the street when no one was looking and banged him over the head with Patti's Fender out of pure jealousy."

"That's a theory." He shifted his gaze to his smartphone.

"Do you have to look so disinterested?"

"Don't worry. Your information was helpful. It confirmed

his boot as if striking up the band for a country line dance. "I had a feeling I was missing something."

An announcement blasted over the loudspeakers, asking the crowd to return to their seats.

"And that's not all I've got." I grinned. "Clay claims he wasn't at the poker game all night. Did you know there was a poker game?"

"Sure. He was playing at Pecos Pete's."

"Says he left the game to get more cigarettes at one o'clock in the morning—said he was gone for forty-five minutes."

"Aren't you one of the judges?" He gestured toward the stage.

"I still have a minute. But—and here's the important part—the bartender says Clay was at the table all night, but Britney left at twelve thirty, not him. Why would he lie?"

"Maybe he didn't. Maybe they both left the table at different times."

The dance hall lights blinked their final warning. I had to make this fast. "The neighbors—"

"—said someone hit the trash cans at Patti's around twelve thirty."

The head judge craned his neck until he found me and then began to wave frantically.

"Don't leave," I whispered. "I have more."

Impatiently, I sat through the last five acts. The final act, an older woman from Arizona, was clearly the winner. Her original song displayed both her beautiful guitar playing and her humorous but poignant lyrics.

We marked our ballots and passed them to the end of the row so that the committee could tally the results with painstaking accuracy. Then my phone started to vibrate, nearly shaking my glass of Dr Pepper off the end of the judges' table before I could catch it. I checked the screen and found a text message from an unknown number. I didn't hesitate. It read, Jason says he didn't see anything.

I pulled Bubba's arm to bring his ear down to my level. "She's never played guitar, or I'm a gourmet chef," I said.

He nodded in agreement. "And we know that is definitely not true."

How had she made it into the show? Had Ken Price pulled some strings? And if so, why?

We compared our score sheets. Her name was printed bold as brass on each one in the same hand. The lights came up, a Stevie Ray Vaughan recording started playing over the speakers, and the intermission began.

As customers made their way to the bar, I spotted Deputy Lightfoot standing at the back of the room, surveying the crowd. I hopped over a row of seats and almost kissed the floor, but I made it past the throng.

"That woman up there was Jeff Clark's ex."

He took me by the arm and pulled me into a secluded hallway away from the din of folks gabbing and placing their orders. "Are you positive?"

I nodded. "Ken Price pointed her out at the hotel, but only after I spotted her hurrying through the lobby with Jeff Clark's guitar case. It was weird. I think there's something going on between those two."

"If she is Clark's ex, what is she doing with his guitar?"

"I asked Price that very question, and he tried to act as if Jeff owed it to her as an alimony payment."

"She can't play," Lightfoot said with a shake of his head.

I pointed to my chest. "Look at me and pay close attention. This is me, sharing vital information with you."

"Humph."

"And I expect you to return the favor."

"Okay," he said, leaning away.

"Her name is Katy Bonham."

"Jeff's ex?"

"I said so, didn't I? And guess where she lives?" I didn't wait for his response. "Across the street from Patti."

Slapping his hands together, the stalwart deputy stomped

judges' table. The Rising Star Contest committee had selected
ten finalists from the video auditions submitted via YouTube,
and then recruited three judges for the live contest. I was
proud of Uncle Eddie; he'd come up with a great way to
promote local artists while raising money to keep the power
and lights on, not to mention keeping pear cider and Revolver
beer in the coolers.

First up was a teenage boy whose hands trembled so hard,
I thought he was going to run off the stage and cry. With
the crowd's support, he made it to the chorus and then sailed
smoothly, if flatly, from there on out.

The other judges and I consulted, wrote down his score,
and added positive comments on the bottom of his scorecard
like *Never give up on your dreams* and *Keep on trucking*.
Bubba insisted both sayings were popular in his childhood
home in Africa.

The next three contestants made me want to follow them
on social media and join their fan club. If I had to guess, I'd
say they were from either Austin or Nashville.

After writing down their scores and adding my com-
ments, I prepared myself for the next contestant. As the stage
crew set up her microphone and stool, my stomach soured.
Live from Patti's neighborhood and the lobby of the Cogburn
Hotel . . . Jeff Clark's ex-wife.

Now I understood her hurry to find Jeff's guitar. With
her back to the audience, she removed her ex-husband's in-
strument from its case; she then turned to the crowd with a
nervous smile and took her seat on the stool provided. The
lights lowered, the crowd hushed, and she started to play.
She began with one chord and stayed on it for far too long.
We judges shot a glance at each other.

"She only knows one chord," Bubba said in my ear.

She had tenacity, I had to give her that. She kept singing
her original song, something about second chances, but in-
stead of changing her fingerings to match the chord changes,
her fingers remained glued to the same strings.

Chapter 21

ᕗᕗᕗᕗᕗᕗᕗᕗᕗᕗᕗᕗᕗᕗᕗᕗᕗᕗᕗᕗᕗᕗᕗᕗᕗ

Wednesday was uneventful and Thursday's lunch shift was downright exhausting. Neither Camille nor Lily had shown up, which meant a long day serving *and* busing tables at Milagro. As a result, I was eagerly awaiting the opening of the Rising Star Contest that evening. Much to my delight, Uncle Eddie had asked me to be one of the judges. I parked around back, crossed through the Two Boots kitchen, and entered the green room—the same one that the Jeff Clark Band used as a dressing room only a week earlier. Determined not to get the heebie-jeebies, I changed into my last calico dress, matching prairie bonnet, and white apron.

I walked to the door and took a final look around, remembering that fateful night Patti and I heard Jeff and Clay arguing outside this very room. Had their fight been over a song? Money? Or something else?

"Take it back," Clay had hollered. My guess was that Jeff Clark said something insulting about the other man's fiancée, good ole Britney.

I made my way through the crowd and settled in at the

"I need to get back to work." He set down his teacup and wiped the tips of his fingers on his cloth napkin.

"Thanks for the interview," I said with sincerity. I wasn't sure why he'd shared so much confidential information with me in the first place. My guess was he either thought it didn't matter what I printed in a paper with such a modest readership or he enjoyed the gossip. If the latter was the case, would he turn around and share our conversation with Britney and Clay, or Jeff's ex-wife, Katy?

With a smile, he slipped his hands in his pockets. "Go do your reporter thing. I can see your fingers twitching."

"And I thought you wouldn't notice."

His eyes registered my attempt at humor. "Don't forget." He pointed a finger close to my face. "You owe me."

Before I could argue that I didn't owe him anything other than a positive mention if and when I ever wrote a story again with his name in it, he stepped into the lobby elevator and was gone.

"Jeff eventually broke free of that quagmire. He was self-possessed enough to prevent breaking up the band or losing his songwriting partner because of her."

I was running out of questions. "Why did you allow her to tour with the band?"

"Believe it or not, she caused more theatrics if Clay tried to leave her behind."

I slid my notebook and pen into my bag. "Thank you for your time." As soon as I left, I was going to do a thorough background check into Ms. Katy Bonham.

He studied me. "I bet you'd like to know before you retreat that Britney approached me about making Clay a solo act long before Jeff died."

"Doesn't surprise me none," I said, but it did.

"Said I'd be a fool to let another label snatch him up, as he writes all the songs—which is not true." He frowned, hit a button, lifted the phone to his ear, and listened to a message.

"No?"

"He cowrote most of them."

"Did you share her request with Dustin Akers?"

With a sigh, he brushed off his pants and stood. "No, and I didn't tell him about her bright idea to cover her new SUV with a sparkly skin advertising the Clay Conley Band either."

We laughed.

"I haven't seen the two of them use any mode of transportation except for their feet," I said. "Did you let her off easy?"

"I told her I didn't care how much she paid for it. Her ride was uglier than— How would you Texans put it? Oh yeah. Uglier than sin." From his wallet, he withdrew a couple of bills and tossed them on the leather-topped coffee table.

I took a deep breath and forced myself to take another sip of tea. Where should I go first? To Lightfoot? To Britney? To Gretchen Cruz?

"Guess our interview is over."

"Sorry." How long had I sorted through the to-do list in my mind?

to talk about Clark's marital problems or who has his favorite guitar. Do you have any more questions about the band?"

With an effort, I drew a deep breath and attempted to set aside Price's officiousness and Katy Bonham's address, at least until I finished my interview. I reached for the phone but left it untouched. Price would talk more if the recording device stayed off. "If your new act, the Clay Conley Band, depends on the sex appeal and showmanship of one Clay Conley, how are you going to cope with his clinging vine of a fiancée, Britney?"

"That's the question, isn't it?"

I lobbed a grenade. "I hear she's pregnant."

He froze. Narrowing his eyes, he studied me for several uncomfortable seconds. "That's what she claims anyway." I couldn't get a read on him.

"Uh, you and she . . . You never dated, right?"

He jerked back as if I'd shot him. "Nooo. He can have her—as long as she doesn't stand in his way to number one on the Billboard country charts."

I tried another tack. "You ever play cards with Clay and his boys?"

"No, I like to hold on to my money." He checked the time on his Rolex.

"I understand why you gave the story to that other reporter, but give me something. Tell me about Britney."

"You'll leave Katy out of it?"

"Sure."

"What do you want to know?"

"How long have they been together?"

He checked his phone. "Who? Clay and Britney?"

"Who else?" I asked, struggling to hide my impatience.

His smile held a sly malice. "Hard to imagine her with anyone else, right? Actually, she and Clay hit a skid a few months ago, and Jeff stepped into the gap. I found out when he let it slip one night after a few beers."

"How on God's green earth did she and Clay stay together?"

with Jeff Clark's guitar case?" I hadn't failed to notice the singer's name in faded but large black letters along the side.

"Because I gave it to her."

"The question is, Why didn't you save it for Jeff's family? What about his daughter?"

His gaze dropped to my phone. "That woman has a right to it."

"Would you care to explain?"

With the back of his hand, he brushed nonexistent lint from his pants. "Katy is Jeff's ex-wife."

The world was a suddenly a minuscule place and shrinking by the second. "You expect me to believe you didn't know she lived across the street from where Jeff Clark died?"

He had the decency to squirm. "I didn't know precisely where he died." He began to drum his fingers on the table. "It never came up."

I was starting to comprehend what, or rather who, was keeping Ken Price in Broken Boot. They probably held their meetings in his hotel room.

"Why do you think she deserves Clark's guitar?" I asked.

"The jerk never paid alimony or support. It's the least I could do."

"Those children at her house—those Clark's?"

"What? No." He crossed his ankle over his knee and pretended to relax into his chair. "Those kids are from her second husband." His expression changed to one of derision. "No, she's not currently married, and yes, she needs the money."

"And the moral support only you can give?" I snapped my head around just to make sure Katy Bonham wasn't standing behind me . . . again. My understanding of the case was splintering into a dozen pieces. Ken Price was seeing Jeff Clark's ex, who lived across from Patti Perez, who the sheriff's office arrested for Jeff's murder.

As Price's cheeks flushed again, he snapped his fingers, which made me want to slug him. "Come on. I'm not here

lobby at a fast clip was the woman: full-figured, platinum blond, and very familiar.

"That women leaving the lobby, the one you were nodding to? What's her name?"

With his thumb and index finger, Price squeezed more lemon juice into his cup. "I don't know her." He sighed. "People always mistake me for someone famous."

"Really? Well, I've met her . . . somewhere." I stood and the memory shook loose. On the day I'd interviewed Patti's neighbors, she was door number 3. The paranoid one with the small children. "She lives across the street from where they found Jeff Clark's body."

He cocked his head as if considering the veracity of my statement. "I guess she could. I really don't know."

"That's a bizarre coincidence." I chomped on my cookie. "Did you notice she was carrying a guitar case?"

"Are you insane?" Ken's eyes darted around the lobby, but the only other person in sight was the desk clerk who played bingo with Senora Mari on Monday nights.

"Did you notice whose guitar she was carrying?"

He leaned in close. "Keep your voice down."

"I wouldn't put it past her to have stolen that guitar." The brief time I'd spent on her doorstep was enough to make me think she was at the very least peculiar. "If you don't know her—and I suspect you know all the musicians staying at this hotel—then I need to have a word with the manager."

"Okay, ssh. Can't you mind your own business?" His words were clipped.

"Not when my best friend, Patti Perez, is in jail for murder." I leaned into his space. "Now tell me her name and who she is to you."

He glanced at my recorder. "Off the record?"

"No promises." I gestured to the table and the inactive recorder. "I'm not recording, if that makes any difference." I tried to appear nonthreatening.

"Katy Bonham is her name. Can we change the subject?"

"Why is your friend Katy walking through the lobby

think Clay is lead-singer material? Will he win over the fans still grieving for Jeff Clark?"

Price hesitated, and then his gaze shifted to something over my shoulder.

I started to turn to find what had captured his interest.

"Well," he said in a piercingly loud voice, "he'll have to learn how to win over the audience. Friday night's concert at Two Boots will give him a chance to practice his powers of persuasion."

"Why haven't I heard anything about it?"

"Why indeed?" He frowned. "Your uncle and I confirmed the arrangements early this morning." Even as he frowned in disapproval, I finished off my cookie. "I have no doubt Clay can pull it off now that I've convinced Dustin to stay with the band for another year," he said, tipping more tea into my cup.

"Is that fair?" I whispered. "The man has cancer."

"Past tense. He's in remission."

I sighed and picked up another cookie, vowing to skip sweets for the rest of the week. How could I make such a pledge? I currently had none in my pantry. When I looked up, I caught Ken Price involved in some kind of drama. His eyes wide and his brow furrowed, he shook his head back and forth in tiny but emphatic gestures as he attempted to communicate silently to someone behind me.

I whipped around, hoping to catch one of the band members. Instead the only person nearby was a woman reading one of the host of tourist brochures.

Price touched my arm. "Callahan, the man needs to keep his mind off dying. Don't waste your time feeling sorry for Dustin. He didn't need much convincing to keep things the way they are." Though he focused his gaze on me, his complexion was mottled.

"How do you know her?" I asked Price.

"Hmm?" He sipped his tea as if he'd forgotten the last few seconds.

Quickly, I glanced over my shoulder. Exiting the hotel

Chapter 20

After that bit of bad news sank into my bones, I drove back to the Cogburn Hotel, called Ken Price, and demanded that he meet me in the lobby immediately. For once, the agent was in a benevolent mood. Whether he felt sorry for me or was merely bored, ten minutes later we sat in a secluded corner of the lobby in Manchester carved chairs with curved backs, scroll arms, and fine leather upholstery. As it was afternoon, the hotel provided us with a pot of tea and freshly baked cookies. Price turned up his nose, but I helped myself to a couple of chocolate-chip pecan cookies.

"The Clay Conley Band, really?" I asked.

Giving me a look of disgust, Ken handed me a napkin. "You have some chocolate just there." He pointed to the corner of my mouth. "Not my first choice for a band name, but the guys suggested it."

"You don't mind if I record this, do you?" I asked, phone in hand.

"Yes, I do. I don't know why, but I want to give you a break."

I placed my phone in the middle of the table. "Do you

"Anything else?" I asked.

He chuckled. "Didn't you hear? It's now called the Clay Conley Band. Said his agent pulled some strings, and they're hitting the road for Nashville in a day or two. "

My heart sank. Pulled strings with whom? Sheriff Wallace? I didn't want to consider that the perfect sheriff of my youth had heels of clay. Lightfoot? No, that I refused to consider. The upright deputy didn't have compromise in him, or my name wasn't Josefina Callahan.

Questioning this dude was starting to resemble a wrong turn on the road to nowhere.

"Anything else?"

"Yeah. She left around twelve thirty."

"You sure it was Britney, not Clay?"

He wrinkled his forehead. "Yeah, almost positive."

Aha. Clay was lying. That meant Britney could've driven over to Patti's and killed Jeff . . . but why?

I perked right up. "How'd he get home?"

"Oh, she came back to get him around one." That shot a hole in my assumptions.

"Does she always do that? Drive him home?"

"No, he usually walks back to the hotel." Hmm. Clay had lied about Britney's staying for his entire poker games. Guess he wanted me to think that she idolized him.

I bolted from the stool and hurried toward the door. "Thanks," I said as I ran to the Prius, too stoked to care if he heard me or not. As I reached the door, I screeched to a halt and retraced my steps.

I opened the front door and stuck my head inside. "She's not back there now, is she?"

He shook his head. "No, Sherlock, she's not."

"Thanks. I owe you."

"You bet your butt you do."

"Tamales?"

"Fajitas."

I tried staring him down, but he didn't flinch from his pricey request. "Fine," I muttered.

"And free admission to Two Boots tonight to hear Clay's band."

"Jeff Clark's not even buried yet. And it's not Clay's band—not from what I heard."

I returned to the bar. If I continued to holler, even the folks in the back would hear me. "What did Clay say?"

"Hmm." He began to retrieve glasses from the dishwasher. "Let's see. . . . He's the man." He grabbed a clean towel from beneath the bar.

I looked at him and he looked at me.

"You think Clay puts up with Britney 'cause she's got pregnancy hormones shooting out her ears."

Shorty cocked a finger at me. "That's what I know."

"And Clay's excited?"

"Oh yeah. He let it slip one night when she left early that they'd broken up, until she told him about the baby."

They wouldn't be the first couple to find true love while pushing a baby stroller. That could keep people together longer than true love sometimes, or so they say.

"You going to order something else or prop up the bar?"

I started to give him what for, as I still held a hard cider in my hand, but then realized he'd had maybe five customers all day. Another drink wouldn't do, as I might or might not be in the same establishment as a killer. On the other hand, I did want to grease the wheels of information, so I ordered oily cheese fries, the sports-bar equivalent of tamales, and a Dr Pepper.

As he entered my order into the computer, I threw out my first live one. "Was Britney here that night?"

"She's here every night."

"She stay in there with the cardplayers or out here with you?" I said it with a smile.

He frowned. "She's wound too tightly for me. End of story."

"She ever complain about Clay?"

"Try asking if she ever said anything nice about the poor guy."

"Did she?"

"Nope."

"That night she was out here?"

"If I'm remembering right, she was inside with Clay. They ordered a BLT on whole wheat, which we don't have, with mayo on the side and extra bacon. She loves the bacon."

I glared at him.

And he lifted his hands in surrender. "What?"

"Speaking of poker games, I'm overdue." He swallowed the last drop and slammed the mug to the bar. "Bring the next one to the table."

"Sure. Why not?" The bartender removed the empty, caught the ten-dollar bill Clay threw at him, and gave the cardplayer a solemn nod.

Shorty stared at me long and hard after Clay left.

"Uh, sorry about that." Of course, he'd overheard our conversation. "He gets under my skin."

"He and his band need to beat it out of town before I'm tempted to beat his . . ."

I chuckled. "You don't see eye to eye?"

"More like fist to face."

I swallowed. "Were they here the night of the murder?"

"I'd love to say no," he wiped down the bar with the towel over his shoulder, "but he's right. I would have remembered if I'd been clear of them even one night."

"Did he do or say anything odd?"

"Nah. He don't say much, and when he does it's about how he's going to take Nashville by the tail and swing it over his head."

"Doesn't sound like him."

"Huh. Guess that was my interpretation of his boring bullcrap."

"What about Britney?"

"Ah, Britney the beautiful."

"Puh-lease."

"She would be if she weren't always tied up in knots about something or other. She's always on his case."

"About what? He's a musician. God knows they only have to look good and play the guitar."

He chuckled. "Bitter?"

"You bet."

"What kind of things is Britney tied up in knots about?"

"She's always eating crackers and complaining that the food gives her indigestion."

"No." I swallowed. "Why would I think that?"

He turned to face me, so close the alcohol on his breath made my eyes sting. "I did exactly what I said." He leaned even closer. "Why you asking?"

What should I do? I closed my eyes and told the truth. "I'm trying to put together everyone's whereabouts at the time of the murder."

"What business is it of yours?" His voice lowered to a growl.

"I'm a reporter with the local paper." My voice cracked. "I'll be out of a job if I don't come up with something plausible enough to please my editor."

"So you say."

"If you're innocent, you've got nothing to hide."

"I have a roomful of witnesses who'll tell you what happened that night."

"What if I told you the bartender remembers differently?" Shorty was on the phone, taking a to-go order, and missed both my taunt and the furtive glances I sent his way.

"I'd say that was more than forty-eight hours ago and he's just trying to get into your pants."

Clay was a horrible human being. I wanted to shove him backwards until he fell off his stool. He wasn't going to make me run scared or stop asking him questions by making me uncomfortable.

"All grossness aside, he said that you were gone for an hour," I lied.

"Well, that's his word against mine."

"He's also given me the names of the guys at the table."

"Look, I don't know why you think I'd do Jeff any harm, especially right now. That's what this is all about, right?" He placed his hand on my shoulder. "My fiancée's not at her best right now. In fact, you could say she's weak as a newborn." He threw his head back and roared, releasing my shoulder.

Whatever had him grinning into his beer had me wondering what was up with old Brit.

"Uh, pear cider?"

The bartender frowned. "How about hard cider?"

Cider was my speed. "If you recommend it." I pasted on a smile and turned to Clay. "I heard tell you're the fellow to beat at cards around here."

He pulled his hat down over his eyes and groaned. "Who told you that?"

"You win big, word gets around, but only to the right people."

After a swig of his beer, he responded. "I win. Sometimes."

"Did you win big last Thursday night?" I held my breath.

"As a matter of fact, I did." He sat up and stared me straight in the eye. "That's why they can't pin that murder on me." He gave the bartender a nod and finished the beer in one gulp. "I was at the poker table all night."

All of a sudden, I wished that Lightfoot, Pleasant, or even Barnes would walk through the door and take over. Interrogation was hard work. "Is your fiancée, Britney, your good-luck charm?"

"Most times." He waved the bartender over. "Give me a cheeseburger with American cheese this time."

"She must've been with you all night for you to win so much." My legs began to shake. I was used to whistling "Dixie" in the dark, but this was more like spelunking without a headlamp.

"I reckon," he said, his words slurring ever so slightly. He sat up straight. "Now that I think about it, she played a couple of hands while I went home to get me some cigs and a fresh shirt."

I took a deep breath to slow my pulse. "Uh, so your luck changed while you were gone during that— what?—thirty or forty-five minutes?"

He stared at me, his eyes narrowing while he tapped his pack of cigarettes on the bar. "I see what you did there. You think I'm lying?"

"Yip."

"I'm married, see?" He raised his left hand in front of his face and wiggled his fingers.

I explained who I was and what I needed. The only information forthcoming was that his name was Shorty. I kid you not.

As I ordered a basket of fries and a mushroom burger with avocado and bacon for Lenny and me to share, Clay Conley strolled in.

"What are you doing here?" I asked in a cheerful way.

He wore his standard uniform of black leather pants and vest, but he'd mixed it up with a white cowboy hat. Not unlike the one Jeff Clark used to wear.

"I'm getting myself a drink," he muttered, and sat two stools down.

"What's up with your band?"

"What's up with that dog under the bar?"

Lenny growled.

"Shh," I whispered.

Before I could answer, the bartender intervened. "He's a service pet."

"Just keep him away from me. I'll take a Coors Light with a whiskey chaser."

"Are you thinking about moving to Broken Boot?" I asked, praying the answer was no.

"Heck, no. We're playing another week at Two Boots. Don't you and your uncle ever say hey?"

"But you don't have a lead singer."

Shorty served Clay his beer and whiskey without comment.

In one gulp, the singer's shot glass was empty. "We're using the place as a tryout for our new lead singer, namely me."

"Congrats." I was anything but happy for the man. I hadn't forgotten that night at Milagro when he'd never said a kind word about Jeff Clark, even after the man's death.

"What are you drinking?" Shorty demanded.

I started to say *nothing*.

"Yip."

"You're coming with me to Pecos Pete's. Would you like that?"

"Yip, yip."

I tried to find Senora Mari, but she was helping Uncle Eddie hire a new cook for Two Boots. After giving Anthony and Camille my prime lunch tables to make amends, Lenny and I marched down the block. We successfully avoided a tumbleweed twice his size and tourists who wanted to pet him, turned left at the post office, and found Pecos Pete's, the sports bar with pool tables that Ryan mentioned.

From the outside, Pete's was nothing to bark about. Concrete blocks held together by crumbling mortar, grime-streaked windows, and a broken neon sign that, unfortunately, declared the establishment's name as PECOS PEE'S.

The interior was a horse of a different color. Modern and bright with a wide bar, vinyl booths, and scattered tables. In the next room, I could make out pool tables, dartboards, and a shuffleboard table. A Luke Bryan tune was blasting from the sound system, and football and soccer games played on giant screens in the four corners and above the bar.

I began by questioning the bartender. "You Pecos Pete?"

He was shorter than me and twice as round. He tossed a menu on the bar. "Very funny. Who said you could bring that mutt in here?"

"No one." I was tired of prevaricating. "He's real sweet. He won't bite or chew things."

The height-challenged bartender walked around the bar to get a good look. "You going to order?"

"No, but we'll be out of here lickety-split."

He frowned. "Wrong answer."

Realization dawned. "Yes." I nodded emphatically. "We are definitely going to order." I thought about the twenty in my pocket. "What do you recommend?"

"Beef," he answered, and returned to his spot behind the bar.

As I studied the menu, I threw out a hook. "They make you work behind that bar every night?"

landed on her trash cans, barely out of the way of oncoming cars. If she said something despicable, she would be lucky if I didn't flatten them with my Prius.

Goose bumps on my arms, I returned to the door and knocked.

"What?" Victoria Pappas thrust her hands on her generous hips.

"Did you see any raccoons that night?"

"Huh?"

"You *said* you heard raccoons in the trash cans and ran outside with a broom."

Her expression softened. "Right. So?"

"So did you *see* any raccoons?" I tried to keep my voice calm.

She sighed and wiped her brow. "No, now that you mention it. The cans were on their sides, but I didn't see any critters."

"Great. Thanks!" In a state of elation, I almost ran back to my car.

"Just 'cause I didn't see them, doesn't mean it wasn't raccoons," she called after me.

Lenny and I needed to take a walk. "Lenster?" I called softly as I entered our apartment.

There was no answer, but I could see him hiding behind the gold-tasseled throw pillow on the love seat. He was ignoring me. I had left him alone quite a bit the past few days while I played crime journalist.

I bent down and gave him a belly rub. "Will you forgive me, buddy?"

"Yip," he said.

Scooping him up in my arms, I carried him to the kitchen. With my other arm, I dug under the sink for a dog biscuit. "Friends?" I begged, offering the treat.

"Yip," he said, catching the treat with his teeth, which set his tail to wagging on its highest speed.

"Don't worry. I'll take care of it. Let me go so I can get there sooner." Senora Mari needed a strong talking-to. What would happen to the girl arriving on the bus? Anthony had enough mouths to feed.

I drove over to Patti's neighborhood. When Victoria Pappas answered the door after a good minute, I asked about both a Land Rover *and* a Range Rover.

"I don't remember seeing anything like what you're describing." This time she'd forsaken the water for a twenty-ounce bottle of diet soda. "It was dark except for the light through the windows, like I told you."

"What about your husband? Could he have seen anything else? Like a four-by-four or some other vehicle?"

"A four-by-four?" She curled her lip. "I doubt it."

She studied the notebook and pen I held at the ready. "Look here. I'll ask him if he noticed anything unusual that night when he came in and get back to you."

"I thought you met him at the door with dinner and a smile."

"True, but I'm kind of forgetful." She waved a cell phone the size of a deck of cards at me.

I opened my mouth to supply my number.

"Oh, I know who you are," she interrupted. "You're that niece of Eddie and Linda Martinez. I'll call you at Milagro after Jason responds."

"Call me anytime," I pleaded. I dug around in my bag and found a Milagro business card, scribbled my cell number on the back, and handed it to her. "It's that important." I shoved my unused notebook and pen inside.

"You think you can get her off?"

"I'm praying I can."

Victoria glanced up and down the street and then she leaned in close. "She's a mess, what with all those piercings up and down her ears."

"She's good people."

I didn't wait for a response from Patti's neighbor, too afraid she'd make a crack about my best friend. My gaze

Chapter 19

◄◄◄◄◄◄◄◄◄◄◄◄◄◄◄◄◄◄◄◄◄◄◄◄◄◄◄◄

Ignoring that little voice reminding me that I ought to call Lightfoot first, I followed my baser instincts and called Milagro.

"Anthony, be a sweetheart and cover my tables until I get there."

"Miss Linda's going to be angry," said our newest full-time waiter.

"If she says anything, just tell her I'll be there soon."

There was a long pause on Anthony's end. "Miss Josie, I will do this for you, but you must talk to Senora Mari for me."

"I thought I told her to let you choose your own bride." I was afraid I had forgotten.

"She has bought Lucinda a bus ticket."

"Oh no."

"And she is to arrive today."

"I'll talk to her, I promise, as soon as I get there."

"Please, Miss Josie. I am an American. I don't want an arranged marriage with a bride I have never met. Would you?"

I looked up and found Ryan bearing down on me from forty yards away.

"What's your number?" I held out my notepad and pen.

He gave me a look as if he suspected I had designs on his person. Finally, he scribbled down his digits.

"Thanks." As I headed for the gate, I turned and waved to the entire team. Only Niles Williams waved back.

"Tamales on me," I called to Niles.

"Yeaaaaah," twenty male voices answered.

Senora Mari was going to have my head on a skewer. I left the field and walked over to inspect the Range Rover. It had a beautiful coat of new paint and a broken taillight. Who would dish out the money for a new paint job and fail to make such a simple repair? Only someone who was desperate to make a quick sale.

My heart sang with possibilities.

"Did you have it painted, by any chance?" Someone nearby whistled.

With a frown, he scooted away. "No, but the owner claimed the paint job was new."

"Who sold it to you?" I held my breath.

With a nervous glance at his friends, he mumbled, "Some woman who met me at Brookshire's."

"You didn't get her name?" I sensed we had become an object of great interest for the other players. *Time to wrap it up.*

"I don't remember much except she refused to lower the price when I pointed out the broken taillight."

I made a note. "It's on the title, isn't it?"

"I guess."

With great effort, I refrained from raising my voice. "You don't remember her name, not even her first name?"

"No." His brow furrowed. "Uh, Katie something?"

"Don't you have the title?"

He huffed like a bull. "She said she'd give me the title when I gave her the final payment."

"Why the delay in paying her?" He didn't seem too concerned about the expense.

"I gave her a deposit. My dad transferred the money to me the next day . . . like she asked." He eyed me suspiciously.

"It's okay. What happened next?"

"I told her I wouldn't make the final payment until she fixed the taillight, like my dad said."

"Callahan," Coach Ryan bellowed from across the field. "Cut your interview short or suit up! You're distracting my team." Masculine laughter from several players followed.

I shot to my feet. "When will you meet her again?"

"I don't know yet. She's supposed to call me."

"Do you mind if I call you, so you can tell me whose name is on the title? This Range Rover may have been driven by a person involved in a crime."

"No kidding."

"You betcha. It's serious business."

"Not that kind of friend." I swallowed, trying to add moisture where none existed. "Let me get right to the point."

"Yes, ma'am."

Close by, an assistant coach began to call players to the field. I was going to have to project if I wanted Williams to hear me. *So much for privacy.* "Is that your gold Range Rover in the parking lot?"

"Yeah." His heavy brow lowered dramatically as if I'd come to tell him I'd damaged it with my car.

I chuckled. "Everything's fine, but I, uh, want to buy one just like it."

"Okay." The frown remained.

I smiled sweetly. "So where did you get it?"

"I bought it." With a grunt, he looked away to follow the action on the field.

"Craigslist?"

"No," he said in disgust. "It was parked at the school with a For Sale sign on it."

"Didn't you think that was strange? An expensive vehicle left in a school lot for anyone to steal."

"No. Well, yeah, but I see them in New Orleans." At this point, his teammates lost interest and rejoined the ranks of players huddled around the coaches.

I stepped closer. "Have you seen any others like it in the area?"

He stared at me intently. "Just this one." A ghost of a smile crossed his face. "I've always wanted one, and this one was dirt cheap."

Inside my head, alarm bells rang. "Do you mean to say you bought it recently?"

"Sunday."

"This past Sunday?" I cried. "As in, three days ago?"

Helmets turned our way.

"Tamale Tuesdays, be there or be square," I said with a smile, my nerves getting the best of me. What an eerie co-incidence. Not wanting to be overheard, I sat beside him.

Five pairs of eyes looked at me with sudden interest.

"Good to see you, Miss Callahan." The coach nodded, and we were off.

I smiled, showing both dimples. "For helping me out, you five guys can claim a dozen tamales at our to-go window for free."

"A dozen?" a broad-shouldered Hispanic player asked.

"Two dozen would suit you better?"

They nodded.

"Two it is. Just tell them Josie sent you."

They led me down a dark hall, and I clamped a hand over my nose in an attempt to block the stench of dirty socks, sweaty bodies, and nauseating disinfectant. When we finally exited into the bright sunshine and sparkling air, I nearly fainted with relief.

Like a marching band, we paraded in a straight line through the gate and onto the grass. Players crowded the sidelines, some watching the field and others pressing close to the coaches. Every muscle in their bodies telegraphed their yearning to play.

We arrived at a row of benches near the back. Two were empty, but a third was markedly not. The massive young man before us sported a shaved head and a tribal tattoo around each bicep. As one, my escorts nodded to him and then turned to wait for me to do the talking.

"Coach Marquez said I could ask you a question."

With small moss green eyes, Williams checked out my wardrobe. "Huh," he grunted. "Guess so." He shot a quick glance at his fellow players and waited.

I'd planned on pulling him aside to talk to him in private, but he wore a blue ankle cast and had stowed his crutches under the bench. "I'm a friend of Coach Ryan's."

The other players glanced at each other, and then nonchalantly gave me the once-over.

"And she owns that restaurant with the tamale to-go window on Main Street," said the shortest player in a quiet, authoritative voice. He made a gesture that I should continue.

"Some crazy kid from New Orleans. Name of Niles Williams."

"I've never seen one around town. Has he always had it with him?"

His brow as furrowed as a field of cotton seedlings, Juan was studying the useless machine in front of him once again. "He's only had it a day or two. You could ask him."

He raised his whistle.

"No, don't."

"It's okay. He's on the field riding the bench today, recovering from a broken ankle."

Juan Marquez raised the whistle again, and I covered my ears. In spite of the piercing sound, nothing happened for several seconds. I laughed. Did he really expect this Williams kid to hear him from the practice field? "That's okay. I'll find him on my own."

He studied me for a moment. "Must be a big deal for you to find your way into the field house with Coach Prescott nowhere in sight, but have it your way."

"Thanks. I'll find him." After a wrong turn that led me into an odorous room filled with industrial washers and dryers, I finally found the trail back to the coach's office so I could start again.

"Looks like you found him," Marquez said with a straight face. Inside his office, five very tall, muscular young men of various ethnic backgrounds stood at attention, holding their helmets in their hands.

Marquez stood. "These gentlemen are going to escort you to the field. Isn't that right?"

"Yes, sir," they said in unison. If they were surprised at his request, it didn't pierce their serious expressions.

"Ms. Callahan's family owns Milagro, the best Tex-Mex restaurant in Big Bend County. Y'all be nice to her, and there could be free tamales in your future."

Boots." With a grin, he snatched his cap from my head, climbed over the front railing, and walked onto the field.

I pulled out my phone and dialed my uncle's number. It rolled to voice mail, and I left him a message to call me as soon as possible.

I hurried out toward the Prius, started to dial Uncle Eddie once again, and froze.

Under the shade of a live oak tree was the vehicle of my dreams. *Thank you, Lord.* Then I took a closer look and my bubble of bliss burst.

A gold Range Rover. *Dang it.*

Slowly I circled it, studying the paint, the size, and the emblem on the back. Did the neighbor with the Doberman know one car from another? Like the difference between a Land Rover and its cousin? This four-wheeled answer to my prayers was mighty close to the mark.

I hurried back inside the field house and found Juan Marquez, another one of Ryan's assistant coaches. Juan had leathery skin and a quiet smile. He'd played football at West Texas with Uncle Eddie.

"Hey, Mr. Marquez," I cried, trying my best to sound nonchalant. "Who owns the Range Rover out in the parking lot?"

"Hey yourself, Miss Callahan." Juan glanced up briefly and then continued to study his computer screen, his finger tapping a steady rhythm on the mouse.

I tried again. "Sorry, Juan. What are you doing playing hooky in here by your lonesome?"

"Trying to find the e-mail address for that Patrick kid's high school coach over in El Paso." He shook his head in disgust. "Useless machine. It was here last week." He pushed the keyboard away and swiveled toward me. "What was it you asked me?"

"The Range Rover outside. Who does it belong to?"

"What night?" I repeated.

Football, the queen of Ryan's life, was demanding his undivided attention.

I hurried after him. "Hey!"

"I'm not sure. Friday, maybe," he tossed over his shoulder.

By the time I reached the spot where he stood talking with his assistant coach, the two were deep in conversation about a passing route.

"Thanks," I said with a wave.

He kept his eyes on the other man and a raised a hand in farewell.

Another woman would've been irritated, but I understood I was lucky to catch Ryan in a talkative mood. Too bad his information was as helpful as a makeup consultation without a mirror.

A poker game on Friday? If the murder took place on Thursday or early in the morning Friday, that was no help at all. The big lughead had probably confused his games, since the Broken Boot Bears played their high school football games on Friday nights.

I sighed. In truth, Ryan hadn't sounded too sure about any of his answers. Perhaps he was trying to keep me out of trouble. I frowned. There was nothing for it but to do what I should have done all along. I had to get over to Pecos Pete's to do some reconnaissance myself.

I headed for the exit when Ryan yelled, "Hey, Josie."

It took me a sec to find him in the glare from the metal bleachers. "What?" I asked, squinting into the sun.

"Are you still looking for that truck?"

"Truck?"

He began to climb over four rows of bleachers, which was no problem with his long, muscular legs. "Yeah," he said with no obvious sign of being out of breath. "Weren't you trying to find a Land Rover?"

I perked right up. "Where? Where'd you see it?"

"Eddie mentioned he spotted one last night at Two

"What?" He whipped around as if I'd touched him with a cattle prod. "We don't date."

I scooted out of reach. "You see each other, don't you?"

His look of consternation cleared. "Oh, you saw us together the night of the murder."

"Maybe." I shrugged.

"Jealous?"

"No." *Relieved* was more like it.

"Cool." He gave me a friendly punch on my upper arm. "You and me: no strings, no drama."

"You and me." I gestured between the two of us. "Drama-free zone."

"Yeah, that's what I need." His ready smile evaporated.

"Before we plan a trip to Austin, I need your help." Something had been bugging me.

"What's the question?"

"Why'd you leave the poker game early that night?" Winning or losing, if Ryan played poker, he played all night.

"That guy—what's his name with the red hair?"

"Clay Conley."

He shook his head. "What a braggart."

"Has he played in Vegas?"

"Are you kidding? No, he was bragging about what a great musician he was. How he could write songs better than Jeff Clark and anyone in Nashville." Ryan took off his sunglasses and wiped the lenses.

"And that made you leave?"

"I split because he wouldn't shut up about his band."

"His band?"

"You got it. Kept saying how soon everyone would be talking about the Clay Conley Band."

Jackpot. "When's the next game at Pete's?"

"Evans!" He jumped to his feet. An assistant coach with wraparound sunglasses halted in midstride. Ryan started down the steps, waving the man toward him. They met a few rows from the bottom.

Patti's pale face and atrocious jumpsuit abruptly came to mind. I reined in my impatience. Coach Ryan Prescott was used to being in charge, so I played the game his way. I placed a hand on my heart. "What—tamales and margaritas don't cut it anymore?"

His gaze returned to the field. "I'm in the mood for a night at the White Horse, listening to real music and drinking cold beers."

"Which you do here in Broken Boot . . . frequently."

"Not as often as I like, because I have students and their mommas watching me at every turn."

I was a bit confused. "You want me to drive you to Austin so you can line dance with a bunch of honky-tonk hipsters?"

"Let's shake the dust of this town off our boots and hang out like we used to."

Though we'd spent hours on end at the White Horse during college, I was surprised. When Ryan broke up with that diva, beauty queen Hillary Sloan-Rawlings, I was so happy I nearly threw a pool party—even though Casa Martinez only had a quaint, aboveground version. My ex was a genuinely nice person, and she was so not his type. Had another local beauty refused to go out with him a second time? Or was he being genuine about just wanting an opportunity for two old friends to hang out, like he said?

It might sound strange, but I liked Ryan enough not to want to date him ever again. I glanced his way, trying to read his expression and intentions from his profile.

"Ha ha, very funny," I chortled. "You had me thinking you meant a date or something."

He shook his head and gave me a slow smile. "Do you think I'm half-crazy or just completely nuts?"

I chuckled. "Both." In spite of the heat, the view from the stands was breathtaking. The mountains in the background, the big blue sky above. I studied the field before us as the quarterback hurled the ball more than forty yards, only to have the receiver run the wrong route. "What about Jayda? Aren't you and she almost a thing?"

His eyes remained on the field. "No. Why? It's not like you to be so nosy."

"We are talking about me, right?"

Then he grabbed my knee and squeezed. "I meant when it comes to where I am, what I'm doing, and who I'm doing it with."

Busted. "Look, whatever. As long as you go to work every day and church on Sunday, you can date whomever your heart desires . . . within reason. I'm worried about Patti, so shoot me if I skip the pleasantries. But if you need to share your feelings about how your new gal doesn't appreciate you or answer your text messages, we can do that instead."

After a laugh so loud it had the closest players on the field turning their heads, Ryan wiped his eyes. "Boy, howdy. I didn't think you'd come all this way to watch practice."

I ducked my head and grinned. "Remember the other day, when I asked you about the poker game at Pete's?"

"Have you finally gotten around to asking what you need to know?"

"I'm *working* on it."

"Continue."

"Have you heard of any other card games in town?"

"I could've sworn you already asked me that." His head snapped toward a tackle running up the field so slowly, Senora Mari could have passed him. "And I told you no."

"Right. You also said you left early."

"Beacon," Ryan shouted, nearly bursting my eardrum. "Get your tired butt down the field twice that fast, or you'll be running the bleachers after practice."

The skinny player froze in midstride.

"You hear me, son?"

"Yes, sir," the young man bellowed like a boot-camp private, and flew down the field to the line of scrimmage as if his hair were on fire.

With a slight turn of his head, I could feel Ryan staring at me from behind his shades. "Is there something in this for me?"

as to the source, and found one gray cloud floating lazily on a backdrop of blue. A brief sun shower was the likely source.

We found seats halfway up. The metal bleachers were sizzling, and I was glad I'd worn jeans. I pulled my sunglasses over my eyes and raised my hand to shield me from the blinding sun. Still I could barely make out the activity on the field.

"What are you doing out here without a hat, city slicker?"

He removed the West Texas cap from his head and plunked it down on mine. A sudden cool breeze flirted with his hair, but he'd worn the hat too long for any breeze to win out.

I started to argue, but he didn't act as if he minded the heat or the glare. "Trotter," he yelled to one of three assistant coaches wearing a blue polo and white shorts on the field, "tell Patrick to break the huddle twice as fast. Josie could call plays faster than what he's doing."

I shoved him. "Watch it."

Trotter blew his whistle and proceeded to pass along Ryan's comments to the quarterback decked out in all white.

"Patrick's got a good arm on him," I said, as the quarterback threw a fifty-yard pass into the skilled hands of his receiver, a player wearing the number 10. He followed it up with a series of short passes to two other players and then another bullet down the field again to 10, passing forty to fifty yards as we watched.

"In practice, he's lethal," Ryan continued. "In a game situation, he's like jelly. Too sweet."

I considered the best way to begin.

"When's the last time you came to one of our games?"

"This Saturday?" Truth be told, I hadn't seen a game since my return to Broken Boot nine months earlier.

"Uh-huh. You're already thinking of a way to weasel out of it, aren't you?"

"No." With Ryan, it was usually best to come right to the point. "You weren't up late playing cards by any chance?"

The fact that he himself wasn't clean-shaven made me wonder what was up.

"Late night?"

He tried for his usual devil-may-care grin, but the corners of his mouth barely lifted. "The team's not jelling," he said, pulling off his West Texas cap and ruffling his hair. "You know we lost our first game last week, which was a fiasco. Thank God we have a bye this week."

Everything he said was true, but the team's difficulties usually made him fighting mad, not worn-out. If memory served, that smile usually accompanied a dating fiasco. "What'd you do now? Refuse to meet her mother?"

A frown appeared across his brow. "How'd you know I was dating someone?"

"You're always dating someone."

"Am not."

"Was it or was it not you who told me that you had ants in your pants and you're born to dance?"

He hooted with laughter until he was red in the face. "How old was I? Eighteen?"

I frowned. "You were a freshman. That's all I know."

"What makes you think I didn't mean just what I said? That I liked to dance?"

"Huh. Context, my friend. I remember the context even if you won't admit it."

"Huh." He stood, stretched his long arms above his head, and started for the door. "Come on, I want to show you what I'm working with."

Not being a football fan in Texas is like rejecting your mother's milk. Back in college, Ryan's endless talk of game strategy and his endless dissection of his opponents' plays wore me out. Now that we saw each other less often and had both mellowed, I didn't mind being taken into his confidence.

In fact, it was a huge compliment.

As we climbed the stands, the air was redolent with the smell of sagebrush and creosote. I glanced skyward, curious

Chapter 18

After taking Lenny outside and tossing some kibble in his bowl, I drove to the West Texas University field house. I found Coach Ryan Prescott with his athletic shoes on the desk and his hands laced behind his head—which made it difficult to ignore the fact he lifted weights alongside his players. When he failed to look my way, I decided the blackboard and the plays that covered it had hypnotized him.

"Why, Ryan Prescott. Who said you could hide in here from your responsibilities?"

With a bit of a delay, he roused himself and removed his Nikes from the dented metal desk. "Look what's come home to roost. I haven't seen you inside this place since—"

"Never," I interrupted. "It smells like armpits in here."

"Yeah, that's right. You never did breach the walls of . . . What was it you called this place?"

I grinned. "The Temple of Meatheads."

"That's it!" He chuckled but his red eyes drooped, and he wore at least a two-day-old beard. Ryan's requirement that his players remain clean-shaven was one of the many regimens he'd introduced to turn them into fighting machines.

my voice with saccharine. "I get it. Don't let little old me stand in your way."

He inched his hat back from his forehead with his thumb and smiled. "Thank you kindly, Miss Josie."

I was so shocked to see the white of his teeth that my mouth fell open. Before I could encourage him to use that line on Patti, he jerked open the door, set the cowbell jangling, and strode out to the parking lot.

Well, shoot. He'd distracted me on purpose with that toothpaste grin of his.

One day Patti was going to thank me for sacrificing my dignity, or else.

"No. We don't want to place all of our focus on Dustin."
His jaw clenched. "Because . . ."

"Dustin has cancer," we said in unison.

I leaned forward and smiled. "And he's quitting the band
after this tour."

"You sure?" Lightfoot was genuinely surprised.

"That's what he told Uncle Eddie. Why would he say it
if he wasn't actually going to do it?"

Lightfoot just looked at me. "Of course, he could be tell-
ing a lie, trying to throw us off his scent."

"If you really want to get Patti off the hook and look like
a hero, you should be asking one question: where was Clay
the night of the murder? That's what you should be asking."

He closed his notepad and shoved it in his shirt pocket,
slid from the booth, and placed his cup in the tub we used
for dirty dishes. "And why do I need to look like a hero?"

I opened my mouth to respond.

He held up a hand. "Don't answer that."

"Where are you going?"

"Sheriff Wallace wants to ask me some questions."

I hurried to put away my cup. "I'm coming with you."

"No. Stay here, keep your eyes and ears open, and then
report back to me. That's how you can help me without
getting in the way."

"Wait a minute," I cried. "You'll still impress her even
if I help you."

"What?" He turned from the door. "You know I can't
bring you with me. This isn't television."

"You've said that before."

"I could lose my job if I don't follow the book on this
one."

He had a point. Broken Boot needed Lightfoot's solid
grasp of right and wrong. How could I ask him to compro-
mise on that one integral part of himself, his very founda-
tion? Patti, when she found out, would understand and
respect him for standing his ground.

"Fine." I crossed my arms, pasted on a smile, and laced

"Huh." His brow creased. "No. That guy with the red hair and black leather."

"Clay and Britney." I tapped my finger on his notepad. "If you ask me, they're a bit too helpful." I told him how they'd accused Dustin Akers of murdering Jeff.

He lifted his cup, and then set it down without taking a sip. "That's garbage. Akers has an airtight alibi."

"Which is?"

After a weighty pause, he continued. "He has more on his mind than murder." He studied my face. "Cancer."

A lump formed in my throat. The poor guy was fighting for his future, and I'd mentally accused him of murder. I glanced up from my coffee cup to find Lightfoot watching me.

"You know him?"

"I've met him. He asked me to show him downtown, so we went for a walk. He told me about his music, and how that snake Ken Price refused to give him a shot as lead singer of the band."

It was my turn to ask the questions. "What do you know about that couple, Britney and Red?"

He didn't immediately respond, which told me he knew plenty. He remained quiet for several seconds. Was he organizing his thoughts or deciding what he was willing to share? "What do you know?" he asked, sidestepping my question.

"You'll give me something in return?" I asked.

"Okay. Yes. Didn't I say I would?" With his finger, he loosened the back of his collar.

In spite of Lightfoot's calm and steady demeanor, he wasn't fooling me. He was worked up about this case because the wrongful arrest involved Patti. It all made sense once I put two and two together. He had a thing for my best friend. "They want us to think it was Dustin Akers because he should have had Jeff's job, et cetera, et cetera."

"But that's not good?" Lightfoot began to tap his index fingers on the table.

"She says she heard a raccoon in the trash cans around twelve thirty and Patti's jeep start up at around one or one thirty."

With an absent gesture, he lifted the cup in his hand while smoothing his long hair back behind his ears. He circled something in his notes. "Why would Patti threaten to kill this Jeff guy? I've never seen her riled up about anything."

"She's a slow burner."

A frown line appeared between his eyes. "You mean she has a long fuse."

"Exactly. Her anger keeps burning and burning until finally it explodes all over everybody and everything."

He made a note.

"Uh, well, she can get loud, but I've never known her to strike out at anyone." I forced a laugh. "She's all scary Goth Princess and nothing else."

He nodded thoughtfully. "Why did she explode all over Jeff Clark that night?"

"He was drunk and coming on to her." I sipped my coffee. "Sounds like a good enough reason to me."

"Why was she angry *before* he was drunk? Before they even reached her house?"

"Well, who says she was?" My voice rose in frustration. It was clear as the nose on his face that Patti was the injured party here. "And how do we know they're telling the truth?"

His eyes narrowed again. "Why would they lie?"

Before I could stop it, my cheeks flamed. "Depends on who we're talking about!"

"You know I can't disclose that information."

"I don't give a flying fig what you can or can't do. We're talking about Patti—not some hardened criminal."

He sighed, gave me a mock glare, and flipped back through his notebook until he found the correct page. "The couple that tours with the band?"

"Wilhelmina and Heather?"

"That's pretty common," I said.

"But murder is not." His eyes narrowed in speculation.

I raised a hand. "Don't say, *Murder wasn't common until you moved to town.*"

"Fair enough." He gave me a nod. "Now, I'd appreciate it if you'd tell me exactly what the neighbor told you."

If he was ignoring his strict code of confidentiality, he must be disturbed. "I'm glad to help." And I suddenly meant it. I gave him a smile, and he gave me another unblinking stare.

"At first he said a blue vehicle that was *definitely* not a truck. He was rude. And I have a good idea Pleasant is the reason he slammed the door in my face."

"Any dent on the end of your nose is your own doing." He dug the pencil out of his pocket. "Tell me what the other neighbor said."

Busted. "Which one?"

"That's what I thought." He glared.

I sighed. "It wasn't a long conversation. I asked if she witnessed anything the night of the murder, and she said yes. She'd seen Patti and a man drive up around midnight." My best friend had told me that same thing at the station, which was a plus in her column.

He made a note. "And?"

"When I asked if she got a good look at the man, she described a guy with boots and a cowboy hat."

He nodded and kept scratching on the paper. "Which could have been anyone."

I opened my mouth to argue.

"But there's no reason Patti would lie about being seen with Jeff," he interrupted. "She's on record as saying the same thing."

I wanted to ask him about his date with Patti, but I could wait. I didn't want Lightfoot to get distracted by my nosiness.

Wishing I could read his notes, I continued. "I asked if she saw or heard anything else."

He covered his writing with his hand. "Go ahead."

cheekbones and dark eyes. It was if I were staring into a black-and-white photograph from the turn of the previous century.

He stared at me over the rim of his cup. "What?"

Unlike my ex-fiancé, here was a man's man—a bit on the solemn side, but woven of honesty and integrity. "Why are you ready to talk to me about this case? Is your belt on too tight today?"

One side of his mouth rose. "My belt's just fine. Thank you." He set down his cup and pushed it away. "I need your help."

His solemn gaze met my incredulous one. "Would you repeat that? I could have sworn you said you needed my help."

He removed his hat and flung it onto the seat next to him. "Something's going on at the station." He averted his gaze, as if mesmerized by the Sugar Rush ice-cream truck parked across the street.

My heart went out to him. His way of looking at things was so black and white; it had to be difficult for him to criticize his superiors. "Are they painting the men's bathroom? Or do you mean something's not quite right in the sheriff's office?"

His lips tightened. "The investigation into this case is being rushed. Details are being overlooked." He raised his cup to his mouth. "I pointed out to Wallace we needed to canvass the neighborhood."

"I thought you said Pleasant spoke with the guy in the pink house."

"He's *one* neighbor. The whole block should have been interviewed."

"Did Wallace actually stand in your way?" I knew Sheriff Mack Wallace through his daughter, Crystal. As young teens, we'd played on the same softball team, the Chisos Mountain League Cactus Flowers.

"No, but he assigned the other deputies to an incident of suspected cattle rustling."

"You're a deputy. You like it black."

"No. I take it black when there's only artificial creamer around."

That wasn't very coplike, taking cream in his coffee. "You'll probably find some milk in the kitchen." Anything to delay our little talk.

But then my hostess genes kicked in. "Be right back." I dragged my feet in the kitchen for as long as I dared.

"Sit down," he called. "You're evading the consequences."

I placed the small metal pitcher on the table. "What consequences?"

"For obstructing justice." He stopped glaring at me long enough to add milk to this coffee.

"I wasn't obstructing anything. I was trying to help."

"By talking to a witness before he was interviewed by law enforcement."

Lightfoot was someone I respected. He was the strong, intelligent type. And he did his job without being all puffed up and arrogant. He had a way of looking at me, as if he knew what I was thinking and wanted me to be nobler.

He stared at me and I stared back.

Finally I broke. "You're right."

Silence again. He was really dragging this out.

"I apologize." I was *mostly* sorry.

"Who did you talk to?"

Coming clean was good, but I thought it would be best to divulge my secrets in small increments. "The neighbor in the pink adobe house next to Patti's."

He nodded and flipped to a page in his notebook. "He told Pleasant that he didn't see anything that night."

I was lower than dirt. Lightfoot was sharing information. I had to make amends.

"He told me that he was positive it was a blue Land Rover, but he couldn't make out the driver." Even as I spoke, I noticed how straight Lightfoot's nose really was. It was perfect, if a bit too prominent. It worked nicely with his sharp

I lunged for my phone and ended up doing a belly flop on my bed.

"You up?" Deputy Lightfoot demanded.

"No. And if that was you downstairs, trying to break down the door, you can come back later, after you go buy some manners, mister." Lightfoot had no right to wake me up at seven thirty in the morning.

"Open up. You and I need to talk."

I didn't like his bossiness, but I was intrigued that he was so desperate to speak with me. Maybe he needed my help with the investigation, or perhaps he'd viewed a recent episode of *Castle* and changed his tune about needing a part-time journalist to tag along with him and brainstorm ideas.

Hurriedly, I threw on a sweatshirt and a pair of boots and hustled down the steps.

"Yip," Lenny said, hurrying along beside me. "Yip, yip."

"That's just what I was thinking."

I raised the blind at the front door and unlocked the bolts with the keys hidden beneath the cash register. "This had better make my day."

"Got any coffee?"

I frowned. "What do you think this is—Waffle House?"

"Point me to it. And don't look so put-upon. I'll make it."

"You'll do no such thing." I flounced over to the coffee urn, set up the coffee, and hit the button. "Sit down."

We found a booth. "What's going on that you're here so stinking early?" I rubbed the sleep from the corners of my eyes.

"Have you been harassing Patti's neighbors?"

Ah, sugar snap. I forgot to call Lightfoot with an update. "Define *harassing*."

I could tell fire and brimstone were about to pour from his mouth. "Wait. I need coffee before you bring down the fist of doom. Wait." I fixed us both a cup. I remembered he liked his black, deposited the cups on the table, and slid back across the vinyl seat.

"Where's the cream and sugar?"

Chapter 17

The next morning my eyes sprang open without their usual blurriness. In fact, I was so wide awake I immediately noticed a crack in the ceiling above my bed—which led me to Jeff Clark's cracked skull and who the murderer might be.

On the way to pick up Lenny from Wilhelmina and Heather last night, I mulled it all over. In truth, I hadn't met anyone in my interviews who struck me as the murdering type. Who else could have done it? And why?

"Yip, yip," Lenny said in his outside voice.

"Okay, let me get dressed."

Then I heard it. Someone, an angry someone by the sound of it, was banging on the front door of Milagro. As we received our deliveries on Mondays, and we weren't scheduled to open for another three hours, I ignored it. "Tell me about it."

"Yip," Lenny complained.

As I hopped on one foot, one leg in my jeans and one out, the banging stopped. Immediately my cell began to ring.

"You're the best." I hugged him back. He smelled of Old Spice and beer, and he was the closest thing I'd had to a father for more than ten years.

Ty sprung through the door. "How about a group hug?" he asked, his arms thrown wide.

"I suggest you keep your hands to yourself unless you know how to play guitar with your feet."

into the palm of the other. "They're not going to offer him Jeff's job. He'd never expect them to."

I wasn't buying it, not completely. "If I were dying, I might want to settle old scores."

"You'd do no such thing." Uncle Eddie chuckled. "You'd be praying for your enemies and making peace with your soul before you climbed that stairway to heaven."

"Say what?"

"The song by Led Zeppelin? Oh, forget it. You know what I'm trying to say here."

"Hm." If Uncle Eddie was correct, there went my only real suspect.

He continued. "Dustin Akers told me over two double scotches that he's retiring at the end of the tour."

"Bless his heart," I said, and meant it. I couldn't imagine dying or suffering such a horrible illness. What if I were a singer and found out I had cancer? What then? How would I feel to realize I'd never be able to sing again or not with the same musicality? To see my dreams of fame and fortune go sailing off in a cloud of pain and frustration?

"I hate to burst your water tank, Jo Jo, but what can I say? Even if I don't want Patti to stay in that jail one more minute—and I don't—Akers didn't do it."

I glanced at my uncle's order form. "You missed the Coors."

"Since when?" he demanded.

I pointed to the bottles of Coors hidden beneath the Budweiser at the very bottom of the tower of brews.

While he knelt to count them, I continued. "Someone's putting pressure on Wallace to stop looking for other suspects. Who would do such a thing?"

"I'm not sure," Uncle Eddie mumbled. "Cogburn, maybe?"

"That's what I was thinking."

"I'll find out." Uncle Eddie stood and placed his arm around my shoulders. "Don't worry. We'll get her out of there."

toward me. "Hold on for a special bulletin from yours truly: Jeff Clark not only owed a guy money, but slept with his wife. And that fella killed him deader than a cell phone in Carlsbad Caverns." He pointed to his rather expensive footwear. "Betcha my new alligator boots on it." Would wonders never cease? Ty Honeycutt had either recently won at the poker table or managed to save his hard-earned cash.

"I'll dump that in my circular file," I said.

He frowned and thought about my comment. "Huh. Well, don't forget it was me who helped you find the killer." He bent down, brushed an imaginary speck of dust from one boot, and then exited the storeroom, headed for the office. How he and Uncle Eddie never tired of passes, fumbles, tackles, and touchdowns for hours on end was a mystery to me. Cavemen and gladiators. Enough said.

"One of the members of Jeff's band was hoping to take over the spotlight from Jeff," I said.

"Enough to kill him?" Uncle Eddie asked.

"The job was supposed to belong to Dustin Akers. Ken Price, their agent, told him the lead singer position was his, but Price gave the job to Jeff."

Uncle Eddie shook his head. "You want to find someone who's guilty, I understand, but Dustin Akers isn't that guy, no matter how badly you want him to be."

"How can you be so sure?"

"The other night I was tending bar and he was warming a stool."

"And?" I asked.

"He told me just what you said. The job was supposed to be his, but he's at peace with that."

"Well, he would say that, wouldn't he?"

My uncle just stared at me for a long moment. "He's got throat cancer, Jo Jo. He's finished his chemo, but he's only been in remission three months."

"Oh, Lord."

"You said it." Uncle Eddie slapped the back of one hand

"Hey." He backed away, staring at me as if I were out of my mind.

And maybe I was. "This is Patti, in jail, arrested for murder. Did you actually see one, are you pulling my leg, or were you too drunk that night to know what you were seeing?"

He had the decency to look sheepishly at the two of us. "Probably the latter."

"Jo Jo, you haven't figured this out yet?"

"I'm trying." I studied Ty. "But it's hard to find any solid information."

"Any suspects?"

"Yes, a couple." I wasn't about to unload my innermost observations to Uncle Eddie in front of Ty Honeycutt, card-player, country musician, and freeloader.

Ty smirked. "And you're not going to tell him with me around, that right?"

"What gave you that idea?"

He shook his head. "Look, little sister, you should know that Jeff Clark wasn't no saint. In fact, he was a bit of tom-cat. I met a couple of women on his tour bus who are more than ready to put a bullet in his you know what."

"You met them? Do I dare ask under what circumstances you met these women?"

Like the country boy he was, Ty crossed his arms and stuck his thumbs under his armpits. "You hang out in bars, you hear every gal's sad tale of woe. Ain't that right?" he asked Uncle Eddie.

My uncle nodded. "Reckon so."

Ty was just warming up. "He was horrible at cards, lost a pile of money. If you need a suspect, I'd wager on someone he owed money to." Without warning, he slapped his hands together. "Eddie, the new game film in your office?" He headed off without a good-bye.

"You betcha."

Just when I thought I'd heard the last of him, Ty spun

Instead of driving back to Milagro, I headed for Two Boots. I found Uncle Eddie in the storeroom, counting bottles of beer.

"How's Patti holding up?"

"Okay . . . I guess. She's keeping her head high, but you should see her. That place has worn her confidence down to a nub."

Waving his pencil in the air, he finished counting a towering pallet of Budweiser and entered the total on his order form. "Has that brain of yours come up with any suspects?"

"Not unless you know someone who drives a Land Rover."

"Ty was talking about buying one until the bank tried to repossess his El Camino."

I perked up. "Any chance he bought one in the past week?"

"Why don't you ask him yourself, darlin'?"

Ty Honeycutt strolled in, and I hurled my question into the air. "Did you buy, borrow, or steal a blue Land Rover over the past few days?"

He wrinkled his forehead. "I wouldn't be caught dead in a blue one. What am I? A sissy? Mine would be black with gold trim, a sweet leather interior, and a hundred fifty-two horses under the hood." He sighed and stared off into the distance with a dreamy smile.

"Have you seen anybody driving one in town?"

He paused, looked back and forth between us. "Maybe?" He grinned and scratched the blondish growth of beard on his chin. "Seems like I saw one a few weeks ago."

"Nothing the night of the murder?"

"No."

"What color was the one you saw a couple of weeks ago?"

"Geez, I don't know. Black?" His eyes darted around the room as if the answer lay hidden in one of the corners. "But it might have been green."

I walked over and grabbed him by the shoulders.

I interrupted, not wanting Patti to hear the worst. "Could they withhold our evidence?"

"I don't expect any shady business." Gretchen Cruz waited for Patti's full attention. "It isn't like what you see in the movies."

"Time's up." Deputy Pleasant moved to the table, towering over us like a professional female wrestler.

"You can't kick us out." I folded my arms across my chest. "She's allowed to meet with her attorney twenty-four/seven."

"You don't have a law degree, Callahan, last time I checked." Pleasant unlocked the cell door and held it open.

"I'll walk her out." Cruz placed the slender folder in front of her client. "You can read through your file while I'm gone."

"I'll be back soon," I said, wishing I could give my friend a hug. "Don't eat anything fried. You know how it gives you reflux."

Patti's mouth twisted as if fighting a smile. "Don't forget about me, okay?"

"How could I do that? You have to play in that contest on Thursday so you can pay me the twenty dollars you owe me." I gave her a two-fingered salute.

Once we exited the cells and stood alone in the waiting area, Cruz moved closer. "Sometimes things in this town don't go according to the strictest interpretation of the law."

"This is insane," I said. "Wallace knows she's not guilty. Cogburn does too, if he'd just get his head . . ." I forced myself to stop. My voice had risen until it was echoing down the hall.

"Someone wants this to go away and quick. Any ideas?"

Ken Price came to mind. How much influence could a smarmy agent from Los Angeles, and a midlist one at that, have on a small-town sheriff? Not much . . . not unless he offered Cogburn something in the way of money or influence that would benefit his campaign for reelection.

* * *

"Oh."

Leaning forward, Patti's lawyer lowered her voice. "Someone's leaning on him to settle this case, and fast."

Patti and I looked at each other. "Mayor Cogburn," we said in unison.

"Did you have a motive to kill him?"

"No," she answered.

"How did your relationship end when you two were previously together?"

"He was seeing other women on the side, so I kicked him down the road with the rest of the tumbleweeds."

Cruz nodded. "You don't think it's suspicious that you would go out with him again after he humiliated you so badly last time?"

Patti's cheeks flamed. She swallowed. "He said he'd changed, but he lied."

My hands began to shake beneath the table. She wasn't guilty. Why was this happening to her?

"And that made you want to do him harm?"

"But I only *wanted* to kill him." Realizing too late what she'd said, the color drained from Patti's face.

"I'm taking your word for it." Gretchen Cruz lifted a finger to her lips, her eyes wide. "That's what I do."

"Thank God. I've explained twenty times to the sheriff that I wouldn't kill anybody. I'm"—she shot a glance at me—"all talk and no action."

"Can they make the charges stick?" I asked.

"We hope not." Cruz turned to a blank page in her legal pad. "A lot will depend on their witness."

"What about a hearing? Don't we have a few weeks to prepare?" Patti owned the first ten seasons of *Law & Order*. She was nobody's fool.

"You'll have a hearing. That's the law." Patti's attorney glanced at the deputy. "As far as how long we have to prepare, that's up to the judge."

"What do they have on me? Why am I still here, putting up with this crap?"

The hair on my arms rose. "That or someone didn't like the way Jeff Clark played guitar."

One of Cruz's eyebrows rose ever so slowly. "They also have you driving Clark to your place in *your* jeep."

"Which I never denied."

"Why would she kill him? They hadn't seen each other in years." I demanded.

Cruz closed the file. "You admitted to arguing with Jeff Clark. Did you hit him?"

Patti's eyes narrowed. "I should've kicked him where the sun don't shine. That would've kept him from reproducing any other misogynists like himself." She placed her fists on the table, her hands red from gripping so tightly. "He was too drunk to believe that I wouldn't want to pick up our relationship right where we left off."

Honestly, after some of the things she shared about her past dates, I found her reaction surprising. . . and refreshing.

Cruz raised a hand. "Don't say that, even in jest."

"She had no reason to kill him," I said.

"The sheriff's department has found a witness who heard you and Clark arguing in the parking lot," Cruz continued. "Says she heard you say you would kill him if he touched you again."

"Yeah, but that's stupid." Patti ground her knuckles into her temples. "Why would I say that out loud if I was about to help him meet his maker?"

"That's what I said. The county prosecutor thinks otherwise."

"Who?" I asked.

"Jackson Cline, head prosecutor for Big Bend County."

"I've never heard of him." Pretty much everyone who was anyone had graced one of our tables in Milagro at least once a month.

Cruz glanced at Deputy Pleasant, who pretended to ignore us and continued to stare at the opposite wall. "He was elected about a year ago—after his father retired."

"Nope." She sat up in her chair and pulled her hair behind her ears. "There's no cure for being sick of the food, the bedding, and this god-awful, atrocious striped jumpsuit."

I opened my mouth to argue that her outfit suited her black hair, but then I caught her raised eyebrow. "You're right. It hurts my eyes, it's so ugly. At least you're ready for Halloween."

"For which I am eternally grateful," Patti quipped.

"You know, I think that jumpsuit is even uglier than that bright green bridesmaid's dress you wore for your sister Claudia's wedding."

"Way to make me feel better, Jo Jo." To defuse her comment, she reached across the table and we bumped knuckles.

Pleasant stepped forward. "If you touch the prisoner again, you will be escorted from this cell and deposited in the parking lot, at which time you will be issued a citation for failing to follow the posted procedures of the Big Bend County Jail."

"Uh, okay." I placed my hand over my heart. "I promise . . . sincerely."

"Let's review for Josie's sake." Cruz opened her briefcase and removed a legal-sized folder. Though she referred to the report inside, it was obvious she'd rehearsed her speech. "They have Patti's fingerprints on the guitar."

Goth Princess curled her lip. "Of course they do. I play it every day!" She threw her hands into the air. "Can you believe some idiot destroyed my Fender Blacktop Stratocaster?" On a road trip to the Buddy Holly Museum in Lubbock, Patti and I'd found her guitar next to a ukulele in a pawnshop.

I ignored the windowless, concrete walls around us—walls that closed in more and more as we talked. "Why didn't they use a frying pan or a shovel?" I was trying desperately to hide the fact that I was scared for her.

"Perhaps the guitar was symbolic," Cruz said, making a very good point.

me—we reached the visitor's room. Inside we found a quiet, withdrawn Goth Princess. She sat on one side of an old, warped wooden table, its one leg not close to touching the ground.

"Patti." Without thinking, I started toward this pale, bent version of my friend, intent on giving her comfort with a hug or a touch.

"That's far enough." Deputy Pleasant, Big Bend County's only female deputy, stepped between us.

"Over here." Cruz gestured to the opposite side of the table.

"How you holding up, girl?" I asked.

At first, Patti stared right through me as though her inner fierceness had burnt out, leaving only a lifeless, weak creature. "About time you got your sorry butt in here to see me," she said with a hint of her old fire. She attempted to smile, but the corners of her mouth barely lifted.

"I had to stop by to make sure you've been rehearsing your songs for the singer-songwriter contest."

"Ha. How am I supposed to do that? Accompany myself with an imaginary guitar?"

"Hm. It might help you make a case for temporary insanity," I said in a stage whisper. I smiled at Deputy Pleasant to show my comment was all in good fun.

The female officer raised an eyebrow.

"Watch that," Cruz said as she took her seat next to my friend.

I trotted around to the other side of the table and joined them.

"You okay?" Patti couldn't stay in this dank place with no windows nor sunlight. Like any girl from the desert, she would dry up and then disintegrate into a million pieces.

Her eyes filled with tears, but then she swallowed hard, eviscerating any signs of weakness. "Sick."

"Oh no." Was that code for someone had hurt her? Stuck her with a—What was it called? A shiv? "Did you demand to see a doctor?"

she's the visitor and I'm the lawyer, we can both go inside at the same time."

His mouth slammed shut. His eyes narrowed. After a pregnant pause, he drew a deep breath. "Come on." A guard opened the metal door to the cells, and we stepped into a small, narrow passage. As the door clanked shut behind us, Barnes removed a large, heavy set of keys from his belt.

We walked down a wide aisle with rows of cells on either side. In my peripheral vision, I could see that about half were empty, while the others contained only one female prisoner each. I didn't know what to do. Should I look at their faces? Or pretend I didn't notice them in their black-and-white-pinstriped pajamas? I was frankly more than a little scared that they'd try to grab me or spit in my face. What did I know? I'd never been inside a jail before. I'd only seen women prisoners on cable.

I made the mistake of turning my head to the right. The giant of a woman's dark eyes scorched my skin like simmering asphalt against my feet on a hot summer day. In spite of my elevated pulse, I managed to lift the corners of my mouth and give her a nod.

I'd spent that first summer after the death of my parents in Broken Boot, roaming the streets with Patti Perez. I learned that a girl with facial piercings and black combat boots could be your friend, in spite of her appearance.

"Cruz, help me," whispered a short, dark-haired woman with tattoos up and down both arms. "Come on, *chica*, this lawyer they gave me sucks."

Gretchen Cruz looked neither left nor right. Was the miserable inmate one of her old clients? Or simply attempting to get a rise out of the strong yet feminine attorney?

With a slight movement, I adjusted my path to the far side of the aisle. I didn't want the prisoner to bite a tattoo into my arm just to prove she could overpower a *gringa* without working up a sweat.

Without any physical violence on the part of the prisoners or fainting spells on the part of Patti's best friend—namely

She placed the cigarette behind her ear. "Wouldn't it have been too dark to see?"

"No. Apparently not."

Keeping her comments to herself, she made a note. "What did he see?" She removed the cigarette from her hair and began to work it through her fingers like a majorette twirling a baton.

"A midnight blue Land Rover."

She broke the cigarette in half. "Darn it," she muttered, staring at the two pieces as if surprised at what she'd done. "That sounds like he made it up. Who drives a Land Rover in this part of the country except for tourists?"

"That's why it could be true."

"Did you tell the sheriff?"

"I was going to tell Deputy Lightfoot while I was here today."

She looked at me in disbelief.

"So I forgot. I remembered when it counted."

"Right."

"Let's go see Patti."

"What about the other neighbors?" She poised her pen. "What did they see?"

"Not much. Someone heard a trash can being knocked over. That's about it."

She threw out the broken cigarette and wiped off the loose bits of tobacco on her skirt with a tissue she pulled from her briefcase. We wandered through the bowels of the building until we made it to the visitor's entrance. A certain familiar freckle-faced deputy dared to scowl at me. As usual, he was sporting a sunburn. He was so fair that he never tanned—the curse of the redheads.

"What's she doing here?" Deputy Barnes asked Cruz.

"She's a visitor." She pointed a long-nailed finger toward the gigantic sign on the wall behind his head.

He grabbed his belt with both hands and opened his mouth to complain.

In a loud, confident voice, Cruz took the floor. "Since

"You make quite a case. Didn't I mention that I think she's innocent?"

I collapsed onto the window seat. "That's a relief."

"How could she possibly be guilty? The evidence is too pat, too perfect." She pulled out a cigarette and held it between her fingers without lighting it. "Don't worry. I'm just flirting with it."

"That's what I figured."

I thought about that Land Rover. "Did the sheriff and his deputies interview her neighbors? Didn't any of them see someone else that night?"

"The sheriff's office says they canvassed the neighborhood. They admit that a few of them weren't home. The ones that were claimed they didn't see or hear anything."

"Well, that's predicable. Hear no evil and see no evil."

"The evidence is circumstantial, which isn't good enough. Between you and me, they're desperate for a motive. Are you sure there's not some hidden reason Patti would have for killing Jeff?"

"I thought you said she wasn't guilty."

"I said I didn't *think* she was guilty. Regardless, if they unearth even the slightest motive, even if she admits to having *considered* killing him in her sleep in the middle of a bad dream, they're going to find her guilty."

I ignored the coward inside of me and plunged ahead. "I interviewed the neighbors."

"Uh-oh." Cruz lowered her briefcase to her lap.

I frowned. "I did it under the guise of writing an article for the *Bugle*."

"Okay," she said, her expression remained skeptical.

"I was the consummate professional each and every time."

With a sigh, she opened her case and removed a legal pad and pen. "Give me all the details. Don't leave anything out."

"One of the neighbors remembers seeing a vehicle driving away that night. One he'd never seen on the street before."

Chapter 16

I found Gretchen Cruz in the waiting area. She was talking to her cousin, who was once again typing her way through a leaning tower of paperwork.

"How's it going?" the cousin asked.

"That's what I'm here to find out."

Cruz picked up her briefcase and led us to a window seat at the end of a long hallway I had missed on my previous visits. "They charged her."

"I guess we knew this day was coming."

"She needs to see you. She's not doing well."

"Tell me another one."

Cruz didn't crack a smile.

Trying to shake off my emotions, I stood. "You won't meet anyone like Patti Perez. Come on. Who do you think runs the Feed and Supply now her parents are dead? Who do you think remodeled it and kept it from going under when the economy went belly-up? This may knock her down for a spell, but you wait. You'll see. She's going to rise again, stronger than ever."

"Look-a there, he's a two-timer," Heather crowed.

"Can he help it if he loves people?" I asked.

"How will you get him back?" Wilhelmina studied the two of them as Lenny bathed her daughter's face in wet kisses.

"I'll come get him." I handed Heather the leash. "Where will you be a couple of hours from now?"

"Oh," Heather sighed. "Can't I keep him longer?"

"I don't think the Cogburn Hotel takes pets. You'll have to sneak him in as it is."

"I don't care." She hugged him to her breast.

"Yip," Lenny said in agreement.

"Don't squeeze him too tightly. He may look tough, but under all that hair he's as delicate as a baby bird."

Wilhelmina slowly shook her head as if stunned at her predicament. "Thanks, I guess."

"No, it's me that's truly appreciative. I have to go see a friend. Kind of like an emergency. It would bring Lenny so down in the dumps if I took him home, only to stay by himself when he could be outside enjoying the fresh air." I glanced at the hotel. "He's going to love your room at the Cogburn Hotel—don't you worry." Oh, boy. The hole I was digging was getting deeper by the second.

"Okay. Fine," Wilhelmina said.

We exchanged information and I jogged back to Milagro and my Prius. Within minutes, I was on the highway and headed for the county jail.

down, put a finger in his water bowl, and pretended to sip from it. "Drink and then we'll go on a walk?"

"Yip." In spite of my poor acting skills, he drank.

On the street, the railroad depot and surrounding businesses basked in the setting sun's hot pink glow. The cool evening breeze flirted with my hair even as the heat soaked through my shirt. We walked and greeted those we knew around us. Across the street at the Cogburn Hotel, Clay and Britney exited the building and turned left. Even though I pretended to watch Lenny sniff a loose ball of tumbleweed that had ventured down Main Street, I noted in my peripheral vision that they headed toward Pecos Pete's.

As we started off again, Wilhelmina and Heather walked out of Elaine's Pies. "Fancy meeting you here," I said.

The mother and daughter shared a furtive look between them. "Guess so," Wilhelmina said with a ghost of a smile.

"This is Lenny."

"Yip," my Chi said in greeting. Heather knelt and cautiously patted his nose, as if touching a hot stove. Not too proud to grovel, Lenny rolled over and gave her his belly. "Sweet doggie," she whispered.

"She loves dogs." Wilhelmina looked on with bemusement. "Always begged Jeff to let her bring one on tour, but he refused."

Heather scratched Lenny's belly. "Said it wasn't fair to make everyone else put up with my dog."

Hmm. Jeff Clark was no fool.

Once Lenny and I started on one of our walks, I hated to stop. He loved greeting his neighbors and tending to the smells he discovered along Main Street with first one sniff and then another. He needed our walks together to keep his creative juices flowing. How could I turn around and head for home so soon? I couldn't disappoint him. Heather was petting him and cooing over him as if he were her long-lost child. "Would you like to walk him?"

"Oh yes," she said picking him up to kiss his nose.

He responded by licking her face.

I choked back a laugh. "In your dream?"

She broke eye contact with Lenny and slung him to her side so that their faces were nearly side by side. "He sang a beautiful country song."

"Yip," Lenny said.

Aunt Linda was doing an admirable job of keeping a straight face. "Was it 'Your Cheatin' Heart'?"

"No, but it filled me with sweet sadness and heartbreak."

This time I could hear Aunt Linda's impatience. "What did Jeff Clark tell you with this song?"

"He said the person who killed him was not sweet, but rotten with bitterness and envy. He asked me to draw."

"Draw? With pencils or crayons?"

"Ssh." I wanted to hear what she said. There was often a seed of truth in her dreams, somewhere, if you listened hard enough.

"No, that's not it." Senora Mari raised her chin as if she might challenge her daughter-in-law to a duel. "Poker. Draw a card, like poker."

"What do you think that means?"

"Yip," Lenny said.

"Yes, yes, he's right." Senora Mari handed him to me and immediately wiped her hands on her apron. She was wearing one we had given her for her last birthday that read *Stir it and die.*

"Come on, what did it mean?"

"Five-card draw." It was all we could drag out of her.

As I was changing out of my uniform, I received a text message from Patti's lawyer, Gretchen Cruz, asking me to meet her at the jail. Patti wanted to meet with both of us now that she could have visitors. Before I ran out the door, I called the jail to double-check on the actual times. A bored operator, doing an excellent impersonation of a recording, said ten to five o'clock. If I hurried, I could combine two errands yet again. Efficiency to the max.

I clipped on Lenny's leash. "Drink, Lenster." I knelt

to the vet for his shots. With gentle hands, she turned him around so that she was conversing with him face-to-face.

"Yip, yip, yip," Lenny said.

Senora Mari maneuvered the troublemaker from my aunt's arms so that she could hold him like a prized grand-baby. "He has been very brave. He has unmasked Jeff Clark's killer."

"Was that smart?" Aunt Linda asked me.

"Lenny's his own man. Why should he be the one guy who ever listened to me?"

Senora Mari usually went to great trouble to convince us of her great dislike of Lenny. In fact, she usually chased him out of the kitchen with her broom when he managed to make it downstairs from my apartment and into her domain. Now she dropped the act and began to rock him in her arms. In return, Lenny stared lovingly into her eyes, batted his eye-lashes, and gave her his heartwarming doggie smile.

"Last night I had a dream."

I shook my head and Aunt Linda struggled to contain a grin.

Senora Mari didn't see either one of us, or she chose to ignore us, because she kept her focus on Lenny. "This mu-sician guy with the cowboy hat . . ."

"Jeff," I said.

"Yes, Jeff Clark. Like the Clark Bar."

That caught me off guard. I might've seen one of the antiquated candy bars in my entire life. Was it popular in Mexico—a treat from her childhood? For me, it was some-thing found on the convenience store shelf when they were out of my ten favorites.

"So, what wisdom did he impart this time?" There was only one way to go when it came to Senora Mari's dreams: let her get on with it.

"He didn't say much."

"Yip," Lenny said.

"No, it's true." She spoke directly to Lenny. "He sang."

"I read it," I lifted my hands as if in surrender, "and I don't see the problem. It was just a lot innuendo and general silliness."

"If it goes viral, the fans that would have bought Jeff's record and any records that came from his surviving band aren't going to support their music. Look at what happened to that girl group from Texas. They never made it back after their comment went viral."

"That was a gecko of a different color."

"As they say in Texas, bullcrap."

He marched over to Senora Mari. "I bet you know where he I can find him."

My *abuela* drew up her to her full height, threw back her shoulders, and raised her fists like a prizefighter. "I do, but you're not going to touch a hair on his head. You understand?"

Price nearly fell on his head, backing over the step stool Senora Mari used to reach the back of the grill. "Once I press charges, the sheriff will rout him out. You tell that little coward what I said."

We followed Price as he huffed toward the exit and jerked the door open. Senora Mari and I shot a glance at each other. If he slammed the door against the wall, the decorative pane would break into pieces. Again.

As if he'd heard my thoughts, Price stepped outside, glared at me so hard I thought his eyes would fall out, and then slowly closed the door.

"What did our little friend write this time?" Senora Mari hurried to the window and peered through the blinds until the agent was out of sight.

"Lenny said Price was a deceitful, immoral jerk. He also accused him of protecting the band from prosecution in spite of the fact that one of them clearly killed Jeff Clark in order to lead the band to fame and glory."

Aunt Linda joined us from the back. "What did you say this time, you handsome troublemaker?" She held the Lenster in her arms, having just returned from taking him

"Right?" Anthony nodded sagely. "He must have said something terribly cruel."

"What did this older man look like?" I asked.

Anthony went on to describe Dustin Akers to a *T*.

The cowbell over the front door banged against the wall.

"Who left the front door open?" I walked into the restaurant and found Ken Price carrying some crumpled pieces of copy paper in his hand.

"What's going on?" Senora Mari hurried in from the office, holding her gold cross in her hand. "Are you trying to wake the dead?"

Which I thought was a strange comment, as no one was asleep. Come to think of it, her hair was lopsided, one side flat and the other puffed up like a bag of cotton balls. Price had obviously woken her from a short siesta in the office.

He shook the papers in his hand. "Who wrote this drivel?"

"What drivel?" An old-fashioned word, for a young professional like himself.

"Who is Lenny?" Price's skin had turned an angry purple.

Senora Mari and I stared at each other. "Why?" I asked.

"Because I'm going to sue him for libel."

My throat constricted and I tried unsuccessfully to swallow. "Libel for what?"

"You know who he is, or the hotel wouldn't have told me to ask you where to find him."

Senora Mari stepped up. "Lenny is cagey. No one knows where he lives. Some say behind the old cemetery, and some say he lives in an abandoned mine on the edge of town."

My *abuela* had seen too many old Westerns.

"How did you happen to read Lenny's blog?" I asked Price, smiling in spite of the tension in the room. One more reader was, after all, one more reader.

"Someone in the bar at the hotel was reading it." Price crumpled the pieces of paper into a ball. "They made a point of telling me I should check it out."

answered in his patient way. "He thinks it was that Dustin character."

"No, he doesn't." Lily hurried over to me. "Tell him, Josie."

"Lenny doesn't share his ideas with me. He doesn't want me to get in trouble for interfering with an investigation."

"It's not interfering to state your opinion."

"If I know Lenny," I said on my way to the cooler to check the vegetable prep, "he'll post again tomorrow with even more opinions."

"It's not funny, Miss Josie," Anthony said. "Patti Perez does not need to be in jail one more second. I wouldn't wish that on a dead man, even if his name was Jeff Clark."

"That's a strange thing to say. What do you know about Clark?"

"I know I saw him at Two Boots the night he was murdered."

"Were you working that night?" I asked.

"No, but I was dancing that night." Anthony grinned sheepishly. "Eddie let me in for free."

"Dancing with Vanessa." Lily sashayed from the refrigerators to the storage closet and back again.

"Hush." Anthony's brow furrowed like a bull preparing to charge a bullfighter's cape. "No one asked you."

"Vanessa?" She was the afternoon sales clerk at Wicks of the West candle store, next door.

Anthony knew all too well what Patti was going through. Three months earlier, Sheriff Wallace arrested him on circumstantial evidence for the death of Dixie Honeycutt, one of Broken Boot's premier jewelry artisans. With the help of Patti, I'd proven Anthony was innocent. "What happened?"

Anthony placed his Mexican-style bow tie around his neck. "Before the show, I saw Jeff Clark leaving the men's room. He was arguing with an older man. He grabbed the man by the shirt collar and started yelling in his face." The young waiter created a lovely bow and then tied a white apron around his waist. "The old man started to cry."

"Men don't cry," Lily said.

"Go." I smiled. "I'm sure." I waved him away. "You've got important things to do." I prayed he wouldn't see through my mock bravado.

He stood. "Can't keep the band waiting."

I must have reacted, for he raised a hand. "It's a private meeting."

"What do I look like—paparazzi?" A girl could hope for an invitation, but that didn't mean she was a stalker.

He gave me the once-over, his mouth twitching. "Definitely not." He started toward the hotel and then made a right, heading off in the direction of Two Boots.

If I called Sheriff Wallace and broke my word, I might alienate Price—but that didn't mean Lenny couldn't print something in his blog about the whole stinking mess.

By four o'clock that afternoon, Lenny had written a blistering account of Patti's arrest. He'd taken a bite out of the sheriff's department, Sheriff Wallace, Ken Price, and Jeff Clark's band. He had mentioned all the innuendo that Britney, Clay, Wilhelmina, and Heather had passed around like mono at the prom.

Right away folks started chiming in with their reactions. Most were in favor of Patti's release, but there was a crackpot or two who thought she was guilty.

I headed downstairs to check on the dinner prep.

Carlos was cleaning the griddle with a wide metal spatula. "Patti might have done it. You tell Lenny that Perez is one tough chick, like Michelle Rodriguez in *Avatar*."

"Tell him yourself!" I had no clue our cook liked to read, let alone Lenny's blog.

"I did, but he hasn't commented on my comment."

"I'll make sure he gets right on it. Where is everyone?"

The back door opened, and Anthony and Lily came in. "You don't even know who these people are," Lily argued. "What makes you think you can tell if they're lying or not."

"I can tell in the way Lenny described them," Anthony

ing that I was sure sales of "Sweet Thing" would skyrocket without his help now that Jeff's murder had hit the national newswire.

"Why won't you call Wallace and tell him what you just told me? Patti's innocent. You know it, but you won't do anything about it."

"I'll make the call," he checked his phone, "though I don't think he'll listen to anything I have to say."

"But will you try?"

He straightened his tie. "I said I would."

"Thank you."

"Uh," he kicked the dirt with his leather shoe. "I'll tell the Sheriff in a day or two."

"What?"

"The song's almost at the top of the charts now. If word gets out that Dustin killed Jeff . . ."

"What about your word is your word?" I studied his expression, trying to comprehend whether or not he had lied from the first. "Isn't any publicity good?

"One day," he said, taking my hand. He had a much better manicure than I did. "That's all I ask."

"Forget it." I pulled away. "How would you like to be in jail with prostitutes and heroin addicts?"

"You get those here?"

"We aren't completely bereft of hardened criminals." A plan was brewing in my brain. "Okay." I nodded. "I won't tell Sheriff Wallace until tomorrow that Dustin had a good motive for killing Clark."

"What's the catch?"

"You mean, what'll it cost you?" This guy was the absolute limit. Slimier than a puddle of kitchen grease and smellier than the slime in the bottom of the ice machine at the Gas & Guzzle. I had a plan that would cook his goose six ways from Sunday. "It's free. I don't want to benefit in any way from Jeff's death."

Relief shone from his face like the sun emerging from a bank of clouds. "Well, if you're sure—"

"I couldn't very well say that in front of those two, could I?"

"You shouldn't say that. That could ruin his reputation."

"Why not? You won't print any of your wild theories in that local rag of yours. You can't afford to lose your job and become a financial burden on your family."

"It's called a newspaper last time I checked." It was a weak comeback, but I refused to let him intimidate me or get the last word.

"What about Clay? Couldn't he have done it? And what about Wilhelmina? You have to admit, she's overprotective when it comes to her daughter."

"Like I said. If it *is* a member of the band, then it has to be Dustin. He did time for assault and battery back in his youth." Smiling smugly, he added. "He carries a grudge for all to see."

I wanted to argue, but I was enjoying this chatty Ken Price. The article from the AP journalist had appeared on the Internet yesterday. Ken had made no actual accusations. And wasn't it interesting that he still managed to imply that a local had killed Clark, not one of his band members? If the goober had done his homework, he would've discovered that some of them were born and raised in Big Bend County.

"What's with you giving my story to that AP reporter?"

He stared. "You're serious. It was an über-sensitive matter that required delicate handling."

"And you didn't think I could give it the care it deserved?"

"I think your readership is about . . . what? Twenty thousand? Five?"

"I have contacts in Austin. They would've found a national audience for my piece."

"I couldn't take that chance. Jeff may have died in near obscurity, but he won't stay there. Not as long as I have the power to promote his music all the way to the top of the Billboard country music chart."

I bit my tongue and barely managed to refrain from say-

of information out of Wilhelmina and her daughter. I couldn't blame them. It wasn't their fault they needed to stay on his good side. Or file for unemployment.

"How long did the sheriff say the band has to stay around? Especially if they have the killer, as you say," I asked.

"Sheriff Wallace wants them to stick around a couple of days—that's true. No problemo. I'll use that time to audition new lead singers."

"Aren't the crowds coming to see the Jeff Clark Band? And wouldn't that be strange if no Jeff turned up to their concerts?" I'm good at making a nuisance of myself.

"We have customers who love the sound of the band. Tickets that have been purchased well in advance for the rest of the tour."

"What are you going to do? Have a sing-off?" I couldn't help it. I'd asked that question to watch his reaction.

"I want to audition," Heather said, opening her eyes wide.

"Not interested." He looked back and forth between the mother and daughter. His countenance took on a conciliatory shade. "Work on your songs and your guitar playing. I'll give you an audition next time."

She beamed at her mother. "Told you."

"Thanks, Ken," Wilhelmina said, throwing her arm around her daughter.

Heather shot to her feet. "Let's go, Mom. I want to practice."

"Sure thing, sug." They tossed their trash, waved good-bye, and hurried out the door. Wilhelmina climbed behind the wheel of the tour bus and drove away, without ripping the siding off the building or knocking down the nearest telephone pole. If you ask me, that was mighty impressive.

"You aren't fooling me with that butter-wouldn't-melt-in-your-mouth routine."

I counted to ten in my head and turned slowly. "What?"

"You're not going to find a single band member who would have killed Jeff except Dustin."

"But you said—"

"True," Heather said.

Price had waited at the counter for his food. Now he headed our way. He drew back a chair and said, "Mind if I join in?" His phone rang again.

I prayed he'd leave us to our conversation. Instead he checked the screen and placed his phone in his shirt pocket. "Ladies, don't stop gossiping on my account."

I licked my lips, my mouth as dry as the banks of the Rio Grande in August. I frowned, hoping to convey that I had no earthly idea what he was talking about.

"You must be Josie Callahan." He extended his hand.

"Yes, sir, Mr. Price. That's me." His palm was sweaty, but I didn't want to insult him by pulling my hand sanitizer out of my bag.

His eyes narrowed as he studied my face. "Wilhelmina's right," he said after a moment.

"I am?"

"She wouldn't have killed Jeff for flirting with her daughter, who's no longer underage, by the way, no matter what story you've concocted in that crazy brain of yours."

I opened my mouth to argue.

"You're desperate to find anyone other than the killer already incarcerated in the county jail, aren't you?" He turned to the mother-and-daughter pair. "Why do you think that is?"

"We're good friends," I interrupted. "That's true."

He snorted, which obliterated his smooth persona. "From everything I heard, you and Patti Perez are thicker than thieves."

Ignoring his tired cliché, I pointed at him. "You understand the guys better than anyone. Do you think one of the band members killed Jeff?"

His expression froze, and then he snorted again. "You need to get out of this town more often. Women are the ones who go crazy over Jeff—crazy enough to want to marry the guy and murder him at the same time."

After Ken's pronouncement, I could get only a smidge

most up my nose. "And don't you forget it!" Wilhelmina took a big swig of her tea and a bite of her brisket sandwich.

Ken Price turned and stared. With a bemused shake of his head, he made his way to the counter, placed his order, and paid, all the while keeping his phone glued to his ear.

Heather bit her bottom lip. "Oh, Jeff was real nice to me. We used to talk about his daughter, Chrissy. She's six."

"Some jerks started spreading rumors that Jeff was coming on to Heather. If you ask me, they were hoping to get him fired from the tour."

"Why would they do that?" Heather asked, her cheeks bright red. "Jeff's a sweetheart." Her hand flew up to her mouth. "I mean, he was . . ."

My pulse quickened. This was exactly what I needed. "Who'd want to get Jeff fired?"

The two women looked at each other, but remained quiet. On cue, they both took a bite of their brisket sandwiches.

I leaned forward. "It's okay. I know how much Dustin wanted Jeff out of the picture." I had to tread carefully. If I offended them, they might give me the boot. "But he sure is a nice guy. What do you think? Could he have done it?" During our walk together, he'd been charming—except at the end. Had I only imagined the dangerous rage in his eyes? Perhaps a trick of the light on the dark street had transformed everyday frustration into a malevolent glint.

Wilhelmina glanced over her shoulder at Price and then whispered, "Dustin wouldn't hurt a fly. He's like the father Heather never had."

Drenching a fry in ketchup, the girl nodded. "He's cool. He's teaching me how to write songs."

"But he told me that he should've had Jeff's position." My argument was weak, even to my own ears.

"I can't believe he'd tell you that. He must have trusted you." She gave me a reproachful look. "He shared that with you because he liked you. He doesn't confide in just anybody."

"That's a heavy load of disappointment for one man to bear."

accused the wrong person, a good friend of mine. And she didn't do it."

They exchanged glances. "How do you know?"

"I've known her since we were in seventh grade together. I've known her since she bought her first bra and choked on her first cigarette."

I wasn't sure what to do, so I did the unthinkable: I told a half lie. "I didn't want to tell you this," I said to Wilhelmina, "but I heard a rumor that you killed him because of something he did to your daughter."

An avalanche of guilt tumbled to the bottom of my stomach.

Wilhelmina's eyes narrowed, her face flushed, and I thought for a few seconds she was going to come across the table and throttle me. "Tell me who said something about Heather, and I'll gouge their eyes out of their head." Like mother, like daughter.

Me and my chair scooted backwards just in case. "Uh, I promised not to repeat their name."

Heather, on the other hand, merely smiled as if remembering a pleasant occasion.

I was an idiot for lying—I almost always got caught. And I was a stupid jerk for getting Wilhelmina all worked up. "I'm sorry. I can't tell you exactly what they meant, as they didn't go into details, but I probably misunderstood the whole thing."

"That's all behind us. A big misunderstanding. Jeff apologized." She reached for her daughter's hand and gripped her fingers. I was guessing that if Jeff had a reputation for being a ladies' man, a girl like Heather would have had a bit of a crush on him—even if he was several years older.

"You don't have to give me details." I gave Heather an apologetic smile.

"You'd think we had wild sex in a pasture under a full moon." She laughed.

I waited, but I wanted to scream, *Well, did you?*

"Which they *didn't* do." Wilhelmina stuck her finger al-

"He's on guard duty right now, keeping our apartment safe from geckos."

She giggled. "And I bet he's good at catching 'em, isn't he?" With a smile, she picked up their baskets and made her way back to their table. Gone was the jealous schoolgirl.

I started to follow, but my stomach overruled. I spun on my heel. "I'll take a number 6, the turkey, no fries. Add beans, extra pickles, onions, and jalapeños."

Bubba nodded his approval. "Coming right up."

Price had parked himself at a table in the corner and was deep in conversation, muttering agreement to whatever the caller was saying. If he was waiting for table service, he was out of luck.

Dang. What was he doing here? I needed to talk to the mother-and-daughter pair without him overhearing or stifling their gossip with his presence.

"Mind if I join you?" I smiled.

"Come on," Wilhelmina said with a wave. "Who would have thought we'd still be stuck in this," she wrinkled her nose, "town."

"You can say it. Won't hurt my feelings none." I pulled up a chair. "*Rinky-dink* describes it best."

"It's awfully charming." Heather smiled and salted her fries.

"I'll get right to the point." I hesitated. Technically, I didn't know for a fact that these two hadn't killed Clark, but I had serious doubts. I would have to be cagey, which wasn't something I'd excelled at previously. "Jeff Clark was murdered." I leaned in close.

"And?" Wilhelmina glared at me as if I'd done it myself.

"That's old news," Heather muttered.

I glanced over my shoulder at Price. Fortunately, he had turned his back to the room. "Jeff had enemies. Why do you think that was?"

"Are you going to print what we say in the paper?"

"Of course she is, Mom. What do you think?"

"No." I met the daughter's eye. "I'm here because they've

me. I discovered with some dismay that it was Ken Price. He gave me a nod and held open the door for us both.

"Give her two weeks to make up her mind. She dyes it red and gets a perm or she finds another agent." He lifted one corner of his mouth at my surprised expression, and pointed to his Bluetooth-enabled earpiece.

Was the brilliantly crafty Price determined to make country music fans forget about the iconic older singer by supplanting her with his own version? Had Reba McEntire retired from country music?

I avoided making more than brief eye contact. His gaze made me cringe, as if an iguana had licked my skin. Believe me when I say I know what that feels like. Uncle Eddie's iguana, named Eric, lived to the ripe old age of fifteen before drying up into a dusty doorstop.

"Right." Ken Price continued as if everyone in the place was on the conference call with him.

"Josie, you looking good." Bubba's rich, melodious voice bore only a sweet hint of flirtation. Taller and darker than any other man in town, he'd escaped a terrifying childhood in Chad and found a new life with Jerrie and Bill McAllen in Broken Boot.

"Not half as good as you, my friend."

I found the costumer and her daughter in the corner next to a giant metallic sign that read, PIG'S FEET, JOWLS, AND EARS, ONLY TWO CENTS ON THURSDAYS. They'd acquired two 32-ounce red plastic tumblers, along with one of those long metal spikes with the number 27 written on a playing card clipped to the top.

I gave Bubba a look. "Don't you think you could remember who ordered what without giving them the number?"

He slammed his cleaver into a beef brisket. "That's the way we do it. Don't go getting into my business."

Assembling the meat into two red plastic baskets lined with wax paper, along with slaw, sauce, and French fries, he called out, "Number 27!"

"Hey!" Heather called upon seeing me. "Where's Lenny?"

Chapter 15

It was late Monday morning. I was bound and somewhat determined to find someone else, another band member perhaps, who would confirm or deny that Dustin Akers had reason to harm Jeff Clark.

Britney and Clay had been completely too eager to put the blame on the forty-year-old guitar player and songwriter. I had no proof, but I trusted the two lovebirds about as much as I trusted a coyote guarding a henhouse.

I'd run by Two Boots, only to be told by Vince that the tour bus and its passengers, namely Wilhelmina and her daughter, Heather, had left to scout out the best barbeque joint in the county. Without a second thought, I headed over to Bubba's.

I found the tour bus, complete with its airbrushed painting of the desert sky, stars, cacti, and a comet whose tail spelled out *The Jeff Clark Band*, taking up the empty public lot across the street. The patio was deserted, and there was no sign of activity.

As I approached the front door, someone came up behind

With relief, I opened the F150's passenger door, and Lenny catapulted into my arms. "Hey, Lenster."

"Yip, yip, yip," he chided.

"Ssh. I know," I murmured, rubbing behind his ears. "The strange man is gone. Let's go home."

"You all right, Josefina?" Uncle Eddie asked.

I slid across the seat and slammed the door. "Things are looking up."

Beneath Dustin Akers's friendly exterior hid an angry man. Was that man capable of killing Jeff Clark? One thing was clear: I had my first suspect.

and turned around. "Want to get a drink?" he asked with a grin like a little boy asking for candy before suppertime.

"No, thanks. Maybe some other time."

"I'll take you up on that. Now I've got your number, there's no getting shed of me."

His words should've sounded threatening, but his jovial delivery made me laugh. We stopped in front of the Cogburn Hotel. "I don't know how much longer I'll be in town," he said in a singsong tone.

I considered our conversation. From what he said, he had more than one motive for killing Jeff Clark. On the other hand, his words sounded genuine. Was he a superb actor or just a man fallen on hard times, like me? I hedged my bets. "Call me the day after tomorrow if you're still around?"

"If that's what you want." He smiled and shook his head.

With a deep rumble, a familiar F150 with a Milagro decal drove around the corner and squealed to a stop. "Well, good night."

He leaned in.

I backed away and pointed to the truck. "Remember my uncle? And that bit about a dog? If I'm not mistaken, he's got Lenny in there right now."

He forced a sound that resembled a laugh. "Day after tomorrow then."

Something in the tone of his voice turned my head. In his eyes, a fury made my bones grow cold. Then he blinked and once again his eyes shone with warmth and goodwill.

He gave me a smile, waved at Uncle Eddie, and then pushed his way through the hotel's revolving door.

Up until those last few moments, I'd subconsciously crossed his name off my list of potential suspects. Now chill bumps lifted the hair on my arms. Was he as harmless as he seemed? Or was that flash of cruelty his true nature?

I forced my admiration for him to the side. I'd find out what he was all about, and without placing myself in harm's way.

He and I wrote songs together that we wouldn't have written apart."

"Did you write 'Sweet Thing' together?"

"That one was written by Jeff and Clay."

"Won't Ken give you the band now that Jeff's out of the way?" I was leading the witness, letting out the rope.

"Not likely," He shook his head, "but if he ignores me again, I'm walking. Nashville's full of decent agents."

"Speaking of walking . . ."

We crossed the street and spent a few minutes staring in the window of Barnum and Hailey's, an emporium filled with handmade toys, magic tricks, novelty items—not to mention college fan gear and university apparel. The curiosity shop held sweet memories for me. When I'd first arrived in Broken Boot to live with Uncle Eddie and Aunt Linda, Mr. Hailey had presented me with a flea circus. The cigar box and my mother's copy of *Where the Wild Things Are* still sat on my nightstand.

"What's a young, pretty gal like you doing unattached?"

I groaned. "You've got to work on that line."

"Old school?"

"Older than dirt."

He narrowed his eyes and studied my face. "I'm still curious."

"I'm recovering from a bad breakup. What about you?"

"You're catching me at the right time."

"Divorced?"

"Twice."

"Oh."

"Kick me to the curb. I can take it."

"That's sad."

"Being with a musician sounds exciting until I'm on the road five weeks out of seven. Not many women can take it."

I hadn't been able to handle my ex playing venues every week around Austin, forget being on tour.

We continued down to the last corner with streetlamps

Leaning back, he turned to stare at the shops on the other side of the street. "Someone told him I wanted Jeff's job."

"Lead singer?"

"Star." He removed his cowboy hat and straightened the brim with his fingers.

I waited.

"I've been in this business twenty years. I've spent ten long years on a label with only one hit to show for it."

"That's one more than most folks will ever have."

He didn't appear to hear me. "When I met Ken Price, he was excited to hear my new stuff. Promised me a tour and a band and an album."

"Oh no."

"You guessed it. Shows you how stupid I was. Price said all that was required of me was to tour with Jeff and use my downtime to polish my songs, maybe even help Jeff write some new ones while I was at it."

Under the pale illumination of the streetlight, I could see his Adam's apple bob up and down as he struggled to remain calm. "Now I'm under a contract I can't break."

"How long had you been touring with Jeff?"

He sighed. "Three years. Stupid, right?"

"No." Why didn't it surprise me that Ken Price was a scoundrel? I contemplated the alternative. Perhaps Dustin wasn't a great songwriter or potential star.

"Every year, Price had the perfect excuse: the market wasn't right, the songs weren't ready, I'd make more money touring with Jeff."

"That's awful."

"What's sick is that I let him manipulate me. Each time I vowed to leave, I'd back down. He was an expert at infusing his voice with just that hint of a threat that he was going to let me go."

That sounded like a recipe for jealousy, if not murder. "Did you and Jeff hate each other?"

"It was hard to get past his talent. The man could sing.

We stopped again in front of the hotel to gaze into a window that held a display of antique pistols and rifles against a collection of pioneer furniture.

"Fishing for a compliment?"

I laughed. "Maybe." I walked down to look in the next window on the other side of the grand entrance. This one was a display made to look like a scene from an old television Western, with figures dressed as bartenders, saloon girls, and cowboys. "Aunt Linda was my mother's sister. We're related to the Martinez family by marriage, not blood."

"Miss Kitty means business." He pointed to the female figure that wore a red silk dress with white pantaloons peeking out from underneath. The mannequin pointed a pistol at a shifty-looking cowboy, who held his hands high.

"Huh, Miss Kitty could give me a lesson or two." *Maybe.* I still wasn't sure I wanted to learn how to handle firearms. I continued down the sidewalk. "You must be going stir-crazy now the sheriff's refused to let you leave."

"Nah. It's a nice break."

I stopped and stared.

His mouth twisted. "Things are a bit slow around here. The folks are friendly. Makes it bearable."

Past the hotel was an antique-looking streetlamp and bench. I led us to it and sat down. Time to dig for the dirt.

"Sheriff Wallace can come on a bit strong."

"You got that right. Acts like somebody pis—" His eyes widened. "Uh, like somebody spit in his corn flakes." His jaw clenched. "I apologize. That was rude."

I waved it off. "It's okay. I won't sic my dog on you for something so piddly. Senora Mari might, but I'd protect you."

He wiped the back of his hand across his brow in mock relief. "Whew."

"I don't know why Wallace would give you a hard time. What was his beef?" I held my breath as I waited to see if he'd take the bait.

I placed a hand on her arm and gently pulled her away. "He's got it, *Abuela*."

She pointed a finger and shook it at him. "Don't forget what I said."

Uncle Eddie peered out Milagro's front door and glared at Dustin Akers as if he had a price on his head. Instead of adding a threat of his own, he engaged the country musician in a stare-down before finally giving him a curt nod. He opened the door wide enough for his mother to pass through, and then closed the door and locked it, staring at the two of us the whole time.

"They're not going to stop until we cross the street at the corner, and maybe not even then." I started toward the Cogburn Hotel.

"Tough crowd," he murmured, catching up with me in three strides.

"Family. Can't live with them; can't exchange them for puppies."

His laugh invited me to join in, which I did. "I was surprised to hear from you."

I glanced in the window of Wicks of the West, the candle shop that stood next to our restaurant. I removed the elastic band from the end of my hair and ran my fingers through my braid until my hair spread over my shoulders.

"I don't get it."

I could see him standing behind me in the reflection from the plate-glass window. "What? Why don't I look like the rest of my family?"

"No. Why don't you wear your hair down more often?" From someone else, that line would have been cheesy. His voice was matter-of-fact and, more importantly, it didn't get on my nerves.

I chuckled and started walking again. "Probably because I don't have great hair like the rest of them." Uncle Eddie and his mother both had thick, gorgeous hair. My hair resembled Aunt Linda's, but where hers was all silky waves, mine was straight and lackluster.

Oh, heck. I hated this new and inferior version of myself, which reared its cowardly head after my breakup with my stupid-idiot ex-fiancé.

Fifteen minutes later, I met him outside Milagro, Senora Mari by my side.

"Howdy," he said, and leaned in for a brief hug.

My *abuela* stepped between us. "Who are you?"

His eyebrows rose into his hat.

"This is Uncle Eddie's mother, Senora Marisol Martinez."

With a nod and a polite smile, he stuck out his hand. "Nice to meet you, ma'am."

She crossed her arms and gave him the once-over, ignoring his outstretched hand.

Dustin took it in stride, looking from one to the other of us as if trying to figure out the nature of our relationship. I shot a glance at her, but I couldn't decipher her mood. No, she could take the lead.

"Josie is family. She is a good girl."

He removed his hat and met her gaze. "She'll come to no harm, ma'am. We're going to take a stroll down Main Street in front of God and everybody."

Senora Mari peered up and down the street. Only a handful of folks were out and about. The local business owners had rolled up the sidewalks, but the antique-style streetlamps glowed.

"You feel safe with this man?"

Too bad the lights did little to illuminate the dark alleyways between the buildings. I took the bit between my teeth. "Absolutely."

He smiled and placed his hat carefully on his head. "Thank you, ma'am."

Senora Mari stepped up close to him, tilted back her head, and narrowed her eyes to give him her most ferocious stare. "You treat her right, or I'll sic her dog on you. He'll tear a strip out of your hide so wide, you'll think you've been skinned alive."

There was a long silence.

It took Britney only seconds to find his number and rattle it off. With a cat-that-drank-the-cream smile, she allowed her man to escort her out the door and down the sidewalk toward the Cogburn Hotel.

While counting out my tips and wiping down the tables and chairs, I pondered how to best meet without placing myself in a compromising position.

At first I'd considered a late lunch tomorrow at Elaine's, but I immediately scratched that plan. I'd recognized on my last visit, albeit a bit too late, that I wasn't ready to meet Suellen face-to-face. Even though it was not my fault her mother, Elaine Burnett, turned out to be a murderess—and I certainly didn't think Elaine's oldest daughter had anything to do with her mother's kind of crazy—it was way too much too soon.

So if not Elaine's, we could meet at Black Creek Bagel or simply take a walk down Main Street, as he suggested. Somewhere we could be outside and still be private would work best. I didn't want him to worry about being overheard if the conversation should happen to include Jeff Clark.

At the last minute, I chickened out and sent him a text.

Usually I hemmed and hawed over every minute decision pertaining to giving a man a bit of my time, unless he was one hundred percent in the friend zone, like Coach Ryan, Deputy Lightfoot, and my uncle Eddie. Only this time, I didn't prevaricate. I thought only of his smile and a walk on a beautiful night. And, yes, curiosity had me by the tail. Call me single-minded, but I was going to relish picking this guy's brain, even as we soaked up a bit of moonlight. If I could give Lightfoot something substantial the sheriff's office didn't already have, perhaps—just perhaps—he'd give me a crumb of information in return.

He responded immediately. Can we meet tonight?

My first thought was to refuse. Though he appeared to be the perfect gentleman, polite and handsome in an older-man way, what did a guy his age think was going on when a woman texted him at nine o'clock at night?

Chapter 14

As the two carnivorous lovebirds started for the door, I realized I had no idea how to reach Dustin to plan our rendezvous.

"Thanks." Britney's voice bounced on the walls of the now-empty restaurant, high and loud.

"Excuse me," I said, meeting them at the door. "Dustin Akers asked me to call him, but I've lost his number."

The two looked at each other with knowing glances. "He's a real sweet talker, ain't he?" Britney winked again.

"Is there something in your eye?" I asked in a sympathetic tone.

She glared. "No."

I deflected her anger with a smile. "He was awful nice." I am not a hick, but it helps to know how to talk like one. It distracts folks from the truth, makes them think you're not too clever.

She chortled behind her childlike hands. "He must really have taken a shine to you if he forgot to get your number." She elbowed Clay. "Right, hon?"

Clay unwrapped a smile. "No doubt."

I pulled up a photo on my phone.

He squinted his eyes in thought as he studied the image. "I might have. Some weird metallic color. Purple? Midnight blue?"

"Yes." I wanted to pump my fist. "Where did you see it?"

"I'm not sure." He glanced first at me, then Senora Mari, and then back again. "There were tons of cars and trucks parked at Two Boots that night." He handed back my phone. "Why?"

"Someone was in Patti's neighborhood that night in a blue Land Rover. And it wasn't someone who lives on that street."

His phone buzzed. He answered with a quick text.

"Anyone I know?"

"What?" he asked, as if he had no idea what I was saying. Playing dumb was Ryan-speak for *I'm never going to tell you, so quit asking.*

"Jayda?"

"What?"

"I knew it." Another beauty. And why not?

"Thanks so much, Senora Mari," Ryan said, taking the to-go bag in one hand as he gave her a quick one-armed hug with the other.

"*Buenas noches*, Ryan. You come back soon."

He headed for the exit and then turned on a dime. "Where's Eddie?"

"What is it with you? If it's not food, it's football."

Ryan ignored me. "Where's your uncle hiding?"

"He was in the office the last time I checked."

Ryan leaned close and my face flushed. At the last second, he rubbed the top of my head with his knuckles. "See you later."

"You wish," I called after him, as he loped toward the office. I rubbed my head and any crazy, romantic notions out of my brain until the feel of his hand in my hair disappeared.

Though I'd relegated Ryan to the friend zone years earlier, he was like double-fudge Blue Bell with chocolate sauce, real whipped cream, and toffee sprinkles. Deliciously tempting.

But always in the back of my mind, like liver pâté that leaves a nasty taste in your mouth that never quite goes away, was the hurt and mortification I experienced when Brooks had left me at the altar on his way to the Great Barrier Reef nine months earlier.

"What about the night of Jeff's concert? Did you see anything out of the ordinary, or were you preoccupied?"

He gave me a wicked grin. "Are you asking for your article or because you want to know who I was out with?"

"Come here," I said, gesturing for him to move closer to the order-up window. "I want to punch some sense into you." Sometimes I remembered too clearly our days as college sweethearts. He, on the other hand, did not have any trouble putting the past behind him.

With a *"tsk, tsk"* in my direction, Senora Mari bagged his to-go containers. "Tell her," she said with a flick of her wrist, "that she will catch a man when she learns how to cook."

A gleam in his eye, he opened his mouth.

"Don't. You. Dare," I said. "I'm asking because Patti's in jail."

Immediately, he was all business. "Dang it." His shoulders tensed. "Of course." He walked over to where I stood, reached through the window, and gave my hand a squeeze. "I'm an idiot." For a few seconds, he screwed up his face as he tried to remember the events of that night. "I don't remember seeing anything strange, but it's hard to say. There were a lot of folks in town for the concert that night from out of town."

"What about a Land Rover? Did you see one of those that night?"

"A what?"

I gestured toward Britney. "Was she playing too?"

"Nah. She was railroading and playing games on her phone."

I cocked my head.

"Railroading? Observing?"

"Gotcha. Could he play?"

Ryan frowned. "Who cares? I left early."

"Was he a serious player?"

"Took the whole thing way too seriously." Ryan shook his head and grabbed a Dr Pepper from the cooler. "Told me to shut my piehole."

"Were you telling more of your lame jokes?"

Ryan raised his can to my face and lifted the tab. "Your mother's lame."

"Boys." I rolled my eyes and walked away. After a quick check on Britney and Clay, I returned to fetch them another round.

I found Ryan in the kitchen, wrangling some tamales from Senora Mari. "Want to make this peach-lime surprise for me?"

"Josie Callahan," Senora Mari chided. "Take care of your own customers. Ryan is busy telling me all about Jeff Clark's concert on Thursday night—which you have not cared enough to do." She was filling an aluminum to-go container with pork tamales, rice, and beans.

Leaning into the kitchen window, I asked, "Did you see anything strange the night of the murder?"

"What?" He paused to drain his Dr Pepper can. "Patti being hauled onstage by that dude like a sack of potatoes wasn't strange enough?" With no inhibitions, he lifted the cover off a tray of beef enchiladas.

"You like these?" My *abuela* found another container, filled it with beef enchiladas, followed up with savory ranchero sauce, and sprinkled them with cheese.

"*Gracias*, senora." Ryan smiled that slow, cute grin of his. To my delight, her stern countenance transformed as she rewarded him with a genuinely fetching smile.

nuts and refilled the bowls on the bar before tossing a handful into his mouth.

"What are the experts saying?"

"Seven and five."

"Not bad."

Before I knew it, he had a playful arm bent around my neck. "Not bad?" He taunted, once again turning into a ten-year-old. "Not bad?"

I laughed in spite of myself and ducked out from under his arm. "Okay, okay. At least that's a winning season."

He opened the door to the storage closet and looked around. "Where's the Lenster?" On occasion, I hid my long-haired friend in the storage closet so he wouldn't bark at being abandoned in my apartment upstairs.

"Aunt Linda took him home with her. Something about him being the only grandkid she's ever going to have."

I drew Ryan's attention to the lovebirds in the restaurant.

"Do you know those two?"

"I've seen them around, mostly at Pete's."

"Since when do you go out during football season?" Never. If he'd made time for a drink at Pecos Pete's, then he hadn't done so on his own—or his name wasn't Ryan Nathaniel Prescott Jr.

"All work and no play . . ." He wiped his mouth and tossed the bottle into the empties.

"What night was that?"

"Thursday. Why?" His eyes widened. "Tell me you're not investigating again."

"Heck, no." Energetically, I began to wipe the spotless bar. "I'm working on an article for the *Bugle*. What else?"

"Huh." He lifted my chin, forcing me to meet his eyes. "Yeah, right. And I'm going to run an Iron Man in the spring."

I pulled away. "So? What were they doing at Pete's?"

"Playing poker in the back room."

"Which means you were playing as well."

"Yes, Mom, but only for a round. Stakes jumped too high for this poor cowpoke."

I spun on my heel in surprise. When Coach Ryan Prescott arrived, the weight of the world seemed to lift off my shoulders a smidge. He was his usual tall and handsome self, if a little gritty from the heat. A glance at the UT clock told me he was stopping by for his post-practice tamales.

"How's the team shaping up?"

"I could tell you, but then I'd have to kidnap your dog." With a laugh, he walked around the bar and helped himself to a Shiner longneck from the cooler. As our special-events bartender, he made himself at home—as well he should. He and I dated in college, and though we'd both followed our separate paths to broken hearts, his had mended with the help of more than a few local beauties.

I scurried after him and swatted his West Texas cap into the sink. "Don't you even joke about hurting Lenny."

"Hey, Mike Tyson, watch that right!" He retrieved his cap from the damp basin and shook it at me for good measure before jamming it on his head.

"That is the worst case of hat hair . . . ever." I laughed. And then: "How could you say that after what happened last time?"

"Aw, heck," he groaned. "I forgot." He placed a gentle arm around my shoulders. "I'm so sorry," he said in a baby voice. "Did the little-bitty doggie get an unexpected haircut from a wicked lady?"

I pulled away and swatted him again. "She could've killed him, Ryan." Elaine Burnett had shaved Lenny and written a threatening message on his side before my doggie sidekick had helped me bring her to justice.

"Jos, Lenny and I are old friends. You know I wouldn't harm a hair on his head." After another laugh at the irritated look on my face, he took a swig from his longneck.

I sighed. "What you're not saying is that you hope to God you've got a good team, but you wouldn't stake your life on it."

"That about sums it up." He found the can of assorted

She frowned.

"Tomatillo sauce coming up."

"You are quite the actress too," Senora Mari whispered as I passed her on my way to the kitchen.

When I returned with the *salsa verde*, their heads were close together. As I set the bowl down, she popped upright like a jill-in-the-box. "You may not have realized that Clay and Jeff were old friends, but we want to set the record straight. Do you know who would've killed to have Jeff's position in the band? Dustin Akers. Ken promised him he would be lead singer when the band was first formed a couple of years ago," she pulled down the corners of her mouth in an exaggerated frown, "but Ken never gave it to him. He gave it to Jeff and never looked back." She turned to Clay, as if waiting for him to continue the performance.

"I don't envy Dustin," he said, staring down into his beer. "He's had to swallow his pride on more than one occasion." They both looked at me as if waiting for my reaction.

I swallowed. Did they know I was a reporter with the *Bugle*? Had they heard that Dustin had asked me out? Or was this routine merely their way of steering me away from their true feelings about Jeff and the band?

"Is Ken going to offer Dustin a deal as well?"

"He's been pushing for one." She patted Clay's arm. "As if we don't know what he does behind our backs."

My neck started to sweat. "Can I get you both a refill?"

"Thank you, sweetie." She handed me both glasses with a saccharine smile.

I retreated to the bar, thinking about Dustin Akers and how'd he asked me to show him around town. No warning bells had pealed in my head as I accepted. For all I knew, he was exactly what he appeared to be—a friendly, warm-hearted, dignified soul. What should I do? I sighed. If what these two yahoos said had even an inkling of truth to it, I needed to accept his offer, pronto.

"Howdy, Josie."

tickets hanging on the line as they ate the chips and salsa before them, kissed briefly, and whispered together in a more serious vein.

Did Britney always travel with the group? What kind of life was that? How did Ken Price feel about paying her way?

"She's too cute." Senora Mari said, slipping up beside me.

I glanced down and found my *abuela* studying Britney like a bobcat studying a field mouse.

"Can you be too cute?"

"Look at her," she whispered. "She's acting like she's in love."

Was Britney merely pretending to be the dutiful girl-friend? Was there perhaps a bit of manipulation in the hand she placed on his arm or leg? She would turn her face to stare into his eyes when she spoke to him, and always with a little smile, an extra twinkle in her eye. Maybe she just loved the guy. People still fell in love and found their happily-ever-after. Or so they claimed.

"How is everything?" Clay had eaten half of his fish while Britney had scraped the pecans and sauce from hers, until it looked like a chicken breast on a diet.

"It's great, but do you have some of that green sauce?" A line formed between her eyes, as if the answer would determine the outcome of the next Super Bowl.

"Tomatillo?"

She tilted her head to one side. "Sure."

I turned to Clay. "I heard the band the other night. You were awesome. Are you thinking of forming your own band now that Jeff's dead?"

"He's going to be a superstar. Ken's working on a recording deal for him as we speak."

"I heard about that Jeff," I ventured. "Were you about to leave the band? I heard he could be a real tool. Not to speak ill of the dead or anything."

"You ask a lot of nosy questions."

"Gee," I said, placing a hand to my chest in mock horror. "I'm sorry. I've lived in a small town too long, I guess."

I took their order and cruised into the bar to consider how best to keep the information flowing. So far, they didn't seem to mind talking about their business.

"Can I get you another drink while you're waiting?"

"This is yummy." Britney took a deep sip of her peach-lime surprise.

"Glad you like it." I wet my dry lips. "Won't you miss touring with Jeff Clark? I bet y'all had a ton of fun."

Clay. The guy's name was Clay. It had all of a sudden come back to me. He stared at me over the top of his glass as he took another swig of beer.

"Yeah, right." Britney gave Clay a glance. He ignored her. "Touring with the band's great. The last stop on the tour was supposed to be Nashville."

"You must really miss him." I tried to load on the awe and wonder.

"As if," she said with a giggle.

I waited and lifted my eyebrows to receive whatever info they would slide my way.

He turned to glare at his woman. "Be respectful of the dead."

She shook her head and raised an eyebrow at him. "I didn't wish Jeff any ill will, but everybody in the band knows that you are the real superstar of the bunch."

"Are you a singer too?" My cheeks were hurting from smiling so much.

He gave me a curt nod. "You going to bring us our food, or what?"

"You should hear him sing." She kissed him on the cheek. "Melts your heart."

I went to check on their two orders of pecan-crusted ti-lapia, which happened to be a favorite of mine, and thought about what I had witnessed. The two seemed to be happy together. Neither one expressed any dismay over the end of the tour or sadness over the death of Jeff Clark, some-one they had both known very well.

From the order window, I watched between the paper

"Ooh, baby." The young woman wiggled her shoulders in delight. "I'll have the peach-lime surprise." She gave me a wink. Guess the fact she was buying liquor made us suddenly fast friends.

"Just give me whatever Mexican beer you got on tap." He gave his partner a disapproving stare while placing a proprietary arm around her shoulders.

"You got it."

I returned with their drinks. "I'm surprised you and the band are still here."

They glanced at each other.

Playing it smart, I took my time as I carefully laid their drinks on their Revolver beer coasters. "I mean, now that Jeff is dead and all."

"It's not like we have any choice."

"Britney," the man warned.

So *this* was Britney, the creature who supposedly heard Patti threaten to kill Jeff Clark.

My blood pressure rose so quickly, I could feel my ears redden like a Tasmanian devil's. I gripped my emotions with both hands. All I had to do was keep my cool to find what they heard that night. *Subtle* was my new middle name. "I don't get it. Not that we don't love the band, but why can't you leave?"

"Ask your sheriff," the man muttered. "It's his party."

Britney leaned her head briefly on his shoulder. "We're not paying for this little vacation, babe. That's all that matters."

"You think Ken's going to pick up the tab? He's through. It's on us from now on."

"Gosh," I said, wearing a dumb look. "Hasn't the sheriff already questioned all of you?"

After a second, Britney slammed her menu closed. "Two of his deputies tried to treat us like a couple of rednecks without any common sense, but Ken provided us a lawyer the second time around." She scored a point in the air with her index finger. "That shut them up. Didn't it, babe?"

We both pulled out our phones and started searching for a photo of said Land Rover.

"Here's a sweet one." He held out his phone. The four-by-four in the photo was a silver Defender model. If the Terminator were to go on an African safari, this would be his ride.

"Would you ask around? See if anyone has seen one?" How hard could it be to find such a strange specimen?

"Why?"

Senora Mari hurried over. "Let him get back to work."

"*Abuela*, I need him to help me find this."

She grabbed Carlos's phone from me. "I have seen one of those."

"You have?"

"Ten, maybe twenty years ago."

I sighed heavily. "Gee, thanks."

"I'll check around. Don't worry." Carlos gave a superior nod, while doing what he did best: ignoring Senora Mari and her attitude.

I was in the process of persuading Aunt Linda to close the dining room early for the night when another couple slipped in. As I seated the slim blonde and tall, redheaded dude at a booth in the rear, I recognized him. I would've been a dolt not to. He'd fought with Clark the night of the singer's murder, and he failed to make a sweeter impression when the band chowed down at our expense. The young woman, judging by her distinctive hair color, blond with chocolate highlights, was the giggling bimbo that had left Jeff Clark's dressing room right before their fight.

Had Lightfoot questioned them? Or was I going to have the first crack at them? "Howdy," I said. "What would you like to drink?"

They ignored me and looked pointedly at the dinner menus I still held in my hands.

I handed them over and pointed to the blackboard on the wall. "Tonight's specials are *chiles rellenos* or pecan-crusted tilapia. Our special margarita is a peach-lime surprise."

Chapter 13

Back at Milagro, our usual Sunday business was off. One table held two couples from out of town, but the only vehicles in the parking lot were our own.

"Carlos," I called through the service window. "Do you know anyone who drives a Land Rover around here?"

He schlepped over. "I don't think so. Wait, my cousin has a hack job. The front's an old El Camino, but the back is a Grand Cherokee."

"That's a jeep."

"*Excuse* me for trying to help a body out."

Thanks to Senora Mari's constant criticism, Carlos' skin was a bit thin. "How's that going for him?" I asked, hoping to calm the waters.

He shrugged. "He can carry six people, two ladders, and all his tools."

"Trouble is, I wouldn't know a Land Rover if it ran me over in the middle of a cow pasture."

"Humph." Carlos gave me a look of disgust. "If you find one in this county, you'll be lucky."

Before I could turn around, she slammed the door, rattling the decorative panes. With a sigh, I left my card on top of the mailbox.

As I suspected, no one was home at the houses on either side, so I decided to pack it in.

If I were a detective, I would canvass the neighborhood, asking questions about a blue Land Rover. But I was a waitress. If I didn't pull a shift sometime today, I wasn't going to be able to pay for Patti's new Latina lawyer.

identification. "I've seen you with Patti," she said in a childish whisper.

I smiled. "Yes, that's true. She and I go way back. I know Patti Perez like a sister. There's no way on God's green earth she killed Jeff Clark." I lay my hand across my heart. "Lord knows she seems tough on the outside, but she's as kind and considerate as everyone else."

The paranoid woman continued to study me with her right eye. "She honks at my kids all the time. I don't know why she couldn't have done it."

"Mommy," a girl's voice broke in.

The right side of her face disappeared. "What?" she hissed.

"I need to go number one."

"Go on and go. I'll be right there."

This time the woman's entire face appeared, her eyes downcast.

"I didn't see anything." She ran her tongue across the front of her teeth. "Don't ask me again. I have my children to consider. Lord knows you don't care what happens to people in this neighborhood." Her eyes grew wide and wet.

As the door closed, I called out, "Did you see anything suspicious that night?"

She glanced over her shoulder, stepped onto the doormat, and pulled the door shut behind her.

"Uh, if you think of anything, no matter how small it seems, will you call me? Please?"

"I already spoke to Deputy Barnes. Does he know you're here harassing us?"

I backed away from the raw emotion in her face. "Uh, I understand your concern. I'm only trying to help my friend." I turned to stare across the street at Patti's house, now abandoned and desolate. Across the front door, the yellow crime-scene tape hung in the shape of a tattered *X*.

I heard the brush of the door closing and a small voice ask, "Who was that lady?"

"Calls herself a reporter."

that *night*. I started to correct him, but thought better about it. "Thanks. What's your name?"

"Don't see how it matters."

"Want to give credit where credit is due."

"Here's my name: mind your own business." He cackled and slammed the door.

Didn't matter. Lightfoot would get it out of him once I passed along the neighbor's identity. Would the deputy be willing to trade some facts in return?

I figured I should hit the three houses directly across the street. Wouldn't that be something if I discovered more than one clue that Lightfoot didn't already possess? All three driveways were empty, but the one directly across the street had two children's bicycles parked haphazardly across the sidewalk that led from the street to the house. One was a purple girl's bike with a pink basket, and the other, smaller one was green with black racing stripes.

I rang the doorbell and waited. Immediately I heard a child scream "Mom!" at the top of her lungs. I waited for thirty seconds without any other sound permeating the expensive dark wood and decorative glass panels. Then a small child peeked out from behind the living-room curtains. I couldn't be certain, but I suspected she was all of two years old.

The door opened on a full-figured woman with platinum blond hair and braces. Her eyes flew to the notepad and pen I held at the ready. "I'm not signing anything or supporting any causes," she squealed. "Take my name off your list and don't ever come back." She moved to close the door.

Normally pink rubber bands on someone's teeth meant they were still too young to drink, but her age was hard to determine—probably because all I could see through the crack in the door was the right side of her face.

"I'm not selling anything." I took out my driver's license and tried to hand it to her. "I work for the *Bugle*."

She didn't open the door or make any move to study my

After a few seconds to scratch his nose and adjust his glasses, he sighed. "No. Wasn't a truck."

I checked my watch. Lightfoot could arrive at any time. "If it wasn't a car, how about an SUV? I bet that's what it was, right?"

I watched as he rolled his eyes skywards. "All that comes to mind is the word Rogers."

"Rogers. Like Roy Rogers?"

Screwing up his lips, he rolled his eyes in the opposite direction. "Land. Rogers." He shook his head violently. "No. Land . . ."

"Rover?" I nearly shouted. "Land Rover?"

"Yes," he said with a prim nod and a finger to the bridge of his glasses. "A blue Land Rover is exactly what I saw the night of the murder."

I wanted to twirl him around like a preschooler. I wanted to give him a high five with one hand and a knuckle bump with the other. I did none of those things because his face contorted into a mask of terror as if he suspected where my thoughts had gone.

"Hmm. Are you sure?" I asked. I had never seen a Land Rover in Broken Boot that I could remember. The last time I noticed one was in Austin, when my neighbor's father came to visit from Dallas.

"Young lady, I used to sell Mini Coopers for a living back in the eighties. I know a Land Rover when I see one."

His logic made no sense to me, but I persevered. "Did you see who was driving it?"

"No."

"What time did you see it?"

"I don't sleep much. I came out to get the paper at five thirty and saw it driving down the road, back toward the interstate."

"Five thirty in the morning?" I was confused.

"That's what I said."

I could have sworn he said he saw the blue Land Rover

confident voice. "I'm a friend of Patti Perez, your neighbor, and I write for the *Bugle*."

"Seen you before," he cried, yanking one of the dogs away from the door. "Get on with it!"

I moved closer and instantly regretted it. In addition to loud canine threats puncturing my eardrums, the odor of unwashed dog and cooked Brussels sprouts assailed my nose. "Did you see any strangers pull up to Patti's house on the night of the murder or that next morning?" Abruptly, the threatening noise and stench dispersed. From somewhere in the back of the house, I could still hear them whining, scratching, and longing for my flesh.

"Didn't see anyone or anything," he said in a nasal voice as he opened the door a measly five inches.

I sighed. "What about on the street? Did you see any unfamiliar cars or trucks?" If he could see my face, it was a miracle. His glasses were thicker than Coke bottles. Made me wonder if he could see his own hand in front of his face.

"Didn't want to help that deputy that came by."

"No?"

"Women shouldn't be in law enforcement. What a crock."

"Deputy Pleasant came by?"

He sniffed. "We didn't get to the introductions."

"Oh, well. I'm Josie Callahan. You know my aunt Linda and uncle Eddie, I imagine. They own Milagro."

"Never heard of it." He tilted back his head as if trying to see me through the bottom part of his lenses.

"On Main Street? Tex-Mex, tortillas? No?"

"I don't eat out. Gives me indigestion."

I started to pull out my notebook and pen, but sensed he might shy away if I did. "I could really use your help."

"Blue. I saw a blue vehicle."

Nodding encouragement and smiling like an idiot, I said, "Great. Was it a truck or a car?"

"No. Was definitely not a car, but it did have four doors."

That was promising. "Was it a truck with an extended cab?"

Michaels had only taken fifteen minutes. Now for the neighbor on the other side.

This house was an unfortunate shade of pink adobe with a roof that had seen better days. In fact, the roof slumped so badly across the front of the house that I could envision rain pouring through the shingles and onto the floor. No flowers sunned themselves in the front beds, but the owner had planted four pink flamingos in different sizes. They clustered near the front door. If I didn't know better, I'd think they were waiting to peck the toes of individuals brave or foolish enough to knock.

I dropped the door knocker twice in spite of the watchful pink fowl and immediately heard the ferocious barking of what sounded like two extremely large dogs. In seconds, they were hitting the door with their paws, scratching, and whining to get at me. "Get back, you idiots!" I heard a man's voice yell through the cacophony of snarling and growling.

I backed onto the sidewalk—the better to sprint for my car if he unleashed the hounds. The door opened a crack and the barking became louder. I saw a black Doberman trying to squeeze his head through the bottom crack of the door. The handsome but ferocious creature began to whine at not being given free rein to remove my ankles from my legs. "I said 'Get back!'"

The dog was jerked away from the opening with a yelp. For a second, I saw a second canine head try to make its way through the doorway. This one belonged to a whiskey-brown pit bull. The second one wasn't whining. Instead, he was growling as if a generator had kicked on inside his throat—a generator that would propel him through the door to remove my ears from the sides of my head.

I backed away just as the second doggie disappeared. A bald head with wizened features; gray bushy eyebrows; wire-framed glasses; a long, thin nose; and full lips, made a brief appearance. "What do you want?" All I could see was the dome of his bald head and the elbow of his plaid flannel shirt.

"Sorry to bother you," I said in what I hoped was a

As if I were a small dog, she shooed me toward the front door, knocking me into her Dallas Cowboys umbrella stand. "Don't write in your article I made jokes about the dead, living or otherwise. Okay? I didn't mean that the way it sounded."

"How do you know it was him the entire time?" I asked, picking up an umbrella from the floor. "Did they leave the blinds open?"

"Well, there aren't any on the windows at the front door, are there?" She threw up her hands. "I could see them walking back and forth. And, like I said, I heard the music." She opened the door and reached for the screen.

All kinds of alarms were going off in my head. I thought she was lying, but what if she had all these details about the hours leading up to Clark's murder for another reason? This was not how I wanted this interview to end. "What about the rest of the night or the next morning?" I asked, unable to hide my growing impatience.

"Look, hon, you have to go." With a nervous glance out the screen, she opened the door.

"Please." I placed a hand on the doorjamb. "Patti's your neighbor. She needs your help."

"I guess it was around one, one thirty when I heard her start up the jeep and drive away."

"How can you be so sure of the time?"

"My husband gets off work at midnight." She smiled like a cat inhaling catnip. "I make a point to greet him at the door with dinner and a smile." She glanced longingly toward the television.

I pocketed my notepad. "Thanks for your help . . . uh?"

"Victoria Pappas." Did that explain the Grecian blue shutters?

"How do you know it was Patti behind the—?"

She didn't answer except to let the door swing shut. As it did, I heard the swell of the instructor's voice and the energetic music playing beneath it.

I checked my watch. My interview with the next Jillian

"Sex on a stick. Jeff Clark's as sexy as they come."

"And you knew it was him from the back of his head?"

For a second, she cocked her head to one side. "I noticed he was lean, with a great butt." She gazed off into the distance, remembering every stitch on his back pockets. "He wore a white hat over wavy brown hair." With a sigh, she settled back down to earth and eagerly brought her water bottle back to her lips. "I guess I didn't know for certain that it was actually Jeff Clark until the police showed up."

If I hadn't been desperate for information, I would've walked. This woman was lying or I was the next governor of the great state of Texas. "You were a fan?"

Her eyes widened. "Not until I laid eyes on him."

I made a quick note. "What about later that night? Did you see anyone else?"

"No."

"You sure?"

"I heard something that sounded like raccoons in the trash cans and went to run 'em off with a broom. That was about twelve thirty."

"Was Jeff still there?" Now, I knew that she would have no way of knowing that unless she had peeked in Patti's windows through the plantation shutters, but I didn't put it past her.

"Girl, you can say that again." She realized her mistake, turned on her heel, and carried her bottle to the faux-marble counter that separated her kitchen from the great room. "I mean, as far as I could tell with that racket going on."

"Were they fighting?" That would align with Patti's story.

With an impatient gesture, she wiped her hair from her forehead. "They were jamming on their electric guitars loud enough to wake the living dead." Her chuckle was forced. "I guess the *living dead* would already be awake, wouldn't they?" She wiped her face again. "I'm sorry, but you need to go. If I don't finish this workout, Jason will never let me hear the end of it."

"Just one more question?"

that adjoined a state-of-the-art kitchen. On a giant-screen TV played a martial-arts workout video that she was just restarting. The instructor's voice blared through her giant speakers before she hit the Mute button.

"Go ahead, ask away," she shouted, as she followed the instructor in a series of kicks and punches.

"Were you home Thursday night?"

"I went to the grocery store for eggs about six o'clock." She paused to spin and aim a kick at the screen. "But I was home after that."

"Eggs?"

"Omelets." She didn't look at me as she answered.

"Did you hear or see anything next door?"

The instructor on the screen took a drink of water and she followed suit. I realized I didn't know her name. Even though *Romo* was on the back of her jersey, something told me that she and the famous quarterback weren't related.

"I heard Patti's jeep drive up around midnight."

"Is that all?"

"I heard two doors slam."

"Two?"

"Yeah. She always slams the door to her jeep when she gets home. I remember there were two doors that slammed that night, so I figured she finally had a date."

This made no sense to me. "If she had a date, wouldn't she be riding in someone else's vehicle?"

"Not necessarily. Her jeep's a nice one." More huffing and puffing. "She purchased it after her parents died, out of her inheritance, I imagine."

"Did you see them?"

She shook her head. "Not really."

"Not even a glimpse out of curiosity?"

Even though the instructor began to kick and punch at a faster pace, my hostess stopped again to drink water from her water bottle and wipe the sweat from her brow with a dish towel. "I saw the back of his head."

"What did he look like?"

* * *

After he drove away, I pondered how long it would take him to drive to Two Boots, find Wilhelmina and Heather, and piece together what information they had given me. An hour, maybe less. What if he couldn't find them? Then again, what if there was no one at Two Boots to interview? He might head over to Patti's neighborhood in fifteen minutes or less.

I promptly drove over to Patti's house. I didn't think the good Lord would mind as long as I stayed out of the crime scene and the path of the sheriff and his deputies.

The Big Bend County Sheriff's Department had successfully covered the porch in crime-scene tape from floor to ceiling. But as no cops were around, I parked in the driveway.

As I didn't know exactly who Lightfoot had spoken to, I started with the houses on either side. I knocked on the door of a white split-level ranch, decked out in sky blue shutters with a front door to match. The front flower beds boasted white azaleas, which went a great deal in the direction of softening the strange shade of blue. A woman in a Cowboys football jersey, which could've been worn as a dress, it was so long, answered the door while jogging in place.

"Yes?" Several dark wavy strands had escaped her ponytail, which was coming undone. Sweaty tendrils of hair stuck to either side of her face.

"Hi. I work for the *Bugle*."

"I know who you are. You're Josie Callahan." She continued to jog in place, but managed at the same time to look me over with blatant curiosity. "Where's Toto?"

"Yes, well." I swallowed a bit of nerves. "I just wanted to ask you a couple of questions about the night of the murder."

"Listen, I don't mind answering your questions, same as that deputy, but you're going to have to ask while I continue my workout. It won't stay on pause forever." She turned and jogged down the hall.

I followed, happy to find someone willing to allow me to snoop to my heart's content. I found her in the great room

"Let me get this straight. You want me to break the rules, willy-nilly, just because you want to ride along."

Instead of being offended, I had the sudden urge to laugh. *Willy-nilly* sounded odd coming out of his mouth.

"Fine. When are you going to question Patti's other neighbor?"

Without answering, he slid into his seat and raised his hand to close the door. "After I head on over to Two Boots to question all the members of Clark's band I can dig up."

While I argued with myself about whether or not I should share my information with him, he shut the cruiser's door and started the engine. I knocked on the window until he lowered it. "I've interviewed two of them."

"Two what?" he asked, his mouth twisting in derision.

I swallowed back my nerves. "Members of Clark's road crew." I watched in silence as his jaw clenched and un-clenched. "I would share with you what they told me in con-fidence, and then you and I could go together to interview Patti's neighbor."

Without prying his lips open, it was hard to be sure, but I could have sworn he was grinding his teeth.

I smiled at him, making sure to give him a dimple.

Like a mirage in the desert, his gaze was empty, and then something magical appeared, something that made me think he had finally come to his senses. He leaned in, real slowlike, gestured for me to move closer, and eased his mouth close to my ear.

My shoulders tensed at the smell of pine air freshener and spaghetti. The hair on the back of my neck jumped to attention.

"Hell, no," he whispered.

I backed away, madder than a turkey on Thanksgiving. "You just wait. You'll be begging me for information."

He chuckled, but it contained no humor. "You stay out of my investigation." Giving me a dead-eyed stare, he de-manded, "Am I clear?"

hind his back. "Have you guys discovered any leads so far? Any clues to speak of?"

"Don't forget Deputy Pleasant."

"Excuse me. Guys and *gal*."

With a thumb and index finger, he carefully tipped his hat back from his forehead. "The pieces are beginning to fall into place." If I didn't know better, I'd say the good deputy was stretching the truth by a city block.

"Have you questioned the neighbors?"

He hesitated. "Yes."

"Uh-huh. You didn't question all of them, did you?"

"Three out of four."

"Well, let's go question number four."

"Why don't you leave it to us professionals and go home and help your dog write his blog or something?"

I beamed. "You read Lenny's blog?"

"I've read it a time or two." He turned away abruptly to watch Lily exit the Laundromat with an overfull black trash bag thrown over her narrow shoulders. "Need some help?" he called.

"Do I look like an invalid to you, Officer?" Lily spat.

"No, ma'am." Lightfoot tipped his hat.

"Bye, girlfriend," I called after her.

Without dropping a hand from her makeshift laundry bag, she gave me a thumbs-up and a wink. One thing Lily didn't appreciate was charity. She would rather help her brother support their younger brother and sister than take a handout, or a hand with anything she was strong enough to manage on her own.

I plastered on a smile. "Hey, why don't you let me go with you? I'd be an awesome resource, like that writer on that television show."

He started for his cruiser. "You aren't a famous crime novelist, and I'm not a detective."

With a skip and a gallop, I caught up to him as he opened his door. "Please. For Patti?"

"I see Patti's lawyer filled you in."

"She told us the evidence against her is circumstantial."

He checked the screen of his phone and returned it to his belt. "True."

"Why'd you arrest her? And don't tell me you're not in charge."

He glanced at the Laundromat's windows and motioned for me to follow. We stopped at the far side of his cruiser. "Cogburn's gunning for a quick arrest and sentencing."

"Why?"

A frown line appeared above his winglike brows. "Tourists don't want to visit a town where they stand a chance of getting killed."

"Shoot. You know tourists are safe in this town—safer than in their beds at home."

"He's trying to get the independent chili-contest folks to hold a competition here next year."

"And they care about two murders in one year?"

"What do I know?" Lightfoot kicked a rock across the parking lot with the side of his boot. "And there's something about the Texas Artists' Guild wanting to visit to evaluate whether or not to hold their annual art show at the university."

"I hate to sound stupid, but why would they choose Broken Boot?"

His eyes narrowed. "Let's see. Maybe the beauty of the land and the national park? Or maybe West Texas University?"

The scenery in Big Bend County was without compare, but last I heard, we had more cattle in the area than students at the university. "Again, why would they care?"

"Seems the artists' guild has already called about the murder. They are asking lots of questions that lead Mayor Cogburn to think we've lost our shine."

If Lightfoot would simply throw me a bone, he could go off and do his investigative thing and I would do mine be-

nodding occasionally as the man gave his side with wild gestures toward Lily.

The deputy called Lily over. The three of them discussed it. Lightfoot had her turn out her pockets. The old man began to yell. Finally, he sent them both on their way.

"She's banned for life," the old man yelled after her.

"Old goat," she muttered between her teeth.

I placed an arm on her shoulder. I wouldn't stake my life on the fact she was telling the truth, but I was willing to give her the benefit of the doubt. Her scruffy appearance made her appear more than ready to steal if the opportunity arose to support her family. Her brother Anthony would have her head if he found out. As he functioned in lieu of parents, Anthony was strict with his younger brother and sisters.

"You okay?"

"Our laundry's in that flea hole."

She followed me over to where Lightfoot stood next to his sheriff's cruiser, writing a report.

"Hello again," I said.

Perhaps it was the angle of the sun, but the deputy's countenance was different from earlier in the day. In his gaze I discovered a camaraderie and respect between equals. For the first time, I stared into his dark, fathomless eyes and believed that he would do his utmost to free Patti. Could it be that Lightfoot was sentimental?

"Lily needs to retrieve her clothes from inside," I said with a nod toward the Laundromat.

"Dale," he hollered in a loud voice, "the gal needs her laundry." I wanted to laugh. Not once in the few months since I'd met the taciturn deputy had I heard him raise his voice.

The old man spat on the asphalt and nodded his head. "Then she better git in there and git it, han't she?"

As Lily ran off to gather her things, I started in on Lightfoot. "I can't believe you'd listen to some woman named Britney."

"Lots of folks say that and don't mean it. I say it at least twice a day." She pointed to her chest. "Am I a murderer?"

Gretchen dropped her notepad into her briefcase. "It's not much in the way of evidence, but it's enough to prosecute when there's pressure from higher up."

"From whom? Cogburn?" I asked.

"Wallace, I bet." Senora Mari poked me in the shoulder with a bony finger.

"My guess would be the mayor's office, but I don't know enough to form an educated guess." Cruz squared her shoulders. "And that's what I have for a hundred dollars."

"Oh," Senora Mari and I said in unison.

"Unless you have decided you want me to take the case."

I caught Senora Mari's eye and raised a brow. She lifted a shoulder. We nodded in agreement.

"How much?" Senora Mari asked.

I placed a hand on her shoulder. "We'll pay it." We had no room to barter, but somehow I'd find the money to rescue Patti Perez, Goth Princess and best friend.

After dropping Senora Mari off at Milagro, I jumped into the shower and forced myself to relax. The hot spray drove out the panic, allowing me to formulate a plan. I'd drive around town until I spotted Lightfoot. Once we were alone, I'd plead for more information on Patti's case. If that didn't work, I'd pry it out of him with a crowbar. Metaphorically speaking.

I found him outside the local Laundromat, settling a dispute between an old, wizened gent and a young teen or preteen—it was hard to know for sure. The young preteen turned out to be the diminutive Lily, one of our bus girls.

"He says I broke his machine and stole twenty dollars in free washing."

"What happened?"

"The crappy machine was already broken."

Lightfoot was standing in the doorway with the owner,

supposedly regretted the way he tomcatted around on her. Said he wanted to apologize and get together for old time's sake—"

Cruz interrupted, "You don't think he was telling the truth?"

"Does a dog lie under the house in the summer?"

She shook her head in confusion.

I continued. "Patti wasn't a hundred percent positive she wanted to see him, but he wore her down."

"That's what she told you."

"That's the truth." Patti and I had no secrets between us.

Senora Mari nodded in agreement. "That is the truth. The two of them, they are like sisters."

With a quick glance around, Cruz continued. "Don't tell anyone else—I'm only telling you because you hired me—but they have a witness who says she heard Patti threaten to kill Clark on the night of the murder."

"Lies!"

I placed a hand on Senora Mari's arm. "I don't believe it. They left Two Boots that night hand in hand, like two lovebirds."

Gretchen studied her notes once again. "A Britney Kincaid overheard them fighting in the parking lot of Lula's Lizard Lounge around one o'clock in the morning on Friday."

"Who?" Senora Mari demanded, as if the young lawyer had dared to utter an unbelievable name like Rumpelstiltskin or Frida Kahlo.

I made a small calming gesture, which only seemed to infuriate her more.

"Who is this B-Britney person?" She jabbed a finger into the air. "What does she know, this girl no one has ever heard of?"

Cruz spoke up. "She's the girlfriend of one of Clark's band members, a Clay . . ." She ran her finger down the report in front of her, "Conley."

Senora Mari slammed her hand on the wooden seat.

Chapter 12

I grabbed the bench on either side of me to keep from flying into a rage. "Patti's had that same electric guitar since she was twelve. It's been in the corner of her living room since I've known her. Anyone could have walked in and bashed him over the head with it."

Gretchen raised an eyebrow and then lowered her gaze to the leather-bound notepad she held.

I continued. "This guy had enemies. A line of folks would have paid to bash his head in. Did the sheriff and his deputies mention that?"

The corners of her mouth lifted in a small smile. "No. Can't say that they did."

Senora Mari and I glanced at each other. "What do they have?" The older woman's voice was calm and deadly.

"Did you know that Patti and Clark had a past?" the lawyer asked.

"Sure," I murmured, "but they broke up years ago."

"If that's the case, why do you think she agreed to see him Thursday night?"

I leaned forward for emphasis. "It was all his idea. He

her head to meet his gaze. "Or did you do whatever that foolish sheriff told you to do?"

In spite of his deep brown complexion, I could see his cheeks flush. "I'm not in charge, if you haven't noticed." His phone buzzed on his belt and he checked the screen with a frown. "I'm sorry."

He turned to me and I read the honest regret in his eyes. "It's out of my hands."

Tears welled in my eyes, but as I watched him exit the building, I knuckled them away.

"Now what?" I asked in a tone that set Gretchen Cruz back.

She recovered quickly. "We try to get her out."

"But what evidence could they possibly have against her that's not circumstantial?"

"You tell us. Right now." Senora Mari's hands clutched the handle of her purse so hard, I thought she was about to knock Gretchen out with it.

With a quick glance over her shoulder, she led us outside to a wooden bench that rested in the shade of a nearby live oak. "For starters, they have her fingerprints."

"Of course they do. She lives there, for pity's sake."

Senora Mari grabbed her knees for emphasis. "Did you tell them that?"

"Yes." She spoke quietly and slowly, as if trying to infuse the older woman with her calm demeanor. "Jeff Clark was killed with Patti's guitar."

from the strain of worry. I took Senora Mari by the arm and gently helped her to her feet.

"These shoes are going in the trash," she said, emptying the Hot Fries bag and a few old tissues into a metal receptacle.

"Shh. Your sandals aren't made to wear for long periods of time."

"And yours are ugly."

I ignored my *abuela*'s exhausted attempt to return my unintended insult. As we reached the exit, we both turned to wave at the female clerk of divine intervention. She wiggled the long nails of one hand in our direction just as her very efficient cousin and a familiar deputy crossed the waiting room from the opposite doorway.

As they approached, the deputy removed his Stetson. "Senora," Lightfoot said with a respectful nod to Senora Mari.

She pursed her lips and gave him a narrow-eyed stare. "So. Did you arrest her?"

He shot a glance my way. The truth was there for all to see.

Not thinking, I grabbed his arm. "Are you crazy? Why did you arrest her?"

He reached out with both hands as if to calm a nervous filly. "Whoa. It came down to evidence, clear and simple."

"Circumstantial evidence, you mean," our new lawyer said with grit.

"You can't arrest her if you only have circumstantial evidence." I was not a complete idiot. I knew my courtroom dramas.

His chest expanded and he drew a deep breath before replying. "It's not all circumstantial"—he cast a suspicious glance at Gretchen Cruz—"which I'm sure her lawyer will be more than happy to explain."

"Did you tell them to let her go?" Senora Mari walked right up into the deputy's personal bubble and tilted back

with the nimble fingers of one hand, lifted a few stray ten-
drils from the back of her neck, and began to fan herself as
if she were about to keel over from heatstroke.

"You sure?" I asked. I was having enough trouble re-
maining calm without worrying about her passing out.

"*Sí.*"

I said good-bye and settled in for a long wait on an un-
comfortable chair. After fifteen minutes, Senora Mari was
fast asleep with her head on her chest and her hands folded
across her stomach. With each exhalation, she made a light
whistling sound through her nose. If she was faking it, she
had my undying respect.

The longer I sat, the angrier I became. Who in their right
mind would accuse Patti of killing anyone? My follow-up
article would be printed in the upcoming edition of the
Bugle, but by then it would be old news. News? What had
I written? Basically a fluff piece on Jeff Clark. Sure, I'd
interviewed a few peripheral people on his tour, so I had an
idea of who he'd potentially hacked off. Cardplayers, old
girlfriends, and their husbands or boyfriends.

Broken Boot was a small town. Would the sheriff bring
in the Texas Rangers? Not if I knew Sheriff Mack Wallace.
He'd do his darnedest to solve the crime, make the arrest,
and gain the glory without involving the rangers, FBI, or
any other law-enforcement bureau besides his own deputies.

Add to that the fact that Mayor Cogburn was up for re-
election and you had a lot of pressure for the sheriff to solve
the crime and make an arrest before he lost control of the
whole kit and caboodle.

Where was Lightfoot? He would tell me what they had
on Patti. And, if I played my cards right, he might let me
help with the investigation. Yeah, right. Flying pigs were
not on the horizon. Still, he had to be sympathetic to Patti's
plight. Maybe enough for a brief share-and-share-alike ses-
sion between the two of us.

Three hours had passed, and we were both exhausted

Watching her walk away, Senora Mari nodded proudly. "A Latina lawyer will save her. You watch."

"From your lips to God's ears."

Senora Mari raised her eyebrows at my phraseology, and then she crossed herself and touched her fingers to her lips.

Over the next hour, a couple of guys came in wearing stereotypical gold chains, wife beaters, slack-hipped jeans, and tats up and down their arms. Scary dudes. They spoke so softly to the booking clerk that no matter how hard I tried to hear what they were saying, I couldn't make it out. Senora Mari had finished her Hot Fries and had spent the last fifteen minutes trying to wipe the residue off her fingers with hand sanitizer.

We waited for an update from Gretchen Cruz until I thought I'd have to run outside and scream. Uncle Eddie and Aunt Linda both called, separately, for an update, and both offered to join us at the jail. "No, thanks." I told them. "There's no need for all of us to waste our time."

I glanced at Senora Mari and raised an eyebrow in question. "Do you want Aunt Linda to come by to pick you up?"

She looked away, considering her options. "No." She straightened to her full four feet, eleven inches. "Tell her to make sure Carlos is checking the expiration date on the meat."

I wrinkled my nose in disgust.

"What?" she asked, chin raised defensively. "Is it my fault he refuses to earn his GED or go to the market?"

I opened my mouth to answer and then shut it again. He was never given the opportunity to shop alone because she insisted he always shop with her assistance. Everyone knew that all tamales, enchiladas, and anything else served from our kitchen at Milagro had to pass her strict standards. The fact that Carlos could put up with her eagle eye and constant criticism spoke to his patience and his need for employment.

On the other line, Aunt Linda asked again.

Senora Mari shook her head vehemently and pulled one of our to-go menus from her purse. She folded it together

suit with black heels. In her left hand she carried a well-made if often-used leather portfolio. "Gretchen Cruz." She gave a nod, but no smile. "Pleased to meet you." Her voice was a pleasing alto with just a hint of twang.

I stood and shook her outstretched hand. "Thanks for coming."

Unlike the young receptionist we had met only minutes earlier, Cruz had tough hands and short nails with clear polish. Her wrists were bare except for a slender gold watch and a simple band that graced her ring finger.

Senora Mari stood as well and broke into a long tirade in Spanish about the inadequacy of the public defenders and the prejudice in the Texas legal system. The other woman listened, nodded, and finally lifted a hand. "I see," was all she said.

"I'm building a business here and few folks know me." She turned and waved at her cousin, who bore no resemblance to her whatsoever, and the other woman waved back. "I'll charge you a hundred dollars to walk in there and say I'm her lawyer. After I meet with her, I will report back to you, and then we'll discuss my fees."

Senora Mari pinched my arm. "Go ahead."

"Wait," I urged. I wasn't one to make important decisions under pressure. The holdup was not whether I should spend the money, but, rather, when did I need to hand it over . . . exactly.

I rubbed my arm and glared at Senora Mari. "Okay, already." As usual, *Abuela* was correct. Patti, Goth Princess, tough on the outside, not a murderess on either side, needed immediate rescue.

"She's innocent. Won't it make her look bad to bring in a lawyer during questioning?"

"From what you've told me, it sounds as if there's a good deal of circumstantial evidence piled against her. And you think she needs an advocate now. Right?"

I nodded.

She reached out squeezed my upper arm. "Trust me."

"Patti has money, right?"

"Some, I guess." I had no clear idea whether or not Patti's parents had left her anything other than their home and Broken Boot Feed and Supply and its outstanding bills.

"Call this lawyer before they arrest your best friend." She pulled the Hot Fries from her bag. *"¿Eres una gallina?"*

My eyes rolled. There was nothing quite like having my almost-eighty-year-old *abuela* accuse me of being a chicken. She was right, of course. What would it hurt to call this woman, Gretchen Cruz, and ask some basic questions?

I called. A woman with a deep, assertive voice answered on the first ring. "Gretchen Cruz, Esquire."

Despite that slightly pretentious opening, she listened as I introduced myself, but refused to answer any of my questions except for commenting with sympathetic humming sounds. "I will be there in ten minutes."

Before she could hang up, I jumped in with my most important question. "Uh, I don't know how this works. Don't you need a retainer or—?"

"I'll meet you there and we can discuss it in person."

"But—"

"Look," she said in a firm tone. "You want me to fight to keep your friend out of jail, right?"

"Yeah." I had to find a knight in shining armor and fast. "Yes, I do," I said, bellying up to the bar.

"Then we will fight, and we will win," she growled. After a brief pause, she continued in a friendlier tone. "You'll see."

The line went dead and I immediately regretted my decision. What had I done? How would I find the money to pay her the retainer she required?

In eleven minutes, a petite woman with a cap of dark hair crossed the waiting area with the same intensity I'd seen in members of the Texas State Guard around the capitol building in Austin. Her mahogany bangs swept across her brow while the sides were super short. She wore a purple linen

and snagged the card. Salmon with black lettering, it read, *Gretchen Cruz, Attorney at Law.*

"She's my cousin, but she's smart."

I reread the fancy bit of cardstock, hoping to discover some hint as to whether or not this woman's cousin was legit. Not that beggars could be choosers.

I wanted to ask, *If she's so smart, why's she here in Big Bend County instead of Dallas or at least El Paso?*

The clerk must have read my doubts in my face. "She's here because my Aunt Diana is very ill and my cousin wants to be near her mother."

The phone rang in a shrill blast. "Hello?" The clerk listened for a second. "No," she answered, clacking her nails on the desk. "Why?" She listened again and rolled her eyes at whatever the caller was saying. "Not today. Ask me again tomorrow." Without a good-bye to soften the blow, she hung up.

After a few moments spent studying my person, with special attention given to the Austin T-shirt, she leaned toward me conspiratorially. "Don't judge my cousin because she's a Latina. She attended Rice University on a full scholarship."

Which was more than I could say for myself. "I'll give her a call."

The woman nodded her approval and went back to typing, her fingers once again flying across the keys, clicking and clacking like castanets. Her eyes met mine for a split second and she nodded infinitesimally.

"What'd she say?" Senora Mari asked, loud enough for everyone on the street to hear.

I handed her the card.

"Looks good. What are you waiting for?"

"We don't know anything about her."

She tried to grab the card from my hand. "Give me your phone. I'll call her."

"And how are we going to pay her?"

she doesn't have any family to take her side. And that ain't right."

I only use the word *ain't* in certain circumstances, like when I think it makes me sound more pitiful.

She stopped typing, adjusted her glasses, and took a sip from her hot-pink water bottle. "What's her name?" she asked in a voice as tired as a ditchdigger's.

"Patti Perez."

A spark of interest kindled in her eyes. She glanced at two other county employees—an older woman nearing retirement and a young man who appeared to be wearing his first tie—who were heatedly discussing the price of gasoline, the curious fact that Texas did *not* have lower gas prices than Louisiana, and why in tarnation not?

"They took her through, but she hasn't been booked." Her fingers raced across the keys, her eyes narrowed in concentration. "She hasn't been charged with anything at this point." She shook her head and looked me full in the face for the first time. "There's nothing I can do."

"Please."

She glanced furtively around again. "Except to tell you that if it were me, I'd find her a lawyer and quick."

"Why?" I whispered.

"Wallace came through this morning. Met her and the deputy at the door. He's all over this investigation. Taking it serious."

"Okay. Thanks." My mind slowed to a crawl. Who else did I know that would take Patti's case and set her free? And why had the sheriff's fill-in receptionist refused to tell me he'd returned from vacation?

Her long nails stopped clicking on the keyboard. She opened her drawer, pulled out a salmon-colored business card, and slid it to the edge of her desk with one pink nail. "She's the best."

With a quick glance over my shoulder to make sure no one was looking our way, I stretched out over the counter

Was he kidding me? I responded as politely as I could manage. Where's Patti?

His response gave me some relief.

"Let's wait over here." I gestured to a few metal chairs with cushioned seats that were propped to one side against a grayish wall. "Lightfoot says she's in an interrogation room."

"Are they railroading her out of town?"

I wouldn't have used those terms, but the older woman's meaning was clear. "No, they aren't." My pulse kicked into a higher gear. Who was questioning her? Lightfoot or Wallace, or someone unknown to her—someone who wouldn't understand that her personality and moral character didn't match her dyed hair and multiple tattoos? Did she have a lawyer?

Surely my Goth friend had watched enough television to know that you should always ask for a lawyer if they started asking you questions about a murder. What if she did ask for a lawyer? Whom would they send? The only public defender I could think of wasn't fit to wash cars at the Spruce and Shine.

After five minutes of waiting, with my pulse rate beating a mile a minute, I approached the clerk. "Sorry to bother you." I smiled my most sweet Southern-girl smile.

The Latina behind the counter didn't look up from her typing. On her well-worn metal desk lay a six-inch stack of reports. "Uh-huh." Her eyes never left her computer screen.

"We think a friend of ours is here being questioned."

"Uh-huh." She flipped over the top page on the stack, realigned the top sheet of paper, clicked a few keys on her keyboard, and kept right on typing.

"We don't know if she has a lawyer."

"Uh-huh."

Friendliness wasn't working. Melodrama might. "I don't know what to do. I've never had to do this before. She's being accused of murder. They're picking on her because

"Is he coming in later?"

Indecision followed immediately by decision flew across her expressive features. "I don't rightly know what I'm supposed to tell you folks, but I'll check with him if possible. You can call me back in an hour or so."

I glanced at Senora Mari. She had trapped Clarissa in a narrow-eyed glare. "Humph. We'll be back." She lifted her chin and spun on the heel of her sandals in an attempt to make a grand exit.

"Nice to meet you," I said, preparing to follow the older woman before she got us both kicked out.

Clarissa's mouth hung open as she watched Senora Mari march down the hall and out the door. "Uh, you too."

As my cheeks had started to ache, I dropped the let's-all-be-friends smile. "We'll be calling back in an hour to see if you called Sheriff Wallace. You can count on it."

I followed the signs that pointed toward the county jail and eventually caught up with Senora Mari. She had stopped at a vending machine and was studying the snacks.

"Hot Fries taste like pork rinds. *Sí*?"

"But they're not the same."

"I like pork rinds. I'll take them."

I learned long ago that Senora Mari didn't buy her own snacks if someone else was available to buy them for her. Not that I minded. It wasn't clear to me how the whole Martinez family managed to support themselves from the earnings of their two modestly successful businesses. Yet they kept a roof over their heads and food on the table, gas in their trucks, and AC blowing from the vents in the summer, which could cost as much as a diamond ring, depending on your jeweler.

We found an even uglier part of the building that housed the jail with helpful, faded signs with arrows that pointed to booking, processing, visitation, and clerk's office.

Where was Lightfoot? Ugh. Had we even called him?

I glanced down and realized I had a message from him on my phone. *What's up?*

"What she means," I said, placing a hand on Senora Mari's arm, "is that we're having a bit of an emergency."

"Oh, heavens." The young woman placed a hand at her throat as if her lungs were failing.

"We want Patti Perez released immediately." My *abuela* shook my hand from her arm. "You have no right to keep her here."

I agreed, but it sounded preposterous coming from the older woman. They were the sheriff's office. They had the right to do most things, given the circumstances.

Shaking her head sympathetically, the young woman made her way back to the secretary's desk. "I'm sorry, but I can't help you. You're going to have to go down to the jail."

"But we don't know if she's been arrested or merely brought in for questioning."

Senora Mari approached her desk. "I am Senora Marisol Martinez." She drew her shoulders back and raised her chin.

"Nice to meet you. I'm Clarissa." Beaming with good-will, the substitute receptionist stuck out her hand.

Senora Mari studied her hand for a moment. The girl's wrist and hand were hidden by bangles, leather bracelets, and henna tattoos. Drawing herself up to her full height, she took the girl's hand by the fingers and shook it for a split second. She lifted the corners of her mouth a scant half inch, her usual way of pretending to smile at strangers, in spite of the fact she had preached to me the importance of making a good first impression only minutes earlier. My grandmother was not going to pretend to be friendly if you were not her friend. Not going to happen.

"Josie Callahan." I, on the other hand, greased the bureaucratic wheel by giving Clarissa a big smile and a hearty shake.

The delicate young woman withdrew her hand and rubbed her fingers.

I glanced toward Wallace's office. "Is the sheriff back from vacation? I know he'd be willing to help us. We go way back."

A look of doubt crossed her face. "No."

"Jo Jo—"

"Josie." No one called me Jo Jo except for my immediate family. He'd better get that straight.

"Uh, yes. Well, I do apologize, but I have to think of our residents and their need to feel secure in their own homes."

"I'm headed over to the county jail now. You'll be hearing from me again if I find they've actually arrested her."

"Don't you worry, darling. It will all turn out all right. Just keep your hat on." His words should've been a comfort, but I heard his doubt, loud and clear.

We slowed as we exited the highway, both of us searching for a cruiser that might be en route with Patti inside. The only vehicles we observed were a couple of white Chevy Suburbans that bore the name *Big Bend Cowboy Church* in gold filigree lettering on their sides.

Inside the station, it was quiet as a museum. The volunteers who staffed the information booth had the day off, as well as the receptionist at the main desk. Signs led us past the public areas of city hall until the only arrows that remained were those pointing toward the sheriff's office and the county jail.

My breath grew short and my pulse raced. Patti Perez didn't belong in jail. She was a part of this town. To bring her in like a common criminal was, well, criminal. We blasted into the sheriff's private reception area and found no one at the desk.

"Hello," Senora Mari shouted. "Who's there?"

A young woman with hair as curly and red as Little Orphan Annie's entered, wearing a receptionist's headset. She swung the disconnected wire in one hand. "Sorry about that, y'all. Nature calls, you know?"

She was probably all of eighteen. This was not the sheriff's weekday Valkyrie, ready to protect him from all comers.

"Where is Sheriff Wallace?" Senora Mari demanded.

The young woman's eyebrows flew up into her hair at the older woman's tone.

"Is everything all right?" he whispered.

"Uh, no, but we can talk later. Shouldn't you get back to the council?" The mayor was running for his second term in office. You would think he'd try to keep his best foot forward.

"They've been discussing new school taxes for the past twenty minutes. How can I possibly support higher taxes and keep my job? Answer me that. I excused myself to the washroom while they hash it out."

Here was someone with the power to help us straighten out this mess. "Well, now that you mention it, they've taken Patti Perez to the county jail."

"Good God!"

"Exactly, and she didn't do it, Your Honor. It's circumstantial, every bit."

"Of course it is." There was an awkward silence.

"Did you know ahead of time they were going to arrest her?"

He cleared his throat. "No, not Patti Perez per se. I called Sheriff Wallace and told him to get back here, vacation or no vacation."

I sensed there was more to it than that. "And?"

"We can't have folks feeling scared to go about their business. For pity's sake, we don't want to be known as the murder capital of West Texas. I told him he'd better make an arrest and make one soon."

I glanced at Senora Mari, who was leaning in to catch every word. *"Loco,"* she whispered as she twirled her finger in the age-old gesture for lunacy.

"Circumstantial evidence doesn't mean they can lock her up."

"Well, now, is that all they've got? That's not the impression I received."

I bit my tongue . . . hard. I was madder than a yellow jacket in a lawn mower. And just like that winged yellow avenger, I wanted to sting the hell out of any man who'd throw my best friend in jail.

she considered my reaction both unnecessary and excessive. "I can do it."

I bit my tongue and waited to see what she would do.

"I hit the button. It's dialing."

Just then, a chicken trailer appeared in the distance, driving slowly. "Blast. Well, tell him to hold on." Confident that no one was on the road, I moved into the opposite lane to pass earlier than needed.

"Hello," Senora Mari said in her most proper voice.

As I passed the semi filled with dirty white cluckers, a red sports car zoomed toward us from out of nowhere. I cursed.

"Who is that?" Senora Mari asked imperiously.

Hitting the brake as hard as I could without throwing us both through the front window, I darted back behind the chicken trailer as the red Corvette raced passed us, tooting its horn in a playful taunt.

"Why are you on this phone? You are not Deputy Lightfoot." Her voice held all the authority her four-foot-eleven frame could hold.

"I'll take that." I reached for it, but she backed away toward her window.

"No, I am not Josefina Callahan," she sniffed, "but she has given me the use of this phone." *So stuff it,* her tone implied. That was as close as she'd come to cussing.

I passed the chicken truck this time without any other approaching vehicles in the opposite lane. Once I changed back into my lane, I reached around her and retrieved my phone.

"This is Josie," I said brightly, as if the person on the other line had called me. "To whom am I speaking?"

"What the devil's going on, Josie? I'm in the middle of a city-council meeting." Mayor Cogburn was on the line and madder than a wet hen in a pig wallow.

"I'm so sorry, mayor. Senora Mari must have misdialed." Why he'd answer his cell during a council meeting was anyone's guess.

"No. I told that female deputy, the one who orders at Milagro so politely."

"Deputy Pleasant? You told her?" I tried without succeeding to keep my voice calm.

"She called the house and asked to speak to your friend." She sighed. "Can I help it if I forgot she was an officer of the law?" A spasm of nervousness crossed her face as she spied the odometer.

To my surprise, the dial indicated I was cruising at a mere ninety miles per hour. I lifted my foot from the gas and drew a deep breath. "Patti wouldn't hurt a fly." I hesitated. It was true that in middle school she had been known as Perez the Punisher, but that was only by pimply boys who thought her Goth mystique meant she was free with her favors. As if she would be willing to walk on the wild side with any of them dumb enough to ask.

"Estupido."

"You said it." Everyone who knew Patti knew that she had done more than take over the Feed and Supply after the death of her parents. She'd brought her own style and artistic sensibilities, turning the Feed and Supply into more of a market of farm goods and local artists' wares: jewelry, clothing, yard art, and high-quality, if quirky, boots and ranch wear.

After five minutes, I squeezed my phone from my pants pocket and handed it to Senora Mari. "Look up Lightfoot's number."

She studied the dark surface of the phone and frowned. Before I could offer an explanation on how to turn it on, she began to pound it against the dash.

"Hey!"

"What? I am waking it up."

Before I was forced to pay yet another phone deductible, I grabbed my cell from her and hit the Refresh button. When the screen reawakened, I managed to tap the Contacts button while keeping one eye on the road. "Here."

A deep furrow appeared between her eyes, which meant

lipstick, Sunday dress, and leather bag all said, *Watch out. I mean business.*

At the next Stop sign, I craned my neck to search the side streets for the sheriff's cruiser that had taken Patti. "How long ago did they leave?"

She shrugged a shoulder and clicked the tip of her tongue against the roof of her mouth. "Ten minutes. Fifteen?"

"How did they know where to find her?" Patti had left my apartment only moments before Lenny and I had set out on our abbreviated run.

No answer. I shot a glance at Senora Mari to ask again, but she had turned her face to the passenger window, as if memorizing every fence post and cactus.

I raced onto the highway, only to end up behind a truck carting hay bales. The vehicle was so old and low to the ground that I expected the hay bales to roll out the back and smash my hood like giant bowling balls.

I honked the Prius's neurotic horn and zoomed around the truck, narrowly avoiding a roadrunner sprinting hell-for-leather across the road. Before moving to *far* West Texas, I'd thought a roadrunner looked like the one in Saturday-morning cartoons, but the real McCoy was quite a different story: no more than twelve inches high, weighing maybe four pounds, and without the signature beep-beep. I turned my head in time to see him disappear through the scrub of tumbleweed and grass.

As we whizzed by the open fields, the play of the sun on the tops of the mountains caught my eye. Like a warm, sun-dappled stream, the peaks danced in the embrace of the sun, adding grandeur to the sparse vegetation on their flanks.

The road stretched on for miles with no sign of anything except for the heat mirage of water already at work on the steaming asphalt.

"Slow down before you wrap this car around a fence post."

"Did someone tell the sheriff's office where to find Patti?"

"You want to make a good impression, not invite him to drink with you at the bar." She nodded emphatically as she reapplied her dark-red lipstick, took a tissue out of her bag, and blotted her lips. Slowly, she raised her eyebrows. "Or do you want to invite a certain deputy to drink with you?"

"I'm pretty sure that's all kinds of not true, at least not in this century."

"You need to use that brain of yours."

When I stopped at the first Stop sign, I managed to raise an eyebrow at her in return.

She pursed her lips and studied my chest again. "Look at yourself the way the sheriff and his men will look at you."

"And I should care what they think because . . . ?" Unfortunately, it sounded as though Senora Mari thought the sheriff and his deputies would consider me a woman of little consequence and nothing more. I was tired of trying to measure up to some masculine ideal. Wasn't my opinion of my appearance the one that mattered?

"Humph. Will they see you as a girl interfering in their business or will they see a strong, respectable woman from a good family with the right to know what they are doing?"

I glanced down at my ensemble. *"Abuela—"*

"No." She raised a hand. "What is my name, Josefina?"

I sighed. Once she decided to play the matriarch card, there would be no budging her unless I conceded to the formalities. "Senora Martinez?"

"Senora Mari will do, *por favor.*"

With a whimper, I bit the inside of my cheek to keep my tongue from lashing out. "Senora Mari, I was dressed for my run. Do you want me to go back and change?"

I'd made sure to match and to wear the colors that suited me best when I'd started out. My clothing had been the furthest thing from my mind when I'd bolted for Milagro, thrust Lenny in Aunt Linda's arms, and driven to Casa Martinez like Dale Jr. on the back stretch of the Texas Motor Speedway.

"Don't worry." She patted my knee. "I am here." Her

better than to reveal it in my speech. Senora Mari required the utmost respect.

"Pick me up by the gate. I'm ready."

"But—"

"I'll be waiting outside in the hot sun." I could have argued. I could have tried to cajole her into doing anything other than accompanying me on my mission to rescue Patti—for that was what I was going to do. But I might as well argue with a goat found chewing up a sheet as it hung on a clothesline.

"Five minutes, but you're only along for the ride."

"Humph. I'm along to make sure justice is done."

Five minutes later, I squealed up to the home of the only family I'd known since I was twelve: Aunt Linda, Uncle Eddie, and Senora Marisol Martinez. It was a '70s ranch in the *far* West Texas style: brick veneer and textured stucco, rustic wooden shutters, a red door with decorative tin imprinting, and a yard full of indigenous plants and grasses. Only a fool or the very rich bothered with the deep lawns of Dallas or Austin on the edge of the Chihuahuan Desert.

Senora Mari wore a cotton dress of bright pink with a brown woven leather belt and woven leather sandals, otherwise known as her summer church attire.

She walked purposefully toward my Prius and slid in, being careful to hold her skirt down as she did.

I made a show of shaking my head. "I thought you only wore that dress to church."

"I am not dressed for church." She sniffed and lowered the visor to inspect herself in the mirror. "I am wearing my flat sandals." She returned the favor by closely inspecting my outfit of teal capri pants and matching tank top with *Keep Austin Weird* airbrushed across the chest. She waved a dismissive hand over my ensemble. "You think this getup will impress the sheriff?"

"I don't need—"

"You will not impress this man with . . ." She wrinkled her nose in disgust as if my clothing smelled of rotten eggs.

Main and Mesquite before Lenny needed to stop for a spell and take a drink—that was my story, and I was sticking to it. As I sat on the curb, waiting for him to finish, my phone began to vibrate.

"Jo Jo," Aunt Linda cried.

"Here." At the panic in her voice, I jumped to my feet. "I'm here!"

"They came to the house."

"Yip, yip," Lenny barked, hearing my aunt's fear mirrored in my own voice.

"Ssh," I scolded.

"That new one," Aunt Linda continued. "What's his name? Barnes? Barnett? Oh, heck fire, if I know."

"Whoa. Who came?" I started flipping in my mind through the names of her friends, most of them members of the Broken Boot Community Church—then it hit me. "A deputy stopped by. Is that what you mean?"

"Yes, yes." She raised her voice in frustration. "They took her. I told him I'd have his job before he could whistle 'The Yellow Rose of Texas.' Your Uncle Eddie didn't play football with Mayor Cogburn for nothing."

"They took Senora Mari?" A few months ago, my *abuela* tried to rescue Anthony from a murder charge by admitting to a crime she hadn't committed.

"No, hon." There was a barely perceptible change in my aunt's voice, but I caught it just the same.

The other shoe dropped. "What does he want with Patti?" Like a flash of lightening beneath my skin, I could feel the blood in my veins surge to the surface. "Are they still there?" I scooped Lenny back into the bag.

"No, but they just left. You can still catch them." There was a pause, and then arguing in the background.

"Josefina?" Senora Mari asked, as if I were an impostor with nothing better to do than pretend to be her almost granddaughter. Or perhaps she thought her daughter-in-law was not to be trusted with knowing who was on the phone.

"Abuela?" I was impatient to catch Patti, but I knew

Chapter 11

I don't run fast, and I don't run often, but running in my stylish purple shoes with orange accents and my sock puppet knee-highs gives me that same uplifted feeling I receive when I listen to the preacher's sermon on Sunday mornings. Makes me believe in the impossible—like jogging down Main Street will make me lose weight and fit into my clothes.

"Lenny, I hope you've got your groove on because you're running too, my friend."

"Yip," he said, bouncing up and down with excitement.

I snapped him into his body harness, grabbed my UT water bottle, and bounded down the stairs. It was always a good idea to bring Lenny along; that way folks were less likely to suspect that I was as slow as a box turtle wearing a brick around his neck. Hopefully, they would take one look at Lenny and think, *She can't run any faster, not with a dog the size of a loaf of bread. Bless his heart—just look how fast his little legs are going.*

And I never challenged Lenny to a race because there were days when I suspected he could outrun me.

We made it as far as the doggie fountain on the corner of

She nodded. "How about you only answer the questions I ask?"

"Isn't that the advice they give parents on how to talk to their children about sex?"

She laughed and hurled a pillow at my head. "Shut up."

I smiled in relief. "I'd tell you where I'm going, but you didn't ask."

"As if I care." She smirked and grabbed the duffel from the floor.

"So, you're really abandoning me for Casa Martinez?"

"You bet your butt I am," she said, walking toward the front door. "Two *homemade* meals a day and my own room? My momma didn't raise no fool."

"Yip, yip," Lenny barked.

She laughed and managed to scoop him into her arms without dropping either the duffel or her striped bag. "I'll see you soon, shrimp." With a rub behind his ears, she handed him to me.

I followed her into the kitchen and watched as she tossed my spare key onto the Formica table. "Keep it real," I said.

She turned in the open doorway. "Uh-huh. You just keep it safe."

"And you, Goth Girl."

Patti closed the door and clambered down the stairs.

in college with my own money, and located my running shorts, UT T-shirt, and sock monkey knee-highs.

"Exactly. Since when do you make exercise your business?"

I quickly changed, found my running shoes in the closet, and proceeded to lace up.

Tightening my hair band, I chuckled. "Need to clear my head."

Her expression clouded as if she understood I was withholding what was actually weighing on my mind. "It's okay."

And she was right. My mind was racing with the desire to discuss the murder. My brain was brimming with questions and facts, as if I'd crammed all night for an exam and had yet to take my final.

I busied myself with attaching Lenny's leash and finding some dog snacks for my pocket. How could I bring up Jeff's murder yet again? Each time I mentioned his name it would stab her in the heart like a spear.

"Josie."

I looked up, realizing her voice was strong, nearly normal.

She dropped her duffel on the end of the bed. "I wasn't in love with the guy, but he was a human being. And he was killed in my home." She pounded on her chest. "My living room. And I brought him there."

I placed a tentative hand on her shoulder. "That's not your fault. You had nothing to do with it."

She stepped closer, her gaze intensifying. "Of course not, but it's too insane being this close to two murders." Her voice faded, her eyes gazing out the window at the Chisos Mountains in the distance.

"And me? Do I make it worse?" Was I a reminder of all the violence too?

"Huh. I don't know which one of you snores the loudest, you or the Lenster."

After a moment of thought I said, "Why don't I play the investigation close to my chest?"

someone had hit him over the head with a guitar, he was a serious gambler and womanizer, his agent was desperate to break even on Clark's tour, and every woman I'd met who knew him seemed to love him in one way or another.

I needed to process what I'd uncovered so far, but as Patti's old boyfriend was the murder victim, I decided to leave her out of it. I rang Lightfoot at the sheriff's department, but his line went straight to voice mail. I called back, hoping the switchboard operator would bend and give me his whereabouts. Though she was hardly friendly, the crotchety woman on duty did manage to loosen her corset enough to admit he was on patrol.

What better way to clear my head than to take Lenny for a run? A little thing like exercise wouldn't kill me. And, besides, burning off more calories would allow me to consume more calories. I raced up the stairs.

"Where are you off to?" Patti removed a pile of clothes from the bedroom floor and stuffed them into a navy duffel bag.

I whistled, and Lenny raised his head from his taco-shell bed. When I'd bought the doggie bed shaped and colored like a crispy beef taco, I'd thought it cute and irreverent. Now it was just plain weird. When he raised his head from the meat-colored cushion, I swear it made me think of ants at a picnic, or worse.

"Lenster, run." He stood and shook his whole body from silky head to feather-duster tail. With a lack of enthusiasm, he trotted over to where his leash lay on the floor near the front door and brought it to me. The handle lay between his teeth and the rest of it dragged along behind.

"Good boy. Who's the smartest boy?" I scratched him behind the ears and he sighed and began to shake his back left leg.

"I know that look." Patti had her duffel over one shoulder and a striped Guatemalan cloth bag over the other.

"You know me—business to tend to." I hurried to my dresser, the first piece of furniture I purchased as a freshman

To be honest, I preferred my own company. "Patti's used to sleeping in an old, quiet neighborhood."

"True, that," my friend said with a laugh.

Aunt Linda glared. "She can't be any worse than you." She grabbed my braid and gave it a yank. "Eating us out of house and home."

"Excuse *me*." I didn't lay a finger on most of the items in the pantry or refrigerator when I stayed the occasional night at Casa Martinez.

"We can't keep guacamole and hummus in the house if Jo Jo's home. And forget about popcorn, Dr Pepper, tortilla chips, and ice cream."

"Not true. I've cut way down on Dr Pepper and cookies 'n cream."

"Since when?"

"Last week." I hadn't had the opportunity to shop for groceries or mooch from my family since the murder.

"You come over whenever you like, Patti. We're glad to have you."

"Thanks." She threw back her rounded shoulders. "I'm opening the Feed and Supply later this afternoon to do inventory." Patti gave me a lopsided grin as she made her way to the stairs. "Why don't I go up and grab my things now?"

"Should I be insulted?" I called after her.

"Nope."

"Should Lenny and I go with you to keep you company?" She was an independent cuss, but I couldn't resist.

"Yip?" Lenny asked.

"The dog can come if he stays out of my suitcase," she called from the top of the stairs.

"Yip, yip," Lenny cried.

"Ah, go ahead." I removed his leash and placed him halfway up to abbreviate his monumental climb.

I'd mulled things over in my mind as I bantered with Patti. Now I stared out the front window onto the street, searching for someone or something that might connect the dots. What did I know about Jeff's murder? A few things:

"*Sí.* We will call it . . . what is the name of that Jeff Clark's song?"

I laughed. "'Sweet Thing.'"

"That's it. Call it that, write it on the blackboard," she shrugged, "and we'll see if these tourists and reporters like it." Her tone said she highly doubted it would be a success, even with strangers.

She straightened her shoulders, gave each of us an imperial nod, and walked back into the kitchen, her domain.

Once the doors to the kitchen closed, Aunt Linda and I laughed. "Well," I said, placing an arm around her shoulders, "you got your wish."

"Sweet Thing." She shook her head. "I'll prove to her how sweet it is."

Patti joined us. "Do you make those at home?"

"I used to make them every Sunday night."

"Would you be making them tonight, by any chance?"

"I could."

Patti broke into a wide grin.

"Would you like to join us?" my aunt asked.

"That'd be awesome." Patti opened her mouth to say something else and hesitated. She'd slept in my room the past few nights, but not well. Sleeping in my tiny apartment was an acquired taste. You had to like the sound of trains passing through town during the middle of the night, and the yips Lenny made as his little legs chased rabbits and mice in his dreams. Not to mention the clatter and bang of the garbage truck as it picked up trash from each of the businesses along Main—at the unfortunate hour of five o'clock in the morning, three times a week.

"What Patti's trying to say is she'd rather stay with you tonight." I raised an eyebrow.

"Did I give you permission to put words in my mouth?" She twisted the iron nail that hung on a leather cord around her neck.

"What do you think?" My aunt turned to me, searching for any sign of hurt feelings.

"Where are you off to?" Aunt Linda followed her husband as he headed for the back door.

"Meeting with Ryan."

"On Sunday?" Why Aunt Linda still acted as if my uncle would suddenly decide to stay home and ignore Coach Ryan and football was a mystery.

"Yes, my little cactus flower." He turned and took her in his arms.

I stepped back, not wanting to interrupt. They had little time for tender scenes such as this one in their busy lives.

"Are you shorthanded?" He kissed the back of her hand.

She laughed like a teen with her first crush. "No, no."

He kissed the back of her other hand. "That's good."

She backed away. "Come home early." Her smile evaporated. "Someone killed this man, and we don't know why or who."

"Okay." He gave her a light kiss on the lips. "I'll come early so that no crazy can hit me with an electric guitar." He chuckled and headed out the back door.

Before I could slip away, Aunt Linda turned and caught me smiling at their exchange. She dropped her soft demeanor. "He needs to come back early, not because I'm afraid, but because he's going to work himself into an early grave if he's not more careful." What she said was true, and tough or not, I knew she was affected by yet another murder in our quiet town.

"I have decided." Senora Mari joined us.

"And?" My aunt's voice was a perfect study in politeness, but after years of living with her and Senora Mari, I could perceive the thin thread of irritation.

"We will add to the specials one of those things you make."

"What? My tamales?" my aunt asked.

"Yes, a sweet one." *Abuela*'s nose twitched in disapproval.

"How about the apple and raisin ones?" These were my and Uncle Eddie's favorites.

The silence was deafening.

Into the tension-laced air, a quiet voice rang with steel. "You, who have only been working here three months, you want us to vote on the menu?"

He opened his mouth to respond, his cheeks flaming a deep red.

Senora Mari cut him off. "You think we should vote on the menu that has existed in this restaurant for fifteen years?"

Someone in the back muttered, "Oh, boy."

With a gesture of Uncle Eddie's hand, Anthony moved to the back of the room. "Please consider it for me, *Mami*."

The older woman adjusted her bracelets and touched the gold cross at her neck with the other hand.

With a chuckle, Aunt Linda stepped between her errant husband and her mother-in-law. "Eddie, you don't spring a matter of this importance on Senora Mari as if you have already decided without her approval." My aunt placed her red lacquered nails on her husband's denim work shirt. "Let her consider it." She turned her head so that her lips were closer to his ear and farther from the audience of employees. "Alone," she whispered.

He nodded. With another big intake of breath, he stepped back. He schooled his expression, wiping it clean of disappointment and frustration. "Thanks, everyone. Back to work. It's up to Senora Mari now."

My uncle was wise in the ways of his mother. She was proud and had created the restaurant's menu from her own sweat and creativity.

"Why don't they name a dish after me?" Carlos muttered as he ambled back to the kitchen.

Everyone else murmured among themselves and went back to their prelunch chores of wrapping silverware, refilling bottles, wiping down the bright and lively oilcloths on each table, and other everyday but important tasks.

I watched Senora Mari as she studied the blackboard of daily specials on the wall.

"What? All ten of 'em?" Carlos looked around, expecting laughter, but this time he received a dozen glares.

As my uncle thrust his hands on his hips in frustration, I wondered if he realized he was the exact mirror image of his mother. "I don't care if it's two or ten thousand. If we make a good impression on the tourists and these news folks, word will spread."

"Eduardo, are you stretching the truth?"

My uncle blew out a big breath. "Regardless, we add this one dish to the menu and customers will love it. It'll be a . . ."

"Talking point?" Aunt Linda shook her head and kicked up one side of her mouth.

"Yes, uh, a talking point." My uncle glanced nervously among the female members of his family as if realizing anew he was outnumbered. "Why don't we go ahead and name the chicken tamale dinner Dixie's Delight in honor of the first victim Josie found?"

Aunt Linda reached over and slapped her husband upside the head with a stack of menus from the bar.

"Hey," he cried, grabbing the menus from her hand. "Seems only fair," he said, rubbing his head as he glanced around the room, clearly expecting each of us to appreciate his black sense of humor.

"You are disrespectful of the dead." Senora Mari raised two crossed fingers to her mouth. "You must pray that their spirits don't come and haunt you in your sleep."

Muttering began among the various groups.

Aunt Linda stared at her husband in confusion. "What made you think that was appropriate?"

"*Ah, Dios*! I won't change the menu for this dead man that I don't know," Senora Mari cried.

"Listen to his music." Uncle Eddie took the phone from his wife and handed it to his mother. "Give it a try, and then you tell me if we should honor him in some way."

"We could vote on it." Anthony stood and opened his arms to the room. "That would be fair."

"Who?" Lily asked.

"Jeff Clark." Anthony nudged his sister with his elbow. "You know, the guy that was killed."

"No."

"Ssh."

"Linda, find that song of his and play it for 'em." My uncle was starting to sweat. Sometimes his good intentions got the best of his ability to express them.

Aunt Linda pulled out her phone, and after only a few seconds of scrolling, found the song. She adjusted the volume and played a familiar—and weren't all country songs familiar?—tune called "Sweet Thing."

"I've heard that one before." Camille looked at Lily as if trying to pass along her love of the song.

"If I ever heard it, I erased it from my memory." The curl of Lily's lip and the disdain in her voice made it clear that Clark's music was not her cup of tea.

"The order of six tamales will now be renamed as the Clark Six-Pack."

"Did he have a six pack?" Lily asked with relish.

"What is this? You do not change the names on the menu unless you consult me."

Uncle Eddie placed a hand on his mother's shoulder. "*Mami*, it's important."

With a look of disgust, she promptly removed his fingers as if they were a dirty dishrag. "He is not a star, this Jeff Clark, like George Jones or Romeo Santos."

"But these aliens from out of town will be hungry for any mention of him."

"I don't see any aliens." Camille leaned in, eyes as round as saucers.

I gave her a smile. "He means the reporters in town to cover the murder."

With a grin, Uncle Eddie pounded his chest. "Don't forget the folks in town for our new Homestead Days Music Festival."

his hotel and the town by giving an extensive interview to the reporters I'd spotted on the sidewalk.

"What's—"

"Not now." Eddie cut me off with a gesture.

I turned to Aunt Linda, but she merely raised a finger to her lips and widened her eyes.

"I've called you all here to tell you what I just saw in front of the Cogburn Hotel."

"Beyoncé." Carlos's voice rang out with sardonic humor and just a touch of pubescent hope. Though it sounded far-fetched, the pop singer had made an appearance at a trendy campground not far from Broken Boot in the spring.

Everyone laughed, even Uncle Eddie. Senora Mari, on the other hand, merely looked at everyone in displeasure, as if Carlos had made fun of her beloved son.

"No, no. Reporters are here. They'll eat in our restaurant. They'll drink in our bar and dance in our dance hall." He raised his arms in triumph. "We've struck gold."

The staff murmured to each other in excited tones.

"Why are they here?" Senora Mari asked.

"To cover Jeff Clark's murder."

"Was it murder?" Camille asked, glancing toward the exits as if the murderer would walk in at any moment.

"Doesn't matter. What matters is that we jump on the bandwagon and make the most of it."

"Eddie!"

"I didn't know the guy, and I'm not happy he's dead. Still, this case is drawing a lot of media attention."

Aunt Linda placed a hand on his arm. "Tell them your idea."

"It is a fine idea, and it has my blessing." Senora Mari raised her chin with pride as she placed her hand on his other arm.

With a start, he disengaged from the grip of the two strong women in his life. "We take one of our signature tamales and we rename it in honor of Clark."

Hailey's emporium and circled back around to Milagro's parking lot. I hurried upstairs, clipped Lenny's leash to his collar, grabbed him up into my arms, and hurried back down again.

"Yip," Lenny said and licked my face.

"I'm sorry, Lenster. Didn't mean to squeeze you so hard."

"Stop where you are." Uncle Eddie's voice hit me from behind.

"Where are you going?" Senora Mari muttered. "Take me with you."

"Mami, you aren't going anywhere." He gently but firmly ushered her into the bar area and tried to lead her toward a table.

"No." Senora Mari pulled away. "I will seat myself."

"Jo Jo!"

I knew that commanding tone. I climbed onto a barstool next to Senora Mari, who was looking none too pleased at being ordered anywhere by her son. Her legs swung in the air as if she were eight instead of almost eighty. Anthony and his sister, Lily, and Camille sat at a nearby table. Around me, seated at the restaurant's bright-colored tables, was all of our staff—even Carlos, though his arms were crossed in defiance.

From across the room, Patti waved from a table near the window. I sighed with relief. It was unlike her to close the Feed and Supply, which meant she needed our company. In her way, she was admitting to being only human.

"But—"

"You might as well take a seat." Aunt Linda walked in from the office, fast on their heels. "Eddie's called a meeting."

"Have a sit, kid," Senora Mari said, patting the last empty stool. Anthony checked his phone and ignored her.

I sat. If I knew Uncle Eddie's meetings, and I did, this one would finish quicker if I sat down and refused to ask any questions. If no one gave him any lip or questioned his thinking, we'd be out of there in a jiff. I could only hope that Mayor Cogburn would do his usual fine job of promoting

Chapter 10

My story on Jeff Clark's murder had pride of place above the fold of Sunday's *Broken Boot Bugle* the next morning when it hit the front yards of our fair city. My bubble of delight burst when I found AP articles in online newspapers throughout the region on the death and suspected murder of up-and-coming country music singer and songwriter Jeff Clark. How did I ever think I could scoop the major papers?

I stopped at Two Boots after church to pick up the limes Senora Mari needed for the day's special soup. I was on my way back to Milagro when I spotted two news vans, one from an Austin station and another from El Paso, parked in front of the Cogburn Hotel. I passed Milagro and joined the other rubberneckers, as reporters with microphones, camera operators, Ken Price, Mayor Cogburn, and various onlookers all huddled in front of the hotel. The media had taken a bite and decided Clark's murder was a tasty morsel.

"Dad gum it!" I slammed on the brake, nearly rear-ending a minivan on its *Don't Mess with Texas Grandmas* bumper sticker as I strained to see who all was being interviewed. I turned right down the alley next to Barnum and

UT clock on the wall behind me. "No trouble, darlin'. I'd wait until the sun comes up."

"I'd love to, another time." I touched his arm. "I have to finish a story I'm working on for the *Bugle*." I wanted to process what I'd overheard between Price and the reporter dude. The iTunes drop was a great factoid.

"You're thinking way too hard. I'm talking about tonight, not forever."

"Order up," Carlos said, ringing the bell at the pickup window.

"In that case, I'll be sure to call you real soon."

His self-deprecating laugh hit just the right note, warm and carefree, with no strings attached.

here chores." I raised the ketchup bottle high. "So sorry. One Dos Equis coming right up."

"Make that two."

"Yes, sir. Two."

"Geesh," the younger one added as I left.

I hurried to the bar, found the beers, flipped off the lids so fast one hit the pressed-tin ceiling.

"What are you doing, Miss Josie?" Anthony was wiping down the tables in the bar. "Who are those guys?"

"Ssh. I'll tell you later."

I hurried through the doorway, a big grin on my face, but they weren't following my progress. Once again I slowed down, trying to catch each word. I was sure I looked like a creature out of a sci-fi movie. You know the ones where everyone starts moving in slo-mo for no good reason?

". . . probably found out he was screwing someone else." Silence.

Two sets of hostile eyes were now riveted on me.

"Here you go."

This time Price waited to speak until I'd not only left their table, but crossed to the back counter.

Was he talking about Heather, the CD Girl, or Wilhelmina, her mother?

While I was lost in thought, the cowbell over the front door jangled to life. In strode the gray-haired member of Jeff Clark's band, his warm smile firmly in place.

"Howdy there, Miss Josie Callahan." He might as well have announced who I was over a loudspeaker at the county fair.

I hurried over. "Hey." I placed myself between him and the two at the booth, praying they hadn't heard.

"Would you care to join me for a late supper?"

"Uh, sure. But not tonight."

"Oh?" His smile dimmed.

"I don't get off work until nine."

I had to give him credit. He didn't check his watch or the

and marketing like he was another Kenny Chesney, but his early releases were amateurish. The audiences didn't buy the songs or tickets to his shows."

"That's tough."

"I'm not saying my career's on the line or anything." Price chuckled. "But this song's got to pay some serious bills. *Capisce*?"

"Sure."

"Take these two women he had on tour with him—one old enough to be his mother and the other young enough to get him into serious trouble if he looked at her the wrong way."

"Yeah, yeah, so what happened?"

I froze, praying they wouldn't notice that I'd run out of things to straighten.

"Well, for one, he doesn't need a seamstress for the band. What is this? The Elton John tour?"

The younger man laughed.

"Sure, she does laundry and whatever, but they can do their own. They're not the Rolling Stones. And this girl, the CD Girl he called her. What a crock. Am I right?"

I heard no response, so the reporter was either in midbite or intent on taking notes.

"Come on. I told him the road manager could sell the T-shirts and stuff, but he complained like a little baby— something about her needing a job and running from a terrible home life. The two of them were probably running from the law and her parents, if you know what I mean."

"Oh yeah." In the young reporter's voice I could almost hear his thoughts: *I won't tell until I need to further my career.*

"Excuse me." Price's tone was icy.

Uh-oh.

I swung around, my simpleton mask firmly in place. "Oh, I'm so sorry. I didn't forget exactly—I just caught up in these

"Sorry about the timing."

"Are you kidding me? It's a gift from the gods."

"Why is that?"

"Don't get me wrong. Jeff Clark's death is a tragedy, plain and simple." I watched as Price pounded the table. "But we've got to honor his memory by getting the word out about his music." Quickly, I glanced away. He must have paused to take a bite, for I heard the clinking of forks. "That's where you come in. Once you post your story on social media, his single could rocket up the charts in a matter of minutes." Price's phony easygoing manner was wearing thin, and I could hear his underlying desperation. Was the band responsible for the losses incurred if they canceled the rest of the tour? Or was Ken Price?

The reporter-looking dude placed the notebook on the table and continued to eat his enchiladas. "Anything off the record, man?"

I froze, waiting to hear the juicy question, when out of the corner of my eye I could see Price waving a beer bottle. I acknowledged him and slowly made my way over, praying they'd continue while I was still within earshot.

"Another Dos Equis."

"Yes, sir."

I turned away as slowly as I could.

"Huh." Price chuckled. "If we're off the record, *man*, then you got to turn off the recorder."

I started walking, straining to hear. Paranoid about missing something, I paused at each table along the way so I could straighten the salt and pepper shakers, which allowed me to hear their discussion.

"Sorry." He must have turned it off. "Go ahead. Whatever you say, man, stops here."

"It better." There was a pause, and I proceeded to checking ketchup bottles. "Jeff was a real pain in the wallet, if you know what I mean."

"Why?"

"He convinced the label to spend money on advertising

The young journalist with the unwashed hair ignored me. "Jeff Clark was a one-of-a-kind, man."

Price adjusted the gold bracelet on his wrist. "True."

"Even so, for those who didn't know his brand of country, who did he resemble on the country scene?"

"Kenny Chesney meets Brad Paisley meets Luke Bryan."

I bit back a smile. Price was comparing Clark to every popular male country singer that was currently making big money. Those names would blow up social media.

"If Jeff Clark were here with us today, what would you tell him?"

"Can I help you?" He rolled his eyes at the reporter as if I couldn't see him.

"Do you need anything else?"

He narrowed his eyes, the better to inspect my insectlike qualities.

"Hey," the young journalist said in a softer tone, "if we need more chips and salsa, we'll let you know."

It took all the acting skill I possessed to give them a nod and walk away. I was actually biting the inside of my cheek to keep from giving Price a sharp piece of my mind.

Perhaps I could pretend to be the simpleton they assumed me to be and riddle Price with enough stupid questions to make him lose that LA sheen—like when you go canoeing on the Rio Grande and find you're a gourmet entrée for a hoard of mosquitos.

I found a clean cloth and the spray cleaner and started wiping down the chairs, starting at the table farthest away but slowly moving closer. I was careful to work as silently as possible so I could hear the questions and answers, hoping for clues as to who would want to kill Jeff Clark.

"Got enough?"

The young guy checked his notes. "Yeah, looks great."

"I almost forgot. Jeff's new song dropped on iTunes yesterday."

"Awesome. What's it called?"

"'Sweet Thing.'"

He took Ken Price's measure. "You deserve better. Maybe the one with the glasses."

"Not in this lifetime." Only if I wanted to mother someone down the aisle and throughout our lives together. Ugh, there I went judging people again. Peccadillos indeed. My *simple* flaws were piling up like pumpkins on the annual Pumpkin Path in San Antonio.

I grabbed his order pad and the pen from his pocket. "Gentlemen."

The Ray Bans were now on top of his head. He gave me a cursory glance that didn't meet my eyes. "I'll have whatever the special is tonight." Was I so easily ignored because I was too curvy or too Texas? Who did he think he was dealing with?

Our special that evening was shrimp diablo, shellfish sautéed in coconut oil and a blistering chile sauce. You could choose your heat level or go with the standard four and a half that Senora Mari and Carlos prepared. My *abuela* preferred a face-sweating seven, while our cook preferred a moderate three. I could warn Price, but, then again, maybe he read the blackboard when they arrived. And maybe he loved scorching-hot food that would leave his mouth inflamed for a few hours.

"And for you?" I turned toward the younger one. He held his phone in one hand while tapping the fingers of his left hand on the table, clearly impatient for me to go.

"Whatever's decent."

"Right," I murmured. Most of our customers thought all our menu was lip-smacking good. I would bring him the cheese enchiladas with a guacamole tostada and a side of black refried beans.

I was itching to address Price, but I'd wait until I'd served the meal to confirm that Ray Ban Guy with the metrosexual vibe was indeed LA's own Kenneth Price.

"Can I get you anything else?" I caught myself before I said *Mr. Price.* I would learn more if I didn't identify myself. They gave me their drink orders.

tor. I was pretty sure that meant she used hot rocks in her studio and not a commentary on whether or not she was attractive. Heck, as I couldn't find a picture of her, it could have been both.

After the evening rush, a short, slight man with dark hair, a perfectly groomed five o'clock shadow, and a killer pair of Ray Bans waltzed through the front door of Milagro, followed by a dude wearing the T-shirt, cardigan, jeans, and wire-framed glasses of every college journalist ever portrayed on the big screen. If the short guy with the perfect smile and pugnacious gaze wasn't Kenneth Price, then my instincts were as out of tune as a fiddle in a leaky garage.

I watched Anthony step forward to greet him. As he started toward the door to the patio, the short guy stopped him and pointed instead to a table in the back near the emergency exit. Lily brought waters, chips and salsa, and complimentary *frijoles borrachos*, or drunken beans. The intense young man with black-framed glasses removed his phone from his man purse, asked Ken Price—for it had to be him—a question, and then promptly took a picture of the agent with his phone.

Anthony and I watched this from the broad archway that led to the bar. He pulled his order pad from his pocket. "Two orders of beef fajitas coming right up." It was our private joke. If a tourist had no idea what to order, they demanded skirt steak, peppers, onions, and tortillas.

I stopped him with a hand on his arm. "I got this."

He smiled. "Oh yeah?"

I chuckled. "Yeah, this guy owes me for standing me up this morning."

"That guy?" Anthony asked with a sneer.

"What?" I asked, poking him in the side with my elbow. "You don't think it's true love?" I'd never seen our young headwaiter so disgusted with another human being, let alone with a stranger.

move. It was time for tamales. Was I hungry? No. Did it matter? Not today.

Without Ken Price's interview, my article would still hobble into print. I edited what I had, adding in the bits about the business of Price's schedule, his upcoming visit to the morgue, and the fact that Clark had a sister in Oregon who was being notified.

I fed Lenny some crunchy kibble and girded my loins to read everything online about Jeff Clark that I should have already read and consulted. I sent the updated version to my editor and explained I had a potential interview with a member of Clark's band—the gray-haired Dustin with the warm smile—and Clark's sister, if I could reach her.

I was hoping for an additional sidebar, though in my heart I feared the AP article would quell any enthusiasm my editor had for my homegrown stories. Of course, if a major catastrophe occurred or a reality show hero changed her hairstyle, the Associated Press might only release an article or two and be done with it.

While I was unearthing research on Jeff Clark's early gigs in places like Ville Platte, Louisiana, and Bell Buckle, Tennessee, the AP article on his death hit the online papers. Their piece was thorough and to the point, stating that his death was under investigation by local authorities. Thankfully, it gave both the Homestead Days Music Festival and Two Boots a brief mention.

Who knew? Maybe that would cause a wellspring of business for our dance hall. And maybe the good Lord would forgive me for thinking such mercenary thoughts in the wake of a man's murder.

I continued with the paper's search engines at my fingertips, pulling all the relevant information together, and added my own brand of sentiment, turning the erstwhile King of Country into a veritable saint. I did eventually have at my disposal a scant number of facts that the AP reporter hadn't mentioned: he had an ex-wife, a cousin in Fort Worth, a sister in Oregon, *and* a cousin who was a hot-yoga instruc-

have to visit the morgue and call Jeff's sister in Oregon so we can transport the body. Plus I have to find the sheriff and get an update on what's being done to remedy this situation."

Could one remedy someone's *murder*? "Oh, well," I said with feigned nonchalance. "I guess I'll have to print my article about Clark's murder with what I have." I dug the knife deeper. "If you don't think there's a need to give me information that will make his cause and his music sympathetic and appealing to our readers, then so be it."

"Is your paper with the Associated Press?"

I ground my teeth. "No."

"Then it doesn't matter, does it?"

"You might want to reconsider. We have a hundred thousand readers from all over the state and the Southwest."

He barked a laugh. "Not impressive by any stretch of the word."

I took my pride in my hands. "You did say we'd meet today, and I did wait at a table, alone, for a long, long time."

"That's unfortunate for you, but I have to leave as soon as possible." He paused, and then his tone changed for the better. "A deal's coming through that needs my attention back in LA."

"Why not right here, right now, on the phone?"

"Hmm. Sorry, but no. That window of opportunity has closed."

My face flamed. I could feel my self-control flying down the stairs and out the front door. Before I could think of a suitable retort, he threw a gauntlet into my face.

"The AP will release an article later today that will include a bio of Jeff. You can do your own research or quote that article in yours. Be my guest."

The line went dead. What was it about me that made him think he could keep hanging up on me?

"Yip," Lenny said.

"You're right. I'm toast."

Lenny licked my chin.

Which I allowed him to do while I considered my next

Chapter 9

After forcing myself to remain long enough to drink a big glass of water, I paid my bill and drove back to Milagro. Hoofing up the stairs to my apartment, I heard the familiar and heartwarming yips of my canine friend.

I unlocked the door and caught him in my arms. "Hello, precious Lenster." I kissed him on the head as my phone started to ring.

"Hello," I said with an effort, raising the phone to my ear as I juggled my long-haired, enthusiastic Chi onto my other shoulder, like the big baby he was.

"Yip, yip," Lenny said in greeting.

"Kenneth Price." The agent's voice was brisk and officious. "You called this number." Beneath his brittle sophistication, I could hear the slight blur of exhaustion or a late-night date with his mini bar.

"It's Josie Callahan, Mr. Price. We were to meet at Elaine's this morning. I waited for over an hour."

A pause. "Oh, right. I had to take a call from the office."

It was my turn to remain silent.

"I'm not going to have time to meet with you today. I

He was Jeff Clark's agent. And he's meeting me this morning to give me a brief interview."

He slapped the table with a hand whose nails were bitten down, neatly but vindictively. "Enough said." He rose and took an extra few seconds to arrange his chair perfectly beneath the table once again. "Don't let me make a fool of myself."

"I won't."

Back in work mode, his face once again took on the aloof expression of a Parisian waiter. "Coffee, madam?"

"Thanks."

While I waited, I watched the tourists on the street. It wasn't difficult to pick them out, as they mostly wore cruise wear or matching shorts sets or clothing that was obviously new and not worn by the modest, let's-get-work-done citizens of Broken Boot. After fifteen minutes of mental gymnastics, I ordered a Western breakfast quiche filled with ham, peppers, onions, and tomato. After forty-five minutes, I began to fear he felt no compunction at leaving me to my own devices. And after an hour of waiting, I decided he was a cretin frightfully prejudiced against journalists and ordinary people from small towns.

Since my recent layoff and breakup, these thoughts rupture my otherwise calm exterior when I am kept waiting or when I find myself in anxiety-laden situations. I pushed away the coffee, recognizing that the caffeine was adding to my anxiety—that or an army of ants had invaded my shirt—and pulled out my phone.

I discovered no new text messages or voice mails, so I called him. And Mr. LA, the hater of small-town journalists, refused to answer.

Suellen looked first at one and then the other of us, her face a study in concentration. Apparently, she wasn't a fan.

"My dog."

"Heavens, I know who Lenny is, but I didn't know he was a writer." She glanced around the restaurant, eyeing in particular the cases for pies and desserts. On the wall near the blackboard covered with the daily specials was an area where customers hung their business cards and announcements on an old-fashioned corkboard. "Why don't you put up a notice?" She gestured toward the corkboard. "People like me could use the diversion."

"I'll do that." What could I use? Lord knows Lenny didn't have his own business cards.

"Don't worry, honey." Andrew patted my arm. "I'll handle it. If I know you, and I have to admit I don't know you well, you already have so much stuff on your plate that things are falling off the side."

"Thanks."

"Breakfast or lunch menu?" Suellen asked.

"Both?"

She handed the menus to Andrew, who led me toward a table that faced the street with a perfect view of the Chisos Mountains—hills, by any other states' standards—and the adobe-style railroad depot.

"So, what's the special occasion?" Andrew moved each item on the table until it was in perfect alignment.

"Keep your eye out for an escapee from LA by the name of Ken Price. He should be here any minute."

This time Andrew nearly hugged himself with excitement. "LA? Here?" He glanced around, but the elderly ladies in the far corner near the antique display of quilts and doilies were lost in conversation. He slid into a chair and leaned in close. "Who is it? And why are they here?"

I smiled at his enthusiasm. Like I said, we're a small town, and strangers are like exotic animals in the zoo, which would make a man from LA on a level with a space alien.

It didn't take long to drive back down to Main Street, parallel the Prius in front of Elaine's Pies, and scramble inside.

"Josie," a familiar voice called in excitement.

"Lily." Anthony's younger sister filled her meager free time with working at both Milagro and Elaine's Pies to help her provide for the two of them, plus their younger brother and sister. Tough cookie, and even harder worker. "Are you busing tables?"

"A bit. I'm mostly hosting this week, but Suellen—I mean, Miss Burnett—said she'd give me a table or two this week if business picks up."

"And you're keeping your grades up?" We had a deal. If she stayed in school and kept her grades up, she'd continue to have a job at Milagro.

She shrugged. "Sure. It's only the second week."

I lifted my fist for a knuckle bump. "That's awesome."

A tall, skinny, elbows-and-knees kind of woman spotted us from the serving window and made her way across the restaurant to us. "Josie? How can we help you?"

I felt the corners of my lips lift in a smile, but I was still a bit overwhelmed whenever Suellen and I came face-to-face. I had helped the police solve Dixie Honeycutt's murder. Unfortunately for Suellen and her sister, Melanie, I had also proven their mother was behind it.

"Josie Callahan," came a cry from behind me.

Andrew, the restaurant host and Suellen's right hand, entered from the kitchen with a wide, toothy grin. As usual, his black slacks and dress shirt were immaculate. His green-and-white-polka-dotted bow tie lightened my spirits.

"When is Lenny posting again? He's been a bit lazy about maintaining his blog over the past two weeks."

I laughed. "He posted last night, as a matter of fact."

"Ah," Andrew said, rubbing his hands together as if he were a villain in a melodrama or a small child looking forward to a double-dip cone. "I await his erudite wisdom and choice of phrase."

The phone rang, and Uncle Eddie paused the film.

With a glance at my uncle, Ty walked into the hall and gestured for me to follow. "What's in it for you?" he asked softly.

"I want my piece for the *Bugle* to be accurate, not a whitewash."

"You trying to solve the murder?" He gave me the once-over, not overly aggressively—just a neighborly sizing-up.

"No. I'm concentrating on my relationship with the *Bugle*, not with the sheriff's department."

"I wouldn't be so quick to assume it was his gambling got him into trouble."

"No?"

"Here's what else I know." He leaned in, and again I resisted the urge to back away. "He had chick problems."

I raised my eyebrows in question.

"Yeah, he was a little too fresh with the ladies."

"You would know all about that."

He frowned. "So you say. I, at least, am a one-at-a-time kind of guy."

"So you say."

"Fine," he said, turning away.

I placed a hand on his shoulder. "I apologize. What was your point?"

"Lots of local girls are plumb crazy, and he knew lots of local girls."

"And?"

"And that's all there is to know about that." He glanced at my hand where it still rested on his shoulder and smiled, his dimples in full view. "Unless I can help you with something else?"

I jumped back as if I'd placed my hand on a hot burner. "Not in this lifetime, buster."

He merely laughed and cruised into Uncle Eddie's man cave, leaving me to digest the new tidbit he'd tossed my way.

* * *

tine poker games and watched as Lightfoot hauled his butt off to jail on suspicion of killing his aunt.

Uncle Eddie peeled his eyes from the football game long enough to give his friend a look of disbelief. "Not once?"

"We might have discussed it, but he only came into town Thursday morning. It's not like we had time to play Texas Hold 'Em during his sound check."

"Did he ask you to find him a game?" I asked.

Ty's jaw clenched. "Yeah."

I threw out a softball to see who would swing first. "I heard he had a gambling problem."

Uncle Eddie nodded his head slowly. "Something somebody said makes me think you're right."

"Did you hear anything about that?"

Ty had returned his attention to the television. The offense was punting and the kicker booted one into the end zone. "Maybe something. Why does it matter, shorty?"

"Just answer the question," I said.

"I'll answer yours if you answer mine."

"Maybe his gambling debts caught up with him?"

"And someone murdered him over them. Not bad, Nancy Drew."

"You still haven't told me where you heard about his gambling."

"One of the guys in my band played in a high-stakes game with Jeff Clark in Tulsa. He mentioned Clark would be looking for a game when he came to town."

"Was there any hint that Clark had a gambling problem?"

He shrugged and took a moment to crack his knuckles. "No, except that I could make big money if I played with Clark."

"Not much of a winner?"

"Or he didn't know when to quit." This from Uncle Eddie. "What? I'm not saying I gamble, but I hear enough to know that's when you get in trouble is when you don't know when to walk away." He gestured toward the television. "Same's true in football. Walk away while the walking is good."

woman had murdered his aunt—who was like a mother to him—only three months prior. But not me. He'd embraced his vices long before that tragic event. Any hope I held that his grief would cause him to clean up his act had gone the way of his Marlboros. Up in smoke.

"Don't tell me." I shook my head in mock amazement. "You were an all-star quarterback in your day."

One side of his mouth kicked up. "Nah, running back. I could run the quarter mile in nothing flat." With a grin, he flopped into the chair and promptly ignored me in favor of the twenty-two men running around in tight pants and space helmets on the screen.

I grabbed the backs of their chairs and leaned in close. "Finding you two together is like birthday cake at Christmas! Couldn't have asked for better."

"Watch out, son." Uncle Eddie took a sip of coffee from his *West Texas* mug. "That means she's about to ask you a barrelful of questions."

Ty chuckled. "I don't have to answer, do I?"

"Nope." Uncle Eddie flung a glance at me over his shoulder. "Not unless you want her to keep pestering you." He raised his eyes to the ceiling. "But she's like a dog with a T-bone. Going to nibble at you until she digs the marrow from your bones."

"Ignore him." I stepped closer, hoping to keep their attention away from the football antics, which bored me silly from too much exposure. "Did you meet Jeff Clark before he died?"

"She gets right to the point, don't she?" I couldn't help but appreciate the way Ty deflected the question with another question of his own.

"Yep, she's cutthroat that way," Uncle Eddie said.

"Yes or no, Honeycutt?"

"Sure. What of it?"

"Did you play cards with him?"

That got his attention. "Hell, no." About three months ago, I'd led the sheriff's department to one of Ty's clandes-

he was sitting in front of the television, watching game film of recent football games. This one appeared to consist of two small colleges, McMurry and Hardin-Simmons.

"Hola." I kissed the top of his head.

His eyes remained riveted to the screen. "Hey, Jo Jo. What's up?"

"Where's Ty?"

"Had to see a man about a dog. Cool your jets." He gestured to the empty guest chair in front of the TV.

"Don't tell me you've recruited him to help you?" Uncle Eddie often assisted Coach Ryan by watching films of other games in the conference. Since the NCAA had named my uncle Rookie of the Year in Division III football as a freshman, an unprecedented honor for a West Texas College athlete, he'd never quite left his cleats behind.

"This is my way of paying him back for extending my contract." Ty Honeycutt stood in the doorway, as if posing for a fashion spread in *GQ*, the redneck edition. His wavy brown hair was uncovered for once, which left it free to form a cloud around his head. On his feet, he wore athletic shoes instead of boots, and he'd exchanged his skintight jeans and Western shirt for a pair of cargo shorts and a T-shirt that read *Hogsbreath Saloon, Florida.*

"That so?" I asked. "You played again last night, I hear."

Uncle Eddie kept his eyes glued to the game.

"And I'm playing again tonight," Ty said with a smug smile. "The crowd just couldn't get enough of this handsome face. Ain't that right?" He slapped my uncle on the back.

"Hmm," Uncle Eddie said, which told me he hadn't discussed the added performance with Aunt Linda.

I caught myself smiling at Ty's good-ole-boy antics and quickly reminded myself that he was well on his way to checking all the vices off his bucket list: women, booze, gambling, lying, and sloth. And who knew what he practiced in his own home?

Someone else might have cut him some slack, as a crazy

"I have to shower and shave. I could meet you in a couple of hours."

"Why don't we meet for breakfast at Elaine's Pies? It's next door to the hotel." Even though Elaine Burnett was currently serving time in Huntsville, I couldn't stand the thought of her family, namely her oldest daughter, Suellen, suffering due to the fact her mother was a loony bird. "Their quiches are to die for." A poor choice of words. "You name it, they've got it."

"Huh. So they carry cage-free egg-white omelets?" His veneer of civility was wearing thin as old boot leather.

"Um, I bet you'll find something you like." His style of breakfast wasn't foreign to me—I'd lived in Austin, for pity's sake. I wasn't going to let the LA demeanor and sense of entitlement I heard in his voice deter me from my objective: a good story. "Want to meet in, say, an hour?"

"You're persistent. I like that." Mr. Friendly had returned. I waited.

"All right. See you at . . ."

"Elaine's."

"Right." He chuckled as if I were some kid in need of encouragement, and hung up.

I found myself staring at the phone in wonder. If I didn't know better, I'd say Ken Price was the stereotypical money-grubbing agent. I sighed. That was being judgmental, and I was trying so hard to put my peccadillos behind me.

"Gracias." I waved to the hotel clerk and headed out into the warm September sun. With the hour I now had at my disposal, I was going to find out more about Jeff Clark and who wanted him dead.

I drove the Prius over to Two Boots. When I spotted the El Camino, I pumped my fist in exhilaration. "You're mine, bucko." I do love it when I can fit errands into tiny increments of time between other chores. Makes me feel all kinds of efficient.

I entered through the side door and into the dim lighting of the hallway that led to my uncle's office. As imagined,

"Have you seen him today?"

She peered at me over her glasses and shook her head with the smallest of movements. I knew that under the hotel's privacy policy she couldn't give out his room number.

A short well-manicured finger pointed across the lobby. "I'll have him call you on the house phone."

With a grateful nod, I crossed to the red leather wingback chair and waited. I couldn't make out what she said, but I witnessed her use of the phone and her lips moving, and a few nods of her head. "Thank you, Mr. Price." I could hear those final words from across the room.

"Thanks."

She gave me a wink and went back to the paperwork on her desk. The lobby was quiet. The buffalo and antelope studied me with their glassy eyes from the stucco walls of their permanent home. I had a moment to study the beams above me and to ponder if they were authentic or added after the fact for atmosphere.

After a minute, the pedestal phone on the leather-topped table beside me rang, quiet and unobtrusive, polite.

"Mr. Price?"

"Ken." The voice was brisk but flat, as if the flight from LA had pressed all the vitality from his vocal cords. "Make it fast."

"This is Josie Callahan."

"Got it in one. As you can guess, I waltzed into a cataclysmic cyclone of chaos this morning."

"Uh, well, when you and I spoke yesterday, you indicated you would answer a few questions for the local paper."

"Absolutely." A forced politeness entered his voice, as if we were fast friends. "I want to talk to you about Jeff—of course I do."

"I wouldn't need but a few minutes of your time. I want to represent Mr. Clark in the best way possible in my article, and you too." He would need to promote his other clients in spite of the murder of this one. As an agent, he might appreciate the interview from a business angle.

Chapter 8

The Cogburn Hotel's distinctive lobby, replete with buffalo and antelope heads, exposed beams, and mosaic tile, gave me a warm Southwestern welcome.

"Hello," I said in greeting to the sturdy middle-aged Latina behind the registration desk. She had to be Senora Mari's friend from bingo night, for they were as alike as two dried chile peppers, except for the fact that this woman was five to ten years younger. She wore her reddish-brown hair in a low bun, plus hand-painted reading glasses, a gold vest, and a matching skirt with a navy blouse.

"May I help?"

"Uh, I'm Josie Callahan." *Should I mention her phone conversation with Senora Mari?*

"Ah yes. Good morning." Her smile was startling white against her tanned face and red lips. Her dark eyes warmed with instant friendship.

"Is Mr. Price available?"

After a quick glance around the lobby, she keyed in a few words and her computer screen changed. "He checked in last night."

"Of course." She gave me a curt nod and headed for the grill to inspect the chicken Carlos was currently cooking, though we both knew he had no need for oversight.

"See you later."

As she sprinkled cayenne pepper over the scintillating grill, her voice rang out. "If they give you the runaround, you call me. I'll knock some smarts into them."

That was a match I'd pay to see: my guinea hen–sized *abuela* socking it to LA agent Ken Price.

I sighed. Only the truth would defend my honor. "It's essential for my story that I interview Jeff Clark's agent."

"The dead guy?"

"Right. And the hotel won't tell me if he checked in last night."

Like a mime on Austin's Sixth Street, she lifted her shoulders in an exaggerated shrug. "So call him."

"It's going straight to voice mail." He hadn't answered the four previous times I'd phoned him. I was lucky if he hadn't already decided to block my number.

She marched over to the old rotary-dial phone on the wall—that had to be as ancient as she was—and dialed. *"Hola."* She paused to listen. *"Muy bien."* Her smile lit up the room.

"What are you doing?" Her meddling could ruin my tenuous relationship with Ken Price, especially with the drama already on his plate. "Shh. Stop whatever it is you're doing." I hung over her shoulder, trying to listen in.

She launched into a rapid conversation in Spanish. "Uh-huh," she answered with keen interest. "Uh-huh," she answered yet again, the interest in her voice—feigned or real—growing in intensity. Again she asked the person on the other line three or four rapid-fire questions. She glanced at me, her eyebrows rose, and she nodded. "Okay." She listened some more. *"Gracias."*

With a purse of her lips, she cradled the phone. "He is there."

"Who was that?"

She lifted her chin proudly, peering up at me from her diminutive height. "The hotel desk clerk plays bingo on Monday nights." She lifted two fingers and pressed them together. "We are like this."

I broke into a grin and hugged her before she could retreat. "Thank you, thank you, *Abuela.*"

"Okay, okay." She backed out of my arms, but a smile played around her mouth.

"You are the best."

"Yes, yes. Well, is he?"

I rifled through my bag, finding my phone and notepad, but no pen or pencil. "You know men."

"Humph. That native ordered—"

"Native American," Aunt Linda said, joining us from the direction of her office.

"When did you two get here?" Any other time I would've heard them in the parking lot, arguing louder than a truck full of turkeys.

"I needed an oil change, so Eddie dropped us off."

"Humph." Senora Mari thrust her hands on her hips. "That *deputy* ordered you to stay home like a good girl, *sí*?"

"That sums it up."

"Who is he to boss you around?" Aunt Linda demanded, a deep furrow of disapproval across her forehead.

"Whoa," I said, surprising myself. "He *is* a deputy, an officer of the law." I might have a hankering for investigative journalism, on a Broken Boot–size scale, but Lightfoot was the real deal, dedicated and humble.

"He doesn't have to be uppity with it, and don't you let him." She pointed a finger for emphasis and spun on her heel, returning to her office and its piles of bills.

I hurried through the kitchen, hoping to slip out before Senora Mari waylaid my investigative efforts.

"Where are you going, *chica*?" My *abuela* was as stealthy as a Mexican ninja.

I swallowed. "Headed to the Cogburn Hotel."

"Your tables are covered?" she demanded, pointing toward the dining room with her chin.

"Anthony and Camille will be here."

Her strong hands found her hips—their permanent resting place. "It's Saturday."

"They can handle it. Besides, they'll be glad for a two-way split."

"Tsk, tsk." She clicked her tongue as she considered my response. "Why are you running up and down the street instead of earning your keep?"

integrity of this investigation and you tell me something that might or might not have any bearing on this case."

My face flamed. "I told you plenty."

He slammed the bar and stepped into the sunshine.

"Hey, what about an even exchange of information?"

"The body was sent to El Paso for an autopsy," he threw over his shoulder.

"What's that? You always send bodies there." I followed him into the parking lot. "Hey, I just gave you that guy with the goatee."

"Nah, I already heard about the fight from Vinnie."

With a grunt, he removed his hat, smoothed his raven hair, and replaced the Stetson so it rode low over his eyes. "Do yourself a favor, *Jo Jo*," he said, adopting the nickname used only by my family, which rusted my spurs. "Stay out of our way. Don't try to help us—we don't need your help. You were lucky last time. What if this time we're not dealing with a crazy local, but a hardened criminal who wouldn't think twice of killing you, Patti, and your dog?"

I struggled to find a witty rejoinder as he unlocked his cruiser, threw it into reverse, and propelled onto Main Street, spraying gravel in his wake. Only now that he'd splattered my mind with our narrow escape from Elaine Burnett, I was slow to the draw.

I hurried to the street. "Says you!" I hollered. His cruiser was unimpressed as it vanished around the corner.

Like a kitten defending her kibble, I'd embarrassed myself by screeching after Lightfoot for all of Main Street to enjoy. There was nothing left to do but head on over to the Cogburn Hotel and grab my interview with Clark's agent by the horns.

I stepped inside to find my shoulder bag.

"Is that Indian looking for trouble?" Senora Mari demanded from the wait station, scaring the bejesus out of me.

"Native American, *Abuela*."

seemed a little out of it, forgetting from one day to the next what we had purchased from the market that week. Senora Mari had hired him, and if he met her high standards and didn't bother the rest of us, I'd leave the details to her. Customers loved our food, so he wasn't going anywhere anytime soon.

"Not sure, but I know Senora Mari found tilapia and chicken breasts on sale this week."

His eyes grew wide. "Uh, that's it?"

"Check the bulletin board. Aunt Linda should have tacked the specials up last night before she left."

His face cleared like a child realizing he wasn't going to have to sit in the time-out chair after all. Without another word, he reversed through the swinging door like a jack-in-the-box.

I swung toward Lightfoot, hoping to catch him up short. "Can I ride along on your next interview?"

"No."

"Not a sound, nor a peep."

"No."

"Not even a question. Silent as a mouse."

"What do you think this is—*Castle*?"

Well, shut my mouth. Deputy Lightfoot watched television dramas.

"Not a fan."

"Humph. Still not going to happen."

I followed him to the door. "I have to write these stories— you know I do."

"Hmm."

"Why not help me to write them accurately?"

With one arm on the push bar, he turned slowly. With an intensity akin to a polecat studying a gopher pup, he studied me in silence.

My pulsed surged, but I held my ground. "We could exchange information."

"You mean I'd tell you something that might hurt the

"Go on."

"But he threw it off once he realized we were there." I hugged the six containers and crossed to a table in the far corner.

I expected him to grill me, but he returned his notebook and pencil stub to his pocket, took another swig of coffee, and walked over to the waiter's station and placed the cup in the gray tub we used for dirty dishes. When he turned, his gaze had softened. "Josie, I don't want you to get hurt."

Surprised, I grinned. "This ain't my first rodeo, deputy."

"It could be your last if you're not careful."

"I learned my lesson," I said, crossing my heart. "One encounter with a killer is enough for a lifetime."

He shook his head in disbelief. "When's this article you're writing coming out?"

"Sunday. I'm hoping to write a follow-up as well."

He nodded. "That's good."

"Why?"

He straightened his badge. "We'll have completed most of the investigation by then."

A door slammed in the back, and I spun around. "Hel-loooo," I called, embarrassed by my lack of composure.

"Just me," Carlos said in a sleepy voice. With a bang on the metal prep table and the slamming of refrigerator doors, our head cook had arrived to start his day.

The door from the kitchen swung open. "Morning— Oh, hey, deputy." Our cook wore his usual combination of jeans, black *Selina Forever* T-shirt, white bandana across his brow to ward off the heat of the kitchen, and unbuttoned white chef's coat. This last item was an attempt by Aunt Linda to remind Carlos that our kitchen had to meet the health code of the great state of Texas. Senora Mari thought it was all rubbish and didn't bother to insist he keep the coat buttoned. He turned his sad, mournful eyes on me as if I held the answers to the mysteries of life.

"What's the special today?" I never asked why Carlos

The show was supposed to start at ten o'clock, but Ty Honeycutt's set went long. We headed backstage when Clark's band failed to take the stage. It couldn't have been later than five after."

He tapped the notebook with the end of his pencil. "And?"

I threw the cloth back onto the shelf where it resided. "Like I said, after we heard something fall, this tall guy with a goatee came shoving his way past us."

"Did you know him?"

"No, but I assumed he was in the band."

"Why?"

"He wore a black leather vest and matching leather pants. Who else would dress like that?"

"You can't assume."

"Don't worry. I noticed him onstage that night." He had to be one of the jealous band members Wilhelmina alluded to before she booted me from the bus. What if Redheaded Goatee Guy had continued their fight at Patti's and ended Clark's musical career with a guitar to the skull?

"What'd Jeff say about it?"

"Huh. Clark said nothing. Changed the subject when I told him they'd have to pay for any damages."

He flipped a page and made a note. "Tell me about Jeff Clark."

I hesitated, remembering too clearly Clark's handsome smile and smooth charm—all for Patti's benefit. "Unruffled." I couldn't explain why I'd disliked Clark from the beginning. I finally managed, "and cocky."

"He wasn't angry, even though you said he and his bandmate had a fight?"

"You're right." I began to gather up the sugar dispensers. "He stormed out of his dressing room ready to skin his own buffalo."

"Thought you were a big-city gal."

"What?"

"We?"

"Patti." I studied his face for any hint of reaction, but he didn't even blink. I'd thought the two of them might become an item, but apparently that ship had sailed for Cozumel.

"What were you two doing there?"

"I assume you mean backstage," I called over my shoulder as I gathered three containers and carried them to the table closest to the kitchen.

Before I could stop him, Lightfoot gathered five glass dispensers and placed them alongside the others. "That's right. Did you know him?" Without hesitation, he gathered the rest and plunked them down next to the others.

"Nope."

His eyes narrowed. "How about Patti?" I'd purposely left my friend out of the explanation for as long as possible. I found the tin of sugar in the storage closet and returned.

"How'd she know him?" Lightfoot asked, lifting an eyebrow.

With a practiced hand, I removed all the lids and wiped them down. "They were a couple a few years ago. He sent her a text message asking her to meet him in his dressing room the night of the concert."

No sign of jealousy marred his intense concentration. With a sage nod, he pulled a small notebook and a stub of a pencil out of his breast pocket and made a brief note. "What was the argument about?"

I topped off the containers and screwed on the lids. "Like I said, I'm not sure. We were standing outside the dressing room at that point. One of them said something like 'Give it to me.' Someone else—I think it was Jeff—yelled, 'Give it back.' It sounded as if they were shoving furniture—that or tossing it. I didn't see the inside of the room; I only heard a crash, and then this angry character came storming out."

With a nod, he made an additional note, this one longer and more detailed. "What time was that?"

I grabbed a cloth from the shelf under the register and began to wipe down the surrounding countertop. "Let's see.

that he'd had a fight with one of his band members the night before that nearly resulted in my being run over like an armadillo in the middle of Main Street."

In my agitated state, I turned on the water with my left hand and stifled a whimper, realizing my mistake too late. Feeling his gaze on my face, I took several slow breaths, kept my eyes on my throbbing hand, and waited for my inner wimp to get a grip.

"Whoa, now." With a light touch, he turned my wrist and studied the red angry patches. With his other hand, he drew my hand under the water with a gentle touch.

I shuffled as far away from him as I could without removing my blistered skin from the water. "I got it."

Abruptly, he dropped my wrist and crossed to the far side of the kitchen. "Uh." He shifted his feet. "I didn't mean to insult you or your article, but Wallace is here and he's riding my—" He cleared his throat. "Let's just say he's leaving no pebble unkicked."

After giving the deputy a nod of forgiveness, I studied the deep lines around his mouth.

He straightened his shoulders and adjusted his cowboy hat so that it hid any emotion in his eyes. "Which band member was Clark fighting? And what was it about?"

Shoot. Me and my big mouth. "I don't know his name." I wasn't about to stand in the way of law enforcement, but I had wanted a chance to consider all the facts I'd gathered before presenting them to him. My plan: first, submit my article to the *Bugle*; second, contact Deputy Lightfoot before the paper hit the newsstand.

We stared at each other, two gunslingers prepared to draw if the other refused to kowtow to demands.

I dried my hands and returned to the dining room to fill the glass sugar containers for the day, which gave me time to consider my words. "The night of Clark's concert, we were waiting outside his dressing room and overheard a shouting match over . . . something. Could have been a song, a guitar, or a toothbrush, for all I know."

It wasn't until he'd finished his three tortillas and I my one that he repeated his question. "Did you finish your article on the Clark case?"

"Yes and no."

He found a bit of paper towel and wiped his mouth. "Go ahead."

I paused to refill our cups, take a big swallow of brew, and burn the roof of my mouth to blue blazes.

"What's your angle?" He watched me over the brim of his own cup, seemingly unfazed by the temperature of our strong coffee.

His word choice was aggressive, but I refused to respond in kind. I had a feeling I knew where this was headed. "Uh, let's see. I tried to keep it simple: where and when. I added a couple of quotes from his band and road crew." I shrugged. "Heartwarming stuff."

"What'd you say about the murder weapon?"

I found the cream in the pie cooler and made a production of adding just the right amount to cool the coffee. "I didn't mention it. Why would I? You're trying to solve the case, right?"

"Did you mention where the body was found?"

"What? Like, in a bowl of guacamole?" In spite of myself, I answered abruptly, revealing my resentment of his need to ask me such a stupid question. What was I—a high-school intern?

"Just answer the question."

Without thinking, I slammed the cup to the counter and sloshed the hot liquid onto my hand. I cursed.

He grabbed my wrist before I could pull away with a strong, leathery-smooth hand and lifted it toward the light. "You better put some cold water on that."

I started to argue but resisted; the skin between my thumb and index finger was on fire. I marched over to the sink with Deputy Do-Right on my tail. "No, I did not mention the electric guitar, the bowl of guacamole, or the fact

cups stacked at the waiter's station, and filled it from the first of many carafes of coffee that would be brewed during the day.

I was glad to see him. It kept me from hunting him down.

"Thanks." He studied the tile, the exposed beams, and every booth and table. "You here on your own?"

"For the time being." Carlos would arrive in the next half hour to start preparing for lunch.

"That wise?"

"Why? You think I'm going to produce another dead body in the stockroom? Or from under the kitchen sink?"

His ebony eyes narrowed. "What time do you start cooking around here?" He raised his head and sniffed.

"Come on," I muttered. From the fridge I gathered eggs, leftover refried beans, and Carlos's awesomely awesome fresh salsa.

"Humph." Lightfoot watched me closely as I turned on the griddle and anointed it with a splash of olive oil. "I thought you couldn't cook."

"Any fool can cook eggs." Much to my eternal mortification, only weeks ago Senora Mari attempted to convince Lightfoot that I would be a worthy mate due to my smarts . . . even if I was lacking in culinary skills.

"Make yourself useful and hand those to me." I pointed to a tub half filled with leftover homemade corn tortillas.

"Why aren't you working on your big article on Jeff Clark's murder?"

With a flip of the wrist, I tossed corn tortillas on the hot griddle. "It's an ongoing work of epic proportions." I cracked the eggs on the sizzling surface and found two spatulas.

"Need some help?"

"No, but I hate to see a body with nothing to do." I handed him a spatula. "Flip those tortillas, *por favor.*"

Within a couple of minutes, we'd produced four mouthwatering tortillas of runny-egg goodness. Our conversation stalled as we ate, the only exchange the sound of satisfaction.

Chapter 7

❧❧❧❧❧❧❧❧❧❧❧❧❧❧❧❧❧❧❧❧❧❧❧❧❧❧❧❧

The next morning was Saturday, Milagro's busiest day of the week. Before the staff arrived, I whipped up one of Patti's favorites, huevos rancheros, and shuffled her out the door toward the Feed and Supply. She didn't put up much of a fuss. In fact, she threw her leather backpack over one shoulder and climbed into her jeep without as much as a sigh. I watched her squeal out of the parking lot, white gravel spitting in all directions, and said a silent prayer for peace of mind and renewed strength in her soul.

I moseyed into the kitchen, glanced at the empty prep tables and cold stove—which would soon be laden with tantalizing peppers, onions, and savory meats—and immediately exited for the coffee machine out front. In spite of the cheerful act I'd donned for Patti, I wasn't ready to meet the day or its customers.

"Josie Callahan." A voice, so deep I was surprised the floor didn't tremble beneath my feet, called from the back door.

"Hey, deputy. Want some coffee?"

Lightfoot emerged from the kitchen, found one of the

into a rocket called social media and send it soaring through every ear, storefront, telephone, and billboard for miles around—or at least the three surrounding counties.

"Okay, buddy, come over here and take a look."

Patti's eyes narrowed. "Oh no, you don't. He's staying right here."

"Yip," he said, still on his back, legs in the air.

"Read it out loud."

I raised an eyebrow in question. *Can she take it?*

In turn, she lifted a dyed-black eyebrow and stud in response.

I began to read. Her facial expression didn't change until I reached the part where Lenny expressed deep sadness for the neighborhood where Clark's body was found. My canine counterpart ended his post with a plea for sympathy and understanding.

"You think that'll play?" she asked.

"Yeah. The ones that read Lenny's blog are already on your side."

"How many followers does he have?"

"Three hundred and thirteen."

Patti didn't say it, but I read it in her eyes. That wasn't many.

"I'm a modern woman, aren't I?" I shook my fist with mock bravado. "I can grow Lenny's readership. I just haven't done it yet."

"Why bother?" Her gaze fell to Lenny, but I caught the blur of unshed tears.

Over the past year two years, she'd lost both her parents and still clung to hope with ten black-painted fingernails. Patti's prickly Goth persona protected her heart, the same way a desert cactus protected its fragile blooms, but Clark's murderer had plucked that flower and ground it under his bootheel.

I glared at her. "Because I'm motivated."

And because even though she was my best friend, I understood why she would be a prime suspect.

"Yip." He began licking her ankle with renewed commitment.

My fingers were building speed as I filled the blank page with my initial ideas. "I usually write the first draft, and then he reads it and makes corrections." I was hoping for at least a chuckle.

Silence.

Her gaze rested on the top of Lenny's head. She switched from stroking his small, delicate head with two fingers to scratching behind his ear. This caused an immediate reaction in his wiry body. He stretched out on his back across her leg and began to kick his back right leg in time with the motion of her fingers behind his ear. She'd found his happy place.

I typed quickly to get myself out of the predicament I'd placed myself in. Stupid of me to think she wouldn't be affected by the blog, the mention of Jeff, the discussion of the murder. With anyone else, I would've been afraid that she'd judge me for being so callous. But she knew me. She understood I processed my thoughts and emotions through the end of my fingertips, through the clicking of the keys, through the rhythm of my thoughts hitting the page.

I kept my phrasing simple so it wouldn't be a quantum leap for readers to believe my dog had written the post, not unless they failed to accept the spirit of this whimsical venture and branded my journey as one of self-aggrandizement or a foolish need for attention.

After including just the barest details of finding the body—due to the fact Lenny didn't want to offend his more sensitive followers—he continued by writing a glowing paragraph about Clark's career. I wanted badly to mention his popularity with the ladies, but Lenny refrained. When I wrote as Lenny, I had no difficulty mentioning items of note and concern in the community, but I did it with a generosity of spirit and forgiveness that had certainly been channeled from my tiny friend to me.

Finally, I concluded without mentioning Patti or her home. If I did, the town gossips would load those tasty tidbits

"Time for Lenny to write his blog."

Patti lifted my writing buddy, the better to stare him in the face. "What will your post be this week—a rant or a rave?"

I had planned to write a tribute to Jeff, but I had made the mistake of including Patti in the process. *Brilliant.*

"Yip," Lenny said.

I nodded and cocked my head to one side as if contemplating the wisdom of his suggestion. "I don't know." I shot a glance in her direction, and then sighed in the longhaired Chi's direction.

"What?"

In for a penny . . . "He wants to write a post with an apology."

Though completely unaware of my maneuvering, Lenny's ears perked up. "Yip."

"You're too kind." I made a show of sending a covert glance Patti's way. "It's too soon, buddy." With another shrug, I smiled sheepishly at Patti, as if I were embarrassed by Lenny's suggestion.

"Enough already," she growled. "What does he want to write about?"

"Yip, yip."

I nodded. "He wants to apologize to the community on my behalf."

"For what?"

"Um, for the fact that since I returned to Broken Boot, I've had the misfortune of discovering two dead bodies." I waited for a reaction to cross her face. And though I held my breath, her expression remained devoid of all emotion for at least twenty seconds.

"What?" Her eyes met mine, daring me to mention her previous, well-deserved meltdown from only a few hours earlier.

I lowered my eyes to my keyboard and started typing. "Nothing."

"Hey, buddy." Patti tilted Lenny's face up so she could look in his bright button eyes. "You okay with this setup?"

Chapter 6

I spent another half hour helping Aunt Linda clean up before I turned out the lights and made my way upstairs.

"Did your enchiladas convince Clark's band to play tonight?" Patti asked.

We were watching highlights from a Houston Aces soccer game on the late-evening news out of El Paso. Patti lay on the love seat with her head at the far end, her inky black hair dangling over the edge like a waterfall of Texas tea, her legs propped on the wall at a ninety-degree angle.

Lenny perched on her lap, and, like a gentleman, he had allowed her to pet him repeatedly on his head for the past fifteen minutes.

He turned his baleful gaze in my direction.

"You're a good boy," I murmured. What a saint. I would have bitten her hand and hid under the bed long ago.

"Yip, yip, yip," he urged.

I retrieved my laptop from the kitchen table and sprawled out in my faded purple recliner. "A capital idea, Lenster."

"Yip."

"What are you two on about?" Patti demanded, back to her usual strong delivery.

He gave me a job." His Adam's apple bobbed. "Best job I could've ever imagined." He dropped his gaze to the floor. I could tell he was struggling.

"That's perfect."

I looked to Dustin Akers and raised my phone toward his mouth to catch every word.

"He wasn't even one percent perfect, but, by God, that boy could sing." He placed his cowboy hat on his head and sighed. "He's probably writing songs for the angels to sing right about now." His face fell. "Let's go, Brady."

The teen gave a curt nod, once again macho and tough.

Instead of following him out, Dustin looked me in the eyes too long for comfort. "Would you be interested in having a cup of coffee with me sometime?"

It was the last thing I expected him to say, and I answered without a second thought. "That would be a bit of all right."

"You could give me the nickel tour before we hit the road?"

"Make it a silver dollar and you've got a deal."

His roguish smile was a humdinger. "Yes, ma'am."

As I watched them go, I realized I was still smiling. He came across as a decent person, and whether he was forty or fifty, it didn't matter. That smile of his made me want to know him better. And that in itself was a strange thing to feel.

The posse reached the door. "How do these *fans* know we're playing tonight?" Romeo asked with suspicion.

Busted. "Uncle Eddie never got around to taking you off the website."

Angry grumbling ensued.

I swallowed. "Folks will be disappointed if you don't show."

They didn't respond loud enough for me to comprehend what they said, but I noticed some heads nodding and shoulders shrugging as the group headed out the door.

The gray-haired man placed his hat across his heart. "Thanks again, for dinner. It was mighty generous of you." His voice carried a quiet dignity. "I'm Dustin Akers." He stuck out his hand. "And that's Brady."

"Josie Callahan." I shook his hand as firmly as I'd been taught. "And you're welcome." I plunged in with both feet, plus the rest of me. "I hate to ask this, Mr. Akers—"

"Dustin will do. I'm not that old." And when he smiled, I believed him.

"I wear a lot of hats around this town. One of them is reporter for the local paper."

A frown line appeared between his eyes.

"It may be too soon—and you can say no—but would you consider giving me a brief statement for my story on Jeff Clark's death?"

"I would," Brady said, perking up at a chance to earn a minute of fame.

"Thanks," I said, giving the boy a smile. I fished in my pocket for my phone and started the video, intending to use it for notes.

"Am I gonna be on television?" he asked.

"Nah, I just use it to help me quote you correctly."

His perkiness dissipated. "Okay, if you're sure."

"What would you like to say about Jeff?" I asked softly.

He looked up at the ceiling for a moment. "I want to thank Jeff, wherever he is, for giving me a chance." He held my eye. "He didn't hold things against me like he could have.

"Eddie'll be lucky if they don't eat themselves into a coma."

It was almost eight o'clock when we cleared away the last of the dinner dishes. The baboons had settled to quiet talk.

"Is there anything I can get you before you head back to Two Boots?" I asked, praying they'd say no.

"Nah, thank you, darlin'," the romantic baboon said in a mellow and more sober voice.

"Who says we're heading back to that lousy joint?" The eighteen-year-old jeered with a look up and down the table for support.

I jumped in. "I was hoping I'd get to hear you play again before you leave town."

Dustin stood. "We thank you for your hospitality. Mighty good eatin'."

The guys stood, three or four of them offering up sincere appreciation for our culinary donation.

"If I'm not mistaken," Dustin said, "your family owns both this restaurant and Two Boots dance hall."

In the dim light, I felt my cheeks heat at being caught. "Yes, sir, we do. We wanted you to know that our hearts go out to all of you and to Jeff Clark's family."

"Who will want to listen to us without Jeff?" the teenager asked in disgust.

Before I could argue, a redheaded man slapped him upside the head. "Boy, what do you mean?" He was the same angry dude who'd pushed past us the night of Jeff's final concert. I hadn't recognized him with half his face covered with his cowboy hat and the other half buried in his plate.

"Ow." The young man rubbed his head as he scooted out of reach.

"I would, and I know the folks in this town would as well." I met their eyes, one by one, attempting to convey my sincerity as best I could. "They'll come out to remember Jeff, some out of curiosity, but most out of appreciation and respect. It's going to be the best show it could possibly be under the circumstances."

I dropped my forced smile. "I'm awfully sorry to hear. I can't imagine how you're feeling right now."

"Ah, gee, darlin'. Why didn't you tell me you wanted to give me some sweet Southern TLC?" The baboon shoved back his chair. "Let's go."

I moved quickly to the other end of the table even as goose bumps rippled down my arms. "You're a funny one." It wasn't often I handled customers this pushy. I handed the gray-haired man his beer. "You must be Dustin."

"Yes, ma'am." When he smiled, my nerves evaporated. His deep crow's feet made him appear kindhearted, like the protective older brother I'd never had.

"Sit your butt down, Calvin." A wiry baboon seated next to the would-be lothario jerked him into his chair.

After a good ten seconds of fierce stare down, the passionate primate pulled up to the table and took a swig of his beer.

"I would, however, like to offer all of you whatever you want to eat on the house on behalf of my family."

"Your family owns this place?" The teen's eyes grew wide.

"Yep. That's my aunt, Linda Martinez, over there at the bar."

Her smile was wearing thin.

"Cool."

"Anything you want to eat is on us."

The gray-haired gentleman raised his voice. "That's mighty kind of you. We appreciate it. Don't we, boys?"

A few bothered to answer in the affirmative while the remainder nodded their heads. After a few minutes of perusing, they requested several orders of appetizers, tamales, fajitas, and Pancho Villa Platters, which included chiles rellenos, enchiladas, and flautas, along with guacamole and queso.

As I passed the bar on the way to place their order, Aunt Linda murmured, "You could have set a limit, you know?"

"Not if we want them to play both tonight *and* tomorrow night."

I glanced over my shoulder and discovered they'd gone back to their conversation, all but the older gentleman. He raised his empty beer glass and shook it at me.

What an idiot. I thought he'd raised his glass before as a gesture of appreciation, but he merely needed a refill on his beer.

"Uncle Eddie needs them to play tonight," I said.

"Good luck with that. They're so drunk, they couldn't float down the Rio Grande on an inner tube."

"Do you think they've put two and two together?" I asked.

"What? Milagro and Two Boots? I don't think so."

"How about we try to win them over with kindness? Give them some entrees on the house."

She pursed her lips and filled a beer glass with Shiner, most likely adding the loss of income in her head. "That might sober them up." She handed me the beer. "This is for the polite one in need of a refill."

"And then we hit them with the connection between Milagro and Two Boots."

Aunt Linda retrieved the menus from the hostess station in the other room and handed them to me. "Go for it, Jo Jo. They say the way to a man's heart—"

I continued. "Is through his stomach." We shared a grin and said in unison, "Unless he's a vegetarian."

Loaded for bear, or in this case *band,* I sashayed over to the table, ignoring the fact my sashaying skills compared to those of a mule. "Howdy, fellas."

"Howdy yourself, darlin'."

I neatly avoided a pat on the seat of my Wranglers from the dark-haired baboon seated at the head of the table. "We heard the concert last night over at Two Boots. You guys were awesome." I gestured to Aunt Linda, who waved and gave them a wide grin.

"You bet your boots we were," said a buck-toothed teenager, maybe all of eighteen. His eyes welled with unshed tears. "I mean, Jeff was awesome. He was the star."

shirts and bolo ties. They ranged in age from the red-headed twentysomething who'd pushed past us the night before to the silver-haired, bespectacled grandfather with a potbelly.

I crossed to where Aunt Linda was tending bar. "That Clark's band?"

"More like a troop of baboons escaped from the zoo. Next thing you know, they'll start throwing feces at us."

I burst out laughing. When I glanced over my shoulder to see what kind of drinks they were imbibing, I discovered at least a six-pack of them watching me. A couple of them nodded and smiled. A gray-haired man raised a glass. I smiled at no one in particular and turned away.

"How long they been sitting there?"

"Too long. An hour, I guess."

"They drinkin' heavy?"

"Don't light any matches within a six-foot radius."

I gnawed at my bottom lip. I needed just one or two measly little comments, but Lord, if I didn't feel like a grave robber.

"I know that look."

"Huh?"

"Yeah, the one where you want to do something but you're not sure it's the right thing to do."

"I need a comment for my story."

My aunt studied my face while she continued to dry the bar glasses in front of her. "You *need* one or you *want* one? There's a difference."

"If I want to cover Jeff Clark's death for the *Bugle*, I need it." I grabbed a lemon from the bar setup with the metal tongs. "I didn't realize I'd feel as low as a gopher hole when it came time to actually interviewing people."

After a moment, Aunt Linda threw her drying towel over her shoulder. "I see your dilemma, but I wouldn't trust those guys not to tip over a table or cuss you out if you were to traipse over there and butt into their business."

first interview for my story, and froze. The mother and daughter roadies had shared a little and left out a lot . . . like their last names. *Hang it.*

After convincing Wilhelmina and Heather to divulge their last names through a crack in the bus door, I flew into town to transcribe my recording and reconnoiter the only two locations in Broken Boot that sold tamales: Milagro and Milagro's to-go window.

It was early dinnertime by then. I strolled inside, my eyes darting to and fro, searching for guys that fit my idea of a country band. Instead I found a restaurant teeming with locals.

"You did it again." Senora whispered behind my back, causing me to start.

"What?" Before anyone spied me, I took her arm and stepped into the office.

"You and your dead bodies," she continued in a hiss. "You've brought in more customers."

I peered around the doorjamb and discovered the restaurant was standing-room only. "That's a good thing, right?"

"Not for the dead people."

With great effort, I avoided rolling my eyes and the subsequent pinch Senora Mari would immediately give my arm. "Have any members of Jeff Clark's band stopped by?"

"Who?" She removed the flower from above her ear and pinned it in my hair.

"You know the dead guy from your dream?"

"Ah," with a small, bony finger she placed my hair behind my ear, "the musician." With a purse of her lips, she considered for a moment. "No," she turned to leave, "but there are some hippies at the bar."

From the doorway to the bar area, I peered around the jamb and spied six guys in country western Harley wear— almost bikers, but a bit more styled.

Only half of Clark's posse wore the requisite leather vest and blue jeans, while the others sported Western

me, I turned off the recorder to encourage her to share more. "Why would anyone want to kill him? I don't understand."

"Jealousy," Wilhelmina said, rising from her seat and pointing a finger at me. "It's the devil's tool." She made her way to the front of the bus, making me wonder what I'd done to shut down the interview so soon. "No explaining it. It's just a fact of life." She wrenched on the silver door handle with her wizened, pink-nailed hands.

I adjusted my bag on my shoulder, buying time. "Women. The original green-eyed monsters."

"Men are worse," Heather muttered.

I raised my eyebrows in mock surprise. *Men?*

Wilhelmina shook her head, her lips pursed. "Band members, friends, other musicians—guys hired to support each other but jealous of Jeff's success."

"His career?"

"Girl, his life." She gestured to the stairs.

I tried to think of one last question, but their faces bore the same closed expression. They'd had enough of the likes of me prying into their business. "Thanks for everything." I stepped down and froze. "Where's the band?"

"Look for tequila and Tex-Mex," Heather called out as the door began to close. "You'll find 'em." I jumped off the last step to the gravel, the door screeching closed behind me.

As I walked back to my Prius, I considered what I'd heard. The two women obviously loved Jeff Clark in distinctly different ways. Wilhelmina wouldn't have touched a hair on his head, except to smooth it with her motherly fingers—or so she wanted me to believe. Heather, on the other hand, reeked of jealousy. Though it wasn't a stretch to believe she'd kill anyone Jeff took a shine to, I wasn't convinced her rage had extended to her crush.

Would the sheriff's office even consider Heather or Wilhelmina as suspects when they already had tough Goth Girl Patti at the scene of the crime? I struggled to swallow the lump of dread in my throat.

I gave myself a mental pat on the back for completing the

"Jeff was taking us with him." Heather leaned forward and grabbed my arm. "He would never have left us behind."

"How do you feel about his death?" I hated to lead these people on—they were obviously hurting—but I needed direct quotes. That's what Sumter Majors, my editor, required.

"Things won't ever be the same without him." Heather nodded, her eyes wide and swimming with tears.

"If we were a family," Wilhelmina paused, drew a sigh, and crossed her hands over her heart, "he was like a son to me." Her eyes remained dry, though she rubbed the corners with a knuckle. "I'll miss him and his music."

"If you had to compare his music to that of another country singer, whose would it be?"

Wilhelmina closed her eyes and smiled. "George Jones."

"Are you crazy? He sounds more like Keith or Kenny," Heather argued.

I grinned at her passionate response.

Wilhelmina's eyes flew open. "Girl, have you lost your mind?" She turned to me and raised her drawn-on eyebrows. "Who does Jeff's music make you think of?"

Under the pressure of their intense stares, my mind went blank. I dug for the only country music star I could remember—the one country star no true Texan could ever forget. "Willie Nelson?"

Heather squealed with displeasure. "That old weasel? Have you lost your mind?"

"Weasel? Willie?" I'd never heard anyone criticize the Texas legend. I paused to consider my words as I recovered from Heather's slanderous comment. She had a point. Clark no more resembled the ancient singer than Lenny resembled Lassie.

"In what way are they alike?" Heather asked.

"Smiling on the outside but sad on the inside," Wilhelmina said. "And they both sing ballads as big as the Grand Canyon." Wilhelmina laid a hand over her heart. "That hit me right here."

Strangely, I understood. My curiosity getting the best of

"He's the gray-haired one," Heather said with impatience. I shook my head.

"Plays guitar?"

"Sorry." I didn't remember any members of Clark's band except the angry guy with auburn hair.

"So Jeff wasn't married?" That much I figured. My conscience did a flip-flop. Did I really want to know *all* the dirt on Jeff Clark? Depending on what I found out, how could I look Patti in the face the next time she mentioned him? Did I actually *need* to know how many girlfriends Clark had in addition to Patti and the giggling beauty backstage, assuming she had been there to see him? After a long, awkward pause, I swayed toward the whole truth and nothing but the truth. "Girlfriends?"

"What'd you say?" Heather was glaring at me as if I were a fly on a fruitcake.

"That's a slippery subject." The older woman wasn't biting. "Let's talk about his good qualities, right?"

"Sure."

"Handsome as Tom Cruise."

"True." I was already formulating how to incorporate her comments into what I had in mind.

"Whatever." Heather moved her self-righteous glare onto her mother. "He was tons more handsome than any Tom Cruise. Try more good-looking than Channing Tatum."

"Cool." I settled back, enjoying their sudden enthusiasm. "And?"

"He had a voice like an angel." Heather beamed.

Wilhelmina chuckled. "Like a fallen angel."

"And he wrote his own songs."

"Well, most of them he wrote with Clay," corrected the girl's mother.

"He was down-to-earth and cared that we all got along like a family."

The older woman pinched the end of her cigarette until satisfied it was out. "He was the real deal." She sniffed and wiped her nose. "He was going to be a star."

I knew what they meant. "Was he an easy man to work for?"

"Yes," the older woman said. "He'd buy you a drink at least once a week. He didn't get angry if you couldn't find where he'd thrown his clothes."

"Huh, not unless he was hungover." Heather giggled behind her hand.

I made a show of stopping the recording. "Do you want me to use that negative stuff?"

She shot a look at her mother and then turned away.

"No, she don't." Wilhelmina shook her head. "She's just upset that he's dead."

I turned the recorder on again. "Did you enjoy working with him?"

The older woman looked away and then a slow smile spread across her face. "He was real sweet. He was a mess, but yeah, I loved being around him and the other guys."

"Did he have any family?"

"No, not really. I think he said his mom lived in Oklahoma."

"He had a brother, lived in Tulsa." Heather leaned toward the recorder when she spoke.

"No family, no wife, no girlfriend?"

Heather stared as if she'd unexpectedly lost her hearing and good sense.

The older woman stood and retrieved a pack of cigarettes from a shelf above the window. "You mind?"

Of course I did. Who wants to inhale secondhand smoke? "No, go ahead."

She lit a long brand and inhaled deeply, blowing the smoke back over her right shoulder. I could only assume that was her way of protecting me from the cancer-causing fumes. "To hear Dustin tell it, Jeff had an ex-wife, but he's the only person I've ever heard mention her." She inhaled again and her foot started tapping. "He wasn't married." She tapped the ash into her hand.

"Dustin?"

Heather stared over my head out the window and eventually nodded. "Go ahead. Ask away."

Her mother dropped into a leather bench seat that folded down from the center section of the wall.

With another we're-all-friends-here smile, I joined her and removed my phone from my pocket. "Is it okay if I record this? I don't want to misquote you or anything."

"Oh, she's going to misquote us." Heather turned up her nose. "That's what happens to celebrities all the time."

"Or so they say." I laughed, but neither woman joined in. "Uh, I won't misrepresent you. I can't afford to be sued for libel or slander." I chuckled, while they refused to crack a smile. "If I had to pay a penalty, I wouldn't be able to afford to keep Lenny."

"Who's he?" Heather looked suspicious. "Your boyfriend?"

I tried not to frown as I bit the inside of my cheek. "He's a much better roommate than any man. He's my long-haired Chihuahua."

"Ooh. I love little dogs." She turned sad puppy eyes to her mother. "And we're going to get one soon, aren't we?"

Wilhelmina reached over and smoothed her daughter's hair. "Sure thing, sweetie. As soon as we finish this tour."

"I'd be happy to introduce you." I waggled my eyebrows. "He really likes the ladies."

"Cool." Heather sighed and gave me her first genuine smile.

"Best get on with it." Wilhelmina gestured to the phone.

I set it up to record. "What was it like working with Jeff Clark?"

They stared at each other, exchanging a silent conversation.

After a moment, Wilhelmina began. "Well, it was fine. He could be real nice and friendly."

"Huh." Heather's mouth twisted in derision. "That's one way of putting it."

teeth. "I'm Wilhelmina. And this here's my daughter, Heather."

"Nice to meet you. Are you in the band?" Now, I hadn't seen these two onstage Thursday night, but I hated to say, *So what the heck are you doing here?*

The older woman laughed so hard she began to cough. "I take care of wardrobe. Heather here takes care of CDs and T-shirts."

"Hats and beer cozies too," the young woman said with pride.

"I see." I nodded and took a quick look around, making special note of the bedroom at the back of the bus—Jeff Clark's, I'd wager.

"Where's the rest of the band?"

"Hard to resist them guys in tight pants, ain't it?" Wilhelmina laughed at my expression.

Sharing my actual opinion on the unattractiveness of skanky male musicians—like my former fiancé—would not produce the desired result. "Um, you said it. I'd like to get some quotes for my article."

"They're not going to give you much, seeing as how they're not here." Heather flipped her hair back over her shoulder, which reduced her age from thirty to at least twenty-one.

"Where can I find them?"

"They went into town." Heather eyed me suspiciously as she plopped down into one of the plush seats.

I'd wow these women with kindness by this end of this exchange, or I wasn't the niece of Linda Callahan Martinez, the strongest, most persuasive woman this side of El Paso. "Do you mind if I ask you a few questions?"

"Get lost." In her eyes, I read curiosity in spite of her terse words.

"Don't pay her no mind." Wilhelmina turned to her daughter. "Tell her the positive things. Don't focus on the negative. Wouldn't Jeff like that?"

thirty. It was hard to tell from her straight, shoulder-length pale hair, unisex jeans, and band T-shirt.

"Josie Callahan." Again, I gestured toward Two Boots. "I'm Eddie Martinez's niece, and I'm writing a piece for the *Broken Boot Bugle* about Mr. Clark's death."

The freckles on the girl's face stood out in stark relief. "What do you know about Jeff? You trying to make a buck off his death, you money-grubbing—"

"Heather. That's enough." The older woman placed a brown leathery hand on the girl's arm and gave it a squeeze. "Let her talk."

"I'm sorry for your loss." I swallowed my nerves. "I met Jeff last night backstage before the show. He is—was—an old friend of my friend Patti Perez. She owns the Feed and Supply."

The two females exchanged glances. "Was she the black-haired witch that joined him onstage?" Heather's freckles threatened to jump off her nose and punch me in the face.

"Ha." Definitely not the way to start off with these two. "She's real nice once you get to know her."

"Did they go out after the show?" I'd made a mistake. Heather's shoulders tensed and her fingers curved like a female wrestler about to rip my hair out by the roots. "What was that girl's name again? I want to pay her a visit."

"Sweetie, you'll do no such thing. Mind your manners." The older woman chuckled without concern.

"Uh, she didn't hurt him—promise." I smiled. "She's cool." I looked to the older woman for support. "They dated several years back."

Heather's eyes narrowed. Any minute she would bare her teeth.

"They were only reminiscing, not starting back up, if you know what I mean." I tried a laugh, which fell as flat as my hair on a humid day.

With a glance at my notebook, the older woman smiled, proudly displaying the wide space between her two front

door with the side of my fist with all my might, ignoring the pain in my hand. "Hey, in there." Nothing. "I need just a minute of your time."

My hand throbbing, I glanced around the parking lot and down the road to make sure no one else was bearing witness to my tomfoolery. I raised my fist again, and the door opened with a groan.

"Darlin', watch yourself. You're going to do yourself an injury." The afternoon sun was in my eyes and the inside of the bus was dark, but as best I could tell, the gravelly alto belonged to a woman.

"Howdy," I said, going for friendly. "My family owns this place." I gestured toward our dance hall with a thumb over my shoulder. "And I'm a reporter for the local paper."

A bank of clouds blocked the sun, revealing a middle-aged woman with straight, iron gray hair. Over her shoulder, a young, pretty face peered.

"Listen, may I come in? It's hot as Hades in winter out here." My shirt was already sticking to my back like a second skin.

She turned to the girl standing behind her. After a few seconds of fervent whispering on the part of the young one, she waved me inside. "Sure, come on."

I stepped into the bus and sighed as the frigid air melted my irritation like a Double Lemon Chill on the Fourth of July. The AC was running full blast and country music—Jeff Clark, by the sound of it—played faintly from hidden speakers. Once my eyes adjusted to the dim interior, I noticed the plaid curtains at the windows were tied back like in someone's country kitchen. I glanced around, taking it all in—the fridge, cooktop, stereo system, large flat-screen, and all kinds of electronics.

I spotted a guitar on a seat near the back and a pile of girly magazines underneath the seat closest to me.

"Who'd you say you were?" asked a soft feminine voice. I turned and found an ethereal young woman of sixteen or

shirt pocket. "I told them they could play a tribute to Jeff Clark and arrange it any way they wanted."

"Hmm." I delayed my response by taking a large bite of my own breadless bacon and turkey sandwich, followed by a chunk of dill pickle.

As if his glasses interfered with his speech, Uncle Eddie raised his readers. "Too soon?"

I wiped my mouth with a brown paper towel from above the industrial sink. "Sounds like it."

"Dang it. I didn't mean to be such a callous clodhopper." A deep furrow appeared across his wide forehead.

"You're okay." I gave him a quick one-armed hug. "It was an honest mistake. What about Ty?" He was many things: gambler, womanizer, and nephew of the dearly departed Dixie, but he was also a good musician.

"Oh, sure. That polecat finally agreed to play until the cows come home, as long as I agreed to give him an open bar tab. Can you believe he made me wait fifteen minutes before giving me an answer?"

I laughed, almost spitting a bit of pickle across the room. "Why? Were you interrupting his Texas Hold 'Em?"

He took a swig from his coffee cup. "Could be you're right on that score."

I finished off the pickle and rinsed my hands. "I'm going to go find those guys. Who's in charge?"

"Some guy named Travis Mitchell, road manager."

"Wish me luck."

He laughed. "I'll wish them luck. Go easy on 'em, Jo Jo."

I straightened my braid and drew it over one shoulder. With my sunglasses firmly in place, I shuffled through the parking lot and cursed the 97-degree heat.

Though I couldn't see anything inside the bus—only my own reflection in the windows and an empty driver's seat—I knocked on the door with the flat of my hand. "Helloo." My knock was as pathetic as a gnat knocking on a stainless-steel refrigerator. I saw nothing, but sensed that the bus and its occupants were laughing at me. The next time, I beat the

twenty-three fruit flavors hit the back of my throat like a drug. I sighed. "Where's Jeff's band?"

Uncle Eddie swallowed and wiped his mouth. "I'd stay clear of those cats. They're not playing nice today."

"They've had a big shock."

"I guess." He chomped again, screwing up his face in thought. "Doesn't mean they have to be downright mean and ornery."

A familiar tantalizing aroma captured my attention. I found the cooked bacon in the fridge along with some turkey slices and a kosher dill. "Ornery how?"

"I asked them if they'd play tonight and tomorrow night, and right nicely too." He tore off a paper towel from a nearby roll with his left hand and wiped his mouth, "They said I was being a jerk."

I could see his side, as it was my side too. We needed to eat, pay the mortgages on a house and two businesses, and meet payroll. "Did you explain?"

"I tried." He continued to chew with such a downcast expression, you'd have thought he was eating the last club sandwich on earth. "Something about needing to contact their agent."

"And did they?"

With a worrisome clanking sound, the camouflage duck clock on the opposite wall began to quack the hour. "I knocked on the bus door fifteen minutes ago." Instead of continuing, he finished off his sandwich with a huge bite that made him look like a puffer fish.

You would think by now, I'd be used to my uncle's need to stretch a story to its very limit, but, in fact, I was imagining myself opening his mouth and yanking out the details like the end of a thread caught in a tangled ball of yarn.

"No one answered." With a contented sigh, he threw his napkin into the trash and picked up his clipboard and the list of grocery items needed for the day.

"Maybe they don't know anything yet."

He dug his wire-framed reading glasses from his denim

Chapter 5

In spite of a smattering of Friday-afternoon tourists on Main Street, Two Boots was taking a siesta until the late afternoon. Standing out from the gravel parking lot like a circus tent in the desert was a luxury bus bearing *Jeff Clark Band* on the side in airbrushed letters that would have made the King of Rock and Roll proud. Next to it was parked a white commercial truck. This was not a huge tour of buses and trucks, but enough to blast the eardrums of those lucky enough to hear the band. Looking back, I realized his look, his voice, and even his whole band had been a notch above Ty Honeycutt's local musicians. Perhaps he was more of an up-and-comer than I thought.

I slipped in the side door and found Uncle Eddie in the kitchen of Two Boots, fixing himself a club sandwich.

"Want one?" He stuffed the first bite in his mouth and chomped like a man on a mission.

"No, thanks." I found a glass-bottled Dr Pepper in the cooler and forced off the lid with the bottle opener attached to the side of the counter. The first sip of carbonation and

"Just try a bite. It'll give you a new outlook."

With a groan, she covered her head with the lovely yellow wedding-ring quilt that my mother had made for me, with the help of Aunt Linda, when I was a baby. One of its multicolored rings rested around her head like a halo. From beneath the cotton and batting she muttered, "Not hungry." She turned away toward the windows that overlooked Main Street. "Go away."

I leapt onto the bed, barely missing her torso, found the top of her head through the quilt, and planted a big smack on it. "Enjoy your wallowing, Perez." I climbed off, grabbed my keys, and lightly tossed Lenny on top of her. "Because when you're through, we're going to find whoever did this and make them pay—for a new Fender."

As I walked away, I heard her chuckle.

On the screen in front of me was a whopping four sentences. "That's not much. Are you positive there's not anything else you can tell me?"

"There is one thing." I could hear him smile. "Wallace left Galveston this morning."

"Thanks!" That was a factoid my editor might appreciate. "That's too bad." I blanched. "Uh, I meant that you're lead on this case right now, aren't you?"

"For the moment."

"This is a rare opportunity for you to gain some experience. . . . Oh, heck. You know what I mean."

He made a grunting sound that almost passed for a laugh . . . from a dried-up mesquite tree. I was finding if I paid close attention, the stoic deputy actually had a sense of humor.

"Okay, well, uh, thanks. I appreciate the info. Gotta go or I'll miss my deadline."

"Wouldn't want that to happen."

Add sarcasm to his list of hidden traits. Maybe he'd brandished sarcastic comments before and I'd missed it. *Hmm.* I'd pay closer attention in the future. Sarcasm was almost humor, and humor was a quality in a man I'd sorely been missing in my past relationships.

I put the phone down and finished the article by tightening my prose and removing the hints of emotion I'd added subconsciously in my word choices. I'd write an emotional story about finding Jeff's body, but I'd pen that piece as Lenny. His blog was the perfect place to let it all hang out—at least all that wouldn't get me sued for libel.

After completing the requisite word count, I e-mailed the article to Majors with an explanation that I would gather some quotes from Jeff's bandmates to include in a follow-up piece. I checked on Aunt Linda and the staff on the evening shift and snagged Patti a Laredo special: two crunchy beef tacos, a cheese enchilada, rice, and refried beans.

"I'm not hungry." She waved her arm toward the yellow Formica table.

"Since when?"

"Since you found a second dead body within six months."

Was it my fault that I made a habit of being in the wrong place at the wrong time? "Come on. I'm not full-time press, merely a wannabe reporter. And I'm never going to be anything else unless I submit this story within the next thirteen minutes. Dad gum it, haven't I earned a few brownie points for finding those dead bodies for you?" I was paddling upstream with a straw, and I knew it.

There was a pregnant pause, and then he began to speak in a low voice. "The medical examiner declared Jeff Clark dead."

"I should hope so."

"Should I continue?"

"My bad."

"The Big Bend County Sheriff's Office is working the crime scene, compiling forensic evidence. More information is forthcoming."

If I weren't a law-abiding citizen, I'd . . . "Can we agree it was murder?"

"No."

"Quint Lightfoot, cut the shenanigans. He didn't hit himself over the head with a Fender."

"We haven't ruled that out."

"Come on. Straight into the guacamole—really?"

"We are not releasing any information at this time that points to murder. And you'd better not hint there's more that does, unless you want me to have a private discussion with your new boss."

I started to argue, but thought better about it. I needed to stay on my editor's good side—if I could figure out where it was hiding.

Quickly I moved the phone to my other ear, the better to type. "So, you're trying to give the murderer a sense of security?"

"Something like that."

Lenny's ears pricked and his silky tail wagged even faster. He smiled with his bright button eyes and twirled in anticipation—the better to show off his beautiful black-and-white markings.

I patted the bed, and up he jumped.

After a moment, Patti lowered her legs and allowed Lenny to jump into her lap. He proceeded to lick her chin, obviously having decided that her chin was most in need of comfort.

"Ugh, dog germs." But she didn't move him out of the way or wipe away the spittle. She hugged him close with his head over her shoulder like an infant. "Thanks, sweetie."

Now to find myself an air mattress and write my article. I checked my watch. "Patti, I'm sorry, but I told Majors at the *Bugle* that I'd write this piece on Jeff in the next few minutes." Forty minutes was all that remained.

"It's okay. Right, Lenny?"

"Yip," he agreed, backing out of her arms to sit in her lap and lick her leg.

I gave her a quick hug and headed back to my laptop and one of the most potentially important pieces I'd ever written. It came easily, like water through a sieve. My fingers flew across the keyboard, refusing to edit my words the first time through.

I dialed Deputy Lightfoot with fifteen minutes to go.

"Yes, ma'am?" His response was right on the edge of brusque. I had obviously interrupted if the somber officer was anything but unwaveringly polite.

I was actually surprised he'd taken my call. "I need a quote for the paper. How does the investigation stand?"

He sighed. "All questions from the press must be sent in writing to Sheriff Mack Wallace, care of the Big Bend County Sheriff's Office."

"I got it, but I have fifteen minutes—make that fourteen—before I miss my deadline. Give me something."

"Not if you're a reporter. Wallace handles all interactions with the press."

"Your whole house is a crime scene. And even if it wasn't, it would certainly require a thorough cleaning."

Her eyes grew wide as tostadas. "Who's going to clean? Me? You?"

"Why not?"

She raised an eyebrow.

"I'm going to find an untapped well of cleaning skills—just you wait and see."

She burst into silent tears, her shoulders shaking and tears streaming down her face.

"What?"

"Things have taken a nasty turn when *you* offer to clean anything."

I laughed. After giving me a shocked look, she chuckled in spite of herself.

Joining her on the bed, I nudged her with my elbow until she scooted over. "Don't worry. You're staying here with me as long as you want."

She lifted her head and glanced around. The tears sprang forth again.

"What's wrong with this place? Lenny doesn't snore." I tried for a joke, but I'm terrible at making jokes.

She sniffed and wiped her eyes with her T-shirt. "I hate this bed."

Shock had set in. "Okay, well, all right. You can sleep on the love seat if you want."

She cocked her head to one side. "And hang my feet over the armrest, I guess?"

"Or an air mattress on the floor?"

"Hmm. That might work . . . if it stays inflated." Her eyes searched for Lenny, finding him sprawled across the bedroom doorway. He caught her eye and stood, wagging his tail like a single windshield wiper on high. She pointed to him. "Won't he pop it with his toenails?"

Probably. "We'll teach him not to."

She gave me a dubious stare.

I grinned and gave a short whistle.

Patti lay still as a corpse, with her hands folded on her chest. Too still.

"You can open your eyes now."

Her eyes popped open. "How'd you know?"

"Who could sleep through all that?"

She sat up and tied her black hair into a knot. "Your family can be a bit much, if you don't mind my saying so."

"I'm right there with you, sister."

She brought her knees up to her chest and placed her chin on her knees.

"Are you going to be okay?"

She blinked rapidly and looked away. "Oh yeah." She attempted to chuckle. "Good thing I didn't like the guy."

"Right," I said a bit too enthusiastically. "But still?"

"He wasn't a complete loser." She wiped the corner of her eye.

I reached over and touched the sheet where it rested on her leg. "Not if he wanted to be with you. How could he be?"

"I keep seeing him on the stretcher in my front yard." She focused down, still not meeting my eyes. "I keep remembering that stupid guacamole on the side of his mouth." Something resembling laughter erupted from her belly, but as soon as it faded away, her eyes filled with tears.

"Ssh." I patted her leg.

"The sheriff's department isn't going to let me back into my own home, are they?"

"Not yet. Believe me, you don't want to see any trace of what I saw on your coffee table."

With a grimace, she pulled my mother's wedding-ring quilt up to her neck. "Nothing personal, but your bed sucks."

"My bed is ergonomically correct." I slapped the futon I'd schlepped home from Austin, which lay upon an old pine platform bed.

"I want my Serta, my kitchen, my clothes, and my cat."

How could I spell it out without upsetting her? "Soon, hon." I couldn't . . . not yet.

"Argh," she groaned, fisting her hands in the sheet.

"Okay. The dream I remember the most was filled with music."

"You heard music," I asked, rolling my eyes on the inside.

"Yes, country music. Like what they play at Two Boots."

"And?"

She frowned. "And that singer was there. You know the one?"

I shook my head, more than ready to write my story. "Was he handsome?"

"Yes, and sad."

"Sad?" I stood and retrieved my laptop from the dining table.

"Yes, big brown eyes and dark hair."

True, Jeff Clark did have both. I opened my laptop and typed in my password. "What did he want?"

"He wanted me to tell you something." She said this with a straight face, but, then again, her face was usually solemn, devoid of a smile.

I opened a new document and typed the header. I looked up and found her staring at me with a hard, narrow gaze. "Are you listening?"

I nodded.

She shot a frown at the laptop and then decided to continue. "He says you know who killed him."

This time I frowned. "I know who killed him? But I barely knew him."

She shrugged and stood. Straightening her dress, she nodded. "I know, but he still says you know who it is, and it's up to you to find them and bring them to justice."

"Them?"

She shook her head and walked out the door.

I hurried after her, my laptop cradled in one arm. "Does that mean 'more than one' or that you don't know if the killer's a man or a woman?"

She ignored me—she loves a cliffhanger—and continued on downstairs.

I walked over to the bedroom doorway and peeked in.

* * *

I hurried through the kitchen, mooched a taco with savory carnitas, onions, and jalapeños, and bolted upstairs. Before my eyes, something odd was taking place. Aunt Linda and Senora Mari sat elbow to elbow on the love seat, discussing the recipes in one of my old *Southern Living* magazines. "Is Patti still sleeping?" I whispered, before taking the last bite of corn tortilla, dripping with flavorful yumminess. If tamales aren't around, tacos are a close second when it comes to comfort food.

"Ssh. Yes, of course. Why else would we be sitting here together?" She rolled her eyes as she waved her hand back and forth between the two of them.

Aunt Linda lifted her head from the back of the love seat.

"Now that you're here," my aunt pushed to her feet, "I'll run to the bank." Slowly she moved her hips from one side to the other, as if practicing her hula. Then she reached for the ceiling and leaned back. "Ah, that's better." She plucked a water bottle from the door of the fridge, waved it at me, and hurried down the stairs.

Senora Mari waited until the last of Aunt Linda's footfalls faded away. "I had so many dreams last night."

She wanted me to say, *What did you dream about?* However, I knew her too well to give her the satisfaction so soon. I would bet my firstborn child that she was going to say that her dreams were about Jeff's murder.

I patted her knee. "I hope they were all good ones."

"Half good, half not so good." She frowned.

I tried hard to wait her out, but if I didn't allow her to tell me about her dream, I'd lose even more of my writing time. *"Abuela,"* I said softly. "The *Bugle* is waiting on me to write about the murder. Me. The former reporter from Austin. Hit the high points, and then we'll discuss it at length when I've made my deadline."

"The digest?"

"Sí."

"A musician playing Two Boots this weekend for the Homestead Days Music Festival."

"Holy guacamole, I have to get someone on that story pronto." His voice rang with excitement.

"Come on, Sumter, choose me. I found the body."

"Yip, yip, yip," Lenny barked at a poodle promenading down the opposite side of the street with Mrs. Cho from the dry cleaner.

"Ssh."

"Callahan, are you kidding me?" He chuckled. "Are you killing people so you can cover their stories? Is that your game?"

"That's sick."

"Huh," he grunted. "It's awfully convenient."

"Oh, please. Wouldn't it be convenient to offer your readers a special edition of the *Bugle*?"

"You've been watching too many old movies."

"But—"

"James Eddleton's in Dallas, visiting his daughter this week. If," he paused, "you can't get it done, I could ask Nancy Connally over in Alpine. She puts out smart stuff. Excellent writer."

"Give me a chance."

"When can you deliver it?"

"I'll start now. When's your deadline for tomorrow's paper?"

"You mean Sunday's paper?" he asked in a low, no-nonsense tone.

"You're going to sit on this until Sunday?" I squared my shoulders, and Lenny sat up. "Someone's going to write this for the bigger papers. We need to get it out there first."

"Write it in an hour, e-mail it, and text me. We'll talk after I've read it."

"Yes, sir, boss." I would whip up the perfect article, one he couldn't reject, show up at his office, and stare him down until he gave it the green light.

over Clark's death. Even if it was purely a business relation-
ship, I expected a larger show of sympathy and horror.

Clearly, Clark had caused his share of trouble in the past.
Maybe that's why Mr. Ken Price wasn't a fan.

Lenny and I trotted round the corner, dodging a boy on
a skateboard and two teenage girls in frontier costumes tak-
ing selfies in front of the WELCOME TO BROKEN BOOT sign.
One girl wore a gingham dress while the other preened in
a buckskin jacket with fringe and a coonskin cap.

I checked my watch. Lenny and I might catch Sumter
Majors, the editor of the *Bugle*, if we walked over at this
hour, but I couldn't leave Patti behind. What if she awoke
scared out of her mind? Or, worse, what if she was truly
heartbroken over . . . whom? Her ex-beau? Her date? I men-
tally slapped myself upside the head. Did it matter what the
exact nature of their relationship was? One night Jeff, a
human being, was alive, and the next morning he was deader
than disco.

And in her house, for God's sake. The very house she'd
inherited after the death of her parents. Now one more death
would be associated with that home she once held so dear.
What would she do? How could she live there again?

Even as Lenny pulled on his leash to scamper after the
skateboarder, I slowed down and dialed the paper, praying
for once that my editor would respond better to an appeal
on the phone than he did face-to-face. He picked up.

"What do you think? Can I write it?"

"If you mean am I aware that True Bell ice cream won't
go back into distribution this week? Yes. The factories still
aren't passing muster."

Oh yeah. That was the story I was supposed to be writing.
Where was our beloved True Bell ice cream? Why had it
been recalled—the real reason? How were locals coping
with the loss?

"I'm talking about the murder of Jeff Clark."

"Who?" His choked and spluttered his coffee. "Here?"

His voice had taken on a syrupy quality. "So, you're with the Associated Press?"

"Uh, not exactly."

Without a glitch in his new, friendly persona, he continued. "Now I know Jeff Clark's dead, I'm torn. I could handle everything by phone. Or at least my assistant could."

How could he handle the fallout in the Jeff Clark Band over the phone? Clark was murdered, by God. Price had to have a sliver of tenderness in his stony heart, even if he was an LA agent.

"If you don't mind my saying so, Mr. Price, you should handle things in person. This is a small community, and the way we do things here may not be what you're accustomed to. We need more direction. Also, what about the band? What are they supposed to do?" I thought about Uncle Eddie's predicament. "Isn't it in their contract to play two more nights?"

"That's none of your business," he said, his tone chilly. "Their road manager can handle it." He paused. "You may be right about my needing to fly down there to see . . . to things myself."

"I understand if you want to reschedule our interview." My courage was drifting away like a stray gray cloud on a sunny day.

"What? You nervous?" His laugh made the hair on the back of my neck dance.

"Don't be silly. Just sounds like you have a long night ahead of you."

"I'll catch a flight this evening and drive to . . . Broken Boot. If you stop by the band's hotel in the morning, we can chat over coffee. That's all the time I can afford."

Weakness morphed into blithering joy. "I will, Mr. Price. I will. You can count on it."

"What?" He sounded far away.

It took me several seconds to realize he'd hung up. *How rude.* Come to think of it, I hadn't heard any sadness or regret

"Has anyone in the band, uh, called you today, Mr. Price?"

There was a nine-months-pregnant pause. "What's he done now?"

With great effort, I attempted to swallow, but the giant ball of nerves in my throat made it impossible. "He's . . ."

He cursed. "Michelle," he yelled, "get me a flight to . . . Where did you say you were?"

"Uh, Broken Boot."

"Is Jeff in jail? Have they posted bond?"

I tried to open my mouth to give him the horrific news. Honestly, I did. "You fly to El Paso and rent a car to Broken Boot, sir." Instead, I could only blather on like a travel agent.

"I'll kill him." He could not have chosen a more apropos turn of phrase.

"What aren't you telling me?" He waited in silence for several seconds. "Is someone else involved? Are they hurt?"

"You can't kill him, Mr. Price. Someone's beat you to it."

I filled him in on what I knew, minus the part where I found his client naked from the hips up in my best friend's guacamole.

"Is there anything I can do to help before you get here?" Silence on the line.

"Who'd you say you were again?"

"Josie Callahan, a local reporter. I was scheduled to interview Mr. Clark this morning and you tomorrow on the phone."

"Well, that's not happening."

This time the shivers ran down my spine. "Um, I do need to cover the story, sir. I thought you might want to help me shine a positive light on Jeff Clark's career. Other papers are going to be saying all kinds of things, but we can hit the news feed early with the positive."

"Michelle, hold on a minute."

There was another long pause. "You have a point, Josie."

in authority to judge my friend by her outward appearance. But if I did a little digging, I could set them straight—point them to the real suspects—before she suffered the bitter sting of any false accusation.

I straightened my shoulders. I would call Ken Price, Clark's agent, and ask him to grant me an interview so that I could write a proper eulogy for his former client. I'd collect enough evidence to keep Patti's name above suspicion *and* my editor happy. It wouldn't surprise me if some people accused me of being mercenary.

I started out the back door, only to stop myself with my hand on the push bar. In my mind's eye, Dixie's dead body lay in that same alley—where I'd discovered her only months ago.

Lenny whined.

"Don't worry. I got you."

Instead, I made my way to the front of the restaurant and parked us on the wooden bench facing Main Street.

"I can do this without being a vulture. Right?"

My four-legged friend ignored my vacillation and turned to greet a haughty tabby in the front window of Wicks of the West. "Yip."

Endora studiously ignored him and continued to clean her long orange coat.

"Yip, yip, yip."

"Shh." I found the agent's number and dialed.

"Ken Price," a brisk, intelligent voice answered without a trace of accent.

"Mr. Price, this is Josie Callahan."

"Who?"

"I'm the reporter from Broken Boot, Texas. We have a phone interview scheduled for tomorrow to talk about Jeff Clark."

"Okay." His tone said, *Get off the phone, small-town idiot.*

With a sinking feeling in my gut, I realized no one had called him about Clark's death.

"If you need to reschedule, get with my assistant."

that could possibly help us out of this mess. I bit back my own misgivings. "You could ask Ty to play again."

One corner of Uncle Eddie's mouth kicked up. "He'd be tickled pink."

My aunt plunked the seat of her Wranglers on the edge of the huge metal desk she'd found in a going-out-of-business sale. "But will customers pay to hear Ty Honeycutt play again so soon?" She shook her head, answering her own question.

I touched my aunt's arm. "Hate to say it, but this crowd would come back if for no other reason than to see the place where the late Jeff Clark played the night he died."

Uncle Eddie removed his hat and placed it over his heart. "Sad thing, that boy dying, but Josie's got a good point."

"That settles it." Aunt Linda slapped her hands on the desk for good measure. "Call Ty before he dives headfirst into another all-night poker game."

"Will do."

I caught my uncle outside the office. "Shouldn't you call Jeff's agent and tell him what happened?"

"Why, Jo Jo? His band's probably gone and done that already." He mussed my hair and strode for the door with springs in his bootheels.

As grisly as the idea sounded, my gut was telling me that I needed to continue the story on Jeff Clark. Or did I? Some reporter somewhere was going to cover the story. Why not me?

For starters, like Uncle Eddie said, some folks would accuse me of being coldhearted. What would Patti say? My gut said my friend would understand. After all, she'd called Clark a jerk and slept in her office last night in order to avoid him.

A prickling sensation danced down my arms. If it had been anyone else, I would've thought that excuse way too convenient. I worried my bottom lip. I'd avoided thinking of Patti as a suspect up to this point, but that didn't mean the sheriff's office had done the same.

My skin grew clammy. It would be too easy for someone

of being a coldhearted"—he shot a glance my way—"you know what."

He twirled his hat on two fingers. "I didn't want to bring this up." He dropped his voice. "He might've been a hotshot on his way to the big time, but he had a few problems."

I had a hunch what was coming.

Aunt Linda leaned her elbows on the desk and rested her chin on her folded hands. "Hit me with it."

"He was a horndog with the ladies, hon."

"Eddie Martinez, what a thing to say!" Her back straightened. "Are you sure you've got your facts straight?"

I refused to speak ill of the dead. In spite of his weaknesses, Jeff Clark had been someone's son. And wrong or right, Patti had loved him once.

Uncle Eddie sighed. "He flirted with more women than you could shake a stick at, and his bus only arrived yesterday."

Aunt Linda's lip curled in disgust. "What are you thinking?"

"What if one of those women killed him?" He shuddered dramatically. "Beautiful women can be more jealous than a herd of alley cats."

"Well, did you tell all that to the sheriff's office?"

"No," he muttered. "I only thought of it this minute."

"You and your thinking." She came around the desk and took his hand. "Go talk to them." With her other hand, she relieved him of his hat and placed it on his head. "Plead our case, how we need the band's help to survive. Then go and find that Deputy Lightfoot and tell him what you're thinking." She planted a kiss on his cheek and directed him toward the door.

After a few steps, he turned back. "Ah, sug. How can I ask them? It's callous as all get-out."

I could see Uncle Eddie's side. Money was tight, and we would take a hit if we hired another big name for the weekend in addition to Clark's. But there was another horndog

* * *

I left the staff to clean up and headed upstairs in case Patti needed me by her side. She was sound asleep. My mind was racing, what with the coffee, tea, and adrenaline pumping through my veins. What could I do? Lightfoot and the deputies had the crime scene in hand.

"Do you think Uncle Eddie has tonight's entertainment under control?"

Lenny whined and placed his front paws on my leg.

"Yeah, that's what I'm afraid of." Last night was only the first performance for the Jeff Clark Band. They were booked to play Two Boots tonight and Saturday as well.

I sprinted down the stairs so fast, I nearly wiped out the Mexican Talavera planter at the bottom.

"Yip?" Lenny asked from his perch on the middle step.

"I'm okay, buddy." I scooped him into my arms. "Let's find the grown-ups."

When we walked into the office, all conversation came to an abrupt halt. It was clear as the frozen expressions on their faces that my aunt and uncle were troubled about my finding another dead body. I pretended not to notice. Since the day I'd come to live with them as a snarky twelve-year-old after my parent's untimely accident, I'd seen that same fearful look from time to time.

"Whose playing tonight if Clark's . . . dead?"

"Good question, Jo Jo." My aunt, the practical one in the family, turned a narrow-eyed stare on her husband and pursed her lips.

He popped his cuffs. "They signed a contract."

"Sure. Why not ask the band to play without him?" I dropped into the guest chair and lifted the soles of my Toms to the edge of the desk. "All they can say is *forget you, old man*."

"Humph." Uncle Eddie removed his Stetson and ran his fingers through his dark hair. "They could also accuse me

After they had all departed, Anthony, his sister Lily, and I cleared their tables and wiped them down.

"I tell you what," Lily said, slapping a table with a wet towel. "This here murder sure was good for business."

"Don't do that." Her brother grabbed the cloth from her hand, threw it into her plastic bucket, and gave her a shove toward the kitchen. "Go on, now. I need to talk to Miss Josie."

Lily puffed up like a bantam rooster, shot a glance at me, and then discarded her angry-younger-sister act. "He's got girl trouble." She threw her hands over her heart in a dramatic fashion and moseyed to the kitchen, probably hoping to wear her brother's nerves down to a frazzle.

Anthony looked around as if expecting to find someone hidden under one of the tables with a recording device. "Uh, Miss Josie. I don't have girl troubles." He straightened his Mexican bow tie. "I've got Senora Mari troubles."

"What's she done now?"

"She wants to set me up with her niece in Juárez."

"What niece in Juárez?"

He stuck his finger in his collar in an attempt to give his muscular neck some breathing room. "How do I know? But she claims we're perfect for each other and that all I need is a good wife to take care of my brother and sisters."

I tried to hide my reaction, but it didn't sound like a bad idea to me. That is, if he knew the girl and liked the girl, the girl liked him, and the immigration services approved.

"Can't you ignore her?"

He shook his head like a depressed basset hound, all sad jowls and sockets. "Every morning when I arrive and every day when I leave, she mentions her, describes her cooking, asks me over and over when I'll call her."

I smiled with compassion. "I'll talk to her. Sounds like she needs an intervention."

"Bless you, Miss Josie."

Lord bless me indeed. Trying to talk Senora Mari out of matchmaking would be like trying to divert a runaway train from disaster.

With a chuckle, Aunt Linda stepped up. "And Lord knows you'd better watch out when he's thinking, 'cause he might hurt himself."

"Doesn't anyone want to know what I think?" Senora Mari was taking the floor.

"Now, *Mami*." Uncle Eddie tried to put his arm around her, but she stepped out of reach.

"It's a case of bad juju," Senora Mari proclaimed.

"Where did she pick that up?" Aunt Linda asked in a whisper from behind my shoulder.

Senora Mari shrugged one eloquent shoulder. "It's true. Before Josie moved home, we had no murders in this town." She pointed at me with her melodramatic tendencies in full view. "Now we've had two in the past three months." She shook her head and pinched her lips. "Bad juju."

"Don't blame this on me." I turned to Aunt Linda. "When have I ever had bad juju? Never."

Anthony, our youngest and most recently acquired waiter, stepped into the conversation with two feet. "Didn't you lose your job and your fiancé nine months ago?"

I caught Aunt Linda turning her head away in an attempt not to laugh.

"See?" Senora Mari opened her arms to the crowd. "I told you. It's getting worse and worse."

Fortunately for me, our friends and neighbors laughed.

Bubba stood and shoved his hat on. "I don't know about y'all, but I've got to get back to work." He bit his bottom lip. "And y'all do too." With care, he bent down to help his elderly mother out of her chair.

"Come on, folks." She lifted a feeble arm, urging them to follow her. "Let's beat it." She shuffled out the door, head high, her hand clenched on her son's arm.

One by one they left. A few were silent, casting curious glances at Senora Mari and me. Others shook my uncle's hand and kept right on gossiping about Clark's road crew and the other bands in town for the Homestead Days Music Festival.

"Uncle!"

With a laugh, he released me and patted me on the back.

Aunt Linda pulled out a chair at an empty table, just as Senora Mari placed my favorite pork tamales and ranchero beans before me with a glass of icy sweet tea.

"Eddie," Fred Mueller called from the back of the room, "who do they think done it?"

With one eye on my uncle and the other on my plate, I inhaled the comfort food in front of me, and even though sweet tea wasn't my thing, I drank it down. The sugar and caffeine would help put me to rights after all I'd seen that morning.

"Well, sir." Uncle Eddie puffed out his chest. "I had a talk with Deputy Lightfoot about the case."

"Where's Sheriff Wallace?" Jerrie McAllen asked in a timid voice. Her son Bubba owned the local BBQ.

"He's on vacation in Galveston this week," Aunt Linda answered.

Fred Mueller rose to his feet. "Galveston shmalveston. He must come home. Now."

Uncle Eddie raised his hands to calm the owner of Fredericksburg Antiques. "As I was saying, Lightfoot and the other deputies are on the job."

Apparently, the grapevine, otherwise known as the switchboard operator at the sheriff's office, had spread the word faster than smoke signals.

Uncle Eddie crossed his arms across his barrel chest. "I told him he should check into that band of Clark's and that road crew he travels with." His mouth turned down in disgust. "That crowd is hell-bent on causing trouble."

I turned in my chair and grabbed his hand. "You shouldn't say things like that," I whispered. "You don't know what you're talking about." I observed our usually calm neighbors murmuring to each other with angry expressions.

Uncle Eddie eyed their heated reactions. "Uh, I spoke too soon . . . I guess. I don't know nothing for certain." He shot me a frustrated glance. "So don't take what I said as gospel. I was just thinking out loud."

widening my eyes, trying to convey how much he needed to change the subject. Now.

He opened his big mouth again. "What do you mean you don't—?"

"I'm sorry, y'all. I'd love to tell you all about it," I paused for effect, "but I need to go lie down."

"But, Eddie," I heard someone say as I left the room, "who was killed?"

"No one we know. Some singer, name of Jeff Clark."

Before I could check on Patti, I met Senora Mari and Aunt Linda at the bottom of the stairs.

"How's Patti?"

"Yip," Lenny said from the landing. According to him, she was doing better than expected.

"She's out like a light." Aunt Linda grabbed my arm, preventing me from flying past her. "Let her sleep awhile." She placed her arm around my shoulders and guided me back into the dining room. "She'll need you plenty when she wakes."

Senora Mari peered into my face. "You need some tamales and sweet tea."

"I'm not hungry."

"Tsk, tsk. When are you ever not hungry? If I didn't lock the freezers at night you'd eat up all our profits."

The assembled neighbors laughed, and the tension in the room broke into tiny pieces and fluttered to the floor.

"That's not true." I threw out my hands, appealing to the smiling faces seated around me. "We never lock the refrigerators."

They laughed even harder.

"And, besides, Uncle Eddie eats more than I do."

"Is that so? He grabbed me from behind and pretended to throttle me, much to the delight of the onlookers.

"Sorry."

"What did you say?"

"Uncle?"

He pretended to tighten his grip.

Chapter 4

After a few swigs of coffee, I turned to Dorothy something-or-other, the manager of Wicks of the West, and Sam from the local thrift store, Play It Again Sam. Both wanted as much information about the crime scene as I was willing to give. As they were neighbors and fellow business owners, their questions deserved honest answers. I gave them one or two gory details, while sparing Patti by not mentioning her date with the deceased the night before.

"Where was the body found?" Samuel asked.

I hesitated and chose to sidestep the question. "The body was found in Kenwood Estates."

"Yes, but which house. Didn't you find the body?" asked Fred Mueller, the owner of Fredericksburg Antiques.

My gaze shifted toward Suellen Burnett, but she'd slipped out. Couldn't say as how I blamed her.

"Whose house was it?" A loud male voice asked from behind me. Uncle Eddie waltzed into the room and gave me a tight side hug.

I wanted to kick him in the shins. "I don't know," I said,

I hugged him to me. "So sorry, Lenster."

"Yip."

"You betcha," I answered. "We can go, right?"

Lightfoot stared at Patti for a moment. "You can go. I know where to find you."

When we arrived at Milagro I expected to find the place quiet, as the lunch crowd usually petered out by this time. Not only was my family and the waitstaff there, but folks from the neighboring businesses. Somehow word had spread that I had found the body, and they'd come over to hear it from my own lips.

"Patti needs to go upstairs and lie down."

The two strong pillars of my family, Senora Mari and Aunt Linda, realized how fragile Patti was with one glance at her face. "Come, *chica*," my *abuela* said. Though she didn't always permit me to call her *Grandmother*, I couldn't help but think of her that way when she showed her soft, caring side.

They disappeared up the stairs to my loft apartment above the restaurant.

"Yip, yip," Lenny asked.

"Of course you can go."

"Yip," he said in appreciation, and headed off after them. In the quiet, I could hear the clatter of his toenails on the oak staircase.

Anthony, our newest waiter, stepped closer. "Are you okay, Miss Josie?"

I gave him a weak smile as I made my way to the coffee urn. "I'm fine except for feeling like I've been run over by a Mack truck."

had dated once or twice. How did it feel to be asking her these intimate questions?

"No."

Eyebrows raised, he lifted his head. "No?"

"I said *no*, didn't I?"

"Why was he here if you didn't spend the night together?"

Without warning, she bolted for the side of the house, reared back her arm, and threw the rake like a javelin over the fence into the backyard. She spun to face him. "He slept here and I slept on the cot in my office." Her cheeks flamed.

His pencil froze above his notepad. "You're telling me that Jeff Clark spent the night here, but you slept in your office."

"Have you lost your hearing? That's what I said."

My pulse jumped to my throat. "That's what she told me this morning. I swear."

"Why would you leave?" Lightfoot asked.

"Because he was drunk and he wasn't in his right mind."

"Why not drive him to his hotel?"

"Why should I? He could sleep it off on his own. I wasn't about to drag his drunk, lazy butt anywhere."

"Did anyone see you at your office?"

"I didn't see anyone, but I couldn't swear that no one saw me."

In spite of everything, I smiled. Goth Girl had returned.

One corner of Lightfoot's mouth twitched. "What were *you* doing over here?"

"I was trying to get an interview," I said. "I thought he stood me up."

"Figures." He pocketed his notebook and pencil. "That'll do for now."

"Yip, yip, yip," I heard from behind the fence to the backyard.

"Oh, Lord. Lenny, how'd you get back there?" When had I dropped his leash? No telling how many doggie footprints had contaminated the crime scene.

Patti opened the gate, and Lenny ran out. "Yip, yip, yip."

A pause, and then, "Who bought the beer?"

"Jeff Clark."

He nodded. "Who drank the beer?"

When she didn't answer, he paused to study her down-turned face. He waited until she took a moment to rest on her rake. "Who?"

"That's a stupid question. Have you ever seen me drink anything but beer?"

To his credit, he remained as cool as a fall breeze. "Who drank the beer last night?"

"Both of us." If he'd been a white-tailed deer, she'd have skinned him alive with her eyes.

He nodded and made a note. "Did you drive separate vehicles or did he ride with you?"

A spasm fluttered her eyelashes. "We rode in my jeep, and nobody drives Priscilla but me." She marched to the other side of the porch and attacked that flower bed as well.

I followed along and reached for the rake.

With a jerk, she turned her back to keep me at arm's length. Her shoulders tensed as she prepared to fight me if necessary.

"How was Jeff Clark planning on getting back to his hotel this morning?"

She sighed. "I don't know. He said something about sleeping in and calling some roadie to come pick him up."

"A roadie," Lightfoot repeated.

"Someone on the tour. I don't remember who."

She began to tap the tines of the rake on the sidewalk, increasing her intensity as weeds and flowers broke free.

Lightfoot and I exchanged glances.

"What happened when you got here last night?"

For a second she froze, and then continued to shake the gardening tool until I was afraid she'd break off the tines and send them flying like so much shrapnel. "You want to hear all about the mouth-to-mouth. Is that it?"

He sighed. "Did you spend the night together?"

I couldn't help but study his expression. The two of them

daisy fleabane along her driveway. "She's right over there, Einstein."

Barnes's pink skin flushed at my remark. Before he could respond in kind, Lightfoot raised his hand, palm out. "Follow the ambulance to the morgue. I'll call you when I finish here."

"That's forty miles," Barnes said.

"Then you'd better hustle." Lightfoot followed the other deputy to his cruiser, where they exchanged a few words. They shot surreptitious glances Patti's way until Barnes slammed his door and headed out.

Patti pulled those weeds with the same concentration I imagined surgeons used when removing malignant tumors. "Can I go inside?" She carefully removed a tall weed from the dry ground, making sure to get both the flower and root.

I glanced at Lightfoot and he shook his head.

"I don't think that's a smart idea, hon." The crime scene had to be secured and photographs taken.

"I think it's a brilliant idea." She gathered the weeds from the driveway and carried them to the trash can. Across her forehead, she'd left a smear of dirt when she wiped her face. Dusty soil cascaded down her shirt like a trail of bread crumbs.

With a deft movement, Lightfoot blocked the sidewalk. "Sorry, Patti, but we're all staying outside for now."

"Fine." She found the rake on the far side of the garage and began raking the flower bed. Vibrant pink azaleas snapped in two.

"Watch out, hon," I cried.

Lightfoot placed a hand on my arm and shook his head. "Tell us in your own words what happened." He removed a familiar small notebook from his pocket and a stub of a pencil.

She continued raking, catching dirt, weeds, and azaleas with the rake's tines. "We went to the show. We bought some beer. We drove to my house. We gave each other mouth-to-mouth."

I could have saved my breath. As I glanced at her one last time before entering the house, she sat staring at her neighbor's pink adobe bungalow, basking in the view of a breathtaking sunset on the Window View Trail.

I found Detective Lightfoot in the kitchen.

"You know I need to question her." His stoic expression remained the same, but I could detect a flicker of sympathy in his dark eyes.

"Are we suspects?"

He hesitated a fraction of a second too long before answering.

"Are you crazy?" I tensed, hoping he'd respond in anger so I could vent the feelings threatening to overwhelm me.

Narrowing his eyes, he took a deep breath and slowly released it, making me suspect he learned that technique for dealing with hysterical witnesses. "Barnes has your statement, but I'd like you to stay with Patti while I question her."

"As if I'd do anything else."

He frowned. "She can stay outside. If she cooperates, it shouldn't take too long."

"What good will it do to question her now? You saw her."

He clenched his jaw and remained silent.

I realized what he left unsaid. As an officer of the law, he needed to evaluate her current state of mind. Questioning her at this vulnerable moment would make it clear how she felt about Clark and the frightful nature of his death. A guilty person might let something slip that would lead to her arrest.

I wanted to punch something. Why did Patti and I have to be in the thick of things again?

"That's the best I can offer."

"Thanks," I muttered. I hated to admit it, but my journalistic side understood.

Lightfoot and Barnes led the way onto the porch. "Where'd she go?" Barnes asked, raising his hand to his holster.

With a hand shielding my eyes, I found Patti pulling up

bors." She dropped her head to my shoulders and closed her eyes.

I patted her hand. "Your neighbors are too busy chasing their tails to care."

After forever and a day, the EMTs brought out what was left of Jeff Clark, up-and-coming Country star. The man who'd once serenaded the Southwest with his melodic voice was silenced forever.

Patti darted from the swing toward the back of the ambulance.

I started to tell her that wasn't such a good idea, but I swallowed my need to take control. If anyone could look death in the face and come out on top, it was Goth Girl.

When she lifted her hand, the young EMT drew a breath to complain, but the older man scorched him with a silent reprimand.

I wanted to be there for Patti, but I wasn't sure I could stomach another glimpse of Jeff Clark's cold, dead face.

Her hand barely hesitated, and then she pulled backed the covering.

"Oh, my," the older man said in sympathetic tones.

Clark could've been sleeping; his expression was that peaceful. No blood or gore oozed over his features, only a thin trickle down one temple. Unfortunately, he wore guacamole down his chin, as if the killer had caught him in midbite.

On the other hand, if someone asked me what I would request for my last morsel on this earth, guacamole would be on the top of my list.

Once Patti saw Jeff's face, she was content to let the sheet fall back into place. She didn't cry. Instead she remained riveted to the spot, transformed into a wax figure.

"Thank you." I nodded at the EMTs, placed my arm around her shoulders, and slowly helped her back to the swing.

"I'll be right back, hon." Where was Lightfoot? I needed to get her away from this place before she let loose a storm of tears again.

Sirens shattered the scene as the ambulance rounded the corner and screeched into the driveway. A young man I didn't know and Clarence Stubbins, a retired elementary-school principal with a cap of silver hair, raced to the back of the ambulance and removed the gurney. "Where's the body?" the young one asked, unable to hide his excitement.

I glared at the young man and pointed toward the front door.

As if someone had unplugged her power cord, Patti burst into tears and collapsed into the nearest Adirondack chair, her head falling to her knees.

I tied Lenny's leash around one of the white porch posts and knelt beside her. As I wrapped my arm around her shoulders, I wished I could do more than next to nothing.

"She all right?" Lightfoot asked me, studying Patti's tears.

I could guess what he was thinking. Ever since Patti's parents left her the Feed and Supply, she'd put her grieving aside and transformed her parents' struggling business into Broken Boot's newest success story. To quote Uncle Eddie, that gal would charge hell with a bucket of ice water.

Watching her cry was like watching the space shuttle: one minute she was awe-inspiring; the next she was exploding into the atmosphere. My guess was Lightfoot, like me, had forgotten she was human.

I turned her shoulders and she fought me. "No, I'm not going anywhere," she said.

My eyes met the impatient gaze of the young EMS worker. "Ssh, we're just going to go sit over there," I said, gesturing to the wooden swing in the far corner of the yard.

Her gaze followed my hand. She relaxed and allowed me to lead her to the place where we'd once shared our adolescent secrets. As we settled on the swing, Lightfoot led the EMTs into the house.

"Can you believe it?" Patti demanded.

"What?"

"Crying like a big, fat baby in front of God and the neigh-

run out of questions to hurl at my head, I heard the one o'clock Amtrak train approaching the tracks at the end of the street. In the distance, Patti's green jeep raced toward the railroad crossing just as the gates started to lower.

"Don't do it," I whispered.

From my vantage point, the train could've been a mile or a hundred yards away. My heart jumped into my throat. Patti flew the jeep over the tracks with nothing to spare. Even from where I stood, I heard the metallic scraping sound as a layer of green paint was lost to the crossing arm. She barreled down the street toward home, through a neighborhood that had never known a serious crime, except for the time Mrs. Trumble's son was picked up for skipping thirteen days of school ten years earlier. I dug my fingernails into my thighs and prayed no car, pedestrian, or three-legged dog would venture into her perilous path.

Neatly taking out her blue recycle bin at the curb, Patti screeched to a halt in the yard and cut the engine. Her hands gripped the wheel as if glued to the leather cover.

Not wanting to spook her any further, I took my time as I approached.

She rolled down the window, keeping her eyes locked on the front door of the house. "You can tell me. I can take it."

"Jeff . . ." I couldn't speak for the large knot in my throat. Even though I thought she had lousy taste in men, she'd pinned more than a few hopes on the guy.

Like a ventriloquist's dummy, her head turned and her body followed a moment later. "Just spill it, for God's sake."

"I'm sorry, hon." I licked my parched lips. "Jeff's dead." Whatever she'd thought I was going to say, that wasn't it.

With a perplexed expression, she studied my mouth as if trying to make out what language I was speaking.

I wanted to snatch my words from the air. "I'm sorry," I whispered, not knowing what else to do.

She blinked several times, shoved open the door, and started toward the house just as Deputy Lightfoot stepped onto the porch, face grim, hat clenched in his fist.

dead?" He removed his hat, pulled a few errant strands of hair behind his ears, and replaced his standard-issue cowboy hat. He held my gaze, not defiant, but ready to take my word.

"That, or he's taken up acting on the side." There was no need to describe the color of his skin, the smell of death.

"Accidents happen."

I fought a strong desire to run away. "You're right. Maybe he decided to beat himself to death with his own guitar." I threw my palm onto my forehead in mock consternation. "Why didn't I think of that?"

He studied me for a moment, the strong, silent wheels of his mind turning too slowly for my taste.

"Please," I said through gritted teeth. "Patti needs to hear this in person."

With a squeal of the siren, another deputy cruiser parked across the street.

Lightfoot gave a quick nod. "Wait here." He crossed to an auburn-haired deputy whose slight frame and freckles made him appear all of ten. They spoke in low voices and then approached.

Lenny tried to stop the trembling that had overtaken me by licking my arm.

"Ssh. It's okay, Lenster."

"Barnes will take your statement while I go inside. The ambulance should be here any minute."

"Thanks," I whispered, and began to tear up. I shook my head to clear my emotions away. "Don't mind me. It's shock."

"Got it." Lightfoot pushed his cowboy hat back from his forehead and lifted the corners of his mouth in the semblance of a smile. "See you soon." After exchanging a stoic nod with Barnes, he laid his hand on his holster and opened the door.

I answered Barnes's questions with what little actual knowledge I had. Unfortunately, I had to admit to the young, officious deputy—while Lenny relieved himself on a telephone pole—that I'd contaminated the crime scene by slipping in the salsa on the living-room floor. As he began to

"Whatever. Where are you?" Worry crept into her voice. "Are you okay?"

Tears threatened to choke down my words. "Close the store and come home. Now."

I disconnected. Should I meet her on the way? How could I leave the scene before the deputies arrived? Before I could make a decision with my addled brain, Deputy Quint Lightfoot parked his cruiser along the road.

With his usual reserve, the long-haired deputy moseyed over to where I stood and gave me a brief nod. His dark eyes studied me long and hard from under coal black brows. Slowly he lifted his right hand to rest on the holster of his gun.

"Who was he?" His gaze left my face and narrowed on the doorway behind me.

"Jeff Clark. His band's playing Two Boots this weekend."

"Yip, yip," Lenny barked, encircling the deputy with his leash.

Lightfoot was six feet minus an inch or so, but graceful with it. He bent down and offered the Chi his hand to sniff. As soon as Lenny licked his hand, he gathered him in his arms and handed him over to me.

"Barnes will be here in a minute to question you. Once he's finished you two need to hit the road."

"Hold up just a minute. Patti's on her way." That's when I remembered that Lightfoot and my Goth friend had gone to a gallery showing of her photography in El Paso together.

I could see the wheels turning as he considered the pros and cons of my remaining. Would I be more suited to comforting Patti after she found out that her past, and possible future, was dead?

"Where is he?"

Unbidden, an image of the dead singer draped across Patti's oval-shaped coffee table infused my brain. I jabbed a shaky finger toward the porch. "He's in the living room. You can't miss him."

Lightfoot drew closer. "What makes you so sure he's

utes of shocked silence, I began to feel guilty. "You think I should call her, right?"

Lenny ignored me, choosing instead to focus his attention on a squirrel perched on the neighbor's fence. "Yip," he said in greeting.

The squirrel merely squeaked a warning.

I closed my eyes. "Dear Lord, if someone else can deliver this news to Patti better than me, feel free to drop this call." I dialed her number.

"Jos, what's up? I got a customer."

Guess I had my answer. "Hey, girl, um . . ."

There was a long pause. "What's happened?" Her good humor evaporated faster than sweat on a cactus. "I told you he was good for nothing. What'd he do? Vomit all over the living room floor? Lock himself out of the house without any clothes on and borrow Bessie Trumble's Vespa without asking?"

If push came to shove, I'd tell her over the phone. But I couldn't bear the thought of her driving like a maniac and putting herself and the community in harm's way. I could have said many things, including the fact that I found him facedown in a bowl of guacamole, wearing nothing but his Wrangler boots, but it could wait. "You sure you got only one customer in the store?"

"What . . . does . . . it . . . matter?" she demanded, spacing out her words as if trying to wring the answer from my lips.

"Count them."

"One! There's only one."

"Close the store." I infused my words with all the gravitas I could locate in my curvy body.

"Jos—"

"I'll tell you if you promise me you won't drive off the road."

"Geez," she sighed. "You're so dramatic."

"Cross your heart." I was dragging my heels, but how could I tell her the man she'd opened her heart to was dead?

Chapter 3

I called 911, my heart beating like a jackhammer in my chest. I was afraid if they didn't hurry, they'd need to bring a second stretcher. I blurted out all the pertinent information and the impertinent, like the fact the body was naked from the hips up. I ended the call before the operator could insist I check Jeff's body for signs of life. Been there, done that, never want to do it again in this lifetime. When the operator called me back, insisting that I try to revive him—same as last time—a wave of guilt washed over me. I'd doubted his integrity and now he was dead. How could I not try to save his life? Less than a minute later, we both realized the truth: Jeff Clark was on a road trip to the pearly gates.

Same as when Dixie died, I found myself waiting outside for an ambulance. "I'm glad you're here, Lenster."

He turned to me, lifting his ears to catch my voice. "Yip," he said, and proceeded to race around the yard, chase a sparrow, and sniff the yucca plants.

I'd called the ambulance, but I hadn't called my best friend. I was a coward, plain and true. After about ten min-

I crossed the living room, hoping to head off Lenny and Norman in the dining room before the oak flooring was carpeted with fur. As I drew closer to the shades, I realized there was a mound of blankets on the couch. I froze, squinting— as if that would prevent me from seeing any uncovered body parts. If he were naked, my retinas were about to be scorched.

"Jeff?" I whispered.

Norman and Lenny continued to hiss and yip in the other room.

This was stupid. I forced my shoulders to relax from around my ears. *I* was stupid for charging in here like some paparazzi wannabe. "Jeff?" I raised my voice and stepped closer. My foot slid on something wet, and I was down.

I reached behind me and discovered my jeans were wet and cold. I drew a small amount of whatever it was onto my finger and sniffed. Salsa never smelled so good. I glanced at the coffee table before me, expecting to find the remnants of a late night snack.

Instead, I found Jeff Clark facedown in what appeared to be a bowl of guacamole, buck naked.

"Yes, ma'am, boss."

I approached the bedroom door. "Oh, Jeff, are you still sleeping?" I called, again using an obnoxious singsong.

Lenny began to whine. "Jeff? It's me, Josie." No answer. "Patti's friend. We met last night?"

I pressed my ear to the door. I could make out a droning sound. Snoring?

"Sounds like he's awake."

"Yip, yip."

"Don't worry, cowboy. I won't look." I opened the door a few inches, the better to be heard.

Now that the door was open, I recognized the droning sound as an oscillating fan. "Jeff, this is Josie Callahan," I said in a sunny voice. "I'm here for an interview your publicist arranged for this morning." The bed frame rattled and I blanched. "Uh, I'll wait on the couch while you get dressed. How's that?"

Lenny disappeared around the door.

"Hey, get back here." Keeping my eyes down, I pulled him back.

"Yip, yip, yip," Lenny complained.

"Sorry about that," I said through the crack in the door. "We're in the living room." The only answer was the rattle of the bed frame.

As my eyes adjusted to the dim light in the living room, I bent down and scooped Lenny into my arms. "You are a naughty boy." I wanted to laugh. "Was he naked?"

"Yip."

Something scraped the floor behind us and Lenny jumped from my arms. Norman sprang for the kitchen while Lenny flew after him like a Chihuahua from hell. "Yip, yip."

This escapade would definitely make Lenny's next blog. Of course, he'd have to share what it was like to meet Jeff Clark. He could also introduce a lively discussion on the pros and cons of cats, which should start a flurry of never-ending comments.

From the kitchen, the caterwauling began.

blanket close to my side, turned the key in the lock, and stepped inside.

"Don't surprise him, whatever you do," Patti said in a panic, which made me wonder what kind of surprise she thought might be in store.

"Jeff," I called in a lilting way.

No answer. From the entranceway, I could make out the silhouette of a sofa, chair, and love seat in the dim living room. Straight ahead, the clock on the microwave invited me in for a look-see. I started for the kitchen, but Lenny refused to budge.

"Chill, Lenster. Norman's going to run and hide like a big 'fraidy cat." In the sink, I found a haphazard pile of plates, bowls, and silverware and a skillet coated with grease. The whole mess smelled like fajitas, and, sure enough, I discovered bits of chicken stuck to the pan. The coffeepot was on. Two coffee mugs emblazoned with skulls and the word *poison* rested in the sink.

"Tsk, tsk."

"What?" Patti snapped.

"I thought you were a neat freak."

Lenny whined and pulled on his leash. "Shh, don't be such a chicken," I said sotto voce. "That cat's too chubby to catch the likes of you." I turned and smiled. There on the refrigerator was a picture of Patti and her parents circa 1995, before cancer had thinned their cheeks, under a magnet shaped like a holly wreath.

"You tell Lenny to let Norman be." Patti's voice was hard to hear over the phone.

"Can I help it if my Chi is friendlier than your grumpy-tailed cat?"

As I passed through the living room, I followed the rays of sunlight that peered through the plantation shutters at the end of the hall.

"Oh, fantastic," Patti whispered. "A customer. You call me right back."

he marked Patti's territory as his own. Norman, Patti's Snow-shoe cat, was going to have an aneurysm.

"He's not answering, Jos. Maybe he caught a ride from someone."

"Who would he call?"

"Gosh, I don't know," she snapped. "He said he would wait for me to take him back to the dance hall this evening."

My inner bullcrap meter was going off. Why would he wait around all day?

Two hours left until my deadline. Some people miss dead-lines, but I couldn't afford it. I was new to the *Bugle* and it had taken way too long to have an article picked up, let alone a column. After complaining that my first few stories weren't folksy enough, they'd eagerly accepted my story about how I'd solved Dixie Honeycutt's murder and barely escaped with my life.

"Where's your key?" I asked.

"In my hand."

"Not that one, smarty pants." Patti always kept her spare key in an obvious place, if I could only remember. I lifted the potted fern and found nothing but a few roly-polies. With a stick from the yard, I foraged in the dirt of the only other plant on the porch, a potted and decidedly decrepit barrel cactus.

"You're trying to find my spare key, aren't you?"

"Hm."

"Cut it out. Someone's going to see you, break in, and steal my Bose."

As Lenny dug another latrine under a light pink azalea, I fumbled under some grocery flyers. When Patti's parents were alive, there was always a key in the mailbox that hung to the side of the front door.

"Got it!"

"Jos, don't go in there. You'll be invading his privacy."

"It's not his house." I whistled for Lenny. "It's my butt on the line for this deadline." I gathered my canine security

tain laurel embraced the short sidewalk that divided her modest lawn. I was glad to see she'd started to make the place her own by adding a red tin roof.

"Yip," Lenny said, breaking into my memories.

"Crud!" I remembered the tacos too late. This was not the way to start out with Mr. Sexy. If food was indeed the way to that man's heart, I would be turned away at the door like an overzealous Boy Scout peddling popcorn.

A gray sedan was headed down the street. It veered into one of the trash cans that littered the end of the driveways, where the sanitation company had left them. The can fell to its side and rolled into a mailbox, causing the metal mailbox door to fall open. I tried my best to pierce the driver with an icy stare, but as I couldn't see him due to the glare, I doubt it made a dent in his driving pride. If I knew the neighborhood, it was probably an elderly driver out for a romp to the pharmacy to get a new pair of eyeglasses.

Once I rang Patti's front doorbell, I swore to wait sixty seconds. But, as usual, my patience slipped. I rapped on the decorative glass pane, winced, and repeated.

No answer. Jeff was gone . . . or in the shower . . . or sleeping it off.

Exasperated for no good reason, Lenny and I proceeded to check out the driveway hidden behind a grizzled live oak on the side of the house. It was empty as a church parking lot on a Friday night. "Lenny," I said, scooping him up with one arm. "Did Patti say she drove her jeep or that he followed her home?"

Lenny tilted his head to one side, his tail swinging madly. "Yip."

"That's what I thought. I don't think she said one way or the other."

I called my Goth friend. "What's he driving?"

"Squat. He left his truck at Two Boots last night."

"Text him again. Sleeping Beauty's not answering."

I dropped Lenny's leash and watched him dart from one azalea to another. First he dug around the trunk, and then

In spite of my question, I knew what was ailing her. Patti had this thing. Some might call it a fatal flaw where men were concerned. If they even hinted that she was to wait on them, especially in the area of meals, her heart would curl up like the toes of the dead witch in *The Wizard of Oz* and retreat into its protective shell.

I threw an arm around her. "Hey, don't get your knickers in a twist. I'll take him some tacos. You stay here and play hard to get."

She grabbed a broom and started sweeping invisible dust bunnies from the floor. "I can't just close up whenever he gets a wild hair up his nose."

Sure she could. She was the sole owner and proprietor since her parents had left her the Feed and Supply. But I wasn't going to argue.

"Stay here and mind your fencing. Lenny and I will take Mr. Sexy some sustenance, and thus win a hasty but fabulous interview."

Lenny ended my attempt at witty banter by bolting for the entrance like a greyhound on speed. As I opened the door, I spied the source of his alarm. A desert cottontail was bounding toward a stand of purple fountain grass for all he was worth.

"Yip, yip, yip." He nearly yanked me into the street before I could lock his leash.

"You'll get him next time." I bent down and rubbed my hand along his trembling back. "Don't you worry yourself, son." Jeff Clark was waiting to give the interview of his life, whether he knew it or not.

After a brisk twenty-minute walk, Lenny and I arrived at Patti's stucco, ranch-style home. The last time I'd visited was the day of her mother's funeral. The house had overflowed with folks offering tearful hugs along with platters of cold cuts, cheesy casseroles, pecan pies, and fried chicken from Wagoner's Thriftway. A dwarf pine and a Texas moun-

him for my article, and I'm running behind. Where's he sleeping?"

She blushed. "On my couch."

"Humph." Was she blushing because he was on her couch or because he was actually in her bed? Enquiring minds didn't want to know, because if they did, enquiring minds would give her a speech that would fall on deaf ears.

"He said he doesn't sleep well in hotels." She sipped slowly. "What was I supposed to do? He has to play again tonight."

"You're a real community volunteer. Would you please send him a text and ask him if I can interview him? Lenny and I'll even walk over."

She screwed up her nose and spluttered her tea. "Don't go over there. I haven't vacuumed or dusted in a coon's age."

"I'm not passing judgment on you or your housekeeping skills."

"No, not going to happen." She was redder than before, which made me wonder what could be so embarrassing. "You could interview him here," she gestured with her chin, "in my office." Her eyes held a hint of dreaminess.

"Okay, but I'm on a deadline. As in, I have to finish this and send it in by three o'clock." According to my watch, it was one. I wasn't SuperWriter. I needed time to edit and polish, like everyone else.

Patti pulled out her phone. "Wouldn't you know it?"

She opened her mouth and shut it again, both sides curled up like the joker in a Batman movie.

"What's he saying?"

"This is a text he sent hours ago."

"And?"

After giving me the stink eye, Patti read the text. "Why don't you come home, baby? And bring some tacos. I'm starving to death in more ways than one."

I laughed when I caught sight of my best friend's expression. She looked as if she'd swallowed a spider. "What's wrong with you?"

Her prairie bonnet shaded the woman's features from the glare of the overhead fluorescents. "Don't mind me. Having too many babies shot my nerves long ago."

As I laughed, I tried to locate Patti with a surreptitious glance around the store. "Nice to meet you," I said.

"Got to run." She hurried to the door and her long skirt swung wide, revealing denim-blue boots, a nice complement to her outfit.

"She just moved to Broken Boot this week." Patti joined us from the back of the store, wearing her version of a costume: black pants, a red-and-black flannel shirt, and a black felt hat. Surprisingly, she'd omitted her typical black liner and ghostly pale foundation.

I gave her a slow once-over.

Without flinching, she met my gaze with a stare that would melt iron, but after a few seconds, her cheeks flushed pink.

"You finding everything you need?" Patti asked the other woman.

"Do you carry rat poison?"

Patti grinned. "Sure thing. It's right over here." While my best friend led the older woman to another part of the store, Lenny and I perused the doggie clothes in the pet section, which consisted of one aisle—one side food and litter; the other side boutique clothing and chew toys.

After the woman paid and left, Lenny and I sidled up to the counter.

"What have you done with Jeff Sexy? Enquiring minds want to know."

"Where'd that name come from?"

"It's my own creation. Don't you like it?"

"No. Makes him sound like a stripper." She reached under the counter to retrieve a big hand-thrown ceramic cup. Over the rim lay the tag of her favorite flavor of tea, sage rosebud. She took a long swig before answering, gazing at me over the rim.

"Last time I saw him, he was asleep," she finally said.

"That's more than I wanted to know. I need to interview

column. "Humph," he said after several seconds, and turned to his computer. His fingers clicked across the keys, rapid-fire. "He's not here."

I was wise to the minor-celebrity mind-set. I untied my prairie bonnet and stowed it in my bag. "I know Jeff Clark's not officially *here*, but would you please call and tell him that I'm here? My name is Josie Callahan, and his publicist, Terry Riley, set it up."

He pursed his lips the way Senora Mari did right before she lost her temper with Uncle Eddie. "He checked out this morning."

"Do you know where he's staying?"

"I'm sorry."

I leaned in. "Please, can you at least tell me where Mr. Clark said he was going?"

Like a cat drunk on ice cream, he shook his head slowly from shoulder to shoulder. "We never divulge the personal information of our guests. Why don't you call his publicist again?" he asked with a smirk.

"Thanks," I muttered over my shoulder as I marched into the revolving door with Lenny and hopped out the other side. I tried to call the publicist, but had to content myself with leaving a voice mail. As I considered my next move, Lenny sniffed the tufts of grass beside the sidewalk. My gaze followed a couple of girls with dyed black hair and tattoo sleeves made of real tattoos across the street.

"That's it! Let's go ask Patti."

"Yip," Lenny said.

Inside the Broken Boot Feed and Supply, the place was dark, but the Open sign was on. I shoved open the door and set the cowbell clanging. A woman in a denim skirt and matching jacket spun in our direction, a plump hand to her heart.

"Woo, you nearly gave me a heart attack!"

"I apologize, ma'am."

"Yip," Lenny said.

who came into town, whether for the Wild Wild West Festival or a gig at Two Boots, stayed in the only downtown hotel Broken Boot had to offer. They could have stayed at a chain hotel out on the highway, but they preferred the ambience of the historic hotel, which dated back to 1883.

With Lenny in my arms, we had no trouble circumventing the rotating door. The lobby, as always, spoke to my inner cowgirl: exposed beams; thick doorframes of the same dark, rustic wood; authentic Mexican tile; and the requisite live game heads on the wall, each with wide horns and glass eyes.

"Good afternoon." The desk agent was an older man with a fringe of gray hair behind his ears and wire-framed glasses. He pursed his lips, peered down his nose at Lenny, and then raised his gaze to the sign on the wall behind him that read:

NO PETS

His look might have bothered me if I didn't know for a fact that you could stay in the Cogburn Hotel with a pet if you paid them enough money under the counter.

"Good afternoon to you. Nice costume." I smiled, and Lenny bared his teeth at the man.

Simpson Crane, according to his name tag, sucked his teeth and waited for me to continue.

With a sinking feeling, I realized that what I assumed was his pioneer attire—a plaid vest and red saloonkeeper's tie—could very well be his normal wardrobe. "We're here to interview Jeff Sexy—I mean, Clark. I'm with the *Broken Boot Bugle*." I had no credentials, so I slapped a copy of the paper on the counter. On the last page above the fold sat my byline along with my picture. It was a good likeness, if you tilted your head and closed one eye.

With the air of a man who had no other joy in life than to drive others to pull their hair out, he eyeballed my latest

Chapter 2

On Friday morning, the town council couldn't have asked for better weather. The sun hung proudly over our desert community, gilding the buildings and railroad tracks with affectionate arms of gold. The Chisos Mountains boasted gorgeous cloaks of pale gray shadow and rosy gold clouds.

"Yip," Lenny said, anxious to show off his pioneer getup. I'd dressed him in a plaid shirt and a straw hat. If I had to meet Jeff Clark, I wanted someone on my side to remind me to remain not only a neutral journalist but an open-minded, kind human being as well.

It was high noon as we promenaded down the wooden sidewalk, past Wicks of the West and Elaine's Pies.

"Come on," I said to Lenny.

"Yip," he agreed.

We continued for another block and a half, treading lightly around the slow-as-snails window shoppers and the locals clogging up the sidewalk with their daily gossip sessions until we made it to the Cogburn Hotel. Jeff Clark's publicist had e-mailed his client's location for the weekend, but I could have saved him the trouble. All the musicians

down into the crowd. His biceps flexed as he lifted a woman with long black hair and multiple piercings from the crowd. Patti.

The crowd hushed. Jeff started to sing, but with eyes only for his companion. As the electric slide guitar led the band into a heart-melting instrumental break, Jeff handed his instrument off to a roadie. While the audience swayed, he slow danced with Patti in a tight embrace beneath a tender blue spotlight.

It was the spotlight that gave him away. Two Boots didn't own a blue spotlight, which meant two things: 1) His crew set it up before the evening began; and 2) the romantic lighting was an integral part of all his concerts. The only thing that changed was the girl.

My stomach was aching from the schmaltz of it all. Where had hard-as-nails Goth Girl gone?

After the dance, the band skedaddled off the stage for a barely earned break, and Patti left the stage with Jeff.

I eyed our basket of chicken wings and dared them to come one step closer. They didn't, and I called it a night before I broke my vow to eat a tad smarter.

The parking lot was full. Some industrious patrons had parked on the grass, in front of the Dumpster, and even created new spaces at the end of rows, to the point that it was going to be a major horn-blowing fest to get everyone's car out without incident.

I spun away from a couple kissing behind a red Dodge Ram and started toward Milagro and home. I didn't miss my ex, the slime bag, but I did miss holding a man close, the smell of his skin, the rough of his beard, his breath on my face.

As soon as that image entered my brain, I thrust it away. Love had done me wrong and love could kiss my queso.

tattoo sleeves? With a whiskey-smooth baritone he greeted the crowd, earning another round of enthusiastic cheers.

I joined in, cheering and applauding like a true believer. I pushed aside my own disappointments and clung to hope. As he began his set, he made eye contact with the front row of fans, mostly women, and tipped his hat. They screamed in response like a crowd of eighth-grade girls at a boy band concert. If anyone else besides my fiercely intelligent friend had decided to make a play for this country girl's fantasy, I'd have chalked it up to temporary insanity and told them to get back on their medication. I sighed. This wasn't about me. It was about Patti finding happiness.

I caught her watching him with laser-beam intensity, the corners of her mouth lifted in a huge smile of anticipation.

And, sure enough, within seconds, the sexy musician's gaze abandoned the front row of adoring fans to lock eyes with Patti. Again, he tipped his hat and widened his million-dollar smile. Heads turned to find the recipient of his attention, but none landed on my companion. It was too hard for them to believe he had eyes for a Goth princess.

"Looks like he's making his move."

"You bet your sweet Aunt Fanny he is." She swigged the final sip of her beer, slammed the bottle to the table, and wiped her mouth with her thumb.

From the stage, Clark gave Patti a come-hither wave of his hand, and the ladies in the crowd went wild, as if his invitation was meant for them.

Goth Girl jumped from her stool. "Here goes nothing."

"Be careful," I hollered as she headed toward the stage and disappeared into the crowd.

When he slowed things down with his next song, couples around our table paired off for a slow dance—if you could call shuffling an inch forward and backward dancing.

"This song is our new single, available tomorrow on iTunes," Clark said over his band. "Hope you like it. It's called 'Sweet Thing.'"

A whoop from the fans rocked the rafters as Jeff reached

Though they'd greeted his opening number with enthusiastic applause and his guitar solos with cheers, it was obvious by the disappointed sighs at the beginning of each subsequent song he wasn't whom the crowd had paid to see. I hoped he didn't notice the crowd's lack of enthusiasm for his music.

"Is this a sellout?" Patti made a sweeping gesture. "And is it legal?" With a glance of dismay, she drank a healthy swig of beer.

"It's an answer to Uncle Eddie's prayers." We needed the additional revenue to cover the night's elevated expenses.

"Huh." She shook her head at my conservative turn of phrase. "You better pray no one has the fire marshal on speed dial."

I lifted my cider. "Here's to paying our debts, expanding our business, and more tourists than we can shake a stick at."

Her pinched lips relaxed and broke into a grin. "Amen, sister."

Due to the success of our Wild Wild West Festival and the popularity of the late Dixie Honeycutt's jewelry designs, Broken Boot was now a slightly bigger blip on the radar. Tourists not only passed through town on their way to Big Bend National Park; they also stopped for lunch and, more and more, stayed the night at the Cogburn Hotel and the Rifleman RV Park.

Nearly giddy with the chance to finally make money and pay his bills, Uncle Eddie searched until he found an up-and-comer for the Homestead Days Music Festival that would draw a bigger crowd. That man was Jeff Clark.

"Good night, Broken Boot," Ty yelled from the stage with a whoop and a screech of his electric guitar. The crowd applauded with more enthusiasm now that the main event was finally within their sights.

Suddenly Jeff Clark and his band stormed the stage to whoops, hollers, and thunderous applause. From the audience, the singer looked handsome and dangerous. Tattoos decorated his well-formed biceps, trailing down to his wrists. Funny, I hadn't noticed those earlier. Had he donned

We chuckled. "This is Vince," I said. "He keeps things from getting too rowdy around here."

With a nod, Jeff shook his hand. "Howdy."

"Head doorman and bouncer," Vince added. Both men's biceps bulged as the handshake turned into a test of their virility.

Jeff grinned as he disengaged from Vince's strong grip. "I'll be sure to keep that in mind if I find someone in need of bouncing." His eyes locked with Patti's until his gaze lowered briefly, caressing her body from the butterfly tattoo at her ear to the black combat boots on her feet.

From the look on Patti's face, I could see she'd cast caution to the wind.

I gave myself a mental shake and let go of my worries. I'd give him the benefit of the doubt, if only for the sake of my friend's happiness. After all, I was jaded from my own disastrous relationship. The truth: my BS meter was kaput.

A young man wearing a Jeff Clark Summer Tour tee and tattered jeans hurried over from the direction of the kitchen. "Jeff, where you been?" He ignored the rest of us. "Less than five minutes, man."

"Right." Jeff transformed from lover to businessman in the flutter of an eyelash. "See you soon, sugar." He kissed Patti's cheek and whispered something that made her blue eyes dance.

"Three minutes." The roadie shifted back and forth on the balls of his feet.

Jeff managed to grace each of us with his oh so sincere smile. "Enjoy the show," he said, and hurried off, already in earnest conversation with his roadie.

We maneuvered our way back to our table, but after fifteen minutes there was still no sign of the charming Jeff or his band onstage. "I hope my eardrums are still intact after this," I said, as we waited at our table.

Ty Honeycutt and his band of local musicians were currently playing his boot-stomping, electric-guitar-wailing blend of country rock for a standing-room-only crowd.

"Can't y'all read?" He slapped his hand on the door, ripping the sign so that it hung precariously from one corner. "I'm not signing T-shirts or cowboy hats or bandanas, nothing. Not until after the show, so beat it."

"Jeff?" My friend swallowed and pasted on a bright smile, which looked a little funny, as her everyday expression was something between solemn and funereal.

His transformation was awe-inspiring. First, the deep furrows across his forehead changed into solid lines; then his hard, down-turned mouth relaxed; and finally the bite and brawl in his eyes cleared into something bright and shiny. "I thought you'd decided to wait until after the show." He smiled at my friend as if she were the best dark lager, tastiest apple pie, and smokiest beef brisket all rolled into one.

I hoped that look was genuine because Patti deserved someone who truly cared for her. She'd seen enough hurt in the past few years to last until she was gray. But my stomach filled with dread, signaling a warning that he wasn't to be trusted.

Ignoring my nauseous reaction, I turned my attention to the room behind him. "Everything okay in there?" I nodded toward the dressing room. I didn't care if he was country singer Jeff Clark or the governor of Texas. He would pay for any damage caused by their testosterone-laden tussle.

His smile dimmed for a brief moment, and I caught the calculation behind his charm. *Dang it.* I didn't want my gut reaction toward him to be correct.

"Jeff, this is my good friend Josie Callahan." Patti placed her hand on his arm. "Her family owns this place."

His expression morphed into one of delight. "What a pleasure, ma'am. Can't tell you how great it is to be playing Two Boots after all these years on the Texas circuit."

I couldn't help but notice that he hadn't answered my question about the state of the dressing room.

"Watch out," the Two Boots bouncer interjected. "Next thing you know the sun'll melt your cell phone right through your windshield."

"Wait a sec." Holding us back with his outstretched hand, Vince eased open the door.

Angry voices assaulted the air. "Take it back, Clark!"

"You better check yourself, son. Who do you think got you this gig?"

"That doesn't mean," a man grunted, as if in the midst of a struggle, "you can take what you want."

"It's mine . . . for the . . . taking." A groaning sound emanated through the door, as if heavy bodies locked in a game of tug-a-war slid across the floor, bumping into furniture on their way.

"Not this time."

Before Vince could open the door, something large and heavy crashed to the floor. "Everything all right in there?" the bouncer called through the opening.

I shot a glance at Patti and found her gaze riveted to the door and her hands fisted as if preparing to join the fray.

Suddenly the door banged open and a redheaded man in a black leather vest and matching pants growled, "Get out of the way." We jumped back as he swung toward Vince and raised his arm high like a bear ready to maul.

"Whoa, there, Cochise," Vince said, jumping back before the other man could make contact. After a tense moment and a glare at the three of us, the man in black stomped off toward the bar.

Patti's brow furrowed. "Who was—?"

Another man, this one in a white hat and a matching, muscle-hugging tee, lunged through the door. He looked every bit the country-music star. Wavy chestnut hair that curled softly along his neck and around his ears. Incandescent blue eyes. A stance both strong and laid-back like he was born to embrace the guitar and sing songs of love to adoring women everywhere. No wonder Patti wanted to give him a second chance. Or third or fourth.

He stopped short at the sight of us, but his hostile gaze pursued the other man as he disappeared into the crowd.

"Says my boss—this young lady's uncle—who happens to be writing your paycheck."

After a quick glance at his wristwatch, the security guard nodded. "In case you weren't briefed, no one goes in the dressing room this close to performance." He studied me as if I were a stinkbug on the bottom of his shoe. "No matter who they *say* their uncle might be."

"Got it." Vince stepped closer until the guard moved out from in front of the door. "Now git. Your break's already started."

For a few seconds, the security guard merely clenched and unclenched his jaw, staring at each one of us in turn. Good sense or hunger finally seeped into his brain and he stomped off toward the kitchen.

"Who died and left him in charge?" Patti, always serene and unflappable, adjusted the collar of her blouse, fidgeted with the leather bands on her wrists, and then began running her fingers through the ends of her hair as if we'd walked inside from a Texas windstorm.

"That would be Jeff Clark's agent. Under his contract, we're required to provide additional security."

Vince flexed his muscles and turned to look at me with his good eye. "Don't know why. I got it handled." My childhood friend lost the vision in his left eye to a piece of shrapnel while fighting in Iraq.

"How do I look?"

I placed a hand on Patti's arm. "You're just as beautiful as you were before that blond bimbo walked out of Jeff's dressing room."

"You bet your butt I am."

I grabbed both her arms and gently shook her. "Girl, you got this."

"Whoever he is," Vince cracked his knuckles, "if he hurts you, I'll break his face."

Patti laughed, stepped out of my grasp, and threw back her shoulders. "Bring on the pain."

The security guard eyed her with a vacant, beatific smile as if the sashaying girl had lobotomized him with her hips.

A deep furrow appeared across my friend's forehead as she watched her go. Without warning, Patti spun toward the door and grabbed the handle.

The security guard pounced, forcing his body between Patti and the door. "Can't you read?" he growled, like a bulldog guarding a pile of week-old steak bones.

"Just a minute," I said, straightening to my full five feet, four inches. "Not only does my family own this place, but Jeff also sent Patti a text message to join him backstage."

Hank crossed his arms across his rent-a-cop work shirt. "I don't care if he asked her to marry him. No one goes through the door thirty minutes before showtime."

"What about that . . ." Patti hesitated. "Lady?"

"She went inside an hour ago." This time a cruel grin spread across his face. Blocking our entry was the highlight of his day, bless his pea-picking heart. "Not to mention, she's got more to offer. Goth and boring aren't on the menu for tonight, girls."

My temper flared so fast my ears started to burn.

"Hey, Josie."

I glanced over my shoulder to discover that Vince Schreiner, our regular weekend bouncer, had joined our little party.

He swaggered over in a Davy Crockett costume complete with coonskin hat, a ready-to-rumble grin across his face. "What's going on, gals?"

Before I could step away, he gave me a one-armed hug, drowning me in the scent of Old Spice and cigar smoke.

The security guard jabbed the handwritten sign with a pudgy finger. "They forgot how to read."

Vince dropped his arm from my shoulder. "Don't you worry about these gals." Flexing his muscles like a Friday-night wrestler, he gave the other guard a curt nod. "Go take your dinner break. I'm your relief."

"Says who?"

ful was another matter—unless you planned to tie them to your fence post. But I was intoxicated by my plans. Her comments fell to the ground unheeded, like grains of rice after a wedding. How was I to know my musician fiancé would abandon me at the altar for the Great Barrier Reef? I sighed.

Her chin rose. "You can leave if you want, but what do I have to lose by giving Jeff another chance?"

"Your dignity, pride, and sense of self-worth." I touched her hand. "Remember how devastated you were after you caught him cheating the last time?" Why my intelligent, fiercely independent friend didn't realize he might be planning to add another notch to his guitar strap was a mystery to me.

A funny look crossed her face. She pulled her cell phone from her back pocket. "It's him," she gushed. "He says he can't wait to see me."

"Just . . . be careful."

She patted my hand. "I will. Don't worry."

I found it impossible not to imagine all the negative things that could possibly go wrong as I trailed along behind her. She maneuvered her way through the crowd of locals in long calico dresses and tourists in straw hats and suspenders, around a couple dancing the two-step, and over a woman kneeling on the wooden floor to recover the contents of her pioneer reticule. I tried to tell Patti I didn't want to go backstage to meet Clark, but Ty's tenor thundering from the speakers made it impossible.

She halted at a door near the kitchen marked by a short, beefy security guard and a sign that read:

KEEP OUT!
YOU AIN'T IN THE BAND!

As she prepared to knock, a blonde with zebralike highlights, dressed in a cutoff T-shirt, Daisy Dukes, and cowboy boots came giggling out the door. "Bye, Hank." She gave us the once-over, sneered, and walked away, whooping with laughter.

to see him face-to-face, I didn't think the hand of fate had orchestrated his appearance in our Homestead Days Music Festival as much as Patti had. Uncle Eddie simply made some calls, negotiated a price, and wham-bam, we had a band.

This new and, frankly, a bit desperate Goth Girl made me nervous.

She frowned and checked the time on her phone. "His set should start in fifteen minutes, if this hillbilly would ever get off the stage." With two fingers, she began to pull pieces of straw from her bottle-black hair.

I ignored her remark. Ty Honeycutt was many things, but one thing the fine-looking country singer was not was a hillbilly. Was he a redneck? His neck was so red you could stop traffic with it. But, friends, Texans aren't hillbillies. After the death of his aunt Dixie, stories of his wild antics faded away. He'd loved her more than his own mother, and I sympathized with his loss. If anything should happen to Aunt Linda, a chunk of my heart would shrivel into dust.

"Is that your way of saying that Ty's songwriting talent doesn't hold a candle to your own?"

"Go on," she said with a disparaging wave of her hand. But when she tipped her head back to take another swig from her longneck, she wore a secretive smile.

I laughed. "I can't wait until Tuesday. The audience is going to go crazy for your songs." In a few days, Patti would join a group of hand-selected amateur singer-songwriters in the final concert of the festival. Social media and word of mouth had done their bit in promoting the performers, *and* the singer-songwriter contest. We were crossing our fingers that talent scouts and record labels from across the state would attend. If nothing else, the five-hundred-dollar cash prize would be a welcome pat on the back.

Still, Patti's sudden interest in her old beau made my stomach roil. "It's not too late to slip out the back," I said. Only last summer she warned me away from serious relationships with professional musicians. With a curl of her lip, she pointed out you could flirt with them, but keeping them faith-

with a few appreciative whoops from the menfolk. I joined in, though I couldn't miss the fact she'd barely escaped hitting the mat face-first.

"Come along, Grace," I said, raising my voice above the wail of an electric guitar. "You don't want to show up the band." The festival's first act was in full swing.

"Just you wait," she muttered. "You're up next."

Ever since a murderous restaurateur tried to put bullet holes in the two of us, Patti and I had forged an unbreakable bond. Tonight, like every other Thursday night, we vented our frustrations with the vagaries of small-town life on the back of Diablo at my family's dance hall.

"Tall, blond, and handsome at two o'clock." I gestured with my thumb to a fence post–thin dude in a pioneer costume, sporting a droopy mustache and a scruffy goatee.

When she laughed, the piercings up and down her ears jingled. "Maybe at two o'clock in the morning." We sat at our elevated table and immediately dove for the basket of buffalo wings, which had arrived during our excursion to the bull riding arena. After our brush with eternity, a strange thing happened. Patti, my not-in-the-least-bit-romantic friend, began longing for a mate. And not just a mate. A husband.

Our weekly excursion to Two Boots was my way of helping her beat the small-town dating blues. In our postage-sized town on the Chihuahuan Desert, if you brought all of the eligible men together in one place, half of them would be older than Methuselah and the other half would look as if they crawled out from under a rock.

I backed away from the wings and wiped my fingers. "When does this Jeff Clark play?" If tonight's headliner would get his boots onstage, I would avoid giving the enthusiastic tourists the added thrill of watching me tossed through the air onto the seat of my britches.

I was looking forward to meeting Jeff Clark. He and Patti had dated for a spell while I was living in Austin, pursuing my big-city journalism career—which unfortunately entailed writing obituaries and classified ads. As much as I wanted

Chapter 1

"Ride 'em cowgirl!"

Diablo lurched, twirled a half turn, bucked his rider, and reeled the opposite way.

"Shut your mouth before I jump off this contraption and belt you one across the kisser," hollered Patti Perez, her jet-black hair flying in all directions.

We might not be real cowgirls, but living in *far* West Texas meant we could play the part when the occasion warranted. And there was no better time to talk like characters from an old Western than when riding the mechanical bull at Two Boots on the first night of Broken Boot's Homestead Days Music Festival.

Patti is the sole proprietor of the Feed and Supply, the only Goth princess in our town of three thousand–plus, and my best friend. With dark-lined eyes wide open, she rode that bull as if she planned to ride it all the way to the weekly livestock show in San Angelo.

Without warning, Diablo shuddered to a halt, causing Patti to slide from the saddle to her feet in the blink of an eye. The crowd near the padded arena burst into applause

Acknowledgments

A book is a jealous companion that often steals my attention from my family and friends when I am least aware. My heartfelt gratitude to my patient family and stalwart friends. I could not have finished this enterprise without your loving encouragement.

It's true what they say. Writing is a solitary affair. That's why I'm so grateful for the broad shoulders, insight, and irreverent humor of my writer friends at NTRWA, SinC, and Cowtown Critiquers. Bless you.

To the mystery writers and fans at Malice Domestic, you rock!

A big thanks to Rebecca Brewer, my editor, and the many folks behind the scenes at Berkley Prime Crime who made this book better. To Kimberly Lionetti, my agent: thanks for always having my back—not to mention the wine and cupcakes.

The far West Texas towns of Marfa, Alpine, and Fort Davis are the inspiration for this series. May their desert beauty remain for generations to come.

For my father,
Christopher Harold Carnley

BERKLEY PRIME CRIME
Published by Berkley
An imprint of Penguin Random House LLC
375 Hudson Street, New York, New York 10014

Copyright © 2016 by Penguin Group LLC

ISBN: 9780425275948

First Edition: November 2016

Printed in the United States of America
1 3 5 7 9 10 8 6 4 2

Cover illustration by Ben Perini
Photograph: limestone background © P. Chinnapong/Shutterstock
Cover design by Judith Lagerman
Book design by Laura K. Corless

The Good,
the Bad, and
the Guacamole

Rebecca Adler

BERKLEY PRIME CRIME
New York

Berkley Prime Crime Taste of Texas Mysteries

HERE TODAY, GONE TAMALE
THE GOOD, THE BAD, AND THE GUACAMOLE

Here ...

"This Southwestern cozy ... flair. Its delightful characters and clever mystery will have you stomping your boots for more."

—Mary Ellen Hughes, national bestselling author of the Pickled and Preserved Mysteries

"Adler's debut sizzles with West Texas flavor and a mystery as satisfying as a plate of fresh tamales. Slip on a pair of cowboy boots, pour yourself a margarita, and kick back to enjoy this Texas-sized delight."

—Annie Knox, national bestselling author of the Pet Boutique Mysteries

"Rebecca Adler's *Here Today, Gone Tamale* is a much needed addition to the cozy mystery genre. Terrifically tantalizing . . . and as addictive as a bowl of chips and salsa. Settle in for a mystery fiesta you won't soon forget."

—Melissa Bourbon, national bestselling author of the Magical Dressmaking Mysteries

"What a tasty idea for a new series! In *Here Today, Gone Tamale*, Rebecca Adler merges the warm and vibrant West Texas town of Broken Boot with a clever murder mystery that kept me guessing until the exciting finale. Josie is an engaging hero who must solve the mystery while helping her delightfully quirky family and balancing trays of steaming tamales!"

—Kathy Aarons, author of the Chocolate Covered Mysteries